# ACCLAIM FOR C

### The Kissing Garden
'A perfect escapist cocktail for summertime romantics'
*Mail on Sunday*

### Love Song
'A perfect example of the new, darker romantic fiction
. . . a true 24-carat love story'
*Sunday Times*

### To Hear A Nightingale
'A story to make you laugh and cry'
*Woman*

### The Business
'A compulsive, intriguing and perceptive read'
*Sunday Express*

### In Sunshine Or In Shadow
'Superbly written . . . a romantic novel that is romantic in
the true sense of the word'
*Daily Mail*

### Stardust
'A long, absorbing read, perfect for holidays'
*Sunday Express*

### Change Of Heart
'Her imagination is thoroughly original'
*Daily Mail*

### Nanny
'Charlotte Bingham's spellbinding saga is required
reading'
*Cosmopolitan*

### Grand Affair
'Extremely popular . . . her books sell and sell'
*Daily Mail*

### Debutantes
'A big, wallowy delicious read'
*The Times*

# The Nightingale Sings

## Charlotte Bingham

**BANTAM BOOKS**

LONDON · NEW YORK · TORONTO · SYDNEY · AUCKLAND

**THE NIGHTINGALE SINGS**
**A BANTAM BOOK : 0 553 40895 X**

Simultaneously published in Great Britain by Doubleday,
a division of Transworld Publishers Ltd

PRINTING HISTORY
Doubleday edition published 1996
Bantam edition published 1996
Bantam edition reprinted 1997
Bantam edition reprinted 1998
Bantam edition reprinted 1999

Set in 10/11pt Linotype Sabon by Kestrel Data, Exeter, Devon.

Bantam Books are published by Transworld Publishers,
61–63 Uxbridge Road, London W5 5SA,
a division of The Random House Group Ltd,
in Australia by Random House Australia (Pty) Ltd,
20 Alfred Street, Milsons Point, Sydney, NSW 2061, Australia,
in New Zealand by Random House New Zealand Ltd,
18 Poland Road, Glenfield, Auckland 10, New Zealand
and in South Africa by Random House (Pty) Ltd,
Endulini, 5a Jubilee Road, Parktown 2193, South Africa.

Printed and bound in Great Britain by
Cox & Wyman Ltd, Reading, Berkshire.

## TO THE LOVING MEMORY OF JANE DUFOSEE

She never made headlines. She made cakes
and picnics, groomed horses, and bandaged
knees, and when she was laid to rest the
little country church was filled to overflowing
with her friends. It is to her memory, and
those women like her, that this book is
dedicated on behalf of the author and
her beloved partner, Terence Brady.

*Hardway House, 1996*

Cover the things that move you,
They glide by.
Cover the things that give you joy,
They are nigh.

# Prologue

When Cassie first was at Claremore, perhaps to drown the sighing of the winter winds and the rains slapping at the ill-fitting old windows, as well as no doubt to turn her mind away from the flaking paintwork and the patches of damp on the walls, Tyrone would sit his young bride on the floor in front of a log fire in the huge but sparsely furnished drawing room and recount some of the old Irish legends, assuming as he did so the sing-song kind of voice used by the traditional itinerant story-tellers who had still been regularly spinning their yarns in the corners of snugs all around Ireland when Tyrone himself was but a gossoon. One of these tales was the famous Legend of Ossian.

'Many is the valley in Ireland that would claim the legend of Ossian for its own, in spite of the fact that this is a tale with a most unhappy ending,' Tyrone would relate. 'For the story goes that after some great period of time Ossian, who had long ago departed for the Land of the Ever Young with his wife Niamh, conceived the desire to see his greatest friend Fionn once more and so, impatient for his friend's company after so many years, set off to meet him. It must have been a fine morning for he sang as he rode, all the while greatly looking forward to the time ahead, and, as may well be imagined, once in the saddle and with the warmth of the sun on his back it was hardly surprising that he soon put from his mind the warnings of his loving wife that he was never in any circumstance to set his foot on Fionn's alien soil, for to do so would surely bring an end to all their joy.

'Now it would seem that all was well until Ossian came across a group of men struggling to move a rock. Being possessed of a good and loving nature our hero at once

9

stooped down from his horse to help them and in so doing the band on his saddle broke causing him to fall to the ground, whereupon all the years he had spent with Niamh in the Land of the Ever Young caught up with him and at once he became a wretched and feeble old man.'

Each time she had heard the story Cassie had thought it too sad, but Tyrone would have none of it. 'Not at all,' he would assure her. 'The legend of Ossian is a most interesting story. It is a moral story and one for all time, the point being not that Ossian left Niamh and the Land of the Ever Young to see his friend Fionn, but what caused Ossian to forget his wife's warnings that he thought himself able to lean out of his saddle and in doing so risk everything. It would have to be nothing more nor less than that old serpent guilt that caused his downfall. For Ossian, do you not see, was convinced that he could help others and stay in the saddle. After all no-one asked him to stop and help them, did they? Not one. Devil the man. No, I would say undoubtedly that his folly was due to the guilt of his great happiness with Niamh that led him to make his fatal error. So when I am gone before you, which being somewhat older than you one day I most probably will be, remember that like Ossian the greatest force of our own destruction is the guilt that lies within us.'

So the time passed and when Tyrone was tragically gathered to his ancestors much sooner than he had expected, Cassie was left to ride alone through the Valley of Life. Unsurprisingly then that long after her beloved Tyrone had been taken from her she forgot his words of warning, just as Ossian had forgotten the warnings of his own beloved Niamh when he too had begun to feel the warmth of the sun once more on his back. Not that Cassie would ever forget her husband's great love, nor his dashing looks or enchanting ways – all Cassie forgot was the moral of the famous legend. Like Ossian in so doing she also leaned too far out of her saddle and at that moment it seemed that she too would be destined to fall to the ground with her happiness lost and gone for ever.

# The Arc

## LONGCHAMPS
### Paris, France.
### October.

For one terrible heartstopping moment he thought he had got it wrong. The gap that he had been waiting for had opened and then just as suddenly closed leaving him with absolutely no way through. He could of course pull out and go round, that he knew well enough, and because his fellow was so very fast and quick-footed he knew it would still leave him in with a whisper, particularly since he had not yet asked his fellow the question and he could feel there was plenty of fuel left in the tank. But what had been five hundred metres a second ago was now a fast diminishing three hundred so, if he did choose to switch to the outside, by the time he extricated himself the leaders would be all but home.

So he waited. And he prayed.

Three strides later and the one right in front of him tired and suddenly rolled away from the rails, leaving the opening for which he had been petitioning the gods, not much of a gap to be sure, barely enough in fact to let them through, but it was now their only choice, now it was do or die. As long as the one in front rolled a little further away from the rails the gap would be big enough, but even when the gap was big enough it would have to keep rolling and start to run in a straight line, otherwise, should it begin to roll back onto his fellow, instead of an untroubled passage through there would be a barging match. If that was the case, then even if Dex did prevail he knew he'd lose the race at the inevitable enquiry.

You did not come up on the inside to make your run unless there was the room.

11

The rules were perfectly clear.

*The rider of any horse who has been guilty of reckless, careless or improper riding shall be guilty of an offence. And when a horse or its rider causes interference or commits such an offence it may either be placed behind the horse or horses with which it has interfered, or be placed last of all.*

*Or even disqualified altogether.*

But that was the chance Dexter had to take, because by now the leaders had passed the distance marker and all he had left were not minutes but seconds. But then as he saw the gap widen and hold rather than close back on him and shut him in, all at once he knew that those few precious seconds had just turned into all the time in the world. It would now simply take what it always took, just one shake of the reins, and the day would be won. One easy, confident go-on-go-get-'em shake, that was all. So with a none too secret smile Dex shook the reins just once, then sat down into his horse and pumped on for the post.

In response to his shout of unbridled joy as the big black horse accelerated away under him, once more The Nightingale flew home.

As the field turned into the home straight Cassie's heart sank as she lost sight of her horse completely, swallowed up in a sea of horses. More even than at Ascot she knew how vital it was if a horse was to have a winning chance for it to be in the first half dozen turning into the straight, particularly since the jockeys had gone no great gallop for the first mile, as this was so often the way the richest race in Europe was run. Instead of being a true test of stamina and speed the contest often became simply a sudden and full-blooded sprint to the line once the field swept round that final bend. For any horse boxed in tightly on the rails or forced to fight its way out of the pack to switch to the outside in order to make its run the race was as good as lost, since by the time it saw daylight the leaders would already be going hell for leather for home.

Yet that is exactly how it was on this glorious sun-drenched October afternoon at Longchamps. The odds-on favourite to win Europe's richest race seemed lost in the *mêlée* and as the horse all but disappeared from the sight of the vast crowd a sigh of dismay arose from the whole British and Irish contingent as it seemed their hero was about to lose his unbeaten record. On the other hand the home crowd began to roar with delight as they saw Esplanade, their own dual Two Thousand Guineas and Derby winner and the clear second favourite in the betting, shooting into what appeared to be a two- to three-length lead at the two furlong pole.

While The Nightingale still seemed inextricably buried somewhere in the *mêlée* behind the leader.

Passing the distance marker the course commentator was calling Esplanade home, his rider having poached what had to be an unassailable lead on the rest of the field. But then with less than two hundred yards of the great race left to run, as the beaten animals began to fall back off the pace, all at once Cassie caught sight of her horse once more and could hardly believe her eyes. Dexter Bryant had him in third place against the rails beside an obviously beaten horse and was sitting as still as a church mouse. The big black horse was simply cruising. In fact so easily was The Nightingale going that even though the horse was still three lengths down on Esplanade, Dexter Bryant had the time to take a quick look around him to see if there was any danger other than the two remaining horses in front.

Then with one shake of the reins the race was over. Despite the last ditch efforts of its jockey Dexter could see the horse which was lying second on his outside was no threat because it was treading water so all he had to catch and beat was the leader. With hindsight Esplanade's jockey was to say never for a moment could he have imagined that he was to be caught so near to home, particularly since his own horse showed absolutely no signs of stopping. So well was Esplanade still going that in any other year the horse would have prevailed, but although at the post mortem the jockey was to swear he sensed nothing coming at him the crowd did. They saw the danger as out of the pursuing pack The Nightingale burst as if from a giant catapult. The tumultuous cheering of the crowd turned in a moment into one massive, anguished gasp as the handsome black Irish colt hit top gear and swallowed up Esplanade. It took just a few strides and the French horse's three-length lead had gone. In fact so fast was The Nightingale flying that there was never even a moment when the two horses were racing neck and neck. The Nightingale simply strode by Esplanade to go first half a length up then a whole length, racing by the French horse so quickly in fact that by the time Dexter eased him up passing the winning post the margin of victory was nearly two lengths.

The moment the big Irish colt flew past the post Dexter stood up in his irons to stroke the horse's massive neck and tweak one of his big floppy ears. While he did so, the roars of the entire crowd swelled in volume as every racegoer present realized what they had witnessed. So mighty was their appreciation that they kept up their cheers until Dexter, having pulled The Nightingale up at the top of the straight, brought him back in front of the packed stands in the company of the course photographers before steering the famous horse through crowds of delirious well-wishers and admirers into the comparative safety of the unsaddling enclosure to be greeted by his owner, breeder and trainer, Cassie Rosse.

As Dexter hopped down from the back of what every-one present knew must surely now be one of the greatest horses ever seen on a racecourse, he was kissed by Cassie's delighted daughter Josephine and hugged around the shoulders by her son Mattie. As to trainer and jockey, however, they just smiled at each other. Both of them had journeyed hard and far to reach this point in their lives and now they were here there was really nothing to be said. Instead they turned their attentions to the big black horse who had just won the richest race in Europe with such contemptuous ease.

Cassie reached up to tug at one of her beloved colt's ears and to stroke his fine neck.

As she did so someone came up behind her and murmured a warning in her ear.

'Mind you don't go getting too successful now.'

Cassie turned round to see to whom the voice belonged, but there was no-one there, and all at once it seemed to her the autumn air suddenly blew cold.

# One

Ireland.
24 December.

For ever afterwards Cassie would remain convinced that Leonora had worn her old white and blue trimmed Chanel suit in order to remind Cassie that the past would never go away, and that in that past she too had loved Tyrone, for it was the very suit she had worn when the newly married Cassie had first brought Tyrone to Leonora's house at Derry Na Loch, the day when Leonora herself had fallen in love with Cassie's now long-dead husband.

That was not all she would remember the day for, because as a newly appointed Oriental butler had opened the doors of Derry Na Loch Cassie knew at once her visit was a mistake. Before she even stepped into the marbled hallway she could hear Tyrone's voice scolding her in the mock tired tone he employed when he most wanted to get her attention.

*How many times have I told you, Mrs Rosse? Isn't it always when we say yes and we mean no that we most learn to regret it?*

*You're right as always, Ty,* Cassie thought, staring around her at the over-ornately furnished drawing room, full of carefully chosen and expensive artefacts, those curious mementoes which the rich seem to love accumulating. She looked too at the collection of new and somewhat overbright paintings that now hung on the silk-papered walls, and at the vast, expensively upholstered sofas on one of which sat four tiny white papillon dogs. Everything was immaculate and luxurious yet from the room Cassie felt nothing but coldness.

*Isn't it always when we say yes and we mean no that we most learn to regret it?*

The thought kept running round and round in her head while she felt herself wishing she might simply turn on her heels and bolt, just the way she had often felt as a child when finding herself at some party she had been dreading. Why she had said yes to Leonora's invitation which she had fully intended to refuse was now beyond her. Initially she had resisted Leonora's pleadings that they must meet up again and bury the hatchet because for once, oddly enough, Cassie found she was right out of clemency. Leonora had tried to steal her husband, and when she had failed in that she had tried to pretend to Cassie not only that she had been innocent of any such manoeuvre but also that Tyrone was the father of their adopted son Mattie by the same young woman who had put the child up for adoption. Finally she had tried to sabotage The Nightingale's chances of winning the Epsom Derby in favour of her own horse, a *coup* which, had it proved successful, because of the side bet agreed between Cassie and herself would have given her possession of the entire property of Claremore. Little wonder therefore that since her horse's famous victory on Epsom Downs until now Cassie had never revisited Derry Na Loch nor once met its owner again, yet here she was not only standing in her bitterest enemy's drawing room but being kept idly waiting as was Leonora's perennial wont.

Finally, after a full ten minutes had elapsed, the door opened and Mrs Charles C. Lovett Andrew, *née* Leonora Von Wagner, sauntered in.

'Darlin',' she drawled, affecting an Irish brogue which failed entirely to mask her own Newport accent. 'Do for God's sake sit down somewhere. You look as if you were back at the Academy waiting to see Miss Truefitt.' She laughed and herself sat down in a huge, deeply upholstered armchair. Her toy dogs as one immediately got down from their own sofa and tried to jump up on her knee, but their mistress was not having it. 'Get down, will you?' she commanded, brushing the little butterfly dogs away from her. 'You shouldn't even damn' well be in here.' Then she smiled at Cassie without a flicker of warmth in her eyes before slowly looking her up and down as if about to interview her.

'Cassie McGann,' she said, adjusting her long blond hair, which she wore swept back from her face. 'You know I still actually can't believe it. Little Cassie McGann we all used to tease so unmercifully at the Academy, who we all voted the Girl Most Unlikely to Succeed – and just look at you. Europe's top woman horse trainer. The first woman ever to train the winner of the English Derby, and then the Irish Derby, and now the Prix de l'Arc de Triomphe. You know something, darlin'? If I were still drinking, I sure as hell would drink to you, Cassie McGann.'

Cassie eyed Leonora disbelievingly, too long used to her boasts of having given up drinking. 'What exactly did you want to see me about, Leonora?' she asked. 'You said it was urgent.'

'Oh, for goodness' sake sit down first, will you?' Leonora replied, unwrapping a piece of Nicotel chewing gum. 'I can't talk to you when you're standing up, and if you're wondering about this ghastly new habit of chewing gum, I've managed to kick the old cancer sticks as well.'

'Next thing you'll be telling me is that you've been born again.'

Leonora looked back at her with an almost imperceptible tightening of her eyes. 'You'd be surprised, Cassie McGann,' she said. 'Anything is possible once you set your mind to it.' She smiled coldly once again, before drinking most of the glass of sparkling mineral water her butler had set beside her. 'So.'

'So?' Cassie echoed, finally sitting down opposite Leonora on a straight-backed chair she swung round for herself from in front of a fine William and Mary escritoire rather than in one of the deep armchairs. 'I would much rather you came to the point, Leonora. I really don't have very much time.'

'No, of course you don't. How awfully selfish of me,' Leonora sighed. 'A woman as famously successful as you.

19

So OK – let's cut right to the chase, shall we? What I want to know, Cassie McGann, is what's next on the agenda for our famous owner and her even more famous horse.'

'You could have asked me that on the phone.'

'You're always too busy to talk on the phone, Cassie McGann.'

'Rosse,' Cassie reminded her.

'Rosse, of course.' Leonora smiled at her. 'It's just that now with Tyrone gone—'

'Tyrone died a long time ago, Leonora,' Cassie replied evenly. 'A very long time ago.'

'Oh, my God, yes. I suppose it really *is* a long time.' Leonora suddenly looked as stricken as if she had only just learned of the tragic news, but Cassie knew better than to remark on it. Leonora had always been singularly adroit at getting fish to rise to her bait.

'Don't look at me like that, Cassie.' Leonora frowned as if Cassie was staring at her which Cassie was not. 'I know what you're thinking. I know you're thinking I have no right to feel as I do about Tyrone—'

'Tyrone was my husband.'

*Don't, Cassie, don't*, Tyrone's voice called to her. *You're always doing this with Leonora. You're like a snake responding to the charmer's pipe. Leave her be. Didn't I tell you anyway never to come here again?*

'You're absolutely right, Cassie darling,' Leonora was continuing. 'I should imagine you'd like to box my ears but really I can't help it. Not now I'm sober and in my right mind again. You know how I felt about Tyrone, and now that he's gone – I mean, where's the harm?'

'To his memory,' Cassie said very quietly. 'I don't want his memory spoiled.'

She knew it was absurd but the thought of having to share Tyrone's memory with Leonora was more upsetting than she could say. Such was her antipathy to her old acquaintance she did not even like to hear Leonora say his name. So, taking a deep breath, she decided to leave the subject and return to discussing the matter of why she had been summoned so urgently to Derry Na Loch.

'There's no use asking where I next intend to go with The Nightingale, Leonora,' she said. 'I make it a rule never to discuss my racing plans with anyone outside Claremore.'

'You make it your *rule*, do you?' Leonora wondered mockingly. 'My. How very imperious.'

'That's the way it is,' Cassie said in her best take it or leave it manner.

'Pity,' Leonora sighed. 'I'm so very interested in just *everything* you do. Particularly how *well* you're doing. I mean you must be simply coining it now. Little penniless Cassie McGann must be worth a not so small fortune. Not just from your winnings, but from the stallion fees that horse of yours is going to command.'

'You didn't ask me here to discuss the health of my bank balance, surely?'

'Well, yes I did, in a manner of speaking. And what am I thinking? You don't have a drink. Just because I'm off the sauce doesn't mean you have to die of thirst as well, darlin'.' Leonora pressed a bell button concealed under the table beside her and smiled her brittle little smile again at Cassie. 'Champagne? I imagine that's your tipple nowadays. One of the many things that's good about being rich, I always say. Being able to drink champagne when and where you feel like it. Most of all when you don't even feel like it.'

While she waited for her butler to reappear Leonora opened a fresh stick of Nicotel gum and, popping it into her brightly painted mouth, crossed one elegant leg and started to swing one beautifully shod foot up and down, watching it for a while with great interest as if she had never observed the movement before. Then she slowly returned her gaze to Cassie who had decided that as far as this conversation went the mountain could come to Muhammad.

'Talking of drink and such related topics,' Leonora continued, 'you do understand, don't you? As I said in my letters, it was drink and the drugs of course that made me act the way I did. Over Tyrone, and then over the Derby. Sober and in my right mind, as you well know, I would

21

never have behaved that way because it is just not me. We've known each other long enough for you to know that what happened between us was not typical of my real character, right?' Cassie said nothing. As far as she was concerned what Leonora had done was totally in keeping with her character. 'Seriously, Cassie,' Leonora continued, 'the way I behaved over Tyrone was mostly to do with what I was taking, not with what I was feeling. I know perfectly well that it was you he truly loved, not me. And I can live with that. Really I can.'

Leonora paused significantly in the way people do who are intent on making it seem that by confessing that they have reformed their ways they are somehow performing a great favour to the whole of humanity. Cassie tried once more to contain her exasperation. The last thing she needed to be told was something she knew better than anyone, namely that her husband had loved her and nobody else, and the very last person she needed to be told that fact by was Leonora.

'I wonder, Leonora, will you get to the point?' she asked, as Leonora's Oriental butler arrived silently by her side to offer her a crystal flute of champagne from a small silver tray.

'This is for Mama's benefit, Cassie, not mine,' Leonora said, holding up her glass for the butler to fill from a jug of fresh peach juice.

'Why in heaven's name would your mother want you to see me?' Cassie asked, remembering how she disliked the mother nearly as much as she did the daughter. 'We haven't had any dealings with each other since she summarily removed her string of horses from Tyrone and frankly I have never had any wish to do so.'

'That's all so long ago, isn't it high time we let bygones be bygones, darling?' Leonora sipped her drink and eyed Cassie over the top of the glass. '*Que sera sera*, as the old song has it?'

'I imagine you mean what's done is done,' Cassie replied, 'rather than what will be will be, and if that's so, then I have to beg to differ, Leonora. In this instance I can't see why in hell I should forgive and forget. Your mother damned near ruined us.'

'She was just doing what mothers do, darling. She was protecting her own. You're a mother. Surely you understand?'

'She was not protecting her own, Leonora. She was protecting her own interests.'

'Because she'd had a fling with your husband.'

'Tyrone was not my husband when that happened, Leonora. It was well before I came into Tyrone's life.'

Leonora just smiled. She smiled the way she always used to do in order to give the impression that what had been said was in fact a lie.

'I think I can guess what your mother wants,' Cassie continued. 'She wants in on The Nightingale.'

Leonora moved her gum to the other side of her mouth and regarded Cassie with steely blue eyes. 'You're obviously going to syndicate this horse of yours, right?'

'What makes you think I haven't already?'

'I'd have heard, that's what, Cassie McGann.'

'Rosse.'

'Sure. OK – you've got it. Mama would like a bit of the action. Why not? She can afford it. And her money's no different from anyone else's.'

'That's a matter of opinion,' Cassie replied, beginning to enjoy herself as she realized how much this was costing Leonora in loss of face. Obviously Mrs Von Wagner had been applying endless pressure to make Leonora make the appeal on her behalf, as she would never have dared approach Cassie directly herself. 'Let's get this absolutely right. Your mother would like to be part of a syndicate on The Nightingale—'

'I think you mean *the* syndicate, darling,' Leonora interrupted.

'No I don't actually, Leonora. I haven't yet formed any syndicate so it's perfectly correct to refer to it in the abstract. So if I may just start again, if you don't mind – your mother would like to be part of a syndicate on my horse and besides that no doubt you're thinking and maybe hoping, I guess,

23

that you too would like to be part of the action and maybe send a couple of your mares to him. Am I warm?'

For the first time since Cassie's arrival Leonora showed signs of the impatience she was feeling, clicking her tongue sharply in response to Cassie's summation and then dispensing of her no longer wanted chewing gum, which she deposited back in its wrapper before throwing it in a waste basket.

'So what would it matter if I did?' she said, her Newport manners suddenly snapping. 'Where in hell is the harm in two friends wanting to do business together? You have to consider the interests of racing here, let me tell you. Mama and I between us have several high-class mares as you well know, and it won't do your financial future much harm, will it, if The Nightingale starts producing quality two-year-olds? You're surely not going to let the past stand in the way of the future. Even you couldn't be—'

'Yes?' Cassie enquired as Leonora stopped herself. 'Stubborn? Stupid? Obdurate? Take your choice, Leonora. I can be all three, if I so wish.'

If Cassie had been feeling less impatient she might have smiled as an agitated Leonora drained what was left of her peach juice in one gulp, just the way she used to empty a glass of vodka when she was drinking. She then sprang to her feet and, scooping one of her lap dogs up from where all four still sat on the sofa, walked over to the French windows to stare out at her manicured gardens.

She must be in terrible debt to her mother to have to humiliate herself like this, Cassie thought, which again would be par for Leonora's course. For the truth was that it would not matter a jot how much money Leonora married for – she would always need more. There had probably never been a moment in Leonora's married life when she had not been in debt to her mother, and since in the eyes of the Von Wagners money could buy anything, even forgiveness, much against her will Leonora had obviously been forced to engineer this meeting.

But for a long time Cassie had ignored her entreaties, and, as she now realized in the awkward silence that

24

followed Leonora's move to the windows, she had only finally agreed to make the visit out of sheer curiosity. In much the same way as motorists cannot help but stare at the outcome of a road accident however hard they may try not to, Cassie had been drawn to come and have a look at Leonora, expecting to find her old adversary much the worse for wear due to her constant abuse of alcohol and drugs. For a moment, when she first saw the new slim and suntanned Leonora, Cassie had almost been pleasantly surprised until she remembered that, despite whatever programme of detoxification Leonora might have undergone, underneath she would still be the old Leonora. When they were teenagers at Miss Truefitt's famous Academy back home in the States Leonora Von Wagner had been a spoiled and dangerous brat. The difference between then and now was that now Leonora was simply an older spoilt and dangerous brat, and that was all.

'If all you want to know is whether when the time comes I will consider any of your and your mother's mares, Leonora, then of course I shall be perfectly happy to do so, once I have all their details and your applications in front of me,' Cassie said. 'But as for the question of any syndicate—'

'Maybe you won't have to go as far as full syndication,' Leonora interrupted. 'Not when you hear what Mama has to offer. She's prepared to invest five million pounds for a one-third share.'

Leonora looked so impressed by the information she was imparting that she poured herself another peach juice without ringing for the butler.

'I'm not in the slightest bit interested,' Cassie said.

'It's a mighty generous offer,' Leonora continued as if she hadn't heard Cassie's reply. 'Your horse is probably worth at top ten million and even that's pushing it, so an offer of five for only a third share – well. You'd have to be crazy to refuse. It would sure as hell secure your future—'

'I said – I'm not interested, Leonora.'

'*And* the future of Claremore. There must be all manner

25

of things you're still dying to do there to keep the old place state of the art – and an investment like this—'

'Even if my life depended on it, I wouldn't take a penny of your or your mother's money, and you can tell *Mama* that from me – OK? And if your new sober self likes to imagine that while there's life there's hope – I am sorry to tell you there isn't. Not where you and I are concerned, Leonora, and most of all not where The Nightingale is concerned, because I am not going to syndicate him. The Nightingale stays where he belongs, in the family. Not only that but he's not retiring to the paddocks. Not yet.' Cassie paused to make sure that she had Leonora's full attention. 'Fact is I'm keeping Nightie on in training as a four-year-old.'

'You're *what*?' Now it was the old Leonora who was looking at her, just the way she had used to look when they were in school and Cassie would come into the classroom to find Leonora sitting at Miss Truefitt's desk surrounded by her cronies, waiting for the target of her taunts to come into her sights. 'You can't be serious.'

'I'm entirely serious, Leonora,' Cassie replied. 'It's what the racegoers deserve. When will they ever get the chance again to see a horse like The Nightingale in action? Possibly never.'

'You're mad, Cassie McGann,' Leonora said, laughing without humour. 'What on earth would you want to do that for?'

'For a very good reason, because Tyrone would have wanted it, Leonora. Why – I really can't believe that you knew him so little that you wouldn't know that?'

'You know that everyone is going to think you're mad, don't you?' Mattie said, pouring them all out some more champagne and looking across at his mother with his usual mixture of affection and condescension. 'On the bloodstock side that is. No-one in their right mind keeps a dual Derby winner on in training as a four-year-old.'

'Vincent O'Brien did so with Roberto and with Ballymoss,' Cassie returned. 'You're surely not faulting the great Dr O'Brien's judgement?'

'Yes, but that was way back when, Ma,' Mattie sighed. 'Roberto was over twenty years ago. And Ballymoss – Ballymoss was some time back in the blasted Dark Ages.'

'1958 to be precise,' Cassie told him.

'That is half a *century* ago. Anyway, neither of those horses won the Triple Crown.'

'The Triple Crown *and* the Prix de l'Arc de Triomphe,' Josephine chipped in. 'And certainly not in the same year.'

'Oh, thanks, Jo.' Cassie turned and smiled at her Titian-haired daughter. 'So you think I'm nuts as well, right?'

'We're thinking of Nightie. We just don't want anything happening to him, that's all.'

'You think I do?' Cassie raised her eyebrows in deliberate exaggeration. 'You don't think I've thought this thing right through? Anyway, it's Christmas Eve for heaven's sake. Don't let's involve ourselves with this now, OK? Let's leave it on the back burner until after the festivities.'

Mattie eased himself into a large chintz-covered armchair opposite Cassie and stretched out his long legs. 'It's nothing heavy,' he said with a reassuring smile. 'It's just that Nightie's a very big star, you know—'

'He's more than a star, Matthew Rosse,' Josephine cut in. 'Everyone says he's the horse of the century.'

'Fine, Jo,' Mattie continued. 'So do you have any idea what his stud value is?'

'Of course I do. I remember you and Jack Madigan discussing it on the flight back from Longchamps.'

'Right. So you know we're talking big money. You'll know that Nightie's probably going to command a stallion fee of £100,000 a throw.'

'Now just hold everything, you two. I mean it,' Cassie cut in. 'Nightie doesn't belong to a set of rules because he happens to be the exception and not the case. I bred him, I train him and I own him. He's not owned by a syndicate that wants to realize its profit nor is he ever likely to be, so if I want to keep him on in training as a four-year-old that's my business. I don't have to consider anyone else's

27

feelings in the matter. Only those of the racing public, and you can bet your last dollar they would just love to see him back again next year.'

'Yes all right, fine, we take your point,' Mattie said, giving his sister a good long look which Cassie picked up as she knew she was intended to do.

'Very well,' she sighed, putting down her champagne glass. Really the last thing she had wanted to do at this moment was get involved in a debate about her horse's future. Christmas Eve was always a special time at Claremore, and already Erin her housekeeper had set about fulfilling their Christmas traditions, piling the fires high with logs and the kitchen table with food before propping open the double front doors, hoping as she did each Christmas that this would be the year Claremore would be the house to which the Holy Family would choose to come. It was an ancient Celtic tradition that Cassie adored and hoped would never be broken as long as the house of Claremore stood, so this did not seem to be the moment to be discussing family business. Yet she knew that if she left the argument unresolved there was a danger it would hang over them for the rest of the evening, which was why she decided it would doubtless be best to put the matter to bed once and for all before they sat down to enjoy their traditional Christmas Eve dinner.

'Your future in the horse is quite secure, Mattie, as is yours, Josephine, so there is no need for you to worry,' she said, taking up their unanswered questions. 'As a racehorse Nightie is going to keep right on belonging to me and to me alone. I don't think you can argue with that, either of you, because you know the reason why. The day Nightie was born I dedicated him to your father and what we've achieved together since then – well. You don't need telling. You both understand it fine.' Cassie paused and looked at the portrait of Tyrone above the fireplace painted as she had commissioned it after his death, mounted on his favourite hack Old Flurry. She loved the painting, but on grey days or black days when she looked up at it all she could see was that most terrible of all moments, just as if it had happened that morning, the moment she turned to see Tyrone lying dead in the grass with one temple of his handsome head kicked in.

'Hel-lo?' Josephine called, prompting her back to reality. 'Anybody home?'

'Where was I?' Cassie said, taking a sip of her wine to give herself a moment more to collect herself and her thoughts.

'You were talking about our future security,' Mattie said, taking out his spinhaler and squirting a shot of Prednisone down his throat. 'That there was no cause for us to worry. But then neither Jo nor myself said there was.'

'There isn't,' Cassie replied, trying to ignore his asthma but unable to quell her usual feelings of anxiety as she watched him inhale. 'When Nightie retires to stud here at the end of next year I shall keep a half interest in him and I intend to divide the other half interest in equal shares between you two.'

'What about Padraig?' Josephine asked. 'Isn't he to get any shares?'

'I've thought long and hard about Padraig, Josephine,' Cassie replied. 'As you know, adopting Padraig wasn't the same thing at all as adopting Mattie. Your father and I adopted Mattie because after I lost my second child I couldn't have any more children—'

'Yes I know, Mums,' Josephine interrupted. 'And you adopted Erin's baby in order to give him a good name. Which was great of you, absolutely. But even so, because he is technically a Rosse—'

'Exactly,' Cassie agreed. 'Padraig is only technically a Rosse. When poor Erin found herself pregnant by Father Patrick the agreement we made was that I would adopt the child and Erin would bring it up as her own and no-one in the village would be any the wiser, seeing the way she helped bring you two up. Which is exactly how it turned out. Everyone thought Padraig was a straightforward adoption just as you were, Mattie.'

'But won't Erin still think Padraig has some sort of

claim?' Josephine wondered. 'Not that it matters because it doesn't. I'm just curious, that's all.'

'That's not how Erin thinks, Josephine,' Cassie replied. 'She wouldn't and doesn't expect anything like that for Padraig. Even so, I've made sure he won't go empty-handed. He'll get a decent present when he reaches his majority.'

'Seriously,' Mattie said after a moment of silence, staring at his beautiful and still dark-haired mother in her much loved pale pink Dior suit, silk shirt and two strands of pearls at her neck. 'I really wasn't thinking about us when I was talking about Nightie.'

'I know that, Mattie,' Cassie replied. 'If you were that sort of person I wouldn't make such a settlement on you. Same goes for Jo.'

'You don't have to do this,' Josephine said. 'Anyway – are you sure it's for the best? I mean taking into account what Mattie said about Nightie's value at stud – that is a serious amount of money.' Josephine suddenly stopped and sighed impatiently, turning around to the door behind her, which had blown open. 'Oh, God, will you just feel the draught whistling in from the Hall?' she asked. 'I do wish someone would get Erin out of this crazy habit of leaving all the doors open every Christmas Eve.'

'Jo darling,' Cassie replied, getting up to close the door. 'I do know a bit about what a lot of money can do and does to an awful lot of people. Which is why when the time does come to capitalize on the horse the money will be put into trusts for you both and will be professionally managed. So that you can't blow it all just like that – or, even more important, so that someone else can't get their hands on it. Anyway—' Cassie put up her hands to prevent further discussion. 'Anyway, that day is still some way off. But I just wanted you to know that was the arrangement. So that you didn't think I was being *entirely* selfish.' Cassie smiled at both her children and put down her empty champagne glass. 'Heavens, will you look at the time?' she said. 'Erin will murder us if we're not ready dead on the dot of half past.'

'So what's your plan, Ma?' Mattie asked as they all got to their feet. 'For next season, I mean. Another tilt at the King George VI, yes?'

'I thought we'd open our account at the Curragh with the Royal Whip Stakes,' Cassie replied. 'Then take in either the Coronation Cup or the Eclipse, preferably the Eclipse, then certainly a second go at the King George. After that we'll give the old boy a short holiday before getting him ready for Longchamps again to see if Nightie can be the first horse since Alleged to win the Arc two years running.'

'You know what your trouble is, don't you?' Mattie sighed, shaking his handsome head in mock sadness.

'Tell me.'

'You will keep thinking small.'

As Cassie well knew while she lay soaking in her bath ten minutes later, most people would have been more than happy to retire their dual Derby winners at the end of their three-year-old career, particularly if their horses had won the listed races which her now internationally famous colt had won. What she did not know quite as surely was why she was so determined to keep The Nightingale in training as a four-year-old. The risks were there for all to see except, it would appear, herself. Yet she knew that if she had in fact over-raced her horse as a three-year-old, which was what a tiny minority of her critics were trying to imply, and that consequently The Nightingale did not train on, then her horse's reputation could be seriously dented. There was no denying this fact, particularly since Tyrone had been in the habit of forever reminding them both how notoriously fickle the racing world was. *And God, they're never so fickle as when they're giving off as to whose fault it is when a horse doesn't train on, particularly a horse they've all been praising to the skies the previous season,* he would say. *You should hear them, Cassie my love. How, when it came to it, Pegasus never really beat anything worthwhile during his reign as a three-year-old. There's little the boys in the grandstands like more than to put up something to be admired and then shoot it down in flames.*

31

So if Cassie's big black homebred had indeed decided he'd had enough of racing and flopped as a four-year-old, even though he would still be able to command a very high fee at stud his fame would have been tarnished and question marks would be raised over the value of his form.

Worse than that, however – far, far worse – would be if he injured himself.

Only two months earlier Cassie had seen the very best four-year filly in training killed on the racecourse. Gunpowder Plot, George Montgomery's lovely dark grey which had won the Oaks the previous year and had trotted up in that year's Eclipse, broke a shoulder coming off the top bend at Goodwood and had to be destroyed. The Montgomerys, who were friends of Cassie's, were inconsolable at the loss of their beautiful homebred horse, George bitterly regretting his decision to keep the horse in training. It was not her value as a brood mare over which he lamented, as he told Cassie afterwards, it was as if he had lost a member of his family. If anything similar should happen to The Nightingale Cassie knew that she would never forgive herself, and neither would her children. Nor too would the legion of The Nightingale's fans.

Yet here she was prepared to take that very risk, she reminded herself as she ran some more hot water into her bath, flying in the face of all the advices she had been given, financial and equine, because that was what she wanted, not for herself but for Tyrone. But why? she asked herself as she lay back in the soft foam of her bath and stared at the ceiling above her. Why should she be risking it all? If she retired The Nightingale now she would be rich for life. If the horse lived for another ten to fifteen years, which it was perfectly reasonable to suppose he would, given the table of average lifespans for stallions, then capitalizing now on the forecast of the horse's covering a book of twenty-five mares a season at £100,000 a throw The Nightingale would be worth £25 million. Neither she nor her children nor even their children nor *their* children's children would ever want again. Claremore would be safe, as would the jobs of all who worked there. Of course there was no guarantee that The Nightingale would turn out to be as brilliant a sire as he was a racehorse, but with his astonishing record as a three-year-old it was a gilt-edged certainty he would have a full book of the best mares in the world for at the very least the next five or six seasons, even if every single one of his progeny turned out to be squibs.

*So why am I not heeding the good advice I'm getting?* Cassie wondered to herself. *I should be thinking of me and my children and my future grandchildren, and of the future of everyone connected with Claremore, surely not of a man who lies dead and buried in the village graveyard, however wildly and madly I loved him. I have to be crazy. It just doesn't make any sense. Nightie won one of the greatest Derbies ever seen on Epsom Downs in the joint fastest time ever recorded, and then for the rest of the season he simply brushed aside any further opposition, winning all his subsequent races without ever being asked a serious question. And only a little over two months ago at Longchamps he did it again, producing that murderous turn of foot of his to accelerate past a really high-class field of international horses to win Europe's most valuable race, so what else do we both have to prove? Tell me, Tyrone, please, please tell me why. Your family's future is secure. I'm richer than either of us ever imagined I would be, even in our very wildest dreams. I am as happy as I could possibly be without you, my love, so will you please just tell me what in heaven's name I am thinking of doing this for?*

*Because, Cassie McGann, of how you are*, an inner voice returned. *Because you want to show them, that's why.*

Closing her eyes in peace now that she understood herself the better, Cassie lay back in the bath, sinking down in the soft hot suds until the water lapped under her chin. Almost immediately the telephone on the chair beside her rang.

'Hello, this is Claremore. Cassie Rosse speaking,' she said mechanically, her mind still on her great decision, which she felt she was now about to reverse. There was a long silence, such a long silence that she finally heard herself asking who was calling.

'Don't worry who this is, Mrs Rosse,' an unrecognizable voice said in her ear. 'This is simply a warning not to run The Nightingale again.'

'What did you say?' Cassie asked after a moment.

'You heard me, Mrs Rosse.'

'You bet I did,' Cassie replied, 'and the answer is go to hell.'

'You're thinking you've had these calls before and so what. The so what is this one is different,' the voice continued, forcing Cassie to go on listening. 'The difference being that if you insist on running the horse next season you will regret that decision for the rest of your life.'

Then the phone went dead. For a moment Cassie sat in her bath just staring at the humming receiver before slowly replacing it in its cradle. *Sure, you bet I've had calls like that before from scum like you, plenty of 'em,* she thought. *And I've ignored every one of them, which is just what I intend to do with this one. I shall simply change my personal number yet again and do precisely what I see and think fit.*

Along with her personal number she would also change her mind, she decided as she lay back once more in her bath smiling grimly to herself at the irony, because if her antagonists had delayed making that call until after Christmas they would not have had to bother making it at all. For the simple reason that prior to the call Cassie had decided to do exactly what they wanted her to do, namely not to keep The Nightingale in training as a four-year-old, and for all the right reasons. He was too valuable to be risked, she had concluded. Family and expert opinion was perfectly correct. To keep the horse in training could well prove to be a Pyrrhic gesture which if it backfired might jeopardize the security of both her business and, more important, her family.

One telephone call had changed all that.

It was not simply that Cassie was not a person to be bullied. However stubborn she might be she was not so obdurate that just because someone warned her not to do something she would go right ahead and do it out of sheer defiance. What changed her mind was the principle that lay behind the threat, namely that unless the honest people involved in racing resisted the forces of darkness which whatever their size were ever present in the sport, then racing would fester. Like everyone else who made their living honestly from the Turf she knew all too well that while corruption was not exactly epidemic it most certainly was endemic, so by refusing to be frightened off and making it known she had resisted the threat Cassie could at least set an example for others, however token it might seem to some.

*Most of all it is important not just for racing itself but for its public, Cassie. The public must always be shown that those in racing who genuinely love their sport are in no circumstances whatever to be frightened into submission.*

*Thank you, Mr Rosse,* she said to herself as she got out of her bath to wrap her slender frame in a thick, soft white towelling dressing gown. *As usual you came through at exactly the right time.*

# *Two*

The news that The Nightingale was to stay in training was greeted with universal delight, even more so once Cassie elaborated on the reasons behind her decision. When everyone learned the full details even the professional knockers had nothing to say because they found themselves disarmed. The horse returned from his winter holiday in Italy sound, well and in high spirits and once back in work the early indications were that he seemed to have lost none of his old zest and enthusiasm, particularly after Liam, Cassie's head lad, had finished his six weeks' roadwork on the horse in the foothills of the mountains which rose behind Claremore and Dexter Bryant, Cassie's regular and fully retained jockey, had ridden him in his first serious piece of work. When Dexter jumped off the horse, having completed a good breeze-up over six furlongs, he announced delightedly to Cassie that if anything the big horse felt even stronger than ever.

'Not only that, guv'nor, but he's coming good early,' the American said over breakfast in the kitchen back at Claremore. 'We'll need to go a tad easy on him to make sure he doesn't peak too early. His first race is six weeks off yet, and the way Nightie worked this morning he'll be ready for action in less than a month.'

Having seen from the ground how easily the horse had worked and how swiftly he had quickened when Dexter had asked him to do so for no more than a dozen or so strides at the end of the canter, Cassie agreed with her jockey's suggestion that they should put the horse's first proper gallop back for at least a week and just keep him sweet until then by letting him stretch out over long, easy canters.

'As a matter of academic interest, Dex, tell me what you'd do if you were going to get at a horse nowadays,' Cassie asked from nowhere, getting up to brew some fresh coffee.

'You had some more not so idle threats, is that it, Cassie?' Dexter wondered.

'I don't know what I get or don't get, Dex. I tell Rosemary to censor the mail every day. What the eye doesn't see, you know? Not that I take much notice of that sort of thing anyway. Even so, now and then you begin to wonder at all the hate there is around.'

'Don't you bother with it, boss,' Liam piped up. 'Sure if people like yourself listened to all the crackpots who write to yous or ring you up you'd never get a horse to the races.'

'The point is, Liam, that whatever I may or may not think of the threats, finally you can't stop someone who wants to stop a horse, and that's a fact.'

'Come on – we have the best stable security system in Ireland, boss,' her head lad protested. 'Besides which there's not a person in the yard who wouldn't lay down their lives for the horse so there isn't. And for you too of course.'

'I know that, Liam, and I'm not doubting anyone's integrity or their devotion. But the point is horses get stopped, and it's not only horses from the little stables. You know as well as I do that certain Derby favourites have been got at even in recent times in spite of the most massive security precautions.'

'You wanted to know what I would do if I was going to stop a horse,' Dexter said. 'Well, I guess if I was up against a security system like the one we have here I'd try to get at him somewhere that isn't quite so well protected.'

'You mean like on the way down to the start on the course,' Mattie said, looking up briefly from his bacon and egg.

'You may not be being serious, Matt, but I sure as hell am,' Dexter said. 'It's a fact that most racecourses do have their vulnerable areas. But I wasn't just thinking racecourses. What about out there on the gallops, on the roads, in the foothills, you know what I mean? There's simply no way you can have round the clock vigilance.'

'Ah, come on, Dex, will yous?' Liam said. 'You're not seriously suggesting the enemy's going to lie in wait with blowpipes and poisoned darts, are yous?'

The rest of the lads round the huge scrubbed table where they all breakfasted every morning after work roared with laughter and began fantasizing about how best to blow a poisoned dart into the right horse in a string of a dozen trotting or cantering animals.

'OK.' Dexter grinned and then shook his head wryly. 'But the state of the art as far as stopping horses goes has been out of the darts and blowpipe stage for quite some time.'

'So what is the state of the art, Dexter?' Cassie asked. 'Do you have any particular gadget in mind?'

'You could try lasers,' Dexter suggested.

The whole table fell silent for a moment with all eyes on the American jock. Then Liam stubbed out his cigarette in a large cut glass ashtray, the very first racing trophy ever won by his late guv'nor Tyrone.

'Lasers, Dex,' Liam said. 'Like as in science fiction. Like as on the teevee?'

'No, Liam,' Dex replied with a shake of his head. 'Lasers like as in fact. Like as in real life.'

'Lasers would leave a mark, wouldn't they, Dex?' Cassie wondered, putting down her cup of coffee to stare thoughtfully at her stable jockey. 'They'd leave scar tissue, surely? And wouldn't you have to be at pretty close range to make sure of sufficient accuracy?'

'I really don't know the details, guv'nor,' Dex replied. 'What I do know is that rumour has it that if you hit the right target on a horse the scar tissue is so small you'd only find it if you were looking for it and then if you were very lucky. Same thing goes for range. The state of the art is pretty well advanced now, as I gathered when I was back home at Christmas. My dad told me about a couple of cases where these horses had mysteriously gone real sick just before their races. One of them was later found to have serious liver damage although all the regulation function tests they'd run up to the time of him getting sick had been a hundred per cent good, and the other horse had some sort of brainstorm it seems. Went berserk when they were walking him back to the barn, ran full steam into the side of the fodder lorry and broke his neck. When they cut him open they found he had this massive scarring of the brain.'

'And nothing else?' Liam asked in wonder. 'No other marks on him at all?'

'A scorch mark the size of one of those freckles of yours, Liam,' Dex replied, pointing to the back of Liam's hand. 'Right between the horse's ears in the middle of his forehead. That was the extent of the visible damage.'

'I don't see why such a thing shouldn't be possible,' Cassie said, in response to the nonplussed looks on her lads' faces. 'For the life of me I don't understand the technicalities but from what I've read in the papers and seen on the television it seems that tomorrow's world is already with us.'

'You don't really have to understand the technicalities,' Mattie said suddenly, looking up at his mother. 'Even if there's only the slightest truth in what Dex says, then what we have to do is pull our fingers out and double our security.'

'I wonder what your father would have done in these circumstances,' Cassie said the next morning as she and Mattie sat on their hacks watching the third string come towards them up the gallops.

'I wish you'd stop forever wondering that,' Mattie replied. 'He's not here any more, so he can't tell us.'

Cassie looked round at her son in surprise. Mattie was usually so patient and sympathetic whenever Cassie fell to wondering about Tyrone.

'I don't think you should have said that, Mattie. You know perfectly well that thinking about what your father would have done is just a way I have of working things out.'

'Yes I do,' Mattie agreed, without changing his tone. 'But maybe now it's time to find some other way of working things out. You can't keep relying on Dad. Not now he's dead and gone.'

'Dead but not gone,' Cassie replied. 'Your father will never be gone.'

'Fine.' Mattie sighed impatiently. 'So he'll never be gone, *fine*. Not from your memory, of course he won't. I realize that. But he can't actually *help* you at times like this. And to my way of thinking—'

'You can think what you like, Mattie Rosse,' Cassie cut in. 'But it has nothing to do with you.'

'It has everything to do with me.' Mattie swung round in his saddle to face her. 'I'm your assistant trainer. I have to help make decisions – and what I decide has to be based on how things are now. Not on what someone who's long since dead and buried might or might not have thought or done.'

'You don't set much store by past experience, then?'

'Not really, Ma. I prefer experience to be hands on.'

Cassie eyed her son steadily, then, gathering up her reins, kicked her hack on straight into a canter.

'In that case you should be watching what's happening on the gallops!' she called back over her shoulder. 'Rather than giving me uncalled for and what is more totally unqualified advice!'

Mattie sighed as he watched his mother ride off to where the string of horses was now pulling up. He knew what he had said had been out of line, but then, as he and his sister had agreed before Josephine had left to return to London, something had to be said, it had to be said soon, and someone had to say it.

Josephine had made one half-hearted attempt, on her last evening at Claremore, but after her mother had quickly and pointedly changed the subject she had chickened out, leaving her reluctant brother to do the dirty work. Mattie had protested, feeling with some justification that the advice that their mother should start trying to live her own life might come better from someone of the same sex, namely his sister, but he had lost the argument as brothers usually do when confronted by older sisters, Josephine managing to force a promise from him to say what they had both agreed should be said. Even so, as he sat miserably watching his mother pull up her horse alongside the string of horses who were now walking off the exertions of their gallops in a large circle a hundred yards below him, he knew he could have timed the giving of his advice a lot better. But then, as his sister was forever reminding him, timing and tact were not his greatest strengths.

With a deep inward groan he gathered his reins up, but just as he was preparing to ride down and join the string, the mare he was riding decided for some reason best known to herself to take a turn before setting off. As she did so, Mattie suddenly caught the glint of sunshine on something metallic in the line of hawthorn bushes which divided this particular section of the gallops off from the road. At first he thought it was just a newspaper scout stealing a quiet look through his binoculars at the line of horses working, but then as he watched he saw the sun was catching something considerably smaller than the lens of a pair of race glasses.

He was a good furlong if not more from the line of bushes but even so he thought he might still have just enough time to catch the trespasser provided whoever it was had not left his car close by. Unluckily, that was precisely what the unknown visitors had done. By the time Mattie had galloped his horse hard up to the bushes he heard the slamming of two car doors and an engine being started. Standing up in his irons to look over the hedge, he just had time to see a small mud-covered black Peugeot GTi shoot past him with two men on board, one of them he could swear holding what looked very much like a high-velocity rifle.

Carefully Cassie picked the still fresh white and buttercup yellow daffodils out of the perforated flower holder on the grave and laid them on the grass beside her before replacing them with a bunch of even fresher flowers.

'These are the first of the tulips,' she said as she began to arrange the pastel pink and pale yellow blooms.

'Remember how much you used to look forward to them flowering? While I was forever telling you that I thought they were town flowers and that I much preferred daffodils. But I know what you mean now, about your "unofficial roses" as you called them. As long as they're planted out as if they're wild, such as under the box hedges and among the trees, you're right – they look wonderful. And they look particularly wonderful this year. I planted this new variety last fall. They're called black but in fact they're more a sort of very dark crimson, and although they look great down at Claremore I thought they might be a bit sombre up here. These colours, these pale yellows and pinks, are wonderful. They're so delicate and so full of spring. And that's something else you loved so much. Coming out of winter into spring. Not that you were ever sad, Ty, not for one moment. I don't ever remember you being really sad, even when things were tough. Like when we lost the baby. I know how you hurt, but you were so strong then. However much you hurt inside you never really let it show, and I'm sure that if you had we'd never have got through it. But now the sun's shining again, my darling, the spring sun is shining through, the earth is warm again and all the horses are through their winter coats.

'And I need your help.'

Having now finished arranging the fresh flowers Cassie sat back on her heels and for a moment looked up at the blue sky above her.

'I had an argument with Mattie this morning,' she said. 'He thinks I should stop calling on you for help, or at least I should stop wondering what you would do in certain circumstances. In other words I should start living my own life. But then he doesn't understand about you and me. How could he? He's barely out of his teens, so how could he even begin to understand what you and I meant to each other? And why I still turn to you. And why you are always with me and always will be. But even so, I suppose it must be a bit upsetting for Mattie – and for Josephine, for that matter, when she's home – to hear me always going on about you in front of them, because it means they can't get

42

on with living their own lives. Not if I'm always referring and deferring to you. So perhaps if I stop doing it in front of them. If I try not to mention you except to myself it might be best. If I just keep you to myself. To my own thoughts only.' Still looking up at the sky, she closed her eyes tight. 'Will you forgive me, Ty?' she wondered in a whisper. 'Will you understand if I just talk to you in my head? When I'm not up here by your graveside, I mean. You'll understand, won't you? Because you'll know I'm not forgetting you. You know I'll never forget you. Because you know I promised you I would never forget you, not even for one second. I promised you that on the day you died. Like I promised that there will never be anyone else in my life, ever. Besides our family, I mean. Because there is no-one who could ever, ever take your place.'

Above her the first lark of spring hovered and sang, just as another lark had sung above them both one day long ago when in the very same churchyard, a few feet away from where Tyrone himself now lay, together they had buried their stillborn baby son.

It was the driest spring in Ireland for as long as anyone could remember. Not only was it dry but it was also unseasonably hot, so that by the second week in May the advance going for the spring meeting at the Curragh racecourse was announced as good to firm, although the *on dit* was that it was more firm than good.

'Sure 'twill not worry him an inch,' Liam kept saying every time the subject of the ground was brought up. 'Himself has won on the good and the good to firm, and with that well-rounded action of his he isn't the sort of horse who won't put down because it's a touch firmer than good to firm. Anyway, just look at the entries. Sure there's only the six entered including Himself, and two of those I know for certain are non-runners. If the others run, won't it only be for the place money.'

Even so Cassie worried. She had never raced The Nightingale on firm ground and had always vowed that she never would. But when it came to deciding whether or not she should run him she was outvoted from the start not only by Liam whose opinion she greatly respected but also by Mattie, who was also certain that due to the lack of any serious opposition the race would only be an exercise canter.

'If you're thinking of sending him to Epsom for the Coronation Cup, then he's going to need this race,' he argued. 'There isn't another suitable race for him before that, and even if there was, who's to say the ground will be right then? The forecast is that this warm weather's going to continue for another two weeks, and if that's the case we'll be looking at firm going everywhere.'

Finally, having learned from racing's bush telegraph that of the five other entries only the two least-considered horses were going to stand their ground, rather than disappoint his legion of fans Cassie decided to run The Nightingale. He looked a picture of health in the paddock, went to post as if he was in love, and duly won without ever coming out of a canter.

'He'd have won if he'd run backwards,' Dexter told the Claremore entourage as he hopped off the horse's back in the winner's enclosure. 'He hasn't just trained on, guv'nor, I'd say if anything this season he might even be half a stone better.'

'If that's the case, Dex,' Liam said as he threw the paddock sheet over the horse, 'then there isn't a horse born who can beat him, even if they start the day before.'

Yet instead of allaying Cassie's worries the result of the race and the very visible proof that The Nightingale had trained on into his fourth year had precisely the opposite effect.

'I don't see why,' Mattie wondered as he drove his mother back to Claremore. 'How can it possibly make you even more anxious? I thought your only worry was whether or not Nightie would train on. But you saw for yourself today that he has, so what's the big problem?'

'What I also saw were the crowds, Mattie,' Cassie replied. 'There was nearly as big a crowd to see him today at the Curragh as there was last year on Derby day. And after he had won they were all slapping him and patting him and trying to pull hairs out of his tail and mane. And what about that lunatic woman who rushed into the parade ring and tried to kiss him? That's what my problem is, Mattie. They couldn't contain the crowds.'

'I see,' Mattie said, turning off into a side road to take a short cut away from the long queues of race traffic. 'You mean if some nutter like that woman can get to him in the parade ring—'

The sentence hung in the air for a moment as they both considered the possibilities.

'It was you who said that Nightie would be at his most vulnerable on the racecourse,' Cassie said, turning to look at her handsome son and thinking as always how amazingly alike his adoptive father he had become. With his dark tightly curled hair and the insouciant set of his mouth with its long upper lip he would have little difficulty passing for the young Tyrone Rosse. 'There was a crowd around the saddling box,' she continued. 'There was a crowd round him coming into the parade ring, there was that lunatic woman in the ring itself, they practically mobbed him on his way out onto the course, and as for after the race—'

Cassie gave a great sigh and lapsed into another silence.

'Yes,' Mattie said thoughtfully after a moment. 'It's a bit of a problem all right.'

'A bit of one?' Cassie echoed. 'It's a king-size one, Mattie. We're talking mania here. The press have been writing Nightie up as if he's some sort of god come back to earth in equine form and he's totally captured the public's imagination. Not just the racing public, but people in general. You saw them today – people who I'll swear have never been on a racecourse before let alone ever seen a thoroughbred in the flesh. Fathers were perching their kids up on their shoulders to catch sight of him, little girls were screaming when they saw him the way they used to scream for the Beatles, and did you see those nuns after the race? They'd lined up all these poor sick and infirm people just outside the winner's enclosure in the hope that even just a sight of the horse would somehow alleviate the despair and the suffering. I never imagined for one moment it would be like this. Not for a moment.'

'No, neither did I,' Mattie replied carefully. 'But then the media have been winding the public up all winter about the horse, and let's face it, they have a lot to go on. There simply hasn't been a horse that's captured everyone's imagination the way Nightie has since Arkle, and I dare say there hasn't ever been a Flat racehorse – at least certainly not in living memory – to attract such a following. Following? Good God, what am I saying?' Mattie laughed and banged the steering wheel with both hands. 'Devotion is what I mean,' he said. 'From what I saw with my own eyes today – well. It was as if they worshipped the horse.'

'Mmmm,' Cassie pondered. 'Worshipped's about the size of it, Mattie. And I'm not sure I can cope with worship.'

'Do you have any choice?' Mattie glanced round at his mother as he slowed down to turn into the lane which led to Claremore's back gates. 'It's not something you can duck. It's not something any of us can. But heck – listen – you have a great team here. Everyone pulls their weight. Everyone knows what Nightie is—'

'No they don't,' Cassie interrupted. 'No-one knows. They can't even begin to know. It's hard enough to fathom out the so-called ordinary horses we all have in our yards. Because horses are something else. They always have been. Horses are something else altogether. But then when you get to horses like Nightie—'

Hearing the distant tone in his mother's voice, Mattie pulled the car onto the verge and cut the engine. For a moment they both sat looking out of the side window across the view that was Claremore, down into the valley of lush green fields, beyond to the gallops and then finally to the house itself silhouetted against the late afternoon sun.

'Did you ever read any Swift at school?' Cassie turned back to look at Mattie. 'Your father was forever reading Swift. He was a mad fan.'

'Was he? I wouldn't remember.'

Cassie noticed Mattie drop his eyes, as if he did remember

ut didn't wish to talk about it. It was only then she realized
ow deep his own hurt ran.

'OK, so if you haven't read *Gulliver's Travels* you should
lo, particularly the Voyage to the Houyhnhms. The Houy-
nhms are horses and they're the gentle, philosophical ones.
And man is an ape called a Yahoo. Society is reversed and
he horses are the higher breed and the apes are the lower.'

'And Dad believed that? Or rather that that's how it
hould be?'

'Let's say it amused him no end. By and large he greatly
preferred the company of horses. He found no difficulty in
eeing why so often they've been worshipped as gods. Did
ou see that look in Nightie's eye today as we were saddling
im up? It was as if he could see things, as if he knew things
hat we'd never know. He suddenly cocked his head as Fred
vas fixing his girth and looked out over my shoulder. I
ouldn't help turning to see what it was he was looking at.
thought it must be the crowd, or another horse going by.
But he wasn't looking at anything like that. He was looking
p into the sky.'

Erin was at hand as always to welcome Cassie back to
Claremore, greeting her as if Cassie had been away for a
month rather than a day.

'I don't want to hear a word out of you until you've
ettled in your chair in Mr Tyrone's study, the way you
always do,' she ordered, and after hurrying out of the room
he shortly hurried back in again followed by young
Padraig and bearing with her a tray holding small snacks,
ome glasses, and a bottle of red wine freshly opened which
he placed on the table by Cassie.

'Padraig – sit there on the little stool, there's a good boy,'
he said, picking the child up and placing him on a
ootstool. 'You be a good boy and eat your biscuits while
ve listen to what happened at the races today.'

The little boy smiled up at Cassie as she handed him
lown a plate of animal crackers and as he smiled Cassie
aw in him the image of his father, their former parish
priest, the handsome and intellectual Father Patrick. He

was lost somewhere now in South America, last heard of working among the poorest of the poor, trying to bring love and comfort to people in places where life was lived at its lowest ebb. He would perhaps be astonished if he could see his son for, even at an age when all children look like one parent one moment and the other the next, Padraig was the priest's living image. The smile that started in the eyes, the over-solemn expression when about to talk, even the very way he clasped his hands carefully across his stomach sometimes when he listened.

'So Himself won doing handsprings, so I hear,' Erin said, pouring out the wine.

'He did, Erin, he won handsomely,' Cassie replied, 'but then he had no real opposition.'

'Ah, but that wasn't the point of the race now, was it?' Erin corrected her. 'The whole point of the exercise was to see if Himself was as good as he was last year and if not better. And be all the accounts carried into my kitchen, and from what I gathered from my wireless, if anything Himself would seem to have improved irretrievably.'

'Let's just say he did everything that was hoped for,' Cassie replied.

'And so he should, for didn't we say enough Hail Marys this morning to last Himself the season.'

As Erin bent over to wipe some crumbs off her son's face Cassie smiled and turned to wind back the tape on the answering machine attached to her private line. There were over a dozen messages waiting to be replayed.

'Mattie said Liam said he's half a stone better than last year,' Erin said, picking Padraig up and putting him on her knee to keep him from fidgeting. 'Whatever that means, because it's double Dutch to me.'

'Now, Erin, you know as well as I do what that means,' Cassie said, pulling a notepad and pencil towards her as she sat down at the desk. 'You've been listening to the double Dutch of horse racing even longer than I have and you speak it fluently. But although it wasn't much of a contest, the horse that was third has won five half-decent races, and the second horse won the Larkspur Stakes as a two-year-old and the Great Voltigeur at three. In an ordinary year they'd both have been given a favourite's chance and Nightie beat them out of sight, so yes – he probably is half a stone better.'

'They're saying there's not a horse anywhere to beat him,' Erin said. 'And do you know what else they're saying? Or haven't you heard?'

'I can't tell you that unless you tell me what they're saying, Erin, can I?'

'Ah sure everyone who knows the horse and who knows you is saying Himself is Mr Rosse come back, that's what they say,' Erin said as if relating the most ordinary piece of gossip. 'What they all do say is that the horse is a reincarnation of none other than your late husband himself, may God rest his soul.'

By the time Cassie had regained her senses Erin was on her feet with her son swung up on her hip, smiling at her before wandering off back out of the room and down the corridor singing softly to her child, back to her kitchen and her preparations for dinner and to her good-natured bullying of poor amiable Dick, Cassie's handyman and Erin's dogsbody. As Cassie looked after her still with a look of astonishment on her face the telephone rang beside her. Before she could reach out and pick up the receiver the caller was intercepted by the answering machine which Cassie had left still operative. *A message for Mrs Rosse*, a quiet and accentless male voice said. *We were not too concerned with the horse's appearance today because a public schooling exercise at odds of twenty to one don't really count. But if you do decide to race your horse in earnest this year just be reminded that it really will be the most regrettable decision you will make in your entire life.*

49

# Three

The decision whether to run or not was taken out of Cassie's hands the next morning when Liam pulled The Nightingale out from his box and discovered the horse was slightly lame, having somehow managed to give one of his knees a good knock during the night.

'That's Epsom and the Coronation Cup out, boss,' Liam said after he'd trotted the horse up for Cassie. 'Given that he had no sort of a race yesterday we'll need a good two weeks to get him back on the road fully wound up.'

'It's probably a good thing, Liam,' Cassie admitted. 'I'd actually rather go straight for the Eclipse anyway. The Coronation Cup could well be all but another walk-over for him but it's never been one of my favourite races, while the Eclipse is in my top six. Besides, it's usually a better race than the Epsom one and I'd rather see Nightie race against good horses than hack up against animals only running for the place money. So I'm sure would all his fans.'

'Ah well – sweet are the uses of adversity, as old Tomas was forever saying,' Liam returned. 'For aren't they often the famous great blessings in disguise.'

So it was with no great regret that Cassie returned to her office to compose a press release saying that her horse had sustained a slight injury and consequently would not take his place in the line-up for the Coronation Cup. She stressed the damage was only very minor but that with the unseasonal heatwave showing no signs of abating she thought it wiser to hope for rain before the Eclipse, which had always been one of the horse's main targets.

*   *   *

The following morning a black and gold painted van drew up in front of the house and delivered two dozen of the finest orchids Cassie had ever seen.

'Who in the hell sent those?' Mattie asked his mother after Erin had brought them into the drawing room. 'I mean, for God's sake what sort of rich lunatic sends orchids in this economically dismal day and age?'

'Read the card and find out,' Cassie said, without understanding quite why she already had a sinking feeling of despair in the pit of her stomach.

Mattie took the card and read it, then looked up at his mother. 'It just says *From a Grateful Wellwisher*.'

'I thought it might say something like that,' Cassie said, taking the card and shredding it.

'Is there something you're not telling me?' Mattie wondered. 'Most women would freak out getting flowers like these.'

'Not if they were from someone who might be intent on frightening you off,' Cassie replied. 'Now call Erin back and send these flowers straight to the hospital. I certainly don't want them in the house, thank you.'

After Erin had removed the unwanted flowers, muttering that she had always thought that orchids were a very superfluous kind of a flower anyway, Mattie poured his mother and himself a cup of coffee and started to flick idly through the latest copy of *Pacemaker*.

'By frightening you off, I take it you mean frightening you off running Nightie,' he said. 'But you've always had these sorts of threats and they've never really bothered you before.'

'There's something particular about this one, Mattie,' Cassie replied. 'I don't know what exactly. Maybe it's because there's so much more at stake now. Or maybe it's the feeling you have when you own a horse like this that there's someone out there watching your every move, someone intent on making you dance to their tune.'

'The only reason someone would warn you off is because that someone stands to lose a lot of money.'

'Or make a lot, Mattie. Bookmakers aren't always the villains of the piece.'

'I don't see who else would have a good reason.'

Cassie finished her coffee and put her cup down beside her. 'Oh, I do,' she said. 'I can think of one or two.'

Leonora seemed to be the obvious choice. Cassie had every reason to believe that her old enemy, having failed to buy into The Nightingale, was now mounting yet another campaign of attrition. Leonora would reckon that if she tried to frighten Cassie out of running her horse early on in the season Cassie would see the folly of her ways, take the horse out of training and send him off to stud, even though the covering season was practically over. More important, she would then reconsider her decision about selling a major share in the horse to Leonora and her mother. It all made good sense, knowing both how determined and how malicious Leonora could be, and yet it made no sense at all. For even should she succeed in this, it still would not guarantee that her wretched mother would be able to buy into The Nightingale syndicate. But then that to Cassie was Leonora all over, illogical, reckless and more than anything else determined not to be outdone.

Particularly since what Leonora wanted Leonora always tried her utmost to get, and if she didn't achieve all her aims she then ran a high-profile spoiling campaign. That was how it had been in the battle over Tyrone. When her pretence at an *affaire* between herself and Tyrone had blown up in her face, she had attempted a *coup de grâce* by endeavouring to make out that Mattie was Tyrone's illegitimate son.

So although she had given up nicotine and alcohol the chances of Leonora's undergoing a really serious character reformation were to Cassie's way of thinking extremely slim. Moreover, given Leonora's new husband's wealth, let alone the continual gifts of money her mother bestowed on her, it would be well within her powers to organize such an operation. Not that a couple of telephone calls and a few expensive blooms amounted to much of a strategy, but then they were still only in the early stages of what Cassie imagined might well be one of her arch-rival's more grandiose schemes. Better than anybody she knew there were no limits to Leonora's Machiavellian ambitions once she had set her mind on something.

Having decided more for her own convenience than anything else that Leonora was behind the warnings not to run The Nightingale, Cassie decided to ignore them and continue with her horse's four-year-old career just as planned. It was not that she took the threats lightly, because she knew from the past that once Leonora was thwarted she was capable of doing anything, but thinking she knew who was behind the intimidation somehow seemed to lessen the danger. Whatever happened she was determined that The Nightingale should be allowed to realize his full potential as a four-year-old in the hope that by the end of the season his achievements would confirm the ever-growing belief that this was the greatest horse of the century, if not of all time.

None the less Cassie was not fool enough to disregard the threats altogether, and hardly were the unwanted orchids exiled from her house than she set about reviewing all the existing security arrangements before summoning Liam, Mattie and Dexter to her office to listen to any further suggestions they might have for improvement.

With good reason, Claremore was considered to be among the best-protected raceyards in Europe, and while it had cost Cassie a small fortune she considered it money well spent even if the lads had renamed it Fort Claremore. The main yard was safely self-enclosed behind a perimeter wall topped with razor wire, gated with twelve-foot solid oak doors which were kept permanently shut once the day's exercise programmes were over, and monitored twenty-four hours a day by closed circuit television cameras. There were only two other entrances to the yard, one used by the lads to come and go between work and their hostel and another which gave direct access only to the muck heap, also enclosed within the perimeter walls so that the muck could only be taken away by a tractor and trailer coming in through the main gates and along the roadway which ran between the back of the boxes and the outside walls. Both these entrances were monitored day and night by security guards, as were the main doors into the yard and the gates into Claremore itself. The boundaries of the estate were patrolled by two more guards with four dogs, the men having been instructed never to follow the same daily routine nor cover the same area of ground. Within the grounds there were more closed circuit cameras which recorded the ingress of every visitor who arrived on wheels, horseback or foot, and at night the entire stable complex was safeguarded by a highly sophisticated alarm system which was triggered by the body heat of any incomer who got within fifty feet of a complex of concealed magic eyes.

'I have an idea,' Mattie said to open the meeting. 'It springs out of what we were talking about before, namely that horses are at their most vulnerable when they leave the yard for exercise. Now although it's all but impossible – or so we think – to get at them while they're being ridden, it isn't *altogether* impossible. I'm not saying that the bushes are going to be crawling with villains armed with state of the art lasers or some such weaponry, but if you remember I did see a couple of fellas lurking at the top of the home gallops only last week and it looked as though they were armed with some sort of gun. And since we don't know exactly what sorts of tricks these guys can get up to nowadays, what I suggest is this. We exercise the horses as they always have been exercised, with this difference. Every horse wears exercise hoods, sheets and bandages so that no-one can recognize which horse is which by any distinguishing marks. All the lads wear the same sort of lightweight black top and the same-coloured pompoms on their helmets. We don't want anyone knowing who is who and from a distance this way there'll be no telling. Secondly, move the lads around from horse to horse much as we have been doing, except don't let anyone know what he's going to ride in advance.'

'Including me?' Dexter wondered with a grin.

'You're the fly in the ointment, Dex, because everyone in the know knows you're the only bloke who rides

Nightie,' Mattie replied. 'Which brings me to my next point. If they're going to be shooting at anyone, so to speak, it's going to be The Nightingale. So he has to be the most secure horse in the yard and in the string. Therefore he can't be allowed to walk up to the gallops any more. We're going to have to box him up.'

'Two objections to that, Mattie,' Cassie said, tapping her pencil on the table. 'One – the horse needs to be walked, and two – as soon as he's seen getting out of the box he can be targeted. Anyone watching will know at once which horse is Nightie.'

'I've thought this one through, believe it or not,' Mattie said. 'First, at this stage of the season any walking the horse needs can be done on the horsewalker or inside the perimeter walls if needs be. Second, when we unbox him on the gallops we screen him from view with all the other horses. Dex will also be riding in the same anonymous black anorak and hat, so as soon as he's up and among the other animals it'll be impossible to spot which one he is.'

'We don't have that many black horses,' Dexter said. 'How many, Cassie?'

'Five including Nightie, but three of them are really only very dark bays. They're not quite as black as Nightie and none of them are quite his size.'

'That doesn't matter,' Mattie said confidently. 'There's no way anyone whatever they're armed with can get at horses on the move. Not with any degree of precision. I mean, suppose they *were* using some advanced form of laser, OK? Which I don't believe for one moment they are. But just suppose they were. To penetrate tissue accurately you'd need to line up the sight on the right target and hope that the said target will stand still for at least – shall we say five seconds? So we keep the horses on the move the whole time. Walking, trotting, cantering, galloping, and at all times we keep Nightie covered up. Particularly getting him in and out of the horsebox.'

'I don't really think this is necessary,' Cassie said with a sigh.

'It's necessary, believe me,' Mattie returned. 'Every single bit of it.'

'Matt's right,' Dexter said with a nod. 'We have to take every possible precaution. Look, whoever's making these threats might not even being doing it for money, you know. It might be someone really sick. Like the nut who shot John Lennon. Someone who sees a chance for fame whatever the price.'

'That changes it, doesn't it?' Mattie asked, seeking the look on his mother's face.

'I guess it does,' Cassie agreed, with a look at Dexter. 'I hadn't considered that possibility. But I guess a horse of Nightie's growing fame—'

'You bet,' Dexter said. 'No-one's ever assassinated a world-famous horse before. And if some crazyhead did manage it, he'd be guaranteed more than his allotted fifteen minutes of fame.'

So security at Claremore was tightened up even more after the review, in line with Mattie's and Dexter's recommendations. As a result during the run-up to the Eclipse Stakes at Sandown Park in England there were no alarms or excursions, nor did the big horse miss the anticipated week's work subsequent to the bang he had sustained in his box, since the setback was nowhere near as serious as had been first thought. In fact The Nightingale was out of his box and perfectly sound after only three days, trotting after five, and had his first good canter at the end of the following week. In his first two years as a racehorse he had been inclined to be stuffy early on in his work, which was why Cassie liked to have as much time as possible in which to get him ready, yet it was obvious from the way the horse quickened at the end of seven furlongs up the all-weather gallop when Cassie worked him at the start of the week of the big race that those days were long gone and that rather than set The Nightingale back, the three days' enforced box rest had probably done him the power of good.

'If anything he seems even more relaxed than ever, Dex,' she said to her jockey after they had loaded the animal back in the horsebox before returning to the yard. 'Is that how he felt to you?'

'He's just brilliant, Cassie,' Dexter replied with a happy smile. 'If anything he's even more laid back this year, with the consequence that he doesn't waste a drop of gas. You just press the button and he goes. God help the opposition's all I say!'

'I haven't run through all the form of the others yet, at least not closely,' Cassie said, climbing up into the cab of the horsebox beside him. 'I know there were twelve in at the forfeit stage, and that Nightie, Hokey Cokey, Whizz who ran second to Nightie in the Derby and the French horses Mot Cambron and Esplanade are the only four-year-olds.'

'Mot Cambron I'd say is the real danger,' Dexter replied, picking up the day's edition of the *Sporting Life* from the seat beside him. 'We have Esplanade well beaten on Arc form, but Mot Cambron who missed the Arc broke the track record for a mile and two at Chantilly in his first run this season. Beat a pretty useful field, too, and he hasn't been beaten yet. His trainer Pierre Duchamps thinks he has a very real chance.'

'Mot Chambron's a front runner, right?'

'So far he's made all in each of his races. And he always finds some at the end as well, so he's not just an out and out galloper.'

'Don't let him out of your sights, then.'

'I don't intend to. We can't discount Whizz altogether either. I saw him when he trotted up in the GalaPrint Stakes at Kempton two weeks ago and he's altogether bigger and much stronger than he was at Epsom. It'll be a proper race, all right. Now let's see what they have to say about it in the *Life*. There's a preview of the race on page four.'

'There's also some news on the front page,' Cassie said, noticing one of the lead stories and bending the page so that she could read it. 'It says Mot Cambron has been sold. "Record Price for Horse in Training".'

Dexter folded the paper back so that they could both read the item on the front page. Which they did, in silence.

'Jeez,' Dexter whispered, just the way he had when Cassie had first met him as a boy of sixteen. 'Will she stop at nothing to try to get even?'

'It seems not,' Cassie said with a heartfelt sigh, as they both sat studying the large colour photograph of Leonora Lovett Andrew holding the bridle of her latest purchase.

Josephine had insisted that the family all meet in London for lunch at the Dorchester on the day before the race, even though she well knew how much her mother liked to spend the time alone in her hotel on such occasions.

'There really is a good reason, I promise,' she had told Cassie on the telephone, barely able to keep the excitement out of her voice. 'I really wouldn't bother you otherwise, but we won't have a chance to talk on the day of the race itself, and then afterwards when Nightie has won—'

'If Nightie has won—' Cassie interrupted.

'When Nightie has duly trotted up we won't have time then either. I mean not just the three of us. So let's just have a quiet lunch somewhere because I really do have to see you.'

'Of course I'll meet you for lunch,' Cassie agreed. 'But even so, sweetheart, surely you can give me some idea of what it is now? You know me and suspense. I can't bear it.'

'I'd much rather tell you face to face,' Josephine replied. 'You know what the phone's like. Some things just can't be said on the phone.'

'Since you said she sounded excited, maybe she's landed the part of a lifetime,' Mattie suggested on the flight over. 'Perhaps Tinseltown has finally called.'

'That she would have told me on the telephone, Mattie,' Cassie replied. 'I think it's a man. I think Josephine's fallen in love.'

'God, not with an actor, I *hope*. I don't mind my sister acting but I do not want some sort of luvvie as a brother-in-law, thank you.'

'It doesn't necessarily have to be wedding bells. I just said your sister has probably fallen in love.'

'God,' Mattie sighed theatrically. 'If you'd been summoned to have lunch every time my dippy sister had fallen in love you would be in serious trouble with your figure.'

'You don't say.' Cassie smiled but then turned away to look out of the aircraft window at the Irish Sea sparkling far below them. Even though Josephine was now in her mid-twenties, Cassie had never given any real thought to the prospect of her daughter's getting married. She seemed so wedded to her career and so happy being footloose and fancy free that somehow Cassie had imagined that was the state in which her daughter would happily remain. Whenever she was home and she was sitting in the kitchen talking to Cassie as Cassie helped Erin prepare a special supper in her honour the talk had always been about her acting career, and how impossible it would be really to settle down with anyone while she was still making her way. It would not be fair on either partner, on the man because Josephine might well be constantly away filming or on tour, or on her because she might feel guilty about pursuing a career which took her away from home. As far as the theatre went, she had decided she would give it until she was thirty and if she had not made it by then she would, as she put it, consider any halfway decent proposal that then came her way which according to her was what most of her friends were doing. None of them was getting married young. With people living to a greater age there seemed no longer to be the need to start thinking about marriage and raising a family the moment a girl stopped being a teenager.

But then out of the blue had come this summons to lunch.

*All I can hope*, Cassie thought to herself as the sea below them gave way to the mountains of North Wales, *is that he is just a little like Tyrone.*

Mark Carter-James was nothing like Tyrone. Whereas Tyrone had been tall, dark-haired, blue-eyed and well built, this young man was small and as thin as a marathon runner with straw blond hair and oddly enough for someone with his hair colour, bright green, catlike eyes. Josephine, who took after her father rather than her mother, was tall and willowy, five foot eight inches compared to Mark Carter-James' five foot six, yet what he lacked in height he made up for in good looks, having a *retroussé* nose, high cheek bones and a double line of thick dark blond eyelashes which would have been the envy of most female fashion models. He was also impeccably dressed in an expensive hand-tailored charcoal grey suit and what looked also like handmade shirt and shoes, and his manners were as polished as his appearance. As soon as she set eyes on him and without beginning to know why, Cassie hated him.

'Please forgive the intrusion on what I understand was to be a family affair, Mrs Rosse,' he said after being introduced to Cassie by Josephine, 'but I was afraid this might be my only real chance of meeting you. I simply had to take this opportunity of coming to say how very much I admire you for what you have done. To have owned The Nightingale would be exciting enough, but to have not only trained him to his remarkable victories but actually bred him as well smacks of pure genius.'

'More of good fortune, I'd say,' Cassie countered with a polite smile.

'Oh, I don't think so,' Mark replied, also smiling. 'On the contrary.'

'Am I right in assuming that Robert Carter-James is your father?' Cassie wondered. 'Or at least that I have your family right?'

'Right first time, Mrs Rosse,' Mark agreed, blinking slowly as he smiled. 'The Mad Major is indeed my father, but now really my intrusion on this occasion simply will not do. Having achieved my ambition – to meet Josephine's illustrious mother – I really should be toddling along.'

'Can't you stay to lunch?' Josephine asked him. 'You wouldn't mind if Mark stayed to lunch, would you, Mums? I know I should have let you know in advance, but that would have sort of spoiled it somehow.'

'Of course Mark must stay to lunch,' Cassie said, watching the eye contact between her daughter and the angelic-looking young man. 'If he is able to, he is more than welcome.'

'Well, I'd *love* to, Mrs Rosse,' Mark replied. 'And in all fairness to Josephine, she didn't actually know I was going to *be* in London today. But of course, I should *love* to stay to lunch. Thank you.'

'Then that's that,' Cassie said. 'Mattie – go tell Maurice we shall now be four for lunch and not three, would you?'

From the look in Mattie's eyes as he ambled off to find the maître d' it was obvious to Cassie that her son was as unimpressed with Mark Carter-James as she was.

Not that either of them could find any good reason to have taken such an obvious dislike to Josephine's latest suitor. Mark Carter-James did nothing wrong over lunch. He was an excellent conversationalist as well as beautifully mannered, and Josephine – to whom he seemed to show just the right amount of teasing affection – was obviously besotted with him. Even his social credentials fitted perfectly, since he was the eldest son of one of the most prominent English racehorse owners and an accomplished amateur jockey himself. Furthermore from his conversation with Josephine it was obvious that he was no Newmarket philistine, for he seemed to take as great an interest in the theatre as he did in racing and bloodstock.

But above all it was The Nightingale and his triumphs which seemed to occupy him most. More precisely, it was Cassie's achievements to which he kept returning at every permissible opportunity.

'You're very flattering, Mark,' Cassie said at one point. 'But I doubt whether your family shares your admiration of my achievement. Certainly not your father. Your father has said in public on many occasions that he thinks women have no place professionally on a racecourse.'

'As anyone who knows him will tell you, you really shouldn't take my father seriously, Mrs Rosse,' Mark replied with a smile. 'A lot of the time when he makes such utterances he has his tongue firmly in his cheek. He rather enjoys, as they say, winding people up.'

'I never *quite* get the impression he's doing that when he talks about keeping women out of the Jockey Club.'

'That is because my father loves women, Mrs Rosse, but doesn't think much of the Jockey Club. Perhaps that explains it?'

Cassie smiled. 'That's very neat. Even so I don't quite buy it.'

'He can be most appallingly tactless on occasions, I do admit. And he has banged on an awful lot about women trainers which I suppose is a generation thing really. I don't actually think he was pointing his gun at you, but if he has ever said anything to upset you then may I apologize on his behalf? Having seen what you have achieved with The Nightingale I doubt very much if he would say the same things now.'

'Of course he wouldn't, Mark,' Josephine said quickly, putting a hand on his. 'The moment your father meets my mother he'll fall madly in love with her. Everyone does.'

'Of course he will,' Mark agreed, crinkling his eyes as he smiled.

'I have already met Mark's father,' Cassie reminded her daughter.

'I meant again,' Josephine replied, smiling shyly.

'Am I likely to do that in the near future?'

'You'd better ask Mark that, Mums.'

As if to try to put off the moment he knew was coming, Mattie signalled to the wine waiter and asked him to bring another bottle. But Mark simply smiled patiently and waited his moment.

'I'm not sure this is the time or even the place, Mrs Rosse,' he said. 'But then as far as your daughter goes perhaps the only time and the only place would be a moonlit midnight at the Taj Mahal. As you may well have guessed by now, Josephine and I would like to get married.'

'I hadn't *quite* guessed,' Cassie said. 'But I think maybe that was the way I was thinking.'

'I'm sure you were, Mrs Rosse,' Mark agreed. 'But the point is that although Josephine is over eighteen years of age—' Mark continued.

'Just,' Mattie added with a teasing smile at his sister.

'Absolutely,' Mark laughed, leaning back and running his fingers through his hair. 'But what I was going on to say was while we do not actually have to seek your formal permission, we would none the less of course very much like to have your blessing.'

'Supposing you don't get it?' Mattie suddenly asked bluntly. Then, catching his sister's hurt look, he added rather lamely, 'Joke.'

'Of course,' Mark said. 'But even if it wasn't, Mattie, and even if horror of horrors your mother did *not* approve of me, it wouldn't actually alter our intentions. Maybe that answers your question.'

'Sure,' Mattie said more to himself than anyone, before taking a good draught of wine. 'It certainly does.'

As the waiter poured them all some more wine and Josephine took the opportunity of this distraction to whisper something to Mark, Cassie glanced across at her son to find a pair of dark eyes glaring back directly at her.

'Now then, Mark,' Cassie said, having frowned back at her son in warning for him not to go any further. 'I don't know how much you know or don't know about me, but as far as my daughter is concerned, and my son for that matter, if they have made their minds up about something then I try not to stand in their way.'

'Good,' Mark said without discernible interest. 'Good.'

'We talk about it, of course, but then the three of us always talk everything out, always have done. So while of course technically you don't need my approval if you are both determined on getting married anyway—'

'Forgive me for interrupting you,' Mark said, looking suddenly serious. 'But in hindsight I can't have put that very well. Look, I would absolutely hate it if you thought I meant that if you withheld your approval we would simply go ahead and marry come what may, because that is not what I meant at all. What I was trying to say was that even if you disapproved of our marrying we would still wish to get married simply because Josephine and I are *very much* in love. What I should have added was that knowing how much your daughter both loves and respects you, Mrs Rosse, I would not want her to marry me until she has won your blessing.'

'Thank you, that's very gallant,' Cassie replied, still wondering why she doubted his sincerity. 'I appreciate that. Just as I hope you appreciate that I would like some time alone with my daughter to catch up on events. We haven't seen each other since Christmas, you see, and well you know what mothers are.'

'And daughters,' Mattie added, looking round at his sister.

'Alas, I don't have any sisters,' Mark said, raising both his eyebrows and putting the flat of both hands on the table. 'My parents got divorced when I was five, after my younger brother was born, but that doesn't stop me understanding that you both will obviously want to talk. And I—' he added, glancing at his gold Rolex, 'I must go, if you will excuse me. I have an appointment out of town and you know what the traffic is like on Friday. Thank you so much for a perfectly delicious lunch and the chance of meeting you and your son – and I shall look forward to seeing you all tomorrow at Sandown Park.'

'I'll come with you to the door,' Josephine said, getting up as Mark did and taking his arm as they walked out of the dining room. Cassie and Mattie watched them go before Mattie turned back with ill-concealed disgust.

'Jeez,' Mattie said hopelessly. 'What has she got herself into now?'

'Obviously you find Mr Carter-James wanting.' Cassie signalled the waiter for some more coffee. 'He seems perfectly charming and very well mannered.'

'If you ask me he's got murderer's eyes,' Mattie growled. 'And he's just so *smooth*. You didn't really like him, did you?'

'We don't really know anything about him,' Cassie said, allowing the waiter to pour her some more coffee.

'You think Jo does? She can only just have met him. Otherwise I would have heard. I'm going to have to have a serious talk with my sister.'

'Easy does it, Mattie. I mean it,' Cassie said, trying to defuse the moment. 'First impressions aren't always the best. Maybe beneath all those perfect manners the problem was the young man was really feeling very nervous.'

'That guy was de-nerved at birth, believe me. What *does* Jo think she's *doing*?'

'Let's ask her when she comes back,' Cassie suggested, putting Mattie's reaction down to fraternal possessiveness. 'In the meantime, let's go through the race.'

While they waited for Josephine to rejoin them, the two of them discussed the various merits and demerits of the eleven horses which had stood their ground against The Nightingale. Both were glad that for once their horse had not frightened off all the opposition and that therefore this particular running of the Eclipse had every chance of living up to its illustrious reputation. Mattie thought that perhaps the fact The Nightingale had only had one not very strenuous run so far might have encouraged the other owners and trainers to take their chances against him, an opinion with which Cassie entirely agreed, adding that the rumour circulating that the knock their horse had sustained had actually set him further back in his work than Cassie had claimed had also given hope to the opposition.

'You sure we were right to leave his arrival until tomorrow morning?' Mattie wondered. 'Nightie's not always been the best of travellers.'

'That was really only at the beginning of his career,' Cassie replied. 'Travelling doesn't get to him at all now, and as far as security goes we were all agreed that the longer he is at Claremore the safer he will be.'

'And you really have had no more threats.'

'Not one. Touch wood.'

By the time Josephine appeared back in the dining room they were both still of the opinion that on form the only real threat lay from Leonora's horse Mot Cambron, although Mattie had been at pains to point out the stable was also running a mare called Tootsuite as a pacemaker.

'And I'll bet you they're doing it for a good reason,' Mattie said as Josephine made her way across to their table.

'Mot Cambron is a front runner, and if the mare's in season, which at this time of the year there's every chance she will be, knowing how The Nightingale likes to hang out at the back of the field all they have to do is make sure the mare stays just in front of him.'

'Like everyone said the French did when they contrived to get Santa Claus beaten in the King George VI,' Cassie mused. 'In that case we might well have to change our tactics tomorrow.'

Mattie got up to pull his sister's chair back out for her.

'Thanks,' Josephine said, before sitting down to regard them both with a widening smile. 'Well? So what do you *think*?'

'He seems to have swept you off your feet,' Cassie told her daughter after lunch when they were alone in Cassie's suite high above Park Lane.

'So what's so terrible about that?' Josephine wondered in return. 'After all, isn't that what Dad did with you?'

'I didn't say I'd marry him right away.'

'Fine – so I did. So what? I'm in love. I've really never been in love like this, really. I'm crazy about Mark and he's crazy for me, so it's only natural to want to get married, isn't it?'

'Maybe,' Cassie replied. 'It's just that you seem to be in a bit of a hurry, that's all. Don't you think you might need a little more time? If rather than rushing things you both took your time you don't have anything to lose. If you feel the same about each other say in six months or even a year—'

'I never thought I'd hear you talk like that,' Josephine sighed, moving away from her on the sofa and crossing her long shapely legs. 'You of all people.'

'What do you mean – me of all people?'

'You're talking straight from the dictionary of clichés.'

'OK, Jose, just try to see it from my point of view. From a mother's point of view, corny though we mothers all may be. We've always been very close, you and I. I really love being part of your life and you being such a part of mine.

And because we're so close all I'm doing is trying to point out to you in all honesty what I feel. Sweetheart – I have only just met the man you think you might marry—'

'The man I am *going* to marry—'

'But why did you spring it on me like this? Like a bolt out of the blue? You could have called me – you always call me about everything. But this time, not a word. Why?'

'I wanted it to be a surprise.'

'You sure as hell succeeded.'

'Look,' Josephine sighed defensively. 'I was worried you wouldn't like him in advance because of his father.'

'Nobody I know likes his father.'

'Mark isn't his father!'

'Mark is the son of his father – and that is something you really have to consider. Your father used to say that a young man should always try to meet the mother of the girl he wants to marry to see what the girl may grow into, and I guess the same goes for young women when they're thinking of getting married. The impression Major Carter-James gives to everyone is that he's not quite a gentleman, shall we say.'

'Mark is not his *father*,' Josephine repeated. 'Come on – you saw for yourself how thoughtful and kind he is. What his father's like really is neither here nor there.'

'As I said, it's just something you should take into account. And what does Mark do for a living? I take it he has got a job.'

Josephine got up from the sofa. 'I don't believe this,' she said. 'I just don't believe what I'm hearing. Of course Mark has a job. He is not after my *money*! Mark has a very good job as a bloodstock agent as it happens and earns good money so you can stop worrying on that particular score, OK?'

'I don't see why. Good money as opposed to what you're worth? Whether you like it or not, Josephine, you're quite a catch.'

'Really? Dad was a bit of a catch too, wasn't he?'

'I didn't even know what your father *did* till after I married him. Until we got on the plane back to Ireland.'

'You see? And you're about to tell me I don't really know Mark well enough to know that I want to marry him.'

'I was actually going to ask you how you met, not when,' Cassie replied, wrongfooted.

'Mark came with a party to see the play, came round backstage afterwards and asked me out to dinner.'

'Yes, but that can only have been quite recently, surely? The play only opened a couple of weeks ago.'

'So?'

'So when did Mark come and see it? Was it on the first night or something?'

'No.'

'So when exactly, Jo?'

'If you really want to know he came to the play last Friday.'

Mattie nearly went through the roof on his return to the hotel when Cassie brought him up to date with events. 'She's making a fool of herself,' he growled.

'We have to be a little careful here, Mattie. Jo's not some immature teenager. She's a grown-up woman now with a mind of her own.'

'And a great deal of bread in the bank, notionally at least,' Mattie returned. 'I rang a couple of chums this afternoon and asked a few questions about Mr Mark Carter-James. Nobody had a good word to say about him.'

'Did anyone have a bad word to say about him?'

'Well – no. Not specifically. The point is, Ma, he is just not *liked*.'

'By how many people is he just not liked, Mattie?'

'You mean how many people did I ring.' Mattie leaned back in his chair and sighed. 'Enough, OK? I spoke to a couple of people who had been at Eton with him and they told me everyone loathed him. I rang another couple of chums in bloodstock – and as for being a successful bloodstock agent? The firm he works for hardly sees him and they reckon he won't hold his place there very much longer. Apparently he spent most of his time at the racetrack.'

Cassie thought for a moment, then shook her head. 'As I said, Mattie, Jo's a grown woman.'

'Fine – well, if you're not going to say something, then I will,' Mattie replied.

'It's really not your place to say anything,' Cassie warned him. 'Besides, you know your sister better than that. Jo's pretty damn' stubborn at the best of times. She always has been. When she was a little girl I soon discovered the best and only way of dealing with her was not to disapprove directly of anything she wanted to do, for the more I disapproved the more determined Jo was to defy me. I always had to come at her from left field, letting her think that the decision we'd arrived at was of her making, when in fact ninety-nine per cent of the time the opposite was true. And as far as I can make out, if ever there seemed to be a time for not taking on Josephine face to face this has to be it. One word of disapproval from anyone and she'll marry Mark the next minute.'

'You may be right,' Mattie agreed thoughtfully.

'I am right,' Cassie corrected him. 'And you know it.'

'OK – but now let's hear what you thought about Mark. Did you like him or didn't you?'

'I told you – as far as first impressions go, I thought he was well mannered and perfectly presentable.'

'Whoa . . .' Mattie laughed ironically. 'Talk about damning with faint praise. What you're saying is you really didn't take to him.'

'There wasn't any good reason why I shouldn't. He behaved impeccably. He wasn't rude, he didn't get drunk or anything.'

'Yet the moment he came into the room, it was fingers down the throat time. I saw you.'

'You don't have to be *quite* so graphic, Mattie,' Cassie sighed. 'At the end of the famous day I guess what I thought was maybe he seemed a little *too* good to be true. You know, sort of altogether too plausible. And when I see plausible I hear your father, I'm afraid. Tyrone always used to say you only need to be plausible if you have something to hide.'

Since as far as the big race went their nerves were beginning to get the better of them both, they had dinner together in Cassie's suite. By the time they had read up all the form yet again and all the printed forecasts for the coming contest they had put to the side for the moment any further thoughts about Josephine's alliance, preferring instead to hypothesize as to how the race might be run, even though as Mattie ruefully remarked at one point it was about as idle a speculation to make as was the possible outcome of a marriage between Josephine and Mark Carter-James.

'If ifs and ans,' Mattie sighed as they were closing up their copies of *Timeform* and *Horses in Training*. 'And you don't have to tell me what Dad always said about supposition because it's practically engraved on my heart.'

'With the help of an *if*—' Cassie began.

'I said I know, Ma, I know,' Mattie interrupted, getting to his feet and stretching. 'With the help of an *if* you might put Ireland into a bottle.'

Cassie smiled at her handsome son and then rose to kiss him good night. As she did so there was a knock on the main door.

'Who is it?' Cassie called after they both had made their way into the lobby. No-one answered, despite a second query, prompting Mattie to look through the spyhole.

'There's no-one there,' he said. 'At least not as far as I can see.'

'I definitely heard a knock,' Cassie said.

'So did I,' Mattie agreed, having another careful look through the optic set in the door. 'But there still isn't anyone there – except – hold on. There isn't anybody, but there definitely is some thing.'

'What?'

'I don't know. It's pushed right up against the door.'

Putting the door on its chain, Mattie eased it open.

'Well?' Cassie asked him from behind.

'Jeez,' Mattie said, once he had opened the door fully. 'Jeez, that is just so *sick*.'

'What is?' Cassie asked again, with increasing

impatience, easing her son to one side so that she could get a clear look at what had been delivered to her suite.

It was a brand new wheelchair.

'Forget it,' Cassie said finally, after they had both stared at it for several seconds. 'I'll have Reception come and remove it.'

There was a card envelope attached to one of the wheelchair's arms by a string tie. Cassie ripped it off before she marched back into her suite to telephone the reception desk, tearing the card open as she did so.

'I know just what this is going to say, so I don't know why I'm bothering,' she announced.

But Cassie was wrong. The card did not contain a personal message to her to heed the previous warnings she had received. What the card said was

*This gift comes to you not for yourself*
*But for your handsome son.*

Unfortunately, before she could pretend otherwise, Mattie had taken it from her hand.

'First thing tomorrow I shall withdraw the horse,' Cassie said as she poured them both a large drink.

'No way,' Mattie countered, accepting his drink. 'You withdraw the horse and you know what you'll be doing. Giving in to the bastards.'

'It's only a horse race, Mattie,' Cassie said, walking over to stare out of her balcony windows at the city lights. 'You're much more important to me. Infinitely so.'

'Look,' Mattie said, coming to stand beside her. 'Listen to me. If you don't run Nightie they will have won. They've been trying to scare you off and if you withdraw the horse they will have scared you off, and scaring you off means they can scare anyone off. So let's look at this sensibly, with a cool eye and a clear head. We know the horse is OK. They haven't got at the horse—'

'As far as we know they haven't—' Cassie chipped in.

'If they had, they wouldn't have bothered with the wheelchair routine. This is eleventh hour stuff, that's all. They're getting desperate.'

'Desperate enough maybe to try to hurt you,' Cassie replied.

'If you're worried about me, guv'nor—'

'Of course I'm worried about you. You're my son.'

'So don't. I'll organize some muscle for tomorrow. I know plenty of guys who'll come and look hard, OK? And as long as I don't go walking down any dark alleys—'

'And what about after the race?' Cassie supposed. 'You can't walk round with a pack of bodyguards for the rest of your days.'

'Oh, that's not how it goes, Ma!' Mattie flopped down into one of the armchairs, setting his drink on the table before him. 'After the race it'll all be over. The horse will either have won or lost and that will conclude the entertainment. If Nightie wins the damage will have been done, and if he loses putting me in a wheelchair isn't going to change things. So there's nothing to be gained in pulling the horse out of the race. Think who you'll be letting down. Not just the tens of millions of people who want to see him race, but people who have never seen him race before and probably right at this very minute are dreaming about what tomorrow's going to bring. So no – you can't take him out of the race because *I've* been threatened rather than you. A threat is a threat is a threat, and since you've always said you're not going to be bullied whatever they try to throw at you, you have to stick by what you said. You're going to stand your ground and so is the horse.'

'I don't know,' Cassie said uncertainly. 'I really don't know.'

'OK,' Mattie sighed before getting back out of his chair and going to his mother, turning her round by the shoulders so that they were looking each other in the eye. 'Try this on for size, then. In the same situation, what do you reckon Dad would have done?'

# *Four*

By the time The Nightingale was being walked round the pre-parade ring there was still an apparently endless queue of cars making their way slowly up the middle of Sandown Park to the enclosures. The grandstands were already packed to bursting as were Tattersalls and the Silver Ring and had been so for a good hour before the first race, so much so that it was hard to believe any more people could be packed in or onto the course. Moreover the weather which was glorious had encouraged even more people to turn out than had been anticipated with the result that the executive had run out of racecards and the bars of anything remotely resembling a cold drink long before the runners and riders were announced for the Eclipse Stakes, a contest which had been billed as the Race of a Lifetime with The Nightingale being opposed by the winners of the French, German and Italian derbies, and eight other horses which between them had won prize money of well over one and a half million pounds. Nor, according to the pundits, was the race the open and shut affair it had once seemed, due exactly as Cassie and Mattie had predicted to the rumours which were circulating concerning the well-being of the Claremore horse. With the exception of the racing correspondent of *The Times*, the rest of the experts were suggesting there was a much harder race in store for the wonder horse than had been forecast, three of them even going as far as to tip Mot Cambron to beat The Nightingale.

For the Claremore entourage this only added to the excitement and failed to dent the unshakeable confidence they all had in their horse. Even Cassie had recovered her inner composure as well as her sense of keen anticipation, thanks in the main part to her son's grit and determination, so much so that she changed her mind and allowed herself to be interviewed before the big race.

'First I have to ask you about the well-being of your horse, Mrs Rosse,' the interviewer asked. 'I know you wouldn't bring him here unless he was one hundred per cent, but since there are still some Doubting Thomases about the place maybe we can silence the rumours by hearing it if not from the horse's mouth itself then the next best thing, from the trainer's.'

'The Nightingale is right on song, John,' Cassie replied. 'As everyone knows he sustained a slight knock one night in his box but it was such a minor bump he really didn't miss a day's work that would matter.'

'So your confidence is undiminished, obviously.'

'If he's beaten there won't be any excuses, I promise.'

'I had a look at him earlier and I have to say he looks a picture. Now to turn to something much more serious—'

'Can we stop the tape here, please?' Cassie requested, turning away from the camera. 'Forgive me, but I wasn't prepared for this. I really would rather not talk about the threats we've been getting, if that's the way you were headed.'

'Well, yes it was, as a matter of fact,' the interviewer agreed. 'Look, I'm sorry, Cassie, perhaps I should have mentioned this to you before we started. It's just that it seems to be common knowledge. After all, that business with the wheelchair was all over the tabloids this morning.'

'Was it?' Cassie wondered with a frown, wondering who had leaked the story. 'I haven't looked at the papers today.'

'If you'd rather not talk about it, I quite understand,' her interviewer said.

'I think you should talk about it,' Mattie said, having come over to his mother's side during the break. 'Think what it'll do for racing. And for all the people who want a Tote monopoly—'

'I'd rather not get involved in that sort of controversy,' Cassie cut in. 'Particularly since we don't know who's behind the threats. I'd rather not go on record accusing a whole body of people most of whom might well be innocent.'

'Listen.' Mattie took her arm and walked her even further away from the waiting cameras. 'You have to say something. It's perfectly obvious who's trying to stop you.'

'No it isn't. It isn't right to jump to such conclusions. So do what you're always telling *me* to do – get real. You've seen the odds. Nightie's four to one *on*. No-one's going to be carrying sacks full of money out of the ring this afternoon at those odds.'

'He's only three to one on in some places. Those are backable odds for the serious player, three grand on to win one. Thirty to win ten. Then there are long-standing doubles and trebles on the horse, and some people have ante-post tickets at odds against, some as long as two to one and seven to four, for Nightie to go through the season unbeaten in all his nominated races. You can still get evens against him winning the Arc a second time. Then there's spread betting. And the ante-post rush from certain quarters on Mot Cambron. It isn't anything to do with what they stand to lose as the result of just today's business. If Nightie keeps passing the winning post first every time, the men on the rails are going to take a seriously heavy drubbing. So go on camera and talk about what happens backstage. You owe it to racing.'

Cassie stood for a moment staring at the winning post as if trying to draw the courage from imagining what was to come that afternoon, whereas in fact she was having a silent dialogue with Tyrone.

'All right, I will,' she said when she had quite finished. 'But only in the most general terms. I'm not going to ask for trouble.'

Mattie put his free arm around Cassie's shoulder and kissed her on the cheek. 'Good,' he said. 'Great, in fact. Go get 'em.'

Cassie gave him a quizzical smile then returned to where her interviewer stood waiting and gave him permission to discuss the topic but not in the particular.

'There are reports, Cassie, that you've been receiving

threats, admonitions not to run your horse *or else* – so to speak.'

'You always do, John. At least you do when you've got a good horse running on its merits. That's racing, I'm afraid, or rather that is a side of racing, a side of racing none of us in the sport exactly like,' Cassie replied as calmly as she could, nervously fingering the gold locket around her neck which Tyrone had given her and she thought she had lost the day he had been killed. 'But then if every owner and trainer gave in to every threat they got, there'd hardly be any racing.'

'So bravely you've chosen to ignore all these caveats.'

'As long as I can keep The Nightingale safe then I shall continue to race him. Even if there are those who would rather I didn't.'

'Do you have any idea who might be behind these threats?'

'None whatsoever. But whoever it is, I hope they're getting the message that we won't be frightened off. Now if you'll excuse me, I have to go and help get my horse ready.'

Cassie didn't stay to hear how her interviewer wound up the piece as she hated to be short of time whenever she was getting The Nightingale ready for a race. So as she hurried away to the stableblock she missed the debate between the various commentators concerning the existence of independent bookmakers versus the possible benefits of a Tote monopoly.

Even more to the point was the news from the ring. Much to the astonishment of the television commentary team's eccentric betting specialist, far from being deterred by the almost prohibitive odds on offer several professional punters had already waded in with astronomic bets.

'One account punter has just walked up to my old pal George Barclay on the rails here behind me and put on fifty thousand pounds to win ten! Another punter walked into a betting shop in Bournemouth and wanted a hundred thousand to win twenty! Ladbroke's the Magic Circle tell me they have taken several similar bets, and one layer has

76

just invested two hundred thousand to win forty grand! The layers are so confident this is a one horse race they are treating the Eclipse Stakes as pay day! And it's not only the professionals! My old pal over here – Terry the Monkey Taplow – Terry the Monkey Taplow tells me he is taking money from you housewives! That you're betting the pin money on the wonder horse! Twenty pounds to win two! Fifty pounds to win a tenner! I tell you, when – not if, mind! – when the wonder horse trots past the post, as far as the *amount* of bets laid goes, this could be the biggest loser for the bookies since the Charge of the Light Brigade! Yes – *come racing*! It's all happening here today!'

In fact racegoers could not remember a day like it ever, such was the atmosphere and the intensity of the excitement, all due to the presence of a single horse. When the stewards had seen the size of the crowd, even more elaborate security precautions were ordered to be taken to ensure nothing untoward should happen to The Nightingale. The officials had already allocated a mounted police guard to escort the horse from the parade ring out onto the track in order to keep the favourite out of the reach of any well- or, more important, ill-wishers and now they also granted permission for the favourite to be walked on the grass in the centre of the parade ring and not on the tarmac perimeter pathway for the selfsame reason.

Meanwhile the object of all the stress and attention strode round the lawn in the middle of the parade ring with his ears pricked, occasionally jog trotting as if to show how fit he was.

'I almost feel sorry for the other poor horses,' Josephine said as the Claremore party which now included Mark Carter-James in its number assembled in the middle of the ring. 'No-one's taking a blind bit of notice of them.'

'It's not as if they're a pack of dogs,' Mattie murmured back to his sister. 'These are the pick of the best horses in England and Europe.'

'Aren't they just?' Mark agreed. 'And I must say Mot Cambron looks the pick of the rest.'

Much as Mattie would have loved to disagree he could

not, because when he turned to have a look at their main rival he saw Leonora Lovett Andrew's big strapping liver chestnut was not just on his toes but looking every inch an eminently possible winner.

'I can't see the owner,' Josephine remarked. 'She's not going to miss this, surely?'

'Of course she's not,' a voice drawled behind them. 'I don't spend all that money to sit at home channel skiing in front of the television.'

Leonora was dressed from head to toe by St Laurent in a suit and hat of the palest spring yellow. She was lightly suntanned, the sort of tan the very rich allow themselves to show they have been abroad but did not spend their time lying on beaches. People only went the shade of designer brown Mrs Charles Lovett Andrew had gone from being at sea on private yachts.

'You'll excuse me but I have to talk to my jockey,' Cassie said, moving slightly away as she saw Dexter striding across the paddock to meet her.

'I only stopped by to wish you luck, Cassie McGann!' Leonora called after her. 'Because it certainly should be some race!'

Cassie ignored her, continuing on her way to meet her pilot.

'Your mother doesn't change,' Leonora remarked with a gleam in her eye to Josephine and Mattie. 'She still gets herself so worked up. And goddammit, it's only a sport after all.'

'I don't know how you dare, Leonora,' Mattie said icily. 'If I was my mother I'd kick you all around the paddock for the way you've behaved. Now if you'll excuse us?' And lifting his hat in exaggerated politeness he caught his sister's arm and made to walk off.

'My,' Leonora laughed. 'If this is what we're like before the race, what are we going to be like if we lose?'

'We won't,' Mattie told her, turning back briefly. 'We're going to leave that pleasure to you. Good luck none the less.'

'You're going to need it, honey, not me!' Leonora called

78

out after them with a laugh. 'Today's the day the bubble bursts!'

'You know who she always reminds me of, Mattie,' Josephine remembered as they hurried across to where Dexter was being legged up on The Nightingale by Liam. 'Cruella de Ville in *A Hundred and One Dalmatians*.'

'You're kidding,' Mattie retorted good-naturedly. 'Compared to Leonora, Cruella de Ville is Mother Teresa.'

Mark turned to follow Josephine and her brother across the paddock but before he left he smiled once at Leonora who returned it in full.

As the horses took a last turn round the paddock before being led out onto the course for the parade, Mot Cambron started to get worked up and tried to lash out at Hedel, the German Derby winner who was behind him. Leonora's pacemaker Tootsuite was also very much on her toes and swishing her tail, but Cassie and Dexter already had her number and had put a barrier of ten horses between The Nightingale and her. The favourite was further cushioned by the phalanx of two large police horses which guarded him as he left the mouth of the paddock past a wall of security guards. Neither was he at all upset by the parade, of which like most others in her profession Cassie thoroughly disapproved since during these promenades the more highly strung horses often boiled over and lost their races before they were even run, thanks to the unnecessarily drawn out proceedings. All The Nightingale did, however, was stare back up at the enormous crowds packing the grandstand before Liam let go the lead rope and Dexter turned the big horse, who was last in line, to canter down to the start.

The crowd applauded him all the way past the packed enclosures on his way to post. From their pitches the bookmakers shouted and signalled the odds, taking most of the money now on betting without the favourite, the books showing Mot Cambron as the 6/4 favourite, Esplanade at 2/1, Whizz at 4/1, Hokey Cokey and Hedel jointly at 6/1, Filmgoer, the most fancied of the longer-priced English runners, at 7/1 and 10/1 bar. With the favourite they bet 2/9 The Nightingale, 8/1 Mot Cambron, 10/1 Esplanade, 16/1 Whizz and 20/1 the rest of the field. The only thing not in The Nightingale's favour was the fact he was drawn number one against the rails, but in a race over a mile and two furlongs it was considered only the smallest inconvenience to a horse who preferred to hang out the back and come to win his races with a late run.

'I'd rather be down there on the lawns,' Cassie said as her party settled into their private box at the top of the stands. 'But if he wins I don't think we'd ever get back to the paddock in that scrum.'

'When he wins, Mrs Rosse,' Mark corrected her. 'The bet is by what distance.'

'Absolutely,' Josephine agreed. 'I have a hundred pounds at five to one to say he's going to do so by twelve lengths.'

'I hope you've told Dexter,' Mattie said. 'He says he'll win by a distance.'

'They're under starter's orders!' a voice over the tannoy announced after the last horse had been loaded in the stalls. 'And they're off!'

As soon as the stalls opened Esplanade, who had been drawn in the number two berth next to The Nightingale, came across the favourite in a perfectly allowable attempt to box him in. But in doing so he accidentally gave the favourite a mighty bump and for one heart-stopping moment it seemed the big black horse would be brought to his knees.

'Jesus Mary he's down!' Josephine cried as the entire party trained their glasses on the Claremore horse.

'No he's not,' Cassie said calmly, even though she was quite unable to hold her race glasses steady. 'Dex has got him. He's just picked him up and now he's pulling Nightie to the outside.'

'Do you think that's wise?' Mattie wondered as the field passed the nine furlong marker.

'Sure. He could take him into the next county, Mattie, and Nightie'd still win,' Cassie muttered, hoping that no-one could hear the pounding of her heart.

'I think he might have heard you,' Josephine said. 'He's taking him miles out of his way. Lookit!'

They all looked and what they could quite clearly see, as indeed could everyone, was Dexter Bryant pushing the favourite on and past the rest of the field.

'Did you discuss this option?' Mattie wondered.

'Yes,' Cassie returned. 'But if we hadn't I'd say it's a bit late now.'

It was Cassie's rule as it was with most thinking trainers not to lay down a hard and fast plan how a race was to be run. Each race was different and, while it was important to know which was the best way to run the horse, needs often had to be adapted when it appeared that the race in question was going nowhere near to plan.

And this was precisely what was happening out in the racing amphitheatre that is Sandown Park. The jockeys had decided the only way to have even the remotest chance of beating the favourite was to deny The Nightingale the chance to run his regular race. It was no good simply trying to slow the pace down as had happened the previous October in the Prix de l'Arc de Triomphe. The Nightingale had such speed that he seemed able to come from anywhere and pick the leaders off whatever the pace, nor could they run him ragged by the use of a pacemaker because when most horses were flat to the boards The Nightingale was still only cruising in third gear. So the plan was to keep The Nightingale trapped in behind a wall of horses, knowing that this was where he liked to be, and then as the field hit the home turn to fan out away from the rails and force the favourite, who they imagined would be waiting for a break to appear on the rails, to make his run on the wide outside. Many a good horse had been beaten this way up the stiff Sandown hill, and so although there was only a tiny chance of this tactic's succeeding it was after all the only chance available.

Happily Cassie and Dexter had imagined this to be the likely scenario and had made provision for it, as they had for all the ways the race could possibly be run. Dexter's orders were that if he thought he was being boxed, instead of beginning to make his run for home at the two furlong post he was to produce the horse long before the field turned into the straight and let everyone try to catch him. It was risky because there was always the chance that with nothing to race against up the hill the big horse might begin to idle and something could come at him out of the pack with a wet sail and catch him before he could hit top gear again. Staying clear of any trouble, however, seemed to be the better of the two options, particularly since Cassie and Dexter knew that Leonora and her trainer would be prepared to try almost anything to prevent The Nightingale from getting a clear run.

So when Dexter saw Tootsuite going off hell for leather in front and the other horses being deliberately checked in front of him, he knew that the only way to show the world how truly great the horse under him was would be to prove that The Nightingale could fly home any which way he liked. As they reached the eight furlong pole he had already pulled the favourite wide to the outside of the other eleven horses, so wide in fact that altogether he must have added a good ten lengths to his total journey. But the big black horse was still cantering, with his ears pricked and his head tucked into his chest.

'You going somewhere, Dex?' one of his rivals shouted to him from the back of Whizz. 'If you are, don't forget to send us a card!'

'I thought I'd go do a bit of train spotting!' Dexter called back, as a train headed for Esher station down the track at the back of the course.

'Might do you some good! 'Cos that's just how I'm going! Like the proverbial bloody train!'

'Oh yes?' Dexter shouted, giving The Nightingale one good squeeze. 'Myself I always prefer to fly!'

By the seven furlong pole the favourite had accelerated so hard he was on the heels of the pacemaker who was still racing flat out. When he got to about a length off the leader, Dexter eased The Nightingale back a couple of notches and, brilliant horse that he was, the favourite at once came out of top gear and back into cruise.

From the stands it looked as if Dexter had asked the horse too early and burned him out in the process, because although by the time the field turned for home the pace-maker was spent, five of the favoured horses were going ominously well behind the new leader. Esplanade appeared to be cruising, poised to make his run on the rails tucked in behind Hokey Cokey who was also still on the bridle. Hedel came next, half a length down, but then his jockey went for his whip and as soon as he went to work the German Derby winner fell apart. Not so Filmgoer who was being brought with a nicely timed run on the outside by Walter Swinburn, nor indeed Whizz whom the masterful Willie Carson had always had handy, but the horse apparently going best of all was the big liver chestnut, Mot Cambron, who was shortening the distance between him and The Nightingale with every stride.

'His rider's got a double handful,' Mattie murmured as the drama was about to reach its climax. 'Do you still reckon Dex did the right thing?'

'Wait and see,' Cassie said. 'If you think Mot Cambron's jock's got a double handful, just look at Dexter.'

All eyes turned now to the favourite as the leading runners came off the bend and began to straighten up for the run up the hill. The Nightingale was less than two lengths clear now and the others were definitely closing. Yet Dexter was still sitting as still as night. He didn't even move when Mot Cambron got to his girths on his near side and Whizz appeared along his off side. While the huge crowd roared for him to go all Dexter did was cock his head and take what seemed to be a good, long look at what else might be a threat before sitting down and shaking his reins once in what was now the trademark of the way he rode the famous big black horse.

With that one shake of the reins the race was over.

Suddenly in a couple of strides the other five horses who had come to challenge the favourite all began to tread water, so that what had seemed to be turning into a close and epic encounter all at once became a procession as The Nightingale simply strode away up the hill from his rivals, increasing

83

his winning margin with every stride. By the two furlong pole he had accelerated to be six lengths clear of the pack, by the furlong marker he was ten and going so incredibly easily that the crowd became delirious with joy as they hollered their hero home. Fifty yards from the post Dexter stood up in his irons, bent his head down to look back through his legs to see where everyone had gone, and, when he saw how far behind the rest of the horses in fact were, eased The Nightingale down to a canter to pass the post.

Whizz was the second horse home, beaten by what was later officially declared to be twelve lengths. Hokey Cokey was a neck behind Whizz in third, Filmgoer was another neck away in fourth spot, Mot Cambron faded to finish two lengths away in fifth and Tootsuite ran on to snatch sixth place from a completely exhausted Esplanade. The rest of the field hacked in another dozen lengths behind. Those who witnessed the race were of the opinion that The Nightingale's triumph had to be the most emphatic victory ever seen in a horse race of this quality.

Even easing up in the last fifty yards he still knocked one and a half seconds off the existing course record.


'What are you smiling about?' Cassie asked Mattie on the plane back to Ireland.

'Leonora's face,' he said. 'Talk about bad losers.'

As always whenever Leonora's name was mentioned, Cassie felt a moment of despair which annoyed her, since she realized that all the adversities over which she had triumphed should at last have liberated her from the hold Leonora had once had over her. Yet back came the old anxiety, like a well-conditioned reaction. So bad was it that even now at the moment of victory Cassie could still manage to feel guilt.

Beside her Mattie started to laugh all over again. 'I actually thought she was going to throw a blue fit,' he said. 'And as for the roasting she gave her poor jockey.'

'Sometimes I think she'll never ever rest,' Cassie said, looking out at the clouds beyond her window. 'At least not until one of us is six feet under.'

Euphoria returned as soon as the raiding party landed back in Ireland and journeyed in high fettle triumphantly to Claremore where, once the hero of the day had been safely transported back from the airport and settled in his stable with a supper of bran mash and Guinness, Cassie threw an informal drinks party for everyone who worked for her, all her nearby friends and colleagues, and everyone who wanted to come and celebrate from the tiny but now world-famous village. They sang and danced, drank and told stories until the dawn broke and it was nearly time to pull out the first string of horses.

Finally tired out by the excitement, the travelling and the revelry Cassie excused herself from riding work and took to her bed where she fell into a deep and untroubled sleep. Erin called her at midday as she had requested with a pot of fresh coffee, a pile of newspapers and a hot bath already drawn. After Cassie had bathed and read the reports of the race in all the main papers she went down to the drawing room to crack a bottle of champagne as promised with Mattie.

He was on the telephone when she came into the room which Erin had bedecked with flowers picked that morning from the gardens. While Dick performed his usual wrestling act with the unopened champagne bottle Cassie waited, pretending to rearrange some roses in a vase on top of the grand piano. Once he had finished taking the call Mattie also waited until Dick had finally managed to win his battle with the recalcitrant champagne cork, poured them some wine and retired muttering mild Gaelic oaths under his breath.

'Who was on the phone?' Cassie wondered as she handed her son his glass of champagne.

'Tony, the guard on duty at the main gates,' Mattie replied, clearing his throat and trying to look at his most relaxed. 'It was nothing.'

'What sort of nothing exactly?'

'Nothing nothing.'

'Come on, Mattie,' Cassie urged him. 'I am your mother,

you know. I've been looking at that face of yours since you were a baby and I know when a cloud goes across it. So what was the call about?'

'Oh, Jeez, it was just some joker. Some silly bugger sent an undertaker's van out from Wicklow.'

Mattie shrugged his shoulders as if it was of no account, but as he turned away Cassie saw him reach into his pocket for his spinhaler and take a long, deep pull on it.

# Five

On her way back from church Cassie stopped in the yard to see The Nightingale. It was lunchtime and with the horses all duly fed no-one except the security guard was about. The horse looked up at her from his manger as she quietly entered his box and seeing who it was went on methodically eating his food. Cassie went over to him and stood beside his head but besides giving one swish of his thick tail in friendly warning he paid no further attention to his visitor.

'You really do like to get stuck in, old friend, don't you?' Cassie said, gently stroking his big, strong neck. 'Since you were weaned for the life of me I can't remember you leaving an oat.'

The horse snorted into his food and pushed what was left of it round his manger while Cassie stood back and took stock of him. When she was away from his stable and not watching him work or race, she found herself nowadays sometimes wondering whether he was worth all the anxiety which he seemed to be bringing with him in ever-increasing amounts. Never for one moment when she had helped Tomas with his foaling four years earlier could she have anticipated what a huge responsibility the birth of that strapping black foal would bring. Like every breeder watching their stock grow, the most she had hoped was that he might win a race somewhere, sometime. Of course like every breeder she had occasionally dreamed that the race in question might be a Derby, but she knew the odds against producing a classic winner were astronomical to say the very least. So as The Nightingale grew into a big, strong yearling she had contented herself simply with thinking that he looked a good enough sort to earn the right to go into training as a two-year-old. But never did she imagine, or indeed could she ever have imagined, that a colt foal born out of her bargain clubfooted mare was on his way to becoming one of the most famous racehorses in the world.

Now, however, with the way his fourth year was turning out Cassie certainly had her doubts and with good reason. With the threats now being directed not at the horse's welfare but at that of her family she was seriously reconsidering her decision to keep The Nightingale on in training. The incidents with the wheelchair in London and then with the local undertaker's van back at Claremore had already made it perfectly plain that there were bound to be more threats and she knew it would be foolish to take these lightly. So although withdrawing the horse now and sending him to stud would disappoint everyone, the move would put her family out of any further danger as well as minimizing the risk of anything befalling The Nightingale. It would also secure for ever the family's and Claremore's financial future.

Yet like her late husband Cassie baulked at defeat, and taking the horse out of training would be an admission that her unknown enemies had her beaten. It would also be an unacceptable precedent since it would mean that no-one who owned a decent racehorse might ever really be safe from villainy. So on that hand it was vital that Cassie should at least appear to remain unaffected by the intimidation, and most important of all she and the rest of the racing fraternity should do everything in their joint power to find out who was responsible for the outrage. Failure to do so could have a lasting effect on the whole racing industry, particularly on the bookmakers, who were the odds-on favourites in most people's minds to be those with the most to gain from scaring off the horse and its connections. But Cassie was old-fashioned enough still to think that people were innocent until proved guilty, and consequently considered it would be unpardonable if the future of the bookmaking profession was endangered purely as the result of rumour-mongering.

'The trouble is I'm frightened,' she had admitted earlier to Tyrone as she had knelt by his grave, fixing an arrangement of roses cut freshly from their gardens. 'I'm frightened. Not for myself but for our children. As well as for everyone who works at Claremore, come to that, since there's no knowing what these people might do. I know it's no good asking you what you'd do in the circumstances because I know perfectly well what you'd do. You'd say *blow the lot of them*, and go right on with what you were doing, but I guess maybe I don't have your courage, or your determination. God, how I wish you were still alive, how I wish every day that—'

She stopped as she fingered the gold locket at her neck that Tyrone had given her and which she had lost that fateful day after the magical birthday party he had thrown for her, when together they had ridden up into the hills behind Claremore, even happier and more passionately in love than they had ever been – only for Cassie to find the locket had fallen from her neck somewhere in that last field across which they had come, so that Tyrone had got off Old Flurry in order to help her with her search. One fly kick was all it had taken Tyrone's faithful old hack to despatch him to eternity. A horse fly or a wasp sting on the horse's soft underbelly, a sudden lashing kick, and Tyrone had been taken from her, there in the fold of the hills where March hares boxed, under clear blue summer skies and where larks rose at dawn.

*There you are!* he had called up to her as he had found the locket. *God is kind!* Only for God to take him from her the very next moment and in an instant, leaving her cradling his dead body in her arms and forlornly calling out his name on the warm summer breeze.

Thereafter everything Cassie had done she had done for him. Her whole life had been and still was dedicated to Tyrone's memory and now that she had reached perhaps the most crucial stage of her long widowhood she missed his counsel and his strength more than she had ever missed them before.

'As I said, I know it's no good asking you what to do,

Ty,' she had told him with a sigh. 'At least everyone tells me it's no good because there is no way you can answer my questions. But I feel it does me good, because somehow whenever I come up here to talk to you I go away feeling so much stronger. And now I need the strength you give me more than ever. Because it's not just the worry about The Nightingale. There's Josephine, too. She's fallen in love with someone – someone she says she wants to marry – and Mattie can't stand him and I'm not at all sure about him either – which isn't really fair seeing we've only met him a couple of times. But then you know what you were like yourself. First impressions were everything to you and if you didn't like someone or something at once that was it. Nothing or nobody could ever make you change your mind afterwards – and that's how it is with this young man. At least as far as Mattie and I are concerned it was. One look at him and it was hate at first sight.' She paused. 'You know, Tyrone, I only wish I could hear you the way I know you can see me.'

Josephine was quite her old effervescent self when she wasn't with Mark. When they had met her with Mark, as Mattie said afterwards, she had not been firing on all six cylinders, yet two weeks after the drama and final triumph of the Eclipse, when the play in which she was appearing in the West End had suddenly closed and Josephine flew over by herself to Ireland for a week's holiday at Claremore, it was obvious she was right back on song. Cassie and she spent as much time together as they could find, which with the King George VI Stakes at Ascot now less than a week away was not as much as both of them would have liked. Happily Josephine was only too eager to ride work and generally help out in the office and the yard, so although hours alone together were hard to come by they still found enough time to talk about almost everything that needed talking about. All that was except Mark Carter-James.

Every time the subject came up, however subtly Cassie introduced it, Josephine buried it. She would talk in general terms about the relationship, including even the plans to get married which much to Cassie's relief seemed very vague and not at all well determined. As long as her daughter's plans remained in such a state Cassie felt that Josephine and her intended were perhaps not as serious about each other as they had first made out, or at the very least that Josephine had decided to be a little more circumspect. So rather than press for details which Josephine was not willing to volunteer, at the same time being aware that too much concern masquerading as maternal interest could rekindle Josephine's determination, Cassie tried instead to be as uninterested in the details of the love affair as she could be without seeming to be indifferent. Josephine seemed more than happy with this attitude, and as the week went by and little time was spent discussing the subject she was quite her old, sunny self.

'Maybe she's frightened of him,' Mattie said on the one morning Josephine slept in and he found himself alone with his mother watching the first string being exercised. 'She's talked to me quite a bit about him, and although she didn't go into any details I got the distinct impression that he dominates her. It's often the way with small guys, or at least so I've heard. They like tall women whom they then dominate.'

'And what about small women?' Cassie wondered. 'Like me? Do you reckon we're bullies as well? I don't think your father would have agreed with you there.'

'You're not a bully, you're just seriously determined,' Mattie replied. 'When you want something, God help anyone who gets in your way.'

'I guess a lot of that comes from the way I was brought up,' Cassie said. 'Maybe having an unhappy childhood is the making of people. If I'd had a perfectly idyllic childhood perhaps I wouldn't be where I am today. In fact I know I wouldn't.'

'I think our childhood was pretty idyllic,' Mattie said, adjusting his reins and resettling his hack who was getting restless. 'All except for not knowing our father.'

'How do you think it's affected you?'

'I don't know, it's hard to say,' Mattie replied. 'I know Jo feels it, even though she does at least remember Dad.'

'It might explain her problem with men,' Cassie said, never taking her eyes off the string of horses coming up the gallops. 'Maybe that's why she just doesn't best know how to be with them. It seems she's always been at either their feet or their throats.'

'Usually at their feet,' Mattie said with a grin. 'Maybe it also explains why – at least according to Jo – I'm so defensive. Particularly in the company of older men.'

'Let's just wait to see what you bring home in the way of a wife,' Cassie replied.

She smiled at Mattie who smiled back at her, both of them knowing that the reason he was so often bullish was because he had a problem believing in himself. He was fine as long as he was around Claremore, but Cassie often feared for the future if he ever found himself cut off from the security of his home.

'Anyway,' she called, preparing to canter off down to where the first string was pulling up below them. 'You're not the person who needs sorting out at the moment. Your sister is our main concern.'

'Just leave her to me, guv!' Mattie called back. 'I'll get to the bottom of it, don't you worry!'

He got further than his mother had done, thanks to the help of a couple of joints he'd procured from one of his friends in Dublin.

'Mums would have a fit,' Josephine said as they lay on their backs that evening in the long grass watching the swallows cooling themselves in the carp pond.

'Do her some good,' Mattie murmured, passing the cigarette back to his sister.

'Might do,' Josephine agreed. 'She sure is uptight *à ce moment.*'

'No she isn't.'

'Oooh yes she is. Is she uptight.'

'Maybe if she met somebody, Jose. Maybe that's what she needs. She needs to meet somebody.'

'Yeah. Maybe. Then maybe not.' Josephine took another deep draw and passed the joint back to Mattie.

'I talked to her about all that stuff with Pa, you know.' Mattie lay back and closed his eyes. 'Like you asked me to. I talked to her all about that. And she lost it. She didn't like it at all – but at least it got aired.'

'You think she's ever going to get over it? I don't.'

'That's why I said maybe if she met somebody . . .'

'I think she needs something more than that,' Josephine said after a long silence.

'She doesn't. She just needs a man who'd sort of – yes. She needs a man to do what whatsisname's done to you.'

'You know bloody well what Mark's called.'

'Fine. So what did Mark do to you?'

Josephine took a last draw on what was left of the smoke before flipping the stub into the reeds.

'I said—' Mattie slowly began.

'I heard,' Josephine replied before exhaling. 'I heard.'

'I asked you what whatsisname did to you.'

Instead of replying Josephine began to giggle.

'God, you're not going to get silly, are you?' Mattie asked, and then picking up the infection started to laugh himself. 'Once you start laughing I've had it.'

As they both continued to laugh, Josephine sat up and bent her head down through her knees so that her long hair fell either side of her face. Then she straightened up and pushed her hair back with her hands, holding it in a bun at the back of her head.

'OK. So you want to know what Mark did, right?' she said, suddenly serious. 'He bothered. He bothered about everything. Right from the word go. He really bothered about me, I mean like who I was, rather than just trying to get me between the sheets which is what everyone else has always tried to do.'

'Maybe he can't do it.'

'That's not even remotely amusing. And anyway he can.'

'Oh. You mean you have.'

'That isn't what I said!'

'OK. *Oh*-K.'

Josephine lay back with a sigh. 'Next thing you'll probably say is what everybody else says. That because I never knew Dad – and because Mark bothers – blah blah blah . . .'

'Suppose it might figure.'

'Yes, well, it goes a whole lot deeper than that. He's about the first man I've known who wasn't after something. Ever since Nightie kind of burst onto the scene, and lo and behold I started getting a *lot* of work all of a sudden, because all of a sudden I came with a story – honestly, after we won the Derby there wasn't *anyone* who didn't call me. There wasn't a place to be seen I wasn't taken to. And God it was awful. No-one was interested in *me*. They were just interested in trying to lay a bit of the glory.'

'And whatsisname's not like that.'

'Mark's not at all like that. Mark's got money, and if you cast your tiny mind back his father won the Derby—'

'I know. With Persian Artefact. I remember,' Mattie interrupted. 'Worst horse ever to win a Derby.'

'He still won it, Mattie. So he's not broke, he's not socially ambitious—'

'And all he really cares about is little old you.'

'Oh, you can go to hell.'

Josephine got up and strode off round the lake. Mattie let her go, rolling onto his side to watch a large mirror carp moving slowly an inch beneath the top of the water. A quarter of an hour or so later when she'd walked round the small lake half a dozen times Josephine came back and threw herself down on the grass once more beside her brother.

'I just wish I knew why you don't like him,' Josephine wondered. 'You don't have any reason not to like him. So what is it? Don't you trust him or something?'

'I don't know,' Mattie said. 'Yes, maybe that's it. I don't know really.'

'You don't have any reason not to trust him,' Josephine replied tartly. 'None whatsoever.'

'I didn't say I didn't trust him, Jose. I just said that might

94

be it. It was you who mentioned it so maybe it's you who doesn't trust him.'

'Trouble with being a man is you don't know what it's like,' Josephine said, carefully ignoring Mattie's last comment. 'You have no idea what it's like when all people want to do is get you into bed.'

'I wouldn't mind,' Mattie replied, poker-faced. 'It wouldn't break my heart.'

'It would if you were a woman. Particularly if you were trying to do something other with your life than just getting in and out of bed with a load of men. I really wanted to act, Mattie. You know I did. You know how much I did.'

'Wanted to? How much you did? Sounds like past tense to me, sis.'

'That's because it is. I can't tell you what it's like. Being an actress. It's not what you do it's who you do. Same thing if you get to be some sort of social number, except it's them wanting to screw you to get on instead of vice versa.'

'You heard about the Irish actress, I suppose,' Mattie said idly.

'Years ago,' Josephine groaned. 'She slept with a writer. *I* told you that. Anyway, I've had it. Seriously. I want to get married, and have a home. And kids.'

'And whatsisname's Mr Right, right?'

'Yes.'

'Oh well,' Mattie said, and then pretended to yawn. 'Long as you're sure.'

'Of course I'm not sure. You know as well as I do there's no such thing as a racing certainty.'

'If you're not sure then maybe you shouldn't be marrying him.'

'I didn't say I was, did I? Anyway you don't marry someone because you're sure. You marry them because you're not.'

'Pretty good but no way good enough, sveetie,' Mattie sighed, adopting a terrible German accent as he suddenly turned and grabbed his sister by the waist. 'You know ve haff vays of making you talk.'

'No don't!' Josephine screamed. 'No don't you dare tickle me! You tickle me, Matthew Rosse, and I shall be sick! I promise you!'

'First you will tell me vot I vant to know, demn you! First you vill tell me—'

'No!' Josephine screamed. 'I'll never tell you! Never ever ever!'

Suddenly they were children again, wrestling around the nursery floor, except in those days it had been Josephine who'd had the upper hand. Now she was screaming helplessly for mercy, but the more she begged the less he listened.

'All right!' she yelled finally, but suddenly sounding more angry than anything. 'All right just stop and I'll tell you! Stop it, OK?'

'No! You tell me zen I vill stop it!' Mattie laughed back.

'All *right*! All right – I want to get married—'

'Yah?'

'I want to get married! Because!' Josephine yelled, louder than ever. 'I want to get married because sometimes! Sometimes I think that if I don't! I'll never be able to stand on my own two feet, that's why!'

Mattie stopped and sitting back on his heels looked at his sister. 'Yes,' he said. 'Go on.'

'I just feel I'll never be free of here,' Josephine said, trying to catch her breath. 'That I'll never really be my own person.'

'I know exactly what you mean,' Mattie said, brushing back the hair which had fallen in his eyes. 'What is it? Is it Dad?'

'It's everything,' Josephine said, putting her hands behind her on the grass and leaning back. 'It's Dad, it's Mums, it's the famous horse, it's Claremore. This place casts a huge shadow, you know, Mattie. Don't you feel it sometimes? And I just don't want to go through life being *Daughter of Claremore*, thanks. Like some sort of story in a pony book. I mean that's not all I want.'

'Yup,' Mattie agreed curtly. 'I know what you mean.'

'Do you?' Josephine turned her head to look directly at

him. 'What about you? You're expected to be some sort of a younger version of the great Tyrone Rosse and you can't tell me that's fair.'

'No, it isn't. But I do love my work. You've got to remember that.'

'To my way of thinking, Mattie, Mums needs to move on. There are other things in life, I mean there are more things *to* life, than just memories. Someone really should tell her that.'

'Well, now it's your turn,' Mattie said. 'You try telling her, and let me know when you're going to do it, because I really have to be there for it.'

'Meaning?'

'Meaning you may be her natural daughter, but it sounds to me as if you understand our mother even less than I do,' Mattie replied, getting to his feet. 'Now I'm going back because I need a long, cold drink.'

Mattie strode off down the hill towards Claremore which lay below them, bathed in the evening sun. After a moment Josephine got to her feet and followed him, and soon both of them were down in the rose gardens and lost to sight in the long dark shadows cast by the lovely old house.

Two days before the King George VI Stakes at Ascot a man who had been specially commissioned by the Sandown Executive to make a statue of The Nightingale to commemorate his already legendary performance in the Eclipse arrived at Claremore to photograph the horse prior to commencing the sculpture. Since there was always a well-regulated stream of visitors to the yard, such as journalists who wanted interviews, photographers who wanted yet another study of the wonder horse at rest and at work, or some of the strictly rationed number of bona fide admirers allowed in, Cassie paid little heed to the arrival of her latest visitor except to note it and ensure that maximum security was in place.

And most of all, that her precious horse wasn't fussed.

'How long has Nightie been out of his box, Bridie?' she demanded when on returning to the yard mid-morning she found Bridie still standing on the grass circle holding her charge's head.

'Not nearly long enough,' said a voice from behind her.

Cassie ignored him and looked at Bridie instead.

'He's being awful good, Mrs Rosse,' Bridie said. 'And he's not been out the whole time. I had him back inside while your man was changing films and lenses and things.'

'I've told you before, Bridie, photographers will go on taking photographs for just as long as you let them,' Cassie replied firmly, before turning back to face her visitor. 'Now if you don't mind, Mr – '

'Benson,' her visitor prompted. 'Joel Benson. You gave me permission to come and photograph your horse if you remember.'

'Of course I remember,' Cassie replied. 'But not all morning.'

'No,' Joel Benson agreed, taking another couple of shots. 'But then I haven't been here all morning. I've been here for precisely three-quarters of an hour and photographing the horse for just twenty-five minutes.'

'I should imagine that would be quite enough time for anybody,' Cassie retorted.

'I'm sure you would, Mrs Rosse,' Joel Benson said, lining up another shot. 'But then you're not me.'

'And you're not me. And this horse has a very important race in two days' time, so Bridie – if you don't mind . . .' Cassie nodded towards the horse's box.

'Mrs Rosse.' Joel Benson took his eyes from the viewfinder and turned them on Cassie. He was a tall man, and one of Cassie's initial impressions was that he was one of those loose-limbed people who give the impression of doing everything at half speed. He wasn't the remotest bit handsome, having a large aquiline nose and a slightly protruding lower lip which gave him the immediate appearance of wilfulness as well as what seemed to be a permanent frown which deeply creased his forehead and imbued his large, dark brown eyes with an intense look. Neither was he the sharpest of dressers, wearing as he was what looked like a very old cricket shirt rolled up at the sleeves, a pair of lightweight blue cord trousers which were so faded and worn they looked like velvet, and a pair of ancient tennis shoes done up with black laces. His long black hair was as untidy as the rest of him, falling in his eyes whenever he leaned forward to look through the viewfinder of his Hasselbad so that every time he stood up he had to brush it back into place with one long, slender-fingered hand. Finally, as if to emphasize a total commitment to lack of effort as far as appearance went, he was also unshaven.

'Mrs Rosse,' he repeated. 'I take it you are Mrs Rosse?'

'Of course I'm Mrs Rosse,' Cassie sighed.

'Mrs Rosse,' Benson continued, ignoring the rebuke. 'You were kind enough to grant me permission to come and photograph your horse—'

'Photograph him, yes, not paint him. He has a very important race the day after tomorrow and I'm afraid enough is enough.'

'I should have thought it was risk enough to let him be sculpted.'

'I'm sorry?' Cassie stared at him deliberately blankly. 'I can't see what someone doing a sculpture of my horse has to do with taking any undue risks. The risk surely is letting someone I don't know into my yard?'

'The risk is, at least according to horse folklore apparently,' Benson continued, beginning slowly to pack up his equipment, 'the risk is having any sort of portrait done of a horse while it's still racing. You didn't know that?'

He looked up at her from where he was stooping over his camera boxes and stared at her from behind the mane of hair which had once again fallen in front of his face.

'No,' Cassie replied, sinking her hands into the side pockets of her jeans. 'No, I did not know that, and anyway it doesn't make sense. How could the fact that someone is painting or sculpting or drawing your horse have anything to do with its performance?'

'I'm just repeating what I've heard. That horses often die if they are painted or sculpted before they retire. You're obviously not superstitious.'

'Not at all.'

'Yet you have a horseshoe hanging by The Nightingale's box.'

'That's always been there.'

'You sound like the famous Danish physicist. I can't remember his name. Bohr I think it was. Anyway, someone was at his house once and teased the scientist for having a horseshoe on his wall. Fancy you of all people believing a horseshoe brings you luck, the visitor said. To which the atomic physicist replied that he didn't believe any such thing. But he understood that a horseshoe brought you luck whether you believed in it or not.'

Cassie said nothing by way of reply. Instead she smiled and looked at her watch by way of a further prompt.

'Maybe if I don't have everything I need I can come some other time?' Joel Benson enquired as he began to pack up his tripod. 'I'm often in Ireland so if it wouldn't inconvenience you, it won't inconvenience me.'

'Of course,' Cassie said. 'Just ring my secretary if you need another visit. Goodbye.'

Then she walked into The Nightingale's box for no other reason than to curtail the conversation, privately hoping that like the horseshoe the old wives' tale about horses' portraits did not also come true whether one believed in it or not.

# *Six*

Up until the eleventh hour Cassie was still seriously considering withdrawing The Nightingale prior to announcing his retirement to stud. Not that there had been any more threatening messages or ominous deliveries made during the week. It was the brief conversation between herself and her artistic visitor that had upset her far more than she had at first realized. She knew her worry was a ridiculous one, but like so many professed non-believers in superstitions she still avoided walking under ladders, and hated seeing a singleton magpie on her way to the races.

But the real truth of the matter was that Cassie was feeling the strain of the past few months more than she had dared admit. The one thing she had always been determined to insure was the safety of her family, and now to feel that she was almost wilfully putting them at risk led her to conclude that had she been able to foretell the consequences of keeping The Nightingale in training she would never have done so. She had achieved more than she could ever have hoped for with the horse, and having done so she blamed herself for not being content and retiring him as a three-year-old. So the nearer she got to raceday, the more she was convinced that she must call her vet Niall Brogan and persuade him to sign a certificate saying the horse had been cast in his box so that she could withdraw him and thus put an end to her anxieties.

But Mattie as always was there first, reading his mother's thoughts long before she even considered expressing them. He told her he knew what she was contemplating, said that it would be no way to end such a triumphant career and then asked her to imagine the disappointment such a sudden retirement would cause.

'I know he doesn't need to establish himself as one of the best horses ever because everyone knows he is,' Mattie argued on the Friday morning as they hacked back together after watching the gallops. 'But you yourself have always said that if you train horses to race and they're fit and sound then they should be raced.'

'You have to admit there are mitigating circumstances surrounding this particular horse, Mattie.'

'Sure,' Mattie agreed, 'but you've taken every precaution possible. And as far as this particular horse goes, I can't imagine one who's ever had better security. So we've *got* to go to Ascot. They're all saying it's the race of the century, with the dual winner of this year's English and Irish Derbies—'

'I know what's entered, thank you very much.'

'You couldn't imagine a better race,' Mattie continued. 'With not only this year's English and Irish Derby winner Changement taking Nightie on, but the French Derby winner Concise as well, *and* Thirtynine Steps the winner of the King Edward VII Stakes, *and* the 2000 Guineas winner Which Way Now, *and* Mrs Mopper – I mean, come on – what a field!'

'You've forgotten Mot Cambron.'

'Probably because on the way it ran behind us at Sandown I would say that Leonora's horse hasn't got a chance.'

'And how do you rate the chances of the others?'

'Nightie's the only four-year-old colt. Except for the mare all the others are three-year-olds, so weight for age we have to give them a stone—'

'And the mare seven pounds. She won our Oaks in record time, remember.'

'Come on, Ma. You know as well as I do we could give them all two stone and still wallop them. They're billing it as the Dream Race which it just has to be, and then if you want to retire him you can do so after the race. You can't retire him now, not when you've come this far. Just twenty-four hours more and honestly, after he's obliterated one of the best fields ever assembled everyone will understand if you say that's enough. And then of course there's Jose.'

*And then of course there was Josephine.* Josephine had persuaded Mark's father to let her ride one of his horses in the De Beers Diamond Stakes, the prestigious race for Lady Riders which opens the racecard on King George VI day. To qualify for that privilege it seemed she had been diligently riding work every day at Newmarket where under Major Carter-James' tutelage she had been deemed more than adequate for the job ahead. Josephine was a brilliant horsewoman, and although the only seriously competitive races in which she had ever ridden had been pony races on various Irish beaches, no-one who had ever seen her ride in those contests would ever doubt her ability, or more importantly her competitiveness. As Cassie had said herself many times, had her daughter not chosen to go into the theatre she could have gone right to the top as an equestrian.

'She won't win for a minute,' Mattie said, taking a quick draw on his inhaler as he and his mother walked their horses back into the yard. 'But she'll go damn' close, and it would well and truly take the edge off her day let alone everyone else's if we were to pull Himself out of the race now.'

But Cassie's mind was now elsewhere so she hardly heard the rest of what Mattie had to say as they walked their horses down the hill. Of course it was perfectly normal to want to ride for your fiancé's stable, but for some illogical reason it appeared to Cassie as an act of disloyalty. She couldn't help it. She wanted Josephine by their side in the Claremore party on The Nightingale's big day, not dividing her loyalties between her family and the Carter-Jameses.

Mattie coughing beside her brought her back to earth.

'You don't sound too hot,' Cassie said as they slipped down from their horses in the yard. 'I noticed you were on the Ventolin early on as well.'

'It's nothing, really,' Mattie said, flicking his irons up over his saddle. 'The pollen count's a bit high at the moment, that's all. So do we go tomorrow or do we not?'

'Sometimes I really wish I'd chucked it all in years ago and taken up growing roses,' Cassie sighed, pulling the saddle off her horse.

'I take it that's a yes,' Mattie wondered, looping his horse's reins forward over his ears ready to lead him to his box.

'It is,' Cassie said wearily, pushing her own horse's stable door open with her foot. 'But then that's it. The King George really is going to be The Nightingale's very last race.'

The horse's departure from Claremore to the airport was as well planned as any military operation. Apart from Bridie nearly forgetting 'Mrs Murphy' as she had dubbed her lucky black hat, and Fred the travelling head lad panicking because he thought his wife had forgotten to pick up his best blue suit from the cleaners, the entire loading of the horse and the flight over to England went without a hitch. While the colt and his entourage travelled in a specially fitted out cargo plane, Cassie and Mattie travelled with the private party being airlifted in Jack Madigan's private jet – Madigan being one of Cassie's richest owners, a man who had made his first fortune from vending machines and who now owned a string of international hotels as well as one of the biggest studs in Ireland. He was a devoted fan of both The Nightingale and the horse's owner whom he tried on practically every occasion they met to get to marry him. It was a running joke, but Cassie, much as she liked Mad Jack as he was known by everyone, had always enjoyed only the most platonic of relationships with her top owner and intended to keep it that way, especially as she kept reminding him because he happened to be married already.

'Ah sure Fiona would understand well enough if you were t'agree, Cassie!' Mad Jack would laugh in return. 'Ah God sure isn't she your greatest fan ever?'

As it was Fiona had become a great friend of Cassie's and on the smooth as silk flight over to England they sat next to each other talking about everything but the forthcoming race.

On arrival in England The Nightingale was to be secretly stabled well before the party from Claremore had landed and so was perfectly composed when Cassie and her family arrived by helicopter from London to see him. They had avoided the risk of travelling him by road and stabling him at the racecourse in case of being followed, the plan being to convey the horse to a large country estate belonging to the friend of another of Cassie's owners near Pangbourne which had been chosen as the colt's 'safe house'. They had even gone to the trouble of leaving The Nightingale on the plane after landing while another black horse was dutifully unshipped, loaded into a waiting horsebox and driven away under escort as a decoy to a different location altogether. The Nightingale had remained on board the cargo plane until it had been taxied away as if empty to another part of the airfield where the animal had been taken off and loaded into a horse transporter repainted in the livery of a frozen food transporter. Besides Liam and Bridie and the immediate family, no-one else knew of the exact protocol, Liam having been designated to give the orders for the transportation of the horse stage by separate stage as yet another degree of security.

So far everything had gone like clockwork.

Until at midnight the heavens opened and the rains started.

'He won't mind it, not a bit,' Mattie assured his mother when they arrived at the Berkshire racetrack to walk the course the next morning. 'With his action he goes on anything. You know that.'

'It's not true ground, Mattie,' Cassie replied, testing it with her special stick. 'With the drought beforehand they've been watering the course. You can't blame them. No-one wants bone-hard ground and I for one certainly wouldn't have run Nightie had they not been watering. But now with this torrential downpour—' Cassie shaded her eyes, looking to the skies to see if there was any sign of a break in the clouds, but there was none. 'I have to say if it goes on like this there's every chance it'll become a quagmire and that can be just as dangerous as racing on the hard.'

'So OK – if you have to withdraw him you have to withdraw him,' Mattie said. 'If it's because of the weather, no-one can blame you for that.'

'Maybe it'll be worse if the sun does come out,' Cassie said, more to herself than to her son. 'Maybe if it just goes on raining they'll slosh through it. What we don't want is for it to get holding.'

'They say the forecast is for rain all day,' Mattie said, himself glancing up at the skies.

Yet despite the forecast being one hundred per cent right, nothing deterred the crowds from packing into the famous course. Like Sandown Park, the roads leading to the racetrack were blocked for over two hours before the first race and the car parks were jammed to overflowing. With no sign of the sun and the rains easing only slightly, Cassie walked the course again half an hour before the first race, this time by herself since Mattie had slipped off to help Josephine saddle up before the De Beers Diamond Stakes.

'I don't know,' Cassie muttered as she reached Swinley Bottom where the ground was particularly soft. 'Should we or shouldn't we, Ty? Yes – I know. It's the same for everyone but I don't want the horse to lose. Not in these conditions. These conditions would be barely raceable if we were jumping, but for Flat horses of this calibre . . .' Cassie sighed deeply and once more stuck her stick into the ground to measure the depth of the going. 'I just doubt if he'll be able to quicken in this, and if the old boy can't quicken, then he won't win.'

'I think he will,' a voice behind her said, startling Cassie so much she slipped on the wet grass and nearly fell as she swung round to see who it was. 'Hi,' said a tall man who was dressed in an antique knee-length Barbour and a large soaking wet bush hat. 'Joel Benson. We met in your yard a couple of days ago.'

'Yes, I can see who you are, thank you,' Cassie replied, pulling her measuring stick out of the ground. 'You startled me. I didn't know there was anyone following me.'

'I wasn't following you,' Joel replied. 'I was walking the course like you when you stopped and I saw no reason to.'

'Why are you walking the course?' Cassie asked, wondering at the same time why this particular man's perfectly innocent presence out on the racecourse should be upsetting her. 'Do you have a runner?'

'No I don't have a runner. I'm a sculptor, not a trainer, remember?' Joel replied.

'And do sculptors normally walk racecourses?'

'I don't imagine so,' Joel said, walking on after Cassie as she began to stride up the hill towards the home bend. 'But then I don't imagine many sculptors are as interested in racing as I am.'

'Fine. But walking the course?'

'You can't really make sense of a race unless you walk the course. I just happen always to walk whatever course I happen to go racing on. Even now I'm not riding.'

'You're telling me now that you used to *ride*?' Cassie asked disbelievingly, turning to glance at the tall figure beside her.

'Only point to point and hunter chases,' Joel replied with a shrug as he ambled along beside her. 'And the odd steeplechase as an amateur.'

'Weren't you a little tall?'

'No taller than I am now. Not as heavy maybe, but I wasn't any taller.'

'That's not what I meant,' Cassie said, smiling only briefly because her mind was fixed on the forthcoming race. 'Now I must get a move on—'

'Of course,' Joel agreed before she could finish. 'Your daughter's riding Huckleberry Finn in the first. I used to be able to do ten stone nine.'

'You must have been living on air.'

'I won the Magnolia Hunter Chase here on a rather good horse called Wingate.'

'I remember Wingate. He was rather useful. Won a lot of good races under rules, including the Foxhunters at Aintree.'

'I didn't ride him that day, unfortunately,' Joel replied. 'I'd injured myself.'

'What did you do?'

'Broke my back.'

Cassie looked at the man ambling along beside her again, but he was busy staring up at the stands.

'He was a good horse, Wingate,' he said distantly before turning to glance quickly at Cassie. 'And I wouldn't worry about the going if I were you,' he added. 'If any horse can handle this bog it's your chap. He'll win easily. Probably given his famous turn of foot by at least two or three lengths. Anyway – good luck.'

With that he ducked down through the running rail and disappeared into the vast crowd which in spite of the endless rain was standing happily packed as tight as sardines in the public enclosures.

Josephine was beaten into third place in the De Beers Diamond Stakes. For one wonderful moment as the field turned into the straight and she produced her horse on the outside of the field to hit the front at the furlong pole it seemed as if Huckleberry Finn might defy those who had said he didn't get the trip and win, so easily did he appear to be going. But as his jockey said afterwards it was not the trip that beat him but the going, and if the ground had been good he would have won by an easy couple of lengths. As it was he was only beaten by a length and a neck and Josephine was as thrilled as if she had won.

So it seemed was Mark, who was there with his father to unsaddle their horse.

'Well done, poppet,' he said, leaning forward to kiss her on the cheek. 'That was a simply tremendous race.'

'I can't help it,' Mattie muttered to his mother as they watched, well away from the party. 'He keeps reminding me of that bloke who was always playing royalty on the box. He is so *unreal*.'

Cassie didn't say anything but privately she agreed with Mattie. Mark Carter-James was exactly the sort of person Mattie and Josephine had always found so funny. Mark Carter-James was a *poseur*.

'Time to go and see the big fella,' Cassie said to Mattie, taking his arm, only to be stopped by a short and stocky red-faced man in a dark suit and a Goodwood hat.

'Don't know if you remember me, Mrs Rosse,' the man said. 'Carter-James. Mark's father. We met some time ago.'

'Of course I remember you, Major, very well in fact,' Cassie said. 'Congratulations. I think your horse ran a splendid race.'

'Thank you. Your daughter rode him very well. Going beat 'em, as you probably heard. What's it going to do to your chap? Any idea?'

'He'll waltz through it, Major,' Mattie said before Cassie could reply. 'Now if you'll excuse us we have to go and start getting our horse ready.'

'Of course you do.' Major Carter-James stood aside and doffed his hat. 'Personally, I don't think he's going to like it, mind!' he called after them. 'Heavy-topped sort of animal!'

'He'll waltz through it, just you see!' Mattie repeated as they made their way to the stables, followed at a discreet distance by a gaggle of Mattie's handpicked friends-as-minders. Then he turned and took his mother's arm.

'This is going to be the greatest day in Nightie's life, guv'nor,' he said. 'Just you wait and see. This is going to be a day none of us will ever forget.'

The race was everything they said it would be. Amidst mounting excitement which moments later was to turn to mass hysteria, the field came off the final bend in a pack with the French Derby winner Concise holding a length and a half advantage over Thirtynine Steps, the very useful three-year-old who had strolled home in the Edward VII Stakes at the Royal Ascot meeting, and the 2000 Guineas winner Which Way Now, neither horse apparently toiling in spite of the heavy ground. Mrs Mopper was right there on the tail of the leaders, tucked in on the rails alongside Mot Cambron who seemed to have run too free in the early stages of the race and was now beginning to drop off the pace, while swinging wide towards the middle of the course were Changement, the Sadlers Wells colt who had won the Derby six weeks earlier with almost contemptuous ease and finally The Nightingale who was being pulled ever wider by Dexter in an attempt it would seem to find better ground.

Then with just over a furlong and a half to run Concise ran out of oxygen and began to drop quickly away, leaving Thirtynine Steps suddenly with a two-length lead. At once his jockey sat down and sensing an historic victory began to ride for his life. Nor did his horse falter. In fact no horse could have run a better or braver race. It was just that on this one especial day he simply was just not good enough.

None of them were. At the furlong pole with the exception of Concise they were all there with a chance, a line of horses headed half a length by Thirtynine Steps with Which Way Now beginning to make a very strong challenge along with Mrs Mopper, the little silvery grey mare who having found a run up the rails had now gone into overdrive and was flying so fast that when with only two hundred yards left to run she hit the front it seemed she had the race won. But the real race was going on behind.

From where he had tucked his horse in behind the leaders, Walter Swinburn now produced Changement with one of his perfectly timed runs. Picking up his reins and changing hands to get his colt really motoring he pulled his horse's head out from behind the flanks of Which Way Now and sat down into the drive position. The sudden increase in the roars from the crowd made Mrs Mopper unexpectedly swerve and almost duck through the rails, causing her jockey to snatch her up and lose what must have seemed to him her winning momentum. In a couple of strides she had gone from first to fourth, her balance and her chance gone, while Changement had in his sights what would be one of the most famous racing victories ever.

Then just as the crowd's roar was about to turn to a corporate moan of anguish as they thought they were going to see the wonder horse beaten, Dexter performed his trademark, shaking his reins once at The Nightingale and once again The Nightingale flew. Right up the centre of the course he came, not because the ground was any better there but because Dexter wanted everyone to see just how fast this great horse really was. Afterwards he said he had known when the field had dropped down into Swinley Bottom and the horse had actually quickened through the worst of the going while the others were visibly floundering that The Nightingale could come and win the race as he liked. There was no sensation whatsoever of running into bad ground. He said if anything the big horse seemed to enjoy it, actually lengthening his stride quite voluntarily as he galloped through the mud, and in fact he was pulling so hard as they began the climb up towards the home turn that Dexter had to take a tug so as not to hit the front too soon, although not because he didn't think he could win from there. Dexter knew from the way the horse was travelling he could win from anywhere. He simply didn't want to hit the front too soon because he didn't want to do another Sandown. He wanted to show everyone that The Nightingale could do it every which way.

One hundred yards from the winning post he was alongside Changement and cruising. He glanced at Walter Swinburn and Swinburn glanced back at him, knowing as the big horse appeared at his window that it was all over.

'Cheerio, Walter,' Dexter called, and for the first time for as long as he could remember he shook his reins for a second time at The Nightingale and the result left everyone who saw it for ever after at a loss for words. There were less than one hundred yards to run, eighty at most, and both the leading horses appeared to be at full stretch. Yet with that second shake and within the length of less than four cricket pitches The Nightingale had pulled three lengths clear and was still actually going away from Changement as he flashed past the post.

In going which the BBC commentator described as unfathomable The Nightingale's winning time was only 1.3 seconds outside his own course record.

In going which before racing began caused the executive seriously to question the wisdom of allowing the meeting to go ahead, The Nightingale's last furlong dash was timed at forty-two miles per hour.

In going which Peter O'Sullevan, the doyen of all race commentators, said would have caused even the stewards at an Irish point to point meeting to call it a day, The Nightingale left a field of five of the best young horses in training for dead, horses which were of such a high class that later in the year they were to go on to win between them the St Leger, the Champion Stakes, the Ebor handicap and the Prix Henry Delamarre, and take second place in the Prix de l'Arc de Triomphe.

It was, as everyone who saw it said, an indescribable achievement.

People cheered till they were hoarse as Fred and Bridie led the horse back to the winner's enclosure. They threw their hats in the air. Men and women. Children were hoisted onto their fathers' shoulders and lovers were lifted off the ground by their young men to catch sight of him so that by the time The Nightingale had reached the un-saddling enclosure, many racegoers were seen to be crying.

For a moment Cassie didn't know what to do as she walked towards her horse with Mattie on one side of her grinning from ear to ear and Josephine on the other. The Nightingale knew what to do, however. Seeing his beloved owner he snorted at her, showering her with spray and sweat before pushing against her with his nose and nearly knocking her off her feet.

'OK! All right!' Cassie said with a laugh, steadying herself as Mattie grabbed hold of her. 'Take it easy! We're just going to tell you how brilliant you are!'

Mattie patted the horse's sweat-streaked neck and pulled one of his loppy ears.

'Well done, old fella,' he said. 'You really are just something other. What I don't know, but whatever it is it's something else.'

As Cassie helped Bridie pull on the horse's sweat sheet she caught sight of Joel Benson in the front row of the crowd thronging the winner's enclosure at ground level. He was so tall he would have been hard to miss at any time, but now he seemed to tower above the people around him. He wasn't smiling. Instead he was looking at Cassie with a deep frown while holding up three fingers on one hand to show the winning margin as he had predicted.

'Horses away, please!' an official called. 'Horses away.'

In answer Cassie smiled back at him, then giving The Nightingale one last pat instructed Bridie to lead the horse away from her and so to begin the most fateful journey of his life.

# *Seven*

Had it not still been raining so hard perhaps someone might have noticed something different. As it was the rain had begun to come down even more heavily as the file of horses were led back after the race to the stableblock to be washed down and dried off, with the result that everyone who wasn't actually in charge of a horse ran for cover. But then the whole scheme had obviously been so well planned that it did not have to rely on vagaries such as cloudbursts which turned almost immediately into vicious hailstorms.

Even so, the storm must have helped the perpetrators of the deed since during the five minutes the hail continued to rocket down from the skies no-one in the horsebox park or the vicinity of the stables could have been clearly visible let alone even vaguely recognizable. Furthermore, because of the freak storm there was a certain amount of chaos reigning as those in charge tried to find shelter for the poor rain-soaked creatures in the stables or horseboxes, and given the prevailing conditions they could be forgiven for not noticing anything or anybody untoward. During those few all-important but rainswept minutes visibility was down to a matter of a few feet.

For security reasons The Nightingale had been allocated a stable for his sole use throughout the entire length of his stay at the racecourse. Since the safety of the horse was everyone's primary concern it had been agreed that he should leave the track as soon as possible after he had been washed down and allowed to cool off, although given the weather it was obvious that both these tasks would for once have to be performed in the stable rather than outside in what should have been the warm sunshine. Roger Harris's travelling head lad Mick Molloy who was drying his own horse off in the next door box remembered calling out his congratulations to Fred and Bridie as they led The Nightingale into the VIP box, just as he clearly remembered that despite the downpour the two security guards were still on duty outside the stable.

The next thing that anyone remembered with any clarity was the horsebox leaving the yard with Bridie at the wheel. Although the official on the gate did not know Bridie personally he was sure the young woman fitted the description given to him by the police, that of a small, slight dark-haired female in her twenties wearing a black and white cap pulled well down to her eyes. There was no-one else in the cab.

The horsebox was last seen turning out of the box park in the direction of Reading. It was not seen again until it was found abandoned early the next morning on a disused trading estate on the outskirts of Woking.

At first the failure of the horsebox to arrive at the airfield was attributed to all those usual things that can go wrong, mechanical breakdown, punctures, traffic accidents and particularly the appalling weather.

'The roads were bad enough when we drove down,' Cassie said. 'We were diverted off the motorway twice because of flash flooding.'

'But if the box had broken down we'd surely have seen it,' Mattie reminded her. 'We'd hardly miss a broken down horsebox on the motorway or the roads we've just travelled on. Particularly one disguised as Madigan's Meats.'

'Of course we would,' Josephine contradicted him. 'For a start it was still pouring with rain, at times so heavily you could hardly see the car in front, and secondly they could have pulled into a layby and that way we'd never see them. Particularly since we weren't looking for them.'

'They would have rung by now if they'd broken down,' Cassie said curtly. 'They'd either have rung me on my mobile, or they'd have rung here to say they were going to be late or that they were waiting for Horsebox Rescue. Fred would not just leave it in the air. God almighty, if Fred's going to be five minutes late he rings me! He always rings me! They must have had an accident.'

'But surely we'd have seen evidence of that as well?' Josephine asked.

'I don't know! Why?' Cassie asked back, pulling anxiously at the locket round her neck. 'Suppose because of the weather they'd been forced to take another route? Supposing they've simply got lost? All I know is that something has happened! And if it has it'll be all my fault!'

'All right,' Mattie said, going and putting his arm round his mother. 'It's OK, guv. There's bound to be a perfectly logical explanation.'

'No there is not, Mattie, and you know that as well as I do!' Cassie retorted. 'We have this whole thing covered! No loopholes, remember? If anything goes wrong, the orders were to pick up the phone! So don't tell me about logical explanation! I'm telling you I know that something has gone horribly wrong!'

Nobody knew precisely what until the next morning when they found the abandoned horsebox and even then it was only guesswork. Once the vehicle and its invaluable cargo had been reported missing they had waited agonizingly all evening and night for news, but none came. The police had no relevant reports of any accidents involving heavy vehicles or horseboxes and every time Mattie telephoned Claremore to see if any news had filtered through to there he drew a blank.

'I don't understand why you're calling home,' Cassie said when he first rang Ireland. 'They couldn't have got back home any other way than to take the plane that was waiting for them, could they?'

'I know that, and that's not why I'm ringing,' Mattie replied.

'You're thinking Nightie's been kidnapped!' Cassie said suddenly.

'Surely the thought has crossed your mind as well?'

'Like hell it has! How the hell could they kidnap a horse from one of the most secure racecourses in the country?'

'By waiting in the lorry,' Mattie replied quietly.

Cassie whipped round on him. 'Never,' she said. 'They could never have got past the security. You have to have passes to get into the stableblock—'

'I know, I know. It's just a theory, that's all.'

They were in the safe house, the big Queen Anne house overlooking a lovely stretch of the Thames near Pangbourne which belonged to Cassie's owner's friend, a wealthy Dutch widow who was away on holiday in Italy and had willingly agreed to turn her house and staff over to the Rosse family, their horse and its entourage. But now, instead of being able to sit down and enjoy the fine dinner which had been prepared for them in celebration of their horse's famous victory, the family had sequestered themselves away in the large and elegant drawing room which looked out over terraces of lawns which ran all the way down to the river itself.

'A theory,' Cassie repeated. 'Right, so let's hear it.'

'There are lots of loose ends,' Mattie said, pouring himself another drink. 'You have to base everything on what we've always said. That you can get in anywhere on a racecourse with a lead rope and a bucket of water.'

'Not past the security on the gate of the stableblock,' Cassie disagreed. 'Those guys see it all.'

'Before the race maybe,' Mattie continued, 'and believe me, I'm not about to slag anyone off. When all the horses are coming *back* from the race, no-one's looking for anyone suspicious. So maybe you could get in at that moment with just a halter and a bucket of water.'

'I doubt it,' Jack Madigan said from the wing chair in the corner of the room. 'Now I know this isn't my affair, Matt me boy, but putting meself in the shoes of whoever it was who planned all this, I wouldn't leave one damn' thing to chance. I wouldn't contemplate even one little *maybe*. The plan would have to be foolproof. Watertight. An open and shut job.'

'Yes,' Mattie said reluctantly, not wanting to lose the floor. 'But even so, Mr Madigan—'

'No, Matt, I'm sorry, me boy, but there can't be any *even*

*sos*, not in this scenario,' Jack continued. 'If they don't get in with the bucket and lead rope scam, then where are they? Up the famous creek, that's where. They have to *guarantee* a place in the stableblock yard. They have to *guarantee* a place in the stables. And how do you think you go about getting that? I'll tell you.'

'You have a runner,' Cassie said.

'Of course you have a runner, Cass,' Jack agreed, holding out his glass for Fiona to refill. 'You have a runner, that's what you have. Or maybe even more than one.'

Mattie swished the ice round in his drink and stared into his glass. 'Of course, if you have a runner or two you come and go as you like. Two of you. And the two of you wouldn't have to be with your horses the whole time—'

'You wouldn't have to be with it at all once it had run, or for a certain time before it had.'

'I'll take once it had run, Mr Madigan. There's always things to do when your race is coming up, and our horsebox left long before the last race. As far as we can gather it left during the second last, in fact.'

'OK,' Cassie said, prowling round the room. 'Right, so whoever masterminded this had a runner today. That means it's another trainer.'

'A trainer or an owner,' Josephine said helpfully. 'The two of them could be in cahoots.'

'It had to be somebody with a horse, Mr Madigan's right,' Mattie said. 'They wouldn't have got access into the yard otherwise. And if we're right, then it had to be somebody with a horse in the first or second race.' He picked up the day's edition of the *Sporting Life* and collapsed backwards onto the sofa to study the racecard.

'There were twenty-two runners in my race,' Josephine said.

'And fourteen in the second,' Mattie replied.

'It could even have been somebody in your race,' Jack Màdigan suggested.

'Let's forget who it might or might not have been for the moment,' Cassie said. 'I want you to tell me how they pulled it off. Because what you seem to be saying is once they were there under official sanction in the racecourse stables they could just take the horse. But it can't have been as easy as that. What about the guards outside the stable?'

'Whoever took your horse must have been in your lorry, Cass,' Jack said, lighting up yet another cigarette. 'I imagine it went like this. No-one was told to check the lorry, were they? I mean there were no specific orders for the lorry to be guarded while the horse was being hosed down and walked off, or to be checked before he was put back in, am I right?' Cassie nodded. 'Good. So anyone can walk into a horsebox. Let's say there are two of them. Armed in all probability. It's a big lorry, I imagine.'

'It'll take six horses herringbone, four square on,' Mattie said from behind his paper.

'And it's got living, of course. Living accommodation for an easy two or three sitting up front in the cab en route. If necessary.'

'So plenty of room to stow away,' Jack continued with a nod. 'They could go two ways. They could get the dirty work out of the way once the horse was loaded and then drive the box out themselves, which is the more unlikely of the possibilities, or they could make that lass of yours—'

'Bridie,' Cassie said.

'They could make her do it at gunpoint from behind the cab. Either way, it worked, because they drove out of the place without anyone turning a hair.'

'What about their own horse?' Cassie asked. 'And their own horsebox, come to that? If your theory is right and they had a runner today they couldn't exactly leave a racehorse and a lorry behind them, could they? With the trainer's name emblazoned on the side.'

'Horseboxes aren't checked leaving the place,' Jack said. 'So either they loaded their own horse up into your lorry and took it with them, or they loaded it up in their box and sent it home that way. If they were sharing transport that would be the safest way. Put their fellow on board and let the transporter take it away with all the others. Alternatively if they came in their own box they could have used it as a Trojan horse. To smuggle in a couple

119

more people and leave 'em in the box to drive it home again. That's probably the most watertight way. In these big state of the art horseboxes you could practically bring in your own private army.'

'I'll buy their own box,' Mattie said. 'It leaves everything covered with no questions asked. Let's say the two who were smuggled in drive the horse home. The man on the gate's not going to notice a change of driver exactly. Leaving the other two to take our box.'

'And our horse,' Josephine added quietly.

'Yes,' Cassie said, standing at the window which overlooked the gardens. 'All right. OK. This is all very possible, I'll grant you that. But will somebody please tell me why? Why? That's what I want to know. *Why?*'

When the police found the abandoned lorry the next morning they did not find the answer to Cassie's question but they did find Fred and Bridie, tied up and locked away in the living quarters of the box.

Neither of them was in very good shape, with Fred suffering from quite severe wounds on the back of his head from where he had been clubbed into unconsciousness and Bridie from the after-effects of a near overdose of chloroform. Nevertheless all they wanted to know was whether or not anything had been heard about The Nightingale and when they learned that not a word had been heard Bridie fell to crying and Fred to swearing fiercely in Gaelic.

'I never got a sight of them,' he told one of the policemen who found them as they waited for the ambulance. 'They must have been waiting in the lorry for us for the next thing I knew I was coming to bundled up like a rabbit in there.'

'I heard voices,' Bridie said in a whisper. 'When I come to I heard their voices when they must have been taking Nightie out of the lorry. I heard a man and a woman.'

'Did you take note of their accents?' the senior police officer enquired. 'Did you hear them clearly enough to be able to notice how they spoke?'

'The woman was English,' Bridie replied, putting the back of one hand to her forehead. 'But I couldn't make the man out at all. He kept his voice very low at all times. Oh, God have mercy on us, for didn't I say, Fred? Didn't I say we shouldn't both of us go up in the lorry together?'

Fred put his arm round Bridie's shoulder but it was small comfort.

'We had it worked out every way except the one,' he said. 'The one thing none of us ever thought was that they'd come at us as we were leaving. After the bloody race was over.'

It was as if a major world figure had been abducted rather than a racehorse. So great were the demands of the media that once the family had returned to Claremore a special staff with its own communication system had to be taken on to deal with the round-the-clock calls requesting updates on the situation. Another room was set up like a police incident room, where Mattie and Jack Madigan who had volunteered his services sifted through the hundreds of letters that came pouring in purporting to have information on The Nightingale's whereabouts. Dublin Castle put an army of detectives on the case, four of whom were posted at Claremore where the two pairs took it in turns to do six-hour shifts through the twenty-four, supervising Mattie and Jack's sifting of the letters and following up any information which had the slightest hint of authenticity.

But over the next three weeks every chase was for wild geese. Every lead ran into a cul de sac. No-one actually knew anything. No-one had really heard a thing.

None the less rumours abounded with everyone from terrorists to extraterrestrials being said to be responsible for the horse's disappearance, but Cassie knew well enough if they had been terrorists she would have heard from them by now.

'They wouldn't know how to keep a horse like The Nightingale, not for a long period of time,' she maintained. 'At least not without running a very real danger of being traced, particularly if something went wrong with the horse. They would want a very quick exchange with no questions asked. But I've heard nothing from anyone, which leads me to suspect that what I've always thought is the truth. That this is the work of professional criminals fired by entirely different motives.'

By this the media thought Cassie meant the villains had to be people with a professional interest in stopping the horse and at once began to point the finger at the bookmakers, who in turn began loudly to protest their innocence to a man, insisting that The Nightingale was to them a 'good loser', with liabilities they could well afford to meet. According to their spokesman there was absolutely no good reason why any bookmaker should wish to harm a hair of the horse. Again to a man they were ardent in their appreciation of a horse as great as The Nightingale and apparently as 'gutted' as anyone else over his abduction.

By and large the public chose not to believe the bookmakers, not because holes could be picked in their arguments but because they could think of no-one else who was as likely to be responsible, despite two apparently serious newspaper reports of unidentified flying objects having been seen first over Watership Down and then Windsor Great Park the night before the race, leading the authors of the articles to suppose that aliens had abducted The Nightingale in order to find out what made him run so fast. One firm of bookmakers even opened a book on the most likely explanation for the kidnapping, only to learn to their astonishment that a punter in Bournemouth had walked into one of their shops and placed a £1000 cash bet at 1000/1 in favour of an extraterrestrial kidnapping.

Within a month the whole dreadful and now possibly tragic affair had been turned into a media circus, so much to the disgust of Cassie that she closed down her own special operations unit, released the extra staff she'd taken on, and redirected all The Nightingale mail to Dublin Castle.

'We are not going to learn one damn' thing this way,' she had told Mattie the day she had decided everyone must go. 'Not one goddam thing. All we're going to get is hurt even more every time we get our hopes raised, only for them to be dashed again.'

'So what are we going to do?' Mattie had wondered in return.

'Nothing,' Cassie had replied. 'What can we do? Except wait and get on with everything else.'

'How? I can't handle this at all. Seriously. I mean this really is doing my head. Yet you – how do you do it? How are you so calm?'

'I'm not, Mattie,' Cassie had replied, suddenly going very quiet. 'I just appear to be.'

No-one could possibly have guessed at Cassie's pain, not Josephine to whom Cassie talked practically every single evening, nor even Mattie who had been with his mother constantly since the horse had vanished. Just as her beloved horse's feat that famous and now notorious Saturday at Ascot racecourse was considered indescribable, so too was the anguish of his owner. When The Nightingale was first gone and everyone was crying, or drinking, or shouting in fury and hatred at whatever sort of people could do such a thing, although it had been not easy it had been easier, for Cassie could hide behind all the noise.

But then night would come, and worse, for morning would follow and she would have to drag herself out of the bed where she had slept only fitfully to supervise the daily exercise routines, which meant she would have to walk into the yard past The Nightingale's box which was now completely shut up, top door and bottom, and into the tack room where on his peg hung his exercise bridle, saddle and embroidered saddlecloth. And every day she would have to ride out on the roads, the tracks and finally the gallops on which every day of the horse's working life he had walked and trotted and galloped, up grassy pulls where all the time he was growing into himself and becoming the horse he was to be. Cassie had ridden him, half standing in her irons with the wind in her face, thundering up the turf furlongs not moving while the big horse swung along beneath her, his breath in perfect rhythm with his stride, his head tucked into his chest and his big ears pricked. Nothing could describe the joy the horse gave her, the thrill he sent through her every time she had ridden him, the love she had in her heart for this big black giant with the heart of an angel. A horse blessed with such an extraordinary turn of foot that it had to be seen to be believed, and when it was seen no-one could believe it.

Yet now he was gone from her, gone from Claremore, and possibly gone even from the world which had taken him to its heart.

'I hope and pray he is dead now,' she told Tyrone when she tended his grave six weeks after the horse's disappearance. 'If the people who took him had wanted anything they'd have asked for it by now, but since they haven't and since there is nothing they can do with the horse, I just pray to God that rather than suffering he is safely dead and buried and up there in the sky with you.'

But he wasn't. Cassie was to be denied even that small comfort. As if to torture her still further a Polaroid photograph arrived the very next day in the post showing The Nightingale standing with his head over a white-painted stable door behind a man in a balaclava helmet who was in turn holding up a copy of *The Times* showing the correct headline for the day in question.

There was no message.

Leonora called. It had taken her this long, but finally she called.

'I should have rung before but here I am anyway,' she said for openers. 'I guess I didn't because I guess I'm there or thereabouts on the list. Am I right or am I right?'

'There's really little point in talking to you when you're in this state,' Cassie began.

'When I've been drinking, you mean,' Leonora cut in, audibly drawing deep on a cigarette. 'You don't think I'm going to call you about something like this stone cold sober, do you?'

'Perhaps it would be better if you hadn't called at all,' Cassie replied, preparing to hang up the phone.

'So I *am* on your goddam list.'

'What list is that, Leonora? If you mean the list of who might have done it, of course you're on it. Who isn't? Since they're even taking bets on little green men from outer space being responsible I'd say you have every reason to be on it. Wouldn't you?'

'Don't be nuts, Cassie. Jesus Christ, you really think I'm capable of snatching your precious horse? What for? You asked yourself that? What in hell would I want with taking your precious racehorse? You mean because you wouldn't count Mother and me in, that it? Well, if that's what you think, you're out of your goddam tiny little head. Right?'

'That all you rang to say, Leonora? Because if it is—'

'Of course it's not all I rang to say, Cassie!' Leonora snapped back. 'But if you're going to start making insinuations, you think I'm just going to sit here and take it?'

Cassie said nothing to contradict Leonora, knowing full well when she was this drunk there was no point in trying to correct any misapprehensions.

'Jesus,' Leonora breathed into the receiver after a moment. 'So much for trying to do the right thing.'

'I have business to attend to, Leonora,' Cassie said curtly. 'I'm sure you understand.'

'Don't you want to hear why I called, for Chrissake?' Leonora snapped back. 'You think I called just to have you insult me? Because you are wrong. You are so – wrong.'

'So what did you call for, Leonora?' Cassie enquired coldly. 'Because as I said, I do have things to do.'

'You can't keep out of the goddam news, can you? If you're not winning every Group One race under the sun, you're breaking everyone's hearts with the story of your kidnapped horse.'

There was another long pause during which Leonora took several noisy draws on her cigarette.

'I really can't be bothered with this, Leonora,' Cassie said, deciding there was little point in prolonging this conversation any further. 'If that's all you called to say—'

'No, as a matter of fact it wasn't, Miss Smartass,' Leonora replied. 'What I actually called to say was that I was sorry about your horse. Really sorry. But there you are. I guess it's a little too bloody late for that now. So why don't you go to hell instead?'

Then the phone went dead.

In the old days, a call like that from Leonora would have rocked Cassie. Now with both Tyrone and The Nightingale gone nothing like that hurt or upset her any more. She was accustomed to pain and suffering, inured to the hurt the world seemed endlessly able to inflict, with only one concern left and that the well-being of her children. As long as Matt and Jo were safe from harm then as far as Cassie was now concerned the rest of the world could go hang. Except for her children everything that mattered had been taken from her, so there seemed little point in trying to care any longer. At least that was what she felt every evening by the time she had reached to turn off the light by her bed.

Even so, that evening as Cassie sat by the fire in her drawing room cradling a glass of brandy she felt the call rankling, not for what Leonora had said but for what it now made Cassie conclude. Before Leonora had made that call she had just been one of the suspects. Now the more Cassie thought about it the more reason she felt she had to make her old adversary the prime suspect, her reasoning being that Leonora had called to try to throw Cassie off the track. She probably wasn't even drunk but only play-acting, Cassie decided as she took a drink of her brandy. Pretence was something else Leonora had always excelled at, having spun web after web of deceit throughout her life causing nothing but misery and insecurity to everyone who had the misfortune to know her, and most of all to count her as a friend. Other than causing her arch-rival unimaginable grief, what else Leonora hoped to gain by organizing the theft of her horse Cassie could not begin to imagine, particularly given the risk she would be running were she indeed proved to be the culprit. But then mindful of what had always motivated Leonora in their previous confrontations Cassie knew spite would once

126

again be a perfectly adequate incentive. In fact by the time she had reached for the decanter to pour herself what she promised would be one last drink and then drunk most of it Cassie was entirely convinced that Leonora had plotted the theft of her beloved horse for exactly the same reasons she had so often plotted her downfall, namely jealousy.

Leonora's jealousy of Cassie seemed to be boundless. For some reason, from the moment Cassie had entered Miss Truefitt's Academy for Young Ladies in Glenville, West Virginia, Leonora Von Wagner had been not merely absurdly jealous of Cassie but obsessively so. Cassie had not been able to understand why. Whereas she was small and according to her mother really rather a plain girl, even in her teenage Leonora was stunning, a tall willowy blue-eyed blonde who, being the only daughter of one of the richest men in America, had everything a young woman needed, from an impeccable background to the pick of society's eligible young men. Yet that had never stopped Leonora from always wanting more, particularly when it came to other people's possessions, animate and inanimate. Even so, Cassie had always wondered what Leonora could possibly have wanted from her then. Later in life after she had met and married Tyrone she understood a little of the nature of Leonora's obsessive jealousy, but at school for a long time and thanks purely to Leonora's machinations, she had no friends and spent most of her time with nobody speaking to her. It was only after the famous tennis final where she trounced Leonora that she achieved popularity with her peers. Cassie sometimes regretted ever having set up that tennis match, particularly now when it seemed that Leonora might have finally exacted the worst revenge possible.

Had she not humiliated Leonora that day Cassie would never have had the courage to go to New York, which meant she would never have met Tyrone. She had only finally run away to escape from all the unhappiness she had encountered at home, culminating in the death of the woman she believed to be her grandmother but who was in fact her mother, and the discovery of her own illegitimacy. It did seem that all this had followed on as a direct consequence of her stay at Leonora's home on Long Island where her so-called new friend had deliberately compromised her by having her discovered in her bedroom with their young stable groom, Dexter Bryant, the boy who had grown into the man who was now Cassie's retained stable jockey.

*Yes, how different things would have been*, Cassie repeated to herself as she put down her empty glass. *Had I gone on ignoring Leonora's hostility at school and not set up that tennis match, I wouldn't have met and married Tyrone, I wouldn't have met Dexter again and helped rescue him from alcoholism, I wouldn't have two wonderful children and I'd never have won the Derby with The Nightingale, because if I hadn't been so set on beating the oh-so-grand Leonora Von Wagner at tennis for the Academy's Challenge Cup then The Nightingale would never have been.*

Cassie sat back in her chair and stared at the ceiling above her.

*If I hadn't taken the stupid girl on The Nightingale would never have been*, she repeated yet again to herself. *There would never have been such a horse. So really rather than hating Leonora maybe I really ought to be grateful to her, because if it hadn't been for her provoking me so much I might never have found this thing I have for winning. I might never have discovered my true self and instead might be locked into a safe but probably dull marriage with someone like Joe Harris, the boy I left behind when I ran off to New York. Hell – things might have worked out so differently. My mother might not have died the way she did, the night of the dance Joe was going to propose to me – at least I'm pretty certain he was – and if I'd accepted, maybe I would have married Joe, and instead of being here at Claremore I'd now be living in the smart part of Westboro with three or four grown-up kids, a moderately successful husband, two cars, a dog and wondering what on earth I'd done with my life? So maybe I ought to be down on my knees thanking you, Leonora, instead of suspecting you of doing the worst possible thing you could now do to me. Because without you I would not have had this life. Without you I would never have met Tyrone.*

*But God almighty, you would have done!* she suddenly said right out aloud, unmindful of the fact that she was now sitting by a dead fire in the pitch darkness. *In fact, what am I saying? You did meet him before I did because Tyrone had been your mother's lover! That's when you fell in love with him, I'll bet! And that's why you felt you had first call – and why you went mad when he fell in love with me! And why you would never let go of him – and pretended you'd had an affair with him in the South of France – and that Mattie was really Tyrone's illegitimate son – I mean long after Tyrone was dead for God's sake you still hadn't given up! Why you still tried to take Claremore from me by the wager you made me make on the Derby – and why now—'*

'Why now you have stolen my horse!'

Cassie shouted the last sentence out loud, so great was the awakening of her rage. Then for a long time, a seemingly endless amount of time, she just sat enveloped in the dark of a moonless autumn night while she realized the depth of her enemy's fury. For to Cassie there was now no other explanation, there was nothing else which could even begin to make sense. Having failed in every other way to destroy Cassie, Leonora had taken from her the one thing Cassie could not vouchsafe for herself and her family. She had taken away their future.

As far away outside in the dark silent grounds of Claremore a night owl hooted a lonely call, Cassie rose and replaced the now only half-full decanter of brandy on the drinks table and slowly made her way upstairs to bed.

Dimly somewhere she heard the telephone ring, somewhere out in the dark. But all she did was moan softly and turn away from the sound of it, burying her face in the softness of her pillow.

Still it rang, again and again and again. Without turning

she reached a hand out backwards and fumbled for the receiver. With a clatter it fell off its cradle and in and out of her hand.

Picking it up blindly she somehow got it round to her mouth.

'Yes?' she said, after drawing a deep, long breath. 'Yes, who in hell is this? Don't you know what time it is, for God's sake?'

'It's a quarter to seven,' a voice said in her ear. 'Don't tell me it's too early. I thought you trainers were always up with the sparrows.'

Cassie looked slowly round her bedroom, trying her best to pull it into focus. Sure enough there were shafts of bright and early summer sunshine lighting up the edges of the windows and walls behind her heavy curtains.

'OK,' she said wearily, rolling onto her back and running the back of one hand across her forehead. 'OK, so who is this?'

'This is Joel Benson,' the voice said, deep and measured. 'You won't remember.'

'Joel Benson,' Cassie repeated slowly, closing her eyes tight against the pain in her head. 'Joel Benson. Yes. Yes I remember you. You're the fellow with all the answers? Who came here to take photographs of—' She stopped and drew another long, slow breath, but this time for a different reason. 'You came here to take photographs,' she finished.

'Yes,' the voice said. 'You got me.'

Cassie raised her head and looking down at herself saw to her horror that she was still fully dressed.

'I'll tell you one thing, Mr Benson,' she said, cupping the phone on her shoulder and sitting up to begin taking her clothes off. 'You sure as hell were right about not having horses' portraits done while they're still racing. Oh boy, were you right.'

'Yes, I was,' the voice agreed. 'And while you may not believe this, I've been feeling pretty bad about that.'

'I assure you – there is really no need.'

'I haven't been feeling guilty about telling you. I've been

feeling terrible about the fact that I had begun my pre-liminary sketches . . .' The voice fell to silence.

'When the horse was stolen,' Cassie prompted.

'It's no good. I can't help thinking that if I hadn't—'

'Don't,' Cassie cut in, screwing her eyes up even tighter against the increase in the pain of her headache. 'Don't even begin to think such things. As my husband used to say, there's nothing so idle as a hypothesis. With the help of an *if*, he would say, you might put Ireland into a bottle.'

'Yes? In that case I'll try not to think it any more.'

'Just tell me why you rang, Mr – Mr—'

'Benson.'

'Mr Benson, I'm sorry.'

'There's no need to be. You must have dozens of people like me crawling round your yard every day of the week.'

'Not quite like you,' Cassie said without thinking, then frowned as she wondered why she'd said it.

'I've found out something,' Joel continued after the briefest hesitation. 'That's what I'm ringing about. The man on the gate at Ascot?'

'The man on the gate at Ascot,' Cassie repeated slowly. 'Which man, which gate?'

'The man who checks the horses in and out of the stableblock.'

'So what about him?'

'He's dead,' Joel replied. 'Which wouldn't mean a thing if he hadn't committed suicide.'

He waited for a moment before adding one word which suddenly got Cassie sitting bolt upright.

'Apparently.'

131

# Eight

He was waiting for her at the arrivals gate, dressed so it seemed to Cassie in the same old white tennis shirt and faded cord trousers that he'd worn on his visit to Claremore, the only visible difference in his appearance being the addition of a battered old panama hat in deference to the heat wave. Even the degree of beard stubble appeared to be the same.

'Good flight?' he enquired, throwing away a half-smoked Gauloise. 'My car's over here.'

Before she had time to respond he ambled on ahead of her towards a filthy and battered car. It was so abused Cassie had no idea what sort of car it was but waited patiently while Joel cleared away the debris off the front passenger seat before she got in and sat down, hoping that the stains she had spotted on the upholstery were as ancient as the car. After several attempts to start the car the engine finally fired, and Joel drove them out of the airport rather too fast for Cassie's liking.

'You look as though you spend your life in this car.'

'Cars are for driving, not washing. Now – this gate man. That's why you're here, after all.'

In response to his glance Cassie nodded her agreement, although that was not the real reason she had flown over to England at the first possible opportunity. Naturally she was anxious to learn the latest developments concerning the theft of her horse but she could do that over the telephone or the fax. There was no real need for her to make a special journey just to hear out some near stranger's latest conjecture based on information which anyhow would eventually come her way via the police. No, the reason she had come was because she could not bear to spend one more moment in her home. The place she loved most in the world had suddenly become like a prison to her and she needed to escape from it. Just for a few days she needed to flee from the pressures, the responsibilities and the memories and try to find the person who she feared might be becoming lost. Never in the whole of her life had she ever thought of drowning any of her sorrows, not through all the grief she had suffered losing her second baby, and not during the anguish of losing Tyrone. Yet the night before she had gone to bed having drunk well over half a bottle of brandy and the act had shamed her, so much so that even had Joel Benson not rung with his news she knew she would have found any excuse to run away, just for a few days.

At least that is what she had told herself before she instructed her secretary to make the necessary arrangements. She was going for her own peace of mind. That was the real reason for her journey. It had nothing to do with anything or anybody else, least of all the tall, dishevelled man beside her or anything he might have to say.

'I don't think you've heard anything I've said,' he was telling her now.

'I'm sorry,' Cassie replied. 'I didn't sleep very well last night. Go on with what you were saying.'

'The police have made no connection between the so-called suicide of the gate man and your horse,' Joel said. 'At least not publicly.'

'But you know something they don't know.'

'A friend of mine's a reporter.' Joel adjusted his rear view mirror which promptly came away in his hand. He sighed and chucked the mirror over his shoulder onto the back seat as he continued. 'He told me there was a note. Said something about taking money to turn a blind eye, how ashamed this guy was, blah blah. And that the horse had been stolen by some totally unheard-of Middle Eastern terrorist group.'

Joel glanced at Cassie and then leaned across her to get at a Cellophane bag of jelly beans in the half-open glove compartment. 'You eat these things?' he asked. 'Help yourself.'

He dumped the bag on Cassie's knee as he returned his gaze to the road ahead.

'That's hokum,' Cassie said, carefully picking out two or three light green beans. 'If it was some terrorist group we'd all have heard about it. They don't kidnap horses just for the hell of it.'

'Good,' Joel said, blindly rifling the bag of sweets. 'That's what I meant by 'apparently'. If there's no Middle Eastern terrorist group, then why did this chap kill himself? And why do I always manage to pick the banana ones?'

Joel cranked down his window and consigned the unwanted sweet to the elements, signalling at the same time his intention to turn off the motorway.

'I'm going to take you to see his bungalow,' he announced. 'I went there myself this morning. Before I came to meet you at the airport.'

It was a small yellow pebbledashed bungalow on the outskirts of Windsor, in a quiet nondescript road near the racecourse. In contrast to the ordinariness of the ugly, one-storey house the front garden had been lovingly tended and was a riot of summer colour, bright red salvias, yellow marigolds and multicoloured pansies precisely arranged in rows at the front of beds planted out with carefully shaped standard roses. After he had stopped the car, Joel got out, stretched slowly and then came round to sit on the nearside wing while he stared at the bungalow. Cassie got out and stood beside him, looking where he was looking but without knowing the reason why.

Joel nodded at a wooden garage attached to one side of the house. 'Scene of the crime,' he said. 'Carbon monoxide poisoning. Tube from exhaust to driver's window, usual scenario. Suicide note in his pocket. End of story. Apparently.'

'And you don't believe one word of it,' Cassie stated.

'I believe a man is dead,' Joel replied, carefully selecting another jelly bean now that he had full charge of the bag.

'But we don't know he killed himself. Police think he did, but I don't. Not necessarily.'

'You as keen an amateur gumshoe as you were an amateur jockey?' Cassie enquired with a smile.

Joel glanced at her, popping a couple of red jelly beans in his mouth. 'Hmm,' he said before pushing himself up off the wing of the car and wandering towards the garage. For want of anything else to do Cassie followed him.

'When did this happen?' she asked as he bent down to peer through the keyhole of the locked garage.

'Day before yesterday.' Joel straightened up and ambled on round the side of the garage into the back garden. Again Cassie followed him. 'You won't have read about it in the papers because it didn't make 'em. And why should it? Some insignificant old bloke decides to end it all – story for the local rag I'd say, rather than the tabloids. Particularly since no details of what was in the suicide note were released.'

'So how do you know there was a suicide note?'

Joel just smiled and tapped the side of his nose a couple of times.

'OK,' Cassie said, accepting another sweet as Joel waved the bag at her. 'So what makes you suspicious?'

'I often get the feeling there's more to things than meets the eye, don't you?' Joel wondered. 'Maybe it's just artists. I don't know. But I get this feeling sometimes. That there are layers. Beneath layers.' Joel carefully pulled a fine rose towards him and bent down to sniff it. 'Bit too much smell for my taste, but even so.' He stood up again and looked round the garden.

'Even so what, Mr Benson?'

'He obviously lived for his garden, the late Mr Waldron,' he said. 'And these roses. They don't look like the roses of someone of suicidal bent. Not unless that someone had sudden good reason. *Won't you come into the garden? I should like my roses to see you.* OK – now let's go and have some lunch.'

*　　*　　*

He took her to a pub in Eton where he insisted she drank a double Bloody Mary while he had a pint of beer and ordered a large portion of sausages and mash.

'How can you eat food like that on a hot day like this?' Cassie wondered, ordering herself a brown bread chicken sandwich.

'Because I'm hungry,' Joel replied. 'The suicide note was typed, by the way.'

'By the way of what?'

'I just think it's odd,' Joel replied, as he lit another Gauloise. 'Would you sit down and type your farewell to the world? I wouldn't. Makes me think he was possibly killed rather than topped himself, gassed somewhere else then driven back to his house and shut in his own car with the engine running. He'd been dead for some time when they found him.'

Cassie said nothing. She just sat and sipped her drink and wondered whether Leonora was capable of organizing such complex villainy. But then such now was the depth of her own paranoia that it took very little time to convince herself that Leonora was entirely capable. As far as she was concerned, Leonora could easily be the Godmother of the entire Mafia.

'You know, you're ridiculously beautiful, Mrs Rosse,' Joel said, snapping Cassie out of her reverie. 'Your pictures don't really do you justice.'

'I take that as a compliment.'

'It's hardly an insult. You've got very good colouring and wonderful bones.'

'Next thing you'll be holding a pencil up in front of me – you know, the way artists do?'

'I'm not talking as an artist. I'm talking as the man sitting here opposite you.' He said it quite factually, without any flirtation. In fact he barely looked at her as he spoke, turning his concentration instead to trying to remove the ash from his Gauloise which had fallen in his beer. Even so, Cassie found herself blushing, and to disguise the fact she pulled her compact from her purse and pretended to check her lipstick.

'How long has your husband been dead now, Mrs Rosse?' Joel asked out of the blue, startling Cassie so much she dropped her compact onto the floor. Joel bent down to pick it up at the same time as she did and their hands touched.

'It's all right,' Joel said, slapping it back into her hand much the way someone would return something to a child. 'It's not broken.'

Cassie straightened up, brushed her hair back from her eyes and took another sip of her drink.

'I was asking you how long your husband had been dead,' Joel repeated, waving to a waiter who was trying to locate the owner of a plate of steaming sausages and mash. 'It must be twenty years, yes?'

'If you know, don't ask,' Cassie replied, trying to control the anger she suddenly felt. Joel caught the tone of her voice and looked back at her.

'I didn't intend to be impertinent,' he said.

'So what did you intend?'

The waiter put down Joel's lunch in front of him and Cassie's in front of her, but this didn't deter Joel from continuing.

'I just wondered if you'd ever thought of remarrying.'

'You don't know me well enough to ask me such a thing.'

'It's because I don't know you well enough that I'm asking.'

Seeing the waiter was listening to their exchange Cassie fell silent until he had gone, taking the opportunity to finish her drink.

'If you don't mind,' she said once they were alone, 'I think I'll wait for you in the car. I really didn't sleep at all last night and I'm feeling a little lightheaded.'

Halfway through cutting all his sausages into four identically sized pieces Joel glanced up at her. 'Don't take offence,' he said. 'I really can't see how enquiring after someone who's been dead that long can be construed as offensive.'

'You're not sitting where I'm sitting. Is your car open?'

'There's little point in locking it.' He watched her as she got to her feet. 'Come on,' he said finally as she pushed her chair back. 'Have another drink.'

'I don't want another drink.'

'Then sit down. I really don't like eating on my own.'

'I'd have thought you were well used to it.'

'Just sit down. Please? You haven't touched your sandwich.'

Cassie glared at the top of his head and then sat slowly back down.

'People who have interviewed you,' he said, pushing a quarter of sausage round his plate in the gravy. 'They ask you all sorts of leading questions. Speculate whether or not you might ever remarry.'

'That's their job. It isn't yours.'

'All right, it's not my job, but it is of interest.'

Cassie idly opened one of her sandwiches and stared at the thin and unappetizing slice of chicken within.

'Let's just stick to the matter in hand,' she suggested. 'Whether or not this poor man who killed himself—'

'Or who was killed.'

'Whatever. What matters is whether or not he really did have any connection with the disappearance of The Nightingale.'

'I don't know. He could be a red herring.'

Cassie said nothing. She just closed her unwanted sandwich up and wearily pushed away the plate.

'Don't you have any theories?' Joel suddenly wondered. 'Or beliefs? You must have.'

'If I do, why should I tell you?' she asked in return. But all the same Cassie did.

Joel hardly said a thing until he had practically driven into London. After he had listened to everything Cassie had to say in the pub and on the journey up the motorway he had just grunted a couple of times, rubbed his stubble and then put on a Joe Cocker tape while he worked through what he had heard. Twice Cassie asked him if he thought she was being absurd, and twice he assured her that she was not, even though he doubted that if her friend Leonora was involved she was in it alone.

'All things are possible,' he said suddenly as he drove off the Hammersmith flyover to join the long line of traffic making its slow way into town. 'It is perfectly possible for someone like your friend—'

'She's not a friend.'

'For someone like whatever she's called with her money and connections to arrange the kidnapping of your horse. After all she's an alcoholic and she's been addicted to drugs and people like that – they get these ideas. But murder.' He petered off into silence.

'That's your theory,' Cassie reminded him. 'The murder thing. You don't really know what happened to that man. It's all surmise.'

'So's your theory about whatsername. Is she really bad enough to arrange or agree to the killing of someone?'

'Maybe she didn't know about it.'

'But say she did.'

'I don't know,' Cassie sighed. 'I guess I really don't know anything any more.' She looked round and now the traffic had come to a standstill she saw he was already looking at her, looking at her in that particular way of his with a deep frown creasing his high forehead and a strange light in his big dark eyes.

'You know more than you think,' he said without taking his eyes off her. 'More than you'll ever know you know.'

There were two policemen waiting to see her when she arrived at the Dorchester, having been told by her secretary when they had rung Claremore where Mrs Rosse would be staying. One of them, a short squat man with glasses, introduced himself as Detective Inspector Bristol and his confederate, a tall balding man who was sweating profusely, as Detective Sergeant Wentworth. In the privacy of Cassie's suite of rooms DI Bristol told her of the latest developments of which Cassie pretended she knew nothing while watching out of the corner of her eye the trembling and sweating Sergeant Wentworth who seemed about to pass out. When she got the chance she asked if there was anything she could get him and he asked for some coffee, explaining that it had been his night off the evening before and he'd probably stayed out longer than he should. While they waited for room service to answer Cassie's call, DI Bristol droned on about the possible Middle Eastern connection while Cassie idly wondered how he ever managed to squeeze his oversize thighs into the trousers of his badly made suit.

She got rid of them as quickly as she could, once the crapulent and badly hungover Sergeant Wentworth had drunk his coffee, most of which he spilt in his saucer, and DI Bristol had droned on further about the thoroughness of Scotland Yard's ongoing investigations into the disappearance of her horse. However, before they finally went it was made abundantly clear to Cassie that the police thought it was undoubtedly the work of not Middle Eastern but Irish terrorists and that regardless of the great esteem they all had for the famous horse, further investigation would be a waste of the taxpayers' money.

As soon as they were gone Cassie rang Josephine to see if they could meet, and when after a short pause her daughter agreed Cassie hurried off to keep an appointment which was to cause her further heartbreak.

Josephine had given her an address in Malcolm Square, a pretty house whose bright shiny yellow door was opened by Mark Carter-James.

'Welcome,' he said with his usual smile. '*What* a lovely surprise.'

Josephine didn't come out to welcome her but waited instead in the immaculately furnished drawing room. When Cassie came in they embraced each other, Josephine kissing her mother on both cheeks and taking both of her hands as she did so, but instead of coming to sit beside her as she normally did whenever they saw each other she went and sat instead on a small pink-upholstered button-backed chair opposite, next to where Mark had positioned himself.

At that moment for some reason Cassie knew something was wrong.

'Now then, now then,' Mark said, affecting a mock comic tone. 'What can I get you, Mrs Rosse? There's champagne? Or there's champagne?'

Cassie agreed to champagne in order that Mark would have to leave the room to fetch it and she might quickly ask her daughter what exactly was the matter, but the wine was sitting already opened in an ice bucket. So instead they all made small talk about Cassie's journey and the lack of any progress in the search for The Nightingale.

'Pappa is convinced it's the IRA,' Mark said, ruffling Josephine's hair before handing her a drink. In return Josephine smiled back up at him. *A lover's tiff*, Cassie thought. *That's all it is. They've simply just had one of those overheated arguments lovers go in for.* 'It has all the hallmarks of their usual botched job,' Mark continued, interrupting Cassie's thoughts. 'He reckons if it had been the work of professionals *something* would have been heard. Right? He says it's Shergar all over again.'

'I don't think so, Mark,' Cassie replied. 'I've said all along that I don't think it has anything to do with the IRA, or any terrorist group come to that.'

'*Really?*' Mark frowned at her, as if this was the first he had heard of it. 'But what else could explain it? Any of these other bastards who like to go round making all our lives a misery would have sent you a demand ages ago. Surely you don't think someone had stolen your horse for a prank? Or even in a simple vendetta, do you?'

'Anything is possible,' Cassie replied, echoing the thoughts of Joel. 'Don't you agree, Jo?'

Cassie's attempt to bring her usually loquacious daughter into the conversation was met with only the briefest of responses from the chair in which Josephine was sitting with her back to the light from outside. To cover up an awkward silence Mark waved the bottle of champagne over both Cassie's and Josephine's untouched glasses and made some more idle talk about the lack of success the police

141

both in Ireland and England seemed to be having in establishing any significant leads.

'This really is a charming house,' Cassie said after she had allowed that particular conversation to peter out. 'I take it this is yours, is it, Mark?'

'Ours,' Mark said. 'Yes, we're very pleased with it. It belonged to a chum, and luckily said chum had the sort of taste we like so practically all we had to do was move our few sticks in, as it were, and put on the kettle.'

'I see,' Cassie said, with a glance towards Josephine who still was giving nothing away. 'So then this is where you intend to live.'

Now it was Mark's turn to glance at Josephine who was looking up at him as if uncertain whether or not to speak.

'Obviously Josephine is still so excited by everything that she can't put it all into words, isn't that right, poppet?' Mark sat himself down on the arm of Josephine's chair and took one of her hands. 'Mrs Rosse,' he announced with a slow smile. 'You wondered if this is where we intend to live and in reply I really should tell you that this is in fact where we *are* living.'

'I see,' Cassie said, endeavouring to keep her face set so as not to show her surprise, a surprise she knew would be quite unwarranted in the times in which they were all living. 'I understand.'

'No, I don't think you do, Mrs Rosse,' Mark continued, refilling his own glass as he spoke. 'The point is Josephine and I were married on Monday.'

'On *Monday*?' Cassie heard herself exclaiming.

'You have some objection to people getting married on Mondays?' Mark asked with a too-easy laugh. 'I do hope not, because myself – I've always thought Monday to be a very hard done by day. I like to think of Monday as a renascence. The start of something wholly new.'

'Yes, Mark,' Josephine said, as if by way of a full stop. In return, Mark put his arm round the back of her chair, as if staking out his territory.

'Why?' Cassie said as she leaned back in her chair. 'I mean, I don't understand. Why?'

'Because we love each other, Mrs Rosse?' Mark replied as if he was guessing at a riddle. 'Why else?'

'I meant why didn't you tell me? Why didn't you let me know, Josephine? And – and Mattie? All of us. I'm afraid I don't understand.'

'I don't see what there is to understand,' Mark wondered before Josephine could reply. 'You knew we wanted to get married.'

'Yes, I knew you wanted to get married,' Cassie agreed. 'It's just as Josephine's mother I would have quite liked to be there.'

'We didn't think it fair. With everything that's happened to you, suddenly to throw our wedding at you as well. So we thought we'd simply just go and get married then perhaps celebrate it afterwards. When all was once more right with the world.'

Cassie looked at the man standing before her, wondering why it was that she found it impossible to believe anything he said. 'Jo,' she said, unable to disentangle her feelings. 'Is this true? Because if it is you know I would still have wanted to be there. That finally you – you and Mattie – finally you both are more important to me than anything else?'

'It's quite true,' Josephine said, unable however to hold her mother's steady look. 'Maybe we read it wrong, but the intention was right. We really thought it would be just one more thing for you to deal with. You wouldn't have just let us get married quietly, which is what we wanted.'

'How do you know?' Cassie demanded.

'Come on. You'd have thrown an enormous great wedding at Claremore, and really that was the last thing you needed. Particularly right now.'

'Look,' Mark said easily, smiling at Cassie. 'I've booked us a table for dinner at Olivar's, by way of celebration. Please. I'm sure you'll understand when we've talked it over fully, Mrs Rosse. Now, Josephine, poppet? Do you need to get anything or go anywhere before we go?'

'No. No, I'm fine, thanks.'

'I'm not,' Cassie said, getting up from her chair. 'I need

to go to the bathroom. Come along, Jo, you can show me the way.'

'Don't be too long, you two,' Mark said warningly from behind as Cassie hurried them both from the room. 'We're running a little late already, poppet. And you know how I hate being late *anywhere*.'

Cassie almost ran up the flight of narrow stairs until they were on the landing. Pushing the half-open door of the bathroom wide she took Josephine's hand and pulled her into the room with her, closing and locking the door behind her.

'So what's going on, Jo?' she demanded. 'And don't tell me nothing. What in hell do you mean running off and getting married without telling me? Let alone inviting me?'

'It's all my fault,' she said, *sotto voce*. 'This has nothing to do with Mark. This is *my* doing, not his. Mark would have waited, I promise you he would. He wanted to wait until you said we could get married, but I didn't let him.'

'Why?' Cassie asked, feeling more wounded and bewildered than she could have believed possible.

'Because I'm pregnant.'

'OK,' Cassie heard herself agreeing, while some other part of her tried to cushion the shock of Josephine's being pregnant by a man she disliked so entirely. 'So you're pregnant. But that's no reason to get married, is it? Least not nowadays. I know you think I'm old-fashioned, but there was no need for you to get married because you were pregnant. If you hadn't wanted to get married I'd have looked after you. You know I would, sweetheart. You know that I'd have taken care of you.'

'Supposing I hadn't wanted you to?' Josephine shook her hair back and turned to look at her mother. 'Suppose when I found out I decided this was something I could handle all by myself for once? Can't you see that?'

'No, I can't see that at all. You're my daughter.'

'And Mark is my husband.'

'He wasn't then. Not when you found out. You didn't have to rush off and marry him.'

'Yes I did. Because of you.'

'But I've just told you,' Cassie insisted. 'There was no need to get married because of me.'

'It wasn't because of you as a person,' Josephine replied, looking her mother in the eyes. 'It was because of what had *happened* to you. Because of what you found out when your mother died, that your father and she had never got married, and that you were a bastard.'

The word lay between them now, bleak and offensive, and there was nothing Cassie could say. All she could think of was herself shouting at Josephine's father all those long years ago. It was New York and she was just twenty.

'*But I'm a bastard, Tyrone. You can't marry a bastard!*'

*And Tyrone's kindness, and his answering laugh.* '*Who says I can't! I'd like to see who'll stop me!*'

'*Everyone will stop you. I'm a bastard.*'

'*So what! So bloody what!*' *And he had married her, notwithstanding.*

'Jo—' Cassie began, wanting to explain, only to be interrupted by a sharp knock on the door.

'Sorry, ladies,' Mark called from the landing. 'But we really do have to go!'

'Call me tomorrow, will you?' Cassie whispered to her daughter, as she pretended to wash her hands. 'I'll wait in to hear from you.'

'There's no point,' Josephine replied without conviction. 'I'm OK. Don't worry.'

'Don't worry,' Cassie repeated with a sad smile. 'You just wait, Jo. Just you wait till that baby of yours is born, and then try telling me not to worry.'

# Nine

These were the times Cassie found it hardest being alone, the times when she had to close the door on yet another empty hotel room in yet another town or city. These were the times when she longed for the company of a man, not for what he could do for her physically but metaphysically. Certainly there were times when she also wanted to be made love to but somehow by turning her mind back to the years she had spent with Tyrone she could put that want aside more easily than she could the need for male companionship. She loved male company. The right man could bring out the best in Cassie as even the most sympathetic of her women friends could not, which of course was the way it should be, Cassie always reasoned. As far as she knew from what she was told by her men friends and what was written about her in newspapers and magazines she was still both attractive and eligible, not just financially but as a woman, although Cassie knew as well as any woman that success and money added greatly to their allure. It gave women a patina, a gloss and a desirability because it gave them a majesty and an independence which seemed to act like an aphrodisiac on men. It also brought women like Cassie into contact with the type of men they would rarely if ever otherwise meet, the men who were at the top of their own professions, the men who headed their own empires, the men who were stars in their own rights.

Not all of them were acceptable company. Many of them were quite the opposite, vain, aggressive men whose only interest was in their own history or their next move, but others were very interesting, dangerously so some of them, able to imbue the atmosphere of their encounters with a sense of risk that was intoxicating, and while Cassie never allowed herself to be either fooled or carried away at these moments none the less she took great enjoyment in them. They were yet another challenge.

But of all the men she had known since Tyrone had died, only two had been lovers, and only one of those had she loved. The man she had not loved but by whom she had been so nearly duped was the sadistic Jean-Luc de Vendrer, while the man she had loved but not enough to marry had been Frank, the eldest brother of her dearest childhood friend Mary-Jo Christiansen who was now a nun somewhere out in Africa. All her other encounters had been part and parcel of long-established friendships and although deeply felt had never for one moment looked like evolving into affairs let alone marriage.

But now for the first time for a very long time she wished she had someone by her side again, someone who would have guided her through the difficulties she had encountered that evening and then taken her back to their hotel first to talk her down and then to take her to bed. She had spent too much time on achievement in the last years, she thought, looking round her beautifully furnished hotel room, and too little on living, but then perhaps since Tyrone's death achievement for her had become a replacement for living.

The phone rang as Cassie was sitting staring at the unopened bottle of Martell cognac she had placed in front of her ten minutes earlier.

'Hi,' the voice said. 'I've been ringing you.'

'I've been out, Mr Benson,' she replied, recognizing the deep, drawling voice immediately. 'I do have a life, you know.'

'Thought you might like to hear the result of the autopsy. Carbon monoxide poisoning, time of death about six p.m.'

'Yes? So what's new?' Cassie moved the bottle six inches closer but left it unopened.

'There could be a little more to it than that.'

'I don't suppose you'd feel like telling me over a drink,' Cassie wondered, and then wondered why she'd asked. *I can't be that lonely*, she told herself. *It can't be that bad that I have to ask someone I barely know let alone hardly like to come and drink with me. Surely not.*

'Suits me. I do most of my telling over a drink,' she heard Joel reply.

'On second thoughts maybe it's a little late.'

'Half past ten? This is the time I wake up. Hold the front page. I'll be with you in about fifteen minutes.'

The cork was still in the brandy bottle when he arrived in her room. The first thing Cassie noticed about him was that he'd changed his clothes and was now dressed in a faded pair of old black rather than blue cord trousers and a much darned blue wool crew-neck jumper. He still had his old tennis shoes on, however, only now he was wearing them with socks. He'd also washed his hair and obviously only recently because it was still damp and slicked straight back.

'I used to stay here as a kid with my grandfather,' he said as he walked in. 'It was very good in those days.'

'It's very good now,' Cassie assured him as she closed the door behind him. 'I never stay anywhere else.'

'Don't you have any Scotch?' he asked when Cassie offered him cognac. 'I don't drink that. Stays with me for too long.'

Directed by Cassie to a sideboard Joel fished around in its contents and found an unopened bottle of whisky.

'Actually it's not true about cognac,' he said, unstopping the whisky bottle. 'The reason I don't drink it is because it's too easy. I drink too much whenever I drink cognac. Which is why I don't drink it very often. Is that what you drink?'

'I don't usually drink anything, except wine really,' Cassie replied. 'And champagne.'

Joel looked at her but didn't ask. Instead he poured her a glass of cognac, himself a large glass of whisky, and then sat down in a chair opposite her with his long legs stretched out wide apart in front of him.

He raised his glass in silent toast, drank, and then stared

148

at the ceiling. 'OK,' he said. 'So if you were going to kill yourself, would you do it at tea time.' He made it a statement, not a question, as if it could only be answered one way.

'If I was going to kill myself I don't suppose it would matter what time it was,' Cassie replied.

'No, it would,' Joel argued. 'Because it does. There's a study on suicide, several in fact. Prime times are midday, early afternoon, but most of all and hardly surprisingly night time. Late night, middle of the night. Even first thing in the morning. Very few at tea time. Hardly any at all, in fact.'

'How do you know this, Mr Benson?'

'I know it. And call me Joel. No, I think if Mr Waldron deceased was planning his own deceasement he wouldn't have done it at tea time. Tea time he'd usually be having his bacon and eggs. Not at all the sort of time methodical rose gardeners like him do it. I'd have put him down as a late night or a first thing in the morning job. The first more likely. Half a bottle of whisky, some pills maybe, then into the garage and goodnight world. Wouldn't you?'

He suddenly stared at Cassie, catching her eyes directly with his. For a moment Cassie couldn't speak.

'I don't know anything about suicide,' she replied.

'Never felt like trying it?'

'Yes. Maybe. No, not really.'

'I'd be night time. I couldn't do it when the sun was shining. Or when it was light.'

'Have you ever been tempted?'

Joel thought for a moment, sticking his tongue in one cheek and then the other. 'When my mother died I was a bit chewed up. She was good news, my mother. Used to ride point to point without a hat, blond hair streaming in the wind. Won the Ladies race at the South and West Wilts four years running. Taught me everything I know about horses. And race riding. But I didn't actually want to kill myself. I simply *felt* suicidal.' Joel raised his thick eyebrows very high and drank some more whisky.

'Anyway,' he went on after a moment. 'To get back to

Mr Waldron. I get this feeling he was bumped off. Somewhere else around about the unholy hour of tea time, then taken back *chez lui* dead of night, *et voilà.*'

'You mentioned your theory to the police?'

Joel shook his head and stretched his legs out even further. 'They've always managed without me before,' he said with a sudden short smile. 'You see the point is, no one saw Mr Waldron deceased come home that afternoon. None of his neighbours, most of whom are net curtain detectives.'

Cassie smiled. 'I never heard that before,' she said. 'Net curtain detectives. That's neat.'

'People in roads are like that. They see everything yet no-one saw Waldron's car. So I'm told. Someone heard a car though, according to my source. Sometime after midnight.'

'Could have been Mr Waldron deceased.'

'Dead men don't wear plaid and they don't drive cars. By midnight, Mr Waldron had been deceased for at least six hours. Now, much as I take your word about this place, I don't really like drinking in hotels. So let me take you to this club I know. In Covent Garden. It's very good. You'll like it.'

Cassie did. There was a small dance floor by a bar in a dark brown panelled room, every available inch of whose walls was hung with black and white sporting prints. The bar was like an American bar, high stooled and highly polished, stocked with drinks it seemed from every corner of the world. There was food to be had too, fresh sea food, home-made pasta, chilli con carne or well fried or grilled steak, with what Joel informed her were excellent French fries. There was also *crème brûlée* among the half dozen puddings, one of Cassie's admitted weaknesses, and since she had eaten nothing at all earlier and now found herself ravenous she was only too happy to agree to eat. As they ordered they sat up at the bar drinking whisky sours and listening to the music being played by a first-class piano trio accompanying a tall pale-faced singer with raven black

150

hair and an hourglass figure wondrously contained by a sparkling red sequinned body-hugging long dress.

'You're right, this is good,' Cassie said after they'd ordered. 'London's all too short of places like this.'

'Yes,' Joel agreed. 'There really aren't enough clubs, are there? Bars, whatever – where people our age can go out to enjoy themselves and feel comfortable.'

'This feels comfortable.'

'I hate hanging out in places where everyone's the same age as your children.'

'Do you have children?'

'Not that I know of.'

'Then why the reference?'

'I was being emblematic.'

'You never married?'

'I married. My wife – ex – she didn't want children. Just a career. Want to dance?'

'Would you have liked to have children?'

'Yes. Now come on out and dance.'

He was a good dancer. Cassie thought he might be because underneath the apparent shambles she had already sensed a natural elegance, but even so she was surprised at quite how good he was. She was also surprised at quite how much she enjoyed dancing with him, and how much she liked the way he held her, with his arm held just firmly enough around her waist and her right hand held up against his left shoulder.

'How come everyone here's wearing ties?' she said, leaning back to look at his face. 'And that there's a notice to that effect but they let you in as if you own the place?'

'Probably because I do,' he replied. 'The pianist is my brother. We own this joint jointly.'

Over a mouthwatering dinner of the best calamari in a provençal sauce Cassie had tasted in an age, followed by a small and succulent beef fillet cooked in brandy and shallots, they talked. Or rather Cassie talked. Even more accurately, Joel got Cassie to talk. Although naturally taciturn, he was extremely adroit at steering conversations in the direction he wanted and then in making the other person stick to the subject. Not that Cassie was aware for one moment of the skills he was deploying. She talked because the ambience was right and because she suddenly felt at ease with the man sitting next to her on the banquette. At first she had been deterred by his somewhat abrupt manner and almost monosyllabic responses, but the more they talked the more she found him to be much more honest company than many more loquacious men that she knew. She liked the way he never let her off the hook. If she hinted at something he would persist until the hint became a theory, a fact, or an opinion and if he considered anything she said an exaggeration he would quietly but persistently make her re-examine her claims until they assumed more realistic proportions.

Cassie talked about everything and anything until before she even realized it she found herself telling him all about Josephine and her sudden marriage. 'I shouldn't be saying this,' she confided, but Joel just grunted that it was hardly an official secret and poured them both some more wine. Encouraged, she told him more, about her three children, how Mattie and Padraig had been adopted although for very different reasons, and finally about how in light of losing her second baby Josephine had become so especially precious. Joel said nothing here, but simply looked at Cassie and nodded to show his understanding, and so after a short silence while they both stared at the half dozen or so couples still dancing in front of them she began to talk about her missing horse and wonder to him why anyone should steal him and keep him without a word and without placing any demand before her.

'You believe it's out of jealousy,' Joel suggested. 'That green-eyed monster that mocks the meat it feeds on. Being a man I say money's behind it. Someone who stood to make or lose did it. With things like this, money's always the root cause.'

That wasn't necessarily the reason behind the other famous horsenapping case, Cassie argued. Some said the other Derby winner that disappeared was stolen as *vendetta*, a revenge for a wrong done to someone's woman, and although it was never proved it had to be given serious consideration since just as in her case there had been no word of the horse and no demand from its captors.

'But you haven't crossed anyone in love, have you?' Joel wondered, lighting a cigarette as the waiter poured them coffee. 'Or have you?'

'Of course not,' Cassie said, reminding him that he knew her theory was not based on that sort of need for revenge and he stood corrected, agreeing out loud that if indeed it was revenge, then it stemmed not from the theft of someone's husband or lover but from the result of a teenage tennis match that had taken place about thirty years earlier.

'Let's dance again,' he suggested after they'd drunk their coffee. 'We've done enough talking for a while.'

Cassie agreed, but no sooner had she stood up than she sat back down again. 'I'd rather not dance to this,' she said quietly, looking up at him. The band was playing 'Stardust', Tyrone's favourite tune.

'Yes you can,' Joel said, taking her hand and pulling her gently but firmly to her feet. 'According to the motto in the cracker, it takes time to heal the heart but that is all it takes. And I'd say nearly twenty years should just about do it for anyone.'

'How did you know?' Cassie asked as he led her back onto the dance floor.

'From the look in your eyes,' Joel replied. 'It would have been impossible not to know.'

One of Joel's studios was above the club, the one he used for doing his smaller work, heads, racing trophies, people's children and pets and so on. Cassie couldn't remember how it came about he took her up there for one minute it seemed they were downstairs dancing and the next he was unlocking the door at the top of the second flight of stairs and letting them both in. He'd knocked two rooms into one, he explained, as well as putting in a large window in the roof for extra light, and the result was a decent sized and airy studio. Off it was a small kitchen which was a mess of clutter, a bathroom and a small room which from the visible jumble of papers and notebooks spread over an old rolltop desk looked as though it was used as an office while above was a large gallery bedroom dominated by a king size old brass bed covered in a multicoloured patchwork quilt.

'It used to be a sweatshop apparently,' Joel told her as she shut the kitchen door. 'Twenty or thirty women crammed into these two rooms. Hardly bears thinking about.'

Cassie was less interested in past history than in the work she could see all around her, in particular an absolutely stunning head of a young girl in bronze.

'I do all my big stuff in an old coachhouse I rent out in Barnes,' he said. 'And I use a foundry down in Basingstoke.'

'This is so beautiful,' Cassie said, unable to take her eyes off the bronze head. 'Really so fine. So beautiful. I thought you did mostly horses. And animals.'

'That's my niece. My brother's daughter by his second marriage. His first wife ran off with his drummer.'

'With the guy I take it who *used* to be his drummer,' Cassie said, smiling, but still looking at the bronze.

'Nope,' Joel replied. 'With the guy who still is his drummer. Bro says it's a lot easier finding a wife than it is a decent drummer.'

'I wish I'd known about you before,' Cassie said.

'I agree.'

'I meant—' Cassie broke off and went to look at another of Joel's works, this one a small carving of a foal lying asleep. 'What I meant was I'd have loved you to do my children's heads. Mattie and Josephine. For some reason I only have watercolours of them when they were small. I'd have loved a couple of bronzes.'

'It's not too late,' Joel murmured, picking up a notepad to check some agenda or other. 'I've been asked the same sort of thing before. As long as you've got plenty of photographs and the subjects are available for a couple of sittings, I can do it.'

'You're on,' Cassie said, looking at him. 'I mean it.'

'Good.' Joel chucked the notepad down and pulled a

half-full whisky bottle out of a drawer in a sideboard covered in sketches and small rough plaster models. 'Be warned though. I'm not cheap.'

He held the bottle up towards Cassie, who shook her head.

'No thanks,' she said. 'I've had quite enough to drink.'

'You can never have enough to drink,' he corrected her. 'You can either have too little or too much, but there's no such thing as enough.' He poured himself a shot and then collapsed on an old sofa along the wall behind him.

'I should go home,' Cassie said. 'I had no idea of the time.'

'I'd rather you stayed here,' Joel said, not looking at her but lighting a Gauloise Blonde instead.

'Do you think I'll pick up a cab outside? Or should you call me one?' Cassie asked, pretending she hadn't heard him. 'I think probably you should call one, don't you?'

Joel took a deep draw on his cigarette, then exhaled the smoke upwards. 'If that's what you'd rather,' he said, reaching for the telephone. As he called, Cassie said nothing further. Instead she walked round the studio looking again at his work.

'It'll be about ten minutes,' Joel said, draping his long legs over the arm of the sofa and picking his drink back up.

Cassie continued to prowl around the room examining all Joel's wonderful work in detail, with the result that by the time the cab finally arrived Joel was fast asleep. Cassie picked up the intercom as soon as it buzzed and told the driver she was on her way down. Then she let herself out, closing the door quietly and carefully behind her.

Once again the telephone woke her early. Once again it was Joel.

'I know it's early,' he said. 'But I'm sorry about last night.'

'That's OK,' Cassie said, closing her eyes and lying wearily back on her pillow. 'We both had too much to drink.'

'That's not what I'm sorry about,' Joel said. 'I'm sorry you didn't stay.'

'I had a lovely evening,' Cassie said carefully, after a moment. 'I really enjoyed myself.'

'What are you doing today?'

'I have to see my daughter. If she'll let me.'

'And then?'

'That depends.'

'You don't have my number. Here it is.'

He gave her two numbers, the studio above the club and the number of his house and workplace in Barnes. Then he rang off.

Mark said she couldn't speak to Josephine since she'd gone off to the hairdresser's. Cassie asked for that number only to hear Mark laugh and say that he hadn't an idea where his wife had her hair done. But he'd give her any message she liked when he picked her up on their way to the station. It appeared they were off to Paris for a belated honeymoon and wouldn't be back for ten days. Cassie said there was no message but just to send her love, then she hung up.

Her telephone rang just as she was running her bath. She hurried to answer it, hoping that it was her daughter.

'Mrs Rosse,' a man's voice said factually. 'You should return home at once. And tell that friend of yours to stop snooping.'

'Hello?' Cassie asked hopelessly. 'Hello? Hello?' But the line was long dead.

Joel was still at his studio in Covent Garden. When Cassie rang and told him about the anonymous call he said he'd take her to the airport as soon as she'd booked a flight. The hotel got her on the first plane in the afternoon and Joel picked her up from the hotel in his terrible old car. As she walked towards it she noticed a sticker in the back window which read *My other car is a Lada*. She smiled to herself and got in, Joel having leaned over from the driving seat and pushed the passenger door open.

'The age of chivalry is not dead,' she remarked.

The car had stalled, but after another bout of groaning and coughing from the engine Joel finally got it to start.

'You look as though you'd just come from a health farm,' he muttered.

'I don't feel it,' Cassie replied.

Joel gave a sigh and without paying much attention swung the car out into the road, causing a taxi to brake sharply and practically run up on the kerb.

'I remember when hangovers used to make me feel sexy,' he said. 'Now they just make me feel hungover.'

'Maybe you should cut down on your drinking.'

'You don't know me well enough to suggest such a thing.'

'And you don't know me well enough to suggest that I should spend the night with you.'

'Hmmm. *Touché*.'

As they drove out of town they discussed what the meaning of the anonymous telephone call might be. Cassie said she didn't know but rather than take any risks she'd rung her staff at Claremore to alert them and also the detective from Special Branch who had been assigned to the case. She had taken particular care to speak to Mattie to make sure he was aware of the latest threat.

'Maybe it's good news,' Joel suggested, dumping a fresh bag of jelly bellies on Cassie's lap.

'No chance. I gave up believing in fairies long ago.'

'I booked a seat on your flight,' Joel said after they had driven in silence for some five minutes. 'Only provisionally.' He looked round at her. Cassie stayed looking ahead.

'There was no need,' she said.

'You never know. If something did happen you might be glad of some dispassionate company.'

'Dispassionate?'

'All right – disinterested. I'm not involved like you are. I can still see the wood in spite of the trees.'

'There's really no need,' Cassie said, but there was now a weakening in her voice and she turned to look at him.

He was looking back at her and when he saw her looking at him, he smiled.

'I packed my toothbrush,' he said. 'On the off chance.'

As always, the sight of Claremore filled Cassie's heart with happiness. The moment the car her secretary Rosemary Corcoran had arranged to meet her turned into the long drive, even though she had only been away a matter of days she felt such a sense of homecoming that for a moment her breath caught in her throat.

Joel, too, had been talking quite animatedly until faced with Claremore he had fallen into silence. Together they both looked out of the windows at the late autumn landscape, the beeches gone to copper, the acers to deep red, and the huge oaks to a papery pale gold while behind the woods and finally the house the great Wicklow mountains rose to view, clothed in a pale swirl of grey mist.

'*And the autumn weather turns the leaves to flame,*' Cassie heard Tyrone's voice singing, as Joel murmured, 'This is one hell of a lovely place, Mrs Rosse.'

'I always mean to plant more late colour,' Cassie said thoughtfully, studying the landscape. 'And then when autumn comes, it seems it's all there anyway.'

Joel stopped and looked up at the house when he got out of the car, and for a moment Cassie stopped too, afraid that he had seen something wrong, but when she turned to look at his face she realized he just wanted to look at the house. While he gazed she looked again at the place where she lived, her handsome stone Georgian house with the lights already on in most of its long sashed windows, and the smoke from the many fires curling slowly up to the misty sky. Then as she began to walk up the stone steps the front doors were opened and Wilkie her devoted lurcher, escaping from the clutches of Erin, leaped out of the house and bee-lined for his mistress who caught him just in time to prevent him from jumping up all over her best suede overcoat.

'Wilkie, you sausage,' she said, bending down to hug the dog's head to her. 'You're a right old Houdini, aren't you?'

Glancing over her shoulder she saw Joel was still standing with a deep frown on his face as he surveyed the rest of the house, so she went on in ahead of him while Dick hurtled out past her to go and collect the bags from the car.

'And what sort of journey did you have?' Erin asked automatically as she took her mistress's coat, her eyes already well and truly fixed on the tall man still standing on the steps outside. 'And who's this you've brought back with you? An architect or a builder I'd say from the way he's surveying the place.'

'This is Mr Benson, Erin,' Cassie said as Joel finally wandered backwards into the hall. 'He's been to Claremore before. He came over to take pictures of – of Nightie. For a sculpture.'

'But not in the front way,' Joel said, slowly turning round and taking in every detail of the lovely hallway. 'Strictly through the tradesmen's gate and up the back drive straight to the yard. I never really saw the house at all.'

'Well you wouldn't from the yard,' Erin said curtly, beginning to pull the coat from Joel's shoulders as if he was one of her charges. 'This would be some sort of place if you could see the old stables from the front winders, now, wouldn't it?'

'Hmmm,' Joel said, submitting to Erin's nanny-like tactics as she half turned him round to get his overcoat off. 'It's some sort of place anyway.'

At that moment Dick crashed back in through the front doors still in his stockinged feet even though he'd been out and down the steps to collect the baggage, only to be collared by Erin's free hand and pushed back to wipe the leaves off his socks on the doormat.

'Come on,' Cassie said to Joel, unwrapping her cashmere scarf from round her neck and draping it on one of the fine Hepplewhite hall chairs. 'Let's go through and Erin will bring us some tea.'

'Erin will do nothing of the sort,' Erin called from the cloakroom where she was busy hanging the coats. 'What

159

I will do is bring you in the champagne I have in the fridge for you.'

'Champagne?' Cassie wondered, as if she'd never heard the word before.

'I thought you might like to celebrate,' Erin said with a sniff and another odd look at Cassie's dishevelled guest. 'Mattie rang to say you had a twelve to one double at Punchestown.'

Cassie settled into the chair by the roaring log fire while Joel prowled around the drawing room inspecting everything from the photographs of The Nightingale winning his great races to the paintings which hung on the walls, very much as Cassie had inspected his studio the night before. Neither of them said anything while the tour of inspection was made, Cassie sitting with her hands held out to the flames and Joel making his way slowly and thoughtfully around the room.

'Hmmm,' he said as he finally came to a stop in front of the portrait of Tyrone which hung above the fireplace. 'That's a Sumner, if I'm not mistaken.'

'You're not mistaken,' Cassie assured him.

'Don't usually much like his work,' Joel mused, pulling his mouth to one side and chewing the inside of his cheek as he examined the portrait first from afar and then close to. 'But this isn't half bad. For once his subject's every bit as well painted as the horse.'

A moment later the door burst open and Dick charged in, somehow managing to keep the unopened bottle of champagne and the two glasses on the silver tray he was carrying despite both the speed of his entrance and the deliberate attentions of Wilkie, who was busy trying to pull off one of the wretched young man's socks.

'Leave that down there, Dick, there's a good fellow,' Cassie asked the now red-faced lad. 'If you just put the tray on the desk I'm sure Mr Benson can manage the bottle.'

'Ah yes, yes, very good, Mrs Rosse,' Dick gasped. 'I shall do precisely that.'

Having safely deposited the tray, Dick then rushed back out of the room but now with only one sock left on his huge feet, Wilkie having triumphantly purloined the other which he now took round the drawing room shaking dead like a rabbit.

Joel collected the champagne and proceeded to open it without incident. He poured it into the two glasses while seemingly never taking his eyes off the portrait.

'It would appear from the look of him Mr Rosse enjoyed laughing,' he remarked. 'He bears the expression of one who sees life as a pleasure.'

'Yes,' Cassie agreed, glancing up at the painting of her dead husband. 'The last thing I remember about him was the sound of his laughter behind me.'

Joel looked down from the painting to stare at Cassie with an even deeper frown than usual. 'Good health,' he said finally, raising his glass. 'Cheers.'

'*Slainte*,' Cassie said, raising her own glass back.

'It was one of the great love matches, right?' Joel asked after he had drunk some wine. 'I remember reading about you two in some magazine or other.'

'I wouldn't know how to answer that,' Cassie said.

'Then don't.' Joel returned to staring at the painting, saying nothing else until he had finished his first glass of champagne. Then he wandered over to the desk, poured himself a second glass, topped up Cassie's, and settled in an armchair directly in front of the fireplace.

'I remember the article quite well,' he said after a silence. 'He was very popular with all his women owners – in fact with women in general.'

'Yes,' Cassie agreed carefully. 'Women seemed to like him.'

'Women seemed to love him,' Joel corrected her. 'Yet apparently you were it. You were the only one.'

'You find that surprising,' Cassie said, for want of anything more audacious.

'I find it amazing,' Joel replied. 'In the world we all live in. Who's this?'

Cassie turned to see where Joel was looking and saw Erin at the door with young Padraig all ready for bed holding one of her hands.

161

'This is Padraig,' Cassie said with a smile as Erin led the child to her. 'Come to say good night.'

She lifted the child onto her knee, allowing him to stand to put his arms around her neck and kiss her.

'Will you read to me tonight?' he asked. 'Please?'

'Ah now sure that's hardly fair, Pad,' Erin said kindly. 'Certain people are just a wee bit tired after their long journey.'

'No I'm not,' Cassie said, kissing the tousle-haired little boy on one cheek. 'I'll come up and read to you in just one minute.'

'And so will I,' Joel said gruffly. 'That is if I'm allowed.'

'He doesn't normally like strange men,' Cassie said after they had sat down to dinner.

'I'm not that strange,' Joel protested.

'People he doesn't know,' Cassie smiled, opening out her linen napkin. 'But he couldn't have enough of you.'

'It's not what you tell it's the way you tell 'em,' Joel replied, rearranging his place setting, before beginning his soup. 'How long were you married?'

'Not long enough. How about you?'

'I wasn't really married. We didn't have children and I don't count that as being married. Not *wanting* to have children, that is.'

'We wanted—' Cassie began, and then stopped.

'Go on.'

'I was just going to say we always wanted a large family, that's all,' Cassie replied.

'But you couldn't which was why you adopted,' Joel said, without looking up from his soup.

'Right.' She looked down the table at him and found him looking back at her. Neither of them smiled, they just looked at each other. Then Joel slowly raised his dark crescent-shaped eyebrows until his eyes were wide open and it seemed to Cassie that she saw him perhaps for the first time.

'I'm very glad you decided to come across here with me, Joel,' Cassie said when they got up from the table.

'Even if that call last night meant nothing, I'm still glad you came.'

'Good,' Joel said. 'I'm glad too.'

But the call had meant something, and when its meaning became apparent Cassie was even more grateful for Joel's presence at Claremore.

*Anxiety came and went to a greater or lesser degree, but never more than at night when Cassie would find that by some miracle whatever tiredness she had been suffering during the day fled and she became as bright as the electric light that burned in the old lamp by her bedside. She would lie propped up against her pillows reading or staring round her at the contents of what had once been her marital bedroom. Everywhere there were photographs of Tyrone, everywhere their gifts to each other, paintings bought for each other, little boxes specially commissioned, everything that told of those years now gone and of Tyrone taken from her so early, leaving her alone.*

*It was then that questions came endlessly into her head leaving her mind reeling sometimes with the thought of her own stupidity. Of course they had all been right. Never should she have taken up the challenge and run The Nightingale as a four-year-old. Instead she should have accepted the offer from Leonora's mother for a third share in the syndication of the horse, founded her fortunes and been rich for life, but she had not. What she had done was to give in to her intransigence and go right in the very opposite direction, indulging herself in impossible and quixotic dreams, determined to stand up against those responsible for darkness in the world.*

*'Fool,' she would tell herself as she lay in the room built from her past, and then to try to put the thoughts from her mind she would read or sew, longing for morning to come, for the first weak shafts of light to appear at the side of her curtains, for the first sound of the birds, for the fear of night to be replaced by the comfort of everyday things, however mundane or domestic those things may be, however tiresome and endless some of the given tasks.*

But then sometimes she found herself unable to deal with the thoughts that came to worry her so late in the night, and with sleep a seeming impossibility Cassie often took to walking in the grounds in the small hours of the morning as soon as it began to get light. With Wilkie running deliriously ahead of her giving chase to any rabbits he could find to put up she would even take herself up into the hills behind the house to try to clear her head of her doubts and fears. First up the springy turf of the foothills and sometimes on fine mornings up into the rocky terrain of the very mountains themselves, far above where the trees and the shrubs stopped growing, until she stood high on a mountain with the fresh wind in her face and her beloved Claremore still asleep far below.

On these long lonely walks she would often revisit the past, happy moments from her childhood when their neighbour Mrs Roebuck would make her granddaughters and Cassie hot muffins and pile the table high with butter and cream and home-made cherry jam. Moments when she and her childhood friend Mary-Jo would hurry to rise from their bunk beds at Mary-Jo's parents' farm, longing to be the first ones up and out to see Mary-Jo's foal, to see him lying fast asleep in the lush grasses of his paddock or to catch him taking his first feed of the day from his mother.

'Prince!' Mary-Jo would call if the foal was just standing by or following his mother, while Cassie would whistle softly to beckon him, and inevitably he would soon come trotting across to them, his little ears pricked and his bright eyes shining, and stand happily while Cassie stroked his furry neck and Mary-Jo tugged at his ears before rolling his upper lip back in a grin and cantering off to rejoin his mother, performing en route one of those funny half-rears in which foals take great delight, and just to show that he could.

'Wilkie!'

In the woods behind Claremore early on the morning after Cassie had dined with Joel, the antics of Wilkie brought her out of her reverie as she realized the dog was

164

*trying to draw her attention to something ahead of them both something that had already caught his own. First he ran in front and then he circled back to Cassie, until eventually between the early morning mists she saw a shape through the trees and as she did so her pulse began to race. Far ahead of her was a large animal, tethered to a tree.*

*Cassie knew who it was at once. She could feel his presence, even though the horse made no sound nor did he seem to move a muscle as she ran to where he was tied.*

*'Nightie!' she cried. 'Nightingale! Nightingale!'*

*He was tied by a length of rope which was far too short for his comfort to a tree on the very edge of the woods, a place where sooner or later he would be bound to be seen from the road. As soon as he saw Cassie he whickered, but not as he usually whickered. The sound that he made was as if he was dying.*

*'Nightie?' she called again, unable to accept what she was calling. 'Nightingale, is it really you?'*

*Then when she was close she stopped dead in her tracks, hardly believing that the horse which stood before her was the magnificent creature she had last seen in all his pomp at Ascot, a horse which instead of staring majestically down at her with the look of eagles now looked back at her with glazed and sunken eyes. Gone were the pounds of hard muscle and gone was the hide of supple black skin, and instead Cassie found herself looking at a creature which seemed to be nothing but slack skin and protruding bone. She moved a step towards him but when she did so the horse grunted and began to roll his eyes and pull with all his remaining strength at the rope. Cassie put one hand up to steady him but as she did she saw a flash of teeth and only just stepped back in time before the horse snapped shut his jaws.*

*They both stood stock still then, Cassie to allow the horse to see who had found him and the horse to watch and wait to see if yet another hand was raised against him. After a long silence Cassie said his name again, quietly, soothingly, softly, and the more she said his name the less agitated the horse became until he stopped trying to break away from the rope which held him by his head and stood quite still, watching Cassie as she now moved slowly towards him, watching with a dull but wary eye. He held his head half lowered and then just as Cassie finally reached him he slowly turned to stare with both his eyes at the woman beside him who was now holding up one hand.*

*She made no effort to take a hold of the rough rope collar which tethered his head. Rather than make any such move which might frighten him again Cassie just lowered her own head and dropped her shoulders the way she always did when trying to attract a stubborn horse from a field, keeping her hand below the horse's muzzle so that he could smell her familiar scent while she waited for him to make the move. For another minute or so neither of them made any real move other than for the horse to sniff carefully at the person standing beside him enough to slowly lower his tired head until his muzzle rested in the palm of her hand.*

*And so they stayed for some time, the horse putting so it seemed the full weight of his head in Cassie's hand, until at last he lifted it again and slowly turned it to bury his nose in her hair. She in return put her hand to his neck and held it there, the far side of his neck, round and under it, while The Nightingale pushed his muzzle further into her hair until after a while he dilated his nostrils and blew, just the once. When he had done so, Cassie put her other hand up slowly to his mouth and the horse opened his lips onto the palm of her hand to touch it carefully with his tongue. Again they just stood exactly as they were before a long time later with what sounded like a sigh the horse lifted his head and put it over Cassie's shoulder where he left it to rest.*

*'There now,' Cassie whispered. 'There now, my beautiful boy, you're home now and everything's all right and there's nothing to be frightened of now you're home, not ever again.'*

*With his head still resting over her shoulder, Cassie wrapped both her arms now around his neck and gently hugged him to her, the centre of her life restored, the sun returned to her universe.*

166

'Come on, my old love,' she heard herself saying as she undid the rope and with Wilkie at her side began the long slow walk back to Claremore. 'Come on while we get you back to your box, the box we've had ready for your return since the day you disappeared. Come along with me now, and Bridie will wash you off all that dirt and mud, rub you dry, and see to all these cuts and scratches you seem to have collected.'

She talked to the horse every inch of the way, her left hand on the leading rope at first and her right hand on the top of his neck. She walked beside his head telling him all, telling him how much she loved him and of the care that would be taken of him now, she talked to him until there was no need to lead him any more, until there was no weight on the halter at all and the horse was walking freely of his own accord beside her, one pace behind her shoulder with his nose just touching the back of her shirt.

Twenty minutes later she stood below the window of Liam's cottage.

'Liam!' she called. 'Quick now, Liam, and out of your bed as fast as you can! The Nightingale has come home!'

When they got to the gates of the yard, Liam opened them and Cassie led the horse in to where the rest of the staff had hurriedly gathered, some of them still pulling on their clothes while others who had already started seeing to their duties stood by with brooms and pitchforks still in their hands. No-one said a thing at first, no-one except Mattie who had rushed down from the house with Joel in response to a call from Liam.

'Is it really him?' Mattie said as he came to his mother's side. 'Is it really him after all this time? I can't believe it. I can't believe that it's him.'

'It's him all right, Mattie, just look at his markings,' Cassie replied. 'Not that I wouldn't know him anywhere, but you can see his famous markings.'

'I'm looking at his condition,' Mattie said. 'There's nothing on him. He's gone completely to nothing.' Mattie put up his hand to stroke the horse's neck but the moment *he did so the horse reared violently, pulling himself almost free from Cassie.*

*'No!' Cassie cried. 'Leave him – get away from him, Mattie! Don't anyone come near him!'*

*Everyone fell back, those near to him well away from him, and those far from him even further.*

*'You must give him room,' Cassie urged. 'Give him space. God knows what this poor creature has been through.'*

*Yet even as Cassie tried to calm him the horse reared above her again, rolling his eyes and snorting until Mattie and Liam were both driven even further away.*

*'Here, Nightie,' Cassie said, allowing the rope almost to pass from her hand. 'Here, old boy, here – it's all right – no-one's going to harm you. I promise.'*

*Then as suddenly as he had tried to break away the horse was calm, back on four feet and standing stock still, allowing Cassie to raise her free hand and once more to drape it over his neck.*

*'Come on now, old fellow,' Cassie said once she was sure the horse was quiet again. 'Come on while we get you in your box and Bridie sees to you and Liam prepares you your bran mash, with a bottle of your favourite stout in it. Come on now, there's a good boy.'*

*She didn't try to lead the horse by his head in case he was still afraid, still frightened that someone – as someone had obviously done while he had been away – might again raise a hand against him, or hold him back away from them with a pitchfork stuck in his side. She just walked beside his head, slowly so as to lead the way, and as she went so the horse followed, less than a pace behind her with his nose once again touching the back of her shirt.*

*Gone now was his toe, the famous bouncing jaunty walk of his, that flash of a pair of proud eyes, the pricking of his big ears and the rhythmic swing from side to side of his handsome head. Instead on unshod feet he shuffled his way forward in the way a hostage might when he is suddenly released from the darkness.*

*Except that in this instance there had been no miraculous*

rescue. The captive had simply been returned to where he belonged without any demand and without any why or wherefore, which was why Cassie's face now wore such a look of concern, for like everyone else in the yard she was wondering what the point of all this dreadful exercise had been.

And then it came to her.

'Pray to God that I'm wrong, Bridie, but I think I know what they've done.'

'What?' Bridie asked, turning back to Cassie, suddenly fearful. 'What are you talking about, guv'nor? The horse is back here alive and in one piece so what can they possibly have done to him? Other than half starve him and beat him up. Sure in no time at all with care and good feeding we'll have him back—'

'That isn't what I mean,' Cassie said, reaching out over the door to turn the stable lights on before dropping to her knees beside the horse. 'Oh God oh Jesus I thought so!' she cried as soon as she was down on the straw. 'Oh God will you look what they've done! Oh, the bastards – the bastards! They've only gone and castrated him!'

# Ten

The first thing Cassie needed to know after the initial shock had worn off was whether the horse was free from infection. Niall Brogan was up in the yard twenty minutes after Mattie had called him and after giving his patient a thorough inspection the vet pronounced him to be clean.

'The horse is in bad shape, that goes without saying, but at least the castration was done professionally,' he said. 'For that at least one can indeed be thankful. We have to imagine that if this was the purpose of taking him the people who did it had to ensure the animal didn't contract a lethal infection. That way they could be certain of getting him back to you alive in order to make their point. Otherwise it seems no-one cared that much for him. From the slackness of his skin and the tone of his muscles he can't have been given anything much other than hay and grass. I've seen horses in better condition than this coming straight off the hills. Like us all, I'd give a king's ransom to get hold of the sods who did this to him.'

Even so, Niall was confident that under round-the-clock supervision they could nurse the horse back to fitness and so start him back on the road to health. To start the ball rolling he injected the animal with large doses of vitamins and iron, as well as giving him a full antibiotic cover, having first taken some samples of his blood to test for everything from anaemia to liver function.

'It's going to be a slog, Cassie,' Niall said as they walked slowly out of the yard, leaving Bridie to rug the horse up and settle him down. 'But I think he'll make it. He's a big tough sort of horse, with a fighter's determination, so there's every hope that if he husbands his strength we can get him back to his old bonny self.'

'He'll never be his old bonny self, Niall,' Cassie replied flatly.

'That remains to be seen. A lot of horses actually improve when they're gelded. I'm not saying Nightie *will* improve because that would be all but impossible, but there's every chance he will not dramatically *dis*improve. That's what I meant. You could well still have a racehorse on your hands. Not the horse he was perhaps, not the greatest racehorse that in my opinion ever graced a racecourse certainly, but one still good enough to earn his living.'

'Nightie's earned his living, Niall. He's earned his living ten million times over. What remains to be seen is whether he's changed. Whether he's still his wonderful old benign self and I doubt that he is. My impression is that he no longer likes anyone near him. Except me. And Bridie. You saw for yourself. We were the ones who had to hold him for you to get anywhere near him. And you couldn't get anywhere near him till you'd tranked him.'

'It's early days, Cassie,' Niall tried to reassure her, although he had seen for himself the difference in the big horse's behaviour. As soon as the vet had entered his box the animal had bared his teeth and started to wheel round and plunge at him. It had taken all his, Bridie's and Cassie's considerable skills to get a needle into him in order to sedate him and even when the drug had started to work in his enfeebled state the big horse had still tried to have a go. 'I'm sure once he's settled into the old routine he'll be back to himself,' Niall continued. 'Listen – there was never a bad bone in that horse's body, and whatever terrible time he's had I can't for the life of me see him changing character completely.'

'I can,' Cassie said, and said it again to Joel and Mattie when they sat in Cassie's study having an early drink. 'I think his character's changed. He never took fright before because he never knew fright.'

'Give him time, like your vet says,' Joel replied, taking out a packet of cigarettes.

'You can hardly expect an animal who's just been through such an ordeal to come back as if he'd just been having a pick of grass,' Mattie argued, refusing the offer of a Gauloise.

'I'll kill her,' Cassie said suddenly. 'I'll tear the bitch's evil heart out.'

Joel looked at her. 'The bitch being Mrs Lovett Andrew, I suppose?'

'Who else?' Mattie asked.

'But you don't know it was her,' Joel said, with a deep frown. 'You don't have a single shred of evidence.'

'Who else could it have been, Joel?' Cassie retorted. 'Who else would have gone to that particular extreme to get back at me? Don't look at me like that. I'm not mad. Leonora thought she could buy into the horse, on the money-can't-buy-love-but-it-sure-as-hell-can-buy-everything-else principle. She couldn't beat us so she thought she'd join us, and when I told her no way, you should have seen the look in her eyes. You don't say no to the Von Wagners. Nobody has ever said no to the Von Wagners.'

'Except you.'

'Yes.' Cassie looked back at Joel. 'I know you think I'm crazy,' she said, 'but think about it. Anyone else with a grudge, or rather a *liability* as the bookies call it, would just have kidnapped the horse and shot him. Terrorists would have made demands. And it's not going to be anyone else because nobody else would have had the savvy. Or the muscle, or whatever. It was either money, terror or revenge, and I'll take revenge. Look – even if Nightie hadn't made it through the season unbeaten, which is a possibility—'

'A very small one.'

'It's still a possibility. So even if he had got beaten in the Arc, say, he would still have been worth just as much as he was before the race. So short of simply killing the horse—'

'And leaving you to claim the insurance,' Joel interposed.

'Yes,' Cassie slowly agreed, with another look at him. 'So short of simply killing Nightie, much the best revenge would be to geld him, right? With that one simple operation there goes every penny that he's worth.'

'You can still claim the insurance,' Joel replied. 'I

remember from our horse insurances at home there's some clause or other about *wilful castration on behalf of those responsible for the theft*. So since there can be no doubt about the theft or about what happened to the horse, they'll have to pay out.'

Cassie got up and walked to the window to look out at the hills far beyond. 'How much would you have said Nightie was worth before he was taken?' she asked.

'I have no idea exactly. An average to good Derby winner is worth at least one to two million as a stallion, so I should imagine your horse was worth maybe five times that.'

'Or more,' Mattie said. 'As a stallion he could have been worth anything up to twenty mill.'

'Now tell him the rate to insure an entire racehorse,' Cassie said to her son. 'While he's racing and then afterwards as a stallion.'

'Seven to ten per cent.'

'Most insurers wouldn't even offer cover on Nightie. Certainly not at that figure. Most of them wanted fifteen to twenty per cent. Who has that sort of money? Maybe the sheikhs do but I don't. I certainly didn't at the beginning of this year. Two million to insure ten? You're joking.'

'You could have raised it,' Joel said. 'You have the collateral.'

'And if something had happened to the horse, which it did, and they paid out, I still have the interest to pay back on the loan, which could be anything up to three hundred and fifty grand. Just in interest. I really don't have that sort of money lying around, Joel. I have serious cash flow problems. Every penny I make goes back into Claremore. Since the horse belongs to me and me alone and wasn't syndicated, the only obligation to insure was to myself.' Cassie shrugged, and then lapsed into silence.

'The horse doesn't stand insured?' Joel asked, now up on his feet and standing beside her.

'He's insured all right,' Cassie replied. 'But only for what I could afford to insure him for.'

'Which was?'

'A fraction of his worth. One million.'

＊　　＊　　＊

After a light lunch and a long talk Mattie went off to do some business and Cassie took Joel up for a walk in the foothills with Wilkie. At one point Joel offered Cassie his hand as they negotiated a steep path. When she no longer needed it she still held on to it and their pace slowed. They said nothing for a long while, until large clouds rolled in front of the sun casting the whole valley into shadow. Rain began to fall, heavy drops that fell into their faces blown by the stiff wind that had suddenly got up, yet on they walked at the same pace as if oblivious of the weather's sudden change.

'All right if I stay on for a while?' Joel asked out of the blue as he helped Cassie over a stile.

'If you're worried about me, there's no reason,' Cassie replied. 'I can cope. I've always coped before.'

'In that case you won't mind if I stay on,' Joel grunted, following her over the stile. 'Knowing you, the last thing you'd want would be someone around while you weren't coping. Matt said I could shack up in the empty guest cottage. Something the matter?' He looked round to where Cassie was still standing by the stile.

'I'll catch you up,' Cassie said. 'There's something I want to do.'

Once he had gone, lost to sight in a small belt of trees which lay below by the top pond, Cassie turned and headed away in the other direction. She walked hard for ten minutes until she came to the oak tree up which Tyrone had built himself a tree house when he was a boy and where often on a summer's night he and Cassie would sit with a bottle of wine counting the stars. Pulling the rope ladder away from the trunk she climbed up it and into the wooden house, which like everything Tyrone had turned a hand to had been built properly and to last. There were bits and pieces of their life together even up here in the tree house, an old wind-up gramophone with a pile of equally old John McCormack 78s still in their original HMV paper sleeves, some Dashiel Hammett paperbacks which were Tyrone's staple fare, the flyleaf of every one covered in his notes

174

recording his own secret handicap ratings for horses he intended to back. There too was an old crystal set in a plywood box given to him as a boy, and which he had restored to perfect working order, a wickerwork picnic hamper with most of its set of light green cups and plates still held in place with white plastic straps, a teddy bear belonging to Cassie because she had never been given one as a child, a small china horse, a leatherbound copy of *Black Beauty*. Even the old double sleeping bag into which they would climb on hot summer nights and make love was there in its place, rolled up in one corner.

'Dammit, Tyrone,' Cassie said out loud as an old faded photograph of her long-dead husband fell out of a book she had picked up to put back on the shelf. 'Dammit. Tyrone, you're everywhere. And perhaps—' She looked again at the photograph and then shut it quickly back up in the book. 'Perhaps it's finally time that you weren't,' she added, and sat herself down in the doorway to think.

She had no idea how long she stayed up there in the tree, nor did she hear voices calling for her from the gardens and then the grounds, but it was twilight when she finally descended and began her return to the house. She saw a vehicle coming across the fields in her direction with its headlights on, and shielding her eyes against their sudden glare she stopped as she realized it was making for her. Somebody jumped out of the passenger's side and ran towards her while the driver swung the vehicle round.

'Where the hell have you been?' It was Joel. He smelt of French tobacco and wine, a smell which far from offending Cassie made her feel safe.

'I've been up in the tree,' Cassie replied. 'Trying to sort a few things out.'

Joel sighed and looped a hand up to scratch his thick head of hair. 'Any idea of how long you've been gone?'

'Obviously far too long,' Cassie replied. 'But then that's my prerogative. I live here.' She climbed in the jeep behind Mattie who was driving.

'We've been over half of Wicklow looking for you,' Mattie said with studied indifference.

'Sorry,' Cassie said, brushing her hair from her eyes. 'But I just needed a moment or two.'

Mattie shoved the jeep into gear and accelerated back down the hill.

'Careful, Matt,' Joel sighed, hanging on to the windscreen of the jeep. 'There are sheep all over this field.'

'I know,' Mattie replied. 'I can see them.' Then he turned round for a moment to look at his mother. 'According to Joel you said he could stay on for a while,' he called over the noise of the engine as he changed down and swung out onto the track. 'I said he could doss down in the guest cottage.'

'Yes,' Cassie said, looking at the back of Joel's head and thinking what a nice shape it was. 'I don't see why not.'

That evening when it seemed the telephone had finally stopped ringing Cassie and Joel sat alone drinking whisky by the fire until late, Mattie having taken himself off to the village to console himself with some of his friends who lived locally.

'It was just as well you disappeared when you did today,' Joel said as he threw his last Gauloise into the fire.

'So you keep saying.'

'The press were all over the place.'

'So you keep saying.'

'Some of the things they asked.'

Cassie let the conversation hang for a moment, sipping at her drink and staring at the blazing logs. 'You're probably right,' she agreed in the end. 'I probably couldn't have coped. Not the way I feel.'

Joel was searching his pockets for more cigarettes, but evidently failed to find any. 'No point in asking you for a cigarette, I suppose.'

'There are some in the middle drawer of the desk. They're not French, they're Virginian. Extra mild.'

'Any port in a storm.' Joel pulled himself up from the

176

floor and wandered over to the desk. 'Closet smoker, are you?'

'I have one a week, after Sunday lunch,' Cassie said. 'But I'll have one now if you don't mind.'

Joel lit her cigarette and then his. Cassie inhaled and felt a sudden rush of nicotine that made her head spin.

'If only it wasn't so bad for you,' she sighed. 'I really like smoking.'

'*Tobacco is a dirty weed. I like it,*' Joel quoted.
'*It satisfies no normal need. I like it.*
*It makes you thin, it makes you lean.*
*It takes the hair right off your bean,*
*It's the worst darn stuff I've ever seen.*
*I like it.*'

'Who's that?' Cassie asked, smiling.

'Bloke called Graham Lee Hemminger. *It takes the hair right off your bean, it's the worst darn stuff I've ever seen, I like it.*'

Joel held up the whisky decanter which had an inch of whisky left in it. Cassie shook her head so he poured the remainder into his own glass.

'I wonder what's going to happen,' Cassie said, carefully drawing on her cigarette. Joel didn't prompt her, he just let her go on thinking out loud. 'I mean, I wonder what I'm going to do?' Cassie threw her half-finished cigarette onto the fire and folded her hands round the front of her knees. 'It feels – it feels as if I'd been floating on a wonderful warm sea for all this time and now it's suddenly turned to ice, that's exactly how it feels,' she continued. 'I'm trapped under the ice and it's all so unreal. You see, I'd hoped and prayed all the time that somehow I'd get him back, that by some miracle he'd be found and we'd get him home, and I never gave up. Even when everyone said there was no hope, I never relinquished mine. It was the only thing that got me through, that one day they'd find him, that he'd still be alive and I'd get him home. And now that I have, now that he's back, it seems as if there's no point any more. None at all. All this way that we've come, ever since Tyrone was killed, ever since Nightie was foaled. I know what he's done has been incredible – more than incredible, I guess – just as I know nothing can ever diminish his achievement, just nothing. Not ever. But now there's nothing to pass on.'

'I don't think that's true,' Joel said, but more by way of punctuation than from conviction.

'OK,' Cassie continued. 'So there was a chance he might not have turned out to be the greatest stallion in the world, but there was more of a chance he would. And even if he'd just turned out to have average fertility that would have been quite good enough. Everyone who loves breeding horses and racing them would have got a bit of him, and if he'd turned out to be as potent as say Northern Dancer think what that would have done for bloodlines. If he'd just passed on a quarter of his ability he'd have produced classic winners, you bet. Just like Northern Dancer, all over the globe. That way he'd have been truly immortal. Long after the people who saw him race are gone racegoers would still be seeing him reproduced in his offspring and I tell you – I tell you that's only what he deserved. But now – ' Cassie stopped and stared into the fire, unable to continue. Joel just drank some whisky and also kept quiet. 'Do you see now why I mean it might have been more bearable if they'd killed him? Rather than mutilated him and sent him on back home.'

'Yes,' Joel said slowly. 'I think it's a bit like a divorce. Sometimes you hear people say – women usually – you hear them say they wish they were widows because at least then they'd have something positive to remember. Painful maybe, but if the marriage had been good up to the point when one of the partners dies, then as you get over the pain you only remember the good times, not the bad. But with divorce, it's acrimony. Misery. Hatred often, finally. But above everything you have this sense of failure. So yes. Yes, I think I get what you're saying.'

'Is that how it was for you?' Cassie asked, still staring into the fire. 'Or don't you want to talk about it?'

'More or less.' Joel put down his glass and leaned his back against the side of the fireplace. 'Not that I'd have wished Julia dead – but talking in the abstract I reckon I'd have found it easier to rebuild my life if she had dropped dead rather than run off with somebody else, and after only a few years. Besides hurting somewhat, it sort of looks as if it is very much your fault. You have to live with your failure, you can't get away from it.'

'I don't see that.'

'You haven't been divorced.'

'I've lost a husband.'

'Better than being divorced from him. No, think about it, before you go off the deep end. You think you'd have got over being divorced from someone you loved as much as him? Having the life you'd spent together derided? You bet you wouldn't. Look – if you'd suddenly found out your old man had been cheating – you'd still be licking your wounds, believe me.'

'So what do you think I'm doing now?' Cassie looked at him, quietly furious.

'You wouldn't want me to tell you,' Joel said. 'Not now.'

'Go right ahead.'

Joel picked up his glass to check that it was empty and then put it down again. 'Any more whisky?' he wondered.

'You've had enough to drink,' Cassie replied. 'You've been drinking all day.'

'And I intend to go on drinking all night.'

'You drink too much.'

'I know.'

'Why do you drink so much?'

'Is that any of your business?' Joel enquired, closing his eyes wearily.

'Is how I feel any of yours?'

'Yes,' he replied.

'I don't see why.'

'Why do you think?'

Cassie stared at him in amazement, and Joel stared right back before leaning against the corner of the fireplace and closing his eyes.

'You really have had too much to drink,' she announced. 'Far too much.'

179

'Want to know something else?' Joel opened one eye to look briefly at Cassie, then closed it again. 'I think—'

'I'm not interested in what you think,' Cassie interrupted, trying to stop him from saying what she knew he was going to say.

'I think you were over the death of your husband a very long time ago.'

'I'm going to bed,' Cassie said, getting to her feet. 'You really are drunk.'

'I don't get drunk,' Joel said. 'I just tell it like it is.'

'Isn't that every drinker's epitaph?'

'You won't face the facts, Mrs Rosse,' Joel persisted. 'You have got over your husband's death but your problem is you don't want to get over it. You think that getting over the fact that he's dead would be like saying you don't love him any more. I have news for you. It isn't.'

'How in hell would you know?' Cassie said, stopping by the sofa to round on him again. 'You haven't ever lost anyone.'

'You don't have to be a baby to cry,' Joel said. 'You don't have to see an execution to be anti-hanging. You don't have to—'

'OK, I take your point,' Cassie interrupted. 'And now I really am going to bed – and I suggest you do too. Good night.'

'The king is dead,' Joel muttered as she crossed the room. 'The king is dead – long live the king.'

If there had been something worthless to hand, Cassie would have thrown it at him.

Cassie spent most of the following morning trying to restore her newly returned horse's confidence. But despite all her efforts The Nightingale would still allow only Bridie and herself near him, showing his teeth and lunging at anyone else who tried to cross the threshold of his stable.

'God knows what they did to him, guv'nor,' Liam said after he had finally given the horse best and retired the other side of the box door. 'The Lord alone knows what they did to him and why. Why anyone should lift a hand against a horse as Christian as Himself is beyond my comprehension. For he hasn't a bad thought in his head nor a bad bone in his body.'

'Ah sure horses get the oddest things into their heads, Liam,' Bridie said as she and Cassie stood stroking the horse's neck and trying to get him reinterested in his favourite peppermints. 'An uncle of mine was attacked by a mare after he'd broken one of her yearlings. He was always rough on horses and he must have gone too far on this occasion and when he'd put the youngster away and gone to tack up the mare she went for him and bit off one of his ears.'

'There doesn't seem to be any one particular bad cut or lump on him, Bridie,' Cassie said, having run a hand yet again all over her horse. 'And there doesn't seem to be anything about his head at all.'

'It'll be in his old head, that's where it'll be, won't it, old lad?' Bridie said, pulling at the horse's ears. 'That's where it'll be, guv'nor. Locked somewhere inside this wise and wonderful old head of his.'

When Cassie went to the feed room to make up a feed for the invalid, she found Joel sitting on the corn bin drinking a beer straight from the bottle while Mattie and Liam supervised the distribution of the horses' midday meal.

'Haven't you anything better to do?' she wondered as she passed Joel on her way to collect her horse's feed.

'Mattie here says the horse seems to let only women near him,' Joel mused, hopping down off the bin and ambling out after Cassie as she made her way back to The Nightingale's box with a bucket of food. 'That he's gone right off men.'

'I wouldn't blame him,' Cassie retorted, turning back the bar at the foot of the stable door with her foot. 'Seeing what they did to him.'

'They,' Joel mused. 'I thought you were convinced your chum was behind it. Leonora Von Whatsit.'

'If she was I hardly imagine she wielded the emasculator,'

Cassie replied. 'And if I were you, I wouldn't come any further. He very nearly caught Liam this morning.'

Joel shut the door and waited while Cassie gave her horse his specially prepared lunch. Once he had his head in the manger, Cassie came quietly out of the stable and headed for her office. Joel strolled across the yard behind her.

'Good day, Mr Benson,' Rosemany Corcoran said as Joel wandered into the office behind Cassie.

'Miss Corcoran,' Joel said, pushing his hair out of his eyes with one hand as he surveyed the cluttered room. 'You're like me, I see. You believe in the theory of chaos.'

'Only way I can work, Mr Benson,' the tall dark-haired young woman replied. 'If I know where anything is I can never find it. Here.' She picked up some sheets of paper stapled together at the corner and held it out to him. 'As you requested, a copy of all the owners and trainers with horses at Ascot for the King George meeting. Same as we gave the police.'

'The *pol-eece*,' Joel echoed thoughtfully. 'I love the way you say that. The *pol-eece*. Like the way you say the *fill-ums*.'

Cassie stared first at her secretary and then at Joel. 'Wait a minute – ' she began, only to be ignored by Joel.

'None of these names rang any bells?' he asked Rosemary, studying the papers in his hand.

'Not as far as I know, Mr Benson,' Rosemary replied. 'The *pleece* – is that better?' Joel smiled at her, then resumed reading through the list of names. 'The police have had it a good few weeks now and we haven't heard of any arrests.'

'What exactly are you after?' Cassie asked him, trying her best to keep her temper.

'Looking at who owned what on the fateful day,' Joel replied. 'Which owners were running which horses on the day of the kidnap. Your friend Jack Madigan, isn't it? Your friend Mr Madigan's line of reasoning. Mattie told me.'

'As my secretary's already told you, the police have already got that list—'

'The police don't know what to look for. See here—' He held the papers out. 'Two or three European entries in the first,' Joel mused. 'Then none in any other race except the big one.'

'Is that significant?'

'It might be,' Joel replied, shoving the papers in his pocket. 'It's certainly worth thinking about.'

When he found out Cassie was going into Dublin to talk to the detective inspector in charge of the case Joel cadged a lift in with her on the pretext of having to do some shopping.

'Fancy car,' he remarked as he climbed in the Aston Martin.

'It was my husband's,' Cassie told him. 'Mine's away being serviced today and anyway I like driving it.'

'You drive pretty well,' Joel remarked after a few miles which had been passed in silence.

'For a woman, you mean?' Cassie returned.

'The police should be coming out to see you,' Joel said, watching a hawk hovering over the verge. 'Rather than you going to see them.'

'I have some business to do, so I volunteered. Any objections?' Joel didn't reply, fishing in his pocket instead for the packet of cigarettes he'd taken from the desk the night before.

'Not in the car if you don't mind,' Cassie requested.

'Hmmm,' Joel grunted, staring at the pack of Cassie's Silk Cut. 'You'd hardly notice one of these damn' things.'

'I'd notice.'

They drove on for another four or five miles with neither of them speaking, Joel half whistling to himself now and then while turning the pack of cigarettes around and around in his hand.

'If I said anything last night—' he said, breaking the silence.

'You said plenty,' Cassie cut in. 'And if I were you I wouldn't compound the felony.'

''Twas a woman who drove me to drink and I never had the courtesy to thank her for it,' Joel said in a very bad imitation of W. C. Fields.

'As I said, you drink too much.'

'No more than the average sponge.'

Cassie changed gear and swung the car round a sharp righthander.

'You don't smile easy, I'll say that for you,' Joel said.

'I don't think there's a lot to smile about at the moment, that's why probably.'

'Will you have dinner with me this evening? We could stay in town and have dinner.'

'No thanks. Thanks all the same.'

'Busy?'

'No.'

'You just don't want to have dinner.'

'No.'

Joel thought for a moment, then breathed in deeply to show he was starting again. 'No you don't want to have dinner, or no you don't want to have dinner with me?' he asked.

'No I don't want to have dinner with you,' she replied. She then turned and looked at him briefly, as if wondering what he was doing there.

'Obviously I goofed,' Joel said.

'Maybe if you laid off the drink—'

'Most people drink because they have a skin too few,' he mused, tapping his fingers against the cigarette packet. 'Did you know that?'

'Is that why you drink?'

'I drink to make other people more interesting.'

'Thank you.' Cassie gave him another brief look only to find he was looking away from her, staring out of his window.

'Not in your case,' he said after a moment. 'I don't need to drink to make you interesting. In fact with you I don't feel I have to drink at all.'

They were on the main road into Dublin now, so Cassie put her foot down even harder and flew past a line of traffic.

'Did you have anywhere in mind for dinner?' she asked.

'I hardly know Dublin,' he replied. 'You tell me.'

*      *      *

For once unable to get a table at either of the two restaurants she regularly frequented and unwilling to allow Joel to take her any place where she used to eat with Tyrone, Cassie decided they would have to take pot luck, remembering in time a new restaurant her secretary told her had just opened in a street off St Stephen's Green. Possibly in the hope that he could persuade Cassie to dine with him Joel had come to town wearing a hand-painted tie hung loosely round the neck of one of his old cricket shirts, as well as a baggy blue linen jacket and a pair of chinos which had long since seen better days.

'I don't think that tie goes at all with that shirt,' Cassie murmured as they waited to be shown to their table.

'Then I shall remove the tie,' Joel replied, ripping the offending article of clothing undone with one hand.

'The management would rather you did not, sir,' the head waiter put in with an unctuous smile, pointing to a notice by the door. 'As you see there is a strict dress code, sir, that includes neck ties for the gentlemen.'

'OK then,' Joel replied reasonably. 'As a customer I reserve the right to tell you that I don't like the way you've done your hair. Centre partings are absurd.'

'If you would like to come this way, madam,' the waiter said, having finally chosen to ignore the insult.

'Let's just cut our losses and go and get some fish and chips at Baggot Street bridge,' Cassie suggested *sotto voce* as they were shown into the bar area.

'No way,' Joel replied. 'Nothing like a challenge.'

There were two other people in the bar, overdressed and of indeterminate age, the woman sitting staring blankly into space and the man sat bent over a bowl of nuts which he was slowly but systematically devouring. After an inexcusable period of time which he had spent pouring red wine from a jug into a bottle which he then recorked and placed on the shelf the barman came across to take their order. Without consulting Cassie, Joel ordered two glasses of champagne to be told that the house only served champagne by the bottle. Since Cassie was driving she said she would rather drink Perrier so Joel ordered her the mineral water and himself a dry martini.

'Sure you wouldn't rather do fish and chips?' Cassie asked him again.

'You bet,' Joel said. 'This place spells fun.'

The first bottle of wine which was presented to him when they had been shown to their table Joel returned without even tasting it.

'Wrong year,' he announced. 'And wrong maker. Otherwise ten out of ten.'

The waiter duly returned with the correct vintage and label, holding it out for Joel's inspection with a sigh.

'Want a glass?' he asked with a glance at Cassie. 'Since you're driving you're allowed two at least.'

'Yes, I'd love a glass,' Cassie agreed. 'I can't eat without wine.'

'Right. Like making love on the floor,' Joel muttered as the wine waiter poured some wine into a large glass and offered it to him to taste, an offer which earned him one of Joel's very darkest looks. 'No,' he said over-patiently to the waiter, taking the glass and handing it over to Cassie for her to try. 'Women have noses too. Often better ones.'

Flattered, Cassie gave it a good nose and a careful taste before pronouncing it good.

'It had better be,' Joel observed. 'I have precisely this wine in my cellar at a sixth of this price.'

The first course was not as disastrous as the second was to be, but even so it did not go unpunished. In answer to their waiter's standard enquiry as to whether everything was all right, Joel told him it most certainly was not, that the bread was not fresh enough, that Mrs Rosse's warm goat's cheese salad was cold and that his chilled watercress soup was warm. For a moment Cassie thought she was going to be embarrassed, but seeing the fleeting expression on her face Joel instructed her not to be, reminding her that they were not being given the meal for nothing.

As if sensing an impending disaster and wishing to avert the crisis rather than prevent it, the proprietor then appeared to stand for a moment glowering at the two of them as if they were children misbehaving at a school dinner.

'I gather we are not altogether happy,' he announced, staring at them through two bloodshot eyes over a pair of dirty half moon glasses. 'But before we start causing further anxieties among our staff I would remind you that when people drop in unannounced to establishments such as this to take what is described as *pot luck*, that is precisely what is to be expected.'

'Let me guess,' Joel said, placing his soup spoon carefully back into his warm soup. 'This is only your night job. During the day you're a pall bearer.'

'Marcel tells me you are not happy with your soup, *sir*,' the proprietor returned, after heaving a theatrical sigh. Joel then took the menu out of the proprietor's hand, directing him to read the description of the soup. 'Chilled fresh watercress, I believe,' the proprietor answered.

'Good. So tell me what this is,' Joel returned, taking the man's hand and sticking one of his fingers in the soup.

'We are short of staff this evening, *sir*,' mine host replied, removing his finger and also the plate of warm soup. 'Perhaps you would be content if I offered you another helping of soup?'

'Chilled this time,' Joel said. 'And a warm goat's cheese salad for Mrs Rosse.'

Joel's main course arrived first and was wrong, Joel having ordered a wing of skate cooked in black butter, soy and ginger only to be served instead with duck in a pineapple sauce. While the mistake was being rectified, Cassie's spicy pork meat in filo parcels arrived which despite Joel's exhortations for her to start she allowed to go cold while waiting the twenty minutes it took for Joel's correct main course to be produced.

'Mrs Rosse's food has gone cold,' Joel informed the proprietor having summoned him over.

'That is hardly my fault, *sir*,' was the reply.

'It is,' Joel assured him. 'When people come out to eat together, they like to eat together. We have not been afforded that opportunity. On top of that our first courses

187

were not presented properly. That's bad service and an infringement of our rights as customers.'

'I knew you were trouble the moment you walked in the door,' the proprietor replied. 'Now I'm going to ask for your bill to be drawn up, and when I have done so I advise you to pay up and leave. You know, I have people like you coming in here the whole time and all they do is complain.'

'I am not surprised,' Joel said, handing him Cassie's full plate of food and then his own. 'It's a wonder they haven't burnt the place down.' He got up, nodding at Cassie to follow him.

'If you try to leave here without paying I shall call the police,' the proprietor said, breathing in deeply and sticking out his pigeon chest.

'If you come on with any more of that, I shall sue,' Joel said sweetly, handing him a dogeared business card. 'My name and address. If you look, you'll see I'm in the same business.'

'Remind me to go out to dinner with you more often,' Cassie remarked as they made their way to the car.

'None of that was my fault. And I didn't choose the restaurant.'

Cassie unlocked the car door and Joel got in.

'When only the rich had watches,' Joel began as Cassie let herself in her side, 'only a few were made but they were all good watches. Now everybody's got a watch and they're mostly all made in Taiwan.'

'Sometimes I have no idea what you're talking about,' Cassie said, firing the engine. 'Correction, make that most of the time. Not that you were exactly that talkative over dinner, mind.'

'When you make love you don't read a book, do you? Or listen to music?' Joel asked. 'Or do you?'

'Meaning when you go out to eat you go out to eat.'

'Primarily.'

'I go out to enjoy myself.'

'You can't enjoy yourself if everything's wrong.'

'You're right, of course. Just as you were to make a fuss,' Cassie said.

'I didn't make a fuss,' Joel replied. 'I complained. If you made a bet and the bookie shortchanged you?'

'I'd complain. And by the way, I don't either read or listen to music when I make love.'

'I'm glad.'

'I knit.'

Joel laughed. Not a lot, but he definitely laughed, it seemed for the very first time since Cassie had met him. To Joel it seemed for the very first time for as long as he could remember.

'Do you know where Blaneys is?' he asked.

'Why?' Cassie asked, knowing full well since it was one of Tyrone's and her old haunts.

'I read about it in a magazine in the cottage,' Joel said. 'Take us there.'

'Why?' Cassie asked again, playing for time.

'Because when at first you don't succeed,' Joel replied. 'I'm serious. I'm also half starved.'

'I used to go there all the time with my husband,' Cassie said cautiously.

'What better recommendation?' Joel returned and settled back in his seat.

In contrast to the other restaurant everything was perfect from the moment they walked in Blaney's door. They both had the same superb food – courgette flowers stuffed with sweetbreads and fried and fresh Irish salmon *en feuilleté* washed down with a 1971 Gerwutz Traminer, most of which Joel drank. In just as stark a contrast was the level of conversation, Joel being positively voluble for him which meant talking occasionally in sentences with subclauses. Not that he ever talked while he was actually eating, but in between courses he opened right up, telling Cassie more about his wild and brilliantly talented mother and his pianist younger brother who Joel confessed was far and away still the best friend he had ever had. It wasn't a highly detailed history, but what information was put before Cassie was so carefully selected and filleted that it built up a totally coherent and accurate picture of the young Joel

Benson's life, a life which was apparently as sunny and happy as could be expected until his mother's premature death in the plane crash. His father while still alive, and also a painter, was finding his work increasingly difficult, since he suffered from arthritis.

At first Cassie was not so forthcoming about herself, more out of modesty than out of reluctance. Whenever people had asked her before about her life with Tyrone and her existence since she had often thought her listeners must have found her insufferably smug, for apart from Tyrone's tragic death and her long uphill struggle to re-establish Claremore, over which she usually glossed, since she had met and married Tyrone it appeared as if much of her life had been nothing less than a fairy story.

Now of course with The Nightingale's mutilation Joel knew the twist in the tail, and Cassie found that beneath all his apparent prickliness and monosyllabia Joel was a most fair-minded and genuinely curious person.

When they got home it was well after two o'clock in the morning. The moon was full and very bright and for a while they stood on the drive at the front of the house leaning on the car and gazing bewitched at the velvety blue landscape.

'What is it about moonlight?' Cassie wondered. 'Why is it so haunting?'

'According to Joseph Conrad, because it has all the dispassionateness of a disembodied soul,' Joel replied, 'and something of its inconceivable mystery.'

'Look at it tonight,' Cassie continued, slipping her arm through his. 'Tonight it's as full as a summer's rose.'

Two large bats flew suddenly out of the great cedar of Lebanon and swooped silently off into the blue.

'Do you want a nightcap?' Cassie asked, looking at the man staring up at the sky. Joel shook his head. 'You sure?' she asked again. Joel nodded. 'You don't want anything?' Joel nodded again. 'You do want something. What?' He turned and looked down at her for a moment.

'I want to kiss you.' Which he did.

After he had kissed her again Cassie put her two hands on his chest and tried to push him away.

'No. No.'

'No what?' Joel wondered, stroking one side of her hair while he looked at her.

'Just no, Joel,' Cassie replied, keeping her hands firmly on his chest.

'You didn't want me to kiss you?'

'I didn't say that.'

'If you had, you wouldn't be saying no now.'

'It's not as easy as that.' Cassie freed herself and took a step back, turning away. 'I mean, I wasn't thinking.'

'All I did was kiss you, Cassie,' Joel sighed. 'I haven't asked you to go to bed with me.'

'You didn't have to,' Cassie replied, remembering the passion of his kiss.

'And you don't want to.'

'I'm not going to stand here discussing it, as if we were deciding whether or not to go out to dinner.' Cassie began to walk off towards the house and Joel ambled after her. 'Making love isn't something you decide like that. At least I don't anyway.'

'I know, it's just something that happens. Organically. You turn out the light and something beautiful happens.'

'Now you're being facetious.'

'And you're being self-indulgent.'

Cassie stopped and swung round to face Joel only to find herself back in his arms once more.

'The king is dead, Cassie,' he said quietly.

'It just isn't as easy as that. So please – just leave me alone, right? Please just leave me alone!' She pulled herself free, ran inside the house and pulled the heavy old door shut behind her.

# Eleven

The next day she was gone. Joel, up late as usual, had come up from the cottage and was making his way through the house en route for the kitchen and some fresh hot coffee when he overheard Rosemary Corcoran on the telephone in Cassie's study informing the caller that her employer would be away until at least the weekend.

'Where's she gone, Erin?' he enquired of the housekeeper after he had arrived in the kitchen. 'I didn't know she was off somewhere.'

'Neither did I, Mr Benson,' Erin replied, putting his coffee in front of him. 'But then generally I'm the last to be told anything. Sure I'm expected to rely on second sight – and Padraig, love?' She took hold of her child by one hand and lifted him back onto a chair. 'Padraig will you just please sit down and finish that biscuit like I told you and not be climbing all over poor Mr Benson again?'

Joel tried not to smile as the child ignored Erin's strictures, at once climbing down off his chair again and making his way over to Joel's side. When Erin's back was turned Joel lifted the boy onto his knee before continuing to wonder in as offhand a way as he could manage where Cassie might have taken herself.

'Ach she's away to Dingle I imagine, Mr Benson, where she usually goes when she has this sort of mood on her,' Erin replied, turning to give him his coffee and shaking her head at her child when she saw where he had put himself.

'This sort of mood,' Joel echoed, pushing the cup well out of Padraig's reach.

'When something upsets her,' Erin said with a particular glance at him. 'Or somebody.'

Joel ignored the remark and lit a cigarette which predictably enough induced a bout of disapproving coughing from Erin.

'How you can ever smoke them things,' Erin said, flapping a tea towel at the smoke. 'They smell like a burning muck heap.'

'And I don't know how you bake such wonderful soda bread,' Joel replied, pushing away the plate he had emptied. 'I have never eaten bread like it.'

Erin eyed him and at once stopped flapping her tea towel. 'Mrs Rosse has gone to Dingle,' she said. 'Do you know where that is? It's in County Kerry, a sort of peninsula thing that goes out into the Atlantic. As soon as her car was back from the garage, off she went. She has a wee holiday house down there, in a village called Coomenhoule – but sure you'd have little chance of—'

Erin stopped with a shake of her head, for there was little point in continuing now that Joel had placed Padraig back safely on his own chair and fled the kitchen.

Mattie said he could borrow the yard's old runabout if it was for only a day, showing him where the Datsun truck was kept. Joel already had his old Harrods carrier bag packed with the few things he needed and was about to start the engine when Mattie stuck his head back in through the driver's window.

'What's going on, if you don't mind me asking?' he enquired. 'It's probably none of my business, but my mother's last words to me before she left were to make sure you were out of here by the time she got back.'

'I'm out of here,' Joel said, now firing the engine. 'So stand aside.' He would have backed the truck out of the hay barn were Mattie's head not still stuck in through his window.

'So what's going on, Joel?' Mattie asked. 'I thought you two were – well, friends.'

'We are, Matt,' Joel replied. 'And you know what they say about friendship. It's infinitely more demanding than love.'

193

'So where are you going?'

'If you must know, to try to alter the balance.'

The roads were not busy, so driving as hard as the old truck would let him across the tip of Kilkenny, through the heart of Tipperary and the middle of Limerick, Joel was in Kerry within a couple of hours where ignoring the spellbinding scenery which began to build up around him he kept the throttle to the floor until he had reached Dingle itself. Stopping to fill up with petrol he found out from the garage proprietor that the village for which he was searching lay at the western tip of the peninsula opposite a now all but deserted set of islands called the Blaskets. It was raining hard when he reached Coomenhoule, a heavy dense rain driven inland by a strong autumnal gale coming fresh off the Atlantic which was apparently keeping everyone inside. Having of course forgotten to ask Erin the location of Cassie's house let alone its name, at a small all-purpose shop in the village all he could do was ask if anyone of the small group of people huddled in the bar at the back of the shop knew the whereabouts of Mrs Rosse's holiday house. When they saw him and heard his question as a man they all fell to silence.

'Mrs Rosse is a friend of mine,' he assured them. 'And I understand she has a house somewhere round here.'

'I'd have said,' a man replied from the far end of the bar, taking his pipe from his mouth and staring into the bowl as he spoke. 'I would have said, so I would, that were you a friend of this person you mention you would know the name of her house at the very least.'

'I've forgotten it,' Joel replied, with no attempt at charm.

'And I've never heard of your friend Mrs Cross,' the man returned, sticking his pipe back into his mouth.

There was a muttered chorus of agreement from the other men at the bar, who all stood staring at Joel while shaking their heads in ignorance.

'Ah now if it's a Mrs Cross you're seeking there's no-one of that name,' another man ventured out of the gloom of the bar.

'Her name is Mrs Rosse,' Joel repeated.

'Ah God there's no-one here of that name either, sir,' the second man said with a nod. 'Not even adjacent to it.'

'There is, you know,' Joel said, lighting up a cigarette. 'I know for a fact Mrs Rosse has a house here, and this is hardly a very large village.'

'No, it is hardly that, sir,' another man agreed. 'This place is so small sure don't you sometimes expect it's yourself you'll meet turning a corner?'

'Ah God now and isn't that true enough?' the chorus asked variously. 'Isn't that exactly what you'd expect?'

Joel ordered himself a whisky and sat down at the bar. 'Mrs Rosse owns a horse called The Nightingale,' he said. 'You must all have heard of him.'

'The Nightingale,' the chorus mused. 'The Nightingale, you say, sir?'

'The Nightingale.'

'The Nightingale,' the first man who'd spoken repeated. 'Would this horse have run this year at Killarney, sir?'

'Nope,' Joel said, drawing on his cigarette.

'Ah well sure I wouldn't know it then, sir, for I never go near a racecourse except for Killarney.'

'Nor I, nor I,' his friends chorused. 'Nor I, nor I.'

Joel drank his whisky in silence then ordered another. 'What would you say if I bought you all a drink?' he asked.

'Thank you,' the chorus replied. 'That's what we'd probably say, sir, we'd say thank you, and God bless you, sir.'

'Let's try again,' Joel said. 'What would you do if I bought you all a drink?'

To a man they all laughed, one or two of them slapping their knees with their caps.

'God sir, we'd drink it, sir!' they cried. 'God sir what else should a man do?'

Joel shoved a hand into his back pocket, took out a fistful of notes and ordered up a round of drinks which were demolished practically as soon as they were set down. Joel drank his own and then looked up to find a line of faces staring at him in anticipation.

'Same again,' he ordered the old man behind the bar. 'Large ones.'

Four rounds later and considerably poorer he appeared to be no nearer finding out where Cassie lived than he had been an hour earlier. The conversation was certainly flowing a lot more freely thanks to the amount of lubrication he had supplied, yet every time he tried to reintroduce the subject of Mrs Rosse, however casually, every one of the men in the bar became as ignorant as they had been the moment he had set foot in the place.

'OK,' he said, standing up and collecting the few coins he had left. 'Thank you for your company, gentlemen, but not for your help.'

Once again half a dozen pairs of eyes fixed on him, although with no longer quite such a steady focus.

'Good man yourself,' the farmer with the pipe said from the end of the bar. 'You're welcome to drink in here any time.'

'There won't be another time,' Joel said, putting his change back into his pocket. 'Not unless I find Mrs Rosse.'

'God now, 'tis surely not a matter of life and death now, is it?' the barman said, wiping the bar down with a cloth he'd had dropped over one shoulder. 'If 'twas a matter of life and death you'd not have been in here drinking all this time.'

'Ah well it would be a matter of life and death, so it would,' said a tall and gangly simple young man who'd silently joined in the drinking without anyone apparently noticing. 'Ah sure if I was you and yous and lookin' for her, wouldn't I be of just the same complexion? Sure I would. Ah sure I would, I would. I would so.'

The lad jiggled up and down on the spot where he stood and grinned foolishly at the other men in the bar who had now turned to stare at him in stony silence.

'Now get away, lads,' the boy giggled. 'Don't yous all be starin' at me like yous are, for yous all know what a beautiful lady she is, sure you do, you do, you do. For aren't yous all always making sheep's eyes at her, whenever she comes here? So yous are, so yous are. Ah so don't all

196

be starin' at me like that, boys. It makes me feel an eejeet. So don't be starin' at me like that, or I'll tell this gentleman exactly where Mrs Rosse lives so I will, I will, I will.'

Joel said nothing. He just looked at the men who'd just drunk him broke. Then he turned back to the youth but before he could speak a huge man in an old full-length cracked black oilskin who had said nothing at all but had done his share of the drinking coughed into a huge fist of a hand before blinking slowly at Joel.

'The house you want, sir, is about five mile out of Coomenhoule itself,' he said. 'You have to take second right after the last house on the left, sir, till you come to a sign which is now just a post and turn right there, sir, and drive up into the hills. When you come to a herd of sheep grazing—'

'They'll be grazing at a specific point, will they?' Joel wondered, opening his eyes mockingly.

'Where else would they be, sir, at this hour of the day?' the man replied. 'And when you see them drive straight on to the right.'

'To the left,' someone said. 'If he drives on to the right won't he be into the bog?'

'You're right, Mick,' the big man agreed. 'You must drive straight on to the left—'

'Ah no, Donal,' someone else interrupted. 'He must drive on only slightly straight. If he drives on utterly straight sure he'll be into the stream.'

'Thank you, Pat, I stand corrected.' The big man put his hand on Joel's shoulder and nodded at him slowly. 'You must do as Pat said. Drive slightly straight for the next several miles taking care to keep the largest of the mountains in front of yous and not to the left, turn again by a pile of stone you'll see on the right, then right again further on opposite a next left turning which will take you right up to the house itself. Isn't that right, lads?'

'It is, it is,' they chorused. 'You'll not go wrong if you follow what Donal has said.'

'You'll not,' the old farmer said. 'Sure a bat could find it in daylight with instructions like that.'

197

'On the other hand, Tim,' a voice said from behind Joel. 'He could just follow me.'

As one the men all looked to the door and when they saw who was standing there they hung their heads in shame.

'Sorry, Mrs Rosse,' the old farmer said. 'We thought your man was from the newspapers.'

'I'm sure you did, Tim,' Cassie replied. 'But he's not. Mr Benson's a friend. I just wasn't expecting him, that's all.'

Joel didn't look round. He just picked up his cigarettes and lighter and nodded his farewell to the men in the bar. 'Gentlemen,' he said, and then turned and followed Cassie out.

Cassie had been amazed when she had caught sight of him in the bar at the back of the shop. The old Datsun pickup parked outside might have given her advance warning but since in the Irish country such vehicles were two a penny she never gave it a second glance. But then as she was waiting at the counter for Mrs McGovern to load her ordered groceries into some cardboard boxes she had caught sight of him through a window dividing the shop from the snug, sitting at the corner of the bar with his chin propped up on his fists. A moment later her surprise had turned to fury as she realized he had pursued her all the way from Claremore without as much as a word so she had stepped back from the window in case he caught sight of her and allowed Mrs McGovern to do all the talking as she collected Cassie's groceries together.

She had listened while she waited, not to the shopkeeper's prattle but to the conversation which was drifting in from the bar, and the more she had overheard the quicker her anger had abated and she began to smile, realizing the dance the farmers were busy leading Joel. For a moment she had almost let the men have their way as if to serve Joel right for invading her privacy, but then her heart had softened when she understood that far from being furious with him she was in truth quite touched that he had followed her to the west, and with an eye on the weather which was worsening by the minute she had realized she could not possibly disappear and leave the poor man to get lost in the swirling mists and rains which were obliterating the hills which rose up behind the tiny village. So she had rescued him, allowing him to climb into her car beside her after they had loaded up the groceries and supplies and drive back to the house with her, leaving the old pickup where he had parked it.

'You might have said where you were going,' Joel remarked as they battled along the narrow road in the teeth of the storm.

'I did.'

'Not to me you didn't.'

'No, not to you I didn't.'

'Any particular reason, I wonder?'

'Maybe because I didn't want you to know.'

'You just kiss and run, right?'

'Because I kissed you last night—' Cassie said.

'Because *I* kissed *you*,' Joel corrected her.

'That doesn't mean I'm going to let you kiss me today,' Cassie finished.

'Rose kissed me today,' Joel murmured, wiping the condensation off the windscreen with his hand. 'Will she kiss me tomorrow?'

He glanced at her, then got to work on the dashboard, looking for the demister and fan controls. Cassie put a hand out to work the controls for herself and after she had turned the fan up Joel caught her hand, held it for a second, then kissed the end of her fingers.

'I'm trying to drive,' Cassie reminded him, taking her hand away with a glance at him. 'Conditions are bad enough without you making them worse.'

'Conditions are perfect,' he agreed. 'For staying in.'

The house stood on a hill overlooking the windswept Atlantic. It was white-painted and comfortably furnished with old furniture draped with locally woven throws and rugs, its windows hung with rough curtains of bright red tweed. The hand-made bookshelves were filled with old paperbacks and magazines, the paintings on the wall were all obviously executed by keen amateurs, and none of the china and crockery matched. It was in fact exactly the way the ideal holiday house should be.

While Cassie had been out shopping the fire had died in the grate so Joel rekindled it with blocks of well-dried peat while Cassie cooked supper. They ate potato soup and *spaghetti al olio* which Joel relished, the perfect antidote to the amount of whisky he had been forced to drink when trying to discover Cassie's exact location. Afterwards they sat in front of the fire while the storm raged unabated outside, finishing a rough but drinkable Beaujolais and playing a variation of patience called Racing Demon.

'I don't know what it is about you, Joel,' Cassie said after he had beaten her at the game for the fourth consecutive time, and then paused for a moment. What she wanted to say was that when she was with him he ended up infuriating her to such an extent sometimes that she really didn't care whether or not she ever saw him again, but then immediately she was away from him she wanted to see him more than she had wanted to see anyone since she had lost Tyrone.

But watching him slowly dealing out another hand of cards all she actually said was that as far as playing patience went he seemed to be impossible to beat.

'Your problem is a simple one, Mrs Rosse. You keep looking for short-term gains rather than taking the long view. Viz – as soon as a card comes up, you play it. That's why you lose. You have to look at the cards behind the cards. You have to play for what's coming up, not for what you can see on top of the deck.'

They played another round and Cassie lost again.

'Why did you follow me down here?' she asked, as Joel threw some more peat on the fire.

'Why did you come down here?' he returned, lighting another Gauloise from a split of paper.

'I wanted time to think. I wasn't prepared for you.'

Joel shuffled the cards as expertly as a croupier. 'A woman surprised is half won.'

'So how are you going to win the other half?'

'Unhappy the general who comes on the field of battle with a stratagem,' Joel said, laying his cards out. 'Now this time, look to see what all the cards you hold are. And then play to your strength.'

This time Cassie did, and she won.

'Bed,' she said, getting up and stretching. 'You must be exhausted. It's a long drive.'

'It's a bit too early for me,' Joel said. 'I bought some whisky. Have a nightcap.'

Cassie hesitated, then declined, taking their dinner things through into the flagstoned kitchen. Joel followed, carrying the rest of the dishes on a tray and the bottle of whisky under his arm.

'Fresh glasses,' he said, putting the dishes and bottle down on the table. Cassie indicated a cupboard and bent over the sink to start the washing up. A moment later Joel had his arms round her waist and was kissing her on the back of the neck. Cassie straightened up so that he had to stop, but all he did was turn her to him. She leaned backwards, away from him.

'No,' she said. 'Please.'

He kissed her all the same and for half a moment Cassie almost relented, pulling herself away only just in time.

'No,' she repeated, more quietly but just as insistent.

'I think you and I are going to have to have a talk, Cassie Rosse,' Joel said, sitting back on the table and pouring out two large whiskies.

'That's too much for me.'

'It seems it's all too much for you,' Joel remarked, pouring some of her whisky into his glass. 'Look, if you don't want me around, why don't you simply tell me to bugger off?'

'I don't know.'

'Oh, I think you do.' He handed her the glass which Cassie put down on the draining board, returning to her washing up. Joel took a draught of whisky and then picked up a tea towel to start drying up.

'We're about the same age, aren't we?' he asked.

'If you say so,' Cassie replied, handing him a plate.

'You know perfectly well we are,' Joel continued. 'And neither of us have as much time as we once had.'

'Meaning we shouldn't miss an opportunity,' Cassie said wryly, handing him another plate.

'Do you find me as attractive as I find you?' Joel asked, putting the two dry plates to one side.

'How can I answer that?' Cassie sighed. 'I don't know how attractive you find me.'

'If I heard you'd gone to the moon I'd have followed you.'

'Maybe you're after my money,' Cassie said, handing him a soup bowl.

'I'm not interested in money,' Joel replied, wiping the bowl dry.

'So what do you want, Joel?'

'Something more than I've ever wanted something before.'

She looked at him as he looked at her. They stood in silence for a long time, eye to eye.

'Of course I find you attractive, Joel,' she said at last. 'And you wouldn't have dared ask me that unless you knew.'

'So what are we going to do about it?' Joel wondered. 'Because we're going to have to do something.'

'It can't be here,' Cassie said, turning away and busying herself at the sink, draining away the water and starting to dry the last of the crockery. Joel picked up a glass and slowly wiped it dry, then held it up to the light to make sure it was perfectly clean. 'What is it exactly you're afraid of Cassie?'

'In a word? Trespass.'

'No. You're not really afraid of what you call trespass. That's just a smokescreen. What you're afraid of is having a love affair and enjoying it because you think that somehow it might knock a few points off your legendary happy marriage.'

'Look,' Cassie said, taking the tea towel from him and throwing it aside. 'If it's any of your damn' business I've

202

had lovers. Several of them if you really want to know, OK? So so much for your neat little theory.'

'Uh huh,' Joel murmured, picking up his whisky glass. 'But I'll bet they were all safe as hell choices. I'll bet you chose carefully so that none of them would be a threat to the memory of your husband.'

'I don't know how you dare,' Cassie said, rounding on him. 'I really don't know how you dare say such things!'

'Somebody really should have said them to you long ago,' Joel said, getting up and catching hold of Cassie in case she hit him as she seemed to be just about to do.

'Let go of me,' Cassie said, struggling to get free. 'I'm going to bed now, and you can do what the hell you like.'

'I'd quite like to go to bed, too.'

'Then go.'

'Where do you suggest?'

'Try the sofa. And if you don't fit – too bad. You should have thought of that before you came charging down here uninvited. Good night.'

After Cassie had gone upstairs, Joel piled some more peat on the fire, refilled his glass and settled into an armchair. He smoked a couple of cigarettes while he flicked through an old copy of the *Irish Field* without focusing on either pictures or text. All he could see was Cassie and all he wanted was to have her in his arms. Finally he chucked the magazine to one side, threw his cigarette into the fire and finished his whisky, resting his head on the back of his chair to stare at the ceiling above him.

When he woke up the storm had stopped and all he could hear was the sound of the sea somewhere far below him. The fire had died and he was cold, so he got up to see if there was something warmer to wrap around him other than the tweed throws but all he could find downstairs were a couple of stiff oilskins and what looked like an old dog blanket. Stiff and cold he carefully made his way upstairs intending to try to find a spare bedroom, but the first of the closed doors which he opened was Cassie's.

She was asleep in a large cane-headed double bed under a green hand-woven cover. Her clothes lay neatly folded on the chair, and she was curled on her side with one arm bent up to cover her ear and the top of her head in the way children often sleep when they are unhappy. She had left the curtains open so that her outline was lit by the piercing light of the moon whenever it appeared from behind the fast scudding clouds. As he stood there and his eyes became accustomed to the half light Joel could make out two photographs, one on each of the bedside tables. One was of Cassie leading her famous horse in after a race and the other was of herself in the arms of Tyrone.

He turned as quietly as he could to leave the room.

'What's the matter?' a voice asked him from the bed. 'Couldn't you sleep?'

'Couldn't you?' he asked back.

'I was sleeping fine until you burst in.'

'Sorry.' Joel began to close the door. 'I was looking for a spare bedroom.'

'The bed isn't made up,' Cassie said. 'And the mattress will be damp. I wasn't expecting visitors.'

'Fine. Well, if you wouldn't mind just telling me where I might find a couple of blankets,' Joel replied. 'The fire's out, there's no more fuel, and I'm half frozen to death.'

For a moment Cassie didn't reply. Finally she removed her arm from the top of her head, pulled the bedclothes up more tightly under chin and looked round at him in the moonlight, childlike and vulnerable.

'Unless you have horse in you, you're not going to be able to sleep like that,' she said pokerfaced.

'Any suggestions?' Joel wondered.

'This is a perfectly good bed,' she said. 'I mean it's aired, and it's warm.'

'Don't tempt me.'

'I'm not,' Cassie replied. 'I'm inviting you.'

For a while in the bed Joel lay on his back with his hands behind his head trying to work out quite where he was headed, while beside him still on her side and turned away from him Cassie was trying to do exactly the same thing. To Joel their relationship seemed to have its own momentum. Never at one point since he had first met Cassie

204

had he made any definite plans as far as they were both concerned. Everything had just seemed to happen, organically as it were, yet everything that had happened had also been invested with a dreamlike quality, lacking the proper rhyme and reason of reality. For example at this very moment it seemed Joel had been solidly rooted in actuality, in the middle of yet another argument with a woman with whom he was fast becoming convinced he was falling in love, yet the next moment he found himself lying in her bed without really remembering how he had got there, in exactly the same dislocated way things happen in dreams.

So too it was with Cassie, who was also unable to make any sense of what was happening to her. She kept finding herself thinking one thing then doing something altogether opposite. Tonight she had wanted to give him his marching orders and now she wanted him to make love to her.

*This has to be a real love-hate relationship*, she thought, pulling her pillow down further under her head. *Yet I don't really hate him. In fact I don't hate him at all. Yes I do*, she corrected herself, settling her head deep into the pillow. *Of course I hate him. Why? Because he's always so goddamn right.*

*And what about love?* Having made herself comfortable on her pillow, she now turned herself round to face him in the dark, very carefully and slowly, half hoping that he might have fallen asleep so that she could lie watching him and perhaps find out what she really felt. Instead she found herself staring into a pair of large dark eyes.

They lay there for a while, looking into each other, saying nothing and doing nothing. Cassie was the first to speak. 'I thought you had fallen asleep,' she said. 'You were so quiet.'

'I was thinking,' Joel replied.

'I was thinking as well. Snap.' She reached out under the bedclothes and took one of his hands. 'I'm sorry I've been totally unreasonable.'

'You have nothing whatsoever to be sorry about,' Joel replied, smoothing her hair and then her cheek with his

205

free hand. 'Nothing at all. I just think it's time you were happy again.'

'I have been happy.' Cassie frowned, but didn't take her eyes from his. 'At least I think I have.'

'Not really. You've been treading water and there's no need. Nothing's going to spoil.'

'How do you know?' Cassie frowned more deeply, but this time from a different sort of anxiety.

'I don't. It's just a feeling I have.'

Cassie put up a hand to touch his cheek. 'You don't say very much, but what you do say—'

'They put on calendars,' Joel finished for her.

Cassie smiled and moved closer to him, putting her arms round his waist. 'I just didn't want to get it wrong, that's all.'

'You didn't. And you haven't. And you won't.'

Cassie kissed him, briefly, sweetly. He smiled at her and kissed her in return, briefly and sweetly. She moved closer to him and they kissed again, this time longer and more passionately, only for Joel to suddenly resist and pull away.

'Don't laugh,' he groaned, turning on his back and staring up at the ceiling. 'But I can't.'

Cassie stared at him, totally at a loss. 'You can't?' she echoed. 'Why not?'

'I can't,' Joel repeated now with a sigh. 'Not here. There's just too much baggage.' His eyes strayed past hers to the picture behind her head, to the photograph of her in Tyrone's arms, and Cassie smiled to herself and with a kiss to Joel's cheek settled herself down to lie in his different embrace.

For once he was up long before her in the morning, Cassie awakening to the sound of him singing downstairs. When she finally made her way down to the kitchen in her dressing gown she found him busy making the breakfast.

'All we did was sleep,' she said, when she saw the size of the fry Joel was making.

'I know, but it still made me hungry.'

While he cooked Cassie sat in the window seat

206

overlooking the sea. When he had settled her there with a cup of coffee and a rug for her knees, Joel resumed singing. He had a strong, smoky voice, well suited to the old Sinatra numbers he was working his way through.

'Great day,' Cassie said, studying the view. 'I love this time of year.'

'Me too,' Joel agreed, before breaking into 'Autumn in New York'.

The day indeed had dawned fine and gentle, the awakening landscape bathed in that clear but wistful light late autumn brings, with the sea now almost calm after the gales of the day before. A small boat had just set out from the jetty far below to make its way across to the nearest of the Blaskets, carrying some of the last of that summer's visitors to explore the islands and spot the basking seals.

Joel idly asked Cassie how long she was intending to stay down in Dingle. Cassie replied that she had no real idea, particularly now. They then sat in near silence, both of them watching the ever-changing landscape of the sea and shore until they had cleaned their plates with slices of the delicious barnbrack loaf Cassie had bought at the village shop and drunk the last of the freshly ground coffee.

'OK,' Joel said, standing up and taking Cassie's empty cup. 'Time to pack. Pack your things and don't ask where you're going.'

After she was dressed and was locking up Cassie found Joel's pack of Gauloises on the table by the fireplace.

'You forgot these,' she called, tossing him the pack.

'No I didn't,' Joel replied, dropping them in the waste basket.

Joel sang while Cassie drove following his orders, southwards towards Bantry through the beautiful Kerry countryside.

'Where are we going?' Cassie asked.

'Mind your own business,' Joel replied good-naturedly, 'and tell me why it's called the Ring of Kerry – because it goes round in a ring, of course.'

'Since you know all the answers, I won't bother to

ask you if you'd like to drive all the way round it,' Cassie said.

'On the way home,' Joel replied. 'Right now I'd like to get where we're going.'

The weather had improved even more by the time they were on the road, with not a cloud to be seen anywhere in the October sky. It was so mild that they drove with the roof of Cassie's BMW convertible down, although Cassie insisted on putting the heater on for her feet.

'Yes,' Joel agreed thoughtfully. 'Can't have you getting cold feet.'

Cassie laughed as Joel looked out of the window and began singing 'Our Love Is Here To Stay'.

'I just hope you're not known here, that's all,' he said as they drew up in front of a fine seventeenth-century manor. 'Are you known here?'

'Yes,' Cassie replied. 'But it doesn't matter. The owners aren't always in evidence, and since I imagined you booked in your name—'

'I think what I really meant,' Joel interrupted, 'was did you used to stay here with your husband?'

'No,' Cassie told him. 'We never even ate here.'

'OK.' Joel got out of the car and came round to open Cassie's door for her. She resisted the temptation to remark on the unusual occurrence as a boy hurried out to take their luggage from the boot. Joel's reformation did not however extend to allowing her to precede him through the front door of the hotel, which left the boy, struggling with Cassie's luggage, to hold it open for her with his foot.

'Good,' Joel said again after they'd been shown up to their rooms, an elegant first-floor suite with a wonderful view of the sea.

'Oh yes, this is charming,' Cassie said, admiring the hand-embroidered sheets on the bed. 'These remind me of my convent days. The nuns used to embroider linen like this.'

'Did you see the patchwork murals?' Joel asked. 'They're rather fun.' He picked up the bottle of champagne which had been waiting for them in an ice bucket. 'Good,' Joel said again after he'd poured them both a glass. 'So what would you like to do now?'

Cassie almost grinned but to stop herself carefully bit her lip. 'I don't know. What would you like to do now?' she asked in return.

'I'd like to do what I came here for,' Joel replied. 'I'd like to go to bed.'

'That's all right by me,' Cassie told him, putting her glass down by the bedside. 'Because that's exactly what I'd like to do as well.'

Joel raised his glass. 'Long live love,' he wished.

Cassie looked up into his big dark eyes and smiled. 'I'll drink to that,' she agreed.

When she woke he was gone.

'Joel?' she called, sitting up in bed. 'Joel?' Her heart sank when she realized she was alone, for how often had she awoken like this, with no-one beside her any more, no-one to talk with or laugh with. To have made love so rapturously with a man and then to awake to find him gone was not what she had expected.

Pulling on a wrap she got out of bed and knocked on the bathroom door, but the door swung open on an empty room. 'Oh heck,' she sighed. 'Now what?'

She looked at her watch and found to her astonishment she'd been asleep for nearly two hours. Convinced he had gone for food, but without quite knowing what she was going to do, she had begun to get dressed when she heard a car drawing up below. Doing up her shirt she peered out of the window and saw it was her BMW, driven by Joel.

As if he knew she would be watching, he looked up at their window after he had got out of the car and waved the bunch of flowers he had in one hand up at her, before going round to the boot and taking out several large shopping bags. Cassie smiled to herself, undid her blouse and got back into bed with a fresh glass of champagne.

'You were asleep so I didn't wake you,' Joel said, after he'd come in and put down all his shopping.

'That's not like me,' Cassie said. 'I wake up at the drop of a glove.'

'Not this afternoon you didn't,' he assured her, offering her the flowers.

'What have you done?' Cassie frowned, taking the flowers without comment, being more intrigued by the new-look Joel. 'That's a new jacket. And shirt.'

'I needed some clothes.'

'You've had your hair cut as well,' Cassie wondered, widening her eyes. 'And you've shaved.'

'You kept giving me these looks,' Joel said, sitting on the bed and taking his brand new shoes off. 'I thought I'd better do something.'

'Joel.' Cassie sighed and put her arms round him from the back. 'The looks I keep giving you. They're nothing to do with the way you look.'

'They're just part of the tender trap,' Joel replied.

'When I look at you like that,' Cassie explained, 'it's because I like what I see. It's nothing to do with how you look as far as how you dress goes.'

Joel sat quite still while Cassie hugged him then he turned round and kissed her. 'Everything I do—' he began.

'You got me,' Cassie confessed. 'You'll have to finish the quote.'

'I do it just for you.' Then he kissed her again while Cassie began to take off his brand new clothes.


'I've just spent a small fortune to look good for you,' Joel said, propping himself up on his pillows and pointing to his new purchases which lay in a heap on the carpet. 'And now tonight I'm going to look just like I always look. As if I slept in my clothes.'

'Oh, but the *Joel Benson look* is in, didn't you know? The crumpled look is *the* look of the moment,' Cassie laughed.

'My mother used to rearrange me even as a baby,' he said. 'I don't know what it is with me and clothes. We don't seem to be compatible.'

'I love the way you look,' Cassie said as Joel finally

climbed out of bed and began to pick up his discarded clothing. 'Don't ever change, really. Not ever.'

'Not ever?' Joel looked up at her, quizzically.

'I mean it,' Cassie said. 'I really love the way you look.'

'And?'

'And what, Mr Benson?'

'And do you love anything else about me?'

'The way you brush your hair,' Cassie replied evasively. 'The way you sing *in* key.'

Joel looked at her for a moment longer, then continued to pick up his clothes, folding them as neatly as he could before putting them on a chair. 'I'm going to have a bath,' he said, standing up and making his way across the room.

'I'd quite like a bath too,' Cassie said, sensing a mood swing.

'I'll leave it in for you,' Joel replied before disappearing into the bathroom.

'Joel?' Cassie called. 'Joel?'

Joel put his head back round the door and stared at her blankly. 'Mrs Rosse?'

'What's the matter, Joel? Have I said something?'

'No, Mrs Rosse, that's just the problem. You didn't say anything.' Then he shut the door, locking himself in.

While Joel soaked in his bath Cassie slid down her side of the bed and took stock.

*We are incompatible*, she told herself. *It's not just that he says tomarto and I say tomayto, it goes deeper than that. We are utterly and completely incompatible. He infuriates me, and I infuriate him. Well no, no I don't actually infuriate him because he doesn't get infuriated, which is one of the nice things about him. I annoy him. I annoy him because I stand up to him and don't let him get his way and when that happens he starts behaving like a child. He's the same age as I am, damn it, but when he doesn't get what he wants – boy. Talk about little-boy-lost. It's amazing. To look at him and to listen to him you'd think he had the whole thing well under control but not a bit of it. Say sorry no deal and the wheels come off. I couldn't live with that. Not after Tyrone. I mean, what initially attracted me to him was that he seemed so – I don't know. He seemed so absolute. So unconditional. It was either take it or leave it and I liked that. He might look a mess but underneath all that hair and stubble and those odd-looking clothes he seemed to be so resolute.*

Cassie found herself suddenly smiling at the picture in her mind's eye of Joel when she first saw him and at once mentally pinched herself. *That won't do,* she said in her head. *You're trying to make sense of your life so there's no room here for any self-indulgence. This man is a crazy and I really don't have the room in my life to take a crazy on. I don't have the time nor do I have the patience. I can't have someone who keeps turning up in my life and expecting me just to jump to whatever tune he feels like playing. Or singing.* Once again she found herself smiling as she remembered their car journey down from Dingle, with Joel half leaning out of the open car singing it seemed to the whole of the beautiful Kerry countryside. *You make me feel so young,* he had sung as they drove past the famous lakes of Killarney, *you make me feel as though spring has sprung* – just as he had sung 'Night and Day' as they had crossed the great Kenmare river with the October sun high above their heads. *No,* she reminded herself sharply. *It's no good. We're chalk and cheese. We simply are not suited.*

*So what's suited?* she wondered as she turned on her front and lay as she always used to lie on her bed when she was small, with her chin propped up on her fists and her legs bent up back behind her. He made love wonderfully. He had been so gentle and sweet at first, as if he had been anxious not to hurt her, and then he had been so strong and dominant. For all his apparent bad habits he was physically in very good shape, broad shouldered and trim waisted and really very much stronger than he appeared to be from the way he ambled around. As far as making love went they were most certainly not chalk and cheese, which had made her so happy that afterwards she had not known what to say, which was why she had said nothing. There was nothing *to* say. Anything she had said she knew would have sounded facile, so she had just lain in the crook of his arm with her head on his shoulder and stayed silent. Nor had she fallen asleep until he had fallen asleep, which he finally had, after holding her so tightly in both his arms she had thought he might squeeze the life from her body.

*So fine – we can make it in bed, but then as soon as we get up it starts all over again. But why? What is it I do that annoys him so much? I stand up to him. No I don't, I annoy him because I'm stubborn. Tyrone used to say I was stubborn, and he was right. I am. He used to say that like all stubborn people I'd do more for my obstinacy than I would for my religion or my country. But then if I wasn't so damn stubborn I wouldn't still be here. I'd have fallen by the wayside a long time ago. But that's what gets Joel. He thinks I'm intractable, and maybe he doesn't find it all that attractive. So maybe he's right. Maybe I should ease back on the stubbornness from now on. After all on that side of things, at least as far as how I feel about him goes, maybe there's no real reason for it any more. Maybe it's time I started to do what Mattie's always telling me to do. To let it happen, to go with the flow.*

OK, she decided as she now rolled over on to her back to lie staring up at the ceiling. *So now I know what it is about me that irritates Joel, but what is it about Joel which infuriates me? What precisely is it?*

She lay there for an age before she allowed herself to answer the question because she already knew the answer but just didn't want to have to face up to it. Finally she groaned out loud as she realized the thought was not going to leave her head and put both her hands over her eyes in despair.

*All right!* she admitted to herself, sitting bolt upright. *OK – he drives me mad because he's always damn' well right! And the reason he's always damn' well right is because he usually is! It is time I stopped living in shadowland and started to live my life properly again! And why not? Because that's what I want!* She looked across at her image in the dressing table mirror. 'That is what I want,'

213

she said again slowly but this time out aloud. 'I do not want to go on doing all of this all alone. And there is no-one I would rather be not alone with, if that makes sense, than the man at present in the bathroom, the man with whom I would be more than happy to share the rest of my life.'

At that moment the bathroom door opened and Joel came out dressed only in a towel. Cassie watched him for a moment, and then leaned forward in the bed, clasping her hands around her knees. 'Joel—' she began.

'It's OK, you don't have to say anything, it's all right,' Joel interrupted, beginning to pull on his clothes. 'I've run a fresh bath for you so you'd better get out of bed in case it overflows.'

'Seriously, Joel—' Cassie tried again as she turned back the covers.

'I said it's OK, Cassie. Now don't be too long. I'll see you down in the bar.'

When Cassie looked back into the bedroom once the bath was run, Joel had gone.

# *Twelve*

He was sitting in the corner of the bar reading a newspaper, with the barman setting a fresh glass of whisky in front of him, when Cassie came in, bathed and changed into a dark blue jacket and trousers with a collarless piqué shirt which she always kept in her house at Coomenhoule in case the occasion demanded something more formal than sweater and jeans.

'Champagne?' he asked her.

'If they sell it by the glass,' she said with a smile.

After he had ordered her drink, Joel pointed out an item in the paper which he had placed on the table in front of her.

The item was headed OPEN VERDICT IN INQUEST ON ASCOT GATE MAN.

'Interesting,' he said, lighting up a cigarette, which earned him a quick glance from Cassie.

'It's OK,' she said, seeing his face. 'I like you smoking.'

'It seems Mr Waldron deceased liked a flutter,' Joel said, putting his lighter away.

'Occupational hazard,' Cassie said as she read the item. 'The lads give the men on the course tips. Next best thing to the horse's mouth. Hard to resist when you know a stable's backing their fancy.'

'Got to the bit about his credit? Seems he got a little behind with his payments to his turf accountant and then all of a sudden he was in the black.'

'So he got lucky.'

'Very lucky when you read what the police found in the house. Five thousand quid in the famous used notes.'

Cassie glanced up and then returned to finishing reading the news item.

'It doesn't make sense,' Joel mused, after taking a drink. 'If he was back in the dibs, why top himself?'

'You think they – someone – paid off his debts and then some, in return for him turning a blind eye on the gate in case he saw anything?'

'If we run with the theory that whoever did it had a runner that day that's what he'd have been asked to do, certainly. But then once the deed was done, and he was paid off, he kills himself, *apparently*.'

'He could simply have had an attack of conscience,' Cassie said carefully as the waiter set down her champagne. 'Once he realized what he'd been asked to do had led not to the stopping of a favourite but the theft of the most popular horse since – I don't know, since Arkle – well, you can imagine. Maybe thinking they were going to kill the horse he killed himself.'

'Yes,' Joel nodded thoughtfully. 'That is a possibility.'

They sat in silence for a while, Cassie drinking her champagne while Joel smoked his cigarette as if he hadn't smoked one for a decade.

'I imagine that tastes good,' Cassie said wryly. 'After such a long abstinence.'

'Giving up smoking is easy,' Joel replied. 'I should know. I've done it enough.'

Cassie put down her glass, touching one of his hands with a finger. 'And by the way, about what I said – or didn't say, rather—' she began.

'What about it?' Joel cut in, looking at her quickly.

'Have you seen – I don't know – let's say *The Night Watch*. By Rembrandt.'

Joel nodded. 'Of course I have. What about it?'

'What did you say? When you first saw it? When you first stood in front of it?'

Joel frowned. 'Nothing.'

'OK.' Cassie smiled and got up from her chair. 'So now shall we go and eat?'

They dined well in the famous green dining room, eating excellent home-made tomato soup and fillets of freshly caught brill off fine Limoges china.

'I like this place,' Cassie remarked as they waited for their second course. 'It was a good choice.'

'Used to be somebody or other's shooting lodge, apparently,' Joel said, looking round at some of the fine paintings which adorned the lovely house. 'Place was all but burned to the ground not so long ago.'

'How awful,' Cassie said. 'I absolutely dread fire.'

'So if Claremore was burning down, what one thing would you save from it?' he asked, unwrapping his forgotten napkin and now spreading it on his knee. 'One thing. Not person. And the truth, mind.'

Cassie thought for a long time before she answered. While he was waiting, Joel carefully arranged his setting so that once more his pudding spoon and fork were laid at the top of his place mat and not by the side.

'The portrait of Tyrone on Old Flurry,' Cassie answered at last.

'Of course,' Joel agreed.

'You said the truth.'

'I know what I said.' Joel frowned deeply at his fish as if he was trying to make up his mind whether to tell Cassie something or not.

'This probably doesn't mean a thing,' he said, when he was about halfway through his main course. 'But there were two men in the bar. It was their paper I was reading. They left it behind. Before you came down they were talking about your horse – because of what was in the paper, I suppose. One of them had a theory.'

'Everyone has a theory. The wonder is to find someone who hasn't a theory.'

'One of them said he thought whoever had done it – did it to get back at your husband.'

Cassie looked at him in surprise, gave it some thought and then shook her head. 'Tyrone didn't have that sort of life,' she said. 'When he had rows with people – which like everyone he often did – that was it. There weren't any grudges borne on either side. That just wasn't his style.

217

Anyway, he was—' Cassie stopped. 'He wasn't alive when Nightie was foaled.'

'Yes,' Joel agreed. 'But the fact that he was dead mightn't have anything to do with the taking of your horse.'

'How can you get back at someone who's dead, Joel? They're not there to say *ouch*.'

'Much loved wife is.'

Cassie stared at him expecting more, but Joel just nodded back at her, once. 'You're saying that someone has waited this long to get back at someone who's been dead for years? That's ridiculous.'

'You know what they say about revenge.'

'It's a dish better eaten cold.'

'Or a luscious fruit you must leave to ripen. Either way—' Joel shrugged again, and returned to finishing his fish.

Cassie put her knife and fork down and thought for a while. 'No,' she decided, with a shake of her head. 'Tyrone would never have left behind that sort of legacy.'

'Not wittingly perhaps,' Joel agreed. 'But he might have upset somebody without realizing it.'

'But who?' Cassie demanded. 'And how?'

'I don't know. But I intend to try to find out. Now finish up your food.'

After dinner they sat in the elegantly furnished drawing room in front of the log fire and talked of other things, mostly what they were going to do and what they had to do in the immediate future.

'I have to get back home some time. I've got work to do.'

'When are you thinking of going?' Cassie asked, trying not to admit her heart was sinking at the very idea.

'I don't know. In a couple of days' time, perhaps.'

'Then let's not stay here.'

'I thought you liked this place.'

'I do. But I like Coomenhoule even more.'

Joel looked at her steadily, his dark eyes fixed on her. 'You sure?'

'Yes. Absolutely.'

They took their time driving back to Dingle, skirting along the west coast of Kerry to take in Valencia Island and then swing back north-east and cross country to spy the magnificent range of the Macgillicuddy Reeks. It was Joel's idea to take a detour, Cassie having been keen to drive straight up to the house since it seemed they were to be short of time, but then as if to torment her Joel had taken the driving seat so that he could control the pace of the journey and indeed the day.

'You're a sadist,' Cassie had told him, after they had driven over the bridge at Portmagee onto Valencia Island to head for Culloo Head. 'You're doing this on purpose.'

'We only pass this way once, Mrs Rosse,' Joel had replied, 'and I for one have never been this way before.'

But as always the drive was worth it, such was the wonder of the Kerry scenery bathed in soft sunlight on yet another Indian summer day. So intoxicating was the beauty of the land that by the time they had reached their destination Cassie felt as if she had already spent the day in her lover's bed rather than at arm's length in the passenger seat of a motor car.

'I think things of moment deserve an overture,' Joel said as he opened a bottle of champagne he had stopped especially to buy in Killorglin. 'And what better prelude than a drive like that.'

'I'll always remember today,' Cassie said, raising her glass. '*Slainte.*'

'Slainte.'

At which point the telephone rang. They both eyed it with horror.

'You'd better answer it.'

'I don't have to.'

'It'll be on your mind if you don't.'

Joel walked to the kitchen window and looked out at the view across to the Blaskets while Cassie answered the telephone. Above a darkening Atlantic he watched as the first grey clouds of the day gathered.

'That was Niall Brogan,' Cassie told him, putting down

the telephone and staring blankly out of the window. 'Nightie's down with a suspected twisted gut. He thinks he might have to shoot him.'

Joel drained his glass. 'Right. Then you must go home this minute,' he said. 'I'll drive you.'

Mattie was waiting for them when they arrived back at Claremore.

'He went as mad as a wet cat during the night,' he said, leading the way to the yard. 'Then this morning he went down. He tried to attack Liam and myself and if Bridie hadn't intervened God alone knows what might have happened. Niall's with him now. He's shot Nightie up with some new analgesic mixed with acetylpromazine and an antispasmodic, but it's looking pretty grim. The horse was beside himself with the pain.'

The Nightingale was still down when they opened his box door, lying flat out on his bedding bathed in sweat with his neck arched backwards and his head twisted against the wall. Niall was kneeling down by the animal's stomach to which he was listening through his stethoscope while the ever-faithful Bridie sat stroking the horse's head.

Cassie waited until Niall had finished his investigation before speaking. 'I won't have him shot, Niall.'

'You might have to, Cassie.' Niall got to his feet, stuffing his stethoscope away in a pocket. 'I was hoping it might just have been an impactive colic and we could stimulate the gut sufficiently to get relief, but it isn't. It's an intestinal catastrophy, I'm afraid. No wonder the poor chap started going berserk.'

'Intestinal catastrophy. That the same as or worse than a twisted gut?' Joel enquired.

'Same thing, Joel, but its proper name describes the syndrome more accurately,' Niall replied tersely with another look down at the horse. 'It really is catastrophic because not only can it involve volvulus of the intestines, it can also include intussusception – which is when a length of intestine becomes telescoped into the following piece, which as you may imagine isn't frightfully funny – or even in the worst cases the rotation of the intestine about its mesentary, the mesentary being a fold of peritoneum which attaches the intestinal canal to the posterior wall of the abdomen. So you can imagine the agony it causes.'

'And there's really nothing you can do.'

'There is, but it's frightfully risky. Which is why generally in cases as severe as this – ' Niall left the rest unsaid, shaking his head instead then rubbing his chin with one hand.

'I should never have gone away,' Cassie said suddenly. 'It was tempting the fates.'

'That's hardly being fair on yourself, Cassie,' Niall replied. 'A horse can get this sort of attack at any time.'

'I don't know what I thought I was doing,' Cassie continued. 'You fiddle and Rome burns.'

'Cassie,' Niall said, seeing her obvious distress and putting a hand on her arm. 'Cassie, whether you were here or yonder wouldn't have made the damnedest bit of difference.'

'Of course it would, Niall,' Cassie replied vehemently. 'I don't know what I thought I was doing.'

'You were living your life, as we all must. Besides, you're not a vet. I am, and now all we're going to discuss is what we're going to do.'

While they were talking and unseen by Cassie, Rosemary Corcoran arrived and took Joel aside. After she had talked to him briefly, Joel detached himself from the group without anyone noticing and slipped away.

'You know what we're going to do,' Cassie replied. 'You shouldn't even have to ask. I'd rather lose him on the table trying to save him than just destroy him in cold blood.'

'In that case we don't have a second to lose,' Niall replied.

Part of Cassie's investment in Claremore had included the building of a fully equipped and state of the art equine operating theatre where her veterinary team could perform urgent and major surgery without the need to travel horses away from the estate. The move had already saved not only the limbs but the lives of several valuable horses, although to date Niall Brogan had not yet had to call on all his considerable skills to untangle a mess such as he found inside The Nightingale once he had cut him open.

'Jesus God,' he sighed behind his mask when he saw the state of the animal's gut. 'This is going to take some sort of major miracle.'

'You're not dealing with an ordinary horse,' Kathleen his assistant said as she started to position the abdominal clamps. 'With this fellow anything is possible.'

'I think this might be the one contest even The Nightingale can't win,' Niall replied. 'If it's as bad as I think it is there's really nothing we can do.'

A figure appeared beside Niall, dressed in surgical green. 'There is if you'll just listen,' said Cassie's voice from behind a theatre mask. 'Not to me, to someone on the telephone.'

'I don't really have the time for an idle chat,' Niall replied.

'This is a vet I met in America. He's pioneered some form of intestinal surgery for twisted gut and it works because I saw him operate on a friend's horse. Name's Rufus Werner. I suddenly remembered him as you were getting Nightie onto the table.'

'And you have him on the line now? What the hell time's it over there?'

'Bedtime.'

Niall took the call on the extension in the washing up room. Sure enough on the other end of the line was a patient although still sleepy-sounding Rufus Werner. After Niall had listened intently to him for a while he interrupted the transatlantic conversation to say that he was going to transfer the call to the loudspeaker facility in the operating theatre itself so that the California-based veterinarian could talk him through the operation step by step.

'It seems he advocates no-surgery surgery,' Niall said to Cassie as they hurried back into the theatre. 'We don't cut or section, we go in and unravel.'

'Apparently it works,' Cassie said.

222

'I'll have to resection if we have tissue death. Otherwise there's a very real danger of peritonitis.'

'Just try doing what he says, Niall. I know the state of play. I know it's the only chance the horse has.'

'What about your friend's horse? Did he make it?'

'Well enough for him to be covering a full book of mares every year.'

Time was of the essence, particularly since according to Niall he could have done with intervening sooner. Rufus Werner confirmed his apprehension, saying that the quicker Niall now got in and began direct manipulation of the affected gut the better.

'If there's any bowel volvulus or torsion of any significant kind, you're going to be looking at a diminished blood supply and possible tissue death,' Werner advised over the loudspeakers. 'Even so don't panic and start cutting. If you try doing what I recommend and attempt to reposition the affected gut manually and *in situ* you can still prevent any absorption of toxins from the devitalized bowel. Too many times we cut and then look, because we've been expecting a variety of bad things to have happened already. This isn't always the case. I like to take a good look first and have a good feel round before even thinking about enterotomy.'

'Incision into the intestine,' Niall muttered to Cassie, who was bracing herself to watch the entire procedure.

'I know what enterotomy is, Niall,' she said, catching his eye over the top of their masks. 'Now do what the man says.'

'Suppose I lose him?'

'It won't be through anyone's fault, Niall. You're not going to save him now by any standard procedure.'

As soon as Niall began the operation Rufus Werner began talking quietly and persuasively, for all the world as if he was there looking over Niall's shoulder and could see everything that was going on. Everything he told Niall to do, Niall did, plunging his arms into the insides of the animal until he was literally up to his elbows in entrails.

'I've found it,' he said into the microphone hanging

above the table. 'I have definitely got the twist right here in my hand – and I'd say just as definitely it's a volvulus.'

Michael Delaney, another of Niall's assistants, swore under his breath at the news as he struggled to hold up the heavy and bulky structures inside the animal. But Rufus Werner did not panic. Instead he instructed Niall to make sure it wasn't simply a malposition and then to try to positively identify where the twist of gut exactly was.

There was a long silence while Niall did as he was instructed, getting as close in to the affected part as the space around the horse's intestines would allow. 'Colon,' he said at last. 'But not where I first thought. It's the large colon and you may be right. It may well just be a malposition.'

'If it is, we're in business,' Werner's voice said quickly over the loudspeakers. 'What we're going to do is reposition it. We're going to manipulate that length of affected gut back into place and simultaneously try to ease out any obstruction. So put your knife away, we are going to untangle the knitting.'

Again, as if he could see exactly what Niall was doing, Rufus Werner talked him through the entire process, even down to suggesting the exact amount of pressure which should be exerted on the attempted easing of the obstruction.

'Think of a tennis ball full of water, with a very small hole in the ball,' he said. 'And you're going to try to squeeze that water out in just a trickle. If it spurts, you lose the game. You just have to squeeze that water out so it just trickles. That's precisely the amount of pressure required – no more and no less.'

Cassie saw the sweat standing on Niall's brow as he struggled not only to hold up the great weight of gut in his hands but to do as instructed and squeeze the affected portion slowly and gently.

'I'm not going to tell you to hurry,' Werner said, 'because you might start squeezing too hard and we'll have lost the day. Just remember that prolonged manipulation carries its own set of risks and weigh one option against the other.'

At that moment for the life of her Cassie could not see how Niall could possibly succeed, so deep into a pile of tangled gut was he. But Niall just listened and did everything he was advised to do without further query, inspired by the distant American veterinary genius who was seemingly convinced that they were going to snatch a victory from the very jaws of death.

Then suddenly Cassie saw Niall's whole body stiffen.

At first she thought something terrible had happened, but then she saw the look in the surgeon's eyes as he glanced up.

'Yes,' Niall said quietly. 'God is watching us.' Then he called out loudly into the microphone. 'Rufus? I've got it! I've got the length of telescoped gut free! And the section that had all but doubled back on itself! Wonderful! You are a genius, fella! A one hundred per cent sixty carat genius! Now if I can only just pack him all back the way he was—'

'Come on – that's the easy part!' Rufus Werner joked. 'You can do that from your book on anatomy! What's the actual state of the colon that was twisted? Can you see any signs of devitalization?'

'Oddly enough, no!' Niall called back when he'd taken another close look, 'No – it looks as vital as the rest of the gut around it! No sign either of a strangulated blood supply! Not so far as I can see—'

'OK – so what you're going to have to look out for – no, you're a top vet, you know what you're going to have to look out for,' Werner corrected himself.

'We're going to have to watch for shock,' Niall agreed. 'Shock and in the post-operative period any sign of paralytic ileus. We've got to ensure the gut re-establishes its normal mobility.'

'Look out for intra-abdominal adhesions as well.'

'Will do. Rufus – if this chap pulls through we can never thank you enough.'

'He'll pull through,' Rufus Werner replied. 'I've seen that beauty race.'

Niall's team spent the last part of the operation

reassembling the horse's intestinal anatomy unaided by any further telephoned instructions, much to the silent wonder of Cassie who despite her own determination had all but lost hope when she realized what she was asking of her vet. Yet thanks to Niall's considerable skills and the vision of a Californian surgeon 6,000 miles away they had triumphed, at least over the initial and possibly the most lethal part of the procedure.

'Yes indeed,' Niall said quietly as he stood up over the still living animal. 'God was watching us all right. OK – we're all sewn up here, Tony, so how are things your end?' He gave a look to his anaesthetist who as soon as the huge incision had been fully sutured had begun to reduce the concentration of the anaesthetic gas in the mixture the horse had been inhaling. Now it was just oxygen with no anaesthetic mixed in which he then allowed the horse to breathe for well over ten minutes while everyone waited around the table. Finally he detached the endotracheal tube from the oxygen to leave the horse to breathe ordinary air via the tube which was left in the trachea until at last the animal swallowed, when it was at once taken out.

But before the patient was in a position to try to struggle to his feet the operating team moved him by way of the motorized operating table into the deeply padded recovery room which had been purpose built immediately off the operating theatre. Here the horse would remain under constant supervision until he managed to stand unaided, until he had got up on his feet and stood supported by two of the surgical staff, one holding him under his head and the other under his tail, for as long as it took until The Nightingale could once again stand safely all by himself.

'First thing to look out for besides shock is any post-operative myopathy,' Niall said for the benefit of the newer members of his squad as he and the rest of the team washed off. 'As you may remember, horses can suffer muscle cell damage from being positioned on their backs for a long period. Even though the operation didn't take as long as I'd anticipated, thanks to where and what the twist actually was, Himself's not exactly a well horse at the moment so we must be on the look-out for every single possible complication.'

'And the chances of survival?' Cassie wondered as they made their way up to the main house for a much needed drink.

'Realistically I'd say fifty to one.'

'For a moment there I hoped you'd said fifty fifty.'

'I've just been manhandling the most delicate part of a horse's anatomy, Cassie. The risk of post-operative infection is enormous.'

'He's got good cover.'

'We've availed ourselves of the best drugs and antibiotics available,' Niall said. 'But with manipulative surgery like that – fifty to one might be being generous.'

'OK,' Cassie said as levelly as she could. 'And how long before we know one way or the other?'

'The first twenty-four hours will be critical,' Niall replied. 'If there's going to be any serious complication it'll have shown itself by this time tomorrow.'

Once they'd all settled into the kitchen Erin filled the kettle and put it on while Cassie fetched a fresh bottle of whisky.

'Good,' Niall said as he sat wearily down at the table. 'So are we all met?'

It was not until the question was asked that Cassie realized they were not all met, and that one of their number had gone missing.

'Erin?' Cassie asked.

'Don't ask me,' Erin replied. 'All I know is that Rosemary had an important message for him and after that I haven't seen sight nor sound of Mr Benson. Not since I saw him hurrying away off down in the direction of the cottage.'

# *Thirteen*

'That was this afternoon,' Erin told Cassie. 'While you was all seeing the horse into the theatre.'

'Did Rosemary say what the message was?'

'Just that Mr Benson had a number to call in England, that was all.'

'And he left without saying anything?'

'There's a note on your desk.'

It was one of Joel's business cards, pushed inside a large envelope. It just said: *Please let me know how he is.*

She rang him at both the numbers on the card, one his studio in Barnes and the other the club in Covent Garden. She got no reply to her first call and an answer machine on her second, on which after reflection she left a brief message saying that the horse had pulled through the operation but that nothing certain would be known for at least twenty-four hours. That was all she said.

'He's probably jealous of the amount of attention you give to The Nightingale,' Mattie volunteered.

'He probably had something important to get back to doing,' Cassie replied, with a look at her son as if she wondered whether perhaps he was accusing Joel of being afflicted with something he himself suffered from. 'I thought you liked Joel.'

'I do,' Mattie said, picking up the telephone. 'Up to a point.'

Before Cassie could draw breath and find what that point was Mattie had dialled the number of one of their owners with whom he then had a long and involved discussion about possible entries for his horses. In response to the deliberate truncation of their conversation Cassie immediately took herself off to the yard.

She was too proud to return the call she gathered Joel made while she was out doing evening stables. She pretended there was no need since according to Mattie all Joel had done was to leave a message saying he was glad to hear The Nightingale had survived his operation.

'I thought you liked Joel,' Mattie remarked with a straight face as he poured himself a drink.

'I do. Up to a point.'

'The point being?'

'That is really none of your business.'

'It will be, if you stop only liking him up to a point.'

Cassie tried to ignore the provocation, but there was something in Mattie's tone of voice as well as the way he was watching her that made her realize he would not let it rest until he had made her confront him.

'OK,' she said with a sigh. 'Let's have it. You've obviously got something on your mind.'

Mattie drank half his whisky in one draught then looked down into his glass. 'You've already said it was none of my business.'

'And I meant it. But you seemed determined that it is.'

'I'm only thinking of you.' Mattie looked up from his glass straight at Cassie.

Cassie waited, refusing to prompt any further.

'It's just that I was speaking to Jo,' Mattie continued a moment later. 'She rang earlier.' He paused, looking directly at his mother as if to make her challenge him into telling her what he had discovered. Again Cassie refused to be drawn, busying herself instead with arranging the bowl of flowers on her desk. 'Don't you want to know what she had to say?' Mattie asked with a sigh.

'I'm sure if it was anything that concerns me she'll call back.'

'It's not as easy as that,' Mattie said, finishing his drink and at once pouring himself another.

'Obviously not, judging from the amount of Dutch courage required.'

'Jo heard something. About Joel. Quite a lot of things as it happens.'

Cassie's heart missed a beat but still she said nothing.

'Come on, Ma,' Mattie said with sudden impatience. 'You're not making this very easy. Jo and I worry about you. We don't want to see you taken for a ride, which apparently is something at which Mr Joel Benson excels. He's famous for his rich and lonely ladies, it seems.'

'I am not lonely,' Cassie said almost too quickly before Mattie could continue.

'You're rich. And you're a perfect target for someone like that. I remember you saying yourself that most artists were spongers. That they made a profession of living off people.'

'I never said that,' Cassie replied. 'Or if I did I was only quoting your father. And he only meant it as a joke.'

'Joking about things isn't that different from saying things when you're drunk,' Mattie countered. 'You've often ticked Jo and me off for that. For saying we were only joking after saying something provocative. And you're right. It is just another way of telling the truth.'

'I should imagine what Jo has heard falls into the category of idle gossip,' Cassie said, ignoring the philosophical detour. 'Straight from the badmouth brigade.'

'I don't know who told her,' Mattie replied quickly, which made Cassie smile to herself. 'But it must have been a reliable source because you know Jose. She wouldn't say something like that unless she was one hundred per cent sure.'

'Josephine is the same as most of us. She never knows how much of what she says is true.' Cassie finished, rearranging the already perfectly arranged flowers and pointedly looked at her watch. 'Now I have to go and get dressed. I'm going out to dinner.'

By the time she got up to her room Cassie was shaking, whether from anger or despair she was not sure. All she knew was that she hurt.

'They have no right!' she said out loud as she slammed her door shut and started to undress. 'It's really none of their goddam business now what I do with my life!'

Leaving her discarded clothes in a line across the

230

bedroom and still swearing under her breath she went into her bathroom and ran herself a shower. The phone rang while she was in there but she failed to hear it.

Mattie answered it in the drawing room. He told the caller that his mother had gone out but that he would of course give her a message.

'No, there's no further news about Nightie,' he told the caller. 'But then in this instance I'd say no news is good news, wouldn't you?'

When he had finished on the phone, Mattie poured himself another shot of whisky which he drank quickly before leaving the house. Deliberately he left no message on the pad. After Jose's and his conversation earlier he was as determined as his sister that no fortune-hunter was going to get his hands on any part of their rightful inheritance.

Before she left to go out to dinner Cassie sat on her bed with the telephone in her lap. Twice she began to dial Josephine's number and twice she stopped. Finally she put the telephone back on her bedside table and getting up took a last look at herself in the cheval mirror before going out of the room. As she was halfway downstairs she heard the phone ringing but by the time she had hurried into the drawing room it had stopped.

'Damn,' she said, looking round the empty room, having half expected Mattie to be still there. 'Mattie?'

But he was long gone and there was no-one else in the house itself, Erin having taken herself off up to her quarters since she knew Cassie was on her way out for the evening. Again Cassie hesitated in front of the telephone, but this time she gave in to temptation, picking the instrument up and dialling her daughter's number.

As soon as she heard Mark's languid tones on the taped message she replaced the receiver and went out, leaving the telephone switched to her own answering machine which in turn duly picked up all her calls. One of them was Joel, ringing to make sure Mattie had reported his earlier call. When he realized he had got the machine, he too left no message.

\* \* \*

'I hear you're seeing Joel Benson,' Leonora drawled as the guests were being served drinks before dinner.

'I heard you'd gone abroad,' Cassie replied tartly. On arrival at the party she had been appalled when the first person she caught sight of through the drawing room door had been the woman she had sworn in private never to talk to again. Leonora had no such compunction, however, and as soon as she saw Cassie she had made straight for her.

'Abroad was weeks ago,' Leonora said, blowing smoke in Cassie's face. 'Infernally boring it was, too. It must be age or something, but I'm beginning to discover that all one changes when one goes abroad is the climate. Now tell me all about you and Benson.'

'Don't tell me you know him as well?'

'Wouldn't you like to know?' Leonora's smile was about as appealing as an oil slick as she helped herself to a fresh glass of champagne.

'Back to all the old vices, I see,' Cassie said.

'Every lovely one,' Leonora agreed. 'But remember – the vices you jeer at in others laugh at you from inside yourself. At least, that's what Grandpa always said. So. You were just going to tell me about you and Joel Benson. Isn't he *weird*? I mean all that long black hair and dark burning eyes and stuff. He really is a little old for that, I'd have said. But there you go. Women, it appears, *love* it. Right?' Leonora looked Cassie in the eye, this time without the pretence of a smile.

'He was commissioned to do a bronze of The Nightingale,' Cassie replied, looking round the room desperate for the chance of an escape route. 'We've seen each other a couple of times since then, that's all.'

'That's not what he's saying, apparently.'

'I'm sorry,' Cassie said, pretending to wave at someone before beginning to ease herself away. 'If you'll excuse me I've just seen someone I have to talk to.'

'Sure you have. I'll catch you later.'

Having made sure by consulting the placement that she was to be seated nowhere near Leonora, Cassie then did her level best to enjoy the evening but, since the sole interest of both the men sitting either side of her was the welfare of her famous horse, by the time she had finished recounting both The Nightingale's dramatic return to Claremore and his horrific ordeal on the operating table she quite understandably felt the very opposite of entertained. In fact long before anyone else showed any signs of fatigue Cassie found herself to be exhausted, and so having discreetly said her goodbyes she did her best to slip away from the party unnoticed.

As usual Leonora was not to be shaken off quite so easily. On the pretext of going to the ladies she followed Cassie out of the room and across the marbled entrance hall.

'So, when you see Joel Benson again – ' she began as a member of the household staff fetched Cassie's coat.

'If I see Joel Benson again,' Cassie corrected her.

'When you see him again, remember me to him,' Leonora continued, undismayed. 'We met on a mutual friend's yacht a couple of years back. He was doing her kids' heads.'

'Sure,' Cassie said, slipping into the coat which was now being proffered.

'He really is quite a character,' Leonora said with one shake of her blond head. 'You know who else he's seeing now?'

'He can see whomsoever he chooses. It really is *none* of my affair,' Cassie said, unable to stop the defensive tone she had adopted, which she knew at once was a mistake, judging from Leonora's instant Cheshire cat smile. 'Goodnight, Leonora.'

'Whatever you say, Cassie McGann,' Leonora said with a shrug, stepping aside from the front door as Cassie walked briskly past her. 'See you around.'

Over the next few days Cassie had plenty of other things to think about besides Joel, most important the recuperation of her famous horse.

'This has to be the most resolute creature I've ever had to tend,' Niall Brogan said. 'Since we put him together again he hasn't taken one step backwards. To tell you the truth, Cassie, when I had that first look inside him I'd have said he had one chance not in one but ten million. And now will you look at him? Up and eating and moving about his box as if I'd pulled a wolf tooth rather than rearranged the whole of his insides.'

'So what next, Niall?' Cassie wondered as she stroked the horse's head over the box door. 'Obviously he'll need box rest. But I wonder what we'll do with him after that.'

'Are you asking or just privately wondering, Cassie? Myself, I doubt if he'll ever be quite the horse he was, but then even if he's a stone inferior to what he was he'd still be a prodigious racehorse.'

'Maybe he won't want to go on being a racehorse.'

'Maybe he won't. But without his equipment, all that'd be left would be to retire him.'

'Sure,' Cassie said, giving one last pull to the horse's ears. 'But somehow I can't see Nightie spending the rest of his days standing in a field.'

When the subject came up for discussion at dinner, Mattie suggested the horse could go eventing if he showed no real inclination to go on racing. Cassie agreed, adding that even if the horse recovered fully she was still in two minds as to whether or not to put him back in training.

'Jose could ride him,' Mattie said. 'She's always wanted to event properly.'

'Josephine is in England,' Cassie reminded him. 'With a husband, remember?'

Mattie looked at her but said nothing.

'What's that look supposed to mean?'

'Nothing.' Mattie finished his wine and made to get up from the table. 'Now if you'll excuse me, I have to call some of our owners.'

'Mattie—' Cassie said, calling him back. 'I need to know what you meant by that.'

'Ask Jo,' Mattie said. 'I was right. Mark's a bastard. Sorry. But you know what I mean.'

'What's he done?'

'Ask Jo.'

After Mattie had gone, Cassie remained behind at the table where she sat staring up at the portrait of Josephine she had commissioned when her daughter was eighteen, wearing a blue sprigged muslin dress and looking every inch a Rosse. She had hoped so fervently that the girl would make as wonderful a marriage as she herself had done with Tyrone, yet ever since she was a teenager Josephine had mysteriously failed to attract anyone of whom either Erin or Cassie felt they could approve. *She's storing up trouble for herself, Mrs Rosse*, Erin had warned. *The way she's going she won't be able to recognize a dacent young man if ever she meets one*, and now it seemed as though Erin's prognostications were fully realized and that Josephine had married a wrong one.

Moreover if what Mattie had just intimated was true, namely that Josephine might be in a position to ride The Nightingale should the horse recover fully and be turned into an eventer, it must mean that her daughter's brief marriage was effectively over.

*Yet why?* Cassie wondered as she rose from the table to go in search of Mattie, hoping to continue their discussion. But when she made her way through, the room was empty except for her dogs who were stretched out asleep in front of the log fire. Looking then in both the study and the library, she still could find no sign of him, so assuming that he had taken himself either off to the office or up to his own quarters to do his telephoning Cassie sat down in front of the fire for a long time before finally picking up the telephone herself to try to get through to her daughter in the hope of finding out first hand what the truth might be. But as usual she got the answerphone, so with a deep sigh of frustration she replaced the receiver without leaving a message and picking up the latest copy of *Pacemaker* started to flick through it without reading one word.

Besides trying to discover what might be going wrong with her daughter's marriage there were a hundred and one other things she should be doing, yet Cassie felt like doing none of them because what she really wanted was company, and most of all the company of one person in particular.

The telephone was still there right beside her on the sofa and all she had to do was pick it up and ring his number. If he wasn't there she could leave a short message on his answering machine – nothing too personal. All she had to do was call him and that would be that. If he did not want to continue with their relationship then either he wouldn't return her call or she would know by the tone of his voice if he was there and spoke to her personally. If she didn't call all she would do would be to sit and wonder, just as she was doing now.

She even got as far as putting the telephone on her knee and picking up the receiver before once again her all too fierce pride intervened.

'Dammit,' she said to herself. 'I know this sort of thing doesn't matter any more, but why the hell *should* I be ringing *him*? He was the one who disappeared. If anyone's due to offer an explanation it should be him, not me, so why in hell should I ring him?'

She slammed the phone back down again and clattered it back onto the table beside her, before going to pour herself a drink. As she was doing so, the phone rang. Forgetting her pride she almost ran to answer it. 'Hello?' she said, in a low voice. 'Who is this?'

'It's me.' Josephine's voice down the line. 'Can I come home?'

'Of course you can.' Cassie said, her heart sinking, 'Do you want to tell me why?'

'When I get home.'


'He's been cheating on me,' Josephine told her mother and brother. 'It seems he even had someone on honeymoon.'

'Not possible,' Mattie said grimly. 'You're putting us on.'

'No I'm not,' Josephine assured him. 'He boasted about it. Someone he picked up in the hotel bar, apparently.'

'I'll murder him.'

'There's no need to Mattie,' Josephine said quietly. 'It's over now. The whole thing.'

'Meaning I hope that you're going to divorce him.'

236

'It's not as easy as that, is it?' Josephine returned, glaring at her brother. 'You seem to forget I'm pregnant.'

'Why?' Cassie asked carefully. 'What has being pregnant got to do with staying married with a man who cheats on you?'

'Because that's why I got pregnant. Right?'

'No, not really.'

'I agree,' Mattie said. 'Blank.'

Josephine flicked her hair back and then lit a cigarette in defiance of the tears now in her eyes. 'Mark has been cheating on me from the word go,' she said. 'Forget the girl on honeymoon. He was still having all his old girl-friends after we'd met, apparently, even after he'd asked me to marry him. When I found out I thought perhaps if I got pregnant—' Josephine stopped and took a deep pull on her cigarette. 'Oh, it doesn't matter,' she said. 'Really it doesn't.'

'Of course it *matters*, Josephine,' Cassie said. 'If this doesn't matter then I want to know what does.'

'It's just that I thought if I got pregnant it might make him reform his ways – you know, be the faithful husband and father-to-be. But instead it's only made things ten times worse. It seems – it seems he hates kids.'

Cassie frowned and stared hard at her daughter. 'He doesn't like children?' she said, as if reacting to a blasphemy.

Josephine shrugged. 'Can't stand them, apparently.'

'Didn't you discuss all this before you decided to get married?'

'No. I just took it for granted – well. You know, growing up in this family you sort of do. Take these sorts of things for granted. That people fall in love, want to get married, and raise a family.'

'So why did he marry you?' Cassie asked.

'Why do you think?' Mattie sighed, collapsing into an armchair. 'Why do you think? And of course you being a good little Catholic girl, you can't or won't divorce him.'

'I don't *want* to divorce him, Mattie!' Josephine burst into angry tears. 'I told you you wouldn't understand!'

'Of course I don't understand!' Mattie replied forcefully. 'Just give me one good reason why you want to stay married to the sod! Just one!'

'Because I love him! Is that good enough for you?'

Mattie looked at his sister appalled while Cassie took a deep breath and got up to walk about the drawing room, trying to collect her thoughts.

'Look,' Josephine said with sudden sarcasm, wiping away her angry tears. 'Look, I don't expect you to understand, either of you – you, Mattie, because you've never had a serious relationship, and you, Mum – you wouldn't understand because of Dad. Because of your famous fairy tale romance. You couldn't *begin* to understand what I feel, not for a second.'

'You could try me.'

'There isn't any point,' Josephine returned, pulling her hand away to twist it in her lap with her other one. She stared down at them with her head bent, her tears falling unchecked onto her fingers. 'I honestly thought the only way to keep him was to have a baby. I thought he might change if I got pregnant. He can be very kind and loving at times, you see, so I thought if we had a baby he'd change and go back to being the Mark I met. The one I fell in love with.'

'You mean the one you dreamed up you were in love with,' Mattie said from behind her. 'The one who was still bonking all his old girlfriends.'

'Shut up, Mattie! You don't know what you're talking about because you haven't grown up yet! You haven't even started to! And you won't – not as long as you stay here you won't! As mother's favourite darling little boy!'

'Stop it, both of you,' Cassie ordered. 'You don't know what you're saying, either of you. And until you do it's better you don't say anything. Am I making myself quite clear?'

'Yes,' Mattie said quietly. 'Perfectly.'

'I knew you wouldn't understand,' Josephine said, still staring down at her hands, which she was wringing even more frenetically than ever. 'Like I knew this was a mistake.

238

I should never have come home. I knew you wouldn't have time for me.'

'How can you say that?' Cassie asked. 'How could you even begin to think that?'

'Because you only really have time for your bloody horse, that's why,' Josephine replied. 'And as Mark said you've made a right mess of him as well.'

'As *Mark* said?' Cassie wondered.

'As Mark said,' Josephine repeated.

'He said what happened to Nightie was my fault?'

'Well, who else's? You were warned by everyone! Everyone with any sense told you – they all said *don't keep the horse on in training*. I told you, Mattie told you, everyone told you – but you did! You wouldn't listen to anybody because you thought you knew best! Like you always do! You had to keep Nightie on in training, and not only that! You didn't even bother to *insure* him properly! I don't know what you thought you were doing!'

'OK, fine,' Cassie said, trying to take the steam out of things. 'Whatever you and Mark may or may not think, that's another subject altogether, Josephine. It really has nothing to do with why you're here back home.'

'You don't think so?' Josephine retorted. 'You should hear Mark on the subject. Mark can't believe it. He says only a woman could be so stupid. He thinks you're mad, and I'm mad – and you have to be because look what's happened! I mean, our whole future, gone! Just because you wanted to have your own way!'

'I don't think you heard what I said, Josephine,' Cassie said quietly. 'I said this is a subject for another time. What we have to deal with first is you – and what's going to happen to you. What's the matter?' Cassie hurried to her daughter's side as she saw Josephine suddenly double up in pain. 'What is it, Jo? What's the matter, darling?'

'Oh my God,' Josephine said suddenly, leaning forward and putting both her hands to her stomach. '*Christ almighty*. There's something very wrong.'

\*    \*    \*

239

The family doctor was no longer old Dr Gilbert, who had helped deliver Josephine into the world but had long since retired and recently died, but his son Derry, a totally different character. His father had been, in Erin's words, an awful grumpy auld stick, addicted to nicotine and not averse to the odd ball of malt, whereas Derry was fastidious, scrupulous and meticulous, and again according to Erin a terrible loss to the Protestant church. He was also punctilious and as soon as he heard the urgency in Cassie's call he dropped everything and was at Josephine's bedside within quarter of an hour. He subjected Josephine to a long and thorough examination, leaving Cassie to pace the floor of the drawing room below and to wonder to herself how everything had gone so terribly wrong.

*What can I have done?*' she asked herself, watching Mattie outside throwing a frisbee for Wilkie. *What can I have possibly done to invite all this bad luck and disaster? I've done everything I could to hold house, home and business together, and now it's all falling apart. All I've done is kept my head down and kicked on, through thick and thin, and all for this.*

And then she remembered the words whispered at her back that day at Longchamps, after the Arc, when The Nightingale had just raced to his famous victory.

*Mind you don't go getting too successful*, the voice had warned her. *Mind you don't go getting too successful.*

Her reverie was broken by a discreet tap on the door behind her and the entry of Dr Gilbert.

'There's not a moment to be lost, Mrs Rosse,' he said. 'Your daughter has to be admitted to hospital immediately. I shall ring the Rotunda at once.'

# Fourteen

'A what sort of pregnancy?' Erin wondered when Cassie told her.

'Ectopic. It's when a fertilized egg becomes stuck in one of your fallopian tubes,' Cassie explained to Erin the next morning as her housekeeper busied herself in the kitchen making lunch while Cassie sat drinking strong black coffee. 'Apparently it can be caused by any number of things, which is something I didn't know.'

'I thought things like that could only be caused by a termination,' Erin replied, wiping her hands down her check apron. 'Or at least they only happened to women who'd had a termination.'

Cassie waited before she replied, taking a sip of her coffee to buy time. The last thing she wanted at this moment was an argument with Erin about the Church's standing on birth control and the termination of unwanted pregnancies.

'No, apparently ectopic pregnancies—'

'Ectopic indeed?' Erin interrupted, following her interruption with a barely concealed snort, as if the condition itself constituted some sort of sin. 'They give all these things such fancy names, as if to take your mind off what they really are.'

'Be that as it may, Erin,' Cassie continued patiently, 'but apparently this sort of pregnancy can be the result of all sorts of things, so the doctors told me. Of everything from congenital abnormality to perfectly straightforward infection.'

'Or even following the failure of certain types of birth control,' Erin announced with a certain amount of undisguised triumph. 'That's something else I heard. That when pregnancies go wrong, it's more often than not the result of taking the pill.'

Cassie watched Erin virtuously rolling out the pastry topping for the pie she was busy making and bit her tongue. Even though she herself was a Catholic, for the life of her Cassie was unable to understand the mind of a person who on the one hand was capable of giving such love to all those who surrounded her and most of all those whom she had helped raise, while on the other she could forget the humanities and begin pontificating like the worst sort of bigot about matters of doctrine. Much as she loved Erin, Cassie found this difficult to take from a woman who had fallen in love with and got herself pregnant by their local parish priest.

But she said nothing for she loved Erin dearly and knew that these two sides of her character in no way constituted a whole, for the real and entire Erin was the one who loved and cared for them all while the other one was the ghost of a frightened little girl who had been brought up in fear and trembling of the Church.

'I hope that pie's not for lunch, Erin,' she said by way of changing the subject. 'I really only want something light because I have to be at the Rotunda by three if I'm to see Josephine before she goes down for her operation.'

'I cut you some sandwiches ready,' Erin replied, folding the pastry over the top of a dish. 'The pie's for this evening, all being well, please God.'

'Everything has to be fine, Erin. Josephine's being operated on by the best gynaecologist in Ireland.'

'But she still has to lose the babba.'

'I'm afraid so. And it isn't a case of saving the baby over the mother if that's also concerning you. There's no way a foetus can survive being conceived outside the womb, and anyway Dr Gilbert told me that in ninety-nine per cent of these cases by the time they operate the foetus is already dead.'

'Ninety-nine per cent is not one hundred per cent, Mrs Rosse,' Erin replied, picking up the pie and placing it carefully on the side. 'At least it wasn't when I was at school. And you know as well as I do what the Church says about such matters. If there's a chance of saving the baby—'

'There is no chance, Erin,' Cassie said, cutting in quickly. 'None whatsoever. And even if there was, there's absolutely no way I'd ask the surgeon to save its life at risk to my daughter's. Now I have some things to attend to, if you'll excuse me.'

Cassie took her plate of sandwiches from the table and went before anything more was said, leaving a speechless and highly indignant Erin behind her. She ate half the sandwiches while she was getting herself ready to leave and hurried out of the house to drive into Dublin half an hour early.

By so doing she missed the telephone call that came through on her direct line and because in her hurry Cassie had forgotten to switch on her answering machine Erin took the call, and because she was still arguing the pros and cons of the Church's standing on birth control and abortion in her head she completely forgot to write down the message she was given to say that Mr Benson had called.

The operation carried out by the distinguished Mr Theodore Pilkington on Josephine late that afternoon was perfectly straightforward, even though as Mr Pilkington informed Cassie immediately afterwards he had been required to remove the damaged fallopian tube as he considered it beyond repair.

'*Nil carborundum*, however, Mrs Rosse,' he announced as he walked her down a hospital corridor. '*Nil carborundum*. The young lady has another perfectly *good* fallopian tube and given a fair shot at it there is no *logical* reason why she should not still be quite capable of conceiving, provided this conception was the result of post-coital contraception. Yes? And not a uterine infection.'

'Could you not tell when you were operating?' Cassie asked, and then corrected herself. 'That was a silly question. I meant, wouldn't you have been able to see signs of any infection when you were actually doing the operation?'

'Hmm.' Theodore Pilkington removed his tortoiseshell half moons and twirled them casually around between finger and thumb as they continued to walk down the corridor. 'I would say the jury is still out on that one, Mrs Rosse. I did detect some abnormal swelling and tenderness of the pelvis when I performed my *pre-op* examination, but we shall not know for certain until we have the results of your daughter's cervical *smear*.'

Normally Cassie would have been amused by the distinguished surgeon's idiosyncratic use of emphases and charmed by the Anglo-Irish lilt to his voice, but the implications of what was being said far outweighed any other observations. Instead she continued to match the tall surgeon stride for stride as they walked the polished hospital corridor and listen to what he had to say in answer to her few but carefully chosen questions. There was it seemed a possibility that Josephine could have been and indeed still was suffering from a syndrome called pelvic inflammatory disease, and if the tests proved this to be the case Cassie was assured it would explain Josephine's recent malaise.

'PID being?' Cassie wondered.

'Pelvic inflammatory disease,' Theodore Pilkington reiterated.

'How would someone contract such a disease?'

'Hmmm,' the surgeon mused, before all at once exhaling childishly through his lips to distract from what he had to say. 'IUD for instance, though I understand the young lady *in question* does not favour the device. Intrauterine device, yes? The infection can often follow a miscarriage, or an abortion – even childbirth. But generally speaking 'tis *sexually* transmitted. As in chlamydial infection and gonorrhoea. Now. Do you think your wonderful horse will ever race again?' he added still intent on distraction.

Cassie smiled politely and shook her head. 'I really can't discuss that at the moment, Mr Pilkington,' she said. 'I'm so worried about my daughter. If I understand what you're saying—'

'Of course, of course, and I'm sure you understand well

enough what I'm saying, Mrs Rosse,' Theodore Pilkington assured her. 'NSU as in *nonspecific urethritis* is *still* the most common sexually transmitted disease in the United Kingdom.'

'I know my daughter to be perfectly faithful,' Cassie put in defensively.

'Then in that case, Mrs Rosse, we shall soon know the *source* of the infection. I shall naturally keep you fully informed.'

With that he was gone, accelerating his pace to round a corner and disappear into a ward.

Cassie arrived home around midnight, having waited to be with Josephine when she finally recovered consciousness. Erin had left her supper on a tray in the library but she was too tired and worried to eat, so she took the food to the kitchen and put it in the refrigerator, and instead made herself a hot chocolate which she carried up to her bedroom where she slowly drank it sitting on the edge of her large double bed wondering over and over if anything was ever going to start going right again.

She brought Mattie up to date as they rode out two recuperating horses the following afternoon. The news Cassie had received from the hospital at midday certainly heralded no upturn in fortune. Jose was diagnosed as having suffered from PID which according to the evidence had been sexually transmitted.

'Whether she likes it or not, she really should divorce him,' she said.

'She won't divorce him because she loves the sod. You heard her,' Mattie replied.

'That was before she lost the baby,' Cassie said. 'And had to undergo an operation.'

'She's in his thrall, Ma,' Mattie said, taking a pull on his horse who had taken to fooling around. 'They have this thing. Jose told me. It's very good physically, if you know what I mean.'

'No, of course I don't know what you mean,' Cassie said

245

lightly. 'It's been so long since I was married I've forgotten all about it.'

'OK, OK,' Mattie groaned. 'I'm sorry. Anyway, to get back to the question of divorce. How can Jose divorce Creepy Carter-James, being the good Catholic girl that she is?'

'From what we know now, and particularly since he said quite categorically he doesn't want children, she can go for an annulment and believe you me she'll get one.'

'Supposing she doesn't? I really think she's seriously stuck on this guy.'

'Are you trying to tell me your sister will stay with a man like Mark just because he's good in bed?'

'It's more than just that,' Mattie said quietly, breathing in deeply. 'Apparently – well, not to put too fine a point on it, apparently he's the first man who's actually satisfied her.'

Cassie looked round at him sharply. 'OK,' she said after a moment. 'But that's no real reason surely to stay with someone who's not only consistently unfaithful but is so to the point where he infects her with his filthy diseases? In this instance with a disease which could have led to her dying in childbirth and which certainly accounted for the loss of her first baby?'

'I thought we were to refer to it as a *foetus*,' Mattie remarked, keeping his horse at the walk.

Cassie turned and glared at him. 'What's wrong with you?' she demanded.

'There's nothing wrong with me,' Mattie replied, widening his eyes.

'Meaning there's something wrong with me.'

'You're just a bit stressed out.'

'Don't you dare patronize me, Mattie.'

'I am not patronizing you. I just said you're a bit stressed out, that's all. We all are. Jose will have to sort her own life out. You can't do it for her. She's an old married woman.' Mattie grinned, hoping the remark would lighten his mother's mood, but Cassie just stared grimly ahead of her. 'Guv'nor,' he chided her gently. 'You have a business to run.'

'You don't have to tell me that, for God's sake!' Cassie retorted. 'I know what I have to do without you telling me, thank you!'

'OK,' Mattie agreed. 'Then tell me what horses we're running tomorrow. And where.'

Again Cassie glared at him but this time she refused to give him an answer, instead tipping forward in her saddle and kicking her horse on into a steady canter up the grass gallop ahead.

For a moment Mattie held his own now prancing horse back, shaking his head as he watched his mother take off.

'You've never given it a thought, have you?' he said to himself. 'I might have been in a wheelchair now because of you and Nightie.'

Then he kicked on and cantered after the pair ahead.

Cassie thought long and hard about her life as she drove into Dublin, most of all of how as far as her children were concerned she had been building it on assumptions, too wrapped up in her own past to be properly concerned with their futures. She had presumed that because she had been determined to rebuild her own life and ensure her family's security her son and daughter would be content to go along with her plans and accept the life she was mapping out for them. It had all seemed to be so trouble free. Josephine had never shown the slightest signs of any overt rebellion and even when she had decided to become an actress Cassie had been only too happy to encourage her.

Except, Cassie suddenly remembered, it hadn't been Josephine who had decided to become an actress, it had been Cassie who had decided it for her. Josephine had set her heart on becoming an event rider but after she had sustained a particularly crashing fall going cross country and had lain so still on the ground that everyone concerned thought she must have done herself serious injury, Cassie decided there and then she could not possibly stand the strain of Josephine's eventing full time and so before her daughter's nerve had returned Cassie had strongly recommended a career in the theatre instead. It was only logical. Josephine was a beautiful girl who had already shown considerable talent in several of her school's theatrical productions, and the suggestion that she could well become as brilliant an actress as she was a horsewoman had proved a perfectly valid one since once Josephine had finished at drama school her career appeared to take off.

But it was Cassie's choice of life, not Josephine's.

Nor had they ever talked about Josephine's career, not in any depth. Doing her best not to be the interfering mother Cassie had confined her enquiries simply to what her daughter might be doing next, although she had religiously attended every production Josephine had been in from the moment she started at RADA. After she had graduated, because Josephine had rarely been out of work Cassie had naturally assumed her daughter must be fulfilled and happy. Yet she had never once asked her any such question.

Neither had she cross-examined Mattie as to his real state of mind. There had always been a very strong bond between Cassie and him since she had nursed him through all the major asthma attacks of his youth, when he was small always taking him into her bed whenever he had a nocturnal attack and then, when he grew too big for such a comfort, sleeping on the floor of his own bedroom to make sure she would always be right there at hand should he need her. So it was hardly surprising that even once Mattie had grown into a young man Cassie would still subconsciously assume he was dependent on her, although the more she thought about it as she headed for Dublin the more she realized that it could well be the other way round, that without a husband Cassie had become dependent on her son. Meanwhile both Mattie and Josephine had developed along their own lines, lines which Cassie hoped it was not too late for her to understand. By the time she was crossing O'Connell Bridge she had determined that as from that moment she would find out exactly what both her son and daughter wanted to do with their own lives, and let them act accordingly. Once she had reached that decision she felt an immediate sense of release, as if she too was stepping out of the shadows.

Her buoyant mood was soon deflated when she reached the Rotunda and found Josephine in the depths of despair. Realizing that this was not the time to review her daughter's life or dispense bromides about the after-effects of losing a baby, instead Cassie indulged in small talk, chatting to her monosyllabic daughter about the steady progress The Nightingale was making and what a wonderful job Liam had performed on him.

'That's great,' Josephine said finally, her face turned away from Cassie.

'It is, isn't it?' Cassie agreed. 'Liam thinks we'll be able to start turning him out for an hour or so soon, the way the old horse is doing.'

'That's not what I meant,' Josephine said, still staring out of the window. 'I mean that you seem more interested in your horse than you are in me.'

'I was only telling you about Nightie because—'

'Because that's all you ever really want to talk about,' Josephine interrupted. 'He's only a horse, you know, Mum. He's not your husband. Or Mattie's and my father.'

'I don't really think we should talk about this now,' Cassie said.

'Meaning you'd rather not talk about it now. You never really want to talk about anything that concerns me. All I ever hear is Claremore, Claremore, Claremore, and The Nightingale, naturally. Oh and if I'm really lucky how brilliantly my brother is doing. But that's all I hear about. It's as if now I'm married I don't exist any more.'

'You're talking nonsense, Josephine. But it's understandable. I don't know what drugs they're giving you—'

'This has nothing to do with drugs! Or with what I've been through! Or rather it has got *something* to do with what I've been through – because of all people I thought at least you'd understand a little bit of that!'

Josephine began to cry. Cassie reached for the box of tissues beside the bed and pulled a handful out, leaning across to wipe away the stream of silent and seemingly endless tears. At once Josephine moved her face away, as far out of Cassie's range as she could, taking the tissues from her to wipe her face for herself.

'I didn't think now was the time to discuss such things, Josephine, that's all,' Cassie said, as stoically as she could manage. 'I thought once you were feeling a little stronger – perhaps even when I get you back home—'

'Home?' Josephine wondered through her tears. 'Whatever makes you think I'm coming back home?'

'I thought as soon as Mr Pilkington gave the word, I'd take you back to Claremore so that you could get yourself back in shape before – before doing whatever it is you want to do next. That's what made me think you might be coming back home, Josephine.'

'Home is in London, Mum, remember? Home is married to Mark, and that's where I'm going as soon as they let me out of this place. I spoke to him this morning.'

'You spoke to Mark this morning?'

'That's right. *I spoke to Mark this morning*. And told him I was coming home.'

'Fine,' Cassie said. 'But all I'd like to know – and I think I have a right to know – is why you came back to Claremore in the first place. I mean if all the time you intended to go home to your husband. I was under the impression—'

'*Exactly*,' Josephine suddenly hissed, her tears now stopping as abruptly as they had begun. 'You were under the *impression*. And shall I tell you why you were under an impression? Because you never bloody well bothered to ask!'

'No, I'm sorry, Jo darling,' Cassie said, standing up and picking up her belongings. 'I don't think that's fair. I asked all right. I asked plenty, but you didn't really tell. And you still haven't. I can only assume you're talking like this because you're not yourself.'

'You can assume till you're blue in the face, Mum, because that's all you ever do. You assume I'm OK but you don't bother to ask. You assume my marriage is over and that I won't be going back to Mark, but you don't ask.

Just the way you assumed because I'd temporarily lost my nerve that I wanted to give up riding and do something else.'

Cassie ignored the last remark, having already admitted her mistake to herself on the drive into Dublin.

'So now you intend to go back to Mark?' she asked instead. 'After all he's put you through?'

'You don't have to understand,' Josephine said, looking at her steadily. 'What I do or don't do is my business.'

For the first time for as long as she could recall Cassie suddenly felt anger directed against her daughter welling up inside her. She knew that given the circumstances it was wrong of her yet she knew the emotion was fully justifiable. She was trying her hardest to do her best by her daughter, yet ever since she had met Mark Josephine had responded to Cassie with indifference, sarcasm or just plain hostility. Cassie was sure this was because Josephine was both afraid of her husband and guilty about the choice she had made, yet she also knew that this awareness would make precious little difference to the present standing of their relationship.

About to try to open the debate fully Cassie turned when someone knocked on the door and came into the private room.

'*Mrs* Rosse,' she heard Theodore Pilkington's voice saying. 'The very person I had hoped to see. Josephine – *will* you forgive me if I remove your mother for just a few moments? I need a small word.'

Once again he walked Cassie up and down the long highly polished corridor outside Josephine's room while he talked to her.

'Not making the very best of progress so far, at least not up here.' The surgeon tapped his temple and sighed. 'Still, 'tis early days, Mrs Rosse, it's early days – but even so, your daughter has not got what they call now, *as I believe*, a good attitude. She's very hard on herself it would seem, and for what reason I ask myself? No doubt as her mother you will be able to answer such a question far better than I, but then answering the question provides an answer to

251

a question but it does *not* provide a cure. Tell me about the husband, if you wouldn't mind.'

Cassie glanced up at the tall man beside her, who smiled politely back at her with an inclination of his head.

'Do you mind?' he repeated.

'Not at all,' Cassie assured him. 'He's been unfaithful to my daughter since he met her. I can't stand him and I don't think Josephine should have married him.'

'Thank you,' Theodore Pilkington replied, falling into step alongside Cassie. 'Husband's a bad egg then. That would make perfect sense. And in case you think I am going off at a *tangent*, I am not. All these things are interlinked, d'you see? Yes, of course you do, because you are a woman and a mother, so you understand that old bromide *mens sana in corpore sano*. The mind and body are so very interlinked, and in my own specialty I have always considered that a certain amount of infertility can be put down to the patient's mental state of mind.'

The surgeon stopped in front of Cassie and turned, blocking her way. He stood a good eight inches taller than her, every inch the ex-international rugby player, the winner of twelve caps on the right wing.

'Do you know we're near neighbours? I'm quite sure you did not,' he said, removing his half moons, snapping them shut and folding them into his pocket. 'I'm only the other side of the hill from you due west, hardly ten miles as the crow likes to have it.'

Unsure how to take this information Cassie just smiled politely, waiting for anything else Theodore Pilkington might have to say. And as she waited she found the anger that had been troubling her began to evaporate, vanquished it would seem by the kindness in his dark hazel eyes.

'Good,' he said. 'Good. So my idea is that since *you yourself* look in need of a little time out you cross the middle mountain which separates us and come and have dinner with me tonight. The only thing that need stop you is if you have a previous engagement and if *that's* the case – why, we can make it tomorrow night or the night after that, the night after that and so *ad infinitum*.'

'Won't you have to clear it with Mrs Pilkington first?' Cassie wondered.

'No, no, Mrs Rosse,' Theodore replied, 'for there *is* no Mrs Pilkington.'

'In that case, thank you,' Cassie replied without quite understanding why but imagining it might have something to do with those remarkable eyes.

'Does that mean tonight or are we into the infinite here?'

'Tonight would be just fine.'

'Excellent,' Theodore Pilkington said, before inclining himself slightly forward. 'I'm sure I won't regret it,' he said, and then disappeared inside the door immediately behind him to attend to his patient before Cassie had time for any second thoughts.

Theodore Pilkington lived in a large square white Georgian house set in half a dozen acres of Italianate gardens. Even though it was now early winter, because of the formality of the planting of the hedges and shrubbery and the perfect positioning of the various ponds and water features the grounds were still a feast to the eye, particularly set as they were in a small sheltered valley near the foot of the mountains, although Cassie was aware of little of this, arriving as she did well after dark and illuminating only the very edges of the gardens with the headlights of her car.

However, she could see from the paintings and the photographs of the house and its grounds which hung in the comfortable but still elegant drawing room how fine an achievement the creation of Bnooghara, as the house was called, had indeed been.

'It had all but been burned to the ground when first bought,' Theodore said, handing Cassie a glass of the palest pink champagne. 'Or does one mean it had been all but burned to the ground? The latter, I think, the latter most probably – not that it matters *one whit* – the point being that more or less all one bought with the place were a few doorways, some windows, and the odd roof beam. Quite fun, really.'

As her host poured himself a glass of wine, Cassie

perused the photographs on the Blüthner boudoir grand, the Georgian military chest and the highly polished mahogany tables. They were mostly of the house and gardens, often with disparate groups of what Cassie assumed were friends gathered in some part of the grounds or the interior of the house. A few were of horses in the winning enclosure, or jumping steeplechase fences, but there were no single photographs of women or children, or indeed of Theodore Pilkington himself except for an amateurish portrait of him as a young man taken on the side of a lakeside hill somewhere, just a head and shoulders shot of him smiling unaffectedly into camera.

'Now tell me,' he said, coming to her side and leading her by the arm gently away from the array of photographs to offer her a seat by the fire. 'This wonderful *horse* of yours. How is he now? What a quite terrible affair altogether.'

Cassie brought him up to date with The Nightingale's apparently seamless recovery while Theodore listened to her intently, neither prompting her not interrupting her. Instead he just watched her, the smile gone from his eyes to be replaced by a look of studious and genuine concern. Cassie looked back at him and into his dark eyes for as long as she could but found she had to keep breaking the contact, using the picking up of her drink as a pretext, or the straightening of the skirt on her perfectly uncreased black cashmere dress.

'Good,' was all he said when she had finished. 'All I will say to that is 'tis a wonder you're in the apparently good shape you are after all that. I most *certainly* would not presume either to offer a theory based on no judgement whatso*ever* as to who could have been responsible for such a heinous crime, or to ask you to conjecture what the horse may or may not be capable of doing in the future. You must, I feel sure, be quite sick of speculation and hypothesis, so instead I shall offer you another glass of wine before we go in to dinner. There were some others coming this evening, but when you accepted I cancelled them so that I could have you all to myself.'

Cassie did her best not to look surprised and followed him into the dining room where they were served by a near-silent Filipino maid in a room whose walls were lined with faded red silk and hung with a series of vibrant contemporary Irish landscapes apparently executed by a friend of Theodore's called Michael Forster. The food was light and exquisite, the wines memorable, and the conversation unceasing. Cassie found they had much in common besides horses, although Theodore said his winners had been few, very far between, and extremely lucky. They also shared passions for Rossini, Bonnard and Chekhov, the Russian playwright entering the conversation because it emerged that Theodore had seen Josephine in London in a particularly good production of *Three Sisters*.

'Willy Wet-Legs, as Hilaire Belloc called the poor man,' Theodore remarked. 'At least I seem to think it was Belloc. Are you an admirer of Belloc? I am an ardent fan, having always admired people who are masters of the insult since I am so *utterly* hopeless in that department. Belloc perfected the art. D'you know a total stranger came up to him once and said *You don't know me. Oh yes I do*, Belloc replied, turned on his heel and walked off. Ah now how many times hasn't one longed to do just that with certain people? Countless. Countless. And you knew Belloc was an ardent Catholic, of course – and that he once stood for parliament? Around 1906 it was, so to seek election as a Catholic took some doing. But Belloc being Belloc, when he first appeared at the hustings to address his possible constituents, in Salford of *all* places – he took his rosary from his pocket and said that he was a devout Catholic, who went to Mass every day, and *told his beads* every day. If the people rejected him on account of his religion, he told them, then he would go down on his knees and thank God for sparing him the indignity of being their member of parliament. He was of course duly elected.'

The story delighted Cassie as much as it once more delighted the teller. And so they talked on until the clock above the fireplace in the drawing room where they now sat chimed midnight, making Cassie stare at it in disbelief.

'I should have been home hours ago.'

'If you should have been you would have been,' Theodore replied with a smile. 'Now since *as they say* we have the drink taken, why don't you let Paul drive you home? Paul is the other half of Silent Mimosa who served our dinner and he is a thoroughly excellent driver. He can bring your car over to you first thing in the morning and believe you me, Mrs Rosse—'

'Cassie, please,' Cassie insisted.

'Likewise Theo,' Theodore replied. 'And as I was saying, first thing will really be *first thing* since Paul is up and ready to go at five o'clock sharp.'

On the way home, driven by Paul, Cassie reflected on her evening. By the time Theo's magnificent old burgundy Rolls Royce turned in at the gates of Claremore she thought she had not enjoyed herself quite so unconditionally in the company of a man since the last time she had sat across a table from Tyrone.

Having once again forgotten to leave her answering machine on, she found Erin had left a list of messages for her on the silver salver on the hall table. Altogether there had been seven calls for her, and four had been from Joel.

# *Fifteen*

'I wasn't going to ring you, but then this came up,' he said.

'Why weren't you going to ring me? I rang you. What makes you so different?' she demanded.

'Hang on. I rang you because I have something to tell you.'

'Isn't that the usual reason people ring each other up?'

'Don't make this harder than it is, Cassie. You never once called me back.'

'Wait. Wait up, Joel. Give me a such as.'

'Such as the last time. I left a message with Erin.'

'You mean tonight.'

'I mean days ago. You were out somewhere, as usual. I rang, spoke to Erin, and said to make sure you got the message.'

'I didn't get it.'

'Then that takes care of that.'

'No it doesn't. Not necessarily. I might not have wanted to call you back. Not after you just walked out of here and vanished without trace.'

'I'd rather explain that when I see you, Mrs Rosse.'

'If you see me, *Mr* Benson.'

'This can't wait.'

'Then tell me over the telephone.'

'No. It concerns the horse. How is he? I understand he's making a miraculous recovery.'

'Then why ask?'

There was a short but exasperated silence from the other end of the phone.

'I didn't have to make this call, Mrs Rosse.'

'Yes you did. You should have made it the day after you walked out of here.'

'I said – I'll explain when I see you.'

'For *when* read *if*, remember?'

'I'm not telling you any of this over the telephone.'

'Why don't you just give me a clue what this is all about?'

'Very well. How's your vet?'

Now it was Cassie's turn to be silenced.

'I'll be on the early bird tomorrow,' she heard Joel saying while she was still trying to puzzle out his last remark. 'I get into Dublin at nine forty.'

Then the phone went dead.

*How was her vet? How was Niall? What had Niall got to do with it? Joel surely couldn't have meant that Niall Brogan had something to do with Nightie's disappearance?*

*Surely that can't be what he meant?*

From the desk where she had taken the call Cassie stared across to the portrait of Tyrone over the fireplace.

*Oh, God, Tyrone,* she sighed. *This way surely madness lies.*

# Sixteen

'Of course that's not what I meant,' Joel sighed as Cassie headed the car out of the airport and joined the Dublin road. 'Ridiculous.'

Cassie had made sure she got her question in early, just as soon as Joel had chucked his hold-all onto the back seat and settled his long-legged frame in the passenger seat of her car.

'Fine,' she said tightly. 'So what precisely *did* you mean? And where exactly have you been?'

Joel looked round at her and gave a small nod. 'Let's get that one out of the way first,' he said, rummaging in his pocket for his cigarettes.

'No smoking in the car, remember?' Cassie reminded him.

Joel sighed heavily, but all the same left the pack of cigarettes unopened. The traffic was heavy and slow but Cassie was in a hurry, so she changed down from drive to two and shot the BMW past a line of cars.

'And I wouldn't mind arriving at Claremore in one piece.'

'Certain people thought your disappearance might have been because you were jealous,' Cassie said, looking round at him.

'Just watch the road, Mrs Rosse. I really don't want to end up on a slab.'

'Well?' Cassie persisted, even so switching her concentration back to the traffic ahead.

'Jealous as in jealous over your horse, I take this to mean?'

'Jealous of the amount of attention the horse was getting, maybe.'

'I should stick to horse training and forget about

259

psychology,' Joel replied. 'If I'm to get jealous, it won't be over a horse.'

'People get jealous of everything and everyone. Particularly people—' She stopped. Joel waited for a second before prompting her.

'Yes?'

Cassie sighed heavily. 'It doesn't matter, really it doesn't.'

'Fine. So it doesn't matter.' Joel fell to silence for a while, finger drumming a *bossa nova* on his cigarette packet.

'To get back to your vet,' he said. 'Fact is I bumped into that dear friend of yours – Leonora de Medici.'

'You saw Leonora? Where?'

'It's a small world and Mrs Charles Whojit Whatsit knows some people I know and we met in their house. So my remark about your vet was because she said you were having it off with him. Almost for openers.'

'That'd be Leonora. Go on.'

'According to her, Niall Brogan's been the only real thing in your life since Tyrone but it's always been an on-off affair because you couldn't make up your mind whether or not to marry him. The latest bulletin was that it was all on again.'

'Great.' The traffic had slowed almost to a standstill now, so Cassie could take another look at the man beside her in perfect safety. 'And you believed her.'

'I'm just telling you what I was told.' Joel wound down his window, staring out at nothing in particular. 'She's quite a spark, though, your old chum. After she'd put you in bed with your vet, she then tried to pull me into hers.' Joel turned and eyed her, trying to note her reaction, if any.

'That's Leonora all right. Anyway, whatever. That can't have had anything to do with your leaving Claremore without a word. Unless you were nursing a theory about Niall as well?'

'That wasn't the reason I left.'

'So?'

'OK if I smoke out of the window?' he wondered, taking a cigarette out of the packet. 'I won't blow smoke in the car, promise.'

'You can do what you like,' Cassie replied, edging the car forward another dozen yards.

'The reason I left Claremore was because my father was suddenly taken ill,' he said, lighting up his Gitane. 'You and Niall were just deciding what to do and what not to do about the horse when your secretary gave me a message.'

'I forgot about that,' Cassie said quietly.

'My father had been rushed to hospital.' He blew a long curl of blue smoke up out of the car window, holding the cigarette out of the car up above the roof.

'I'm sorry. But even so couldn't you have left a message to say where you'd gone and why?'

'Yes. I did.' Their eyes met as they both looked round at each other. 'I told Dick to tell you. Your handyman cum butler bloke.'

Cassie shook her head once more. 'You might as well have told one of my horses. Dick's a dear, but he has a hole where his head should be. And if he doesn't remember to tell you something and you ask him if there's anything he might have forgotten, he just gets even more confused and runs away.'

'Sorry. But then I wasn't exactly thinking with a full deck myself.'

The traffic began to move on a little more quickly, so Cassie slipped the automatic box into drive and kept apace.

'Tell me about your father. Is it serious?'

'It was,' Joel replied. 'He died an hour after I got to his bedside.'

'Oh, Joel, I'm so sorry.' Cassie frowned deeply. 'I really am so sorry.'

'Me too,' Joel replied. 'We were seriously good mates.' He pinched dead the end of his cigarette and dropped it out of the window then began to rummage through some of the loose cassettes in the holdall between the two front seats.

'The Grateful Dead?' he wondered, holding one up.

'Mattie's,' Cassie replied, seeing the turn coming up ahead for her favourite short cut which would take them through the west side of the city ahead, avoiding most of the rush-hour traffic.

'Joe Cocker,' Joel said, picking up another tape. 'Another of Matt's, I take it?'

'No, the Joe Cocker's mine,' Cassie replied, taking a right and accelerating down a deserted side street.

'Nice,' Joel said, slotting the tape into the deck and turning up the volume, putting an end to any further conversation until the car finally drew up in front of Claremore.

Even had she not known the news about his father, Cassie would have sensed a change in Joel. Rather than abstracted, which was his usual state, he now appeared distracted, saying and doing things by rote rather than with any real sense of purpose while all the time looking backwards as if to make sure the person following him was really no longer there. By now of course she knew enough about him not to try too hard to draw him out when it came to talking about things that mattered. As she had already found out, Joel was a Piscean and like all his particular type of Pisceans he dived down deep into the waters when people came after him too vigorously, but even so, accustomed as she had become to his long, thoughtful silences, she now found a different sound to them, a deep melancholic silence born out of the grief that follows loss.

At first she sat out his silences patiently, knowing that he had things to tell her as well as things that he might perhaps wish to discuss. When they finally reached Claremore she had put him in the charge of Erin who saw to it that he was settled in a room in the house itself this time and not left to his own devices out in the cottage. He did not appear for lunch, nor give any word that he would not be coming down, but since Cassie had to be off to saddle two runners in the fourth and fifth races at Leopardstown that afternoon she imagined him to be sleeping and so took an early lunch by herself, Mattie having already left for the track.

Her run of bad luck showed no signs of abating, at least

as far as the form of her horses was going, for neither of her two well-fancied entries won or were indeed even placed, her first runner, a handsome son of Strong Gale who was having his third run over fences, falling at the last when six lengths in the lead, and her second horse, a previously unraced mare by Orchestra, breaking down at the second last flight of hurdles when well in contention.

'That's her out for the season,' Mattie said as Fred and Bridie were loading the lame horse back into the horsebox. 'In fact from the shape of that tendon I'd be surprised if you get her back into training at all.'

Cassie noted the change from the usual *we* to *you* but said nothing, knowing that anything she said to Mattie nowadays generally sparked some form of argument. Instead once she had made sure that both horses were safely loaded Cassie went to her car and rang the hospital on her mobile, asking to be put through to her daughter's room.

'Your daughter discharged herself at lunchtime,' the receptionist informed her. 'Would you like to speak to Mr Pilkington? He's just come out of the theatre as a matter of fact, and I know he was planning to ring you himself as soon as he was free.'

A moment later Theodore was talking to her on the telephone. 'I did everything I could, Cassie, but you know *your daughter* better than I,' he said. 'She's as unbending as an elephant's leg.'

'I don't suppose she's taken herself back to Claremore,' Cassie asked without much hope.

'Not unless they're running a taxi service between Claremore and the airport, for I gather that was where she was headed. Not that she's in a fit enough state to make her way down half a corridor here let alone fly back to London, I might say. Let us just hope she has someone good looking after her across the water for she's a fair way to go before she's out of the woods yet, not just physically but *mentally*. Perhaps on my way home tonight I might drop by and make a plan of action? Just to ensure there are no loose ends left untied. Although that is probably not the most comfortable of metaphors in this instance.'

Cassie hesitated, a moment of uncertainty Theodore quickly picked up.

'No, no,' he said easily. 'If you've other plans – no, no. No matter. We can do it all on the telephone. I was simply being *social*.'

'It's just that I haven't left Leopardstown yet,' Cassie explained. 'What time were you thinking of stopping by?'

'I'd not be there before half seven.'

'In that case that will be fine. I just wasn't sure what I'd be doing for a moment, that was all.'

Joel was lying stretched out fast asleep on the sofa when Cassie, back from the races, came into the drawing room. Automatically she found herself looking for signs of drinking, an unstoppered decanter or a whisky glass left down somewhere, but the room was just as she had left it earlier, all except for the tall figure stretched out one side of a roaring fire.

The telephone woke him, just as Cassie was tiptoeing out of the room to make all her calls from her study.

'You go back to sleep,' she whispered. 'I'll take that next door.'

'I can't imagine what I was doing falling asleep like that.'

Since he was now awake Cassie took the call at the desk, and while she did so Erin brought in a tray of tea and hot buttered scones piled high with jam.

'I would guess you'll be half starved,' she said to Joel as she set down the laden tray, 'what with no lunch insides you. There's cake and biscuits as well as scones and you can always holler if you're wanting more.'

By the time Cassie was through on the telephone Joel had eaten most of what was on the tray. He looked faintly embarrassed as Cassie came across to pour herself a cup of tea but said nothing, getting up and seeing to the fire instead while Cassie sat down in the armchair opposite the sofa. When he had finished rebuilding the fire they talked for a while first about the races and then about Josephine.

'Hmmm. Maybe it's just as well I didn't have any children,' he said when she finished.

'Really?' Cassie wondered. 'I'd have thought you'd have made rather a good father. You're much more patient than I am, for a start.'

'You're the very soul of patience, Mrs Rosse,' Joel assured her, helping himself to another scone. 'Although I wasn't really thinking of that particular virtue. What I was thinking of were the sorts of responsibilities parents have to face. Would you have children again? I mean, given the choice. Would you have children second time around?'

'I can't, so the question's academic.'

'You know what I'm trying to say. Do you regret having had children?'

'No. Not for a moment. Except when they get in the way of what I want to talk about, in this case why you're here. It must have been something urgent to bring you all the way across here. In the circumstances, I mean.'

'Yes, it was,' he agreed, now lighting a cigarette and staring into the fire while Cassie poured herself some more tea.

'You said it had something to do with The Nightingale. Didn't you?'

Joel did not appear to have heard the question, since he sat staring into the fire in silence, persistently flicking non-existent ash off his cigarette.

'Joel?' Cassie said carefully. 'Has your return here got anything to do with Nightie?'

'That was the original script,' he replied, still not looking at her.

'I don't understand. Either it was or it wasn't. And why couldn't you tell me on the phone?'

'Jesus,' Joel groaned. 'All these bloody questions.' He threw his half-finished cigarette on the fire and then lay back on the sofa, his eyes closed, his face turned up to the ceiling. 'If you really want to know, Cassie,' he said after a long pause, 'the reason I came over was because I couldn't bear not being with you for one moment longer.'

Quite at a loss for words, Cassie rose and went to sit down beside Joel. He sat still staring into the fire until finally Cassie took his hand. As soon as she did, he gripped it hard in return as if he never wanted to let go of her again and when he did all at once she knew that if he asked her anything then she would say *yes*. *Yes* to going upstairs to bed with him, *yes* to going anywhere with him, *yes* to doing whatever he wished them to do, *yes yes yes* even to marrying him, such was her sudden love, such was her pity and her sorrow for the terrible hurt she knew he was feeling. But he asked nothing of her. He asked nothing because at that moment all he wanted from her was there in her hand, warmth, security and love.

So there they sat with Joel's one hand in Cassie's two, in a silence broken only by the crackle of the fire flames and the sigh of the winter's wind outside the house until it seemed that Joel was about to say something, for he took a deep breath and opening his eyes with a start as if he'd fallen asleep turned to look Cassie full in her own. At that moment there was the sound of someone charging down the corridor outside the drawing room, running steps which came to an abrupt stop as whoever it was slid to a halt just in time outside the door of the room.

'It's Dick,' Cassie said with a smile and a quiet groan. 'I'm so sorry.'

Dick's athletic arrival was followed by a couple of healthy bangs on the door and a shout of *Mrs Rosse?* in answer to which Cassie called the flustered and embarrassed young man into the room where he announced she had a visitor.

'*Another* visitor,' he corrected himself with a look at Joel, his happy smile suddenly replaced by a worried frown as if he had all at once remembered something he'd forgotten. ''Tis a Mr Pilkington, Mrs Rosse,' he said, still frowning at Joel. 'He says you were expectin' him to call.'

Before she had time to direct Dick to show her guest into her study so that Joel might be left in peace, Dick stepped to one side and indicated for Theodore, who was standing in the dark of the corridor behind him, to step into the drawing room.

'Thank you, Dick,' Cassie said, smiling at Theodore. 'Theodore – Theodore, I'd like you to meet a friend of

266

mine from England. Joel – this is Theodore Pilkington, Josephine's surgeon.'

Neither man was pleased to see the other, Joel turning round to stare at the tall, distinguished-looking man standing behind him with a large bouquet of flowers but not bothering to get up, in response to which Theo likewise stood his ground, nodding a greeting to his fellow guest rather than offering him his hand.

'I don't see why I have to be your friend *from England*, Mrs Rosse,' Joel said, nodding back once at the man he had sensed at once was his rival. 'I'd far rather simply be your friend full stop.'

'Be that as it may, Cassie,' Theodore said with a smile, 'I have no objection *whatsoever* to being introduced as your daughter's surgeon. And these are for you.' He handed the basket to Cassie with a flourish and an eye to the reaction of Joel who remained sitting poker-faced on the sofa.

'Joel—' Cassie began, but suddenly Joel was on his feet. 'I have some calls to make. *If* you'll excuse me.'

'Theodore is here to discuss Josephine's state of health,' Cassie continued as if she had not been interrupted, just the way she used to with her children when they were small and being petulant. 'We're all rather worried about what's going to happen to Josephine now she's discharged herself early from hospital.'

'Quite so,' Joel replied, making his way to the door. 'All right if I use the phone in the study?'

'Of course.'

After Joel had wandered out, without even bothering to make his excuses to Theodore, Cassie poured them both some wine and sat her second guest down by the fire. Neither of them referred to Joel throughout the entire conversation, concentrating instead on Theodore's suggested aftercare for Josephine. By using the information in her case notes he had been able to contact her gynaecologist in London who in turn had promised to prompt their patient into calling him if she had not herself got in touch within twenty-four hours. 'If she should need it, she will have the best gynaecological care possible,' Theodore concluded.

'I just wish I knew why she wanted to go back to her husband,' Cassie replied. 'My son says she's bewitched, although he used a slightly more modern term for it, which I guess she has to be, because if she was simply afraid of her husband all she had to do was stay here. She'd have been perfectly safe, as it really is quite hard to get to anyone here, and after a while I'm sure Mark would have become bored and turned his attentions elsewhere.'

'As far as love and lust go, Cassie, one thing I *have* learned is that there are no racing certainties,' Theodore said, staring into the fire for a second as if revisiting his past. 'Remove something or somebody from someone else, and it immediately makes them infinitely more desirable. Particularly to those whose own disposition is – shall we say? – *somewhat deformed*. No, no, having had some experience of this sort of situation before, I would say that this is a case where only the patient can effect a cure.'

'I'm sure you're right, Theo,' Cassie agreed, 'but as Josephine's mother—'

'Forgive me, Cassie, but remember when daughters get married they cross over the church to their husband's side. It is the husband who stays with his family.'

'A friend of mine says once you have children you never stop being a mother. Not until the day you die.'

'But then think of the children too. Most children think that they have to go on being children until their parents die.'

Now they were on their second glass of wine Cassie slipped up a gear and worked successfully on Theodore to persuade him to stay for dinner, a move which proved far from popular with Joel who now rejoined them, having finished making his calls. Once they were sat at table he addressed not one question to Cassie's distinguished guest throughout the entire meal, preferring instead to eat and drink in silence. Since it seemed he would rather not converse even with Cassie, answering anything she said to him with either a yes or a no, Cassie chose to ignore him just as Theodore had done, both of them carrying on their conversations as if he no longer existed, behaving as they would had they been forced to sit down to dinner with a petulant child.

'I think you might have made a little bit more of an effort,' Cassie said to Joel after Theodore had gone, and Joel was helping himself to another glass of whisky.

'You can think what you like, Mrs Rosse. And I may think what I like.'

'Such as?'

'That your boyfriend is just a trifle pompous. I hate men who sip their wine the way he does, holding the base of the glass. It's so affected.'

Inwardly Cassie sighed deeply, and then began again. 'Look, Joel. I do have some idea of what you're going through—'

'No you don't. You don't have a clue.'

'Yes I do,' Cassie replied, this time with much less sympathy in her voice. 'Of course I do. I haven't forgotten what it's like to lose somebody. That's something you never forget.'

'Oh, for God's sake—'

'No you just listen to me, Joel Benson,' Cassie came in sharply, so sharply that Joel was forced to reopen his eyes at once, to look at her in surprise. 'I didn't say I know *just* what you're going through because I don't. I don't know what it's like to lose a father because I didn't know my father. I didn't know my mother either, not until it was too late. Not until she was dead, so I don't actually know what it's like to lose a parent. But I do know what it's like to lose someone you love, and even though time is meant to heal those scars and in fact does so, you don't ever forget that actual moment, the moment when someone you love dies. But your father was old—'

'That has nothing to do with it, Mrs Rosse,' Joel cut in, throwing his head back again to stare up at the ceiling.

'It has everything to do with it, Joel. It's nothing to do with appointed time or anything like that, but your father was nearly eighty-four and you can't mean to tell me that you hadn't started to prepare yourself for this moment. He would have done, so why not you? You knew he was seriously ill. You said so yourself.'

'You don't know *what* you are talking about, Mrs Rosse.'

'Joel, will you for God's sake start acting your age?'

Again he looked at her, more slowly this time, dropping his chin back down onto his chest then slowly blowing the deep breath he had taken out through pursed lips.

'I mean it,' Cassie continued. 'I'm not trying to minimize your loss, I'm simply trying to mitigate it. You said you came over here because – because you wanted to see me, and I guess that – well, that part of the reason you wanted to see me was maybe to see if I could help you get through this. I hope it was, because maybe I can. But I can't and I won't, I promise you, if you insist on behaving like a child – and not only a child, Joel, but a hopelessly spoilt one at that. Now do you understand?'

'If you say so, Mrs Rosse,' Joel replied, lifting his chin from his chest to nod slowly.

'And for God's sake stop calling me that. You know how it irritates me.' Cassie stared at him and then got up. 'I'm going to bed,' she announced. 'And if you want some advice, you should go to bed as well. You've drunk far too much.' She walked past him and he caught her hand.

'Please don't go. You're absolutely right, I mean it. But please don't go.'

'What's there to stay up for?' Cassie asked. 'You stopped making any sense hours ago.'

'Fine,' Joel said evenly. 'In that case, go to hell.'

Cassie didn't even look at him. She just pulled her hand away from him and walked towards the door, surprised to find she was feeling more hurt than she could remember feeling for years. Even so, she didn't falter, not at least until she was halfway out through the door when the sudden crash of breaking glass stopped her in her tracks.

She turned round quickly to see that Joel had obviously thrown his glass into the hearth, for the unbroken base of the heavy Waterford tumbler was lying out on the hearth where it must have bounced back off the wall of the fireplace.

'What in hell do you think you're doing?' she cried, hurrying to pick up the glass.

'I am giving up drinking, that is what, Mrs Rosse!' Joel replied, holding on to the mantel above the fire. 'If that is what you want, then that is what you shall have!'

'I don't really care what you do, Joel!' Cassie returned. 'But I do mind you throwing my best glasses into the fire, OK?'

'I will get you *another* glass – OK?' Joel said. 'Tomorrow I will go out and get you *another bloody glass*.'

'You won't be able to replace this one,' Cassie said, straightening up and holding the unbroken base, the only bit of the tumbler which had remained intact. 'I had this one specially commissioned for Tyrone after he'd won his first Group One race. After he'd won the Irish Guineas.'

Joel looked at her, appalled. 'Then what the hell were you doing letting me drink from it?'

'Trying to see for myself whether or not you were right,' she said. 'Trying to see whether or not it still mattered.'

'Yes? And?'

'And yes. You've just proved to me that it does. OK?' She dropped the useless remnant of heavy glass into the waste basket and walked away from him, leaving him where he was, still hanging on to the mantel to try to stop himself from swaying.

This time Cassie was through the doorway and halfway across the hall before she heard the second crash, but this time it wasn't broken glass. What it sounded like was the crash of a body hitting the floor.

Fortunately for Joel the sofa had broken his fall, the crash having been made to sound worse than it in fact was by his knocking a large lamp off a side table on his way down. Having failed to rouse him from his stupor, Cassie called both Erin and Dick to come to her aid and the three of them carried Joel upstairs, half undressed him and put him to sleep under his covers.

'I said he was in trouble the moment he walked through the door, so I did,' Erin said with some satisfaction as they made their way out of the bedroom. 'I said to Dick here there's a poor unhappy soul if ever there was one, and now wasn't I right?'

It was a very different Joel who finally made it downstairs late the following morning. He had been left to sleep it off while the household went about its usual business, not showing his face until Cassie had ridden out with three strings, met with Liam to discuss The Nightingale's progress, supervised the loading of the horses due to run that afternoon at Punchestown and sorted out an exhausted Mattie who she discovered had not returned home until it was time to exercise the first string.

She was still trying to avoid arguing with Mattie when Joel made his belated appearance. Mattie was explaining in an affectedly overweary tone that he had been at a party in Dublin and thought it better not to drive home until he had sobered up while Cassie reminded him that while he was working for her his responsibilities lay with the horses and that returning home sleepless and with an obvious hangover left him in no fit and proper state to ride out.

'In which case maybe you'd rather I wasn't working for you,' Mattie began, only to stop as soon as he saw Joel slowly making his way in through the kitchen door and picking up his copy of the *Sporting Life*.

'What exactly do you mean by that?' Cassie asked, unaware of Joel's intrusion since she was sitting with her back to the door.

'We'll talk about it later,' Mattie said. 'Your house guest's up.' Without another word he brushed past Joel and hurried away down the corridor, leaving Cassie to stare after him and then at the tall bleary-eyed man making his way to the table where Erin had just placed a fresh pot of coffee. 'Welcome to the land of the living,' she said, pouring herself a fresh cup. 'I imagine this is what you need.' She pushed the pot of coffee across the table to him and opened her day's copy of the *Racing Post*.

'I imagine I owe an apology for last night,' Joel said. 'To whoever I insulted and for whatever I might have said, I'm sorry.'

'I can't accept any proxy apologies, I'm afraid,' Cassie said, turning a page of her paper over. 'You'll have to say sorry to Theodore to his face.'

'Theodore.' Joel breathed in deeply and rubbed the palm of one hand across his red-rimmed eyes. 'I imagine you mean the bloke who was here last night.'

'You imagine right. You didn't address one word to him all evening.'

'I must have been very drunk.'

'You were a great deal drunker than I thought you were.'

Erin, who had gone to collect her coat and hat, reappeared in the doorway to announce she was going down to the village for some shopping and asked if anyone needed anything. Cassie scribbled a few items down on a note which she handed to her waiting housekeeper.

'I didn't say anything at all to whatever-his-name-was, did you say?' Joel wondered after Erin clattered out of the kitchen.

'Not a word.'

'Why ever not?'

'You tell me.' Cassie turned over another page in her paper, deliberately studying form so that Joel would have plenty of time to suffer the full torments of his alcoholic remorse.

'Oh, God,' he groaned after a while. 'I don't have an idea why I should have been rude to the poor man. Why do you think I was rude to him, Cassie?'

'The fact that he brought me a basket of red roses could have had something to do with it,' Cassie said without looking up.

'Red roses,' Joel said slowly. 'Yes, I remember the red roses. But even so – I mean – Jesus.'

Cassie offered him no succour whatsoever. She was still as angry with him for the way he had behaved as she was for the way he had simply arrived back in her life at the moment when he needed a shoulder to cry on.

'Did we quarrel?' Joel wondered after another long silence. 'That is, did you and I – was I rude to you as well?'

'You were at your very worst.'

'What did I say? You'd better tell me.'

Cassie told him. Joel said nothing, merely staring in front of him in total silence while Cassie was speaking, as indeed he did for a long time after she had finished.

'Mind if I help myself to some of that?' he asked, nodding at an opened bottle of red wine on the dresser.

'Yes I do,' Cassie replied shortly. 'Last night you said you were giving up drinking.'

'That was last night.'

'Joel, if you want a drink go right ahead and have one. But if you do, you leave my house for good. You go back on your word and you don't see me again.'

'I just need one drink, Mrs Rosse, that's all. To get me over my hangover. Then that's it. Promise.'

'You don't need a drink, Joel. What you need is help.'

Joel looked at her, half closing his eyes and furrowing his already deeply furrowed frown. 'Are you serious?'

'Never more so.'

'I just need one drink, that's all. OK?'

'Have it. And I promise we never see each other again.' Cassie got up, fetched the bottle of wine and a glass and placed them both in front of Joel. Then she sat down again opposite him. 'Your move,' she said.

She had no real idea of how long they both sat there without saying or doing anything. It could have been five minutes, it could have been fifty. Whatever, time vanished as they both stared into the future. Finally Joel reached for the bottle and with a badly shaking hand poured himself a drink, filling the wine glass right up to the rim. Then he pushed the cork back into the bottle and slid the glass until it sat on the table right under his nose.

Cassie waited another lifetime until at last Joel picked up the glass as if to drink from it, whereupon she got up at once and walked as quickly as she could to the door. As she got there once more she heard the crash of breaking glass behind her.

'That's two frigging glasses I owe you!' Joel shouted. 'Now come back here and tell me what the hell I'm going to do!'

# *Seventeen*

Cassie had little idea what to do in such circumstances. Like everyone, she found it all too easy to tell someone they must do something, while giving the right advice was actually a very different matter. What she did was the only thing she knew she could do and that was to get Joel to talk about his problem so that she might at least be able to give it some dimension. They were still talking when Erin arrived back from the village, so Cassie and Joel moved to the library where they sat talking for another hour while lunch was prepared.

Neither of them ate much of what Erin put before them. Seeing the trouble Joel was in, Cassie had cancelled her plans to go racing, sending Mattie off by himself to saddle up their runners despite his protests.

'My being there is not going to make them run any better or any worse, Mattie,' she had told him when he expressed his dissastisfaction, a dismay Cassie thought born from jealousy over the fact that she had chosen to remain behind with Joel.

'What about your owners?' Mattie had demanded. 'There'll be some long faces pulled if you don't show up. You know that.'

'Not in this case there won't,' Cassie had replied, handing him his race glasses and his racing hat. 'Both owners this afternoon are ladies, and they will much prefer the charm of your company. So go on, off you go, and make sure you lead up at least one winner.'

'You shouldn't be wasting your time on me,' Joel told her as she plied him with more strong coffee, sitting disconsolately opposite her across the dining table, propping his forehead up with both hands. 'You have better things to do.'

'Don't you start feeling sorry for yourself again, Joel Benson, I'm warning you,' Cassie returned. 'You were the one who flung himself on my mercies, so don't you go telling me now that I'm wasting my time. Even so, there's only a limited amount that I can do, and I reckon we're just about reaching that limit.'

'Fine. And then what?'

'Then what about AA?' Cassie ventured cautiously and rightly so, for no sooner had she asked than Joel started shaking his head adamantly.

'I'm not that far gone. I don't need AA.'

'Joel,' Cassie said, summoning up her courage, 'on all known form you're an alcoholic. OK, so you're not actually killing yourself yet, but you go on the way you are and sure as hell you will. You need help. Badly. You said so yourself, and no amount of self-delusion's going to alter that fact. If you're afraid of going to AA—'

'Don't be so ridiculous,' Joel interrupted sharply. 'Afraid? Get out of here.'

'OK – nervous then. If you're at all nervous at the prospect, then all I was going to say is that I'll come with you.'

'Oh sure. Rather like the way a mother takes her kid to the dentist and then sits reading *Country Life* while the poor kid's having its teeth pulled.'

'Fine,' Cassie said, getting up from the table. 'I can't make you do anything. You're a grown man, you're not my responsibility, so you have to decide for yourself what you want to do.'

She walked out of the dining room, leaving Joel at the table. *Tough love*, she thought. *I had to practise it on Mattie and Josephine whenever they were behaving badly and every time I did it worked. So let's see whether or not it works on this particular juvenile.*

Five minutes later Joel wandered back into the library where Cassie was busy remaking the fire, hands in pockets with the end of a Gitane clamped between his teeth. He stood by the window looking out at the rainswept winter afternoon and finished his cigarette which he then threw on the fire.

'I never told you about the horse, did I?'

'No, you didn't,' Cassie agreed, having herself forgotten that the first given reason for his visit to Claremore had been to tell her his latest findings on The Nightingale's kidnapping.

'Go back to the day of his last race, the King George VI, OK?'

Joel lit up another cigarette and for once Cassie envied him. 'There were several foreign-trained horses running that day, remember? In the first race, the one your daughter rode in, and then in the King George itself.'

'I remember. We went over that.'

'We did. And we also agreed there was nothing unusual about the fact there were a number of foreign entries. That's the state of the art. Nothing unusual until we get to the photograph they – whoever they might be – the one they sent to prove the horse was still alive. They held up a copy of the day's newspaper. *The Times*, if you recall.'

'Yes. So?'

'I had the photograph analysed. Deciphered, rather, by a mate on *The Times* itself. As I thought, every edition of the paper has an identity mark on it, in between the two horizontal lines on the top of the front page. The edition your horsenappers were holding up was a foreign one. European, to be precise.'

'Do you know what part of Europe?' Cassie asked with a quick glance at him.

'Switzerland possibly. Probably, in fact. At least supposition will be fact by the time the paper's computer's done its job. The batch number, the edition and something to do with a sorting code or some such will establish the actual area of sale.' Joel took another draw on his cigarette, watching the winter landscape slide by. 'Has to be interesting, yes? The horse was obviously taken abroad. And there were five foreign-owned and trained horses entered up at Ascot that day. So I'd say that has to narrow the field.'

Joel took a battered but expensive-looking old wallet from his inside pocket, fished out a small slip of paper and read out the first two names on a list of the owners of that fateful day's foreign entries.

'Both of them are above suspicion, I'd say, wouldn't you? Hardly think either the Sheikh or his brother has an axe to grind. And they certainly don't need the money, if money was ever at back of this. Of the three others – well, you tell me. Your starter for ten. Arnold Weinberger.'

'Big art man, not very nice, changes trainers like I change my shoes, but nothing personal,' Cassie said. 'At least not known. Tyrone never trained for him, neither have I.'

'Von Plunkett? Baron Carl Von Plunkett? He had a horse in both races.'

'Don't know him at all. By name only.'

'Right. So just one green bottle left. Someone else with a horse in both races. Someone by the name of Brandt. Herr Rudi Brandt. Ring any bells?'

'Yes,' Cassie said slowly, getting up and going to sit on the arm of the chair in which Joel had sat himself. 'I used to train several horses for Herr Brandt. If it's the same Herr Brandt, that is. Big gambler. Went to gaol for smuggling currency.'

'You could hardly be blamed for that.'

'I did buy back his best horse, at ten times what I'd paid for it when he commissioned me to buy him a string. But then that helped pay for his defence.'

'Could hardly hold that against you either. Anything else?'

'No, I don't think there's anything else really. Except Tomas, our old head lad. Tomas never liked Herr Brandt one bit. Brandt tried to pass himself off as Swiss, but Tomas fingered him for a German and lo and behold at the trial – wasn't he proved right? Brandt was indeed a German – not that there was any shame in that, but what Brandt was busy trying to cover up was the fact that his father had been a somewhat notorious colonel in the Gestapo.'

'Good. I mean, bad. But that's good.' Joel stretched a hand out to stub out his cigarette and when he did and Cassie saw how much it was shaking she was overcome by pity.

'Let's forget Mr Brandt for the moment, shall we?' she asked gently. 'And let's talk about Mr Benson instead. You want to stop drinking, don't you? And you can. Thousands do every year. It's really not impossible.'

'You can't ever have seen *Lost Weekend*, Mrs Rosse.'

'I saw *Days of Wine and Roses*. Now look, Joel, not twenty miles from here there is the very best rehab clinic in Ireland.'

'I don't need a clinic, Cassie,' Joel said defensively. 'I just need to go somewhere to dry out. It isn't habitual, my drinking. Not like this. It just comes and goes. It's come now because this is a bad time, that's all, and if I could just shut myself away somewhere—'

'You can't do this on your own, Joel. People in your state, they need help to do it.'

Joel shook his head. 'I don't. Once before, when it was this bad, I had my brother lock me in my studio and after a week, I was fine. Really. That's all I need. Just somewhere to lock myself away.'

'OK,' she said, getting up from the arm of his chair, the very chair in which Tyrone and she both used to sit on just such winter afternoons, warm and snug while the rain swept down off the shrouded hills and the winds stirred up the piles of sodden leaves.

'OK, if that's really the case, then suppose we shut you away in the guest cottage and throw away the key for as long as you say?'

Joel looked round at her with his deepest frown. 'You sure?'

'If you are,' she replied. 'We'll bring you everything you need, but we won't let you out until you're well and truly ready to come out. Meaning dried out.'

'Deal,' Joel said, getting unsteadily to his feet. 'Lead on, Macduff.'

\*   \*   \*

Joel had just taken a pile of books and magazines over to the guest cottage when Erin came into Cassie's study and closed the door on them both.

'I emptied the place as you probably noticed,' she confided in her mistress. 'I took away everything that might have just a drop of alcohol in it, his mouthwash, his aftershave, his cologne—'

'I'm sure there was no need to go quite that far, Erin,' Cassie interrupted.

'Get away with you,' Erin said with a sigh, crossing her arms over her ample bosom. 'When they get to a certain stage they'll drink anything. And while I was over there I burglar-locked all the windows and took away the key. He's not going to take this lying down quietly reading the latest edition of *House and Garden*, believe me.'

'Do you think we can handle it, Erin?' Cassie asked, suddenly feeling doubtful.

'Do you think he can handle it more's the point, Mrs Rosse. Now then, Mr Mattie's home and waiting for you in the drawing room to congratulate you on the double it seems you had this afternoon, so go off and celebrate, it'll do you good instead of sitting there worrying. You leave Mr Benson to me. My sister's a nurse in America at a big rehab clinic and she's told me all about what they do. As long as he has the will for it, he'll come through.'

Cassie smiled at the freckle-faced Erin. Many was the time the poor woman had driven Cassie half mad with her dogmatism, and many was the time she had said the wrong thing at the wrong time to the wrong person, but in the end somehow whenever it really mattered Erin always knew better than Cassie did where Cassie should be and exactly what she should be doing. Now she was smiling back at Cassie as if she was her daughter rather than her employer.

'Go along with yous now, Mrs Rosse,' she instructed. 'I know all about this sort of business, it's all right. Sure many's the time we all had to pick our own father off the floor when he'd taken a few too many.'

'Tomas? You're not telling me your father had a problem drinking?' Cassie stared in amazement at Erin, for she had idolized her old head lad whom she had inherited from Tyrone.

'A problem drinking?' Erin laughed. 'No, he certainly had no problem drinking, Mrs Rosse. Me father's problem was not drinking. Ah but then it wasn't really his fault. He only ever succumbed when one of his blessed horses here didn't win.'

'So what are we meant to celebrate with?' Mattie demanded to know, having found the drink cupboard securely locked up.

'I can't risk leaving drink around the place anywhere,' Cassie reiterated, having already outlined the situation. 'If Joel should break his word and somehow get out of the cottage—'

'To hell with Joel,' Mattie cut in. 'Your first double for I don't know how long and we're expected to celebrate it with orange juice.'

'We'll go down to the village later,' Cassie said. 'When I'm sure Joel's settled in for the night.'

'You must be crazy.' Mattie collapsed on a sofa and stuck his legs out in front of him. 'Thinking you're going to dry him out here. He should be locked up in some sanatorium rather than be allowed to run riot round our house.'

'You're being a little over-dramatic, Mattie,' Cassie replied. 'Joel's not that sort of drinker. He's not a hell-raiser or home-wrecker. He just has a bit of a problem that recurs now and then.'

'And I just saw a pig fly past the window,' Mattie snorted derisively. 'A bit of a problem that recurs now and then – *not*.'

'I don't understand it when you talk like that,' Cassie said with a frown. 'What do you mean *not*?'

'I mean you just wait and see, guv,' Mattie replied. 'You just wait till you see what your bit-of-a-problem man does to this place. And to your life.'

'Now where are you off to?' Cassie asked him as he turned and made for the door.

'I'm going on down to the village. Are you coming or

aren't you? As I said, I'm in no mood to celebrate our first double for three months on fruit juice or Diet Coke. And don't you think it might be a nice gesture if you went down to the yard and said well done to the team?'

'I don't need you to tell me how to run my yard, thank you, Mattie.'

'Not everyone would agree with you there, *guv'nor*.'

'Really? Interesting that now we've had some success it's back to being *our* double again and not just *your* as in me on my own. Like it has been recently when things haven't been going that well.'

Mattie stopped by the door, turning to face his mother. 'I wasn't going to say anything about this now, because I didn't really think it was the time,' he began. 'But since you seem dead set on a confrontation—'

'*Me* dead set? Now just a minute, you just hold your fire for one minute, do you hear?'

'No I won't,' Mattie returned, looking her right in the eye. 'You know as well as I do that it hasn't been working out between us very well recently—'

'I don't know what you can be talking about.'

'Yes you do. Me being here. Me working just for you. I've been thinking about this for quite a while – and before you jump down my throat again, this isn't just me. It's Josephine as well.'

'What is?' Cassie asked in some amazement. 'How can this be anything to do with Josephine? How do I know what anything can be to do with, because as I said – I don't have even an idea what you're talking about!'

'I'm talking about where I'm at, that's what I'm talking about. And where I'm at isn't being tied to your apron strings any more!'

'No, not you,' Cassie said quietly, her face suddenly creased with the pain of disappointment. 'Not you, Mattie, not you as well.'

'Not me as well as what, for God's sake?'

'Don't you turn as well.'

At her request she saw the look come into his eyes, the look he used to have when he was a small boy and he had known she was about to cry, a look half fear and half love, but adding up to total helplessness. She wanted to go and put her arms about him, just as she had always done when she saw him get that look, so that she could allay his fears and stem the tears she felt burning the back of her eyes, but even though she made no move she saw him stiffen as if ready to resist and in that moment she knew that he was lost to her.

'What is it?' she asked as calmly as she could, after she had cleared her throat. 'Is it a girl? Is it a job? What?'

'Why should it be anyone? Or anything?' Mattie protested, the rise in his voice giving away his guilt.

Cassie took a deep inner breath and soldiered on. 'Come on – there's been something worrying you for quite some time now, so why don't you tell me. The longer you carry it round in there, the more it's going to rankle. What is it that isn't just you but Josephine as well? I don't understand, so please tell me what all this is about, and then maybe I will.'

Mattie paused, dropping his eyes now from hers and staring first down at the floor then up above him as if he didn't know from where he was going to get the strength. 'Tom McMahon's offered me a job,' he said, still looking anywhere but at Cassie.

There was a silence while Cassie digested what she thought she had just heard. 'Tom McMahon – ' she began.

'Tom McMahon's offered me a job, OK?'

'You mean – at least I take it you mean as an assistant? And if so, OK—' she slowly agreed. 'Fine. I don't see any great problem there. In fact I think that might be a very sensible move.'

'Not as his assistant,' Mattie contradicted. 'He's offered to set me up on my own.'

'On your own?' Cassie echoed. 'But that would mean you'd be in opposition to Claremore.'

'Yes, I knew you'd think that,' Mattie said, with a theatrical sigh. 'I knew you'd take exactly that attitude.'

'I'm not taking an attitude, Mattie. I'm stating a fact. If you're going to train horses elsewhere you will be in direct opposition to Claremore. Period. And under the wing of Tom McMahon of all people!'

'But you like Tom McMahon!' Mattie protested.

'You mean I *did*.' Cassie pushed her way past him out of the room with no idea of where she was headed. All she knew was she had to get out. Mattie followed her at once, close behind.

'Look – I can't just stay here for the rest of my life,' he protested, but having seen the look in his mother's eyes now sounding distinctly worried. 'It's not right that I stay here and play second fiddle to you. It's just not on. Josephine thinks—'

'You've been talking to Josephine, have you?'

'Of course I've been talking to Josephine. Someone's got to talk to her, seeing that you don't bother ringing her any more.'

'*I* don't bother ringing her? I ring her all the time – but all I ever get is her machine!'

'That's beside the point,' Mattie said. 'The point is Josephine thinks—'

'No – as far as this is concerned I don't give a tuppenny damn what Josephine thinks!' Cassie said, stopping in her tracks to turn and face her son, frightening him even more. 'Can't you see that just because Josephine's got herself in a mess she wants to drag you down with her!'

'Come on, Ma! That isn't how it is at all!'

'That's how it is, Mattie, and that's how she is, and that's how everyone is and you have to accept that if you're going to be a grown up! Everyone's main priority is looking after number one and their second priority is to ruin it for everyone else!'

Mattie stood there, looking at his mother with open astonishment, not having seen this side of her since he'd been a boy of ten and had disappeared for over half a day without telling anyone where he was going. 'Ah, come on,' he said more quietly. 'Not everyone's like that. Josephine certainly isn't.'

'Everyone is like that, Mattie,' Cassie replied. 'Everyone. Do you know what I overheard Josephine saying the other day? When you two were talking in the tack room? That I'd been very lucky.'

'Well?' Mattie raised his eyebrows. 'So? You have, have you not?'

'Oh yes,' Cassie said levelly. 'Yes, Mattie, I have been very lucky. All my life I have had nothing but good luck.' *Yes,* she thought to herself. *You bet I've been lucky. I had the good luck to be born illegitimate, never to know my father, to be raised by a sadist who pretended to be my grandmother but was in fact my mother, had to run away from home, lost my second child—*

'Yes, all right, all right—' Mattie said, as if reading his mother's thoughts.

'This whole place has been built on luck,' she continued. 'At least that's what you and your sister seem to think – that all it took was luck to build Claremore—'

'No we don't.'

'You do. Of course you do. I overheard you talking and of course you're right.' *It was luck pure and simple that killed your father after only six years of marriage. Luck that got me running up those hills out there every damned morning come rain, shine, fog, frost or snow. Luck that got me fit enough to ride out like a professional every morning—*

'When did you overhear us?' Mattie asked, his face furrowed by a frown meant to cover his guilt. 'If you mean the first day Jose was back home, that wasn't what we were talking about at all. At least that wasn't what we meant.'

'Of course it was,' Cassie countered. 'Mostly you believe the golden apples have just dropped off the tree and fallen in my lap.' *But luck had nothing to do with it, do you hear? Luck played no part in learning how to train horses and how to get them to win so that you and your sister would have a home with a warm bed, plenty of food and a roof over your heads. Luck had nothing to do with surviving what Leonora put me through, or with trying to find enough strength to believe what she was telling me was lies and nothing but lies. With nearly losing my mind when I lost a baby, with producing Nightie to win his*

285

*Derby. You remember yourself how that had nothing to do with luck, Mattie. How he was damn' near lame on the morning of the race and how you and I saved having to withdraw him by icing his leg – you think that was to do with luck? You think how Dexter rode him was to do with luck? Just as it was luck that made him win all his other races? And get kidnapped? And mutilated? Luck that's seen us through standing up to the bully boys? Through not paying attention to their threats? Luck nearly losing the horse on the operating table – or Josephine throwing herself at some adulterous, sadistic son-of-a-bitch and losing her first baby because of it? Or having you now betray me by setting yourself up in competition? You bet it is. Every goddam inch of the way has been a cakewalk, it's been oh so easy every goddam inch of the way.* 'Well,' she concluded, 'if you think it's all only been due to luck, I just hope you don't have quite as much of the sort of luck I've had in my life in yours.'*

Having said it all, albeit only for her inner ear, Cassie found she was no longer mad and angry, just tired and saddened, and a little heartbroken as looking on the face of her son she saw only the child Tyrone had sung to as a babe, the toddler over whom Erin and Tyrone had happily quarrelled every evening as to who should bath him, the little boy in his double-breasted blue coat being handed up by her to sit in front of his father on Old Flurry, the child lying sick in her bed with asthma, the young man bringing home his first girl, the growing man leading up his first winner. She looked at him and saw every part of his younger life and all she could do was shake her head slowly before turning and taking herself off to shut herself away in the library.

'Luck indeed,' another voice added from behind Mattie and he turned to see Erin at another door, come to tend the fires. 'There's precious little luck that your poor mother's had, I can tell you. Lucky, indeed. I have to say that if you and your sister were still in my charge, I know exactly what I'd do to the pair of yous.'

\*   \*   \*

Cassie was just sitting staring into the dying fire when the house phone beside her rang. It was Joel.

'What do you want?'

'What I want, Mrs Rosse, is a drink,' Joel replied.

'Sorry,' Cassie said as firmly as she could, still staring into the fire. 'But if you want a drink, you'll have to go elsewhere.'

'I didn't say I was going to drink,' Joel said. 'I just said I wanted one.'

'So why are you ringing? Do you want me to come over?'

'Of course I do. But you're not to because if you did I'd never let you go.'

'So what do you want?'

'Just to hear your voice.'

'Are you going to be all right, Joel?'

'No. Not for a while. But just give me time.'

'You can have all the time in the world. And ring me any time you want to talk.'

'No,' Joel said. 'No, I think this is something I have to work through on my own. I just wanted to hear your voice once more before – before I face the demons.'

'I'll pray for you.'

'I shall need you to. I love you, Mrs Rosse.'

'I love you too, Joel.'

Cassie replaced the phone.

# Eighteen

She rang him on the house telephone as soon as she'd returned from morning stables. There was no answer. She must have let it ring well over twenty times and was just about to hang up and go over to the cottage to see for herself when he answered.

'Are you all right?' Cassie asked.

'I've heard more sensible questions,' Joel replied in a voice like gravel.

'Do you want me to come over?'

'No. One look from those spaniel eyes of yours and I'd be out of here in a flash and then I'd have to start this all over again – and I don't think I'm man enough. Just send Erin over with some coffee. And a pair of fresh pyjamas.'

Cassie relayed to her housekeeper what was required, instructing her to fetch a fresh pair of Mattie's pyjamas from the airing cupboard on her way upstairs.

'Ah they'll never fit Mr Benson,' Erin said. 'Mr Benson's more Mr Rosse's size than Mr Mattie's.'

Cassie hesitated and sensing it Erin made her employer's mind up for her.

'There's several pairs in the chest on the landing,' she said. 'And if you're still prevaricating, don't. They're only pyjamas, not holy relics.'

Cassie waited until Erin returned from her mission, even though she was already running late for The Nightingale's daily inspection and exercise.

'Well?' she asked anxiously as her housekeeper bustled back into the kitchen bearing an armful of linen. 'Is he all right?'

'The poor soul,' Erin sighed, heading for the washroom

with the laundry. 'He must have perspired half of himself away.'

'Did you go in?' Cassie enquired, following Erin into the washroom.

'I did not,' Erin replied. 'And even had I been asked I still would not have – for you should have seen the state of the room. I saw it through his half-open door. 'Twas as if an army of drunken derelicts had spent the night in there such was the state of it. Bedclothing all over the shop and the furniture everywhere, let alone books and shoes and all manner of other things.'

'But was Mr Benson all right in himself?' Cassie pressed, as Erin loaded the washing machine. 'I mean – oh, I don't know what in heck I mean.'

'You're getting into one of your states now,' Erin warned. 'And you're not to. So by far and away the best thing is for you to leave poor Mr Benson to me, do you see? You just leave that poor wretched creature to me and if you do that'll stop your worrying.'

Cassie agreed, and then having made sure there was nothing else Joel wanted she collected her windcheater and hat to go down to the top yard where Niall and Liam were already waiting for her, stamping their cold feet and blowing on their hands. Cassie apologized for being late and then looked round for Mattie, only to learn that Mattie had left the yard the moment he'd finished riding out. Nor had he left any word as to where he had gone or when he might be expected to return.

'OK, so what's the news on Nightie?' Cassie said, switching subjects. She and her vet were now walking towards the loose school where the horse had been running out daily as part of his recovery programme. 'Is it really all systems go?'

'I don't see why not,' Niall replied. 'He really seems to have mended one hundred per cent so I don't see why we can't start his riding programme straight away.'

'Which is why I have his tack!' Liam called happily from behind as he caught them up.

Niall opened the side door in the loose school to let

Cassie in ahead of him. 'You wouldn't have thought we'd have come this far three months ago,' he said. 'I know I didn't.'

Inside the school Bridie was lungeing the horse who was showing himself off freely and easily, nicely bent and throwing his forelegs out at the trot with precisely the right amount of extravagance.

'I don't know,' Cassie said, after watching him for a while. 'Maybe I should just send him eventing straight away. He's always made such a good shape. Look at him.'

'Now first things first, guv'nor, if I may say so,' Liam said, inclining his head sideways as he too watched the horse. 'First let's see how he likes being under saddle again and then if all goes well we'll see how he takes to leaving the ground.'

'I thought the idea was for Bridie to ride him?' Cassie wondered, seeing Liam pulling on his hard hat.

'And so it was,' Liam replied, buckling up his chin strap. 'But seeing how full of himself the old boy is I thought better of it. He's had Bridie on the floor once or twice, if you remember. When he's in the mood, Nightie can be a right old divil.'

So saying he called Bridie to bring the horse over to him now that she had finished saddling him up and then asked Niall to leg him up, only for the horse to kick out with his near hind and spin round the moment he took hold of the reins, knocking Bridie to the ground and sending both Liam and Niall flying.

'Whoa, boy! Whoa!' Liam called after the horse who had started to bolt off round the loose school. He picked himself up off the ground and called out again, but The Nightingale had got himself into the far corner of the school by now where he was busy flyjumping up into the air while kicking out viciously with both hind feet.

'You were saying?' Cassie asked her head lad now he was back on his feet.

'Ah he's just a wee bit full of himself, guvnor,' Liam said, brushing the shavings off his jacket and breeches. 'And I don't think Bridie had a proper hold of him.'

'Oh indeed I had!' Bridie contradicted him, wiping a thin stream of blood from her nose where the bolting horse had caught her. 'Just as I told yous, I was the one who should be riding him.'

Mick, another of the lads who had been helping Bridie, had run across the school to try to catch the horse, but as soon as The Nightingale had him in his sights he swung round and aimed a kick at the approaching lad who saw what was happening only just in time to duck back and down out of the way of the flying hooves.

''Tis as well Mick's a good boxer,' Liam said, watching the incident. 'That was a neat enough weave, so it was.'

But despite their skilful and careful approaches neither Liam nor Mick could get near the enraged animal, so finally, signalling for Bridie to follow her over, Cassie jumped down from the observation platform and made her way over to her horse.

'The old fella's as foxy out of his box as he was in it,' Liam said, standing well back from the horse who was eyeing him with a lot of white showing. 'When you think what a Christian he used to be. You could put a child on him.'

'I'd say he's taken a not unreasonable dislike to your sex,' Bridie said. 'And after what happened him, sure who can blame him?'

'Oh, is that what you think, madam?' Liam asked, raising his beetle black eyebrows at the diminutive figure of Bridie beside him. 'Well let's see you put your money where your mouth is. You get on him and stay on him and you can pick up me pay packet from the guv'nor on Friday.'

'I was about to suggest the very same thing, Liam, albeit without the side bet,' Cassie said. 'I reckon Bridie's absolutely right. I don't think Nightie likes men any more in or out of his box. So why don't you and Mick – and you, Niall – all of you get over to the other side of the school and I'll leg Bridie up.'

After a moment's hesitation, Liam with a nod of his head signalled the retreat to Mick and the three men ambled back to watch proceedings from the observation platform as bidden. As they moved, the horse gave another nervous squeal and whipped tight round, knocking Bridie this time into the side wall.

'The bet stands!' Liam called when he saw what had happened. 'A week's money says you end up where you'd most like to be!'

'And where would that be, Liam Nolan?' Bridie called back in return, never having let go of the horse's bridle for a moment.

'Why – flat on yer back, of course!' Liam replied, hooting with laughter. 'Good luck now, Bridie Moore! God knows you'll need it!'

'Pay no attention to him, Bridie,' Cassie advised, getting ready to leg Bridie up. 'He's just talking through his manhood. One, two, three – *hup*!'

The moment Bridie was in the saddle the big horse's mood changed, visibly relaxing from total aggression to complete docility, no more the prancing, bucking, kicking animal but back to the Christian saint upon whom so many had indeed put their children to sit.

'What now, guv'nor?' Bridie asked Cassie.

'That's rather up to you, Bridie,' Cassie replied with one hand still on the horse's bridle. 'But I don't see why you shouldn't just school him as you wish. I guess if he was going to have you on the floor he'd have done so by now.'

The big black horse obviously nursed no such intentions, for as soon as Bridie asked him to move off he walked as sedately and obediently as a riding school horse around the perimeter of the school. Five minutes later he and his rider were cantering in complete harmony, as if competing in a dressage phase at a three day event.

'Good on you, Bridie Moore!' a delighted Liam called out. 'Sure if I wasn't married already I'd make an honest woman of ye!'

'You have the ride,' Cassie told Bridie after she'd dismounted and walked the horse to have a pull of grass outside the school. 'You and you alone. Liam?' Her head lad came jogging over, his leather face still puckered up with a grin. 'I'm making Nightie Bridie's ride, Liam,' Cassie said, 'and I'm sure you understand why.'

'If I didn't, I'd have no place here, guv'nor,' Liam replied. 'So what's the plan? Are we to try and get the sausage race fit or what?'

'Let's just call it fit, shall we?' Cassie replied. 'Nightie won't go racing again unless he's completely his old self. And somehow as far as that goes, I have my doubts.'

With a fond pat on her beloved horse's neck and a pull at his big floppy ears Cassie headed back up to the house to see precisely what the rest of her delinquent brood were doing.

For the next few days Joel remained in his room, communicating only via the house telephone. Having taken Erin's advice, Cassie left him entirely alone, realizing how much better it would be for Joel's recuperation to be looked after by someone who would not fuss rather than by someone who would fuss and worry him because she was emotionally involved. All she ensured was that Erin provided him with whatever foods he requested and kept him supplied with seemingly endless pots of coffee and tea and with a fresh supply of clean linen. Over the days the reports Erin made on her return to the house became less dramatic as the patient appeared to be pulling himself through his self-ordained cold turkey treatment.

Not so healthy was the behaviour of the other man in her house, however, for although Mattie still dutifully rode out his allotted horses each morning and attended whatever race meetings Cassie ordained he was absent from Claremore at most other times. Whenever he did spend some time at home it seemed it was only to pick fights with his mother because she remained totally opposed to the idea of him being set up in direct competition to her as a trainer. For his own part Mattie did not seem unduly upset by these constant domestic ructions, treating them as if they were sparring contests rather than serious confrontations, the reason for this being – as Cassie soon came to realize – that his mind was already made up. So no matter how hard Cassie might fight, and whatever arguments she might propose, it seemed her son was already up and running against her.

'Why do you want this, Mattie?' Cassie asked him when at last she realized the full score. 'You know Claremore will be yours one day and if you want more say in the running of it now then so be it. You might not like playing second fiddle but I don't mind. I don't mind at all taking the seat behind you. I might even quite like it.'

'That isn't it. That isn't it at all.'

'Meaning you don't want ready made.'

'Meaning you don't know what it's like. If I stay here working for you or if I go somewhere else as an assistant, that is somewhere you approve of, then I shall always be Mattie Rosse, Cassie Rosse's son. I'll always be OK because I'm a Rosse. Jose felt the same, you know. She thought she was only ever getting decent parts because of the famous family name. Because of strings being pulled and connections being worked. I don't want that, you see. Even if it means not getting this place, I want to do it all myself.'

'But why Tom McMahon?' Cassie wondered. 'Why Tom McMahon of all people? He can barely afford to run his own outfit.'

'Tom McMahon has a very good reason, don't you worry,' Erin informed her later that evening when she and Cassie were discussing the problem over a mug of hot chocolate. 'Tom McMahon is willing to set up young Mr Mattie because young Mr Mattie is walking out with his daughter.'

Cassie looked at her housekeeper in astonishment. 'Mattie is going out with Phoebe McMahon, Erin?'

'He is so.'

'*Phoebe McMahon?*'

'Phoebe McMahon.'

'How long has this been going on, for heaven's sake?'

'Long enough.'

'Long enough for what, Erin?'

'Long enough for it to be serious.'

'So why didn't you tell me?'

'Probably because you had quite enough on your plate at the time. Far too much to be worrying about who your son might or might not be walking out with and that's for certain. Besides, I thought it would blow over. For a start she's a good few years older than him.'

'I know all about Miss Phoebe McMahon, thank you, Erin,' Cassie said, putting down her cup of coffee. 'She's a good five years older than Mattie. She's had quite a history, and like her father she is very ambitious. Not that there's anything wrong with ambition, provided that it soars and doesn't creep.'

'Of course. I was imagining the same. That maybe Phoebe McMahon's ambition is to creep under the very gates of Claremore.'

Cassie said nothing. She had no need in front of Erin.

'Remind me about Tom McMahon,' Erin continued, wiping her mouth with the side of one finger now she too had finished her coffee. 'Didn't he use to ride for Mr Rosse? And didn't he have a bad fall out schooling one day?'

'You don't seem to need very much reminding, Erin. Yes, Tom McMahon broke his back schooling a young horse over the jumps and Mr Tyrone helped him.'

'He trains from a wheelchair, does he not?' Erin asked as she took their two cups away to load into the dishwasher.

'One thing Tom McMahon's never been short on's determination.'

'Uh-huh.' Erin nodded as she closed the machine back up. 'As I remember him, he had a bit of a mouth on him too, at least I seem to remember that's the way he was when he worked here. You could never tell him anything. Sure not even the time of day, for wouldn't he always have it better himself? Least that's what my father old Tomas was forever saying, while sure being in a wheelchair doesn't always turn people into saints now, does it? It most certainly does not. For wasn't I reading only the other day in the paper about this dangerous criminal who was

295

robbing stores with a sawn-off shotgun on his lap under his rug and him a para-*plegic*. There's no good just going be appearances any more. Even though speaking for meself I only have to see someone with a white stick or in a chair to imagine they're halfway to being sanctified.'

'I would think that Tom McMahon's sanctification is a little way off,' Cassie sighed. 'He's never been the kindest of men.'

'Is that right?' Erin asked, idly brushing the crumbs from the table. 'But even so, sure you'd think after all you and Mr Rosse did and have done for him, wouldn't you? You'd surely think he'd know better than to take Mattie from yous.'

'You would, Erin,' Cassie said, getting up and having a weary stretch. 'At least I would have thought that – but not any more.'

'And what's made you change your way of thinking, I'm wondering?' Erin asked, catching the tone in her employer's voice. 'What in heaven's name ever made someone like you change her way of thinking now?'

'The Nightingale,' Cassie replied. 'The Nightingale's done it. Not only has he changed my life but he seems to have changed 'most everyone else I know's life as well.'

Mattie had it in mind to stay at Claremore until the end of spring, but guessing that the person most suited by this arrangement was Mattie himself, Cassie gave him his marching orders.

'I can't! The new yard isn't quite ready yet!' Mattie protested when Cassie made her announcement.

'Then go get it ready, buster,' Cassie replied. 'Buns are either for the having or the eating. *Not* the both.'

'But what about Christmas? It's Christmas in less than two weeks.'

'Christmas will still happen, Mattie. Anyway, wouldn't you much rather spend Christmas with your girlfriend?'

'I have told you before,' Mattie sighed over-patiently. 'Phoebe is not my girlfriend. Phoebe and I are just friends.'

'Oh sure,' Cassie nodded in return. 'But since you're a boy and she's a girl, that makes her your girlfriend.'

'A girlfriend.'

'OK. A girlfriend.'

'You're not really kicking me out?' Mattie asked.

'Of course not,' Cassie replied. 'It's you who wanted to go, remember? All I'm doing is not stopping you.'

'You could wait till after Christmas, surely. And what about Jo? Aren't Jo and Mark coming home for Christmas?'

'I don't think Josephine wants to see me at the moment, Mattie, in fact I'm sure she doesn't. Otherwise she'd ring me. Which she still hasn't.'

'You're just tired, Ma,' Mattie said in an attempt at consolation. 'Josephine's right. What you need is a holiday.'

'My thinking exactly,' Cassie replied. 'So I thought this Christmas I would just shut up shop and go and spend Christmas in the sun.'

Which was indeed precisely what Cassie would have done, had she not received a surprise visit at the end of that fateful week, a visit which as it happened was to change quite a lot of plans.

Every time she returned from the guest cottage Erin had reported to Cassie on the progress Joel was making on the road to recovery, which by all accounts seemed by the middle of the second week to be slow but sure. Even so, neither of them and least of all Erin was willing to speculate on how much more recuperation their patient might need.

'According to my sister it's sometimes a case of not just one step forward and two steps back,' Erin had remarked, 'but of one step forward and ten steps back.'

'But when last heard of—' Cassie had wondered in return.

'When last seen as well as heard of, I'd say things were a whole lot better.'

Nevertheless it still came as an enormous surprise when one morning as Cassie and the lads sat in the kitchen devouring one of Erin's famous after-work breakfasts on a particularly cold and frosty morning the patient finally made his reappearance. Judging from the hush that fell over the table Cassie was not the only one startled into stupefaction at the sight that greeted her eyes as the door opened and the tall, lean figure of Mr Joel Benson materialized. The eyes of every lad were on him as he nodded a greeting to the assembled company and made his way over to join them at their feast, for none of them with the exception of Cassie had ever seen Mr Joel Benson except as a large, shambling and untidy figure ambling around the yard, usually with a half-smoked Gitane in the corner of his mouth.

Yet here was a positive transformation, an immaculately dressed and perfectly groomed figure of a man, his thick dark hair washed and slicked back, clean-shaven, pink-skinned and bright-eyed and dressed in a freshly laundered and ironed blue buttoned shirt and dark blue knitted tie, a Donegal tweed jacket, immaculate cord trousers and polished black shoes, walking across the kitchen with the confidence of a man who has been to hell and back and knows that he has conquered his demons.

'Good morning, everyone,' he said, taking his place at one end of the table.

'Good morning, Mr Benson,' the lads carolled back, after a quick exchange of looks between each other, for there was nothing that went on in Claremore without the knowledge of the entire yard.

'Will you look at yous,' Erin said with undisguised pride. 'You shouldn't be wasting your time painting pictures. You should be in them. Now sit down here – ' Erin pulled out a chair in front of where she was standing. 'The coffee's fresh made, and I'll do you your favourite egg, sausage and potato cake and make you some hot toast.'

Joel looked down the table and smiled at Cassie. 'Mrs Rosse,' he said. 'Beautiful morning.'

'It certainly is, Mr Benson,' Cassie replied. 'One of the very best.'

\* \* \*

'If you're waiting to hear how it was, which I'm sure you are,' Joel said later, after the stable staff had returned to work, 'it was *grisly*, but' – he held up one finger to underline his point – 'I'm still here. And not only that but I have to say I cannot remember the last time I felt as good as this.'

Cassie smiled at him and then up at Erin who was standing behind Joel ready to pour him some more coffee. Erin returned her smile with an overlarge wink.

'So – what are your plans? Have you made any?'

'One step at a time, Mrs Rosse,' he replied. 'We'll take each day as it comes.'

'Anything in mind for Christmas?'

'Have you?'

'I was thinking of taking some time off, as it happens.'

'Anywhere in particular?'

'The Caribbean actually.'

'Hmm,' Joel said thoughtfully. 'Now there really is a notion.'

Nothing more was said about the idea because both of them knew they must wait and see how Joel would cope with his first day back in what he called Real Life. He could not have experienced any proper temptation locked away in his cottage – pain and anguish certainly, Cassie thought, and in spades, but there was no way he would have been able to get a drink. However, they both knew it remained to be seen whether or not the patient was sufficiently recovered and strong-willed enough to continue resisting the lure of the siren alcohol.

Cassie certainly didn't think he was anywhere near strong enough to do what he was suggesting doing, namely accompany her to the races that afternoon.

'No point in standing about the shallow end,' Joel argued. 'That's what the deep end's for. For plunging straight in.'

'You're getting it wrong for once, Joel,' Cassie argued. 'Going to the races would be like taking an addicted swimmer to the seaside and then not allowing him in. The racetrack is not the place for first day uppers.'

'The temptation is always going to be the same. Whether I face it now or later.'

Joel prevailed, much against Cassie's misgivings, and what made it worse was that Well Loved, her good young novice steeplechaser, won the feature race of the afternoon, a contest which was always taken as a significant trial for Cheltenham. After the horse had been led up Cassie had tried to waste as much time as she could in the unsaddling area in order to try to distract Joel from the party of the horse's connections who were all headed for the bar, but Joel was having none of it and followed the Claremore mob into the Owners and Trainers' Bar where much to Cassie's relief he toasted the stable success in ginger ale.

'A doddle,' he said afterwards. 'Once you make your mind up about something, you're home and hosed.'

'You know it isn't as easy as that,' Cassie replied. 'I saw how many cigarettes you smoked.'

'Of course it wasn't easy. If it was an easy thing to do, do you think I'd have had to lock myself away to do it? Things like this – well. A lot depends who you've got on your side.'

'I don't think I was much good to you,' Cassie said in surprise. 'All I did was keep threatening to kick you out.'

'All I did was keep the picture of you in my head,' Joel replied. 'All I really thought about was you. From one minute to the next. If it hadn't been for you – no, no.' He stopped and corrected himself. 'If it hadn't been *because* of you . . .'

Cassie smiled at him and he put his arm around her back as she drove. When the car had to stop at the next red traffic light, she leaned over and kissed him.

So it was they were both in high fettle by the time they arrived back at Claremore, looking forward to the special dinner Erin had promised them in celebration. While Joel took himself off to his cottage to run a bath and change, Cassie began answering some of the messages left for her. It was while she was finishing a call that she heard a car drawing up outside. Since she wasn't expecting any visitors Cassie pulled a shutter aside to see who it might be but it had started to rain very heavily and the window was awash with water, reducing the visibility to zero.

'There's two gentlemen here to see you, Mrs Rosse,' Dick announced breathlessly, having arrived outside the study in his usual fashion, leaping down the hallway and sliding across the polished floor of the corridor to stop with a thud against her door. 'It's the poleece,' he whispered, his eyes rolling around his head in a kind of mixture of fear and wonder. 'Not the local poleece, Mrs Rosse – the poleece from *Dublin*.'

'What is it?' Cassie asked, intercepting her visitors in the hall. 'Has there been an accident? Is it my son?'

'No, no, Mrs Rosse,' the taller of the two policemen assured her. 'There's been no accident, thanks be to God, so you can put that worry out of your mind.'

'That *is* a relief,' Cassie said. 'Whenever the police arrive here unannounced I immediately think the worst.'

'And don't most people, Mrs Rosse,' the shorter policeman replied, taking his hat off and shaking the rain off it onto the mat behind him. 'I always says to Inspector Doyle here that it's the very worst part of our job.'

'I don't know about the very worst part, Eamonn,' Doyle said. 'Although I'm inclined to agree. On the whole yes I'm inclined to agree with you. And here am I forgetting my manners. I'm Inspector Doyle from Dublin Castle and this is Sergeant Moriarty.'

'So if it's not bad news, then what can I do for you both?' Cassie wondered. 'Do you have news of my horse? I mean, have there been developments in his case? Is that why you're here?'

'Ah don't we wish that was so, Mrs Rosse? And with all our hearts I'm sure,' Sergeant Moriarty said. 'For wasn't I his greatest fan?'

'You and twenty million others, Eamonn,' Doyle said with a laugh. 'Yet I seem to remember you saying he'd get beat at Epsom.'

'Now only to make sure that he'd win, sir,' Sergeant

Moriarty replied. 'It's in the nature of a superstition of mine, Mrs Rosse. I always make a strong case out against my fancy and that generally ensures victory. Unless I back it. I never had money on your fella the once. If I had, sure as tomorrow he'd have got beat.'

'I won a packet on him at Epsom,' Inspector Doyle confessed. 'I availed meself of all the sixteen to one I could get about him in the spring before the guineas and took the family to Disneyland on the proceeds. Your horse is a hero in our house, all right.'

'Sixteen to one, imagine,' Sergeant Moriarty sighed. 'You could hardly get sixteen to one about him at odds on be the time he'd finished with racing.'

Doyle gave his junior a quick sharp look, as if to warn him to mind his tongue. 'That is *if* he's finished racing, Eamonn,' he said. 'There's a big world of difference between an if and a when to my mind.'

'My husband used to say that with the help of an *if* you might put Ireland into a bottle,' Cassie heard herself saying, feeling if anything more disturbed by their presence than less.

'Is that a fact, Mrs Rosse?' Doyle wondered. 'Now that's a saying I'd not heard before. And a potent saying it is, too. With the help of an *if* you might put Ireland into a bottle.'

'If she's not well and truly stuck in one already,' Sergeant Moriarty said with a grin.

'That is not the point, Eamonn,' Inspector Doyle corrected him. 'And not only is it not the point, it is also beside it.'

There was another awkward silence as if what they had come to tell Cassie was going sorely to embarrass them and neither of them had the slightest idea of how to broach the subject.

'Look, I don't wish to be rude, gentlemen,' Cassie began.

'No, no, Mrs Rosse, we'll come straight to the point,' Inspector Doyle cut in, having carefully done no such thing. 'For we're well aware of how precious your time is, a lady like yourself, and with a thousand things on her. But this is not a matter we could have addressed to you on the telephone.'

'And there really hasn't been an accident—'

'No, no,' Doyle reassured her, 'it really is nothing like that, I can promise you. This merely has something to do with someone you might know. Now. How shall I put it? Are you at all familiar with a Mr Joel Benson?'

'I certainly am,' Cassie said cautiously. 'Is there something the matter, has he done something?'

'Not here in this country, Mrs Rosse, no, no.' He cleared his throat. 'No, most unfortunately Mr Benson is wanted back in England. By the British police.'

'Wanted?' Cassie repeated the word softly. '*Wanted by the police?* But whatever for, Inspector?'

'I'm sorry to say, Mrs Rosse,' Inspector Doyle said, squaring his broad shoulders, 'that Mr Joel Benson is wanted on a charge of murder.'

# Nineteen

Joel arrived back in the drawing room only a few minutes after the police had left with their mission completed, namely to warn Cassie that the English Home Office had already opened negotiations to have Joel extradited in the case of his refusing to return to England. Inspector Doyle had, however, made no further enquiries as to the wanted man's present whereabouts, other than to inform Cassie that should she see Mr Benson at any time in the 'immediate future' it might be proper to bring him up to date with the exact state of play.

'Just listen and I'll explain,' Joel said, after Cassie had broken the news and indeed demanded an explanation.

'I could have done with one earlier,' Cassie said, stopping her pacing of the room and sitting down. 'Coming here on the run—'

'I am not *on the run*,' Joel interrupted.

'Joel, you are wanted for murder in England and the Home Office is trying to get you extradited,' Cassie contradicted. 'I call that being on the run.'

'What about being innocent until proved guilty, Mrs Rosse? The way you're carrying on you'd think I was sitting here with a still smoking gun in my hands.'

'You are still on the run and I want to know why you came over here. Was it because you knew they'd have to extradite you?'

'I told you why I came over here, Cassie.'

'You told me *one* of the reasons you came over here.'

'I came over here because I had to see you.'

'You don't have to say that now, you know—'

'That is the *truth*. The extradition is purely academic. If

304

I'd stayed in England, once it hit the fan I'd have given myself up.'

'But you didn't.'

'Because I had to see you.'

Cassie looked at him, sat down opposite Joel and leaned forward to look him straight in the eye. 'Right,' she said. 'Tell me about it. I want to hear everything, right from the beginning. What happened to you and what *is* going to happen to you.'

'The truth, Mrs Rosse, is that I have killed someone,' Joel said, raising his eyebrows at her before turning away to look into the fire. 'That part at least is true.'

'Joel,' Cassie said with undisguised shock. 'Joel, who did you kill? What does all this mean?'

'It means that as the law stands I killed someone, Cassie,' he continued. 'But I am perfectly prepared to answer for it. You see, the person I killed was my father.'

'Dear God,' Cassie said, getting up and coming to sit beside him on the sofa.

'He had rheumatoid arthritis, Cassie,' Joel began. 'I don't know how much you know about the disease, but when it takes hold it's a bastard. It doesn't just confine itself to the joints – it can affect practically every part of the body, heart, lungs, blood vessels, your eyes, your mouth, everything – the lymph nodes, the spleen – it's so much more, so very much worse than what it sounds. Some sufferers reach a point where they can't take it any more because the pain is so bad they can't touch or be touched. Their bones are all but through their skin. Quite literally they are in mortal agony. No-one should be left to die in that condition, not nowadays. When it gets as bad as that, life no longer has a purpose. In fact seeing someone like that mocks life. Instead it's a vision of hell. My father had a wonderful doctor who would have put a merciful end to his suffering but he died before my father, leaving him in the hands of one of these modern heartless sods. You know, the health police. This bloke did everything by the book and he expected all his patients to do the same. To live their lives according to the regulations and if you didn't, then your disease was down to you. How rheumatoid arthritis can be self-induced, you tell me. But because my father drank and smoked and ate butter and didn't run up the side of a mountain every morning, according to the health policeman even though rheumatoid arthritis is nothing to do with these things he got what was coming to him. Luckily we had this agreement, my father and I, since being the elder brother I was next in line as it were, my brother and I being the only family left. He never remarried after my mother died, you see. There was just him and me and my bro. He said when it got too much to bear, he and I would have a couple of drinks together and say our farewells. I got the message he was asking to see me just as you were about to operate on your horse. He was at home, where he was being nursed, I'd got what was needed from a medic friend of mine in London several months ago when I knew he was worsening, so I mixed us a couple of drinks, him one sort, me another. Then we had a chat – well, we didn't actually, because he couldn't really talk. We sat there, I drank my drink, and I helped him drink his, through a straw because he couldn't hold anything for himself any more. Then we sat some more and then he died. It was very peaceful really. He just went to sleep and at last there was an end to all his agony. I thought we might have got away with it because both his nurses were very sympathetic and certainly weren't whistle-blowers. But the health policeman was obviously never off duty and if the police are after me then he must have ordered a post-mortem and found the barbiturates. It's not that this guy believed in the Right to Life. He's just the kind of misguided idiot who doesn't only think we shouldn't have a say in how we choose to depart this life but that really we shouldn't have any say in how we live it. That was the old man's favourite joke, by the way. Do you know the difference between God and a doctor? God doesn't think he's a doctor.'

'Oh, Joel,' Cassie said, taking his hands in hers. 'What are you going to do? This is a Catholic country, remember, and for taking a life sure as anything they'll extradite you.'

'They won't have to, Cassie,' Joel assured her. 'I said I

didn't come here to hide. I came here to see you. There won't be the need for any formalities. I'll go back and hand myself in.'

'Why didn't you say?' Cassie asked him, holding herself ever closer to him. 'Why couldn't you tell me?'

'You have other crosses to bear, Cassie, without this one of mine.'

'That's why you were drinking, isn't it? I mean drinking the way you were drinking.'

'Yes. I'm afraid so.'

'*Afraid* so?'

'It really is no excuse.'

'But the reason you shut yourself away – that wasn't to cure yourself from drinking. It was to try to come to terms with what you had done.'

Joel turned to her, taking his hands from her grasp and holding her instead by her shoulders. 'Let me tell you something,' he said, 'I had no idea of the kickback. You think about these things, of course you do. But then when you come to do it – it bears no relation to the abstract. What man is born who ever thinks he'll have a hand in his father's death? But of course because it was all so unreal, I suppose it didn't really hit me for a while, because I was obviously in shock. It was only when I got here – to your home, to this place which is so warm and so full of love and life.' Joel stopped and sighed, opening his dark eyes wide.

'I'm not alcoholic,' he continued. 'I don't have the disease. At least not according to my doctor in London. Sometimes, too often probably, I take refuge in it, that's all.'

The fire suddenly crackled, sending a shower of sparks flying up the chimney. Cassie and Joel both watched them disappear in silence and then Cassie leaned towards him and gently kissed him.

'What you did is the bravest thing I've heard of anyone doing for an awful long time,' she said.

'Things born out of love bring their own courage,' Joel replied.

'I don't think so, Joel,' Cassie replied. 'Not necessarily. I think you really are a brave and a good man.'

'The brave and the good man was my father, Cassie. I wish you had known him, but there you are. I shall go home tomorrow, so don't worry. I won't cause you any more anxiety.'

'I could talk to some people,' Cassie said, pushing some long strands of dark hair from his eyes. 'We could possibly delay your return until after Christmas.'

'Thanks but no,' Joel said. 'I said if it came to this I'd go back at once. I really couldn't stay on with the thought of it hanging over me. And over you.'

'Have you any idea what will happen?'

'I imagine I'll be committed for trial, I hope on a charge of manslaughter rather than murder one, as the Yanks call it. Although while I'm praying I'll be allowed out on bail.'

'And the prognosis? As far as the outcome goes.'

'Dad and I gave this a lot of thought, obviously,' Joel said, leaning back so that Cassie could rest her head on his shoulder. 'We both knew there was a risk. I could still come up before a hanging judge, as it were, a member of the old guard who thinks society's getting out of hand and people should not take the law into their own hands, et cetera et cetera, and he could send me down – but it's an outside chance. The way things are now, a suspended sentence is the most likely, at least according to another chum who's an eminent QC who said if it came to it he'd defend me. He says given the details of the case a suspended sentence should be about the size of it.'

'If they allow you bail. I'll stand it.'

'Thanks, but no need,' Joel told her. 'I have enough collateral.'

'Even so, there'll be a wait between now and the trial, and you won't be allowed back in Ireland – '

'I know. I thought of that.'

'Then I'll come over to England with you,' Cassie said, sitting up and turning to look at him. 'We could spend Christmas together in London.'

'You don't have to do that.'

'I know I don't have to. But I'd like to.'

Then she kissed him again, more slowly this time, much more slowly, until he slipped his arms around her waist and held her tightly to him.

When they got upstairs he led her to her bedroom but she stopped him in the door, turning to look at him as much as to say no.

'It's only a bed, Cassie,' he said, turning her back round to face the room through the open door. 'It's only a piece of furniture.'

'That isn't it. You don't understand.'

'No, I don't,' he replied in some despair. 'So help me to understand. I really thought you were through all this. That finally you'd let him go.'

'Just hold me,' she whispered back. 'Just put your arms around me.' She turned back to him. He put both arms round her and held her.

'You have to let him go, Cassie. Or you'll be like this woman in a story I read when I was shut up next door. In a book Erin gave me. It was some Irish legend or other about two young lovers and one of them died. But the woman wouldn't let go of her lost lover in her mind, so that instead of being a free spirit he was doomed to spend his eternal life as a cloud which was forever blowing around the mountain above where the woman lived, while in the valley below she spent the rest of her own life in tears for her lost love. And whenever it rained on her it wasn't just ordinary rain. It was rain from the cloud on the mountain. It was the tears of her lost love which rained down on her because she would never let him go and find peace.'

'I have let Tyrone go,' Cassie whispered. 'Don't you understand? It's you I'm afraid of letting go now.' She looked up at him, and he saw tears on her face. 'Suppose I lose you too? Suppose something happens to you? I've rebuilt one life. I don't know that I have the strength left to rebuild another.'

Joel looked down into her sad eyes and then holding her to him gently kissed her forehead. 'You won't lose me, Cassie, I promise. Not now we've found each other, you won't ever lose me.'

He kissed her again, but this time as a lover, holding her tightly to him before lifting her up bodily and taking her over to the large double bed where he laid her down to undress her carefully, softly kissing each part of her as it came into view, her shoulders, her arms, her breasts, her stomach, the back of her neck, her feet, all of her. He covered all her body with soft kisses, and while he kissed her she unbuttoned his dark blue wool shirt, slipping her hands inside it against his warm skin, right round his firm waist until she had pulled him to her, down on the bed, on top of her, until they were both undressed on the bed with her hand reaching to turn out the light so that there was just the pale winter moonlight on them. On his skin and on her face as she lay back, his face kissing her face, his mouth on hers and her arms round him and them as one while it seemed all she could hear was the faraway distant sound of a sea somewhere, a sound that began to be thunder while the waves grew until they were crashing over them both as at last and finally the growing storm broke.

The next morning they caught the first available flight to London. Before they left Joel had called Scotland Yard to inform them of his voluntary return.

'That way at least we'll get a free ride into town,' he joked.

They were waiting for him as soon as the plane landed, four of them coming on board with the look of men coming to arrest a dangerous terrorist. Once the senior officer had formally identified him they asked Joel to stand, handcuffing him to another officer as he did so.

'Is that really necessary?' Cassie found herself asking. 'He has flown back here of his own accord, you know.'

'Standard procedure, madam,' said the arresting officer who Cassie noticed smelt rather too strongly of cheap cologne. 'Please nobody move until we're out of the plane – thank you.'

They hurried Joel along the fuselage and out of the main door. The press were waiting as they emerged from the transit corridor and all at once there was nothing but flashlights and reporters shouting their questions at both Joel and Cassie. At long last they reached the police cars waiting outside the terminal where a feeling of dreamlike unreality quickly became hard fact for Cassie as she saw one of the accompanying policeman push Joel's head down below the level of the car roof.

'Why do you *do* that?' Cassie protested. 'There's no need to *do* that!'

'Standard procedure, madam,' his handcuffed companion sighed. 'Just standard police procedure.'

The rear door was slammed shut and the car drove off with all four officers inside it and Cassie was left stranded on the pavement.

'Mrs Rosse? Mrs Rosse?' voices called from behind her and turning instinctively, since for a moment she was lost, she found herself blinded by a barrage of flashbulbs. Putting a hand up to her face Cassie quickly turned away and got into an unhired taxi which had just pulled up alongside her. The *paparazzi* ran alongside the cab as it moved away, shouting more indecipherable questions through the closed windows and holding their cameras aloft to try to catch one more image of her before the taxi joined the stream of traffic pouring out of the airport.

Despite all the press attention at the airport the story of the 'mercy' killing did not make every headline, being third-page news in the heavies and only making the banner headline on one tabloid. It was enough, however, to attract attention and certainly sufficient to allow everyone to ponder as they read their papers on the way to work or over coffee and toast at the breakfast table about the wrongs and rights of bringing a merciful end to unbearable pain and suffering. Such stories were always good copy and it personally delighted Leonora Lovett Andrew who when her maid handed her a freshly ironed copy of the *Daily Mail* actually cried out aloud with delight, such was her sense of *Schadenfreude*.

'My oh my,' Leonora laughed, leaning back on her pile of goosefeather pillows and stroking her Siamese cat. 'Will you just look at that, Kat? What a total mess! What else can happen I wonder to little Miss Primrose Perfect?'

# Twenty

'We're going to Mark's father's for Christmas,' Josephine told Cassie when they met for lunch at the Savoy. 'Since we didn't hear anything from you—'

'No, wait a moment,' Cassie interrupted, with a small shake of her head. 'You were the one who disappeared back to London without a word, not me.'

'I went back to my husband, as I was always brought up to do. Husbands come first, remember?' Cassie got the look she was given but refused to rise. 'I just thought you might have telephoned once or twice, all things considered.'

'I telephoned a lot more than twice but I always got your machine,' Cassie replied. 'When you didn't return my calls—'

'I didn't get your messages,' Josephine said. 'That's why I didn't return your calls.'

'I see.' Cassie looked at her daughter and seeing how tense she still was decided against pursuing the subject. 'Look, to get back to Christmas. I was thinking of maybe spending it in London, but if you wanted to come back home I could change my plans. We should love to have you there.'

'We?' asked Josephine so quickly that against her will Cassie found herself colouring.

'Yes. Mattie and I—'

'I thought Mattie had moved out—'

'Is moving out—'

'We can't. Mark's parents asked us ages ago.'

'It was just a thought,' Cassie said, putting down her knife and fork and looking out over the wintry Thames for a moment.

'Do you mind if I smoke?' Josephine asked.

'No, but some other people might,' Cassie replied, eyeing their fellow diners. 'And I still wish you'd give it up.'

'You smoke.'

'One cigarette a week.'

Josephine sighed impatiently. 'Of course. I was forgetting your famous self-discipline,' she said. 'How after Dad died you taught yourself how to ride work, how you strengthened your leg muscles by doing those simply lethal exercises—'

'OK, that's enough,' Cassie cut in, but with a smile.

'How you ran ten miles each day come hail, rain or snow with lead weights round your wrists and ankles—'

'I said that's enough, Josephine.'

Josephine stopped her sarcastic outburst and just sat smoking her cigarette, again staring out of the window rather than face her mother.

'What's the matter, sweetheart?' Cassie asked out of the silence. 'Why can't you tell me what it is?'

'There's nothing the matter. Nothing at all.'

'Of course there is. You haven't eaten a thing, you've lost weight, you look terrible—'

'Thanks, Mums.'

'Well you do, Jo darling. You look tired and pale, and you've really lost an awful lot of weight.'

'Conceiving in your fallopian tubes isn't exactly life enhancing, you know.'

'Of course. I know.'

'No you don't. That's one thing that didn't happen to you.'

'I can still imagine, Jo.'

'No you can't,' Josephine said bitterly. 'You can't begin to imagine.' She bit her lip, so hard that it looked as if it was in danger of starting to bleed.

'What is it, Jo?' she asked quietly. 'Please tell me what the matter is.' She put a hand out to try to touch her daughter on the arm, but Josephine pulled away sharply and stubbing her half-smoked cigarette out messily on her side plate got hurriedly up.

'I need to go to the loo. I'll meet you in the lobby.'

On her way out Josephine nearly knocked the wine waiter off his feet as he came to top up their glasses.

'I'm sorry about that,' Cassie said. 'No, no more wine, thank you. I guess I'll just have the tab.'

Cassie sat miserably in the lounge outside the River Room waiting for her daughter to come back out of the ladies' cloakroom. Two cups of coffee later Josephine finally reappeared, as pale as ever but with her makeup re-done and her hair brushed. She refused the offer of coffee, her reason being that she had to meet Mark to do some last-minute Christmas shopping. She did however allow her mother to share her taxi back to Knightsbridge.

Cassie attempted to talk to her daughter in the back of the taxi, but Josephine refused to be drawn, preferring to keep the talk to nothing more particular than shopping for presents and the crowded state of London until they were well past the Ritz and heading for the west end of Piccadilly.

'I'll drop you off at Harrods, if you don't mind,' Cassie said, 'because I want to take the cab on.'

'You're not staying at the Dorchester?'

'Yes, of course. I just have to go and see someone.'

'Joel Benson, I take it,' Josephine said without affection. 'Oh yes, I know all about Mr Joel Benson. The man who killed his father. Nice.'

'He didn't *kill* his father, Jo,' Cassie protested. 'He helped him to die, put him out of his agony, which is hardly the same thing as killing someone.'

'Mr Benson is not a very nice person.'

'You don't know anything about him.'

'Oh, I know all about him, Mums, and so does half of London,' Josephine replied, turning to face her mother. The look of unalloyed hostility in her face frightened Cassie. 'He's a fortune-hunter. Why else do you think he bumped off his father? According to Mark his father was worth a small fortune.'

'You don't know what you're talking about,' Cassie said grimly, looking away out of the window next to her and trying to control her temper.

'You bet I do. You should hear your friend Leonora on the subject – she's known Mr Joel Benson for *years*. Ever since he was shacked up with some Swedish or Danish heiress. Nina Von Prost or something.'

Cassie turned back to her daughter with a look of amazement. 'Nina Von Prost?'

'Ask Leonora.'

'Leonora lies.'

'Ask anyone.'

'I shan't ask anyone. I shall ask Joel.'

'You think he's going to tell you the truth? I hear he has a certain amount of trouble in that area. Anyway, he got bail, I take it.'

'Of course,' Cassie replied. 'Why shouldn't he?'

'Exactly. Why shouldn't he? He's white and he's well connected.'

Cassie didn't bother responding to the jibe.

'OK,' Josephine said, preparing to get out. 'Harrods coming up – so have fun.'

As the store loomed into view and Josephine collected her things, Cassie leaned forward and held her by one arm. 'What is it, Jo? Have I done something or what?'

'You haven't actually *done* anything,' her daughter sighed by way of reply, just the way she had when she was much younger, like a child play-acting badly. 'It's more the fact of who you *are*. Think about it, and have a Happy Christmas. *Ciao.*'

With a brief and frosty smile Josephine slammed the taxi door shut, in a moment to be swallowed up in the throng of Christmas shoppers.


Joel opened the door to his house with a Burmese cat on one shoulder and a half-eaten digestive biscuit on one hand.

'I thought you were shopping. Come in.'

Cassie followed him inside as he wandered ahead of her, leaving her to close the front door. It was a large, handsome Edwardian house overlooking a duck pond, the inside of which, Cassie noted, was like an art gallery. There were paintings, drawings and sculptures everywhere, not all by

Joel – indeed far from it. It was an eclectic collection, ranging from small delicate landscapes in oils to huge rough drawings of sheep and horses done on heavy cartridge paper stuck up unframed on the side of the staircase and above a fireplace in one of the rooms she passed by. On the other hand, much to her surprise, the house was not only well furnished albeit in a highly individualized style but it was also tidy, orderly and clean.

'I know,' Joel said with a smile as he faced her once they had reached the large terracotta-tiled and buttermilk-painted kitchen where he had been having his tea. 'I can see by your face. You thought I'd live in a slum.'

'I admit I didn't think you'd live in a small Tate Gallery,' Cassie replied.

'Things I've picked up over the years,' Joel said, pulling a chair out for Cassie at the large scrubbed pine table. 'Some by mates, but not a lot. Most of it's by total unknowns. Least they were when I bought them. The girl who did the large sheep and pigs and things you were looking at is very well known now, and so she should be. So what happened to the shopping?' He felt the teapot, and having decided it was still hot enough poured Cassie a cup without asking her before topping up his own hand-painted mug.

'What happened to the shopping,' Cassie said, taking off her favourite long St Laurent topcoat and draping it over the back of another chair, 'was that I wasn't in the mood.'

'Don't blame you,' Joel said, sipping his tea. 'Can't stand Christmas shopping. By the way, trial's set for the third week of March.'

'That's Cheltenham week.'

'I know,' Joel sighed, looking at her over his mug. 'What's up? You look as though someone stole your bun.'

'Why didn't you tell me about Nina Van Prost?'

Joel barely reacted to the question other than put down his mug of tea and stare into it. 'I suppose because I didn't think it was important,' he said finally. 'It shouldn't be, because it didn't matter to me. I suppose Leonora told you.'

'My daughter told me.'

'And who told her?'

'Leonora.' Cassie shrugged, matching his steady gaze.

'How that woman must hate you,' he said. 'And all because you beat her at tennis. Except that's not the real reason she hates you. As you well know.'

'I'm not in the mood for any crackerbarrel philosophy, thanks.'

'This isn't crackerbarrel. The reason why Leonora hates you has nothing really to do with the famous school tennis match. As you said, she was after you from the word go, and I reckon the reason for that was because she instinctively knew you were always going to have it over her, that whatever happened to the two of you you'd always come out best. Now that's the worst kind of jealousy, the totally irrational sort. No one wants to be on the end of that kind of resentment.'

Cassie looked at him, trying not to betray her sudden interest but obviously without success judging from Joel's expression.

'Worse, you got happy, and that's a bird people just love to shoot down, Mrs Rosse. The little bluebird of happiness.'

Cassie pulled the initially unwanted cup of tea towards her now to cover her confusion. Her intention had been to beard Joel, not to be subjected to a session of pyschoanalysis. 'Fine,' she said. 'Then if we're into whys and wherefores, I'd quite like to hear why you find it necessary to lie. Don't you know how much lies hurt?'

Joel shook his head once and then shrugged. 'Sometimes telling lies stops the hurt. Not only the hurt the truth might bring to other people but also the hurt it causes you yourself. I didn't tell you about Nina because I have tried to forget it, and the reason why I have tried to forget it is because it still hurts. It's got nothing to do with love, so you can take the worried look off your pretty face. The fact of the matter is I had an affair with Nina a year after my wife left me. It was what they like to call a *whirlwind romance*.'

'I still would have rather you'd told me,' Cassie insisted. 'Nina Van Prost is such a gossip column item, and you and

318

she – well. It puts you in a different light, as if you're not really the kind of person I thought you were.'

'I'm exactly the sort of person you think I am and Nina Von Prost's the main reason for that if you'd just listen,' Joel said. 'When I met her Nina Von Prost was – and still is for all I know – unimaginably beautiful.' He took a cigarette from his pack but did not light it. Instead he just sat tapping it slowly on the table while he talked. 'She was also very rich, and I mean seriously – which is probably what started all the stories about me being a fortune-hunter. I was nuts for her and she said she was nuts for me, although what I think she was nuts about was the artist lover bit, being painted in the nude, sculpted in the nude and then put on show for all to see. All that sort of thing. She loved seeing people looking at a drawing or a sculpture of her and only her and me knowing the circumstances of its genesis. She got a kick out of that, for a while, just as she did out of going to jazz clubs and smoking the odd joint now and then. *Très outré*. It was just all very different from anything the spoiled little rich kid had done before. Then, and don't ask me why, I asked her to marry me and she said yes, much to my surprise, I can tell you. I think she'd thought it would be dead sexy living in a studio and pretending to be poor because she was always going on about how *bored* she was with being so rich and how at last she'd found Real Life with me. Which of course was just complete toss. But the most pathetic part about it all was I believed it. Having this incredibly beautiful broad allegedly in love with me, I suppose I just totally lost it, but not for long. You have never seen anyone get bored so fast. One moment we were going to live this wonderfully sexy and exciting *vie Bohème* and the next moment she wanted out. That's where it hurt. It would have hurt a lot less if it had been something physical, or psychological maybe, but not boredom. Having someone getting bored with you, and so *quickly*—' Joel shook his head and sighed. 'It's pretty soul-destroying, believe me,' he continued. 'When somebody thinks you're boring and tells you so, it's an absolute killer. After that it's practically impossible to think of yourself as interesting. Let alone *act* interesting.'

'How long did she stay with you?'

'Six weeks. Not altogether unsurprisingly I lost my nerve a bit after that. Everyone said forget it – put it out of your mind. Pretend it didn't happen. Call it an accident, not a failure.'

Cassie reached across the table and took Joel's hands. 'The one thing I'd say people couldn't ever be with you, Joel, is bored,' she said with a smile. 'Exasperated, yes. Infuriated, certainly. Bored – never.'

'Nina Von Prost was,' Joel replied.

'No she wasn't. What people like that are bored with is life. Or most probably themselves. Is there anything else you should tell me that you haven't?'

Joel thought for a moment, rubbing his face one-handed with finger and thumb down his cheekbones to the point of his chin. 'I have a thing about high heels,' he said very seriously.

'What man doesn't?' Cassie replied.

'Do you have anything you feel you should tell me that you haven't?' Joel asked in return, straightfaced.

'Yes,' Cassie nodded. 'I have a thing about men who have a thing about high heel shoes.'

Instead of falling asleep, after they had made love they just lay on their sides looking at each other without talking. Outside the early evening traffic hummed by and rain began to fall against the bedroom windows.

'There's a wonderful poem that exactly describes this moment,' Joel said, still looking into Cassie's eyes. 'But I can't quite remember it.'

'How does it go?'

'If I knew that, Mrs Rosse, I wouldn't be lying here trying to remember it.' Joel rolled onto his back and stared up at the ceiling. 'It's something about love hanging still as crystal over the bed and filling the corners of the enormous room.'

'Joel—' Cassie began, slipping an arm across his bare chest. 'Joel, what's going to happen?'

'Happen as in what, Cass? If you mean as far as the trial goes—'

'Yes. Yes that's exactly what I mean.'

'I suppose if I'm realistic about it, a suspended sentence is too much to hope for. I expect in the end I shall go to prison,' he said after a moment, still looking up at the ceiling. 'Not for long, but I can't see them not sending me down for a while.'

'No, Joel.' Cassie raised herself up in the bed and looked down at the man beside her. 'No, Joel, surely not,' she said again. 'Surely they won't send you to prison.'

'Will you stop calling me Shirley?' Joel said lamely, attempting a joke only to change his smile to a frown when he saw the concern on Cassie's face. 'My barrister chum still holds by a suspended sentence, but he says if they do send me down it'll be six months at most.'

'I don't want you to go to prison, Joel,' Cassie replied, lying back down in the cradle of his arms. 'I couldn't bear it.'

'No,' Joel agreed. 'Neither could I.'

They made love again, this time as if for the last time, as if they were never going to see each other again, as if Joel was going off to war. They never took their eyes from each other's, looking into each other the whole time, as if to imprint every moment of this loving on their minds so that the memory would always be there whatever happened in the days that lay immediately ahead.

'*Voices will hector, and your voice become a drum in tune with theirs,*' Joel said afterwards in the darkness.

'What's that?' Cassie whispered. 'What are you saying?'

'It's from the poem,' Joel told her. 'When they finish making love he says he will lose her, that she will go back to being the person she was before, that the very voice which avowed their identity will become *a drum in tune with theirs.*'

'Never,' Cassie said. '*Never ever ever,*' she added, a little too forcefully.

\* \* \*

It was late when they reached the club, much later than they had intended, Cassie having insisted on going back to the Dorchester to change despite Joel's assurances that she looked just fine the way she was. The place was packed and smoky, the crowd having been attracted by the notable booking of the Gene Harris trio who according to Joel on their arrival were already *well and truly cooking*.

'Diet Coke,' Cassie said in answer to his enquiry at the bar as to what she wanted.

'You'll need something a little stronger than that,' he replied with only the suspicion of a smile. 'And don't worry about me, OK?'

He ordered her up a whisky sour which he knew she liked and a Coke for himself and was about to order them both some dinner when his brother came over and muttered something in his ear before hurrying away.

'He wants me to sit with his quartet that is now a trio,' he explained. 'His drummer's had an accident. Nothing serious, but he's not going to make it here tonight.'

'You play the drums?' Cassie asked.

'You'd better reserve judgement on that.' Joel smiled, drumming out some double time on the bar with his fingers. 'I can keep time.'

He did more than keep time, Cassie observed once the quartet had taken over from the guest group. As far as she could see and hear Joel was a halfway decent drummer since the group swung nice and easily, earning an approving nod from both his brother and the bass player. While Joel played through the set, Cassie sat on up at the bar enjoying both her drink and the music while wondering where exactly her growing relationship with him might lead. From nowhere all at once it seemed to be going somewhere, and going there so fast now that Cassie had not really taken the time out to think about what actually might happen to them both. Even when they had finally become lovers, that was as much as Cassie would let herself think their relationship might be, a love affair pure and simple, and thinking like that gave the affair some sort of finitude. Where she was now in her life Cassie didn't want to think in terms of a *till-death-do-us-part* relationship. She had done that, she kept telling herself, she had been there with Tyrone with whom she knew she had been lucky enough to experience the greatest sort of *till-death-do-us-part* association of which anyone could ever have dreamed, and that once death had indeed parted them there was never the remotest chance of meeting anyone else with whom she would feel the same sort of consummate affinity.

Yet now with Joel she was beginning to sense that it wasn't going to be quite as she had imagined it might be. She and her best friend Mary-Jo Christiansen's brother Frank had loved each other very much but not deeply enough to want to get married. They had talked about it once when they had both concluded perfectly amicably that neither of them was suited to the state of matrimony, mostly because they both had burgeoning careers which neither of them wanted to give up, although the real truth was that even then, so long after Tyrone's death, his shadow still hung heavy and neither Frank nor Cassie was willing to try to step out from it.

Joel had forced her hand. He had come at her head-on and made her look at her life anew, obliging her to realize that falling in love again or even just having a physical affair was in no way a betrayal of a man who had been laid to his final rest. For that she was grateful to him, yet that was not why she loved him, which was what had stunned her. What she loved about Joel was the man himself. She was attracted to him not because he brought her comfort and kindness as Frank Christiansen had done, but because he excited and provoked her. She felt stimulated by him, engrossed by the complexities of his character as well as physically attracted to him, more physically attracted than she had been to any man since Tyrone, but in an altogether different way from how she had been drawn to her husband. Tyrone had offered her a deep and romantic love which had been almost mystical in its power. Ever since the day she had first met him Cassie had been swept along by what she felt was the force of their mutual destiny, as if their love had been written long,

long ago in some ancient Irish legend, as if they had always been destined to meet and were part of something ordained so that when he was lost to her the size of the tragedy seemed to assume an epic proportion.

Joel was different, so different that there could be no comparison. Whereas everything about Tyrone had seemed classical, Joel was totally modern, not someone dreamed up in some cloud-shrouded Irish mountains by mystical gods and goddesses who liked nothing better than to shape people's destinies. Tyrone had been a horse trainer who was also a poet, tough and fearless, yet sweet and gentle. Joel was an artist who was also an artisan, kind and considerate yet intense and demanding. The boundaries crossed nowhere yet the two men seemed to run into each other, because they each gave Cassie something very different yet what they both gave her fulfilled her every need.

Or so it seemed now, particularly as Cassie sat watching Joel drum, with a lock of his thick dark hair falling over his high forehead, his eyes half closed and the tip of his tongue stuck in his cheek, and she realized that if she was not in love with him already she was well and truly on the way.

The very moment she thought that he opened his eyes and looked at her, as if he could feel what she felt. Throughout the rest of the number, appropriately enough called 'I'm Beginning To See The Light', he never once took his eyes off her until the end, until with a sudden great flourish around the three drums in front of him he cascaded the number to a volcanic halt, finishing with a swishing splash on a thin golden cymbal.

As the nightclubbers clapped, Joel nodded in return and was about to get up from his drum stool to come back across to the bar when a waitress handed him a message which he read with a frown. When he looked up he was still frowning, and as he rose he held up one hand with the fingers splayed to signal to Cassie he'd be gone for five minutes. She smiled and nodded back, ordered herself another whisky sour and thought nothing more of it.

Until the five minutes had become twenty.

She found the waitress who told her someone had asked to see Mr Benson in private.

'In private being?' Cassie wondered.

'I'm not sure,' the waitress replied without much concern. 'Maybe you should try the manager's office?'

Cassie did but only found the manager, deep in conversation with two men with black slicked back hair and expensive silk suits. Surprisingly the two silk-suited men got up after Cassie had knocked and was invited to enter the office but despite their over-polite manner the blank looks on their faces made Cassie fully aware that all they were really interested in was her going.

'Yes,' the manager agreed, 'there was someone to see Mr Benson but since this office was about to be occupied he chose to take his visitor up to his apartment. Would you like me to ring up for you? And tell him you wish to see him?'

'That really won't be necessary,' Cassie said quickly, not understanding why her suspicions were aroused. 'Mr Benson had sent word for me to join him and I know my way around, thanks. I'm sorry to have interrupted you.'

'No problem,' one of the silk-suited men said. 'Really no problem.'

Cassie hesitated at the foot of the stairs which led up to Joel's apartment. She knew perfectly well she had no right to interrupt Joel's meeting since what he chose to do and whom he chose to see was still very much his own business. Yet something compelled her to do so, some inner voice urged her to climb the stairs up to Joel's studio and go uninvited straight into the room because the person in there with him had no right to be there either. She started to climb the uncarpeted wooden stairs, slowly and quietly as if to make sure her approach would not be heard.

*Why am I doing this?* she asked herself, stopping halfway up. *Joel has a perfect right to see whoever he wants to see. Besides, whoever this person is, they asked to see him so it's obviously business. And if it's the kind of business I imagine they're doing down in the manager's office then*

*he certainly won't be pleased to see me because let's not be
naive here, Cassie Rosse. Whatever town or city you're in,
clubs like this pay to stay open.*

Convinced at last that she had no right to be where she
was, Cassie turned and went back down the stairs. Then
as she reached the bottom she heard the door above her
open, and the sound of a distinctive female laugh. And
voice.

She drew back into the shadows, not because she was
afraid of being seen, but afraid of what she might see. She
didn't want to see the woman on the landing above her.
All she wanted was to cross the passage and get back into
the club unseen, but she couldn't do that because by pulling
back into the shadows at the foot of the stairwell she had
cut off her line of escape. If she made a dash for it now
there was no way her flight across the uncarpeted and
brightly lit passageway could go unnoticed. So she flattened
herself against the wall praying that she was wrong until
she heard that unmistakable languid laugh, a laugh she had
hated since the first time she had heard it directed at her in
the classroom of Miss Truefitt's Academy. Leonora.

'Thank you,' Joel was saying, although how he looked
when he was saying it or whether or not he was touching
or holding Leonora Cassie could not tell since she now had
her back to them, hidden as she was under the very staircase
itself, the last four steps of which were on a turn, facing in
the direction of the fire door opposite. 'You're *hombre*. I
mean it.'

'Nonsense, you darling man. You know I'd do anything
for you. *Anything at all.*' Leonora replied, giving a small
throaty laugh after the innuendo.

'Even so—' Cassie heard Joel stop at the foot of the
stairs. 'It might have been a little more tactful if you'd called
first.'

'She won't have seen me, lover boy,' Leonora replied
teasingly. 'I made sure to come in through the back way.'

'Even so—' Joel sighed. 'Forewarned et cetera et cetera.'

'Nonsense.' Leonora laughed again. 'All adds to the fun,
I'd say.'

326

'That depends on your sense of humour, I'd say,' Joel replied. 'Come on.'

They passed within inches of where Cassie stood hidden, close enough for Cassie to catch a waft of the particularly cloying scent Leonora loved to wear. Then she heard the pass door into the club close and when she looked out from her hiding place the passageway was once again empty.

Nevertheless she waited, still hidden in the half shadows while she wondered quite what she should do as distantly the music began again, muffled by the doors and the length of the intervening corridor. She felt more alone than she had ever felt before, deserted it seemed by everyone, and betrayed by those closest to her. There was nothing to do, she thought, except leave. She had to get out of the club as fast as possible, back first to her hotel and then to somewhere where no-one could reach her. There was no point in confronting Joel. He would only spin her another web of lies. Why he would she couldn't now begin to understand because she couldn't begin to understand what it was he had wanted from her. It must be that he was just someone else bent on wrecking her life.

Worst of all, it now seemed certain that Joel must be part of the complicity that surrounded her, Cassie thought, as she stumbled blindly down the darkened side alley into which she had escaped, a garbage-strewn passageway which took her back into the street where at once she began to look for a taxi, running away from the club entrance, further and further away from Joel and whatever mischief he and Leonora were now making. She found a cab finally at the bottom of Garrick Street which at the last moment she ordered to take her to a hotel on Sloane Street and not to the Dorchester where she knew Joel would find her.

*That is if he can be bothered to look*, she thought, sitting back in the cab and watching the Christmas lights of London pass by. *Maybe he won't bother. Maybe he and Leonora will just sit down when they find I've gone, crack open a bottle of champagne and laugh themselves sick, about how oh-so-easy it was to dupe and make fun of poor little Cassie Rosse.*

327

'Damn them,' she said under her breath. *Damn them all anyway. Damn them all to hell and back. I'll show them. Just as I did before, I'll show them. I'll show them all, every single ungrateful, deceitful damned one of them.*

The hotel was full of noisy revellers, which suited Cassie fine. No-one would come looking for her here. This was the last place they'd expect to find her, in a small room high above the street outside, drinking brandy from the minibar and watching a soundless television from her bed until at last in spite of the endless noise she fell into a deep and weary sleep.

The next day she rang her contact at Aer Lingus and asked him to book her on the first flight back to Dublin. Then she sent a taxi to collect her things from the Dorchester, having first rung the hotel to ask room service to pack up her belongings. When the taxi driver arrived at the hotel reception desk to ask for Mrs Cassie Rosse's luggage he missed Joel by no more than a matter of minutes, all that it took for Cassie's set of Louis Vuitton luggage to be despatched by a porter out of the hotel and into the waiting cab.

# Twenty-One

On her return Cassie found a string of messages on her private answerphone, mostly from various owners who wanted to talk to her rather than Liam or Rosemary about their horses' prospects over the Christmas holidays, some from friends inviting her to various dinners and drinks parties, a couple from Mattie trying to find out exactly when she would be back and a brief but angry one from Joel, wanting to know what in hell she thought she was doing walking out on him without any explanation and all but ordering her to call him the moment she got back. Once she had listened to all the messages and jotted down the important ones Cassie then erased the tape and sat down to answer what she considered to be the vital calls. At the moment this did not include making one to Joel.

*You can go whistle for the moment, Mr Benson*, she said to herself as she was dialling Mattie's number. *You have no right to be mad at me. I'm the one who should be and is mad at you, so you can go whistle.*

She got Mattie's answering machine and Cassie could tell from the sound of his voice as he instructed any callers to leave their messages that he was thoroughly fed up, but then such is the nature of tough love, she concluded. Nothing good comes easy, she reminded herself, and as far as her son was concerned, too much had been coming his way of late far too easily.

Even so she left a message saying she was back and that she hoped he would still join her for Christmas at Claremore, even though no doubt it would mean she would have to entertain Phoebe McMahon as well. Such, however, was the joy of Christmas at Claremore that Cassie reckoned entertaining the McMahon daughter would only be the smallest of sacrifices if it meant seeing her handsome son's face across the festive table, just as she would have shut up and put up with her supercilious son-in-law if only she could have somehow got back on the right side of her daughter and persuaded her to come over at some point during the Christmas holiday.

As it was when her call to Mattie was returned it was by Phoebe McMahon who explained that Mattie was unavailable because he was out holding a horse for the visiting Niall Brogan. Furthermore and with sinking heart Cassie learned that Mattie and Phoebe had accepted an offer from Phoebe's parents to spend Christmas week with them in Antigua as guests of one of their owners, to which destination they were due to fly out from Shannon that same afternoon. When Mattie called Cassie back half an hour later to explain, Cassie found she had not the heart to try to talk him out of such a glamorous invitation, instead she urged him to go off and enjoy himself in the Caribbean.

'You'll be all right, won't you? I mean you're not going to be alone or anything? Erin said you've a pile of invitations and I take it Joel will be coming over, won't he?'

'I'll be fine, Mattie, don't you worry,' Cassie replied. 'And sure, I have a whole pile of invites.'

The only problem was all Cassie's summonses were for the week up till Christmas and for the week after it. She had no actual invitation to spend Christmas Day with anyone, since everyone assumed that like themselves Cassie would be spending Christmas with her family.

Instead, as a result of quarrels, misunderstandings and in one case betrayal, for the first time in her adult life Cassie faced the prospect of spending Christmas Day alone.

However, rather than face the time which had always been so important to her in solitary splendour, Cassie repacked a couple of suitcases with everything she would need for the week which as it happened she had initially intended spending abroad in the sun, and then went to tell Erin of her plans.

'You don't have to stay here, Erin. I know you were planning sometime on taking Padraig down to see your brother in Macroom so why not go and spend Christmas together? He's forever asking you down, so this is the perfect opportunity. I've already told Dick he won't be needed at all for the six days I'm away, so we'll just shut up shop and all of us take a well-earned holiday. A bit of time away from here will do us all the good in the world.'

'Should I have a number for you in case of an emergency?' Erin wondered. 'I have no idea even of where you're going.'

'Nor will you,' Cassie told her. 'I don't want to be disturbed unless it's a matter of life or death. I'll leave a sealed envelope with my contact number on the board in the tack room and I'm going to tell Liam the same thing. No-one's to call me unless it's absolutely imperative.'

Liam fully understood the instructions but said the same applied vice-versa. 'You're not to call here to make sure everything's all right, for if you do it'll be no sort of break. We're all organized. The Christmas Day rota is arranged as usual, with everyone working in shifts, so there's absolutely nothing to concern yourself about at all, guv'nor. We know which horses are running where and when, and all the arrangements are taken care of. So God bless you and away with you now to have a wonderful Christmas with your friends. For if anyone ever deserved it, Guv, you did.'

Cassie had let them all think she was going off to the Caribbean as she had previously indicated she might, but as she drove westwards she ignored the signs for Shannon airport and headed the car on towards Kerry, out along the wild and beautiful Dingle peninsula until at last she turned off the road and pulled up the steep rise outside her little house in Coomenhoule.

It was now late on the day before Christmas Eve. So having unpacked her belongings and stored away all the provisions she had managed to smuggle out from the kitchen at Claremore without Erin's knowledge – just as she had taken Wilkie with her on the pretext of leaving him with her usual dog-sitter, Niall Brogan's mother, Cassie set about putting hot water bottles in the bed, lit a fire in the sitting room then cooked herself a simple and instant meal of soup and a pasta dish washed down with half a bottle of Rioja, before taking Wilkie out for his last night walk and collapsing into bed.

On Christmas Eve it rained all day, heavy sheets of water blown in from the Atlantic which washed away the view and kept Cassie and Wilkie indoors by the fire where Cassie read the whole of *Rebecca* with Wilkie stretched out on the sofa beside her. At midnight she drove into Dingle to attend Midnight Mass and when the time came to drive home the skies had cleared leaving the coast and hills lit by a bright winter moon. Before going back into her house, Cassie stood on a high rock nearby and looked out over Coomenhoule Bay, to where the great Blasket Islands slept, giant whales under a night sky studded with stars, while the sea below lay calmed, and instead of thundering onto the beach the waves now broke with the sound of muffled drums.

'At times like this there is no place I would rather be,' she said to Wilkie who was standing by her side with his nose pointing out to sea. 'At times like this, here is the only place to be.'

Overnight the skies stayed clear so that Christmas dawned blue and bright. The sea was as calm as a mountain lake and the day so mild that rather than sit inside eating a lonely Christmas lunch Cassie decided to eat in the evening and packed herself a picnic lunch instead. And so with Wilkie on the passenger seat beside her and the hood of the BMW pulled back she drove up the western coastline of the peninsula to the Three Sisters where she left the car to walk along the spectacular headland past the ruins of Fort del Oro and a tiny church perched on a hillside just above the sea until they reached the strand of Smerwick Harbour which ran up to Murreagh. Perched on a stone of granite worn smooth by centuries of pounding surf Cassie sat with her thoughts, while Wilkie rollicked along the beach, putting up seagulls and chasing them into the sea or running into the sandhills in search of non-existent quarry.

She sat there until the tide had rolled far out and then with Wilkie running round her in delirious circles she pulled on her old dark blue hooded mackintosh which she had been using as a groundsheet, fixed the white-lined hood over her hair to stop it curling in the sea air, then walked the length of the strand, through puddles of clear cold salt water left by the retreating sea, along wet sands dark and soft beneath her feet. She walked as far as an inn which stood on a loop of road above Murreagh where she found the front door wide open, held back by a heavy stone.

Looking in she saw a man and a woman she assumed to be the landlord and his wife preparing to sit their family down for their Christmas dinner. One of the children who was helping her parents set the table suddenly noticed Cassie on her way past the door and stopped dead in her tracks, her eyes widening and her mouth slowly opening. Cassie smiled down at the young girl and the look of wonder on the child's face grew greater.

The pretty dark-eyed little girl said something softly to Cassie in Gaelic, bobbing a deep curtsey to her as she did so. Behind her, her mother called to her from the darkness of the room, again in Gaelic to which the child replied, curtseying again to Cassie before running back to fetch her mother.

'I'm so sorry,' Cassie called, 'I saw the door open, and I couldn't help but look in.'

Now the father stood in front of her, a tall kind-faced man with a stoop to his back, dressed in his Sunday suit and an immaculate white shirt from which he had already removed the collar. Around him all his children slowly gathered, the smallest with their thumbs in their mouths, the eldest wide-eyed in wonder, their ages ranging Cassie guessed, from three or four to nine or ten. Three were girls dressed in what looked like home-made velveteen dresses and two boys in spotless white shirts, red ties and black jackets, all of them staring at the stranger standing in the doorway silhouetted against the winter sun.

By now their pinafored mother had come to join them in greeting so Cassie addressed her apology to her.

'I'm sorry to disturb you,' Cassie said again. 'It's just that seeing the door open—'

'Please now,' the woman said, with a look to her children before wiping her hands carefully on her apron. 'Please, there is no reason for ye to be sorry now, for we was only just putting out the meal, and isn't that what the door would be open for? So as ye may avail yourself? Are there others with ye, or do ye come be yourself?'

'No, I'm all by myself,' Cassie replied, putting a hand down to touch her dog's head as he settled happily in the sunshine on the step. 'I've come from over the hill behind, up there.'

As Cassie pointed to the headland the man nodded once and then stood aside in welcome. 'We have dinner all cooked,' he said, and indeed past him in the bar Cassie could now see that the table was fully laid, lit by six candles in jam jars and set with satin red and gold crackers.

'Have ye made provision to eat this lunchtime, milady?' the landlord's wife asked Cassie.

'Well, no,' Cassie replied a little unsurely, uncertain as to what to say next. 'I'd bought a small picnic I was going to have on the beach—'

Again that was as far as she got, the landlord stopping her politely once more. 'Then we should be honoured if ye would sit down with us,' he said, holding up one hand. 'Haven't we a fine bird cooked and four bowls of potatoes? We have my brother's home-made pork sausage, our own home-made mince pies, and as fine a home-made plum pudding as ye would find anywhere in the west.'

'I couldn't possibly,' Cassie replied, overwhelmed by the strangers' generosity. 'I really had no wish to intrude on your family at Christmas.'

'There is no intrusion, I do assure ye. So please, now that ye are come to our house, we would only wish for ye to come and share our feast.'

The landlord stood even further aside so that the doorway was clear for Cassie to enter. The small room was spotlessly clean, with a polished dark wood floor and bar and a peat fire burning well in the stone fireplace. Beyond the bar, through a half-open door, Cassie could see the living room where a small and simple Christmas tree stood in a corner, much tinselled and hung with small, cheap winking lights.

'This is really very kind of you,' Cassie began.

'Good – so 'tis agreed,' the landlord said, before Cassie had time to continue. 'Margaret?' he commanded his wife. 'Set our guest of honour in her place now so that I may start carving the bird. Children? Come here and introduce yourselves to our visitor now, the way ye know how, and see to it that she has everything she may want. For ourselves, I am James Murphy himself, as ye may have seen sign painted above the door, and my wife is called Margaret.'

'How do you all do?' Cassie asked. 'I'm very glad to make all your acquaintance. I'm—'

'Ah sure there's no need to introduce yourself, ma'am,' the landlord interrupted. 'For as certain as it is Christmas we all know who ye are.'

Cassie was about to wonder why, then remembering what a small community lived on Dingle most particularly at the far western end, she realized that while she might not know everyone by sight or name they very probably all knew her. So she said nothing, instead shaking hands with each of the children as they all presented themselves to her in a line, as if queuing up to meet a visiting dignitary. Cassie could barely catch what they said as they announced themselves in whispers, but even if they had called out their names she would still probably not have been able to take them in, so bewitched was she by their looks. They were all of them handsome children, the girls dark-haired, dark-eyed and peach-complexioned and the two boys with noses well peppered with freckles, heads of copper-coloured curls and green eyes.

Placed to the right of her host in a place already set,

Cassie was served with a fine Christmas lunch, fresh, succulent, home-made and home-grown. Even the turkey, so she was told, was home-produced, coming from her host's brother's farm in Cork, and far from the usual overcooked vegetables and overdone meat Cassie had so often experienced eating out both in public and in private in Ireland the potatoes were perfectly steamed or roasted, the sprouts were firm, and the turkey as succulent a fowl as she had ever tasted. When she commented on the excellence of the food, Mrs Murphy thanked Cassie shyly before her husband offered the explanation.

'Mrs Murphy here is a ferocious reader of the magazines, do you see,' James Murphy said, adjusting his table napkin which he wore like a bib. 'She devours all magazines concerning the home with a great eye for the receeps. So there's hardly a week goes by in the calendar when Mrs Murphy does not present us with some new offering or other, with the result that I have to walk further and further up the mountains each afternoon in order to prevent further personal inflation.'

It was an extraordinary occasion, for no sooner had the introductions all been made and the family and their guest seated than the day continued as if Cassie had always been a part of it. The conversation flowed, and whenever it touched on anything or anybody local that Cassie might neither understand nor know, a brief explanation was added to put her in the picture before the dialogue continued. Yet never once did anyone ask Cassie a personal question. No enquiries were made as to where she came from or what she did. She was simply treated as if she was someone whom either they always entertained at their Christmas Feast or they had certainly been expecting.

Only once was something said which Cassie failed to understand and which was not explained to her. Moments after they had all sat down at the table and after the only brief silence that fell during the meal, the youngest child, an angel-faced little girl with permanently wondering eyes, asked her mother something in Gaelic, a question which was immediately echoed by her sisters but not by the boys who were both still sitting watching Cassie with half-bowed heads. Their mother listened kindly to the question and its repetitions before glancing down the table at their father who nodded back at her once, after which Margaret Murphy answered her children's enquiries briefly but obviously in the affirmative. Whereupon the eye of every child was turned to Cassie in even greater wonder, before their father very kindly but firmly issued what Cassie took to be a serious but gentle scold to them all, also in Gaelic, after which everyone once more relaxed and continued to enjoy their feast.

After a rich but magically light plum pudding served with a traditional and perfectly made custard, crackers were pulled, paper hats were put on, mottoes were solemnly related and riddles were gravely asked. James Murphy then sought the permission of his guest to smoke his pipe, and, having been granted leave so to do, sat in the chair by the fire he had skilfully replenished while the children helped their mother clear away. Cassie was banned from raising a finger to help, invited instead to sit the other side of the fire where for the full half hour it took to clear away and wash up the lunch things she listened to James Murphy's legends and stories of the most western part of Ireland. Tales of the heroic, of mysteries and of humour until the children and their mother returned and gathered themselves around the fire whereupon urged on by one of his sons James Murphy related his favourite story, a tale which concerned two English women taking their holiday on Dingle.

'They had hired one of these old caravans of which yous have no doubt heard or indeed seen now,' he said. 'The traditional sort that is drawn by a horse. So these two fine English ladies who we must say were not too well versed in the art of such caravans took a two week holiday on the peninsula, but when the time came to return the caravan far from being well rested they were found to be in a state of total exhaustion. Although they had greatly enjoyed the countryside and the weather had been kind and good, it appeared they had found it all but impossible each night to get the horse up into the caravan.'

After the genuine gales and hoots of laughter had subsided, the youngest girl, whose name Cassie had now discovered to be Maire, tugged at her father's sleeve and whispered another request. At once James Murphy stood up and lifting the child in his arms walked through to the living room, followed in line by his other children, his wife and finally, as bidden, Cassie.

In the tiny and simply furnished room the children all sat down in a circle around the foot of the Christmas tree while their father picked up five of the eight parcels piled neatly on the floor. These he handed in turn to his children, first calling out their names and then bestowing on each of them a kiss as he gave them their present. When the children had received their gifts, James Murphy handed his wife a parcel and in return she took a package from the floor and handed it to him. This left one present unoffered, the largest packet of all, flat and two foot square. In response to a nod from her father, Maire picked it up from the floor and shyly gave it to Cassie with a small curtsey.

'For me?' Cassie wondered. 'Are you sure, Maire?'

'Yes, milady,' the girl replied. 'We had it ready for ye.'

As the others carefully unwrapped their gifts, Cassie looked to see if there was in fact a tag on her parcel as there was on every other one, but unable to find one she assumed the family had some tradition of always leaving a spare present at the foot of the tree for any unexpected visitor, just as there had been a place already set. So, seeing that everyone was now waiting for her to open it, Cassie carefully undid the blue crepe paper in which the gift was wrapped and took out her gift.

It was a picture, a painting of the Nativity, done by all the children. At the top of it in someone's very best writing was the dedication: *To Our Blessed Mother Mary, Mother of the Lord God Jesus Christ.*

Cassie frowned and looked up, catching at once the eye of James Murphy who looked straight at her behind the backs of all his children and nodded at her several times as if to tell her *yes*, while in front of him five pairs of shining young Irish eyes looked up at Cassie, waiting for her verdict.

'It is beautiful,' she said. 'It's the most beautiful painting I have ever been given.'

'I did that, milady,' the eldest boy child said, carefully pointing to his contribution. 'I painted the stable.'

'And I painted the sky and the stars, milady,' his younger brother said.

'I did all the animals,' the oldest girl said, 'because I'm the best at the animals.'

'And I did you and Joseph, milady,' the next girl said. ''Tis quite like ye now that I see ye.'

'And I did Baby Jesus, milady,' Maire said, climbing on Cassie's knee, 'with the help of me mam.'

Cassie said nothing, but she put her arms round the shoulders of the shyly smiling children and hugged them.

'Can I kiss ye?' Maire asked from her lap. 'And will ye kiss me back?'

Cassie kissed them all and was kissed by them all in return. Then in answer to a look from their father, they sat down at Cassie's feet and showed each other the gifts they had been given.

While they played and talked, the three adults in the room said nothing. James Murphy, his pipe relit, sat in an old rocking chair gently pushing it back and forth, while his wife Margaret sat with her hands folded in her lap, her eyes never leaving Cassie's face. Finally, when Wilkie, who had been left to sleep in front of the snug fire, pushed his nose round the living room door and the cuckoo in the little clock above the fireplace called six o'clock, Cassie got up carefully from her chair, cradling the now sleeping Maire in her arms.

'I really must go now,' she said. 'I've far overstayed my welcome.'

'Ye have not,' James Murphy replied. 'Ye're welcome to stay as long as ye wish.'

'I have to get back. I really do.'

She kissed Maire on her warm pink cheek before handing her carefully to her mother, then kissing all the others goodbye on their insistence she took her leave of the family, thanking Mrs Murphy from the bottom of her heart for all her kindness and hospitality. Mrs Murphy thanked her in return while James Murphy insisted on fetching her dark blue mackintosh with its white-lined hood, helping her back on with it and seeing her to the door, ordering all the children now to let be and stay where they all were.

Closing the living room door behind him, he followed Cassie across the dark bar which was lit now only by two guttering candles which he extinguished before opening the front door onto another moonlit evening.

'Thank you, Mr Murphy,' Cassie said, turning to him. 'Thank you for the most memorable Christmas I ever had.'

'No, ma'am, with respect,' her host corrected her, 'I am to thank ye for the most memorable Christmas we have ever had. 'Tis a day my childer will remember the rest of their lives, thanks be to God.'

'Nothing will ever match your kindness,' Cassie said.

'Ah no sure the day will be remembered for your goodness, not ours. Now, do ye have your picture safe?'

'I do.' Cassie held it up, rewrapped as it was in the blue crepe paper. 'And when I get home I shall hang it in pride of place.'

James Murphy walked with Cassie from the inn to the side of the road. 'I should have asked you earlier now,' he said. 'But did ye walk all the way or do ye have a car parked somewhere?'

'On the headland up there.' Cassie pointed in the direction of the Three Sisters. 'But don't you worry, I shall enjoy the walk. It's a wonderful evening and I have Wilkie beside me.'

'Now ye'll come to no harm here,' James Murphy replied. 'Even so, if I may, I would like to walk to the beach beside ye.'

Together they walked down the road which led back to the strand where the full tide was once more retreating.

'We have always observed the same tradition at Claremore, where I live,' Cassie said as they reached the end of the looping road. 'My housekeeper to this day always leaves the front door open at Christmas in case the Holy Family calls.'

'Pray God she may have the great fortune herself one day, like the fortune ye have brought to our house. For even when they are grown up, the childer will never stop believing in today.'

'I hope not, Mr Murphy,' Cassie said, stopping to make her farewell. 'I myself shall certainly never stop believing in Christmas after today. Goodbye, Mr Murphy, and thank you.'

'God bless you, ma'am,' James Murphy said, taking her outstretched hand. 'But if I might perhaps know your real name. In case one day we meet on the other side of the hill.'

'Cassie Rosse. But don't worry,' Cassie added. 'I shall never come back here, I shall make sure of that.'

''Twould make no difference if ye did, Mrs Rosse,' James Murphy replied. 'The childer would never recognize ye. For the person they saw today was not yerself.'

Once the Christmas holiday was over Cassie plunged back into the work that lay waiting for her on the run-up to the big Festival meeting at Cheltenham, the highlight of jump racing's year. The good news was that as far as The Nightingale was concerned his return to work was so far proving to be successful. The horse was now doing daily road work with Bridie and from his progress Liam and Niall were both convinced he could start cantering in a fortnight at the most. On the racing front the further good news was that the stable had led up five winners over the Christmas holiday, a number which included two strong Cheltenham fancies, Don't Say That and Sauce For The Goose.

'Ironic, really,' Cassie observed to Niall as she inspected her steeplechasers and hurdlers at morning stables. 'I only started training jumpers for Mattie's sake, because he said that's all that he was really interested in.'

'Leave him alone and he'll come home, Cassie,' Niall laughed. 'More to the point, Well Loved's got a bit of a nose, and if you want to get another proper race into him before the Festival, then I'd say we're going to have to keep an eye out. There was spot of coughing in the botton yard while you were away. A couple of the two-year-olds were at it, but we isolated them straight away, and so far – touch wood – we haven't heard another sound.'

'You're quite right, Niall,' Cassie agreed. 'That is much more to the point. We'd better go and have a good look at him, just in case.'

The bad news came after Cassie and Niall had finished doing their rounds, having found much to their relief that the discharge from Well Loved's nose seemed to be greatly improved.

'Your lawyer's been on the phone,' Rosemary told Cassie as she came into the office. 'He's rung twice already, and wants you to ring him as soon as you can.'

'It can't be anything important,' Cassie muttered half to herself as she ran her eyes down the list of entries, and as her secretary dialled the number. 'After all I only had lunch with him just before Christmas.'

But it appeared she was wrong. Michael Irwin wanted to see her at the earliest possible opportunity, and when they met late the next morning at his office in College Green she pretty soon understood the nature of the urgency.

'They're refusing to pay,' he told her. 'It's as simple as that.'

'They've been refusing to pay since the horse was stolen, Michael,' Cassie reminded him.

'But now not only are they refusing, Cassie,' her lawyer returned, 'they are telling us to sue them if we want the money.'

'Then sue them.'

'Of course we shall sue, but it will cost, and it will be difficult.'

'But we will win,' Cassie insisted. 'Insurance companies do this by rote, Michael. You know that better than I. But they have no business refusing to pay out on the horse. He was stolen, he was wilfully castrated, and that is that.'

'You know what their defence is,' Michael Irwin reminded her. 'They say you arranged to have the horse stolen and gelded because there was something wrong with his gut. They quote the operation after his return—'

342

'*After* his return, precisely.'

'And as precedent the time he had bad colic earlier in the year.'

'It wasn't bad colic.'

'It was bad enough for you to claim the veterinary expenses on your insurance.'

'Worst thing I ever did,' Cassie sighed. 'I can't imagine why I did it.'

'You didn't,' Michael Irwin said. 'Your secretary did. But whatever, there it is as a precedental claim, and the underwriters are now arguing that having discovered something wrong with the horse's gut – and remember at the point of the policy renewal they inserted an exclusion clause concerning any further attacks of colic – you had the horse kidnapped and gelded in order to claim the insurance you couldn't get if the horse died from colic.'

'Which he then damned near did do. Except it wasn't colic – technically it was a twisted gut. But of course the insurers will claim—'

'That it was colic. Which indeed they are, claiming that this last illness helps to prove their point, the fact that you went to so much expensive trouble to save him, knowing you couldn't claim on death through colic.'

'This is sheer nonsense, Michael, and you know it!' Cassie said angrily, getting up from her side of the lawyer's desk to stare pointlessly at the traffic flowing past the Bank of Ireland and Trinity College. 'This is a perfectly valid claim and they're going to have to pay out whether they like it or not.'

'Then be prepared for a long, dirty and expensive fight,' Michael Irwin warned her. 'Remember how they opposed Vernon when he lost his Derby winner with cancer.'

'He won in the end.'

'It cost.'

After her interview with her lawyer Cassie crossed the road and asked to see her manager Dennis Fairchild at the Bank of Ireland.

'I need to know how I stand,' she said, having explained the impending litigation. 'How far can I afford to go?'

'How much do your insurers owe you?' Dennis Fairchild asked.

'One million pounds exactly.'

'Litigation is an expensive affair, as you know – particularly at this level.'

'I'm not going to let them get away with it, Dennis.'

'Of course you're not. But you need funds, and funds are a little low at present, Cassie. Should you lose—'

'I don't intend to lose. Now please, you know me and money,' Cassie said. 'I never look at my bank statements until it's too late and I leave all the books to Brian, my accountant. So I need to know, in John and Jane language please, exactly how I stand at the moment.'

Dennis Fairchild removed one pair of glasses to replace them with a pair of gold half moons before carefully opening the folder containing the Claremore *résumé* which lay on the polished table in front of him. Excusing himself to Cassie for a moment, he read the first two pages of the document in order to refresh his memory of the facts before removing his half moons to replace them with his tortoiseshell-framed pair.

'Good,' he said. 'Good. Just as I thought. After your horse's victories in the English and Irish Derbies you embarked on an ambitious plan of modernization for Claremore.'

'A highly necessary one, Dennis,' Cassie reminded him.

'Indeed, indeed, Cassie,' her manager agreed, 'and done with the blessing of the Bank. However, the programme was an expensive one, running to three point five million pounds, two million of which was financed by Claremore Racing and Claremore Foodstuffs, the other one point five being provided by a bank loan, secured against Claremore as collateral. Claremore Racing has paid off five hundred thousand of the outstanding loan through capital, leaving a balance of precisely one million pounds outstanding, earning the Bank interest at two points above current base rate, that is to say approximately one hundred and twenty five thousand pounds per annum. So far with the exception of last year all interest has been paid, leaving a sum of one million one hundred and twenty five thousand pounds in debit to the Bank.'

'So if they continue to refuse to pay me the million pounds they owe—'

'There's no need for immediate concern, Cassie,' Dennis Fairchild assured her. 'You have your usual cash flow problems, but these are symptomatic of businesses such as your own and obviously if your stable runs anywhere near to form once the Flat season starts, provided that your boxes are full, you should be able to process the interest on the loan out of earned capital. However—'

'However,' Cassie interrupted with a grim smile. 'In the event of the underwriters' winning the case, I shall either have to continue paying the interest for much longer than planned, or be left having to find at least another one and a quarter or possibly one and a half million in order to settle the loan.'

'Correct,' Dennis Fairchild said, taking his glasses off to clean them slowly on a new white handkerchief.

'As you know, the plan was to stand The Nightingale at the end of his four-year-old season,' Cassie said. 'One year's quota of mares would have seen to what Claremore owes the Bank. But since his kidnapping and castration, obviously this is no longer possible.'

'As impossible I take it as for the horse to return triumphantly to racing and win sufficient in prize money.'

'Exactly so, Dennis. So what's the clock on this? How long have I got?'

'That I cannot say without reference to my colleagues. It very much depends on the anticipated income from Claremore Racing and the company's ability to meet its liabilities. As far as Claremore Foodstuffs is concerned, the well is pretty dry there at the moment due to your subsidiary's helping with the initial financing of the modernization scheme. None the less, provided Claremore Racing profits more or less to the degree it has been profiting in the last three years, and provided your underwriters cease their foolish resistance and pay you what you are owed, underinsured though you might have been, I can see no reason for the Bank to worry at present.'

'But should none of these things pertain, Dennis,' Cassie enquired, clenching her two hands into tight fists out of sight beneath the table.

'In that very unlikely eventuality, Cassie, the Bank might well call in its debt. Were Claremore Racing unable to repay the loan, we would be forced to foreclose.'

In this particular hour of need, it seemed there was no-one to whom Cassie could turn. She could not confide in Erin because, however dear and fiercely loyal her housekeeper was, like most of her fellow countrymen she always had the greatest difficulty in keeping anything to herself for long. Even when Erin was doing her best to keep a secret she wore such a hangdog expression that every acquaintance knew at once something was wrong and finally, either by sheer pressure or more often aided by a couple of glasses of *the creature*, the secret would be revealed. Cassie had to keep this secret from her housekeeper since she could not possibly risk the chance of any rumour that Claremore was in trouble, which it most surely was.

The profits over the last three years to which Dennis Fairchild had alluded had indeed been healthy enough, but the vast percentage of the monies earned had been won of course by The Nightingale with his hugely rewarded victories in his Derbies, his King George VI Gold Cups and his victories in the Eclipse Stakes and the Arc de Triomphe. It had made sense for Cassie to invest Claremore Racing's profits straight back into Claremore Racing, building new stable blocks, putting in a new equine swimming pool, redraining the gallops, and building a veterinary operating theatre and horse hospital. A massively expensive undertaking but one which had been carefully costed and approved both by her financial advisers and by her bank. The only assumption she had made was that The Nightingale would survive the rigours of the few races she had planned for him as a four-year-old and would then retire to stud, where unless he proved to be either impotent or infertile he would secure Claremore Racing's future. Indeed, in order to assess both the potency and the fertility of the horse Niall Brogan had run a series of tests, the results of which confirmed The Nightingale's future as a successful stallion.

The only possibility Cassie had not taken into account was that the horse might be stolen and castrated.

But then no-one could possibly have imagined such an eventuality, so no-one blamed Cassie for that tragic event. They did blame her just as she now blamed herself for underinsuring the animal, although the more understanding of them appeared to appreciate why she had done so, given the prohibitive cost. As for the others, however hurtful their censure it was really purely academic, since a team of underwriters who were trying to get out of paying one million pounds in compensation would most certainly baulk even more at a ten million pound indemnity.

As a result, however, whichever way she looked at it Cassie seemed to face ruin. Unless the underwriters paid up almost immediately, with her greatest money winner sidelined as a racehorse and out of contention entirely as a stallion, thanks to the escalating interest on the finance from the Bank she was going to find herself further and further in debt. That the yard would produce winners she had little doubt. Already Claremore had enjoyed the best start it had ever had to the National Hunt season, but the prize money for races won over timber and birch was absurdly small compared with the riches to be won on the Flat. Besides, none of the horses which ran from Claremore over the jumps was owned by Claremore Racing, with the exception of a novice steeplechaser and a couple of novice hurdlers which Cassie was bringing on slowly to sell at the end of the season. All Cassie could rely on winning was her percentage of the purse, which as she said would scarcely keep the horses in stable rugs. It would certainly go no way towards helping to pay off a one and a half million pound debt, and at this stage of the season all the training fees did was cover the cost of training.

Then there were the legal fees waiting to be incurred once litigation against her recalcitrant underwriters was duly authorized. If the case dragged on anywhere near as long as the notorious Vernon case quoted to her by Michael Irwin then more tens of thousands were going to have to be found in order to retain silk. Should she lose her case, then she would not only be in for her own costs, but most likely the costs of the opposition as well.

So now it was small wonder that more than ever she needed someone by her side to help her. Joel would have been perfect. Yet because of her fierce pride she still refused to get back in touch with him. She had spoken to him once since her return and only then because he had managed to trick her into answering her private line directly rather than through the shield of her answering machine by pretending to be Mattie.

'That was a dirty trick,' she had told him, about to hang up.

'No, wait—' Joel cut in, sensing she was about to replace the phone. 'Just hear me out, will you?'

'I don't see why,' she had replied, but having heard his voice for real and not on the answerphone tape she had hesitated, waited just long enough to allow Joel in. But she had given him no prompt for his explanation, preferring instead to see what conclusions he himself had reached concerning her sudden departure from his life.

'Phil – my manager at the club – said you were trying to find me after we'd played that set,' he had begun. 'That you were heading for my studio.'

'Yes,' Cassie had agreed. 'But in the end I didn't need to go all the way.'

'Meaning?'

'I heard you coming out of your studio. I heard you both – you and your friend.'

'I thought as much. Look – I can explain.'

'Not *again*. Spare me yet another of your you-have-to-believe-this explanations, please.'

'Why are you so *suspicious* of everyone and everything?'

'I wonder.'

'Some things have a perfectly innocent explanation.'

'Nothing concerning Leonora comes with that tag, I assure you.'

'Obviously you've convinced yourself that your old sparring partner and I were up to no good.'

'Obviously. Not that I took a great deal of convincing. I heard what you had to say to each other as well. *Lover boy. She won't have seen me. I made sure to come through the back way.*'

'There's a perfectly logical explanation,' Joel had said wearily.

'There always is with you,' Cassie had replied, equally wearily. 'You know what I think about Leonora. You know perfectly well how things stand between the two of us—'

'Which was why I was anxious you didn't bump into her that night.'

'So why had she come to see you? You're meant to hardly know each other, *lover boy*!' Cassie had demanded, a little bit of her hoping that the explanation would be short, simple and easily acceptable. It wasn't.

'That's my business, Mrs Rosse,' Joel had returned. 'I don't see why I should account to you for every move I make. You don't own me.'

'You bet I don't!' Cassie had replied, stung. 'You double bet I don't, Joel Benson! And as God is my witness I have no intention of filing for adoption! I have quite enough children of my own, thanks!'

She had slammed down the phone then, so hard it had bounced out of the cradle and hung humming on its wire at the side of her desk. She had let it hang there for the rest of the evening, only replacing it an hour later when she had gone to bed, switching it straight onto the answering machine as she did.

The following day she had instructed the telephone exchange to put her private line on a new ex-directory number and issued orders to the rest of her personal staff that if a Mr Benson rang on any of the other lines she was never to be available.

349

How she wished she had countermanded that direction, and never more so than now as she lay awake alone in the middle of yet another rain-lashed January night with what seemed like all the worries of the world sitting on her. Never for one moment had she believed that when faced with a claim for the wilful castration of The Nightingale the underwriters would actually stand their ground. Knowing insurers of old, and particularly livestock insurers, Cassie had thought the move they were making was simply the usual one to delay payment and that once they realized the depth of her resistance they would pay out the amount due as had always previously been the case. Not unnaturally she had banked on them paying out, particularly since the income upon which she had been relying to keep herself solvent in the near future had disappeared with the mutilation of her stallion. Now everything teetered on the verge of collapse, with her bank debts mounting, and the only creature who would have been capable of making good her losses standing all but valueless rugged up against the winter in his stable.

*Tyrone*, she groaned, turning her face down into her pillow, *Tyrone, you would have throttled me and quite right, too. I counted the chickens before they were hatched, and now even if they do hatch there's every chance they'll all be boobies.*

'Mr Irwin is trying to persuade your underwriters that to proceed would be folly, Mrs Rosse,' said the young dark-eyed man sent by Cassie's lawyer the following week to run over the full details of her claim. 'However, they appear to be determined to stand by their guns, indicating that they have evidence which will substantiate their argument that the horse was not truly kidnapped.'

'They're talking through the back of their corporate head,' Cassie said, with no little irritation. 'What sort of evidence could they possibly have, unless someone's willing to perjure themselves?'

'It's been known,' Gareth Plunkett replied. 'When there's

this sort of money at stake it's amazing the games people play. A lot of their argument seems to hinge on the fact that the horse had suffered from colic previously.'

'The Nightingale is different, I would have thought that was obvious,' Cassie replied. 'If it had been any other horse in the stable I wouldn't have bothered calling in my vet, that's how *un*serious the so-called attack was. But since it was The Nightingale, well – you can understand. I wasn't prepared to take any chances.'

'And your vet will testify to that.'

'Of course. In fact by the time Niall Brogan got to the horse he was up and shaking himself. He hardly had to attend to him at all.'

'Good-good,' Gareth Plunkett said, all as one word. 'Like Mr Irwin, I feel they will settle long before we get to court—'

'But if they don't?'

'Then we go to court.'

'Which takes a long time.'

'Invariably.'

'I don't think I can wait that long,' Cassie said, half to herself. 'I'm not sure I can afford to.'

'That, Mrs Rosse, is precisely what your opponents will be hoping,' Gareth Plunkett replied. 'On the bright side, having reviewed the file thoroughly, my impressions are that Claremore Racing are far and away your insurance company's biggest client. Bar two, they insure every horse standing in your yard, with of course your most famous horse as far and away their biggest liability.'

'Thay have other valuable stallions insured, I would imagine,' Cassie remarked.

'Apparently not, Mrs Rosse, strange to relate. Horses in training certainly, as well as mares and foals at stud, but no other stallions, certainly not of significant value, a fact Mr Irwin and myself find more than a little surprising. In the instance of an eventuality, in order to meet any liability on your horse, you would imagine a brokerage like this would have shored up enough reserves from other sizeable premiums. Such was not the case. It seemed that

Claremore Racing was their milch cow and they will continue to delay at any cost. At least that is our impression, I have to say.'

Cassie stroked Wilkie's head as he sat devotedly beside her and then smiled at the handsome young man who was busily collecting up his papers. 'There's no point in worrying, is there, Mr Plunkett? No point at all. So instead of worrying I shall have to do something else altogether,' she said.

'Which is?' Gareth Plunkett politely enquired.

'Why, do what I'm good at doing. Lead up some winners.'

Since he found he was unable to reach her by telephone, Joel wrote to Cassie. Landlocked in England because of his bail, that was the only way left open to him to keep in contact, and sure enough a letter soon arrived at Claremore addressed to her personally in his scrawling, stylish hand. At first Cassie wasn't going to open it, afraid either that the letter would contain yet more excuses which she would refuse to believe or that it would contain yet more excuses which she would find herself unable not to believe. For the more she thought about it the more Cassie realized that she was afraid of Joel, not of him as a person but of what he had come to mean to her, and she was no longer sure she could handle such a highly volatile relationship without some hurts being inflicted on one or the other of them. So for three whole days the letter remained in the top drawer of her desk unopened. Finally she summoned up the courage and cut it open with an old ivory paper knife. The letter read:

*Mrs Rosse*

*I can't write letters. I can paint pictures, I can draw people, I can carve creatures great and small out of stone. I can play the drums, I can whistle through my fingers, I can walk on my hands, but I can't write letters. If I tried to say what I want to say it would*

come out all wrong. Worse, you might not believe
me. To me seeing is believing. See a person and you
can see whether or not they lie or tell the truth. Even
the telephone won't really do because you cannot see
what is going on at the other end. I need to see you.
I can't get over there, but you could come over here,
if you need, want or even vaguely feel like seeing me
(maybe just out of curiosity). It isn't a good time, all
round. I don't like waiting for trial, but then this I
brought on myself. I'm not sure I brought what has
happened between us on myself but that I might be
able to sort out if you would let me see you. Just once
more. There is a perfectly good explanation (I can
hear you saying 'there always is') but there is. But
I'm not going to write anything down on paper. I
know it will just sound like yet another excuse, rather
than a valid explanation.

Joel

'This is the moment, Cassie Rosse,' Cassie thought to
herself after she had re-read the letter for a third time, 'this
is the moment when movie heroines turn to their best
girlfriends to find out what to do. Or to their mother. Or
maybe even to their daughter. But you don't have anyone
to turn to except yourself. And right now, as far as making
value judgements go, you don't even trust yourself.'

What she did instead of rushing to a decision was put
the letter back in the desk drawer once again so that she
could consider her response calmly and logically considering this no time for either fury or passion. As Mattie
would say she really needed to get her head round this one,
because to her way of thinking once she had decided which
way to go there would not be any turning back. Whatever
she decided this time about Mr Joel Benson and herself was
going to be for good and all, as Tyrone would have said.
No more maybes, no more perhaps, no more just-this-
onces. This time it was all or nothing.

She felt better immediately she had come to that

realization, as if making the actual decision was something that would take care of itself or be taken care of by someone else, perhaps even by something else such as an outside force. As far as Cassie was concerned she had finally made up her mind, namely that when she did make up her mind her decision really would be final.

Then she took herself off to the office to put the finishing touches to Claremore Racing's Cheltenham campaign. She might have only started the jumping side of things in order to keep her son's interest, but such was Cassie's determination, and now that she had not altogether unexpectedly produced some very likely candidates for National Hunt's greatest racing festival, she was resolved not to come home empty-handed.

'Well Loved is our best chance, guv'nor,' Liam said to her one fine dry February morning as they sat on their hacks watching the Cheltenham bound horses thunder up the gallops. 'Unbeaten in his three races now he is, and it'll take something else to beat him in the Arkle.'

'Agreed, although as we all well know there's no such thing as a racing certainty.'

'There wasn't till Himself came along,' Liam said, pointing to The Nightingale who was lobbing up the gallop easily keeping his place alongside the steeplechasers. 'And now isn't he going nicely?'

'He's certainly striding out,' Cassie agreed. 'He's beginning to look his old self.'

'Bridie says he's beginning to feel his old self.'

'You know the saying, Liam,' Cassie remarked, swinging her hack round to head for the top of the gallops where the string was pulling up. 'They don't come back, right?'

'With all the respect in the world, guv'nor,' Liam replied, 'they does not include The Nightingale.'

Together they cantered across the top field, the sharp February wind stinging their cheeks and bringing water to their eyes.

'So what's the long term plan, guv'nor?' Liam called over

to Cassie. 'Are you thinking of giving Himself a run come spring?'

'Come on, Liam!' Cassie called back. 'You know as well as I do, there's one heck of a way to go yet! At the moment my sights are on Cheltenham!'

Cassie talked to the work riders about the performances of their various mounts as the string circled round, their hot breath hanging on the chill of the winter morning. Passing her, The Nightingale snorted his well-being and then gave himself a good hard shake under Bridie who laughed, nearly taken out of her seat by the vigour of the horse. Little Teddy Elliot who was riding the Triumph Hurdle hope Don't Say That turned scarlet when Cassie pulled her hack alongside his horse to talk to him.

'Now then, Teddy,' she said, eyeing the muscular young bay horse beneath him, 'what sort of feel did he give you?'

'Sure and there's no comparison between the harse he was last week, guv'nor, and the harse he is now,' Teddy replied, staring up at the sky above him. 'He's like a great big curled up spring, he is. Ready to go soon as you press the button.'

'He's jumping his hurdles better too, wouldn't you say?'

'The harse has a lep in him like a toad in a thunderstorm, guv'nor. Sure I just wish I was goin' to be in the plate this time two week.'

'It's not an impossibility,' Cassie replied. 'The horse goes better for you than for anyone.'

'Ah Jeez, guv'nor,' Teddy gasped, looking at Cassie quickly for the first time. 'I wouldn't let him down if you gave me the chance. Nor you neither, ma'am.'

'Then we'll pencil you in, Teddy. I'm not promising, mind, but since it doesn't look like I can get Christy Lynch or Terry McGuire there's a good chance you can ride him. Now then, Jimmy—' Cassie wheeled her horse round to go and talk to Sauce For The Goose's work rider, who was having a bit of trouble keeping his charge at a walk. 'He still won't really settle, will he?'

'No, guv'nor,' Jimmy Kelly replied, bouncing in the

saddle as his horse trotted on the spot. 'If he does this at Cheltenham he'll leave his race in the paddock.'

'Let him lead tomorrow. Give him his head and let him bowl along up in the van. I think maybe I've been getting it wrong, trying to save him. Maybe he's just one of those who's happier making all. It's worth a try anyway.'

Jimmy Kelly topped his hat to Cassie in response as she swung round now to Bridie. Under her, The Nightingale stood as cool as could be, watching everything around and about him with a bright eye and his ears pricked.

'Well?' was all she asked.

'It's as if he hasn't missed a day, guv'nor,' Bridie laughed, and then patted her horse on his neck. 'He could take them all going backwards.'

As the string walked back across the top of the field to join the track which led to the yard, Cassie and Liam held back, intending to canter down the gallops and across the bottom fields once the string was safely out of sight.

'Have you thought about who'd ride Nightie if we do decide to give him a run?' Cassie wondered, watching the big black horse sauntering back under the relaxed hands of his beloved Bridie. 'He's not going to go for a man, you know.'

'Ah now with the greatest respect, guv'nor,' Liam replied. 'Once he and Dex get reacquainted it'll be an altogether different story.'

'I doubt it, Liam,' Cassie said, turning her horse to face back down the gallops. 'I very much doubt it.'

'So who'd you put up then? In the unlikelihood of that being the case?'

'In the unlikelihood of him racing at all, Liam,' Cassie replied, shortening her reins, 'then I'd put up a girl.'

As she cantered off before him Liam nearly fell off his horse, and not because he had been caught unawares. At least not as regards being ready to canter on he hadn't.

'You'd put a *girl*?' he shouted across to Cassie as he ranged his horse up alongside hers. 'You'd put a girl up on *The Nightingale*?'

'You don't pull faces whenever I ride him, Liam!' Cassie

called back. 'And you've even come to terms with Bridie riding his work now!'

'Ah but not on a racecourse, guv'nor! With the greatest respect in the world women were not put on this earth as jockeys!'

'Oink oink, Liam!' Cassie laughed. 'I guess we're man enough to have your babies, but not to ride your horses! At least not on the racecourse! Come on – race you to the bushes!'

Even though theoretically she was on the slower horse, Cassie had got first break and she was still a good half length up by the time they galloped past the clump of rowan bushes in the bottom fields where they always pulled up.

'You've certainly lost none of your old ways, guv'nor!' Liam laughed, pulling his horse back down to a trot. 'You're as neatly balanced as a pair of scales!'

'Thanks, Liam,' Cassie returned with a grin. 'Getting a compliment out of you as far as riding goes sure is something.'

'Not at all, guv'nor,' Liam said as they dropped to a walk. 'But to be serious now—'

'You mean you weren't being serious then?' Cassie teased.

'Sure of course I was. What I want to be serious about is what you said up there. About putting a girl up on Himself.'

'Think about it, Liam. If Dex can't stay on, and if we do race the horse, then only a girl will do.'

'Ah well 'tis no wonder the bookies are quoting what they are about him running again, let alone winning,' Liam said in disgust. 'For if that sort of rumour's already in the air—'

'Wait a minute, Liam,' Cassie said, turning half round in her saddle to look at him. 'I know the bookies will lay odds on most anything – but Nightie running again? And winning? What sort of odds are they quoting?'

'When Himself was first returned here yous could get what yous wanted about him ever racing again,' Liam replied. 'Some of the lads who'd never stop believing in him even if the old horse was pushing up the daisies which God forbid, they waded in at sixty-six to one and sure didn't that wipe the price off the boards overnight? Best ye can get about him racing now is two to one against, although there's still plenty of ten and twelve to one about him winning again. Didn't Jimmy Kelly get thirty-three to one about him winning first time out?'

'Thirty-three to one?' Cassie echoed. 'Is this generally available?'

'It was last week, guv'nor. But if they had the spies out this morning, even though the old fella was only hacking up, they mightn't be quite so generous any more.'

Cassie walked her horse on in silence across the wet fields before popping him over the hedge bordering the empty home paddocks. When Liam had done the same and once more caught up with her, Cassie half turned again in her saddle to address him. 'How do you think the horse has come on, Liam?'

'Ach it's impossible to tell, guv'nor, until he's had a couple of really decent gallops. Sure you know that as well as I do.'

'Yes I do. But I also know as well as you do what your eye tells you. About the horse's condition, about his attitude, about his fitness.'

'If I hadn't known the history—' Liam stopped and shook his head once.

'If you hadn't known the history?'

'I'd say he'd be cherry ripe be the middle of April.'

'My thoughts exactly.' Cassie turned away and walked her horse on once again in silence, musing on the various possibilities. 'OK,' she said suddenly. 'Let's get real.'

'Let's get real indeed!' Liam laughed. 'I've never known ye to get otherwise, guv'nor!'

'The main problem is to get the horse race-fit without the world and his wife finding out.'

'And his bookmaker,' Liam added.

'And particularly his bookmaker,' Cassie agreed. 'But say we managed that – and don't ask me how yet, we'll work out the details later. What would we run him in? If we run him in a stakes we'll get no price, will we?'

Liam eyed her. 'You're thinking of having a touch, are ye?'

'We'll get the odds ante post, of course. At least a proportion of the odds you say are on offer at the moment,' Cassie continued, ignoring Liam's observation. 'But as soon as any sizeable bet's down, or as soon as we attempt to get a sizeable bet down, they'll wipe the board.'

'If any real money goes down on the horse, guv'nor, ye'll be lucky to find a bookie to give you a slip.'

'Then we're going to have to help ourselves quietly to what's on offer now, Liam,' Cassie said, 'and then wade in on the day at SP.'

'At starting price? Ah well you're talking of a coup now, guv'nor, aren't ye?'

They were nearing the stable blocks now, so Cassie reined back to a halt and pulled her horse across the front of Liam's.

'I'm not talking at all, Liam, understand?' she said, looking him in the eye. 'We've been talking nothing but Cheltenham and Nightie hasn't been mentioned once.'

'Of course he hasn't, guv'nor. Divil the once.'

'But just suppose we do find him a race, Liam, and particularly with a girl up—'

'Ach now, guv'nor—'

'Think about it, Liam. Think of the odds. A girl up on The Nightingale? Particularly someone as untried as Bridie.'

'Guv'nor—'

'Think of the odds, Liam,' Cassie persisted. 'With Dexter Gordon up the horse will have winner stamped all over him. But with Bridie Moore up—'

'Ah yes, with Bridie Moore up—'

'And maybe even in a handicap?'

'A *handicap*?'

'Forgive the blasphemy – or is it sacrilege, Liam?' Cassie laughed. 'Whatever – if we entered him up in a handicap, with an untried female jock – listen. If he's back to even two stone of his former self, let alone a stone, Nightie could win a handicap even with top weight which he'd be sure to get.'

'And an inexperienced woman rider?'

'He could win with the parish priest riding him, Liam. You yourself know that particularly in that sort of company, The Nightingale is a steering job. But first things first. First we have to start really checking on his fitness, then we pick up some ante post vouchers about him racing again, then some about him winning again. And if we want this to come off, then you and I forget we ever had this conversation, OK?'

'I never heard a word that we said,' Liam agreed. 'Divil the word.'

'Neither did I,' Cassie laughed. 'Divil the word.'

Both of them walked their horses on in silence to the yard, both of them imagining how they might best pull off the proposed coup and what they both might make out of it, Liam wondering how best to spread the three hundred pounds he always had stashed away in his mattress ready for a good touch, and Cassie how she could invest her only available five thousand pounds to make the best part of a million and a quarter.

# Twenty-Two

Finally Cassie wrote to Joel.

*Dear Joel*
*I'm sorry for the delay in writing back to you but*
*things have been a little fraught this end for reasons*
*I won't go into now. Nothing to do with The*
*Nightingale who continues to astonish us all by his*
*recovery to what seems like full strength. Time will*
*tell, however, and we still haven't decided where to*
*go with him next. Maybe I'll just keep him as a hack!*
    *Anyway, I don't wish to burden you with my*
*worries when you have quite enough of your own on*
*your plate (although from what I read in the papers*
*it seems you're more likely to be charged with*
*encouraging a suicide, because your father asked for*
*a drug and you helped him procure it, rather than*
*murder or manslaughter. And even if they do try you*
*for murder or manslaughter informed opinion says*
*because of precedent you'll walk away. I know this*
*won't remove your anxieties, but it surely must relieve*
*them?) – anyway as I was saying, there have been a*
*few things amiss here which have kept me occupied*
*which is why I am so late in replying to your letter.*
    *Of course I will come and see you. The trouble*
*is I'm not quite sure when. We're running up to*
*Cheltenham now, as no doubt you realize, and what*
*with one thing and the other – and there's plenty of*
*'other', take my word for it – I can't see myself finding*
*a day free to fly over before the week of the Festival*
*itself. But I can't really wait that long to hear what*
*you have to say, just as I'm sure you can't wait that*

long to say it. Can't you really write it to me in a letter? Now that time has passed, all I really want to know is what L. was doing in your studio and why you couldn't tell me on the phone when I asked. You can't blame me for being suspicious and/or jealous or whatever. L. has set out on more than one occasion deliberately to try to wreck some part of my life. So when she now starts cropping up not only in my life but in yours what am I supposed to think? You see, what I find difficult is knowing what to believe. So many things with you seem to be a contradiction, or seem at least to be contradicted by a later turn in events. You say you had a reason for L. to be in your studio, and that the things I overheard are easily explicable, so surely you could just write these reasons in a letter? It can't really be that hard to understand, or, if it is, then maybe we'll have come to the end of this particular road.

Is that what you're afraid of? I am. So much has now happened between us and we seem to have got so involved with one another that I know I don't want it to end, believe me. But since we can't yet meet up, something has to be put down on paper. I just don't understand why you got so incredibly hostile when I asked you on the telephone what L. was doing seeing you that night, and why she had to come to your club to do so. So since you couldn't or rather wouldn't explain, not unnaturally I jumped to some sort of conclusion and it wasn't very favourable to you. Of course I know that I don't 'own' you. That you have a life quite separate from mine and the right to see whomsoever you choose. And sure, I'm paranoid about L. Who wouldn't be? She's capable of anything.

So here's how it is – we're not going to be able to settle back and feel comfortable (at least I'm not) as long as we have yet another mystery clouding our relationship. So we're in a kind of stand off, right? If there's nothing to explain, then just tell me why not

*and that'll be that. If there is something to explain*
*and I can live with the explanation then that's OK*
*by me as well. If I can't, well, we'll just have to say*
*goodbye and thanks for the memory. Don't write if*
*you feel you can't. Call me on my new number which*
*I've written on the top of the first page. If you don't*
*get me, leave a message to say what time you'll call*
*(between 6 and 7 in the evening is always a good*
*time) and I'll be there. I'm going to leave the calling*
*up to you because I think it's better that way. If you*
*call, I'll know you mean business.*

*As always,*
*Love,*
*'Mrs Rosse'*

In a hurry to leave for the races and finding she had no
stamps in her desk in the drawing room, Cassie broke one
of her golden rules which was always to mail her own
letters and called out to Erin as she was passing by to ask
if she would take the letter down to the village with her
when she next went and mail it for her at the post office.
For some reason, for a very good reason as it later emerged,
Erin put it in the pocket of her old tweed coat and neglected
to post it.

# Twenty-Three

Hearing nothing back from him Cassie thought she would ring him, then she thought not. What she did instead to make sure he was still in residence at his house in Barnes was to ring his number from her car phone. As soon as she heard his voice, she hung up. She didn't even wait for him to say *Hello?* more than once, in case hearing his character-ful tones she might weaken and say *Hello* back. If she had, she knew she would have lost the battle.

Instead she pressed END on her car phone and drove on to Peter Nugent's private gallops on his estate north of Kilkenny, where they were due to give The Nightingale his first serious piece of work. The operation had been shrouded in secrecy as previously agreed, protected it was hoped by a rumour put about by one of the lads that the big horse was due to work in earnest that particular Friday morning in the third string on the home gallops at Clare-more, ridden by Dexter Bryant. Sure enough Dexter had duly turned up for work and under maximum security had been put up on The Nibbler, another big black horse and an early type of three-year-old due to race as soon as the Flat season opened. He was the ideal choice, for apart from three big white socks the horse was as good an understudy for The Nightingale as could be found any-where, particularly once Bridie had carefully bandaged over the tell-tale white socks and got him ready for the gallop wearing an exercise hood.

The understudy horse was to work with a handful of other early horses which were also pencilled in to run at the end of the month, the instructions being for the others to pull easily away from The Nightingale's double when they hit the final furlong marker and asked their mounts to get serious. The plan worked to perfection, with Dexter really looking as if he was stoking up the big horse under him to keep pace which in a way he was, for The Nibbler for all his fancy breeding was a bit of a slowcoach and had already been earmarked by Cassie and his owner to have more potential as a three mile steeplechaser.

'If our boys are up there where they usually are in the bushes,' Liam had laughed as Cassie had met him at the top of the gallops, 'by lunchtime you'll be naming your price.' But by now, much later in the morning, Cassie was getting ready to watch the real article at work. Liam and Bridie had slipped him and Dorin's Mist, his galloping companion, out of the back entrance of Claremore in Cassie's old trailer, the one she had always used to take Joesphine's ponies to compete. Five miles down the road at a house belonging to Niall Brogan's mother they had transferred their precious cargo to a proper but unmarked horsebox which had been used for the rest of the journey to the estate belonging to Peter Nugent. Nugent was an old friend of Tyrone and now also of Cassie, a gentleman farmer whose greatest joy was the breeding and production of event horses, an occupation which he had been following with increasing success for the past twenty years. Hence his superb facilities, and also, Cassie thought with relief as she drove up the tree-lined drive to his large and handsome Georgian house, hence his lack of competitive edge as far as she and Claremore were concerned.

He was, however, one of The Nightingale's most devoted fans, as also one who believed implicitly that if the great horse did fail to find his feet racing again, both his breeding and his conformation indicated he could well turn into a successful eventer.

'So in a way, Cassie, you'll understand I won't be that displeased if this particular plan of yours backfires,' he said with a smile as Cassie and he walked towards his Range Rover for the drive up to the gallops. He was a stout, red-faced man with a shock of thinning ginger hair, known less for his looks than for his dress sense, which was always immaculate. He was also deceptively fit and active for a man of his girth. 'You know, I'd not be entirely heart-broken to have the horse here for his further education,' he said to Cassie with a nudge. 'In fact I'd not be entirely heartbroken to have him as a gift.'

'Let's first see what the old fellow shows us this morning,' Cassie replied with a smile, taking her friend's arm. 'He's been working like a train at home.'

'And who are you working him against today?'

'Potentially our best three-year-old, Dorin's Mist. He wouldn't be in the same league as the old Nightingale, but we've weighted the old boy up within a stone of his best against him so we'll see.'

'And what weights exactly *are* they carrying, Cassie?'

'Wouldn't you like to know?' Cassie replied with a laugh.

'Well, there's no-one here today to see him anyway,' Peter Nugent said to reassure her. 'Everyone's off hunting down in Wexford except myself and my dogs. So we have the place to ourselves. Has Dexter sat on him before today? I mean since you've started bringing The Nightingale up? I'm only asking that because the horse is giving him an awful funny look.'

They were standing by the rails overlooking the main yard now where Bridie and Liam had been getting the horse ready. Dexter, who had arrived shortly before, was making his way across to his old equine friend with whom he had shared probably the most memorable moments in the history of racing, pulling on and buckling up his crash hat while calling out friendly greetings to Liam and Bridie as well as his intended mount.

'Hey there, old boy!' Dexter called as he slipped on his riding gloves. 'You are looking just a picture of health, aren't you, you gorgeous fellow? Let's just hope you can still go as well as you look.'

While Dexter had been chatting him up, the big horse had just stood looking at him and hadn't moved. But Peter Nugent was right. There were looks and there were looks, and the one The Nightingale was giving his former jockey was baleful to say the least. Dexter noticed it and came to a standstill a few feet from the horse's head.

'Hey – what is it, fella?' he wondered, putting a hand slowly up to stroke the horse's neck. The Nightingale would have none of it, suddenly shying away and standing back on his hind legs to avoid the jockey's touch. 'It's OK, old pal,' Dexter said soothingly. 'It's OK, you know I wouldn't hurt you. Here. Here—' He put up his hand again but again the horse shied away from him, this time much more violently, pulling Bridie with him halfway across the yard, his shoes sparking against the cobbles.

'Maybe if Liam got hold of the other side of his bridle,' Peter Nugent suggested.

'He won't let Liam near him,' Cassie said. 'I'll try holding him with Bridie, but I warned Dex this would probably happen. Didn't I, Dex?'

'He'll be OK once I'm up,' Dexter said. 'Once he feels me up on him again everything will be back to normal. I'm sure it's just he doesn't trust anyone down on the ground.'

'Anyone male you mean,' Bridie corrected him. 'He used to let Liam crawl all over him, Dex, but as I told yous, Liam can't even come near his box now let alone in it.'

'I don't doubt you're right, Bridie my love,' Dexter grinned at the diminutive Bridie. 'But my job is to ride horses and the greatest part of my job has been to ride this particular horse. And I tell you – I don't give up the ride on this fella without a fight. OK? Now hold his head and hold it real good.'

With Cassie holding the horse's bridle on his offside as well as the stirrup iron to give Dexter the bext chance of getting up and staying up, and with Bridie taking a grim hold of the nearside and the left rein, Liam got ready to let the jockey up.

'Easy now, Liam,' Dexter whispered. 'On the count of three as usual, but as light as a feather. I don't want him to know I'm even in the plate. *One. Two. Three.*'

It was as if Dexter was suspended for a moment in air, so lightly did he get up and then land in the saddle. For a moment everyone thought they were there. Everyone stood holding their breath, not daring to speak or move, but they all thought they were there because the big horse had not

367

turned a hair. Dexter was in the plate with both hands on the reins, reins of which he cleverly had not yet taken proper hold so that the horse would not suddenly panic and take off.

Then suddenly and without warning the horse exploded into a frenzy of action, leaping off all four feet into the air and twisting, bucking and flykicking as he did.

'Dear Jesus God!' Liam shouted. 'Bale out, Dexter! Bale out, man, or ye'll be killed!'

Cassie had been knocked flying as had Bridie, although fortunately neither of them had been kicked. Liam had thrown himself clear when he saw the horse go up and was lying on the ground as were Cassie and Bridie while above them the horse continued to rear, buck and flykick. Somehow, miraculously, Dexter was still in the plate, sitting out everything the horse could throw at him as if he was riding the big one in a rodeo. In keeping he even had his left arm thrown out to keep balance as The Nightingale did everything in his power to dislodge him.

'In different circumstances I'd say ride him, cowboy,' Peter Nugent observed as he helped Cassie to her feet. 'What in God's name has happened to the horse?'

'In the Devil's name, you mean, Mr Nugent sir,' Liam said, getting to his feet and dusting his cap against his leg. 'If I only knew who done this to him and what they done—'

'Look out!' Bridie called. 'He's going to make a bolt for it!'

Having failed to dislodge his jockey, the horse was now cantering on the spot with his eye on the fence that contained the yard.

'Ah good and sweet Jesus,' Liam sighed, slapping his forehead with the palm of one hand. 'Sweet Jesus we'll soon see now whether or not the old horse can jump.'

Sensing The Nightingale still had the upper hand even though he had sat the bucks, the rears and the flykicks, Dexter was cool enough to sit still with a loose rein and let the horse do his worst. After all if he did clear the four-foot rail and Dexter still stayed in place all there was ahead of them both was the magnificent Nugent estate around which the horse could bolt himself silly until he was too tired or too bored to go on. So once the horse had rolled back on his hocks and started to plunge towards the fence, Dexter just got into position and waited for the outcome.

Off no more than three paces The Nightingale soared over the fence and was gone.

'Yes, yes, guv'nor,' Liam said, pulling his cap back on. 'Yes, I'd say the bugger can jump all right. He can most certainly jump.'

All four of them ran out of the yard now to see which way the horse was headed. They did not have to run very far, for no sooner had The Nightingale jumped out of the yard and looked to be taking off for the far mist-shrouded horizon than he put the brakes on, dropping a shoulder as he did so and shooting Dexter over his head to land with a heavy thud on the grass where, as the party ran towards him, he lay for a moment motionless before slowly sitting up with a hand to one shoulder.

The Nightingale, meanwhile, having at last rid himself of the man on his back, stood still on the exact spot where he had fired Dexter off, put his head down and contentedly began to take a good chew of grass.

'Goddammit!' Dexter swore. 'I think I've done a collarbone.'

While they were waiting for the ambulance Cassie had to decide whether to abort the whole exercise, which would leave her none the wiser about the horse's present capabilities, or once Dexter was safely taken care of to go ahead with Bridie riding the gallop in his place. Sensing her hesitation Dexter made her mind up for her, recommending the piece of work went ahead as planned.

'But don't let's go drawing any other conclusions,' he said with a grin. 'I've been on the ground many times. Not with Nightie, OK, I'll grant you that. But the horse could have something wrong in his back, or his pelvis. Who knows? He was as good as gold when I got up on him, then something set him off. So I say let Bridie ride the gallop and give the horse the benefit of the doubt. If it had been later in the year we'd all just think something had maybe stung him. Or maybe he simply needs a little bit of re-educating. Either way, if he works as good as he looks, I'll live to ride him on the racecourse. Don't you worry, guv'nor.'

So once Dexter had been removed by ambulance to have his collarbone attended to, the rugs which had been thrown over the two waiting horses were pulled off and Cassie legged Bridie up onto The Nightingale without the big horse's moving a muscle, much to the apparent disgust of Liam. With Liam legged up on Dorin's Mist the two horses were sent on ahead at a gentle canter to the foot of the gallops, followed by Cassie and Peter Nugent in the Range Rover.

They parked halfway up the gallop, the best vantage point to see where the serious work was to be done. Like most successful trainers Peter Nugent had two sets of gallops, an all-weather one and a grass one laid on old turf. The piece of work was to be carried out on the grass stretch since the ground was well drained and the land was drying out, it now being the second week of a fine but windy March.

'I've told Bridie just to come up alongside for the first three furlongs, and then as they start to climb to shake the horse up there—' Cassie pointed to a large white-painted pole on the side of the gallop. 'So that they'll really be stretching as they pass us. I mean it to be a proper test. If the horse is even halfway fit, at these weights he should be two to three lengths up when they reach your red marker up there, which I guess is seven furlongs?'

'Absolutely, Cassie,' Peter Nugent replied. 'As you know it's a good haul up to there, so when they pull up you'll know by how much he's blowing. You can't swing the lead galloping up here.'

As she put her race glasses up, Cassie found her hands were trembling with excitement, just as if she and her great horse were back on the racecourse again, ready to run and to thrill millions of people all around the world. She could see the horses circling at the foot of the gallops as they prepared to strike off, The Nightingale nearest her now dancing on the spot with pent-up excitement while the big bay next to him was plunging and turning as Liam tried to settle him down and get him ready.

A moment later they were off.

Exactly as instructed the two horses cantered alongside at a sensible hunting pace, their riders allowing them to settle and relax. Already Cassie could hear the sound of their pounding hooves in the still morning air, coming nearer and nearer as they swung right-handed round the first crook on the gallops and began to take the slight incline that rose up to the white marker. As soon as they passed the pole the sound of the pounding hooves quickened, a noise joined now by the audible snorting of the two galloping horses and the creak and slap of their tack. All at once they were nearly on top of Cassie and Peter Nugent, matching stride for great stride, the two big horses now really beginning to stretch as their riders asked them for their effort. The Nightingale's nostrils were flared red and his head was tucked down and cocked slightly to one side, just as it always was when he began to race in earnest, yet he hadn't shaken off the big three-year-old who was still going easily enough beside him and as the horses thundered by seemed in fact to have it over The Nightingale until Bridie shook the black horse up and called out to him, words Cassie couldn't make out and wouldn't have understood even had she caught them, for Bridie was calling to the great horse in Gaelic. As she threw him a foot of rein and pumped him just twice from the saddle, the miracle happened and the great horse picked up his bit and flew, suddenly finding another yard in his stride, kicking on up the hill and past the other horse who all at once was a spent force, an also ran, a no hoper, gone in a second from looking like a potential classic winner to looking like every other horse trounced and humbled by the mightiest racehorse in the world.

Cassie could see no more. Surreptitiously wiping tears from her eyes with the back of one hand she ran ahead of her friend after the horses whom she could see pulling up at the top of the gallops. Faster and faster she ran so that the winds would dry her eyes and bring the colour back to her cheeks. *You may be soft, my dearest love*, Tyrone had often said to her, *don't I know you're as soft as feathers, but never ever let an outsider see just how soft you are.*

'Well?' Cassie asked Bridie. But it was no good asking Bridie anything. She was in tears.

It was left to Liam to sum the gallop up. 'He's barely half fit, guv'nor,' he sighed, shaking his head. 'Listen. He's blowing like a forty a day man. Yet he's given my fella – who's no slouch now, is he? He's given my man here a stone and a half, and half fit he's buried him. I tell yous, if anyone gets wind of this, you can forget twenties. You can forget tens. You can forget odds against. If anyone gets wind of this the best price you can expect before you even enter him up is two or three or maybe even four to one *on.*'

But as Cassie stood at the top of the gallops looking at the big black horse, who despite having a good blow was still full of himself – walking easily round the circle Bridie was asking him to make, ears pricked and snorting his good health for all to hear, the odds she might or might not now get were the last thing on her mind. What was in her mind's eye now was a dream, a dream she barely recognized but a dream none the less, and the longer she stood and looked at the horse standing above her on the top of the hill, where his rider had finally pulled him up, the clearer the vision became, so clear in fact that just as the sun coming out of the clouds after a rainstorm can suddenly irradiate the entire landscape, all at once as the eye of the horse caught and looked into her own the reality of her dream was clear to her and she knew they were both on course to meet their destiny.

'Well now, Cassie, what next I wonder?' Peter Nugent said to her, having finally caught her up. 'Because I have to say here and now that what we have just seen constitutes nothing short of a miracle.'

Cassie turned to him, finally managing to break the look

between her and her magical horse. 'You're not to say a thing to anyone, Peter,' she said.

'Now I know that well enough, Cassie Rosse,' Peter replied.

'I know you know, Peter, I'm just saying it as a reminder. To remind us both. Not a word must be said of this to anyone, and most of all you're to say absolutely nothing about what I'm going to say to you, nor of what we're going to do next.'

'Done,' said Peter Nugent. 'There's not a man alive who would dare betray a woman who has a look like yours in her eyes.'

'Right,' Cassie said, trying to keep the excitement out of her voice. 'Because this is what we're going to do.'

They followed her plan exactly, her small private army of Liam, Bridie, Peter Nugent and herself, and two days later when they had the Nugent estate and gallops once more to themselves, Bridie did another piece of work with the horse, an altogether different piece of work, and Liam riding not Dorin's Mist this time but Don't Say That.

Cassie and Peter Nugent watched the schooling session from either end of a four-furlong stretch on the all-weather gallop which had been specially selected for the exercise, Nugent standing half a furlong up from the bottom of the stretch and Cassie at the top slap in the middle so that between them they could observe the two horses from behind and in front. At the very last moment as the two animals thundered towards her Cassie stepped smartly to one side and watched as they galloped safely by her, both of them going easily on the bridle but on Cassie's strict orders not taking them on.

'OK,' Cassie called as matter-of-factly as she could as Bridie and Liam swung the two horses back to face her. 'Let them have a blow, then walk them down and let them come up again, please. Exactly as you've just done, same speed and no racing.'

Just to make sure it wasn't a one-off wonder, Cassie thought to herself, pushing her hands deeply into the pockets of her padded jacket. Just to make sure what we have all seen and experienced wasn't pie in the sky.

Five minutes later the two horses came up again and this time Cassie, instead of training her race glasses on them, recorded the entire piece of work on Liam's camcorder for later analysis. Don't Say That didn't do a thing wrong, working even better than Cassie had expected he would and bolstering her hopes even more that he would give a good account of himself next week in the Triumph Hurdle at Cheltenham, but spectacular as the bright bay horse was all Cassie could finally watch was The Nightingale, who this time up not only improved on his first piece of work but was now almost pulling Bridie's arms out, so obviously unbridled was his enthusiasm.

'I have never in all my born sat on anything like that, guv'nor!' a flush-faced Bridie called after she had finally managed to pull her mount up and swing him back round to where Cassie was waiting. 'Jeez – we could have taken Liam's chap any time we wanted! We were cantering over him all the way home!'

'So you should have been,' Cassie replied, again trying to be as factual as possible. 'You're sitting on a Dual Derby winner and Liam's riding a four year novice. Now walk them both down, please, let them pick some grass down by the box when they're cool and then straight home. And not a peep out of either of you. Understood?'

What nobody understood was what happened next, nobody that is except Cassie and her friend and confidant Peter Nugent. Not even Liam or Bridie herself could comprehend what they both privately considered was their guv'nor's one moment of total insanity.

She had warned them, of course, because she felt it was the right of her loyal stable staff to hear the news first, but what she did not do was tell them one thing more than they needed at the moment to know. Since taking over the reins at Claremore, apart from the deaths of old Tomas and Sorcha, her best girl work rider leaving to get married,

374

Cassie had managed to keep her staff, an unbroken record which few stables could boast, particularly since other trainers were forever on the poach, trying to lure lads away with the promise of more money and better riding opportunities. The team at Claremore had christened themselves the Clan, which was how they thought of themselves, so proud were they of their guv'nor who, unlike other trainers, always ran her horses on their merit. They were never put in races at the wrong distance to fool the handicapper and get their weight down, nor were they ever out for the exercise. Every time a horse ran, the instructions to the jockeys were the same: put the horse in the race and give it every chance. So if a horse got beaten, it was beaten because it wasn't quite either fit or good enough. Since this was how the stable worked, when a horse was expected to win the Clan knew it and they put their money down, often helping themselves at good odds when there was an ante post list on the race, or at 'early-bird' prices, first thing in the morning when the market was forming and the bookmakers were still busy trying to pre-guess the possible favourite before the punters waded in. As a consequence there were never any complaints in the yard, nor was there any need to sell information either to rivals or, more important, to bookies.

Yet after the announcement Cassie made to them all on the eve of Cheltenham itself, even the Clan were shaken to the core and for the first time they questioned the wisdom of their governor.

Cassie knew this. Indeed if she had been in their place she would have felt exactly the same. But she also knew it was the only way forward. She knew that one more word of explanation would be too much, not because she felt that possession of all the facts might prove too much for whoever might be the weakest member of her devoted staff but because as always she believed that once something was out and made public it was up there in the ether, unseen maybe but there none the less, there for somebody who *sensed* something was up – which Cassie had always believed the phrase to mean, namely *up in the ether* – to search for until they found it. Therefore, the less said the better.

Almost everything she said to her stable staff the evening before those involved left for England and the Cheltenham Festival Cassie put in her statement to the Press, which was issued in time for the Tuesday editions of the sporting as well as the ordinary newspapers. It read:

As you know, it has always been our policy here at Claremore to keep both the press and the public up to date with all our developments. Over the past three years these have been especially concerned with one particular racehorse, The Nightingale. Because of the intense public interest in this horse we have endeavoured to keep everyone fully informed of his well-being, particularly since his kidnap. I am delighted to say that physically the horse seems to have made a full recovery from his ordeal, thanks to the skill of our veterinary surgeon Mr Niall Brogan and the love and attention of the staff here at Claremore. Without everyone's patience and devotion I doubt whether the horse could have survived. However, complete as his recovery appears to have been and while the horse is back in full work now, as his owner I feel that to ask him to return to the scene of his former triumphs in the hope of winning again would smack of going to the well once too often. I do not doubt that we could find a race for him somewhere, but I am sure his millions of fans will agree with me that what we do not want to see is this remarkable horse back on the racecourse as a shadow of his former self. I feel he has more than earned not just his living but his place in the record books, and so this is why rather than run the risk of tarnishing that record I have decided to take him out of training. In light of this decision I would like to thank everybody who has supported The Nightingale whenever and wherever he ran, and for their concern, and their good wishes when he was stolen, after he was returned, and when he so nearly died. Without you all there would have been no such horse. Everyone who loves racing creates the arena wherein our sport may take place. You have all been a vital part of The Nightingale and because you have been I feel sure you will understand why I have made this decision.

The only thing Cassie omitted to include in her statement to the Press were her final words to the Clan on the matter. *I think I know how you must be feeling*, she had said. *Probably just as I feel. Afraid, and as if all hope has gone. But just remember hope and fear are inseparable. There is no hope without fear, and no fear without hope. As my own guv'nor used to say – if hope were not, your heart should break.*

After Cassie and Liam had supervised the loading of the Cheltenham-bound horses into the aircraft which was to carry them to England, Cassie took her head lad aside and bought him a drink before it was time for him to embark.

'How has everyone taken it?'

'Ah well how would you expect, guv'nor?' he returned, sadly but without any implied criticism. 'I doubt if there was a dry pillow in the lads' hostel, and sure poor Bridie's still piping away at every given moment. But in their hearts they knows you're doing the right thing. It'd be a terrible day for the old horse if he got beat. But with respect what *I* don't understand, guv'nor, is—'

'Don't, Liam,' Cassie warned, cutting across him. 'Don't try to understand and don't ask me any questions. The decision has been made and there's no going back.'

'I don't doubt that for one moment, guv'nor,' Liam replied, turning the glass of whisky in front of him round and round on the bar. 'It's just that having come this far and with the horse working the way he was working, and then—'

'No, Liam, you're not to say one word more.' Cassie looked at him, not to warn him or to put him in his place,

377

but to make him see it wasn't necessary. Liam frowned back at her, not quite getting it yet, but beginning to hear something different in his employer's tone. 'Let me ask you something,' she continued, having called two more drinks up, another whisky for Liam and a Diet Coke for herself. 'Are you what my husband used to call a dreaming man? Do you think dreams have any value, or do you believe they're just a clearing house? Your mind getting rid of what it doesn't want?'

'The Irish aren't meant to dream until they're exiled, guv'nor. But that's not really what you're talking about, is it? To judge from the look in your eyes.' Liam finished his first whisky and pushed the glass away. 'What you're talking about is visions. Things coming to you from out of the nowhere. Somebody telling you what to do, or something showing you what's going to happen. If that's what you're referrin' to, then I am your man.'

'The trouble is, Liam, I don't see how such things are possible, yet there are all these things which people claim happen to them, out of body experiences, voices, telepathy, spiritualism. I mean, there just have to be too many stories about all these phenomena for there *not* to be something. I'm not making much sense, I guess, but what I'm trying to say is that I've seen something. I don't know where, I don't know how. I don't know whether I dreamed it, whether I imagined it, whether someone suggested it to me somehow, whether I auto-suggested, or what. All I know is that I have this conviction, a really strong conviction, and that it's propelling me on a particular course of action, and that I don't doubt what I'm doing for one single moment. Does that sound mad to you? Do you think perhaps I am mad?'

'You might have gone mad not telling anyone about it, guv'nor,' Liam replied with a grave nod. 'This concerns the horse, does it not? For there can be no other explanation.'

'I don't know what it concerns, Liam,' Cassie replied. 'Other than the future. Which, believe me, is precariously balanced, so it had all better be true.'

'So will the horse ever race again or won't he, guv'nor?'

'Come on now, Liam,' Cassie said with a quick glance at the man beside her. 'Even if he is one hundred per cent back to himself, what else is there for him to win?'

'So we're not going to get rich, then?' Liam asked with a half smile.

'We'd never have got rich that way, Liam,' Cassie replied. 'You know that. They'd never have let us get enough money down. Would they?'

'They would not,' Liam agreed, and he looked at Cassie and she smiled back at him, a sudden and very different smile, a smile that told him the heart should not yet break.

# Twenty-Four

The rains had come for Cheltenham and the raiders' hopes were high. There were twenty-two Irish entries, five of them in the first race – the Waterford Hurdle – after which hopes were even higher since the Irish horses filled the first three places. Cassie was interviewed by various sports channels regarding her own particular aspirations and while she said she considered that Well Loved had the best credentials of her three runners and therefore the best chance of adding another pot to the trophy shelf at Claremore, she thought the home-trained horses seemed a particularly talented lot this year and that she would be more than happy to take part and return home with her three entries unscathed.

In her private box while the rest of her party were down in the paddock, Cassie tuned the television to the BBC to catch the news. There was only a brief report on the trial which had opened that morning but there was film of Joel arriving at the court in the company of his lawyer. A few paces behind him, unaccompanied, in dark glasses and a huge headscarf, was the unmistakable figure of Leonora.

Cassie switched channels immediately, turning back to the racing before getting up and going down to the saddling boxes to help saddle up her first runner at the meeting, Sauce For The Goose, who was due to run in the Grand Annual Steeplechase over two miles. Terry McGuire had been booked for the ride and although he and Cassie had already talked at length on the telephone that morning about how the horse should be ridden, the two of them were still good-naturedly arguing over tactics right up to the moment Bridie folded the paddock sheet off the saddle and back onto the horse's quarters and Liam stood by to leg the jockey up.

'Even though the rain's got in the ground, Mrs Rosse, they're still going to crack on,' McGuire said. 'You saw the pace they've been going already and I'm afraid if we let him run too free he'll have nothing left for the hill.'

'On paper I know you're right, Terry,' Cassie agreed, eyeing up the opposition. 'But the only way this lad's going to be in with a squeak is if he runs them ragged. Drop him out early on and he'll sulk, I promise you. Keep taking a tug and he'll waste himself. I'll take the stick if it doesn't work, but just for me – pop him out first and let him stride on. The other thing this fella can do is jump.'

McGuire grinned, tipped his hat and, agreeing that he'd take the trainer's word for it, let Liam leg him up. The horse whipped round once, jog-trotted on the spot and then fell into line behind the other horses as the field circled the paddock once before being allowed out of the course.

Sauce For The Goose was a 10/1 shot early on, but by the time they were off, due no doubt to the lather of sweat the horse had got himself into before cantering down to the start, he had drifted to 12/1 and by the time they were running he was fairly friendless at 14/1. But McGuire was as good as his word. As soon as the starter let them go he kicked on, and coming to the first the big bright bay had already pulled himself two lengths clear.

The two of them, jockey and horse, gave a model display of jumping, meeting every one of the stiff Cheltenham fences spot on and kicking away from them as soon as they were safely landed, so much so that when they turned for home at the top of the famous hill with three left to jump Sauce For The Goose was still three lengths up on the favourite, Eddie's Treasure, who was showing every sign of finding the pace too hot, and another length clear of the second favourite, the grey Somerset Legend who had suddenly found another gear and was looking the principal danger. Of the other eight runners, four had fallen and the rest, unable to live with the pace, were all but tailed off.

Cassie could not look. She found the jumping game much harder to watch than Flat racing where once the race was on in earnest it was easier to read the action because there were no obstacles to jump. Not here, not in this game, not in the great grand sporting coliseum that was Cheltenham, where now with only two fences left to jump the crowd, particularly the Irish contingent, were beginning to go mad with excitement as three superb steeplechasers produced at the peak of their condition stood off from the penultimate fence to jump it in line. So great was the din that the racecourse commentator could hardly be heard as the leaders swung for home, Sauce For The Goose tight on the rails just where Cassie and Terry McGuire had wanted to be and was still on the bridle. And then.

Just as the Claremore horse once more began to forge ahead, Tony Gilpin, who was riding Eddie's Treasure and had somehow managed coming down the hill to conjure another run out of a seemingly beaten horse, went for his whip once more and his horse took a dive towards the rails, catching Sauce For The Goose just behind his saddle and knocking him temporarily out of his stride so that for one awful moment it looked as if the Irish horse was going to be driven into the wing of the fence. To prevent this McGuire took a pull, straightening his horse as he checked him and miraculously still finding not only a stride but the right stride into the last fence.

But the big bay had lost his advantage and jumped the last half a length down on Eddie's Treasure and almost a length on Somerset Legend who landed full of running. Still the crowd roared the Irish horse on, refusing to believe he was beat, and once again the horse Cassie had considered might be a little short on guts rallied, sticking his head and neck out to gallop for all he was worth up the hill, the famous hill that for generations had sorted out the men from the boys. Ahead of him Eddie's Treasure was suddenly beaten, and as the steam went so he veered sharp right across the broad course, leaving McGuire and his mount a clear run after the still galloping grey who by now was all of two lengths up with less than half a furlong to race. How the home crowd cheered their horse home and how the raiders cheered the challenger, with a noise that must have echoed to the top of Cleeve Hill and beyond. With less than fifty yards to run, Sauce For The Goose was half a length down, with twenty to go he was a neck, with five a short head and as they passed the post no-one could separate them.

'Photograph!' the racecourse commentator called. 'Photograph between numbers three and nine! Photograph!'

So close was it the judge called for a second print and didn't announce his decision until both horses were back in the unsaddling enclosure, steaming like kettles under their sweat sheets. Neither of the two trainers nor their jockeys had the slightest idea which horse had prevailed nor for once did the bookmakers, who went 9/4 on either horse getting the race. Still no announcement came until the crowd began to chant *dead-heat! Dead-heat!* Just as it seemed that must indeed be the result a voice over the tannoy announced the judge's final verdict.

'Here is the result of the photograph for the Grand Annual Steeplechase Challenge Cup. First number three, second number nine.' The rest of the announcement was all but lost in the uproar as the English horse was announced the winner. Cassie smiled at Fred her travelling head lad but he only shook his head with disappointment as she went forward to pat her gallant loser on the neck and to give a hug and a kiss to her equally gallant losing owners, John and Mavis Finnegan.

'The distances—' the voice on the tannoy continued, 'the distances were a short head and six lengths.'

Michael Bird, one of the senior Lambourn trainers who had done a remarkable job to produce the apparently accident-prone Somerset Legend to win in such an exciting fashion, was the first to commiserate with the Claremore party, saying that in a race such as their horses had just run there could be no losers and inviting Sauce For The Goose's connections for a celebratory drink in his party's box, as the officials called *Horses Away!* and the two protagonists were led off by their lads to yet another round of generous applause.

*     *     *

When Cassie finally arrived back at the house outside Stow where she was the guest of two of her owners, Willoughby and Dorothy Manderson, it was snowing.

'Hope we're not going to have a repeat of that farcical Gold Cup day a few years ago,' Willoughby said, pouring Cassie a drink with one eye on the television news. 'Remember? Delayed the race for hours then ran it in a blizzard. What a business.'

'Turn that wretched thing off, Willy,' Dorothy ordered her husband as she piled yet more logs onto the fire. 'All it is nowadays is news, more news and yet more news. As if there wasn't enough to worry about.'

'I don't know whether this chap's going to get off or not, you know,' Willoughby replied more to himself than anyone as he stood right in front of the tiny television set which was balanced precariously on a pile of books. 'The one who's meant to have helped his old man shuffle off the mortal coil. Not as clear-cut as it appeared, so it seems.'

'Don't you know him, Cassie dear?' Dorothy wondered, trying to find some space for them both to sit on a huge sofa covered in dogs. 'Isn't he that chap they commissioned to do your horse or something? For Sandown?'

'Yes he is,' Cassie answered as lightly as she could before turning her attention back to her host. 'Why don't you think he's going to get off, Willy?'

'Slimy Simon Watkins had a go at him today, that's why,' Willoughby answered.

'Once a judge always a judge,' Dorothy sighed, finally shoehorning two lurchers off the sofa and settling herself down.

'Don't like Watkins one bit I have to say,' Willoughby continued regardless of his wife's observation. 'But he is a damn' good counsel when he's found a bone.'

'Exactly what sort of bone has he found, Willy?' Cassie asked, trying to catch a glimpse of the flickering television screen past her portly host.

'I used to much prefer it when they only had the news on at eight or ten or whenever it was,' Dorothy sighed, throwing a dog-chewed rubber duck onto the floor. 'I can't stand it on the hour every half hour. Really I can't.'

'Hmmm,' Willoughby mused for a moment before switching the television off altogether. 'Yes,' he said, turning to Cassie and looking at her over his spectacles. 'It won't add up to much but it'll give the jury food for thought. Depending on his lordship's summing up, natch, and there's another thing. I wouldn't have said he was the ideal man for this particular job anyway, come to that.'

'Please,' Cassie said, breathing in deeply to try to calm the sudden feeling of fear inside her. 'First things first, Willy. The bone the prosecuting counsel found.'

'Ah yes. Yes. Yes. Indeed. Seems—'

'Jolly good sculptor as it happens, Willy, but don't let that stop you,' his wife interrupted.

'Seems like he has this nightclub, you understand. And it ran into some financial difficulty, as these places do indeed, as indeed they do. Slimy Simon argued that's why this painter laddy—'

'Sculptor, Willy,' Dorothy sighed hopelessly, putting a wildly trembling whippet on her knee.

'Slimy Simon argued that's why this chap slipped his old man a mickey,' Willoughby continued. 'Seems his father was worth enough to get him out of his debt. Seems he stood to inherit about a quarter of a mill. Think it's hooey meself, but it's bound to cast some doubt, one would have to say. Depends of course what his side comes back with. They've already denied it, of course, but we'll need to see proof of some sort which will discount profit as a motive. But it's not looking as open and shut as one would have thought. Particularly not with old beaky Bower presiding.'

'He's an anti-Exit man, is he, Willy?' Cassie wondered. 'You know, against anyone lending a hand.'

'He's against most things I'd say,' Willoughby laughed. 'Particularly anything *après circa* 1900. If we still had capital punishment he'd be hanging chaps for loitering with intent.'

'Well all I can say is that I jolly well hope there's someone like this chap round me when my time comes,' Dorothy said, stroking her still trembling whippet. 'Now come along, drink up, you lot. Time to get the head in the manger.'

For the rest of the evening Cassie tried to put all thought of Joel from her head. After all, since he had not bothered to reply to her letter and she had seen him arriving at his trial with Leonora apparently in attendance, it would seem that he had little or no need of her. Yet try as she might she could not put her concern to one side, particularly once she was alone in bed – except for one of the whippets who was determined to share her eiderdown.

*This is preposterous*, she thought as she lay with her light still on, stroking the dog's head. *Either Joel is out of my life altogether or he's not. I made a vow, did I not? That if he didn't answer the letter or give a good reason for Leonora's being there that night, then that was it. So what in heaven's name am I doing lying here and agonizing about what happens to him? At the very worst he'll get a suspended sentence and that will be that. Then he can go back to his precious club, his studio, and his obviously precious Leonora.*

She put her bedside light out and turned on one side, her bed companion happily settling into her with a deeply contented sigh. *Oh, if only men were as easy as you dogs*, Cassie whispered to the animal, who at once stuck a paw up to be held. But tired as she was after the excitement of the day, sleep would not come, and unfuriatingly enough all she could see whenever she shut her eyes was Joel. Joel at Claremore sitting in front of the fire, the glass of whisky in his hand catching the glint of the firelight, Joel walking the course at Ascot, Joel returning from his shopping spree in Bantry, Joel routing the restaurant owner, Joel at the kitchen table in her house on Dingle, Joel in bed asleep with his face half turned to her, one arm crooked up over his head, Joel in bed face down and her in bed face up with one of his arms draped over her waist.

Most of all, she saw Joel in her dreams, mangled, tangled, sometimes only half himself, wholly unreal, but he was with her all night long.

When she woke and was bathed and dressed she found Willoughby already up reading the morning papers.

'Do you have such a thing as a fax machine?' she wondered. 'As well as some sort of legal directory with the numbers of law firms in it?'

Her host took her into his study where from underneath a pile of papers and documents he uncovered an early model of a telephone fax before handing her the required directory.

'Don't ask me how it works,' he said as he left the room. 'I only ever use it for incoming whatsanames.'

Cassie found the number she needed and then wrote a fax on a plain sheet of notepaper she found in a desk drawer.

*I am thinking of you*, she wrote. *Whatever you are thinking of – and it must be a considerable amount of things – I am thinking of you throughout your ordeal and praying for the just and proper outcome I know you deserve. Cassie.*

She put no number or address on the sheet which she then faxed under a header sheet to Joel's QC, marked for the attention of Mr Benson.

When the message had been transmitted she read it back and sighed.

There were eleven runners for the three mile Sun Alliance Steeplechase, for which Well Loved, the Claremore runner, was firm favourite. The snow had stopped during the previous evening, leaving just a light mantle on the distant hills around the racecourse, a powdering which very soon melted in the sudden warmth of full sunshine just before racing started. Terry McGuire had been once more booked to ride, but Cassie saw little need for long instructions since he had ridden the young horse to each of his three victories.

'Theatre Royal will probably make it, according to Frankie Taplin his jock,' Terry McGuire said as he adjusted the silk cap covering his crash hat. 'But I'd say the danger is Sheepshank. That's who I'm going to keep tabs on, anyway.'

Fully in agreement with her pilot's assessment Cassie

wished him good luck and a safe journey as Fred legged McGuire into the plate.

'If I were you, Terry,' Fred said back over his shoulder as he took hold of the bridle, 'I'd also keep a look-out for Good On You, the McMahon horse. I heard they're queuing up to collect already.'

Cassie looked round to take another look at her Irish-trained rival and saw Mattie for the first time during the meeting, legging Tom Collins up and then standing back to talk to the trainer who was beside him in a wheelchair. She thought she had caught his eye, but apparently Mattie hadn't seen her for a moment later he had turned away to follow McMahon out of the paddock.

'On all form we must have the beating of the McMahon horse, surely?' Leslie Unwin the owner of Well Loved asked Cassie. 'We buried Next in Line at Leopardstown and he had Good On You ten lengths adrift in Punchestown.'

'I agree with Terry,' Cassie replied. 'I'd say Sheepshank's the real danger.'

As the race unfurled they might as well have saved their predictions since Sheepshank clouted the second fence so hard his jockey had no chance of maintaining contact and was catapulted yards clear of his mount on landing the far side of the fence where he was duly trampled on by most of the pursuing horses. Happily the jockey got up almost immediately, throwing his whip to the ground in enraged despair as he stood helplessly watching the field disappear away from the fence. Coming down the hill for the first time Good On You almost slipped on landing at the fence before the turn into the straight, Tom Collins losing a leather and a good six lengths as a result and leaving Terry McGuire just where he didn't want to be, namely in the lead by a clear three lengths.

'He can't make all,' Cassie groaned as she watched through her glasses. 'He hates it out front.'

'Take a pull, Terry,' Leslie Unwin shouted at the top of his voice. 'Take a pull, you ejeet!'

Almost immediately McGuire did as told, as if out of all the thousand roars assailing his ears as they jumped what would be the last fence next time round and began the climb up the hill and away from the packed grandstand he had picked up the owner's single instruction. In return Well Loved did as he was bid and steadied, allowing two of the unfancied horses to charge up past him and give him a good tow going to the next which he jumped fluently if somewhat flamboyantly. Behind him Good On You was second to last and apparently to judge from his action not liking the soft going.

The field which were still all on their feet bar Sheepshank streamed into the back straight almost in a line, with Bishop's Mitre leading, followed by Draughty, Pile On The Cash, and then Well Loved who was back on the bridle and going well within himself, Terry McGuire perched up on him still as a field mouse with a lovely loose loop of rein.

'Bar a fall,' Leslie Unwin said in Cassie's ear. 'We have them bar a fall.'

To the Claremore party this seemed to be completely the right assessment since their horse was literally lobbing along while the rest of the field were already being hard ridden to keep in a race which had been run at a cracking gallop for a three mile steeplechase. Over the last open ditch they lost Draughty, who simply seemed to miss seeing the notoriously difficult fence altogether and crashed to the ground just in front of Well Loved who simply sidestepped him without losing impetus as the field then turned and swept down the famous hill for the last time. Now McGuire began to make his move, creeping up on Bishop's Mitre with every stride until as they lined up for the fence at the bottom of the hill he was half a length off the leader. Into the air they rose almost together, but even before they landed Cassie could see Bishop's Mitre had met it all wrong, having been forced by McGuire's tactics to take off half a stride earlier than perhaps the horse had wanted. As a result he caught the top of the fence, twisted in the air and plunged to the ground as his front legs buckled under him, bringing Well Loved down with him in the process.

A huge wail went up from the Irish contingent as they

saw their banker for the meeting brought down just as it seemed he had the race won, while past the two horses who were still on the ground came Pile On The Cash and going best of all Good On You, whose jockey had got him right back in the race along the back straight. But Cassie wasn't watching the race any more. Her glasses were trained on the accident on the landing side of the downhill fence where neither of the jockeys not their horses showed any signs of moving.

'He may well just be badly winded,' Cassie said to her owner who had gone as white as a sheet.

'He's not moving,' Leslie Unwin replied. 'There's not a sign of any movement at all.'

'Really,' Cassie tried to reassure him as well as herself. 'He really could just be very badly winded.'

Somewhere beyond there was a sea of noise cascading around and over the Claremore party, but they heard and saw nothing except the casualties. Already the St John's Ambulance men were on the course with the jockeys as were some officials, one of whom was waving a flag to summon the veterinary surgeon in attendance, while on the inside of the course an ambulance proper sped its way to the scene.

'I'm going down,' Cassie said to her owner. 'You stay here.'

'I'd rather come with you,' he replied. 'Hell or high water.'

The two of them fought their way down through the crowd, which was moving in the opposite direction now that the race was over. Somehow they got down to the track leading from the course up which the victorious and the vanquished would soon be coming, and made their way over to the far side before they were swept away by a tide of Irish supporters who were all shouting their throats raw. Cassie paid them no heed, her mind only on getting to her horse, and grabbing Leslie Unwin's hand she pulled him after her, shouting for everyone in front of her to make way. For some reason the crowds fell away from them, as if reading on their faces the disaster that Cassie and her owner thought must await them, and the next moment they were on the racecourse proper, bolting on towards where Cassie now saw the dreaded screens being pulled around the site where the stricken horses lay.

'Leslie—' she began, half turning to the man beside her, determined once more to turn him back.

'Hell or high water, Cassie,' he repeated grimly. 'Owning a horse means just that. Come hell or high water.'

There were still people on the rails, leaning over as far as they could to get a better view of the death which was to come. Other more sensitive racegoers led each other away. As Cassie and her owner drew nearer, Cassie could see the vet opening the box which she knew contained his humane killer when from behind the screens she suddenly saw the mud-splattered figure of Terry McGuire appear, with Well Loved's racing saddle draped over one arm.

'Terry!' she called. 'Terry – tell them to hold on!'

But even as he caught sight of her it was too late. The dull thud of the bolt being fired into a horse's skull carried downwind to where Cassie and Leslie Unwin had slowed suddenly to a shocked walk.

'Oh Christ no,' Leslie Unwin sighed from the bottom of his heart. 'Oh Christ no please no, Christ please no.'

Cassie looked at him but his eyes were fast closed to try to prevent the tears which were still managing to trickle out between the lids. Then with a squeeze of his hand she left him and walked on up the hill to where her jockey was waiting, bent over double now as if caught again with a sudden pain.

The vet stepped out from behind the screen. 'Are you the owner?' he asked quietly, but then seeing who was confronting him he corrected himself. 'I'm sorry, Mrs Rosse,' he said. 'I didn't see who it was.'

'Obviously you had no option?' she asked in an empty voice.

'Broke his back, I'm afraid,' the vet replied, fetching a pack of cigarettes from his pocket. 'Poor old chap.'

'And the other horse?' Cassie asked.

The vet looked up at her and smiled briefly as he lit his

cigarette. 'Your horse?' he said. 'He was just very badly winded, thank God.'

Why she had not seen him Cassie failed to realize, for when she looked the other side of the screen there large as life and looking doubly sorry for himself was Well Loved with a great slide of mud down the side of his face, another along his flanks and blood trickling from a cut somewhere above his nearside hock. Lying on the ground between Cassie and her horse was the corpse of poor Bishop's Mitre covered with a heavy green tarpaulin with his heartbroken lad sitting on the grass still holding the dead horse by its reins, weeping his heart out.

'Come on, guv'nor.' Terry McGuire had come back to fetch her, putting a muddy-mittened hand on her sleeve to ease her away from the tragic sight. 'Come on, there's no point in you standing there now. What's done is done.'

'And you're coming back in the ambulance with us, McGuire!' one of the ambulance men called. 'You jocks – you think you're made of cast iron! Come on, Terry!'

'It's OK, guv'nor,' her jockey said, squeezing her arm. 'These things happen. The other side of coin, you know?'

Cassie nodded. She did know.

Later, after the Claremore horse had been led back, washed down and put away in his box, Cassie finally learned the result of the race. It had been won by Good On You, trained by Tom McMahon, assisted by Mattie Rosse.

At once she went in search of her son to congratulate him on his mentor's success, finding him after a brief search in the crowded Arkle Bar where he was still drinking with the horse's connections which naturally included Tom McMahon.

'Ah, so there you are, Cassie!' the trainer called from his wheelchair in the corner of the bar. 'Come on and let me buy you a consolation jar!'

Mattie glanced round from where he was leaning on the bar when he heard his mother's name called and nodded back in acknowledgment of her wave.

'Well done, Tom,' Cassie said after she had fought her

way across to the party. 'I didn't see the actual finish, I'm afraid, because I was haring off to see how our horse was. So did he win nicely?'

'An ever-diminishing neck,' Tom McMahon replied, 'but he's a battler if nothing else, and once he has his old head in front, he likes to try to keep it there. But we'd never have won it if your chap hadn't been brought down. Here – have some champagne.'

Cassie accepted the glass on offer and turned to congratulate her son.

'Thanks,' he said without much grace. 'But thanks for nothing really.'

'I don't understand,' Cassie said, as Mattie looked over her shoulder to raise his glass to someone behind her. 'Everyone says he's your horse in all but name. That Tom gave him to you to train on as soon as he'd set you up, because the horse was a rogue. So you must take a lot of credit.'

'Oh sure,' Mattie said, still without any semblance of enthusiasm. 'I straightened out his jumping all right, but we should never have beaten your horse. Our horse isn't within a stone of yours.'

'Maybe not,' Cassie agreed. 'But that's racing, particularly racing over the fences. Maybe if Terry hadn't taken him on into the fence—'

'Too right,' Mattie interrupted, knocking back his whisky and calling for another. 'Was that his idea or yours?'

'I don't see that matters,' Cassie said with a frown. 'I'd have thought you'd have been delighted to beat our fellow.'

'I would have been. I would have been thrilled sick if I hadn't backed him.'

'You backed Well Loved?'

'Come on,' Mattie replied, taking his fresh drink and handing over the money for it. 'You knew as well as I did he couldn't get beat.'

'But he did get beat.'

'Only because McGuire took him on at the wrong time! If you'd told him to wait until the last, your horse would have won doing cartwheels up the hill! He had gallons left in the tank!'

'You're talking through your pocket, Mattie.'

'Of course I'm talking through my pocket. I've just got very badly burnt. Roasted, in fact.'

Cassie stared at her son. She had never seen him so furious, nor quite so obviously determined to become belligerently drunk. 'Come here,' she said, taking his arm and pulling him away from his party so that she could talk to him in confidence over by the doorway. 'How much did you have on?'

'More than I could afford,' Mattie replied. 'I backed him before he even ran, after we'd finished schooling him. Liam said he was the best young jumper of fences he'd ever seen with the toe of a Flat horse. If ever there's a Sun Alliance horse that's him, he said, so we both went and got a price for a run at Cheltenham and waded in. We got thirty-three to one and I don't know about Liam but I backed him all the way down to starting price.'

'So how much did you have on?' Cassie persisted grimly. 'You know what I told you about betting, Mattie. Whatever your father might have done or not done.'

'Like father like son, eh?' Mattie said with what Cassie thought was more than a trace of irony.

'How much did you have on?' she repeated, ignoring her son's tone.

'If you really want to know,' Mattie sighed, looking down at her over his glass, 'I lost the lot. I have just lost two thousand quid.'

For a moment, a long moment, Cassie was unable to believe what she had just heard. Sensing this, Mattie nodded at her and widened his eyes. 'No,' he said, in a tone of mock reassurance, 'it's true. You are looking at someone who has lost every last penny of his savings.'

'You're mad,' she said quietly. 'Stark staring mad. You know far too much about racing and horses and what can go wrong to have gambled like that. You're mad.'

'Like father,' Mattie repeated with that same look in his eye. 'Anyway, it's all gone. Thanks to you and your jockey.'

Cassie was just about to tell Mattie that Tyrone had been the modicum of sobriety when she suddenly remembered how wild and reckless Mattie's real father had been.

'So what are you going to do?' she asked instead. 'I can't bail you out.'

'I don't want you to *bail me out*, Ma,' Mattie returned sarcastically.

'So what are you going to do?'

'I'm going to have to stay in nights, aren't I? Until I can afford to play around again. Now if you'll excuse me, *Mother*, I have a party to attend to.'

Mattie tried to push past her, but Cassie grabbed him by the arm and held him tight. 'You're not going anywhere until you tell me what all this is about,' she said angrily. 'I will not be treated like this. I mean it.'

'Like what, *Mother*?'

'Like this, Mattie. Like the way you have been treating me recently. I won't have it, do you hear? What have I done to deserve it, you just tell me that?'

'I'm not really too well placed to answer that, I'd say,' Mattie replied, trying to shake himself free of her hold.

'I can't think of anyone better,' Cassie said, holding on to him fast. 'And what for instance is all this *mother* bit for? I know you've lost a lot of money, Mattie, but at the same time I'm quite sure you haven't taken leave of your senses.'

'No I haven't,' Mattie replied coldly. 'But in the circumstances it wouldn't have been any surprise if I had.'

'In what circumstances? I don't understand what you mean,' Cassie said.

'In that case, *Mother*, why don't you ask your good old friend Leonora? Now if you'll excuse me?'

This time Mattie managed to wrench his arm free from Cassie's grip and, with a last look at her through narrowed eyes, he fought his way back through the crowded bar to rejoin his party.

Hurt and bewildered, Cassie stood for a moment watching as the boy she had loved and nursed since he was six weeks old hurried to get away from her. Realizing this was neither the time nor the place for anything further she turned to go, only to come face to face and almost collide with a large red-faced woman who was standing right behind her.

'I'm so sorry,' Cassie said, standing to one side.

'And so you ought,' the woman replied belligerently. 'Mrs Win At Any Price Rosse.'

'I'm sorry, do I know you?' Cassie asked, looking carefully at the quite obviously drunk woman. 'I don't think I do, do I?'

'I know you all right,' the woman assured her. 'Mrs Win At Any Price Rosse.'

Cassie looked round behind her, longing for some protection but too proud to enlist it from a stranger. 'Excuse me,' Cassie said, trying to get past the woman. 'Will you please get out of my way?'

'Like you wanted our horse to? At the second last?' the woman wondered. 'What are you going to do? Same sort of thing, eh? Barge us out of the way? Because I'd like to see you try it.'

'Will you just tell me what all this is about?' Cassie asked, looking from her reddened face to that of her equally drunk companion with a sickening feeling that she knew already.

'Your bloody jockey half-lengthed our horse, that's what it's about, you stupid bitch,' the woman seethed. 'Riding to orders, no doubt, because that's the way you like to run your horses, Mrs Win At Any Price Rosse, isn't it?'

'If you're talking about the fall at the second last—' Cassie began.

'Too damn right she is,' the man said, pushing his way alongside the woman. By now their altercation was attracting considerable attention in the blocked doorway of the bar. 'Like my wife just said, your bloody jockey half-lengthed us. If he hadn't – and sod the result, I'm not talking about the bloody result—'

'Quite right, Bri,' the woman agreed. 'Sod the bloody result.'

'Like I was saying,' the man continued. 'If your bloody horse and smart-arse jockey hadn't forced that mistake out of us by half-lengthing us at that fence, our old chap'd still be alive now.'

'I'm sorry about your horse,' Cassie said, knowing for sure she was being taken on by the owners of the late Bishop's Mitre.

'You're sorry,' the woman snorted. 'Sorry, indeed. The only thing you're ever sorry about is when you get beat, like all Americans.'

'I am genuinely sorry about your horse,' Cassie continued. 'But I assure you Terry McGuire was not riding to instructions, and of all the jockeys riding over fences right now Terry McGuire's the last man who'd half-length anyone.'

'You know, if I was a man and you were a man I'd bust your bloody nose.'

Her companion put a restraining hand on her shoulder.

'I'm really sorry about your horse,' Cassie said once more. 'But that's steeplechasing, I guess. It could just as easily have been my horse, you know. And if you really think I'd risk a horse as good as Well Loved by asking him to be ridden like a point to pointer, I have to say you have it all wrong.'

'No, lady,' the man said, looking at Cassie with hard cold grey eyes. 'No, you're the one who's got it all wrong. This is a man's game. Women should stay behind in the kitchen with their pots and pans. Come on, Dor.' He put his arm round his wife's waist to lead her away, but the woman wasn't quite finished.

'Mrs Win At Any Price Rosse,' she repeated once more. 'God knows what you stuffed into that famous horse of yours to get him to win all those races, but you know what I think? I think whoever stole him off you was doing the horse a favour.'

They were gone now, pushing their way through a crowd of people who had turned to watch the confrontation. Cassie looked at the ocean of faces and all she could see was backs. As she herself turned now to go she wondered who, if anyone, would have come to her aid had she been attacked.

*I guess no-one*, she said to herself as she walked out of the famous bar. Perhaps not even her son.

The day wasn't quite done with her yet, however. When she got back to the Mandersons' it began to pour with rain, a fall which continued all night and into the morning, changing the going on the racecourse from good to soft to heavy. Knowing how much Don't Say That hated the mud, as soon as she woke and saw how the rain had got into the ground Cassie rang the horse's owner and reluctantly they both agreed to withdraw the 3/1 favourite for the Triumph Hurdle.

# Twenty-Five

With no runners on Gold Cup day, and because the memory of her altercation the previous afternoon had somehow managed to sour the whole meeting for her, Cassie decided to give the last day of the Festival a miss and go to London instead. When he heard her reason for going, Willoughby Manderson offered to accompany her. Since neither the Mandersons nor Cassie had a runner that day and because the weather had turned so particularly foul her host was glad to forgo the doubtful pleasures of being soaked to the skin and Cassie was only too happy to accept his offer.

'I've always hated courts at the best of times,' Cassie admitted as they began the drive to London. 'Even just as a spectator I always feel as if in some way I'm on trial as well. You know, one false move and you're in contempt.'

'Good,' Willoughby agreed, trying it seemed to remember how to work his car's demister. 'Anyway I'll be able to open a few doors, get us the best seats, all that sort of thing. As well as help you understand the old fool's summing up. Because today's the day. All things being equal Lord Chief Justice Bower should get to his summation after lunch.'

'What's the betting?'

'On the outcome? Mmmm. As I was saying last night at dinner, the defence kicked the killing for profit theory well and truly into touch for sure.'

'By showing that the debts on the club had all been settled before the defendant's father died,' Cassie recalled.

'Certainly caught the prosecution on the hop,' Willoughby agreed, giving a happy sigh as he found the correct way to work the demister, much to Cassie's relief since for the last half a mile or so the car had been veering all over the road. 'Sloppy homework by Slimy Simon's team maybe,' the former judge continued. 'Either that or the defence simply had it up their sleeve all the time. Anyway, certainly doesn't look like a hanging job.'

'That isn't funny, Willy,' Cassie said, 'and you know it.'

'Certainly wouldn't have been in the old days,' Willoughby agreed. 'Best thing that happened, abolishing the death penalty. Like I said, Bower's the sort of chap who if he had his way would hang shoplifters.'

For some reason Cassie's heart sank. Having listened carefully to everything her host had said over dinner the previous night she thought the prosecution had little or no case left in their pursuit for a conviction either for man-slaughter or murder in any degree, so watertight had been the case for the defence so far, yet still she felt less than optimistic about the possible verdict. She knew enough about the law to realize that even if Judge Bower was finally convinced that this had not been in any way a murder for gain, profit or revenge he might still decide to instruct the jury to regard the case as one of suicide by arrangement, and if he did so Joel would not leave the court a free man.

'I wonder who the anonymous donor was who bailed the club out of trouble,' Cassie thought out loud as Willoughby looked for a way to join the motorway traffic.

'Doesn't really matter, you know,' Willoughby replied, finally entering the motorway via the hard shoulder, a move which earned him a cacophony of screaming car horns and a light show of flashing headlights. 'Academic, really. All that was necessary was to prove by way of bank statements and the club's books that the money had gone through prior to Benson's demise and Bob was the famous uncle.'

'Even so,' Cassie muttered, 'I have a pretty shrewd idea of who it could have been.'

Mrs Charles C. Lovett Andrew, however, was not called as a character witness. There was no need for her testimony. Joel's defence had already organized some influential and highly respectable names to come forward and testify as to the character of the accused, depositions to which Cassie sat and listened with a well-concealed but ever-growing interest.

'Chap's a saint from the sound of it,' Willoughby muttered beside her. 'Shows how deceptive appearances can be. Looks more like an ageing new age traveller.'

Cassie smiled and leaned forward in her seat, hoping once again that Joel would finally sense her presence and turn to look her way. But he was sitting absolutely still beside his counsel with his arms folded, staring up at the ceiling high above him as if trying to detach himself from the events going on around him. From somewhere he had managed to conjure up a dark suit but judging from the fact that it was far too large for him and seemed to fit him nowhere at all it appeared not to be one of his own. On the other hand the old crumpled dark rust-coloured shirt was very much his own as Cassie well knew, having wondered out loud often enough whether Joel had anything else to wear except the same old pair of chinos, same old dark blue sweater and same old rust-coloured shirt. But the tie, dark blue with slender sky blue stripes, she had never seen before, at least not on him. She had seen it many times on genuine Old Etonians, but not on Joel who she seemed to remember had been to a considerably more liberal school.

He had also made an effort to control his famously unruly mop of hair, brushing it back away from his forehead and watering it into place. Unfortunately despite his obviously good intentions the end result was more or less as Willoughby Manderson had described a moment before. Far from looking a respectable pillar of the Establishment, Joel had somehow succeeded in making himself look the very opposite, which was obviously the conclusion Justice Bower had also reached, to judge from his summation.

'Thought your pal was home and hosed, Cassie,' Willoughby said as they wandered the streets outside after the jury had retired. 'Now I'm not so sure. Old fool's gone and directed them to find for assisted suicide exactly as one feared he might, and he couldn't have made his wishes known more clearly to the jury. Not over bar a fall by a long way, I'm afraid.'

'Yes, but surely, given the climate of opinion nowadays, Willy,' Cassie argued, 'as well as the quite considerable amount of precedent, as you were saying—'

'Nothing on the statute book as yet, old girl. Far as the law goes, with the exception of a proper directive being given to turn off life support, yes? As far as the law goes, taking a life even in mercy is still agin it.'

'Only technically, surely?' Cassie asked, trying to keep the anxiety out of her voice. 'In a case like this, even if the jury follows its instructions and finds against the defendant, surely the judge is only going to impose a suspended sentence? Leastways that's the way cases like this have all been going in the last few years.'

'Don't count your chickens, old girl,' Willoughby returned. 'As far as the law goes, don't count your chickens until they're cooked and on the table. Particularly not as far as old booby Bower's concerned.'

The jury were out for just under two hours. While they were waiting Willoughby went to pay some courtesy calls to some old colleagues who were in attendance at the Law Courts while Cassie, leaving word where she was going, found a nearby betting shop and watched two races from Cheltenham on SIS. The clerk Willoughby had deputized to act as their runner came to tell her the jury were on their way back in as the runners for the Gold Cup were leaving the parade ring. Cassie and Willoughby both made it back to the court just in time to hear the verdict.

'On the charge of first degree murder we find the defendant not guilty,' the foreman announced, a decision which was immediately greeted with a victorious whoop by the euthanasia lobby up in the gallery. Judge Bower immediately banged his gavel and demanded complete silence.

'That was a given,' Willoughby whispered. 'No-one was going to convict your chum of murder. Not even his nibs.'

'On the charge of manslaughter,' the foreman continued, 'we also find the defendant not guilty.'

This verdict was greeted with even larger whoops of joy from the group above Cassie and Willoughby, an outbreak which took a quite considerable amount of energetic gavel banging by Judge Bower to silence.

'On the charge of assisting a suicide—' the foreman paused and glanced at his fellow jurors with what looked to Cassie like a perfectly obvious expression of regret.

'Yes, Mr Foreman?' Judge Bower prompted. 'And what is your verdict, please?'

'On the charge of assisting a suicide we find the defendant guilty as charged.'

During the ensuing uproar Willoughby turned to Cassie and put a hand on her forearm. 'It's still only a technicality,' he said over the noise. 'Whatever my doubts, it really will be most unfortunate as well as highly unfair if the old fool decides to try to make an example. Believe me.'

But far from feeling reassured Cassie felt only fear. While everyone around her was vociferously denouncing the verdict she was watching Judge Bower, watching his face tighten as he banged his gavel relentlessly, watching his eyes narrow as he observed the disorder in his court. She knew even before he got the silence he demanded and spoke that a token sentence was the thing that was furthest from his mind.

'Prisoner at the bar,' he began. 'You have been found guilty by a jury of your peers of assisting in a suicide and according to the letter of the law for this you must be punished. The law states unequivocally that it is wrong to give assistance to anyone who wishes to take their own life, whatever their circumstances and whatever their physical condition, and for those found guilty of such a crime the maximum recommended sentence is one of fourteen years.' Judge Bower paused, as if to make quite sure his message was getting home as indeed to judge by the utter silence of the courtroom it most certainly was. 'However,' he continued, looking back once more at Joel who was still staring up at the ceiling above him. 'However, taking into account the conditions of this particular case, along with the notable testimonies as to your good character collected on your behalf by your learned counsel, you may be relieved to hear that I have no intention of passing any such sentence on you.'

Willoughby nudged Cassie in the arm as if to reassure her while everyone in the court room seemed to exhale audibly with relief.

'None the less—' Judge Bower continued, raising his voice above the murmurs, '*none the less* I do not intend to allow you to walk away from this court a free man. I will not countenance people taking the law into their own hands without qualified guidance, as you did in this particular instance. You have broken the letter of the law and those who stand *in flagrante* must expect some form of retribution, otherwise the law will stand mocked. I therefore sentence you to four years in gaol—'

The rest of what Judge Bower had to say was lost in the uproar which immediately followed on his shock pronouncement. While an attempt to restore some order was made, Cassie found herself on her feet staring down at Joel who was still sitting exactly as he had been for the past few minutes, staring up at the ceiling with his arms folded across his chest.

The usher as well as the judge was calling for silence, but the order was lost and ignored in the furore that had broken out. Finally, in response to a good ten seconds' worth of gavel hammering a semblance of silence fell as the outraged public retook their seats as directed by the judge, who also advised everyone that he considered all present to be in contempt of court. Undeterred, someone shouted a well-deserved remark at the judge questioning both his intelligence and his birthright.

'He'll need an armoured car to get out of this place,' Willoughby muttered. 'But there you are. Some mothers have the brutes, yes?'

'As I was saying, prisoner at the bar, before I was so rudely interrupted,' Judge Bower continued, fixing Joel with what Cassie took as an ironic smile. 'The sentence I have chosen to pass on you is that you shall be detained for a period of four years, with the recommendation that you serve one of those years in a prison to be selected, and that the other three years be suspended, the further time only to be served should you be found to be in any breach of the regulations governing the behaviour of criminals in Her Majesty's gaols. Take the prisoner down. This court is now dismissed.'

In vain Cassie tried to catch Joel's eye as he stood up slowly, but unsurprisingly instead of looking up he was now staring down at the floor and slowly shaking his head in seeming disbelief. In desperation Cassie called out to him, but such still was the noise that he could not have heard her because as the police on either side of him began to lead him down from the dock he was still staring downwards. At the last moment, just as Cassie was about to call him at the top of her voice, he looked up and catching sight of her stopped. The escorting police stopped too, realizing that their prisoner had caught sight of someone, and then they too looked up so that all three men were staring up at her at once.

But only one looked at her with any emotion other than idle curiosity. As Joel stared back into her eyes Cassie felt her breath catch in her throat. Neither of them did anything except look – they made no gesture, mouthed no message. They just stared into each other's eyes, but momentarily, before Joel disappeared from view, he suddenly smiled at Cassie, a smile such as she had never seen him give before, a smile so broad and so warm that she felt as if much needed warmth was pouring back into her life. As if she had been cured of an illness.

Then he was gone from sight, gone before Cassie could return the smile, before she could mouth the words she now knew she wished to whisper to him.

'You need a drink,' Willoughby said, bending down and taking her arm. 'You most certainly do. And looking at you, I can tell you so do I.'

*   *   *

She was allowed to visit him the following afternoon in Wormwood Scrubs where he had been taken pending his transfer to an open prison just outside Oxford. The dull institutional smell could be sensed even outside the gates, but once inside the actual buildings it became the stuff of Cassie's nightmares, a cloying, gagging composite of floor polish, disinfectant, boiled vegetables, stale nicotine and sweat. The visitors were mostly women, the few males among them being a handful of teenagers doing their best to look hard and uncaring and three or four worn-out-looking older men, fathers obviously come to give weary solace to sons following in their footprints. As they waited Cassie could hear in the distance heavy doors banging closed, raised voices and the faint echoing thud of approaching footfalls. Finally the prisoners arrived and looked round the room to spot their particular visitors.

Joel was one of the last to come in, ambling along by himself at the rear of the queue, his hands clasped behind his back, his face, much paler, lit as ever by the brilliance of his dark brown eyes. In response to Cassie's wave he raised his eyebrows and without any increase in his pace he wandered over to the table where she was sitting, pulled out the chair opposite her and sat down as if prison was the most normal place in the world to find himself with Cassie.

For a moment they just sat looking at each other in silence, eye directly to eye, a look which said so much of what needed to be said before Joel once again raised his eyebrows and smiled.

'Hello,' he said.

'Hi,' Cassie replied.

He drummed the top of the table with the fingers of one hand. 'You didn't by chance bring any cigarettes, I suppose?'

Cassie opened her bag and took out a pack of Gitanes Blondes which she slid across the table to him.

'It's only while I'm banged up, you know,' Joel explained, 'I shall give up again the moment I'm out. As I

406

think I told you before – giving up smoking's easy. I should know—'

'You've done it so often,' Cassie finished for him.

'Fancy you remembering that,' he said, staring at her as he began to undo the pack.

'Fancy,' Cassie agreed.

Having got the pack open, Joel took out a cigarette and looked at it as if he had never seen one before. 'I didn't think I'd ever see you again,' he said. 'Not in person, at least.'

'You nearly didn't,' Cassie replied. 'But I guess I still haven't learned which knob works the head and which one the heart.' Joel looked up at her again but before he could say anything Cassie went on, 'It might have helped matters if you'd bothered to reply to my letter.'

'Which letter?'

'Which letter? The one I wrote in reply to the last one you wrote to me, after that night. The night at your club.'

Joel shook his head. 'I never got it,' he said. 'Promise.'

'You never got it?'

'I never got any letter from you in reply to mine. I swear it.'

'I gave it to Erin to post,' Cassie said with a frown. 'Erin would never have forgotten.'

'Then it must have got lost.'

'I wondered why you hadn't replied.'

'I'd have replied, Mrs Rosse,' Joel said slowly. 'I would have replied.'

'What would you have said?'

'If I never got the letter—' Joel looked at her, eyebrows raised.

'Of course,' Cassie agreed. 'Sorry.'

'So am I.'

'Anyway.' Cassie smiled and then glanced quickly round at all the other inmates and their visitors. 'So how are you? I mean – I mean, how is it? Are you OK?'

'If you mean how's being in gaol, you must know what they say about the English, surely? If you've been to a public school, gaol's a picnic.'

'You didn't go to that sort of school. You told me you went to some sort of high class cushy co-ed. Where you bathed naked in the rivers with the girls.'

'So maybe it's just as well I'm being sent to an open prison.'

'Yes,' Cassie continued. 'Talking of which, what was with the Old Etonian tie?'

'My counsel's idea,' Joel said, now lighting his cigarette. 'The beak was an OE and you know – when you have your back to the wall, every little helps.'

'You are going to appeal?'

'Maybe. Maybe not.' Joel raised a quizzical eyebrow and blew out a plume of smoke which evaporated above Cassie's head.

'Joel—' she began.

'I didn't do this to become some sort of *cause célèbre*,' Joel interrupted. 'The judge was right. I took the law into my own hands and for that I must pay the penalty. I did what I did with my eyes wide open.'

'Oh, for God's sake, Joel,' Cassie retorted. 'You don't have to martyr yourself for some sort of cause, you know.'

'On the contrary, Mrs Rosse. There's quite a queue forming behind this particular bandwagon already.'

'But surely if you believe in what you did—'

'Which I most certainly do—'

'Then isn't it also part of the manifesto to help other people in similar situations?'

'I think I've done my sharing and caring bit, Mrs Rosse,' he replied, tapping the edge of his cigarette on the ash tray. 'After all, I'm the one who's been sent to gaol. I imagine what's happened to me will suit some people right down to the ground and I don't like that. What I did wasn't inspired by any sort of reforming zeal. I did what I did because I loved my father. Others can make what they like of it. But I'm no crusader, caped or otherwise.'

'So you're not going to appeal.'

'Maybe. Maybe not.'

'You'd rather spend a year of your life in gaol.'

'I have a lot of reading to catch up with. I'll be able to get a lot of work done, too.'

Cassie looked at him, long and hard. 'You are the most impossible man I have ever met,' she said. 'In fact you're probably one of the most impossible men in the whole world.'

'True,' Joel agreed, leaning back as he put out his cigarette. 'So how are things back at the ranch?'

Cassie brought him up to date with everything, telling him all about Cheltenham, Mattie's defection, and the reasons behind her retirement of The Nightingale.

Joel told her he'd managed to take in that particular piece of news, even though it broke on the very eve of his trial. 'It would have been hard not to. It made quite a few news bulletins. I was actually quite surprised. When last heard of the horse was working so well.'

'There was nowhere left for him to go, nothing more for him to prove. Besides, he doesn't owe me anything. He doesn't owe anyone anything.'

'What about the kidnapping?' Joel wondered, changing tack. 'Any further developments?'

'My insurers are still refusing to pay out. It looks as though we're going to have to go to court.'

'Good luck. You'll need it.' Joel stuck his lower teeth out over his lip and sucked in some air, drumming his chin with two fingers as he did so. 'OK,' he said. 'Here's how it is. I'm here for a while, and I'll need something to occupy me. So why don't you send me everything you have on the case. Make up a file. Put anything in it which you think might have some relevance to the kidnapping, anything, doesn't matter how wild a card it may be. One thing I have learned not to mock is a woman's intuition, so bung it all in. Everything, and send it to me as soon as you can. I'm going to have a lot of time on my hands over the coming twelve months, more than the police are going to have, and anyway I'm a lot more interested in this case than they are.'

'I won't know where to start.'

'Yes you will,' Joel retorted. 'Just look for connections. Find out if there are any connections between anyone on the insurance side and anyone else involved. Other owners, trainers, rivals, anybody. Old lovers even.'

'What about young lovers?'

'Young lovers even,' Joel replied, looking into her eyes once more. 'Young lovers, old lovers, middle-aged lovers.'

'You know the score, Mr Benson.'

'I think I do. Mr Rosse, the French count, and Mr Christian.'

'Mr Christian*sen*.'

'*Et moi*. We can rule three of those out straight away.'

'Leaving—?'

'Monsieur the count. The sadist from the Loire. We can't rule him out. Hell might have no fury like scorned women, but men can run them pretty close. What was his name?'

'Jean-Luc de Vendrer,' Cassie replied quietly, remembering her close encounter with the wrong kind. 'You're right. I wouldn't put anything past him.'

'What exactly was the problem there?'

'The problem was I got him completely wrong. I thought he was gentle and intellectual and he turned out to be the very opposite. Sometimes I really do wonder what he intended to do to me that night.'

'The night you locked him in his closet and did a runner from his château?' Joel grinned.

'Believe me, Joel, it was no laughing matter,' Cassie replied grimly, remembering the look in the Frenchman's eyes as he had told her to lie where she was on the bed and wait for him.

'What do you reckon he was into? Flagellation maybe? Or something worse?'

'I have no idea, Joel. All I knew then was I didn't want to wait to find out.'

'But you really did shred all his silk designer ties while you were waiting for the housemaid to unlock the bedroom door? I just love you for that.'

'I wish I'd trashed the whole damned room,' Cassie said. 'Only he had some really rather lovely pieces.'

'He has to be on the list of suspects. Nothing is fair in love and war, thank goodness. Put it all down.'

'What about Leonora?'

'I thought you'd never ask. What about Leonora as in the night at the club?'

'I didn't actually mean that. But since you insist – yes. What about Leonora that night at the club? As well as the day she arrived at the trial at your side—'

'Leonora being at the court was her idea. It had nothing to do with me. Leonora at the club, well, that was her idea too. But that had a lot to do with me. You must have worked that one out by now, surely?'

'She bailed you out.'

'She bailed the club out when we hit the rocks, or rather she and her old man did. Charles, her husband, was one of the original investors, and when we hit a bad patch we asked the original money if they had any more. And they did.'

'So you did know Leonora before?'

'Not really. I only really knew her husband and him only slightly. Someone else brought him in as an investor, the mutual friends I once told you about.'

'Even so—'

'Even so, once I knew who she was exactly – this was after you had started on about her, about your lifelong enmity et cetera et cetera – it was a bit late to come clean. I thought you'd misconstrue it so I didn't say anything. Not that there was anything *to* say, but then that only made it worse, if you understand me. If I suddenly said *oh yes, I know who you mean now – I do actually know her*, you'd only have thought I was hiding something. Think about it. I mean you and Leonora. Big wow.'

'All right,' Cassie said with a nod after she had considered Joel's defence. 'I'll buy that. Provided you've exhausted the bag marked *Leonora surprises*.'

'It's empty. There's nothing else you need to know.'

Behind Cassie a warden called an end to visiting times. When the announcement was finished everyone around her began making their farewells.

'I'll come and visit you. As often as I can.'

'It's a long way from Tipperary, and nearly as long from

Wicklow. Look, I'll be fine. The time just flies by when one's enjoying oneself.' He got up, pocketing his cigarettes and going round behind his chair to push it back under the table for all the world as if he were back at school. 'Send the stuff as soon as you can,' he said, getting ready to leave. 'And thanks for the cigarettes.'

'Joel?' she said as he turned away from her.

'Mrs Rosse?' he said, half turning back.

'You take care of yourself,' she said, which wasn't what she meant to say at all.

'I will,' he replied, which from the look of him wasn't quite how he'd imagined their parting either. 'You take care of yourself, too.'

Then he was gone. He didn't turn to look back at her, he just ambled off, hands behind his back again, head in the air just as if he was going back to work in his studio rather than be banged up with someone who probably had never once known any feelings of compassion, someone who, instead of helping someone they loved end a life which was nothing but anguish and despair, had possibly ruined a life which was happy and pain-free by some brutal, callous act. As Cassie watched Joel disappear from her view in the company of people who might have determinedly helped to brutalize the world they lived in, she realized for the first time that there really were some things that could not be cured just by work or dedication. She had to come back to see Joel, and soon.

But first there was someone else with whom she knew she had to deal.

# Twenty-Six

He walked straight past her the first time she saw him on her return home. She knew he had seen her from the way whenever she looked in his direction he quickly turned his back on her, and then finally when the last race was over and Cassie made her way towards him as the crowd began to drift to the car parks he quickly changed tack and accelerating his pace walked in a diagonal past her, raising his voice in conversation with the young woman by his side.

'Mattie?' Cassie called after him. 'Mattie?'

Still he didn't stop, walking on for all the world as if he hadn't heard, but Cassie knew from the half turn of the young woman's head that Phoebe McMahon had heard her well enough.

'Mattie Rosse!' Cassie called again, this time so loudly she knew he could not help but hear her since a group of racegoers ten yards ahead of him turned to see who was doing the calling. Rather than lose any more of her dignity by being seen to hurry after her son, Cassie stood her ground and willed him to stop and acknowledge her. In response to a visible prompt from his girlfriend, he did so.

'Hi,' he said as he wandered back in Cassie's direction. 'At least I take it that was you doing the shouting?'

'Yes, I was calling you,' Cassie corrected him, 'since I seem to have become invisible.'

Mattie looked round at Phoebe McMahon with a *what-on-earth's-she-talking-about-now* look before turning back to shrug at his mother. 'I didn't know you were here,' he said. 'I didn't see you.'

'Even though I had two runners,' Cassie replied patiently. 'One of them in the same race as one of yours.'

'You know me before a race,' Mattie said. 'Sorry. Aren't you going to say hi to Phoebe?'

Cassie greeted the tall and heavy-set Phoebe, who smiled politely at her.

'I need to see you, Mattie,' Cassie said, preferring not to get involved in any small talk. 'What are you doing this evening?'

Again Mattie looked round at Phoebe as if he were a ventriloquist's doll being worked by her. 'We're not doing anything as far as I know,' he replied finally. 'What had you got in mind?'

The last thing Cassie had in mind was asking Phoebe McMahon back to Claremore to discuss the state of her relationship with her son, but rather than antagonize Mattie further Cassie tried to remain as tactful as she could. 'It's really family business,' she said.

'OK,' Mattie nodded. 'Phoebe can sit and have a drink while we talk. We could come back with you now if that suits you.'

'It doesn't actually,' Cassie said, eyeing Mattie the way she had always eyed him when he had decided to play wayward. 'Not at all.'

'Then we'll come over later. No problem. We can go into your study and Phoebe will be fine as long as she's got a large whisky in her hand.'

'This might take a a bit longer than that,' Cassie persisted.

'Longer than it takes Phoebe to drink a large whisky?'

Cassie nodded.

'Then we'll give her two large whiskies.'

'This won't do at all, Mattie,' Cassie said crisply. 'It really won't. Do you read me? The very least you could do is spare me half an hour of your time. Understood?'

Mattie shrugged, but Cassie knew from the look in his eyes he had already conceded. 'OK,' he said. 'But in that case it can't be tonight.'

'That's fine,' Cassie retorted. 'You just ring me when you find you have the time, and I'll work round you. Goodbye.'

She hurried on to her car, grabbing the keys from her

pocket as she did so and crushing them in her hand until she almost cried out from the discomfort, so furious was she with herself for so nearly losing her grip.

For the next two days Cassie spent all her free time collecting the information as requested by Joel. She compiled a detailed list of everyone who had ever had any connection with Claremore, Tyrone for as long as she had known him, herself, Claremore Racing and Claremore Foodstuffs. She included details of anyone who had ever defaulted on their training bills, anyone who had ever taken their horse or horses away either for a given reason or simply in a fit of pique – a list which included Leonora's mother who had removed her entire string from Tyrone's management in an attempt to ruin him – owners who had changed their allegiance, owners with a known criminal background – a small but important group of suspects since it included Herr Brandt – anyone with a grudge however big or small for whatever sort of reason, be it an alleged unfair dismissal or an accident on the schooling grounds, as well as everyone who had or had once had any sort of vested interest or investment in Claremore or the Rosses, everyone from absconding accountants to resentful bookmakers.

'It made rather depressing reading,' Cassie told Theodore over the dinner he had persuaded her to have with him at the end of the week. 'I thought I had more friends than enemies, but it doesn't seem to have panned out that way.'

'Only because you're not looking for your friends, Cassie,' Theodore replied. 'You are *looking* for those who would do you harm.'

'Even so, it made me wonder how we ever got even this far, Theodore,' Cassie said, accepting the offer of a second helping of wild salmon. 'When you pull the curtains right back, it's really pretty dark out there.'

'Do you think your friend Mr Benson will unravel the mystery?' Theodore asked, helping them both to some more. 'Or do you think the *trail* – has gone cold. As I believe they say.'

'I guess there's no harm in his trying,' Cassie said wearily. 'Nothing ventured et cetera et cetera.'

'He's an *odd* sort of cove, wouldn't you say? Or would you? Joel?'

'You could call him that, I suppose,' Cassie replied. 'At least you could if you knew what a *cove* was.'

'Slang for a chap, a fellow.'

'Then yes, Joel Benson is an *odd sort of a cove*, you're right.'

'How do you feel about him?' Theodore enquired cautiously, sipping just as carefully at his glass of white wine. 'Obviously you feel as though you can trust him.'

'As though I can trust him? Now I do. Yes.'

Theodore raised one eyebrow almost imperceptibly and smiled. 'There was a time.'

'There was a time, but that time's over now.'

'He's a very brave sort of cove, too. That's why he decided not to appeal?'

'He's worried they'll turn him into some kind of folk hero.'

'I'd have thought he'd taken that route by languishing in *gaol*, surely?'

'My thoughts exactly.'

'Ah well. *Chacun à son* ideals. Your beautiful daughter. Now how is she?'

'Pass.'

Theodore gave her another slightly quizzical look, then shrugged, as if to let the matter rest. 'Not a very happy time all round, then,' he concluded. 'Not a very happy time at all.'

'You could say that,' Cassie agreed.

He waited until the next course had been served before continuing. It also gave him a chance to bring the conversation back to the subject which most interested him. 'Cassie – might I ask you something, do you suppose?' he enquired after his Filipino housekeeper had left them alone once more. 'You don't *actually* have to answer because in a way it really is none of my business, but I shall ask just the same. How best to put it, that is one's main *concern*.

416

Now then.' He fell to silence as he stared down at the noisettes of lamb on the plate in front of him, which he then proceeded to cut carefully up as if performing the most delicate surgery. 'I suppose really the point is that you have no proper idea of how I feel about you, *if I may say so.*' He looked up at her as he finished the sentence. 'There's no real reason why you should, of course,' he hurried on, lest Cassie should interrupt him and say something to the contrary. 'There's no real reason because of course I have never said anything to you about the feelings I might or indeed might *not* have. How*ever.* The point is that it has become uncommonly obvious – to me at any rate – it has become uncommonly obvious that a woman as charming and as lovely as you, Cassie, should not be living alone. The whole thing – *is ridiculous.* You there one side of the hill and me here the other side – to my mind that makes it even more ridiculous. Utterly so in fact, utterly so. What I am trying to say is this. No. No – no, what I first need to know is this – not what I am trying to say at all. Not at all. *Not at all.* No no no, no, let me start again altogether, because I am making a right hog's breakfast out of this, so I am, so I am. To start from the beginning again, you see I don't even *know* – in fact to be completely truthful, I haven't an idea what you think about me. Not a clue.'

'I think – you're a saint.'

'God *forbid* – that you should ever think that, Cassie. The last thing a man wants to be thought is a saint. A very devil, yes. But a saint, never.'

'I'm not at all sure I know how to answer that,' Cassie said, suddenly confused. 'You're a very kind, gentle, funny, adorable man—'

'But a bit of a *wildflower*, yes?' Theo smiled. 'That's what most people think. Nice enough, but – what they call – a friend of Dorothy's.' Theodore smiled again, which only made Cassie frown.

'A *wildflower*?' Cassie wondered. 'A friend of *Dorothy's*?'

'It's perfectly all right if you thought so,' Theodore continued, for all the world as if Cassie understood. 'That

417

is what most women think, that the reason I've not been married is because I'm one of these people described in their obituaries as the sort of man who *remained a bachelor*. Don't tell me that wasn't what you thought as well, for I won't believe you for a moment.'

'I did no such thing,' Cassie tried to assure him, knowing the opposite was true, particularly when she remembered Josephine's laughter at the thought of her mother going to dine with her gynaecologist. *He's as gay as the famous bee, Mums*, she'd told her later. *Surely you can see that for yourself. He's as camp as a row of bell tents.*

There was a long silence, during which time Theodore looked at Cassie as if expecting her to say something further. But at this point Cassie had nothing more to add, so she too waited for the next development.

'I'm sorry,' he said. 'Our food will be ruined. We must eat.'

He began to eat, almost mechanically as did Cassie hardly noticing how delicious the food was. When they were more than halfway through the course, he put down his knife and fork, drank some claret and then cleared his throat.

'Cassie, I must tell you something no-one else here knows,' he said, 'and it is very important that I do so. I have been married, d'you see. Not only happily married, but ecstatically so. Indeed. *Indeed.*' The second *indeed* was more of an echo, a small lament at some long-standing memory. Cassie quietly put down her own knife and fork and waited for the unfolding of the tragedy she knew was to follow. 'I qualified here, at the College of Surgeons of course, then finished my studies in America, do you see. There I worked until fifteen years ago – and there I lived with Bryony, my wife. Then of all things—' Theo stopped and cleared his throat quietly once more, as time carried him back across the years. 'Then of all things Bree became pregnant at long last. We'd simply not had the luck till then. There was nothing wrong with either of us, we just simply hadn't had the luck. So after twelve years of marriage Bree became pregnant. Now, she wouldn't let me attend her – some sort of superstition she had. She went to another man and the long and short of it is I lost her in childbirth. Child and mother died. They both died. The child, a boy, lived for an hour, but Bree never regained consciousness. It was *absolutely* nobody's fault, the surgeon's least of all. Bree suffered a massive stroke which killed her within minutes, the miracle being that they got the baby delivered at all. But there you are. Some things are meant, and some things are not. And there you are.'

'I'm so sorry.'

'There is no need to be sorry, Cassie, no need at all. Why I'm telling you this is that once she was gone, the point is I could only come back here. I couldn't stay over there, it was quite impossible, so I came back here to my father's house. Now the long and short of it, as I was saying, was that I never had any intention of getting married again, nor even thinking *about it*. I simply had no wish to, which was why I never did anything to discourage people from seeing me as the sort of man who never married. Never did anything about it, that is, until you came along.'

'Theodore—'

'No, no—' He inclined his head on one side and smiled to stop her. 'No, there is no need for you to say anything here at this juncture, that is other than whether or not you're going to marry this Benson chap. I know in a way it's really none of my business, but then in another way, do you see? It is.'

'I haven't even considered marriage, Theodore,' Cassie replied none the less. 'No, that's not true. I'm sorry. Joel has made me consider marriage—'

'Then he has asked you.'

'No – no, he's made me consider marriage in so much as he's made me look back at the marriage I had and consider whether or not that is all the marriage I might ever want.'

'And your conclusion? Have you reached one?'

'No, not yet. That's why I have not considered marrying Joel.'

'In that case, enough said.' Theo drank some more wine

419

and looked at Cassie over his glasses and gave a shake of his handsome grey head. 'Truth to tell, Cassie, even if you do marry your Don Quixote – in fact even if you marry two dozen men in a row – I would still be there waiting. Now – enough is more than enough, so drink some more of this wine of which we have *not* had enough, because it's far too fine to leave to go brown in the decanter – and let us talk of other things. Such as shoes and ships and sealing wax. And whether pigs have wings. The last most particularly.'

Having poured them both two more large glasses of claret, Theo tapped the top of the heavy cut glass decanter back in place and sat back to begin a long and learned discussion on the social subtext of his favourite opera.

If nothing else, Theodore Pilkington's intimations forced Cassie to review her situation afresh. With Joel locked away in prison on the other side of the Irish Sea and her financial and family affairs in such disarray she had been feeling more vulnerable than she had felt since she had lost Tyrone. There had been many occasions since when she had wondered whether or not she could manage not only her family life but the whole of the Claremore Racing enterprise by herself, but somehow she had always found the strength to conquer her doubts and the resolution to overcome those particular difficulties. Yet always at the back of her mind there lingered one major concern, whether or not alone she would finally have the strength to cope with disaster on a far more major scale.

She had good reason to worry, because people were always feeding her concern. As she had put her life slowly together again after Tyrone's death and begun to produce winners from a yard which everyone connected with racing immediately assumed had seen its day, so the acclamations which began to be offered to her instead of bolstering her confidence began to undermine it, since behind each congratulation Cassie sensed an expression of surprise, as much as to say that what she had done was even more astonishing for not only was she a woman, but she was a woman alone. *And how long would that last?* seemed to be the general wonder. How long would that particular streak of luck (for that was surely only what it was) last? In the highly competitive and chauvinistic world of horse racing unattached women were not meant to last. On the very few occasions when they did stay the course, their survival was always put down either to sheer luck or the fact that behind them they had the support of a man.

Such thinking only strengthened Cassie's determination to go it alone. She hated the notion that when it came to the crunch without a man by her side a woman would give in, just as she hated the much put about theory that women were not finally physically strong or capable enough to race ride. To her way of thinking both theories had gained ground simply because women had not been offered the same chances as men because men did not want them as equals. As far as being neither strong nor capable enough to race ride went, Cassie knew otherwise. Thirty years earlier there was no doubt that the theory of the weaker sex held more water because women did not keep themselves anywhere near as fit as they did now. For women riding was intended basically as either a recreation or a social asset. Since they were not allowed to race ride professionally their only experience of the track was point to pointing, and whereas no doubt many of the leading women riders before and immediately after the war were both dashing and fearless their fitness could in no way be compared to the level of athleticism reached by contemporary women jockeys. Cassie knew this from personal experience because when she had been forced to take over the reins at Claremore, before she would allow herself even to ride work she had got herself as fit as a marathon runner, fitter in fact than ever she had needed to be. But she had done that deliberately, since the last thing she wanted was to be found lacking in strength and stamina by her lads when she was riding out on the gallops three times every morning of the week come hell or high water.

She kept herself fit now, not quite as fit as she had been twenty years ago perhaps, but she still worked out in her private gymnasium for an hour a day whenever time allowed, she walked or ran whenever she could, she rode out every day and she swam in her indoor pool at least three times a week. As a result her figure was very little different from what it had been when she was a much younger woman. Her back was strong as were her legs and arms, her hips were still slender, her backside shapely, her breasts firm and her stomach flat. In fact, although she was not in any way a conceited person, Cassie was secretly very proud of the shape she was in, and knew that in the unlikely event of her ever being called upon to race ride, a month's intensive training would bring her to about the same level of fitness and strength of most of the male jockeys she knew and employed. Certainly Dexter Bryant was always impressed by the shape she kept herself in, particularly after a bout of arm wrestling on the kitchen table one morning only the summer before after they had been riding out. Being well and truly beaten three matches in a row in front of all the stable lads had been enough to make him now refuse any further challenge from his guv'nor at that particular activity.

But as far as her inner strength went, Cassie was not so sure, even now at this stage of her life, after masterminding the career of possibly the most famous racehorse ever. She had no idea how men coped with the sort of difficulties with which she now found herself faced, although she had a suspicion that in most families men expected their wives to cope with any real domestic upheaval, particularly ones which affected their children. All she knew was that as things stood at present she felt both inadequate and lonely, and her feelings made her long for the company and the support of a man – but which of the two men in her life? she wondered. Theo was the epitome of kindness and concern, while Joel was tough, determined and certainly understood the workings of Cassie's world better than the considerably more intellectual Theo. He also seemed to understand how Cassie herself worked, at times it would appear even better than she, whereas for all his sensitivity and compassion she felt that Theo might worship her rather than partner her and what Cassie needed most of all was what Tyrone had always been to her. Besides lovers and best friends, Tyrone and Cassie had been partners.

Yet finally she could not as yet see herself married to either man, although she thought that both of them might make good if not indeed wonderful husbands. Theo was successful so he would not resent her own success and Joel was talented so he would not resent Cassie's great gift. Both were undoubtedly brilliant and original men. Both of them loved her. As for her own feelings, as things stood at present, while she knew she loved both men, she felt she was actually in love with Joel, yet still she could not see herself married to him. Joel was a wonderfully exciting love affair, so she thought. Or so she thought she thought. Or perhaps she chose to suppose she thought. What he wasn't was the man in the armchair opposite her every evening, the man at her table every meal, the man in her bed every night, the man in her thoughts every moment.

*Dammit, you've grown selfish, Cassie Rosse!* she scolded herself in her head. *You've grown set in your ways, so set that you don't wish to share your life with anyone any more. You want people to help you out, but you don't really want to let those selfsame people in. But then maybe you have your reasons after all,* she would add on reflection. *Maybe it wouldn't be altogether fair to expect someone to share a life you seem to have now made a real mess of – a family life that's all in pieces and a financial one that's faced with ruin if you don't find a way to bail yourself out. Maybe I'm flattering myself to think that either of these men if it came to it would really want to share this chaos full time. Maybe they're just flattering me. Maybe they're kidding themselves. Maybe we all are.*

*Maybe first things should come first. And that means sorting all this out. That means finding out who wanted me down and out, why my daughter wants to stay married to a sadist let alone why she wanted to marry him in the first place, and what I have done to my son to alienate him.*

*First things first. The affairs of my heart I can and will return to – but first of all I must face my son.*

For a while it seemed there was no way Cassie could persuade her son to come and see her unaccompanied by Phoebe McMahon. She would ring him and either get his machine or indeed Phoebe, but never Mattie himself. Nor in spite of all the messages she left for him did he call her back, and since she knew the racecourse was probably the only place where they would actually see each other and that the racecourse was no place for any sort of private conversation, Cassie finally decided that if she wanted to get to the bottom of this particular mystery she would have to beard the lion in its den.

Guessing his training routine would be pretty much the same as her own at Claremore, and since there was no racing on the particular day she chose to surprise him, Cassie reckoned the best time to catch Mattie would be after morning stables when he would probably be attending to his paperwork and ringing owners and prospective jockeys. She also gambled on the fact that Phoebe McMahon might have to go out sometime that morning, either shopping or perhaps even to her hairdresser's, remembering her own routine on a Monday after a busy weekend. Sure enough, at a little after ten o'clock, from where she was waiting in her own car across the road from the bungalow that was now Mattie's home, Cassie saw Phoebe climb into her little blue Nissan and drive off in the direction of Dublin. As soon as the car had sped out of sight across the Curragh, Cassie hurried on foot across to the bungalow and let herself straight inside.

There was no-one else in the place, just Mattie. He was on the phone in the kitchen with his back to the door, standing by a table covered in racing papers and form books.

'Hello, Mattie,' Cassie said in her best matter-of-fact manner. He swung round to her, his eyes widening in genuine surprise. 'The door was open so I let myself in. I hope you don't mind.'

'I'll call you back in a few minutes, Tim,' Mattie said into the telephone. 'Someone's just turned up uninvited.'

While he concluded his telephone conversation Cassie looked round the untidy kitchen until she found the electric kettle, and filled it under the tap. 'I'm dying for a coffee. I hope you don't mind. And even if you do, you can save your breath. I've had it with you not returning my calls. So if the mountain won't come to Muhammad or whatever the saying is—' She plugged the kettle into the switch on the wall and turned it on.

'I've been busy,' Mattie said lamely. 'I'd have thought that was obvious. What with trying to get this place up and running—'

'I said save it, Mattie.' Cassie stared at him for a moment, then, clearing some more papers and books off a chair, sat herself down at the uncleared kitchen table. 'Sit down. I want to talk to you.'

'Look, we're not at Claremore now,' Mattie protested. 'This happens to be my house and if anyone's going to tell someone what they can do—'

'I said – sit down.'

Mattie sat down.

'Good,' Cassie said, pushing a set of dirty breakfast crockery to one side. 'Seeing how valuable your time is, I'll come straight to the point. I want you to tell me what's going on.'

'Nothing's *going on*. Why should anything be going on, for Chrissake?'

'Really? So if asked you'd say things between us are the way they've always been.'

'Yes. Sure. Of course.'

Cassie eyed him with a degree of contempt and in return Mattie shifted uncomfortably on his chair. 'The kettle's boiling,' she said. 'And while you're making the coffee, perhaps you'd like to reconsider your answer to my question. And no more bull, because I really have had enough.'

Seeing how serious his mother was, Mattie turned quickly away and busied himself making the coffee. Cassie said nothing while he did so, determined not to give him any help.

'OK,' Mattie said as he sat back down at the table with a *cafetière* full of strong coffee. 'I'll admit I've been a bit preoccupied of late, but that's hardly surprising is it? Suddenly being kicked out of home—'

'You weren't kicked out,' Cassie interrupted. 'You'd already made provision to leave and come here. And since I don't believe you can serve two masters, I just hurried the process up. I didn't see why I should be expected to provide board and lodgings for Tom McMahon's *protégé*.'

'Christ – if that's all that's bugging you—' Mattie began, only to be stopped once more by Cassie.

'No, that's not what's *bugging* me, Mattie,' she retorted. 'What's bugging me is you. You in general. And your attitude in particular. I'm not going to give you a lecture about all I've done for you, although God knows how much I'm tempted to, because all that is down to me. You're my son—' Mattie looked up sharply at this, and for a moment Cassie foundered, surprised by the look in Mattie's eyes. 'You're my son,' she continued after a fractional pause, 'and what I chose to do for you is totally down to me. So I'm not going to throw that up in your face because I don't reckon that's fair. You didn't ask to be brought up in any particular way and while I think you have some reason to be grateful I still don't think it's on to throw it back in your face.'

'So what do you want, then?'

'I want to know what's wrong with you.'

'I told you,' Mattie said, looking down into the coffee cup he was stirring. 'It isn't anything.'

'I don't believe you,' Cassie said quietly. 'It's as if you hate me, and don't try to deny it because I'm not dramatizing, and I'm not exaggerating. I'm not the only one who's noticed it.'

'OK,' he said, taking a deep breath and staring up at the ceiling. 'Very well. I don't know how you thought you'd get away with it. I don't see why you thought no-one would tell me. You must have known sooner or later somebody would say something. You must have done.'

Now he was looking at Cassie good and hard, and Cassie

put the coffee cup which she had just picked up back down, almost missing the saucer in her anxiety. 'Tell you what?' she asked. 'I don't understand what you mean – sooner or later somebody would say something. Something about what?'

'The lie you told,' Mattie said, still watching her. 'Because that's what's at the bottom of all this. *The lie you told. The lie you've been living. The lie you made me live.*'

'I haven't told you any *lies*, Mattie,' Cassie protested. 'Never once. Not ever. What lie do you think I've told you?'

'About Dad,' Mattie replied with deadly calm. 'About my father, about my mother, and about who I am.'

Without quite knowing why, Cassie began to shake. But rather than have Mattie see the effect his announcement was having on her, Cassie clasped both her hands together as tightly as she could below the table, at the same time digging her fingernails into the back of each hand in an attempt to regain her self-control.

'If you're talking about your adoption—' she began.

'I'm talking about my adoption,' Mattie agreed.

'You've known for a long time you were adopted. As soon as you were old enough, right at the very moment I was told to tell I told you—'

'But you didn't tell me the truth, damn it!' Mattie was now on his feet, leaning on the kitchen table, banging it with one clenched fist. 'Oh sure – yes! You told me all right! But what you told me was all lies! All that business about some poor girl who got herself banged up and—'

'What I told you was the *truth*,' Cassie pleaded, looking up at him from where she still sat at the table. '*What I told you was the truth.*'

'No it was not!' Mattie yelled, throwing his head back and closing his eyes tight. 'You couldn't tell me the truth because you didn't dare! Never in a million years would you have *dared* tell me the truth!'

'Then why accuse me?' Cassie wondered. 'Why damn me for not doing so? Except that I did. I did tell you the truth and I always have done.'

'I saw Leonora in London, you know? She came round to see me.'

'What's Leonora got to do with it?' But even as she asked Cassie already knew the answer, and for a terrible moment everything swam. The room began to disappear from her view, Mattie's face began to blur and his voice started to sound as if it was coming from the middle of a huge mountain. To steady herself she grabbed the edge of the table with both her hands, but still she felt faint, still everything was happening somewhere out there in the distance.

'I saw Leonora – and Leonora told me the truth. She said she had to, otherwise she wouldn't be able to—'

'To what?' Cassie heard herself asking faintly. 'I don't understand what you're talking about – or perhaps I do. Leonora could not tell you the truth because Leonora is not capable of telling *anyone* the truth. Not even herself.'

She could see Mattie more clearly now, and most of all what she could see was a look of terrible hurt in his eyes, a look she could not begin to understand. For a moment neither of them said anything, then, turning to reach down a bottle of whisky and two glasses from the dresser behind him, he sat down at the table opposite her, pouring them both a drink.

'It was the other week, when I was over staying at Jo's,' he said. 'Remember? She and Mark were away and seeing I had to be in London because Jo asked me to house-sit. Leonora rang up – don't ask me how she knew I was there—'

'She just would,' Cassie half whispered in return, reaching for her glass of whisky. 'Leonora knows everything.'

'She must do, because she knew I was there. She said my name as soon as I answered the phone. *Mattie,* she said. *Mattie, I have to see you. It won't take long. I'm only round the corner from you at the Knightsbridge, so if it's all right I can be with you in five minutes.* People don't ring you up out of the blue and say they have to see you unless it's urgent—'

'So you asked her round.'

'Of course. You'd have done the same.'

'Probably,' Cassie agreed wearily. 'But I wouldn't have believed a word she told me. Why should you? Why should you believe her rather than me, your own mother?'

'That's just the point,' Mattie said ominously. 'So it's better you just hear me out before you go telling me the rights and wrongs. So ten minutes later Leonora came round to the house and I tell you she looked awful. The worst I've ever seen her. I know she's never taken the very best care of herself and everything, but I mean she was so thin, and *grey*. I asked her if she was all right and she said no. She said no, she was dying.'

'Leonora's not dying,' Cassie said, sitting up in her chair. 'Leonora's not *dying*.'

'She'd just come from the hospital where she said she'd had the result of some tests,' Mattie continued, before taking a deep draw on his spinhaler. 'She didn't actually say, but it's pretty obviously the dreaded.'

'Cancer?'

Mattie shrugged. 'Obviously.'

Cassie frowned, searching for her feelings, wondering how she felt about the person whom she knew to be her worst enemy dying, appalled to find at the moment she felt nothing. 'But she didn't actually say,' Cassie recapped. 'You know Leonora. Everything is always for the worst—'

'You should have seen her,' Mattie interrupted. 'There's nothing of her. Not that she had very much weight to lose anyway, but Jeez – I mean you'd only have to have seen her. Anyway, if it wasn't true, then why did she come and see me? She said she had to see me because she had something to get off her chest before—' Mattie breathed in and out slowly. 'Before it was too late,' he said. 'Because she's – because she's dying she said she wanted to set the record straight, that she owed it to me to tell me the truth. She *said* – she said it is an impossibility to go through life without knowing who you really are. It isn't fair on a person, according to her, and I agree. So while she understood why you had told me what you did—'

'No! I told you the *truth*, Mattie!' Cassie insisted. 'I told you the truth!'

'You told me the truth as you wanted to see it,' Mattie said. 'While what Leonora told me makes *sense*, besides she says she can prove it.'

'Does she *never* give up? This is only about revenge. That's all it's ever been about. As far as Tyrone and you and Josephine and me are concerned, all that's ever interested Leonora is to revenge herself on us. But don't ask me why, because reason stepped out of the window years ago.'

'You're wrong,' Mattie said, shaking his head. 'Leonora was genuinely upset when she told me.'

'Go on. Surprise me.'

'She knew the story you had told me about who my parents were because Tyrone had told her.'

'Really? And when would that have been?' Cassie demanded to know. 'He couldn't have told her. We never even discussed when we should tell you, let alone what. So why should your father have told Leonora, for God's sake? Your father hated Leonora.'

'Not according to Leonora. But you're right about one thing. He was my father.'

'He was your *adoptive* father,' Cassie countered. 'You know who your father was. I told you. He was a man called Gerald Secker, the man you met in the bar the day The Nightingale won the Derby.'

'I thought he was called Anthony Wilton.'

'His real name was Gerald Secker. He changed it to Anthony Wilton after an almighty row with his father, when he found out Gerald had got someone pregnant.'

'Antoinette Brookes. I know the story. How those two were my real parents and you and Dad adopted me from birth. With the agreement of my real mother.'

'It isn't a *story*, Mattie. That is the way it was. It's the truth,' Cassie replied.

Mattie took another puff on his spinhaler before putting it back in his pocket and clearing his throat.

'According to Leonora, Dad really was my dad.'

'Oh for goodness sake, she tried to pull this stunt once before, Mattie. On the eve of the Derby. She wanted me to pull The Nightingale out of the race because she was convinced her horse would walk it if The Nightingale didn't run. So she tried to make out she had these letters—'

'She does have letters!' Mattie interrupted, putting his glass down on the table. 'She has letters from Dad which according to her prove he's my father. I asked to see them but she said I couldn't until after she's dead because she doesn't want any more trouble over them. But she said they prove quite categorically that Dad really was my father – and that Leonora—'

'Yes?' Cassie wondered.

'That Leonora is my mother.'

On her lonely drive back to Claremore Cassie replayed the end of their conversation over and over in her head as if it was on tape. She had done her best to convince Mattie not only of the monstrosity of Leonora's lie but of the impossibility of it, but to no avail. In Mattie's mind it was now *une idée fixe* and nothing short of his father coming back to life and shaking the truth into him would apparently suffice.

None the less, as the road into the Wicklow Hills unwound before her, Cassie played their end game over one more time.

'*One of your greatest problems is that you never really knew Tyrone,*' she had said. '*If you had known him never for one second could you have believed what Leonora told you. Tyrone was many things. He was hot-headed, but he was incapable of deceit, and his integrity perhaps more than anything was what infuriated Leonora most. He never lied or cheated as she has. She's done all the lying and cheating for him, and because he's dead she thinks she's safe since he can't answer for himself. But I can, and so can the facts. And the facts are exactly as I told you. Gerald Secker had an affair with a girl called Antoinette Brookes whom he then abandoned. Antoinette wanted to have the baby but didn't want to keep it and when Dad heard about it since I couldn't have any more babies and we so very much wanted to have a boy as well as a girl we arranged to adopt*

431

you. Leonora tried to make me believe that your father really was the father because you looked so alike – finally even I believed her and I made it not matter one bit. If it was true that Tyrone really was your father, then in you I still would have some part of him to keep. I really made it not matter, I promise you, I would not let it wreck my life and yours, and because there was no way of disproving what Leonora had told me—'

'What about Antoinette Brookes? What about my real mother? Why couldn't you ask her?'

'I tried to, Mattie. I finally tracked her down and went to see her. But she'd had a terrible riding accident and – well. She no longer had her senses. The only way you can prove paternity, you see, is by disproving it. Tyrone and you were the same blood type.'

'AB rhesus positive.'

'AB rhesus positive, exactly. But even if we knew what your real mother's blood group was it doesn't prove anything. As they say, you can't get a positive ID from blood groups the way you can from fingerprints. Which is what I meant by disproving it. Proof is only conclusive if the blood samples differ.'

'Meaning all you can really do is prove whoever it is isn't the child of two people.'

'You got it. That's why I went looking for Antoinette, but of course the way things were when I found her there was no way I could ask her to submit to a blood test.'

'You could have got it from her doctor.'

'Her own mother, who was all she had left in her family, knew nothing of her daughter's pregnancy. And as a total stranger I could hardly just walk into her doctor's surgery and demand to know the blood group of one of his patients. Anyway, I didn't have to, because your real father confirmed the whole story. That he'd got your mother pregnant and then abandoned her, taking off for India for ten years. He actually volunteered the information.'

'But you don't know that I was the baby of that particular pregnancy, do you? Antoinette – my mother – she might have had a miscarriage, or she might not even

432

*have been pregnant after all. And then really got pregnant by my father.'*

'You want Tyrone to be your father. And believe me, he is, he was in every way. You don't want some no-good ex-hippie. It's understandable.'

'It's not that. Knowing I was adopted – I mean, it's never been a problem, really it hasn't. Until now.'

'But it doesn't have to be. There's no reason why it should be any problem now because nothing's altered. Everything's the same. All that happened was that Leonora tried yet again to put a bomb under us—'

'But that's the whole point!' At this point Mattie had got to his feet and walked to the kitchen window where he stood facing out. 'That's the whole point, don't you see, for God's sake? You don't know, and I don't know, do we? Neither of us really knows that Antoinette Brookes was my mother. Because we can't prove it!'

'I was there when she told me who the father was. I said to her why don't you marry this boy? And she said because I don't love him. I was there when she said it, and so was your father.'

'But she could have been lying, don't you see? She could have been making the whole thing up!'

'But why? Why?'

'I don't know why! Maybe because Tyrone really was the father! Or because someone entirely different was and she had to go along with the story she'd already invented! How do I know? How should I know! I wasn't there at the time, remember? So you could be making all this up for my benefit, right? God knows I've looked at the pictures of Dad often enough to wonder why I look so much like him – yet here you are still telling me this guy Gerald Secker's really my father! And that some poor woman who's now a vegetable is my mother! Which is easy, isn't it? Because there's no way I can ever check it all out!'

'Yes there is. There is a perfectly good way you can check it out. Blood tests. They may not be conclusive but they can tell you something.'

# Twenty-Seven

Cassie was wrong, of course, as Theodore explained to her that evening when she invited him across for dinner. It appeared techniques of blood typing had advanced to such an extent that with extensive tests parentage could actually be proved as well as disproved by the use of what was known as *genetic fingerprinting*. He patiently explained how it worked, how by taking blood samples from the mother, child and father in any given case as well as some DNA from each, the DNA was then studied for banding patterns.

'DNA's *hereditary* material,' Theodore revealed. 'It's actually called deoxyribonucleic acid and it's the principal molecule carrying genetic information in almost all organisms, containing these unique what they call *bandings* we all have, bandings which are readable by X-ray after they've come back from Boots after processing.'

'Come on, this is serious, Mr Pilkington.'

'I know, I know,' Theodore sighed, sipping his dessert wine. 'So to continue, the child's DNA bands, d'you see, they come from both *biological* parents. So first we take the bands from the mother and identify them, then we compare them with the father's or the *suspected* father's bands. If they match – *hey presto*! Paternity proved. If they don't, if the other bands in the child besides the ones *identified* as coming from the mother do not match, then it's no match. Neat, yes?'

'Very. But surely you need all three people for the tests? Father, mother and child. We only have mother and child. Without Tyrone's blood and DNA we can't prove a thing.'

'Well, yes, we *can*.' Theodore raised his eyes from the napkin he was busy making into a rabbit. 'We could – if we can get hold of a blood sample from the woman who says she's the mother – we could at least begin by finding her type but also we could see if it contains any banding which matches up to banding in your son's DNA. You see.'

'So how do we go about it? How on earth do we get a sample of Leonora's blood for starters?'

'Obviously this is where I come in.' Theodore had finished making a rabbit of his napkin which he now placed carefully in front of him on the table. 'You say Mrs Lovett Andrew is ill, Cassie. Yes?'

'Apparently. She's been attending the Farm Street Clinic, Mattie tells me, for examination and tests. She gave Mattie the impression that she was seriously ill – but then as I've already explained, Leonora is more than a little liberal with the truth.'

'We can soon find out, because we are in luck,' Theodore replied. 'I know that particular clinic well, as it happens, although it's news to me that they have an oncology unit. And the luck is that it is administered at the moment by an old chum and fellow graduate of mine, so there really should be very little difficulty in getting the details we require concerning Mrs Lovett Andrew, nor indeed a sample of her blood. Now you haven't heard anything I've said, you understand—'

'I've heard every word you've said,' Cassie protested innocently.

'No you have not, Cassie Rosse,' Theodore contradicted. 'Tonight we have talked only in the most general terms, d'you see. For higher medical matters are way above that pretty head of yours. Yes?'

'You mean this is against medical ethics, don't you?'

'Only if someone finds out. But don't worry – they won't. This sort of thing goes on all the time, you mark my words. Even so, you haven't heard one word of what I've just said. Have you?'

'Not one,' Cassie replied.

A week later Theodore telephoned Cassie from his home to say that everything was organized and that a sample of

Mrs Charles Lovett Andrew's blood would be with them shortly, processed and banded as requested.

'That's the good news,' he said. 'Now I have some other news for you, but I don't know whether you would describe it as good or bad.'

'Come on, Theodore,' Cassie said, recognizing the tease in his voice. 'Let's hear it.'

'Again, you haven't heard this, you understand – but Mrs Charles Lovett Andrew has indeed been attending the clinic as a patient,' he replied. 'Quite obviously, or otherwise we would not have been able to obtain a blood sample. However . . .' Theodore paused, giving Cassie the distinct impression he was trying to control his laughter.

'Yes?' she prompted.

'How*ever*,' Theodore continued after a deep inhalation of breath, 'all is not as bad as it might have first seemed. It seems Mrs Lovett Andrew has been suffering from certain symptoms which led her to believe there might be something seriously wrong, and so she was admitted for routine tests which included a proctoscopy and a colonoscopy. Are you with me so far?'

'I may well be ahead of you,' Cassie replied. 'Go on.'

'The patient was suffering quite severe anaemia which would account for her ashen appearance as described by your son, as well as high anxiety caused by the nature of her other symptoms. However, the results of the test which were not known until after she had paid her *infamous* visit to your son—'

'Which would explain her mental state—'

'Precisely,' Theodore agreed. 'Since she had herself totally convinced she was no longer for this earth—'

'And so was going to cause as much chaos as she could before leaving it—'

'Obviously – but thankfully the results of all the internal examinations revealed that far from suffering from cancer, Mrs Charles C. Lovett Andrew was merely suffering a more severe case of a condition which notoriously plagues one in three people. The self-same condition which they say caused Napoleon to lose the Battle of Waterloo since on the vital day in question he was unable to leave his tent.'

'Leonora had—?' Cassie wondered wide-eyed.

'Mrs Charles C. Lovett Andrew has strangulated haemorrhoids, Cassie, and while normally I'm not one to find the condition in the slightest bit amusing, I can't help admitting that every time I think of it a huge smile spreads across my face.'

'Me too, I'm afraid,' Cassie admitted, dissolving into laughter. 'I know I shouldn't laugh, but in this instance I have to say that I just can't help it.'

'So there you are, Mrs Lovett Andrew is not going to die just yet. But as I said, you have to make your own mind up as to whether this is good news or bad, or perhaps neither.'

But much as Cassie hated Leonora, she still could find no disappointment in her heart that her old adversary's days were not yet numbered, probably, she imagined, because she was actually too concerned about her son's welfare to give Leonora any more thought than was absolutely necessary.

More seriously, Leonora's mischief had awoken Cassie's own doubts about Tyrone, doubts which she had long thought buried, but now that the case had been reopened, as it were, once again Cassie found herself constantly worrying whether the story she had been told by Tyrone and Antoinette Brookes, which she had told as the truth to Mattie, was indeed genuine. Perhaps Cassie had been duped after all, persuaded by Tyrone away from believing what she had instinctively believed in the first place, that her beloved husband had indeed had an affair with Antoinette and, since Cassie herself had been unable to bear him any more children, had been only too anxious and determined to adopt what was after all his natural son.

'We really need to prove this thing beyond a shadow of a doubt, you know,' Cassie told Theodore when he called by for a drink at Claremore on his way home that evening. 'Mattie's the original Doubting Thomas. We shall have to prove his paternity beyond question.'

'The banding should do *just* that,' Theodore replied, with an anxious glance at Cassie. 'What is it, Cassie? You seem to have got yourself into a rare old fret since we spoke earlier.'

'Have I?' Cassie asked absently, unable to collect the thoughts still spinning in her head. 'No I haven't, Theodore. It's just having to go through this all over again. I really thought this particular spook wouldn't come back to haunt us any more.'

'It hasn't, Cassie.' Theodore took one of her hands in both of his and smiled at her. 'Believe me, we shall be able to lay this ghost once and for all, so you're to stop your worrying. We could do so *quite* categorically, of course, had we say a sample of your late husband's blood, but since this is out of the question—'

Cassie put her drink down suddenly. 'No it isn't,' she said. 'It isn't out of the question at all, Theodore! Dear heavens, what can I have been thinking? We do have a sample of Tyrone's blood! But I'd forgotten altogether about it!'

Theodore regarded her steadily, then still holding her hand led her over to the sofa where he sat her down beside him and waited for her explanation.

'Long before the scare started in proper about blood transfusions, Tyrone had developed a major worry that infection could be passed this way,' Cassie explained. 'He was convinced of it because of certain anomalies he had noticed in horses after they had been transfused and he even used to proselytize about it but because he was a horse trainer and not a doctor no-one paid him much attention, except Niall Brogan our vet. He thought Tyrone was talking sense, so much so that because Tyrone and I both rode so much and were therefore at high risk if you like, Niall suggested to Tyrone that we should all store some of our own blood. Niall was very strong on blood conditions as well, in fact he was one of the very first vets ever here to start carefully monitoring all the horses' blood, and so when he persuaded Tyrone to bank some of our own blood it seemed perfectly sensible.'

'And so it was,' Theodore agreed. 'It's known as auto-logous transfusion – but then when Tyrone and Niall decided on the move, this would have been quite some time ago.'

'Yes. But I really *had* forgotten all about it, and by that I mean that after he died I never issued any instructions to the blood bank to dispose of Tyrone's deposit. They still have mine, of course, and I take it they still have his – *but even better than that* – ' Cassie suddenly got to her feet in the excitement. '*We still have some here!*'

Together they hurried out to the veterinary block down in the stable yard, Cassie explaining as they went that besides the blood Tyrone had assigned to the blood bank, he had also kept a supply carefully and properly stored under the correct conditions on the premises.

'This was long before I built this veterinary block, of course,' Cassie explained, hurrying into the building ahead of Theodore. 'But even so Niall knew how to store blood correctly, so when this was all built every sample was simply transferred into this new banking unit.'

Cassie threw open the doors of what looked like a super refrigerator to reveal a vast store of pints of banked blood.

'Most of this belongs to horses, of course,' Cassie said, consulting a list on the unit door. 'But there should be a smaller section somewhere containing the samples we want – and here it is.'

Cassie tapped a category on the list which read: *Batch 0001 Tyrone Rosse/May 1966.*

'Excellent,' Theodore said with quiet delight. 'All we have to do now is have a sample processed and banded and Bob will be your famous uncle.'

Cassie was so relieved and delighted that she threw her arms around Theodore and kissed him.

Thanks to Theodore's connections the second sample arrived even more quickly than had Leonora's, so that by the end of that week all that remained was to await the report of the genetic engineer Theodore had commissioned to interpret the data on their behalf.

'You understand exactly what this will mean?' Cassie asked Mattie once again as they waited for Theodore to arrive at Claremore with the findings.

'I do,' Mattie replied. 'Do you?'

'Yes,' Cassie said. 'I think so.'

She had found it impossible to watch as Theodore had gone through the samples to find the batch number belonging to Tyrone, once the delight at being able to prove Mattie's paternity beyond any shadow of a doubt had been replaced by the realization that if she had stayed where she was she would have to witness a sample of Tyrone's life force being removed from its cold storage.

*I'm not too good with blood at the best of times*, she had said, excusing herself as Theodore began his search. *If you don't mind terribly, I'll leave you to it.*

So yes, she thought to herself as she checked her hair in the glass of a picture hanging on one wall. Yes, I'd say I know exactly what this will mean.

Theodore arrived bearing a buff folder. In keeping with the importance of the moment Cassie thought that he looked if anything even more distinguished than ever, in his immaculately tailored dark suit and hand-made shirt and shoes.

'Really all you need read are the findings of the expert,' Theodore told Mattie, handing him a single sheet of paper. 'They prove without a doubt that Mrs Charles C. Lovett Andrew is not your mother.'

Mattie took the sheet but glanced at Theodore before reading it. 'Beyond any doubt?' he asked.

'Backed up by the findings of genetic fingerprinting the chances of Mrs Charles C. Lovett Andrew *née* Leonora Von Wagner being your mother are precisely one in thirty thousand million,' Theodore informed him.

'One in thirty thousand million?' Mattie echoed. 'I'll take the odds on offer.'

'That's how categorical genetic fingerprinting is,' Theodore replied.

Mattie read the single sheet of paper, sitting down at the desk to do so, while Cassie looked at Theodore. In response, Theodore held up one index finger behind the folder he had clasped against him as if to indicate that what Mattie had in front of him was not all. Cassie frowned, but again Theodore said nothing, raising instead the same index finger to his lips to indicate silence.

'Well?' Theodore enquired when he saw that Mattie had finished reading the document.

'Thank you, Mr Pilkington,' was Mattie's polite response. 'Yes, that certainly seems to be it as far as Mrs Lovett Andrew's claim goes.'

'Might I see that?' Cassie wondered, picking up the document. 'Not that I need any such proof.'

'You'd have done the same if you'd been me,' Mattie said.

'No I wouldn't and I'm not you,' Cassie said, remembering her own mother's long term deception. 'My mother brought me up to believe what she told me. I don't think I would ever have dared do otherwise. But that doesn't mean I think you were wrong. You've been brought up very differently from the way I was brought up, believe me.'

'It's not that I doubted you,' Mattie said. 'It's just that the whole thing has never quite made sense.'

'Because you look like Dad.'

'Yes.'

'But that's been laid to rest now, Mattie. You don't have to pursue that one any more.'

'You're wrong,' Mattie replied, looking at her with big dark eyes. 'This piece of paper only proves Leonora wasn't my mother. It doesn't prove Dad wasn't my real father.'

Cassie stared back at him, unable to believe her ears. As far as she had been concerned once Leonora's claim had been so absolutely disproved the case was closed. She certainly had not anticipated this particular twist.

It seemed Theodore, however, had. 'Meaning,' he began, reopening the folder once again. 'Meaning that in spite of what your adoptive mother here has told you still believe that your adoptive father was actually responsible for getting Miss Antoinette Brookes pregnant.'

'It's still perfectly possible is all I'm saying,' Mattie replied.

'Even though Mr Gerald Secker otherwise known as Anthony Wilton has admitted paternity.'

'He disappeared to India after he thought he'd got her pregnant,' Mattie said. 'That's as far as he *knew*. We don't have any sort of time scale on this.'

'Oh, but we do, we do,' Theodore contradicted him. 'Being a surgeon is a bit like being a detective. You have to anticipate, if one is to be any good as a surgeon that is, naturally. And having gathered from your adoptive mother here just what a Doubting Thomas you are, young man, I did a little detective work on all our behalfs. Here.'

He handed Mattie two more sheets of typed paper from the folder which Mattie took from him and again sat down to read.

'That is your time scale on the events in question,' Theodore said with a quiet smile at Cassie who was staring at him. 'I got in touch with Mr Secker stroke Wilton who was only too pleased to co-operate with me, being a thoroughly decent sort of chap, as well as an ardent fan of your adoptive mother's. It took him a little while to reconstruct the exact chain of events with their precise chronology, but happily he kept a journal at the time because such was his habit. I understand in fact he still does, since he has always nursed an as yet unfulfilled ambition to be a writer, so as you will see if you read on his claim to have got the young lady in question pregnant in March 1966 when she was living in Dublin and working for Gerald and his father Alec, who was *then* head of Irish Bloodstock Incorporated, has to be *exact*. He even annotates the date he thinks you were conceived because for a moment he did apparently contemplate marrying Antoinette Brookes, but then thought better of it. They also discussed an abortion – but happily for you, young man, and your adoptive parents, your real mother would not contemplate the idea. More to the point, much *much* more to the point is the fact that at the time both of them were out of the country. Alec Secker had sent his son abroad for three months to learn the ropes on a friend's stud farm in Kentucky at the *beginning* of that year, which was actually where he met Antoinette Brookes. And where in fact you, Mattie, were conceived. Read on and you will see that you were born precisely *nine months later* on the seventeenth of November that very year. It simply would not have been possible for Miss Brookes *still* to meet your adoptive father and become pregnant by him because by then she was quite definitely pregnant by Mr Secker stroke Wilton. It's all down in his journals, including a note from Miss Brookes about the result of a pregnancy test run in May of that year, and the fact of the matter is your adoptive father did not *actually meet Miss Brookes* until the Irish Derby meeting at the Curragh on June the 29th, which after all is only five months before you were born. That too is recorded in Mr Secker stroke Wilton's journal, because that too was the first time he had met the famous Tyrone Rosse in person, fresh back from America the Brave as both he and Miss Brookes indeed were. Lastly – at the foot of the second of the pages you have in your hand you will see the results of two other DNA processes, one taken from your late adoptive father from an emergency supply of his blood kept in a blood bank and the other from a blood sample belonging to your real father Gerald Secker, who understanding your concern readily agreed to a test. So there it is, young man. You will find from your readings that there is no chance whatsoever that your adoptive father could possibly have been your real one.'

'It doesn't matter that Tyrone wasn't your real father,' Cassie said to her son after Theodore had tactfully left them alone and returned to his home.

'What do you mean?' Mattie said, the edge back in his voice.

'I may only be your adoptive mother, Mattie, but I'm still your mother,' Cassie said, patting the sofa for him to come and sit beside her. 'I've known you since you were a baby, I've known all your moods, your joys, your woes—'

'My highs, my lows,' Mattie sighed, doing as bidden and sitting down beside Cassie.

'And one of your lows was and still is the fact that Tyrone was not your *proper* father,' Cassie reiterated. 'Although he was a father to you in every sense of the word in every other way.'

'I know, I know,' Mattie said, not without rancour. 'It's just so weird. And always has been. I mean, look at my hands—' He held out both his hands to her. 'Everyone says they're just like Dad's. You can even see it in photographs of him.'

'My mother was always telling me I had hands just like Joyce Hart, who was a well-known American concert pianist when I was a child. But I can't play a note. And I'm absolutely certain she never knew my father.'

'Even so, you have to admit that it's weird.' Mattie lay back on the sofa, putting both his hands on top of his head.

'Maybe all these things, the things you think are like Dad's,' Cassie ventured, 'maybe it's because you want to be like him, and so taking it to its logical conclusion you made yourself want nothing more than that he should actually be your father.'

'Maybe,' Mattie said thoughtfully. 'Yes, maybe. Who wouldn't want to be like Dad?'

At that moment there was nothing Cassie wanted more than to put her arms round her son and hold him, but she resisted the urge because she knew how much it would embarrass him. So instead she just smiled, more to herself than to Mattie, and pretended to brush some of Wilkie's hairs off her skirt. 'So,' she said.

'Why didn't you tell me then?' Mattie asked with a deep frown. 'I mean when I met my real father at Epsom. Why didn't you tell me afterwards who he was?'

'I suppose because I was waiting to see if one day you would ask,' Cassie replied. 'Some adopted children do, and some don't. You didn't say, at least not until now, so I didn't volunteer. Why? Would you like to see him again? Your real father?'

'I don't know. I think so. We certainly got on pretty well

when we did meet. In fact I liked him a lot. So yes – yes, I suppose I would like to see him. If it's all right with you.'

'Of course it's all right with me,' Cassie assured him. 'It won't change anything, at least not anything that's gone before. But it might change things in the future and for the better even, who knows? We'll ask Theodore where he is right now. Apparently he spends most of his time in America.'

'There's no hurry,' Mattie said. 'Maybe I'll write to him first. See if he wants to see me. He might not want to.'

'Of course he will,' Cassie smiled. 'Now he knows who you are.'

'You mean he didn't before?'

'Of course not. We adopted you straight from your mother. Gerald was the other side of the world if you remember, and when he met you at Epsom he had no idea he was your real father. That's why it was so nice you two hit it off straight away.'

'Even so, I still think I'll write to him first,' Mattie said, looking away. 'It'll give him an out, just in case he needs one.'

'He won't, don't you worry,' Cassie replied, smoothing out her skirt once more. 'Now – I have some more news for you, or rather I have a deal I'd like to propose. I want you to have Nightie.'

Slowly Mattie turned and looked at her in wonder, tipping his handsome head to one side. 'Nightie as in The Nightingale?'

'You got it.'

'Why? Has something happened to him?'

'No, nothing's *happened* to him—'

'I mean, not that I mind if something has – no I don't mean that. Of course I'd mind if something's happened to him, I'd mind like hell. What I meant was that if you've decided to retire him and you want to give him to me—'

Cassie patted Wilkie a couple of times on his head and shook her own. 'Nothing's happened to him, I'm not retiring him and I'm not giving him to you,' she said. 'I want you to have him as in to train him – and don't say one word until you've heard me out. Understand?'

'Understood.' By now Mattie had dropped his hands and sunk them in his trouser pockets, turning to give his mother his full attention. 'Shoot.'

'I've thought this through to the last detail,' she told him. 'And when you hear what I have to tell you, you'll see exactly what I mean. I want you to have The Nightingale in your yard and I want you to train him.'

Mattie shook his head. 'Seriously,' he said. 'I thought you really had retired him.'

'I have.'

'Then how can I train him?'

'If you listen, I shall tell you.'

'*If you build it, he will come.*'

'Right. In fact this isn't altogether unlike *Field of Dreams*,' Cassie agreed, picking up the film reference. 'Because when you and I have done our work, you wait and see. The roads everywhere for miles around will once again be choked by people coming to see him once again, come to see the magic of Himself.'

But when Cassie had finished outlining her plans to Mattie, before they could indulge themselves fully in their day-dreams, the telephone suddenly rang.

'Hello?' a familiar voice whispered in her ear. 'This is Josephine.'

'Josephine?' Cassie sat bolt upright, knowing at once something was wrong. 'What is it? Where are you?'

'I'm all right,' her daughter replied, again barely audibly. 'But I'm in hospital. I'm in the Charing Cross, and I'd give anything, Mums, anything, I promise, if I could just see you. Just anything.'

Cassie caught the very next flight over.

# Twenty-Eight

'How and when did this happen?' she asked, for want of something to do fruitlessly rearranging the flowers she had bought Josephine at the airport, anything rather than look again on the sight that had first greeted her.

'It doesn't really matter, Mums,' Josephine replied through bruised and swollen lips. 'What matters is as I said – you were right and man was I wrong.'

'The moment I'm out of here, I'll have my lawyers on him,' Cassie said, once more removing all the roses from the vase and beginning again. 'When I think what this man has done to you, while poor Joel is marking out time in gaol for an act of clemency – I mean, what sort of world is this that we're living in anyway?'

'You're not making any sense, Mums,' Josephine said, with a crooked smile. 'And for heaven's sake leave those poor flowers alone. They were perfectly all right till you got your hands on them.'

Cassie glanced at her daughter, then immediately closed her eyes, holding on to the back of a chair on which she then finally sat herself down. 'Anyway, thank God you called me.'

'I hardly dared to, Mums,' Josephine whispered, turning a black-eyed face towards her. 'I've been so ashamed.'

'There was no reason to be ashamed.'

'Of course there was. I've been so ashamed of the way I've behaved towards you.'

'You really don't have any reason to be, darling.'

'I must have been completely mad. Or as Mattie said, possessed.'

'Whatever,' Cassie muttered. 'I don't care what you say,

447

Jo. Whether you like it or not I'll see that sonofabitch in court.'

'The only court we'll see him in, Mums, is the divorce one,' Josephine answered. 'I should have known better.'

'Don't you go blaming yourself again.' Cassie's eyes flashed a fierce warning. 'I won't hear any more excuses on behalf of Mr Mark Carter-James, do you hear?'

'I'm not making excuses,' Josephine replied. 'I'm just thinking aloud. I knew the moment I came into the house he had someone upstairs in the bedroom. And I should have just turned on my heel, walked out, and got the first plane back home. But no, no, I had to go and have it out with him—'

'And that of course gave him a perfectly justifiable reason to beat you up,' Cassie interrupted. 'Mr Mark Carter-James can count himself lucky your brother was finally persuaded to stay home or he might well be lying in a morgue by now.'

'I am going to divorce him, you know,' Josephine said, shifting her broken arm into a more comfortable position. 'So it's just as well we weren't married in a church.'

'No you're not going to divorce him,' Cassie said. 'What you are going to get is an annulment, and what I am going to do is make sure the mud that flies sticks to him. You just leave this to me and my lawyers. I mean it.'

'An annulment, fine,' Josephine whispered. 'But not the police. *I* mean it. Even if he did go to gaol, when he got out he'd come after me. He's totally mad, really mad. He is right off any given map. I know. And as for marrying him, I *must* have been mad. I can't explain it, really. It was like being hypnotized. It was like being under some kind of awful spell.'

'We'll talk about this when you're yourself, darling, OK? At the moment you're going to need all your strength to get better.'

'There's really nothing more to talk about, Mums.'

'You bet there is,' Cassie said grimly.

\* \* \*

On her way out, having left Josephine in a deep sedative-induced sleep, Cassie asked when she could take her daughter home. She was told that they would need to keep Josephine in and under observation for at least another two or three days, but provided there were no unforeseen complications or as yet undiscovered injuries there was no reason Josephine could not go home after that.

'Fine,' Cassie told the nurse. 'Then please tell my daughter I'll be in to see her first thing tomorrow, and that all being well we'll have her back home for the weekend. And thank you. I mean that. For all that you've done,' she added, but the nurse had already moved on.

True to her word, Cassie flew out of London with Josephine late afternoon on Friday. Mattie met them at Dublin airport in Jack Madigan's chauffeur-driven S class Mercedes, laid on specially for the occasion.

'It was all I could do to persuade Jack not to buy an ambulance specially,' Mattie said, once they had Josephine comfortably settled in the back. 'So what's the damage, sis? Any plans for the return match yet?'

'Don't make me laugh, Matt,' Josephine pleaded through bruised lips. 'Not yet, at least.'

'If you thought I was mad, Ma, you wait till you see Jack Madigan,' Mattie said as the car pulled away. 'If I were you, sis, I'd tell that husband of yours to change his identity and his nationality, unless he wants to end up in a deep hole in a field somewhere in Roscommon.'

'Let's not dwell on such unsavoury matters, shall we?' Cassie said with finality, sliding the glass partition shut between themselves and the driver. 'We'll draw a line under this, just until we know more, that is.'

During the first few weeks of Josephine's recuperation, Cassie spent a good deal of time with young Gareth Plunkett helping prepare their case against her bloodstock insurers. He was a frequent visitor to the house, since given Cassie's phenomenal workload now that the Flat season was beginning to get into full swing it was usually easier to get round the table out at Claremore than it was for Cassie to dash into Dublin at a moment's notice. He was an exceptionally nice young man, very clever without being smart and naturally funny without ever being facetious, something Cassie always found irritating.

'Are you married, Gareth?' she found herself asking him suddenly one day as they broke from working to have coffee.

'No, I'm not married, Mrs Rosse,' Gareth replied, putting down his coffee cup beside his wonderfully neat notebook. 'I was to be married, but in the words of the song, somebody stole my girl.'

'Your best friend, no doubt.'

'Worse,' Gareth sighed. 'My father.'

Cassie looked up from reading her latest brief. 'Your father? That's every son's nightmare, surely?'

'Doubly so, Mrs Rosse. He went and married her.'

'Oh dear,' Cassie said sympathetically. 'There's not a lot you can say to that, is there?'

'I can tell you I certainly didn't find a thing,' Gareth agreed. 'In fact even now when I come to think of it I'm speechless. Talk about not losing a daughter but gaining a son. I not only lost a *fiancé*, I lost a father as well.'

'You poor fellow,' Cassie said, trying to imagine such a thing. 'Sometimes when I hear things like that, I wonder whether family life is all it's cracked up to be.'

'I know what you mean,' Gareth agreed. 'But then there are families and there are families. If I may say so, I wouldn't have thought that you need have much to fear in such directions.'

Cassie nearly told him then. She longed to tell him because she longed to tell someone just how terrible the past months had been as far as her own family relationships had gone. She had refused to tell Joel because he had enough causes for concern of his own, and although she had told Theodore as much as he needed to know about Mattie and his doubts, she had not told him everything because again she had thought it unfair since in a way Theo was still trying to rebuild his own life. In the end she did not unburden herself on Gareth either, simply because she thought that would just be plain unfair, particularly now she had just learned that he had his own particular misery.

'Well, let's hope you meet someone really special,' she offered instead. 'Someone who'll help make good all that hurt.'

'I think I already have, Mrs Rosse,' Gareth said a little shyly, 'but now we really ought to get back to business. After all, you're paying for this time.'

He was back again the very next day, but this time after business hours. Cassie found him standing in the hallway when she came into the house after evening stables, dressed not as he normally was for work but informally in a good pair of blue jeans, a cream-coloured polo shirt and a worn but well-cut suede bomber jacket. He was also clasping a small bunch of spring freesias.

'Gareth?' she said, puzzled and suddenly worried when she saw the flowers. 'There's nothing wrong, I hope? I mean, we don't have a meeting scheduled, surely? Not at this time of day.'

'No, of course not, Mrs Rosse,' Gareth replied, blushing slightly. 'I didn't know I was coming out here myself, until—'

'Until I asked him,' came a voice from the stairs above both of them.

'Jo?' Cassie looked up and saw her daughter coming down the stairway, still with the aid of her walking stick, but freshly made up and looking well on the way to recovery. 'I didn't know you two knew each other.'

'We don't. That is, we didn't,' Gareth offered.

'But we do now,' Jo said, arriving at the bottom of the stairs.

'Your daughter was outside the house yesterday when I arrived, Mrs Rosse,' Gareth explained, smiling round at Josephine as she came to his side. 'She was in the garden and we got talking—'

'And Gareth asked me out,' Josephine said impishly,

451

looking now at the flowers in Gareth's hand. 'Are those for my mother?'

Gareth looked nervously from mother to daughter. 'Yes, yes of course,' he said. 'Mrs Rosse, I'm sorry – these are for you.' He handed the freesias to Cassie who accepted them with a smile.

'Thank you, Gareth. I simply love freesias. When Josephine was born her father filled our entire bedroom with them.'

'I really should have asked you, I think, Mrs Rosse,' Gareth continued in some confusion.

'You should have asked my mother whether or not you should give her flowers?' Josephine teased.

'Whether or not I could ask her daughter out.'

'I'm a bit past that stage, Mr Plunkett,' Josephine said. 'Anyway, supposing she'd said no?'

'Then I would have respected your mother's wishes.'

Josephine sighed and smiled at the handsome young man. 'Who ever said chivalry was dead, eh, Mums?'

'Not me,' Cassie returned with a smile, carefully unwrapping the cellophane from round the freesias. 'So where are you two off to, Gareth? If you don't mind my asking.'

'Not at all, Mrs Rosse. I shall take her wherever she would like to go.'

'It's such a lovely spring evening, why don't we drive down to Killiney and have dinner at the seafood restaurant?' Josephine suggested. 'Do you know the one I mean – Blakey's, isn't it?'

'I know it,' Gareth replied. 'It's owned and run by my Uncle Daniel, and if I may say so he's a fair old cook.'

Cassie watched them drive away in Gareth's old but immaculate red MGB sports into the fine spring evening, past where the mares and their newly born foals were being carefully shepherded out of the home paddocks to be led away and up into their stables for the night, past the racing yards and the loose school and away down the long drive towards the main gates until they disappeared from sight.

'Please God,' Cassie said to herself as she made her way

452

towards the kitchen to put the sweet-smelling flowers in water. 'Please God.'

Then she took the flowers up to Josephine's room where she put them by the bedside, where they had obviously been destined to go in the first place.


A week later Cassie drove her daughter down to Kilkenny.

'You might tell us where we're going,' Josephine wondered yet again as the burgeoning landscape passed in a blur of spring green past the car windows. 'What is with all this *secrecy*?'

'You'll see,' Cassie told her. 'But remember, I meant what I said to you before we left. You are not to say one word of this to anyone. Not a soul.'

'I know where this is,' Josephine announced as Cassie turned the car up a long drive leading to a fine Georgian house. 'This is where that friend of yours Peter Nugent lives. The eventing genius. I didn't know you were into eventing.'

'I'm not.'

'So why are we here?'

'Wait and see.'

'Please, Mums, I can't bear it. It's like being a little girl again. I know when you're hiding something, so please, *please* tell me.'

Cassie glanced round at her daughter and then pulled the car up in a small layby on the long drive under the budding chestnut trees. Beyond the paddocks which lay on either side of the drive several horses could be seen doing grid work in an outdoors *ménage*. The two of them watched the horses work for a moment in silence before Cassie spoke.

She told her daughter everything that had happened until now which was relevant to the scheme, and all that she intended to happen from this moment on. After she had finished Josephine stared at her mother. 'You're serious, aren't you?'

'I have never been more serious in my life.'

'And you really think you can pull it off?'

'No. No, I really think *we* can pull it off, Jo. You, Mattie and I will do it. The three of us will pull it off, with a little help from our friends.' Then she started the car again and drove up the drive to initiate her stratagem.

'The horse is remarkably well,' Peter Nugent told them as they drove in his Range Rover across his cross country course to the nominated fences. 'And not only is he well, he's also one of the brightest chaps I've had the pleasure to work with. You only have to tell him something once and he's got it. Furthermore, Cassie, although it's early days, he still seems to have plenty of toe.'

'Certainly he has. The monkey all but tanked off with me last time I rode him. Obviously your girl hasn't had any problems or we'd have heard about them by now.'

'Mo gets on with him fine, but Mo has her limitations,' Peter replied. 'And of course just as you said, the old boy won't let anyone of my sex near him. Talk about Jekyll and Hyde. Right—' Peter stopped the car and opened his door. 'Perfect timing,' he said. 'Here they come now.'

All three of them stood on the side of the hill on which the car had stopped, watching two horses canter up the slope towards them. One was a bright bay, a good strong eventing type who moved well enough but even at the canter was finding it hard work to keep up with the big black horse upsides him who was positively floating over the ground.

'My God,' Josephine whispered. 'I'd forgotten his sheer power. And as for the way he moves – but you're all mad. There isn't a hope in hell.'

'No negative thoughts, Jo,' Cassie replied. 'I told you. All you need is to get fit which won't take you long. It's not as if you stopped riding altogether.'

'Hacking's a long way from what you're asking me to do.'

'You were still race riding up to the end of last season,' Cassie reminded her. 'It won't take you long to get fit again, once you're fully mended. It never does. It's just going to hurt a bit at first, that's all. I should know. I talk from experience. Now then, Peter – is this the jump you had in mind?'

Cassie deliberately walked away from Josephine to join Peter Nugent by the first of three large newly built fences which had been erected at intervals of about a hundred metres on a specially prepared strip of level grass.

'These are the ones, Cassie,' Peter confirmed, pushing the birch with his hands to demonstrate how tightly packed the fence was. 'As you can see they're a good four foot, with ground rails and another rail halfway up. We didn't put top rails on because although we'd seen him flip over those fences on the schooling ground, these are altogether much more solid, rather like the French hurdles, rather like the ones at Auteuil, yes? And my own feeling was that if there were top rails and he hit one, knowing how bright the old horse is he might just go off the whole enterprise. Either that or start ballooning his obstacles which is not what we want either. Correct?'

'Totally. And you haven't put him at these yet.'

'As agreed, we were waiting for you. After all, seeing is believing. OK, Mo!' he called to the girl riding The Nightingale. 'Show them the first fence, and then in your own time pop 'em over 'em!'

'Alongsides, Mr Nugent?' the girl asked as the two horses circled around them. 'Or do you want Sam here to give us a lead?'

'Alongsides, please, Mo! I doubt if you'd settle him in behind!'

'She would,' Cassie told Peter privately as the horses walked up to look at the first fence. 'You can put him anywhere. But then he's such a show-off he just might on the other hand start fooling about. So absolutely. Send them both at the first one together.'

The three of them positioned themselves in a line halfway down the flight of jumps as the horses were turned away from the fence and trotted back a good hundred yards. Suddenly Cassie felt nervous, more nervous even than she had felt watching the horse on the day he won his first Derby. So much depended on the next few moments, whereas when the horse had lined up at Epsom, even though he was expected to win, Cassie had nothing to lose except her pride. But now, now if the house she was building in her dreams turned out to be made of straw she could face not just ruin but complete ignominy.

As if sensing this, Josephine slipped her arm through Cassie's and held it tight. 'What exactly are we looking to see? Just so as I know.'

'I can't tell you exactly, Jo. All I can tell you is that if the horse has got it, we'll know all right. You can bet on it.'

Even as she spoke the two horses kicked off from the start, settling into a good steady gallop as they headed for the first of the three fences. As always The Nightingale had his head tucked down in his chest, his ears pricked and his bright eyes fixed on the solid looking black obstacle that lay in his path. There were no wings at the fences to guide the horses into their takeoff or to stop them running out and for one awful moment as the two animals shaped up at the first fence The Nightingale seemed about to duck out, causing both Cassie and Josephine to gasp in dismay.

But it was only a check. The horse was in fact changing his legs in order to get his stride right which he did in plenty of time, taking off a full length earlier than his companion, who as a result of The Nightingale's prodigious leap plunged at the fence. Had the animal not been such an experienced eventer he would have almost certainly fallen but instead he fiddled it, correcting his error just at the last moment, and although he pecked on landing somehow he managed to land on his feet and scamper away from the obstacle.

But The Nightingale had flown. He had taken off a good ten feet in front of the fence, cleared it by another foot, and landed at least another eight feet beyond.

Even more important, as he had landed he was already running on.

'*That's* what we wanted to see!' Cassie exclaimed excitedly, turning to watch her horse attack the next fence. 'He picked up the moment he touched down! That's *exactly* what we wanted to see!'

By the time The Nightingale had reached the second fence he had pulled himself three lengths clear, but Cassie wasn't interested in distances. She knew Sam was an eventer, and even though he was an Advanced horse he could not be expected to be a match for a racehorse of The Nightingale's calibre. Sam was being used to quantify The Nightingale's ability to jump because Sam was one of the most prodigious jumpers on the circuit.

And The Nightingale was making him look like a novice. He stood even further off at the second fence than he had at the first, again clearing the obstacle with a good foot of daylight between him and the birch. Everything about him seemed to be correct, the way he found his stride into the fence, the way he tucked his forelegs neatly up under him as he met it, and most of all the way he came away from the obstacles, as if he could hardly wait to get to the next one. In fact so great was his enjoyment in jumping that after he had cleared the third and last jump as perfectly and as effortlessly as he had cleared the other two and Mo had pulled him up easily and sweetly at the end of the nominated stretch of ground, he gave a squeal of delight, two good-natured bucks, swung round and tanked off with his rider to hurl himself over a very solid and daunting-looking log pile that was part of Peter Nugent's event course.

'That does it!' Peter laughed. 'Badminton here we come!'

'First things first,' Cassie said, having calmed herself with a deep breath. 'We have a very long way to go yet.'

'What about Mo?' Josephine asked as Peter Nugent was driving them back across his estate. 'She's not going to take kindly to being jocked off Nightie.'

'I don't suppose she would,' Peter replied, 'if she wasn't leaving to get married to her American boyfriend next week.'

'OK,' Josephine asked her mother as they were driving away from the house. 'So supposing I hadn't come home.'

'So supposing. I'd have found another lady rider.'

'Let's start again,' Josephine nodded. 'Why me?'

'Oh, because,' Cassie said, accelerating quickly away from Nugent land now they were back on the road. 'I guess because I reckon you might just have one or two unfulfilled ambitions left.'

'Suppose I fail.'

'You won't. You're not into failing.'

'Look at my marriage. If that wasn't a failure, I don't know what was. And as for – I don't deserve this. Really.'

'On the contrary, sweetheart. You deserve this all the more. And if we don't pull it off, it will have had nothing to do with you. This one's down to me. Now tell me something. I haven't asked you before because I wanted to wait until you were better – but what did you mean exactly about Mark marrying you to get back at me?'

Josephine looked round at Cassie then turned away to stare silently at the countryside flashing past her before she replied. 'It's just a theory, that's all,' she said. 'He was obsessed by you and Nightie, so was his father. I just don't think they could take it, not in their world. A woman being that brilliant and successful. They both absolutely hate women, that I do know, and to my cost. I just think you represented everything they both hated. And I was there ready for the taking.'

'I'm sorry, sweetheart,' Cassie said, reaching out a hand to take one of Josephine's. 'Sometimes it seems as if Nightie's brought us nothing but unhappiness.'

'Oh, come on, Mums,' Josephine said with a wry grin. 'What happened to me was hardly the horse's fault. I'm old and ugly enough to know better. Right?'

Cassie and Josephine went into training together, once Josephine had been given the all clear by Dr Gilbert who gave her a thorough examination to make sure all the breaks were well and truly mended and all the internal bruising was completely healed, following Cassie's tried and true get-fit regimen.

'It's hardly state of the art, I know,' Cassie grunted as they pounded up the hills behind Claremore in three layers

458

of running clothes with weights attached to their wrists and ankles, 'but it does the trick.'

'It's those dreadful half-crouching exercises I can't stand,' Josephine groaned back. 'I could hardly put one leg in front of the other yesterday.'

'Tomas taught me that,' Cassie said, swinging left now they'd reached the top of the hill and running along the level track that stretched out for a quarter of a mile ahead of them.

'The only way to get your calf muscles, your thighs and your back strong enough to race ride.'

'You can do it in a gym half as painfully,' Josephine replied.

'And about half as effectively. Being women, we have to work twice as hard in those areas as men because we just don't have the muscles there. Particularly in the lower leg.'

'I don't want them, thank you,' Josephine returned. 'Gareth says I've the best legs he's seen.'

'This getting serious between you and that young man?'

'Would you mind if it was?'

'Not at all. You've seen him practically every day since he began taking you out.'

'I don't think I've ever met anyone quite as nice as Gareth. And you're fifty-three times as fit as I am.'

'I've been riding out every day, sweetheart. And swimming. And walking. I have to keep myself fit.'

'Then maybe it should be you riding the horse, not me.'

'Hey!'

Cassie had stopped running and called out to her daughter. Josephine turned and came back to join her and both of them stood for a moment with their hands on their hips, catching their breath and looking down at Claremore which lay stretched out in the spring sunshine far below them.

'Hey,' Cassie said when she had got her breath back. 'Don't you really want to do this? Because if you don't—'

'I think you're mad. Quite quite mad. And of course I want to do this, because I'm your daughter. I'm mad as well. Now come on – last home has to do twenty extra sit

459

downs!' Cassie smiled to herself and gave her daughter a headstart. None the less she made sure she caught her just in time before they collapsed against the back door of the house, because as she well knew Josephine's need to do the twenty extra sit downs was even greater than her own.

At the end of the week Cassie got a long-awaited letter from Joel. It arrived second post, brought to her by Dick in his usual slip-sliding fashion.

'One day Erin will polish those floors even more than ever and you'll end up sliding all the way down the corridor and into the cellars, Dick,' Josephine said with a grin as the shoeless Dick shuffled back out of the drawing room where Josephine, Mattie and their mother had met to have tea and an update on Cassie's stratagem.

While Cassie drew her legs up and tucked them under her on the sofa to read her letter, Mattie and Josephine played a game of Fish at the table. 'I see,' said Cassie after she'd finished reading the letter and was tucking it away back in the envelope.

'Something the matter?' Josephine wondered.

'I was meant to visit Joel this week,' Cassie replied. 'But now he says he doesn't want to see me. He says he thinks it's probably better if we don't see each other until his release.'

'Maybe he's thinking of you,' Mattie ventured, tapping the deck of cards into shape on the table. 'It is a hell of a way to go for an hour's chat, particularly with the sort of life you lead.'

'I shall miss not seeing him for another nine months.'

'Maybe that's also part of the reason,' Josephine suggested. 'The absence makes the heart grow fonder routine?'

'Or the reverse,' Cassie said gloomily. 'It could be the I get along without you very well number.'

'Doesn't he say anything as to why?' Josephine wondered. 'He must give some sort of reason.'

'That's not Joel's style, Jo,' Cassie replied. 'By his own admission he's not the world's greatest letter writer. He's inclined to leave the all-important bits unsaid.'

'Maybe it's there in the you know – subtext.'

'Sure.' Cassie shrugged and passed her daughter Joel's letter to Josephine. 'There's nothing in it that's unsuitable for anyone of a nervous disposition, I guess.' She sat sipping her tea and Mattie layed out a game of patience for himself as Josephine sat on the floor by her mother's feet reading the letter.

'How's Joel as gumshoe getting on?'

'It's hard to say, Mattie,' Cassie replied. 'He's only had the whole file a week or so, although he does hint he's made a couple of connections.'

'I've always reckoned it was someone with a serious grudge. I go along with the theory that whoever was behind taking the horse was talking through his pocket, in which case it has to be a bookmaker. One of the big boys, too, because Honest Joe Finnegan in the village could hardly have afforded the heavy mob, could he?'

'No. But then I've been right through Tyrone's betting books, and although he had some pretty good coups over the years like all gamblers he also had some pretty heavy losses.'

'But Dad's records don't show exactly *who* he hit,' Mattie stated, carefully watching the cards he was slowly dealing out for himself. 'We don't know if any one bookie took a hammering or whether Dad spread his bets around. He could have once done some serious damage to a small bookie and put him out of business.'

'OK – but then by your reckoning if it was only a small bookmaker who'd got hurt he couldn't afford such an expensive revenge. Because let's face it, kidnapping The Nightingale was no bargain basement job.'

'Maybe the bookmaker popped up through another hole, some time later,' Mattie surmised. 'He could have made money some other way and decided he'd finally get his own back. It's only an idea, but – you know – ' Mattie shrugged and began to pick up the cards from his aborted game. 'Half the time you have no idea which way people are coming from. That's what makes making sense of it so difficult.'

'You could well have something. Write and tell Joel that. You never know, it might just trigger something off.'

'You should write to Joel as well,' Josephine said, handing the letter back to her mother. 'And ask him directly what he means, because you can forget any subtext. That's like a letter from a friend, rather than – well, you know.'

'As I said, Jo, Mr Benson does not write great letters.'

'He writes very honest ones. But his idea of you not seeing each other until he's released, maybe it's not so daft. Of course it's great for him to have you visit, but as Mattie just said it is one hell of a long way to go to see him. It's not as if you can just drive up from London, say, or hop on a train from Birmingham down to Oxford. You have to drive into Dublin, take a plane—'

'I know what I have to do, thanks, Jo.'

'All I'm trying to say, Mums, is you might start resenting the journey. You're just really getting into the Flat racing season, you've got a yard full of good horses, you have to be here all the time – and then if you have to miss a couple of visits because a horse is lame, or one starts to cough or something, then Joel might feel bad about you not making it. You see, maybe what he's trying to say is that in the circumstances there's less danger in you not seeing each other for nine months than there is in you trying to make regular visits.'

'Besides the expense,' Mattie mumbled. 'As Jo said, it's not exactly a short drive.'

'Jo's right,' Cassie replied with a sigh, knowing full well she had to keep a tight rein on her expenses. 'You're both right. And maybe so is Joel. Perhaps we should both just get on with what we have to do, and then before you know it, he'll be released and we can just carry on where we left off. Maybe in the long run that is the best thing to do.'

Sensing that neither Mattie nor Josephine had any further interest in discussing Joel she put away her memories of him, filing them away mentally under 'pending', just as she had filed away Tyrone's death for so many long years, the years until she met Joel.

'OK,' Mattie said, snapping Cassie out of her reverie. 'So

now let's hear about the main plan. How's everything panning out?'

'So far so good,' Cassie replied. 'But it'll only stay that way as long as everyone's lip stays buttoned.'

'It's not in anyone's interest to talk,' Mattie said. 'Least of all any of us three.'

Cassie nodded her agreement and then began to go over her stratagem down to the very last detail. For the next three hours, over drinks and then dinner, the three of them took the whole plan to pieces to examine it for flaws and then rebuilt it, nut and bolt by nut and bolt. By the time they got up from table they imagined they had covered every possible exigency which of course as Fate would have it they had not. But then they could hardly be blamed for not foreseeing the events on the horizon which come the following January were going to make them face a seemingly insoluble crisis.

Any thoughts of failure, however, were far from Cassie's mind that evening when she finally reached her bedroom. She could not afford to think of failure, because if the plan foundered then Claremore would be lost. She knew that now she had to watch every penny, for although all the yards were full of horses, a complement which included some very promising two and three year olds, she would need to produce at least one winning Group One horse in order to generate any real profit on the season's racing, because for the Grand Plan to be successful she must not be seen as trying to supplement her income by gambling. Come what may Cassie Rosse must keep being seen as a non-betting trainer, and because she had to watch every penny, she knew Joel's suggestion that she should not continue visiting him was an eminently practical one. Even to fly over and visit him only twice a month would still prove to be a costly enterprise, so not to do so would represent quite a considerable saving over the next nine months. As far as her feelings were concerned she harboured no great fears as to their survival. The span of time they were not going to be able to see each other was by no means a long one and with a busy racing season ahead of her Cassie was hardly going to have either the opportunity or the inclination for any involvements other than those she already had. As for Joel, even if he did have the inclination he certainly was not going to be afforded the opportunity.

Besides, the couple of visits Cassie had made so far had not been altogether successful. Both Joel and she were agreed on that fact, Joel comparing it to one of his most dreaded routines, namely being seen off by someone at a railway station, for despite herself Cassie had found that she kept watching the clock, dreading the moment when they would have to say goodbye while at the same time realizing that any delay in leaving might mean a missed connection back to Ireland.

So by the time Cassie at last put out her light to go to sleep she had quite made up her mind about two things. She would follow Joel's suggestion about not visiting, and only an act of God could stop her pulling off her *coup*.

# Twenty-Nine

By the end of June, thanks to Cassie's old-fashioned training routine, Josephine was beginning to feel fitter than she had ever felt before. The plan was for her to ride in the Diamond Stakes at Ascot, the same race she had ridden on the day of The Nightingale's kidnap, an aim which would satisfy the curiosity of anyone who was wondering why exactly Cassie Rosse and her daughter could be seen every morning pounding along the roads and up the hills around Claremore. In fact so strong was Josephine becoming that Cassie no longer had to pretend to let her daughter beat her. It was taking all of Cassie's fitness to keep anywhere near abreast of Josephine.

By now too news of the break-up of Josephine's marriage to Mark was also abroad, but once the *paparazzi* had contented itself with picking the bones clean, life at Claremore settled back into its well-ordered routine. Cassie had sent Josephine to see her lawyers in Dublin for advice as to the best way to end the marriage, and the lawyers had assured her that since her husband had openly declared that he had no wish to have children it would be highly probable, just as Cassie had surmised, that an annulment based on this determination would be granted. Most important as far as Josephine was concerned, this would mean that as a Catholic should she ever wish to get remarried she would be fully entitled to do so in a church.

At first Mark had tried to put up some token resistance, possibly in the hope of making some sort of financial arrangement with Cassie, but as soon as it was made perfectly clear that if he stood in the way of Josephine's getting an annulment he would find himself facing charges for grievous bodily harm and possibly even statutory rape, no more was heard from him. He was particularly silent after Jack Madigan paid him a courtesy call in London.

'What in heaven's name did you say to him, Jack?' Cassie had asked after learning of the visit.

'It's not what I said, Cassie my love,' Jack had assured her. 'It's what I didn't say that did the trick.'

The result was that suddenly Josephine was happy again, happier than she had ever been since the day she had left Claremore to start trying to earn her living as an actress. Her contentment was due, however, not just to returning to the warmth of her family home, but also to the ever-growing attentions of Gareth Plunkett who since Josephine's return to Claremore had barely let one day go by without seeing her. It came as no surprise to Cassie when the young man finally started to join them on Saturday mornings for their daily ten-mile run.

Mattie, meanwhile, his confidence and self-belief restored, was shaping up into a training force with which the best would have to reckon. At Naas in the second last week of May he saddled not just his first winner but his first two, pulling off a 74/1 double with the victories of a two-year-old in the first and a six-year-old handicapper in the last, backing both horses singly and in a double and thus leaving the course with his pockets metaphorically speaking stuffed full of cash. As Cassie knew, this was more than he could have dared hope for in only the second month of racing in his first season as a trainer and more than Cassie could ever have dreamed of him achieving, for as they both well knew the greater Mattie's success in his first full season, the greater would be the credibility of their intended strike.

'Now the next bit of the jigsaw is getting you home first past the post at Ascot,' Cassie told Josephine one morning the following week when they were alone out running. 'We've got six weeks before the King George meeting at Ascot and I'm going to run your intended mount Dormie One in the big handicap at Leopardstown this coming Saturday, then if all goes well in a conditions race at the

Curragh on Derby Day. Dexter will ride him on both occasions.'

'But—' Josephine began.

'No buts, remember?' Cassie cut in. 'If you're worried about not getting a race on him, you don't have to.'

'I can hardly get a race ride on him if Dex is riding both races!' Josephine gasped as they raced up the final slope of the hill. 'I know he's meant to be a steering job, but it's rather a different matter when there are twenty-odd horses either trying to bulldoze a way through or dropping back on you! Particularly at Ascot with its short straight!'

'It's all right, Jo! You really don't have to worry!' Cassie called back to her daughter over the noise of the wind that buffeted them the moment they breasted the hill. 'You're going to get a race on him! A private one!'

Cassie refused to be drawn any further, waiting instead to see how Dormie One performed at Leopardstown, where predictably enough for such an honest performer the horse ran precisely to his handicap mark, finishing third a neck and a fast diminishing length behind the flyweighted favourite, Crystal Diana.

'The race'll really have brought him on,' Dexter told Cassie as he was unbuckling his girth in the unsaddling enclosure. 'One more run and he'll be spot on.'

'I was thinking of giving him a couple,' Cassie said discreetly. 'But not if you think that'll overcook him.'

'We'll have to wait and see how he comes out of this one first, guv'nor,' Dexter said, slinging his lightweight saddle over one arm. 'He's a tough horse and likes his racing but you wouldn't want another one coming too quick. Mind you, that all depends on precisely what race you had in mind for him next, doesn't it?'

'Let's put it this way,' Cassie replied, standing to one side as Bridie threw a paddock sheet over the sweating Dormie One. 'The race I have earmarked for him you won't find in the Racing Calendar.'

In fact even the most knowledgeable of racegoers would not only have been unable to find the race Cassie had mapped out for her horse but also the very racecourse where it was to be run. For good reason, too, since the last official meeting held there had been back in 1906, well before the Troubles. The owners, however, had never allowed it to fall into complete disuse since it lay on land within their estate walls, and although it had been used to grow hay until the beginning of the Thirties, during the last years before the Second World War it had been fully restored as a private course and used by the family for private race parties.

Now Peter Nugent used it as part of his own training gallops for his event horses, its only other use being the occasional letting to trainers who were close friends of his when they wanted to give any wayward racers they had a school round a track away from the public or to teach wide-running three-year-olds to handle sharp bends.

'Otherwise I'd rather it wasn't in use because let everyone and his wife in and it'd be cut up in no time at all,' Peter explained to Josephine on the Monday two weeks after Dormie One had run at Leopardstown. 'Consequently the course is in perfect order. We maintain it as well as most full time courses and a lot better than some others which tact forbids me to name. So you won't find any potholes or slippery bends, have no fear of that. There's a really good covering of grass as you can see and we keep it well watered from the lake in the middle so the horses'll put down on it all right. Except for the lack of a crowd you might as well be at any decent course in the country.'

Naturally Cassie knew the course of old, having been privileged to use it on certain occasions to school some of her own more difficult horses, and it was just as Peter Nugent had described it, every inch a racecourse except for the attendant crowd of racegoers. Even the old grandstand was still in place as indeed were the running rails, the old-fashioned starting gate, the distance markers and the winning post. It lay in the fold of a valley, no longer accessible from the far distant road which had been deliberately closed by the family in the Thirties when it had been decided the track should be for their private entertainment only. Now it could only be reached by way of a long potholed track which led up from the back of the house around the side of the event course and finally through a long stretch of woodland which hid it completely from the sight of anyone walking or riding by on the east side of the copse. So well concealed was it that the uninitiated would never have known what lay beyond the densely planted woods.

To compete in the unofficial race that day Cassie had shipped down altogether eight of her horses to Kilkenny, all of them weighted exactly to their handicap mark with Dormie One getting weight only from one other, the top weighted Lovely Grub which had already won twice that season. But the horse Cassie knew Dormie One had to beat at the weights in order to be anything approaching a racing certainty by the time the stalls opened at Ascot was a very useful four-year-old handicapper called Big Wallow who was getting nearly a stone from Dormie One. If Dormie One could finish within a length of him, let alone beat him, then the form line would suggest the Diamond Stakes would be his for the taking.

Not that Josephine was kept as fully informed as this. Quite deliberately Cassie briefed all the other jockeys separately and well in advance of the privately held contest, giving them instructions as detailed as those she would have given them on the racecourse proper. The orders she gave to her daughter were also meticulous, above all stressing the fact that although Dormie One was a remorseless galloper he did not exactly possess vivid acceleration and so consequently could not be held up for a late run. His method of victory was to run his rivals ragged so there was no point in keeping him covered up or even handy.

'Remember – he has to be there or thereabouts from the off,' Cassie reminded Josephine as she legged her daughter up into the plate. 'And by the time you pass the three marker, you'll want to be a good three or four lengths clear. Except for the climb up from Swinley Bottom, this track isn't altogether unlike Ascot. You come off the final bend here as I told you with just two furlongs left to run. So whatever you do, don't get boxed in.'

Yet despite all Josephine's best efforts, boxed in was precisely what she got, just as Cassie had ordered her other riders to make sure she did. There being no starting stalls, only the sort of old-fashioned starting gate made of stranded wires which shot upwards when released by the starter and would certainly have scared the stall-trained horses half to death, the race had been started from flag and due to the horse drawn beside her whipping round at the off, through no great fault of her own Josephine missed the break. Consequently by the end of the first half mile instead of lying handy she was ten lengths adrift of the leaders with all to do. The horses up front weren't taking any prisoners either, having set a scorching pace from the drop of the flag, so Josephine knew that unless she made up her ground now she'd be well and truly beaten for toe if by the time they turned into the straight she was still being towed rather than doing the towing.

Happily just when she was looking to make a move the two horses right in front of her moved off the rails as if to try to improve their own positions on the outside since the way ahead was well and truly blocked by the leading trio who were galloping in line abreast, with the inside horse so tight on the rails he was practically taking the paint off them. Knowing that to go round the outside from where her own horse lay would add another three or four lengths to his journey and thinking that by the time they swung into the straight the leaders by the sheer momentum of their gallop would have to swing a couple of lengths wide of the running rail and thus present her with another gap through which to pounce, Josephine took a pull and swung Dormie One right of the flanks of the horse now cutting across her to fill the opening which had been presented to her.

Now he had the rail to run against her horse lengthened his stride and began to find top gear. In fact he was so full of running by the time they hit the three furlong from home marker his head was practically catching the quarters of the horse racing right in front of him which now began to swish its tail, a sure sign of distress.

'Move over, move over!' Josephine shrieked at its jockey,

who was already hard at work with his whip. 'You're beat so get out of the bloody way!'

But the beaten horse was momentarily trapped by the horse on its outside, Dexter Bryant's mount Big Wallow which looked as full of running as Josephine's own mount felt. Next to Dexter's horse Lovely Grub was also still in the bridle, with Liam sitting on it as still as a mouse, which meant that with Dormie One lying right up its backside the beaten horse had nowhere to go except straight into Josephine's horse.

Leaving Josephine – unless a gap miraculously opened in front of her – with no option but to pull out and try to overtake the leaders on the outside and get first run.

That too was easier said than done as she discovered the moment she tried to switch her horse, since a big grey called Damascus with his jockey hard at work on him was less than a length adrift of Lovely Grub, leaving Josephine no choice but to pull out round him as well in order to make her run. Cursing herself at the top of her voice she managed to steer Dormie One clear of both the two beaten horses but by the time she saw daylight on the outside they were past the two furlong marker and both Dexter and Liam were three lengths clear and had gone for home.

Despite riding the strongest finish she had ever ridden in a race and despite the fact that Dormie One was making ground with every stride he took, Josephine's horse was beaten into third place by two half lengths.

Cassie said nothing to her about her performance until they were driving home, and even then it was left to Josephine to bring the subject up.

'Look,' she began. 'It won't happen like that at Ascot because we'll be coming out of the stalls. It wasn't my fault the horse next to me whipped round.'

'I never said it was.'

'You haven't said anything,' Josephine retorted. 'All we've had since I got off the horse has been the sound of silence.'

'That's because I've been thinking.'

'About what a pig's breakfast I made of it.'

'About best laid plans going astray. It wasn't your fault the horse beside you whipped round, but it was your fault you hadn't already pressed the start button.'

'I don't believe what I'm hearing!'

'I haven't finished yet,' Cassie returned. 'If you don't mind waiting until I finish before you agree or disagree, I'd be very grateful. Because as sure as hell you're not going to learn anything by getting in a temper. So as I was saying, you missed the break not because the horse whipped round but because you weren't already going forward. The other jocks anticipated the break. I had my glasses on you. You were caught flat-footed.'

'Fine, so I was caught flat-footed,' Josephine agreed ungraciously. 'But if we'd been in starting stalls it would have been a different matter.'

'No, not necessarily,' Cassie argued. 'It's all too easy to miss the break in the stalls as well. I've seen jocks a thousand times more experienced than you miss the break. Watch guys like Eddery, and Carson, Reid, and Dettori just for beginners. By the time the gates open ninety-nine point nine per cent of the time their horses are already *in motion*. And that's what you have to do, Jose. You've got to have your horse going the moment you see daylight. *Jockeys?* the starter will call you.'

'I know,' Josephine agreed wearily. 'I have race ridden before.'

'*Jockeys?* he'll call you,' Cassie continued, ignoring the interruption. '*One two* – and you're running. I want to see you out of those stalls and a length up while the other ladies are still adjusting their goggles.'

'Fine.' Josephine sighed and looked sideways out of her window as if her mother was still teaching her to suck eggs.

'*Jockeys? One two* – bang. You're out,' Cassie repeated, just to hammer her point home.

'So,' Josephine said, before giving yet another sigh. 'So I get a flyer and I lie up handy. But supposing the same thing happens at Ascot that happened just now? Suppose I'm lying handy and I get boxed in on the rails? With that short straight there's no way I'm going to pull him out in time for a run.'

'No, that won't happen at Ascot, Jo,' Cassie replied. 'Not if you're where you should be, namely first, second or third by the time you hit the four marker, first or second by the time you hit three, in the lead by the time you pass the two. You got boxed in today because you had to make up your ground on the inside. I told the others to slam the door on you and keep it shut if that happened. Just as I told Ted to swing his horse round beside you at the start.'

Josephine turned and looked at her mother with amazement. 'You did what?' she said.

'I told Ted to whip his horse round to see if you'd take your eye off the ball,' Cassie said. 'You lost your focus. You can't do that at the start of a race. You can't do it at any point of a race. You have to stay entirely focused, even in the stalls. You never know what's going to happen. It might look for a dreadful moment as if the jock next to you isn't going to get his horse's blindfold off in time, *but that's his worry*.' Cassie glanced back at Josephine. 'You don't worry about that, not one bit. All you think about is having your horse running the moment those gates swing open.'

'Right,' the chastened Josephine agreed. '*Jockeys? One two* – I'm running.'

'OK,' Cassie replied. 'And where are you running?'

'I'm running first, second or third by the time I hit the four marker, first or second by the time I hit three, and in front by the time I pass the two,' Josephine told her.

'You got it,' Cassie said. 'That way you win by an easy four or five.'

The next move was to pull the horse out of the conditions race at the Curragh which Cassie did at the overnight declarations stage.

'Nothing wrong with the horse, I hope?' Mattie asked when he rang after seeing the runners listed on Ceefax.

'Where are you speaking from?' Cassie said immediately. 'Not in front of anyone I hope?'

'No, I'm on my car phone on the way into town.'

'And Phoebe's not with you?'

'I'm on my way to pick her up as it happens. Now about Dormie One.'

'He got cast,' Cassie said quickly, crossing her fingers in advance of telling the lie, and already asking God's forgiveness. 'He got a bit of a knock and I don't want to take any chances.'

'Quite right too,' Mattie agreed. 'But all being well, Ascot's still on.'

'All being well,' Cassie said. 'But now listen, Mattie. If you're thinking of having a touch—'

'Thinking of it?' Mattie laughed. 'I've thought of nothing else.'

'No,' Cassie said. 'This is not your pension policy. I mean it. You're not to lay the horse ante post. You do, and the deal's off.'

'There must be a reason,' Mattie protested. 'Now that you've pulled him out of the Curragh race, with a bit of careful shopping we'll probably be able to get sixes or sevens. Maybe more.'

'Then wait till the day,' Cassie said. 'You'll get as good if not better on the day. And no on course betting. If you're going to have a touch, put it on in the shops, in small bets, and not personally. None of it must be traced back anywhere near here, you understand?'

'Of course,' Mattie thought for a moment before asking his last question. 'Just one thing,' he wondered. 'What makes you think I might get better than sixes or sevens on the day?'

'Never you mind. Yours not to reason why. Just do as I say,' Cassie said, and put the phone down.

Four days before the Ascot race Cassie gave the horse his last serious piece of work. Dexter rode him in a gallop against Lovely Grub, Big Wallow and Damascus with the horses weighted the same as they had been for the Nugent race. It was a fine, clear summer's morning without a breath of wind, so still that the thunder of the horses' hooves could be heard long before they appeared over the crest of the first hill to sweep along flat for four furlongs before swinging right to climb the last two furlongs which rose in a gentle pull towards where Cassie and Jo were sitting watching on their hacks. Dormie One was swinging along in front with the other three horses packed in a bunch two lengths adrift.

But as they met the rising ground the picture suddenly changed, and Josephine, holding her lightweight race glasses one-handed, leaned forwards in her saddle.

'They're coming at him,' she said in surprise. 'I mean Dex is getting serious, but Dormie's not getting away from them!'

'He doesn't seem to be striding out the way he usually does,' Cassie observed. 'For all Dex's encouragement.'

'He's stuffed,' Josephine said succinctly. 'Grub's got to him and so has Wallow.'

'So has Damascus,' Cassie said, picking up her horse's reins. 'I hope nothing's amiss. Come on, we'd better go see.'

By the time Cassie and Josephine had reached the end of the gallops, a worried-looking Dexter had got off Dormie One and was leading him round away from the other horses.

'How was it, guv'nor?' he asked quietly.

'First there was Laurence Olivier,' Cassie replied, bending down to check the horse's tendons. 'Then there was Dexter Bryant.'

'I could have played the Fool, maybe,' Dexter said, straightfaced. 'And Puck – no problem. The heroic parts, I'm not so sure.'

'Paul Newman's not so tall,' Cassie said straightening up and frowning as if unhappy with what she'd found. 'Now. You see anything I can't see?'

'Just the summer sun glinting on half a dozen pairs of race glasses,' Dexter sighed happily. 'We should have gone crooked years ago, guv.'

'One word, Dexter Bryant,' Cassie said looking at him in the eye, with a gleam in her own. 'One word and you're walking the bottom of Glendalough in a pair of concrete riding boots.'

Both the weather and the going for the King George VI meeting at Ascot were perfect. Claremore was represented twice on the Saturday card, with Dormie One in the Diamond Stakes and Jack Madigan's Big Wallow in the Hardway for which he was second favourite at 3/1. Dormie One, on the other hand, was easy to back all day, opening at 8/1 and drifting out as far as 12/1 at one point.

'I can hear Mattie licking his lips,' Cassie muttered to Josephine as they made their way to the changing rooms. 'I just hope he does as he's told.'

'Blow Mattie,' Josephine groaned. 'I think I'm going to be sick.'

While Josephine was changing into her race clothes, Cassie sat on a bench in the weighing room with Dexter Bryant going through the list of runners one last time in case there was a dark horse somewhere whose form she might have overlooked. It was a big field, twenty-two runners in all, the likely favourite being the northern trained horse Wilstach ridden by the season's leading lady rider, Sue Dorman. To Cassie, much as she respected the horse, its trainer and its rider, they posed not nearly such a threat as another well-fancied horse, the useful Freemason colt War Poem, trained at Lambourn by Attie Bewes and ridden by his daughter Jane. The combination had won a hotly contested amateurs' race at Goodwood earlier in the season, and word was that the horse had been laid out specially for the race.

'But then that goes for about ninety-nine per cent of the field,' Dexter remarked, tapping his whip on his highly polished riding boots. 'As far as lady riders go, this is the race to win.'

'Sure,' Cassie agreed, putting her racecard back in her pocket. 'The difference being that when Attie lays a horse out, he does it better than most. I saw War Poem in the pre-parade ring. He looks awful well to me.'

'So does your fella, Cass,' Dexter said. 'I don't know

anyone who can turn a horse out the way you do. And on all known form—'

'I know, I know,' Cassie sighed. 'Trouble is, as you well know, horses don't read the form book.'

'I tell you, Cass,' Dexter said as they stood up to greet a white-faced Josephine who was making her way out of her changing room to meet them. 'I tell you after what we did to this young lady down in Kilkenny, that diamond necklace is as good as hanging round her pretty little neck.'

'I must be crazy,' Josephine muttered as she and Cassie made their way into the paddock to be greeted by Dr and Mrs Tatlow, Dormie One's owners. 'I thought I was nervous the first time I rode in this race, but that was nothing as to how I feel today.'

'You've only got one problem,' Cassie said as Liam turned the horse on to the central lawn ready for Josephine to mount up. 'He can pull his way to the start and if he does take hold, he could waste too much gas. So get him right up against the far rail and practically tuck his head over it. Don't let him fight you, just tell him who's boss, and once he's got the idea, give him some slack and let him go down nice and freely.'

'And who should I look out for?' Josephine asked to be reminded as she checked the buckles on her helmet straps and then cocked one leg ready to be thrown up into the saddle by Fred.

'Yellow and red,' Cassie said. 'That big chesnut carrying number nine. Remember what I said. He comes with a rattle late and he's got plenty of toe, so you're just going to have to run him into the ground.'

'First, second or third by the time the four marker, first or second by the three, and first by the time we pass the two,' Josephine reminded herself.

'That's my girl,' Cassie said as Fred legged her daughter up. 'See you in the winner's enclosure.'

The stalls were barely open and Dormie One was a length up. At the end of the first furlong Josephine had pushed him on to make that two, and by the time the field had covered the first half mile the Claremore pair were six lengths up with the field already stretched out in Indian file behind them. Behind Cassie someone laughed with delight.

'I didn't know it was Christmas!' the punter cried. 'I've got him at twelve to bloody one!'

Watching her horse through her race glasses, Cassie couldn't help but agree. Even though Josephine was giving the horse a breather, they were still four or five lengths clear of the second horse who was some six lengths clear of a bunch of horses fighting for third place. Wilstach, the favourite, was in a hopeless position a long way off the pace with only four horses behind him, while War Poem would have to prove to be Pegasus to win from where he was, namely leading the bunch of tail enders. Coming to the home turn Josephine stole one look over her left shoulder to make absolutely sure there was no danger and even though War Poem was beginning to make a late run through the field, according to the course commentator it was beginning to look as though Josephine could dismount, lead her horse home and still not get caught. Nevertheless, remembering her orders and mindful of the fact that in horse racing anything could happen, Josephine sat down and rode her horse home as if the rest of the field were within half a length of her. Only when she was less than a hundred yards from the post did she begin to ease up, slowing Dormie One almost to a walk as they coasted past the post.

'First number three, Dormie One, second number nine War Poem, and a photograph for third place between number sixteen Armoran and number seven Wotwilitbee,' a voice announced over the loudspeakers as Cassie made her way down to the winner's enclosure. 'The distances were twelve lengths and a neck, and the starting prices were as follows. Number three Dormie One was returned at eight to one, and War Poem at six to four joint favourite.'

'Eight to one, Cassie,' the man from the *Sporting Life* said as the circle of journalists closed on Cassie after she had greeted her victorious horse and daughter. 'That should pay for the winter break.'

'You know me, Tony.' Cassie smiled back at the journalist. 'I never back. Most of all my own.'

'Somebody knew something, though, wouldn't you say? The horse was all but friendless when they were forming the market, then suddenly – whoosh. That's a pile of money to bring him in that quick to eights,' another voice asked her from the throng.

'Probably the gallop watchers,' Cassie laughed. 'They don't miss a trick.'

'By all reports your chap did a bad piece of work this week,' someone else volunteered. 'There were even rumours he mightn't run.'

'He's a funny old horse,' Cassie said, still smiling. 'You don't know what he's going to do one day from the next.'

'So what is he going to do next?' the *Sporting Life* enquired.

'Go up about two stone in the handicap, I'd say,' Cassie replied. 'Wouldn't you?'


After the trophy presentations, Cassie took her owners up to Jack Madigan's private box for some champagne where Theodore was amongst the guests waiting for her. As she was showing the Tatlows into the box and as Theodore came out to congratulate her a stocky, heavily featured little man in an expensive silk suit and with dark, slicked down hair who was making his way down the corridor stopped when he saw her, staring at her with cold, ice blue eyes before suddenly smiling at her in recognition.

'Mrs Rosse,' he said, in a noticeably hoarse voice from which practically all trace of a Dublin accent had been ironed out. 'Mike Gold. We have met, I don't know if you remember? At the Racehorse of the Year Awards, the first year your horse The Nightingale won.'

He put out a pudgy gold-ringed hand and Cassie took it, remembering very well who this short, heavy-set, dead-eyed man who was standing smiling at her was. Even though they had only met once, like everyone else in racing she had seen the bookmaker's picture often enough in pages

479

of the ordinary daily newspapers as well as those devoted to the industry.

'Yes, I remember you, Mr Gold. You very kindly sent over a magnum of champagne when we won.'

*Which I very nearly sent back.*

Mike Gold smiled, the smile of a man who knew perfectly well that a celebratory gift of champagne was not the only thing for which Cassie Rosse remembered him. And when he smiled, Cassie noticed he suffered from a pronounced *tic* in his lower left cheek.

'May I offer you a glass of bubbly now, perhaps?' he enquired, still holding Cassie's hand in his. 'Your horse certainly did the business, did it not? Got the day off to just the sort of start I like.'

'You had heavy liabilities on the race?' Cassie enquired as if she couldn't believe it, at the same time slipping her hand from his grasp. 'I wouldn't ever have thought that was a big betting race.'

'You know Attie Bewes, Mrs Rosse. Attie laid that horse of his as if it couldn't get beat. And when Attie lays a horse, there are always liabilities. So for coming to our rescue, I would be delighted if you would join myself and my co-directors for a drink.'

Cassie hesitated. There was no way she was going to abandon the Tatlows who were not only loyal owners but also personal friends of hers for a drink with one of the enemy, yet now the opportunity had presented itself for her to get momentarily under the wire she found it hard to refuse.

'Would you think me very rude if I postponed it until after the next race?' she wondered, giving the bookmaker a brief but sweet enough smile. 'Our second runner's not until the fourth, and I really must have a drink with my winning connections.'

'But of course.' Mike Gold smiled back, but hard as he tried to match Cassie's charm it was still the smile on the face of a tiger. 'We're in box F. Come and watch the next race with us if you like.'

'Thank you,' Cassie said, re-opening the door of Jack Madigan's box. 'If I can I will.'

'Mmmm,' Theodore mused as he followed Cassie back into their box. 'Remind me to tell you something interesting about that gentleman sometime.'

When Cassie finally excused herself from her own party and joined the much larger and noisier party in Box F, the second race had already been run and the bookmakers' spirits were running high since the contest had been won by a rank outsider at 33/1 with the odds on favourite not even placed.

'I don't suppose it will matter if Biography wins the King George now, will it?' Cassie asked as her host poured her a glass of vintage champagne.

'We'd always rather a heavily backed ante post favourite didn't oblige, Mrs Rosse, naturally,' Mike Gold replied, clearing his throat and then carefully handing her an expensive fluted glass. 'But certainly these first two results have helped the books considerably.'

A small sharp-faced man standing by the window handed a telephone to Gold without saying a word. Gold excused himself for a moment to Cassie and took the call without moving away. Cassie sipped her champagne and looked round at the roomful of expensively suited men and their ornately costumed women who were busy helping themselves to a mountain of food and a bar stacked with vintage champagne and expensive spirits. The women were all suntanned, designer clothed and covered in modern jewellery while their escorts were muscular, dead-eyed men in equally expensive Italian suits and hand-made shoes. Some of the women eyed Cassie with interest at first but seeing that she was evidently not one of their number they rewarded her with a brief smile before continuing their raucous conversations.

'No,' was all Gold said, right at the end of the one-sided conversation, before handing the telephone back to his minion and turning his attention back to Cassie. 'Now where were we?' he enquired.

'Balancing the books,' Cassie replied. Gold smiled, taking a Havana cigar from a box on the table beside him and snipping the end off with a solid gold cutter.

'Your horse could put a cat among the pigeons. There's been a weight of money for Big Wallow since the office opened and it looks as though he's going to start a very short priced favourite.'

'He'll give a good account of himself,' Cassie replied, turning her attention to the runners who were now making their way down to the start for the next race.

'Not too good, I hope,' Gold said, giving a laugh to show he wasn't really serious, a laugh which soon turned to a hacking cough.

'Tell me,' Cassie wondered, deliberately switching the subject. 'What's the biggest single bet you've ever laid, Mr Gold? Or would you rather not say?'

'Why do you ask?'

'I've always been curious. Not being a gambler myself, I've always wondered just how much one individual is prepared to risk.'

'Good enough.' Gold lit his cigar and also turned his attention to the runners going to post. 'As a single bet, five hundred thousand to win five hundred thousand,' he said after a moment.

'Who won?'

'Not the horse.'

'Who was the horse?'

'Now that wouldn't be very professional of me, Mrs Rosse,' Gold replied, catching the reflection of Cassie's eyes in the plate glass window and smiling. 'Anyway, enough of business and back to pleasure. As a small token of my gratitude for seeing off Attie Bewes' horse in the first, I'd like to offer you a free fifty pound bet on your runner in the fourth. What price Big Wallow now, Mike?'

The thin-faced man in the corner checked the electronic notepad in his hand and looked up. 'In to six to four, Mr Gold sir,' he said. 'We just laid another five thousand to win seven and a half.'

'Mrs Rosse will take the six to four, Mike,' Gold said. 'Fifty pounds to win seventy-five.'

'I'll accept your kind offer only if the money goes to

charity should the horse oblige,' Cassie stipulated. 'The Injured Jockeys' Fund.'

'Done,' Gold nodded. 'In that case we'll make it a hundred to win one hundred and fifty. In keeping with our famous slogan – *Turn Your Bet To Gold*'.

Cassie was about to say something when she stopped, as if the words had been knocked from her, like a blow to her solar plexus. *Turn Your Bet To Gold*. She must have seen the maxim a thousand times but because it was part of the fabric of racing and since she herself was not a gambler, it had registered only fleetingly in the conscious part of her mind. But now it had awakened something deep inside her, the memory of something she had seen over and over again and always taken to mean something entirely different. *Gold!* was the word she had seen and so often. And *Gold Again! Gold! Gold! Gold!* Written in the margins of red leather-spined ledgers, the ledgers in which Tyrone had so carefully annotated every tilt he'd had at the ring. *How could I have been so stupid?* she thought as in an effort to conceal the feeling that she had suddenly stumbled on the way out of what had seemed to be an impenetrable maze she turned away to stare without really seeing at the racecourse far below where the last runners made their way down the track towards the starting stalls. Then she turned back to face Mike Gold.

'You're doing this because you don't think my horse will win,' she said with a sudden smile. Gold held her look, his cigar clenched between two rows of expertly reconstructed teeth, and finally shook his head as if sadly disappointed.

'That's a little cynical, Mrs Rosse,' he said, taking the Havana from his mouth and examining the length of ash. 'My offer is in good faith.'

'In that case lay me the first fifty on offer on the first horse past the post at starting price.'

'You want a *charity* bet? You want me to pay out on *whatever* horse wins?'

'You don't pay out, Mr Gold. You *donate* the winnings to the Injured Jockeys.'

Having finished the examination of his cigar ash, Gold smiled without humour and stuck the Havana back between his teeth. 'I'm a turf accountant, Mrs Rosse,' Gold replied evenly. 'Not some goddam punter trying to buy a knighthood.'

'Very well, let's try it another way,' Cassie said, opening her purse and taking out five twenty pound notes. 'You lay me my hundred on the first horse past the post, the money to go to charity as agreed.' She turned to face him, holding the money out for him to take.

'There's only one loser here,' he said. 'And that's not you.'

'Maybe I've done my share of losing, Mr Gold,' Cassie returned. 'Look – if my horse wins, and is returned favourite, right – you lose. But you'll probably have backed him yourself to shore up your losses or whatever, so the wound won't be exactly grievous. More of a scratch than a cut I'd say. You have similar liabilities every day of the week and if I may say so, you aren't exactly walking round with the seat out of your pants.' Gold smiled as if he had just been awarded the ultimate compliment as Cassie continued. 'But if a long price horse wins, let's say at twenties – with the favourite beaten you'll be only too happy to send a couple of thousand to the injured jocks.'

'I see, Mrs Rosse,' Gold said, nodding slowly as he puffed on his cigar. 'I think you've just made me one of those offers I can't very well refuse.' He took the money from her hand and offered it to the cadaverous-faced man standing in the corner of the window. 'Mike – a hundred pounds the winner of the fourth at starting price.'

'Thank you, Mr Gold,' Cassie said, putting down her champagne glass. 'Now I must get back to my own party. This has been fun. It really has.'

Cassie hurried back to Jack Madigan's box to find Jack already on the telephone.

'Have you backed your horse yet, Jack?' she asked. 'Because if you haven't, don't.'

Knowing Cassie as well as he did, Jack must have sensed

her anxiety because he immediately cupped his hand over the phone. 'I backed him at two to one when the offices opened, but I haven't got stuck in yet,' he replied. 'I intend to do that on the rails, because there's money now for this horse Dequadan. They've backed him solid all the way in from six to one to twos, and if they let our fella drift to seven to four I shall help myself in a big way.'

'Don't,' Cassie said succinctly. 'You know where I've just been. And I reckon they know something we don't know.'

Jack Madigan frowned at Cassie, then killed the call he had been busy making, giving Cassie his full attention.

'They think Wally's going to get beat,' Cassie said, using the horse's stable name. 'If he drifts it'll be for one of two reasons. Either the serious money is going elsewhere and they're trying to trawl in a few punters by a show of generosity—'

'Huh,' Jack Madigan snorted. 'The day I meet a generous bookie is the day that pigs fly.'

'OK,' Cassie agreed. 'My thoughts exactly. So if we don't start five to four or shorter somebody knows something. Believe me, I felt the vibrations. Look, on all known form we should be clear favourite. When Wally ran second to Mockingbird at the Royal Ascot meeting, he beat Haleys Done by three lengths and Haleys Done had Dequadan ten lengths behind him at Newmarket. As for the Howard horse Shantaak, on a line through Strip The Willow and Mashood we're six pounds better. So how come you can still get six to four about him? Seven to four in some places – I just saw a show on the television.'

Jack Madigan picked up his racecard. 'You think I should hedge my bet?' he asked Cassie.

'I certainly don't think this is the time to try to get rich,' Cassie replied.

'Rich*er*,' his wife Fiona laughed. 'I don't know what the hell he wants to bet *for*.'

'For the hell of it,' Jack growled. 'To beat the scumbag bookies.'

'Look – what's this race worth—' Cassie quickly consulted her own racecard. 'It's worth just under seventeen thousand to the winner, so if Wally does win, you're not exactly going to go home empty-handed, are you? But if he loses, how much were you going to lay out?'

'Far too much,' Fiona chipped in, pouring herself more champagne. 'More than he lets me have for clothes I can tell you, Cassie.'

'I've invested five grand already,' Jack said. 'I backed him ante post from four to one downwards.'

'Then shore up on Dequadan,' Cassie urged him. 'If Wally's taking a walk in the market and they're laying the Newmarket horse, somebody knows something. And Dequadan comes from a big betting yard.'

'More women's intuition, eh?' Jack smiled at her.

'At least it comes free and you don't get charged it as an extra on your training bill, Jack,' Cassie replied.

'But they can't have got at Wally, surely?' Fiona asked. 'No-one could get through your security, Cassie.'

'We'll see, Fiona,' Cassie replied. 'But if he doesn't run his true race it certainly won't be Dexter's doing. Now I'm off to check the horse. I'll see the rest of you down there.'

'I'll come with you,' Jack said, following her out. 'I'm going to go to the rails and see what they're offering on this Dequadan. If those bastards are trying to hurt us, then I'm going to try to inflict a big hurt in return.'

While Jack went to lay the possible new favourite with the rails bookmakers, Cassie hurried across to the pre-parade ring where Bridie was walking Big Wallow round in company with some of the other runners for the fourth race.

'How is he?' Cassie asked anxiously, half expecting to find the horse visibly out of sorts.

'He's fine,' Bridie replied happily. 'He travelled great, had a roll as soon as I put him in his box, and is his usual old laid-back self.'

'You haven't turned your back on him for a minute, Bridie, have you?'

'Not for a second, Mrs Rosse. Either Phelim's been with him all the time or I have. You know me. I'm not one to be running any risks now.'

'Phelim?' Cassie asked uncertainly, walking alongside the horse. 'Teddy was meant to be travelling with you and the horse.'

'Teddy was bucked off yesterday, Mrs Rosse,' Bridie replied. 'Liam said he wasn't well enough to travel so brought Phelim instead. And believe you me, Phelim's stuck to old Wally like a leech.'

Bridie smiled at Cassie then led her charge off to the saddling boxes where the waiting lad was signalling to her. Cassie stood for a moment, unable temporarily to put a face to Phelim before she suddenly remembered he was the quiet whey-faced lad they'd taken on with a new batch of lads on the month. She knew little else about him except that according to Liam he'd passed his term of trial with flying colours as had the three other youngsters who'd had to be taken on owing to the arrival of eight more horses in the yard. Even so she was surprised that after such a short period of time Liam should have thought the lad experienced enough to travel as second lad to a well-fancied horse, but any further musings were put out of her head by the sudden and huge crescendo of noise which welled up from the grandstands behind Cassie as the vast crowd began to roar the favourite home in the big race.

'Photograph!' a voice announced over the public address. 'Photograph between number one Biography and number seven Avant!' But even before the result of the photograph was announced with Biography given as the winner, and despite her own horse's seeming rude health, Cassie sensed a growing feeling of despair, as if as far as the fourth race was concerned the day was already lost.

As the field rounded the home turn and swept into the straight Jack Madigan certainly did not share Cassie's pessimism.

'I should have paid no attention to you, Cassie!' he shouted as everyone in his party stood with their race glasses fixed on the race. 'I shouldn't even have begun to listen to you! Will you look, you daft woman! Wally's still on the bloody bridle!'

Cassie didn't want to contradict or discourage him, nor indeed anyone else in the private box who was shouting the Claremore horse home, but even though Dexter hadn't yet asked Wally for an effort, the trainer's expert eye could see that although the horse seemed still full of running he wasn't striding out with his usual confidence. Big Wallow normally had a stride to go with his name but this afternoon on the perfect Ascot going his stride was foreshortened, and as soon as Dexter shook him up coming off the home turn, when it must have seemed to all his supporters the race was his for the taking, sure enough the horse's head came up, his tail went round and his effort petered out to nothing. After giving his mount a couple of slaps to make sure he hadn't just gone to sleep on him, Dexter must have sensed his horse wasn't right because he dropped his hands and allowed Big Wallow to drop right back through the field to trail in last of all the nine runners.

By the time Cassie had hurried down from the top of the grandstand and across the enclosures to where the beaten horses were being unsaddled Big Wallow was very distressed. Bridie and Phelim were in attendance, the boy leading the horse round while Bridie kept a weather eye on the horse in case he went down, but although Wally stayed on his feet there was no doubt about how afflicted he was. He was lathered in a foam of sweat, his eyes were dull and rolling and his legs seemed as if they were made of rubber.

'Jeez, Mrs Rosse,' Bridie said, barely able to control her tears, 'you don't think he's had a heart attack or something, do you?'

'No, Bridie, I'd say he's just badly amiss,' Cassie replied, rolling back the horse's bottom lip to look at his gums before pulling one of the animal's eyelids down to inspect the membranes there as well. 'But what it's due to – we won't know that until they've run a dope test which I shall go and ask for now. And even then we might not know.'

'But surely if he's been got at, Mrs Rosse—' Bridie began.

'According to Niall some of the state of the art dope they're using nowadays doesn't show up in tests,' Cassie said, anticipating the question. 'And that's before you even come to how they get to the horses anyway.' She stood back from Big Wallow and stroked his sweat-soaked neck affectionately. 'And this horse has most definitely been got at,' she concluded.

Just then another trainer whom Cassie knew only by sight arrived with an oxygen cylinder and ancillary apparatus which he offered to Cassie for her stricken horse. Apparently one of his own horses suffered from an oxygen deficiency and so he never travelled to the races without a couple of cylinders on board. Grateful for his kindness Cassie stood by while the trainer and Bridie got her horse to inhale a sufficient quantity of the vital element, happy to see that as soon as he had Wally began visibly to recover, so much so that after another three or four minutes of being walked around he was sufficiently strong to be removed to the stables to finish his recovery in comfort and privacy, away from the curious crowd which had gathered to watch his distress.

'I didn't even see what finally won the race,' Cassie said grimly to a stone-faced Jack Madigan as they made their way back up to the row of private boxes. 'I was too busy watching Wally.'

'Dequadan trotted up, at even money,' Jack growled. 'Wally drifted out to two to one.'

'The way he finished he should have been a hundred and two to one, Jack,' Cassie returned. 'What sort of a person can do that to a horse?'

'Scum,' Jack replied. 'That is the work of the scum of the earth.'

As they passed Box F where the party was in even fuller swing, Mike Gold who was standing by the half-open door spotted the Claremore party.

'That was hard luck, Mrs Rosse!' he called after Cassie from the doorway. 'What happened to your horse?'

Cassie stopped, took a quiet deep breath and then turned to face the bookmaker with a resigned look on her face. 'He spread a plate,' she replied. 'Bryant thought he did it coming into the straight.'

Gold clicked his tongue and shook his head once. 'That's

racing for you,' he said. 'Hard luck. 'Here.' He put his hand in his pocket and taking out a wad of money peeled off four fifty pounds notes, folded them in two and gave them to Cassie. 'One hundred to win a hundred at evens. And whatever you might be thinking, we'd much rather your horse had won.'

'Come on into the box, Cassie, will you? I need a drink badly,' Jack Madigan said from behind her, 'so come in and shut the bloody door, will you? My nose tells me there's something wrong with the plumbing!'

Jack disappeared inside his own private box and as he did so the smile also disappeared off Mike Gold's face. He just stood looking at Cassie as she hesitated before following Jack Madigan, looking at her as if she was the thing he hated most in the entire world. Then with a mock polite smile, he too disappeared back into the privacy of his own box.

# *Thirty*

The first thing Cassie did on her return to Claremore was to check Tyrone's betting ledgers. She had only let Joel have photocopies of all her records, since she was loath as always to let any original Claremore documents out of her sight, keeping the originals locked away in a bookcase in her study. Sure enough there were the entries exactly as she'd recalled them, winning horses with the amounts wagered neatly entered in one column, the prices obtained about them in the next, and then finally in the margin against some of the most successful punts either usually the single word *Gold!* or less commonly the two words *Gold Again!* When idly consulting the ledgers before Cassie had always assumed the words to mean that Tyrone had metaphorically struck gold due to the size of the bet and the generosity of the starting price, since the comments were always only written alongside some quite considerable wagers. But now she realized what *Gold!* really meant, because she remembered Tyrone telling her although not in any detail about a campaign he had once had against a bookmaker in the days when he was a young trainer, long before they ever met and married.

Terry Gold had been the name of the bookmaker against whom he had waged this war.

The father of Mike Gold.

There was something else Cassie knew she should remember but it was gone from her for the moment. So in the hope that something on those few vital pages might serve as a reminder, Cassie reread them all again, over and over and over until she felt she knew the name of every horse backed and the amount of every wager won or lost.

Then the first missing bit of the puzzle fell into place.

The *Gold!* annotations covered only a brief period in Tyrone's betting life.

The campaign had been a limited one, fought over but four months of one Flat season during which time Tyrone had relieved Terry Gold's satchel of a figure in the region of one hundred and eighty thousand pounds. At the end of those four months Cassie found a different remark in the margin of the ledger, the three letters AC C. After that there were no further *Gold!* exclamations, just the ongoing registry of bets laid and monies won or lost.

But some of these entries, which were all winning ones, although not recording especially large touches, were marked significantly with an asterisk, thus: Speedy Cut sp 5/2fav win £75 *, even though the wins were usually at minor meetings, while other more significant and more profitable wins on the leading tracks were not awarded the asterisk accolade. These markings lasted for practically the whole of that season on the Flat, the last annotated win being on October 7th.

Having studied these bets without learning anything new, other than the fact certain bets had been earmarked, Cassie then returned to trying to unscramble the mysterious hieroglyphic AC C. There were only two things Cassie knew AC stood for, and those were alternating current and account.

*Account. Of course,* she muttered to herself, pursing her lips with irritation at her slowness. Tyrone always had a bookmaker's account, just as she remembered him telling her that whenever he was ahead, the bookies were forever closing him down. So AC C must mean *account closed.*

You took Terry Gold to the cleaners, Ty, Cassie said out aloud, running her finger down the entries marked *Gold!* *You hammered him solid until he couldn't take it any more so he closed you down. But then what? And why did you pick on Terry Gold? You usually broadcast your bets just so that they* wouldn't *close you down. So why this guy's jugular in particular?*

There was something else too, something of which Cassie could make no sense at all, yet because it made a very different pattern she knew it was integral to the whole story, namely the history of Tyrone's bets in the last half of the previous season, the one before he decided to hammer Terry Gold. That whole year had been far less productive as far as betting had gone, with the figures at the end of the season showing Tyrone to be a little over five and a half thousand pounds in the red, the equivalant according to Cassie's ready reckoning of about fifty thousand pounds in contemporary money. Tyrone had rarely ended a season down. When he had it had only been a matter of three or four hundred at most. Yet here was a season when his stables had been full of useful horses and when he himself had ended up in third place on the Irish trainers table, where he had lost the sort of money Cassie knew in those days Tyrone could never have afforded to lose. But why?

Significantly, although Cassie could not yet work out the significance, the odds of his largest winning bet were 5/2, whereas in every other year the ledgers were full of entered-up wins at up to 10/1, sometimes even more, touches occasionally having been recorded at odds as long as 25/1 and on one glorious and famous occasion which had been logged surrounded by hand drawn stars Tyrone had landed a coup at Naas of a £100 to win £3300 after a particularly barren run.

Yet this one season when he had ended up so badly in the red, with several well-fancied horses which he had backed as if they could not be beaten, Tyrone had ended up seriously embarrassed.

Why? Cassie asked herself. Why why *why*?

Liam knew why. Not that he'd been working at Claremore that year but his father had and Liam could remember as if it was yesterday his father coming home with the scandalous news.

' "We have a spy, nipper!" he said, swinging me up and putting me on his knee. And I can remember it, guv'nor, as if 'twere yesterday, yet I couldn't have been more than seven or eight at the time. I axed him what a spy was, what's a spy, Pappy? I axed, and he said someone who tells

493

someone else's *secrets*, nipper. And the guv'nor, your late husband that was, Mrs Rosse, God rest his soul, the guv'nor, Pappy said, has kicked him out of the yard. Kicked him right down the drive he did, nipper, and told him and his pal never to set their feet within twenty mile of Claremore ever again. There was two of them, you see, Guv'nor, and weren't they brothers. Mick and Kevin Molloy, they called themselves and they'd been working in the yard since the end of the jumping season, having come well enough recommended, or so the story now goes, from a top yard in Navan, no names no pack drill.'

'You say they called themselves Molloy,' Cassie said, picking up. 'So Molloy wasn't their real name?'

'It was not. Weren't the two of them Terry Gold's brats whom he put about the place under their assumed name to spy for him in certain yards? Certain yards that is which Mr Gold knew liked to have a touch.'

'Got you!' Cassie said, clucking her tongue as if at her own stupidity. 'Of course! That was why Tyrone never got anywhere near a decent price about his horses that season! *Of course.* The Gold brothers would know which horses were going to be backed and when, they'd tell their father well in advance and he'd trim the odds.'

'Trim them, guv'nor?' Liam laughed. 'He'd hack 'em back to last year's growth! And sure you know what bookies is like. I mean that bush telegraph of theirs. As soon as the word was out about one of the Claremore horses you'd be lucky to get your bet on at all. Now don't ask me how your husband, God rest his soul, how he found out what was afoot, but as you knows every bit as well as I does, there was little ever got past the guv'nor. And when he found out all hell let loose. He'd never got rid of anyone like that before, I remember Pappy saying. Like yourself, he liked to choose his lads carefully and he liked to keep 'em. But somehow these two slippery sams got under the wire and cost the yard dear. It cost the whole yard, remember, for like yourself the guv'nor always kept us in the know when a horse was off and when it wasn't. So as Pappy said it was just as well for those two smart alicks' sake, that the guv'nor kicked 'em away out down the drive before the lads all got their hands on 'em.'

'And the year after that my husband got his own back on their father. He went for Gold in every sense of the phrase, and as a result Gold closed down his account.'

'Ah ha!' Liam said with his broadest grin. 'But that wasn't the end of it, guv'nor. Because if I remember it right it seemed that your husband, God rest his soul, he wasn't done with Mr Gold yet. Whenever he had a horse ready he'd let the village know and they'd let their friends know but only on condition they backed it in one of Terry Gold's betting shops. Well you can imagine, can't you.'

'The horses with the asterisks,' Cassie said out aloud but only to herself and then seeing Liam's blank look told him not to mind her but to get on with finishing his story.

'There's not a lot more to tell, guv'nor,' Liam said. 'The stable was getting a good few winners at that time, and since they no longer knew which horses were off and which weren't, they couldn't close down the prices. So some hefty touches were landed, Pappy said. Both on the course and off it. They say that was what killed Terry Gold in the end. The fact your husband – God rest his soul of course – had him beaten.'

Cassie stared at Liam hard. 'They say it killed Terry Gold?' she echoed. 'This was well before my time, remember, Liam. My husband only ever told me the sketchiest version of this story. I don't suppose he thought it would interest me. But believe you me, it does. It most certainly does.'

'Ah sure half the stuff you hear round yards you have to take with a tin of salt, don't you?' Liam sighed. 'Although I'm sure there'd have to be truth in the rumour that was going round even when I first came here.'

'And what was that, Liam?'

'That Mick Gold, the eldest of the two brothers, wouldn't rest till he got even with your late husband, God rest his soul indeed.'

\* \* \*

Everything Cassie had learned she put in her next letter to Joel. In return he wrote back to say the progress he had reportedly been making already was continuing for now with the addition of Mike Gold's name to the list he had been able to establish a full list of all those people with some sort of grudge who had either had some direct connection with Cassie, Claremore or Tyrone. Joel's list read as follows:

Leonora
Leonora's mother
Herr Brandt
de Vendrer
Tom McMahon
Mark Carter-James (?)
Mike Gold

Better still, he had established a correlation between Brandt and Cassie's defaulting insurers. The company was wholly owned by one of Brandt's own subsidiary companies, Brandt having turned himself into quite an active player in the livestock insurance game. Obviously, Joel wrote, like most things to which Herr Brandt turned his hand, it was more in his rather than his clients' interest.

*That makes perfect sense, Cassie wrote back. I've checked the records and in fact when I was training for Brandt it was he who persuaded me to change my insurers, putting all my horses in the care of the company who handled all his business. I had them thoroughly checked out and it seemed to make perfect sense at the time, particularly since they offered such competitive rates with no apparent drawbacks. They paid up and on time, too. I never had one moment's worry with them whenever we had a claim on a horse. Just goes to show, right? You throw back the little fries and sit and wait for the big one.*
*As for your list – Leonora, Leonora's mother, Brandt, de Vendrer, Tom McMahon and Mike Gold – even the Carter-James – yes, it all makes a kind of sense, an awful sense let's face it because every one*

of these people has some sort of axe to grind, but what connects them? And if something does, how do we prove this connection? Leonora we know all about, but yet I can't see her going the full hog and fixing up to kidnap the horse. You were right about that – that isn't her style. She couldn't organise that famous party in a brewery, I agree, and although her mother would have been simply furious to have been denied a share in The Nightingale's syndication, I reckon she'd have looked for vengeance some other way, Von Wagner fashion. Brandt sure – I know he blamed me for not running my horses to suit him, that is either running them over the wrong distances until they'd come down in the h'cap so as he could get a good price about them, or simply not letting them run to their form until he was ready to back. But it wasn't my fault he ended up in gaol, unless he was banking on the money he hoped to make gambling on his horses. He certainly never forgave me when The Donk (a particularly good horse I bought him) won at long odds unbacked.

Then there's de Vendrer. Well I told you all about him. He's a sadist, a fascist and hated it seems by everyone who knows him. He told me his first wife died tragically but in fact she killed herself because he treated her so terribly and yes – I humiliated him in front of his staff by locking him in his closet when I made my famous escape. He has reason enough to hate me, but then my guess is he probably hates all women. But there is one thing which would keep him on the list as a prime suspect and that is where I first met him. I first met him at (wait for it) Leonora's, would you believe? So there may well be wheels within wheels here.

Mark Carter-James: well I have to say I think he's capable of anything, but then I would have to ask why? Jo thinks he and his father have some long-standing grudge against me – which sort of makes sense in an absurd chauvinistic way. Even so he and

497

his father are last on my list because of the lack of any recognizable motive, but don't strike them off at any cost – not yet at least.

Mike Gold: yes well here we have suspect number one, obviously, even though as you always tease me, I maintained that the bookies didn't do it. But who else? We now have a motive for him, revenging the father, and the Golds being Irish we're looking at another form of the Cosa Nostra, wouldn't you say? If you'd seen the way he looked at me at the races, you'd have seen real hate. And by now it won't just be because of what happened his father; it'll be Tyrone's ongoing success, mine, and The Nightingale, because Nightie must have cost the bookmakers plenty of money during his racing career. People like Gold don't like horses. Well, they do – they like losing horses. But what they don't like is winning horses, particularly consistent winners, and particularly the sort of horses whose form is so watertight that as soon as the ante posts lists open the real players wade in. How they must have hated The Nightingale, just think! And I suppose they might even just have had nightmares about the sort of progeny he might have sired. So all in all I'd say somewhere in that list we have the person (or persons) responsible for what happened to the horse. The only thing is, how do we prove it????

And while you're at it, could you put that great mind of yours to work also to find out how they're still managing to get to horses? Even in yards as secure as this, and with travel arrangements apparently watertight they still got to Wally, you bet (we're still awaiting the results of the official dope tests). What are they using? And by whatever method?

By the way – I was really intrigued by your postscript. What made you suspect that the infamous photograph of Nightie when kidnapped was not taken in Switzerland after all? Was it just the logistics?

'It was just a hunch apparently,' Cassie told Niall when they were discussing the subject over coffee at one of their daily meetings. 'Joel got to thinking why take the horse at Ascot, fly him out to Switzerland somehow, either in a private cargo plane or else as substitute for a horse left behind—'

'Why leave a good or even not so good horse behind?' Niall said. 'And where do you leave it? Fine, so it's not such a great horse, it belongs to one of the villains, and they leave it with someone else in on the act, but what you're saying, Cassie, is why go to all the trouble of taking it to Switzerland?'

'There'd be a point,' Cassie replied, replenishing her coffee cup from the *cafetière*, 'if they were either going to kill the horse and bury it without trace, or if they'd been going to hold it to ransom. But they did neither. They castrated the horse and returned him here. So what Joel reasoned was who would go to all the bother to fly the most famous stallion in the world out by plane to somewhere in Europe just to castrate him, keep him for a while from sheer malice and then fly him all the way back to Ireland, box him out to Claremore and leave him turned loose in a local lane. It didn't make sense, not one bit of it.'

'What they must have done was take the horse at Ascot and either hide him away somewhere in England till they thought the heat was off,' Niall surmised, 'then either box him back by ferry or fly him over when one of the bastards was bringing some other horses into the country. That'd be easily enough done, would it not? But then what about that photograph? The one that Joel said placed them definitely in Switzerland because of some tell tale codemark on the front page of the newspaper or whatever?'

'Joel had one of his contacts blow it up to about one foot square to see whether or not it was genuine,' Cassie replied. 'And sure enough, what did they find? The horizontal line that runs under the edition number and the dateline wasn't true. In fact it was very untrue. When the photo was enlarged you could see two lines.'

'Meaning the top of the newspaper as seen in the photograph had been stuck on? Over the paper underneath?'

'Exactly, Niall. To make it look as though they were in Switzerland.'

'Sure. That's perfectly possible, I'll grant you that. But if they really were say in England, or even back over here – how in hell could they get the front page of a foreign edition of that day's *Times*?'

'They could have had one flown in, but given the logistics it would have been much easier to have had a copy faxed to them,' Cassie replied. 'Not the whole paper, just the portion of the banner which marks the edition. Then all they had to do was paste it onto their own edition and if they did it well enough on a polaroid who's going to see the joins? Joel got a friend to try it in his office on a plain paper fax machine, with a nice thin adhesive and a bog standard land camera. He said unless you blew it up to about six times the size, you'd never know the difference. So at least that's one part of the mystery solved. And brings everything a lot closer to home.'

'As far as possible suspects go, you mean?'

'I think as far as suspects go, Niall, we're looking at a conspiracy between a possible four, five, maybe half a dozen people or more. But the more I think about it, the more I get this feeling that the whole enterprise was masterminded by someone who's done this sort of thing before. Or things very similar.'

A few days later they got the results of the official dope test run on Big Wallow. It was negative.

'*How* could it be negative?' Josephine demanded as she and Cassie drove down later that morning to school The Nightingale. 'If a horse is doped, and particularly as doped as you reckon Wally was, then how can it not show up on an official blood test?'

'Because as Niall's always pointing out, nowadays some of the most effective stoppers they use leave absolutely no trace whatsoever anywhere, blood, urine, kidneys, droppings, you name it,' Cassie sighed. 'There was a whole report in one of the racing papers only last year saying that the security officers at the English Jockey Club were completely baffled, although they'd be the last to admit it publicly. The dopers have had various substances for years, so the rumour goes, which are not virtually but totally undetectable.'

'Great,' Josephine nodded. 'So not only doesn't anyone know what they use, they don't even know how they do it. I mean how does anyone get past watertight security? If it was some thriller or something they'd have some fantastic gadgetry or soluble capsules hidden inside the horses' bits which dissolve as soon as they come in to contact with saliva or some such rubbish. But this isn't some piece of hokum, is it? This is serious villainry, with serious guys shooting up decent horses and in so doing almost killing some of them.'

'Your father always said as far as a horse that's been got at goes, forget it,' Cassie remarked.

'Does that mean Wally's no good any more?'

'Probably.'

Josephine swore.

'Joel once said – this was before Wally, of course – this was sometime during the summer. Anyway he maintains it has to be someone on the inside,' Cassie said, turning from the wheel to look at her daughter for a moment. 'Naturally I refused to believe it—'

'I should think so too,' Josephine agreed. 'Particularly with your staff. You couldn't have a more loyal lot.'

'Absolutely,' Cassie said. 'But that's really why I got so annoyed with Joel, because of course I knew he had to be right. If you think about it, anyone really seriously trying to stop a horse isn't going to leave it to chance, are they? They're not going to wait to see if they get a moment on the racecourse to slip the horse a Mickey Finn in whatever shape or form the modern equine Mickey Finn comes. It's too risky. You might not get it done – in fact you probably won't. We're talking about people stopping

501

horses because a lot of money's at stake, thousands of pounds, possibly even hundreds of thousands of pounds. Whoever's behind it, they'll want to make sure that horse is stopped so they're not going to leave one damn' thing to chance.'

'Yes, but someone inside Claremore?' Josephine said in disbelief. 'Come on, Mums – who?'

'Something else your father used to say was follow the man home,' Cassie replied. 'Meaning we think we know everything there is to know about the people we employ. But really we know very little. We don't know what pressures they might be under, financially or personally, nor do we really know how they see us. What they think of us.'

'Your staff think the world of you and you know it.'

'No, I don't. I was thinking only the other day that just lately there are always a few I don't know that much about. I mean I always have to take on at least one or two new faces every season when someone leaves to get married or have a baby, or because they've been enticed away by the promise of much more money at one of the big English yards. And it takes time for them to settle in and for Liam and myself to assess them fully.'

'Who, for instance?'

'This lad Phelim O'Connell, if you want an example. He's new to the yard, yet he was looking after Wally at Ascot. Obviously Liam must think enough of him to give him such a responsible job, but we don't really know everything about him. You can never know everything about the people who work for you. Even their references which we check are often "adjusted", if you like. I'm not saying it was him, Jo. What I am saying is even in a yard like ours which is after all more like a family, you can't follow every one of them home. All it takes is for one of the lads to get into a scrape.'

'When aren't lads in a scrape, for heaven's sake?'

'Precisely. I mean, look – they look at the racecard and they see the owners getting anything up to quarter of a million in prize money. Even some bread and butter race at an all-weather track's worth four or five thousand. Even the horses they look after have a more expensive wardrobe than their own. They're never going to make the sort of money people dream of, which they see people making leading up horses. The only way – and I'm only talking about the ones who aren't satisfied with their lot – the only way they're going to see big money is either by becoming a top flight jockey themselves—'

'Unlikely—'

'There's a chance, but a very outside one,' Cassie returned. 'And the only other way they're going to get rich is by falling off the straight and narrow. They'll be able to justify it, too. They'll tell themselves there can't be any harm in just stopping one horse for one race. So the rich owner misses out on the prize money. So what. Either the horse has collected enough already, or they'll kid themselves it'll come out and win again—'

'Which according to you it won't—'

'Right. But they don't tell themselves that. They look at what they're being offered just to stop a horse once, with a dope that leaves no trace so they're not going to get caught, are they? They probably get offered a good few thousand pounds. If it's a big race like the Ascot one with a lot of money gambled ante post they might even make five figures, provided the horse loses. I pay my stable staff over the odds and I give them every home comfort. But all it takes is one. Just one bad egg.'

'And that's what you reckoned happened to Wally? You think one of the lads got at him.'

'I think someone inside Claremore got at him. I can't see any other possible explanation.'

'That's terrible. That must make you feel terrible.'

'As a matter of fact it does,' Cassie replied despairingly. 'As a matter of fact it makes me feel as though I want to give it all up.'

On an altogether more cheerful note, The Nightingale did a thrilling piece of work, galloping with so much of his old zest that when she got off him Josephine was moved to announce that if such a thing were possible he would win another Derby.

'I don't think so,' Cassie laughed. 'I don't want to pour water on the fire but I'd say just from looking at him he's a good stone inferior to when he had all his equipment. He'd still murder most horses, but there are quite a few around now who could probably take the race off him.'

'You weren't sitting on him,' Josephine retorted. 'I had a ton of horse under me. As soon as you ask him to pick up even just a little, *whoosh.*'

'Well, that's what matters. Even if he's slower than he was, if he hasn't lost the ability to quicken, that's all that matters.'

'I can't wait to do it for real.'

'Well you're going to have to,' Cassie replied, pulling the horse's head up by its bridle from the grass. 'And that's quite enough for you, old boy. We can't have you getting fat on us.'

'You don't want him getting too thin either,' Josephine added.

'No, we don't want that either.'

'Not like the way some of the state of the art trainers produce horses at Lambourn and Newmarket.'

'Certainly not, Jo.'

'Some of those smart-arse young trainers. They think the way to train a horse is to have it looking like a toast rack. That's why I like Kevin England. They all laugh at him for the way he dresses, and because they think he runs his horses out of their depth in Group races, but not only do his so-called pudgy horses win, but they keep on winning. Right through the season – and the next.'

'Now if that concludes today's lecture on Training My Way by Josephine Rosse—'

'All I was saying is we don't want to run Nightie up too thin.'

'And all I'm saying to you is that I've been doing this for so long I could do it in my sleep, but I won't. Instead I'll just simply agree and say *No of course we don't, sweetheart.* And I was only joking about the lecture.'

'Just as well,' Josephine said, and grinned, 'or I'll throw the race.'

Happily for Josephine her relationship with Gareth Plunkett was a lot less argumentative than the one she enjoyed with her mother. Gareth had obviously grown very serious as far as his intentions towards Josephine went and when he wasn't at Claremore to work on Cassie's legal situation he visited Josephine regularly to take her out. Even when he was locked away with Cassie in her study, she often had her work cut out to keep the young man's attention and it amused her to watch his eyes wandering, particularly when Josephine, dressed in her riding out breeches, boots and figure-tight polo-neck jumper, kept wandering past the window.

'You said you had bad news, Gareth,' Cassie said to him one day in late August.

'I have, Mrs Rosse,' Gareth agreed, trying valiantly to avoid looking at Josephine who had appeared to dead-head some rose bushes right outside the window. 'We only heard this morning, but apparently your bloodstock insurers have shut up shop and done a bolt.'

'They've done a bolt?' Cassie echoed. 'Does this bury any chance we have of getting the money?'

'I'm afraid so,' Gareth said glumly, having his eye caught by Josephine at the window who mouthed him an exotic kiss. 'The firm has declared itself bankrupt and the underwriters have, it seems, taken to the hills.'

'In that case,' Cassie said grimly, 'it's time to take the gloves off.'

'How much?' Mattie almost howled with disbelief when he heard. 'You hope to take out *how much*?'

'Keep your voice down, for God's sake,' Cassie warned him, going once again to make sure the drawing room doors were well and truly closed and that there was no one eavesdropping out in the corridor. 'If anyone gets the slightest wind of this—' she began as she turned to make her way back to the drinks table.

But Mattie held up both his hands to signal his interruption and shook his head.

'Now come on, get real,' he said. 'He's not going to let you get that sort of money down. Nobody is.'

'Suppose they don't know it's me,' Cassie said as she poured them both another glass of wine. 'Suppose it looks as though it's coming from several sources? I don't intend to walk into one of his shops, produce a couple of plastic shopping bags and put it on just like that.'

'So how do you intend doing it? On the telephone?'

'Yes. At the beginning,' Cassie agreed, coming to sit down on the faded pink damask sofa opposite her son. 'I organized two new accounts with Mike Gold a couple of months ago so that they could be run in as it were. Established if you like. One was opened by Theodore, and the other in the name of Joel's brother Frank.'

Mattie put his drink down and frowned. 'I thought this was meant to be strictly between you, me and Josephine.'

'It is and it isn't. I've thought a lot about this and initially we must keep any attention away from Claremore. It's no good you having an account, or even Josephine for that matter. We can't have anyone who could be connected with us.'

'OK – but Joel's *brother*?'

'He doesn't know a thing. Neither does Joel yet. At least, no details. I simply told him I was going to have to run an account in someone else's name but that I'd finance it and that was that. No-one's going to make that connection, not until way past post time.'

'And the same applies to Theodore, I suppose,' Mattie wondered.

'Exactly. You couldn't find anyone more trustworthy than Theodore,' Cassie replied.

'If the account's in someone else's name, they could run off with the take.'

'With that portion of the take,' Cassie corrected him. 'Yes, that's true, but I don't think either of them will. Certainly not Theodore.'

'There's nothing to stop Joel's brother from absconding.'

'Yes there is. There's Joel.'

'OK.' Mattie balanced his glass on the arm of his chair. 'So what are your openers?'

'You are, Mattie,' Cassie said simply. 'You and your string. The first thing we have to do – but not quite yet. Where are we? Yes. Around about the end of November, but not until then, our very first move will be to get a price about you.'

Extracted from:
The monthly Claremore newsletter
to
*THE NIGHTINGALE FAN CLUB*
from
Cassie Rosse.

As I told you in the August bulletin *Nightie* has taken to jumping with enormous enthusiasm and skill. During the summer he was schooled over some purpose built fences of about four foot in height to see if he was a natural 'lepper' or just a horse who got over fences because they were in his way. Happily he jumped the line of obstacles correctly and with true precision, leading us all to believe that instead of having to spend the rest of his days as a trainer's hack (and what a hack!) he might have another career after all.

Of course there's a great deal more to eventing than just jumping fences. The discipline of dressage plays a vital part in the correct presentation of the event horse and so with this in mind *Nightie* was sent to an expert instructor to have his paces properly adjudged. His report came back with 10/10.

So since the horse continues to thrive, apparently none the worse for his dreadful ordeal, I have decided to gift him to Josephine, my daughter. When she was a teenager Jo was a successful junior event rider, winning many good trials on her flying grey, Gracie Allen, on whom she represented her country as a junior international, helping to win the team a Gold medal. She then went on to race ride as an amateur and as many of you no doubt will know, Jo won this year's running of the Diamond Stakes at Ascot, having been narrowly beaten into third place the year before. Jo is now back at home permanently, having given up a very successful acting career in order to concentrate on her riding.

So all in all if we choose to follow this path eventing would seem to be the ideal future for *Nightie*, particularly ridden by Josephine with whom he seems to have a special empathy. He still won't let a man near him, not even his old favourite Liam, my head lad, not in his stable and most certainly not on his back, having got rid of every top race rider who has tried to sit on him. Whereas women, and Jo in particular, can do anything they like with him.

And *Nightie*'s not a horse to argue with!

So if everything goes according to plan, *Nightie* will be trained on through the winter and aimed at Novice Event classes as soon as the new season opens in early spring.

# Thirty-One

'What did you get?' Cassie asked Theodore as soon as she had him safely closed away in the library.

'I think they thought I was mad,' Theodore sighed, taking his spectacles off and holding them up to the light to check the lenses.

'I don't mind what they thought you were, Theodore,' Cassie urged. 'Just tell me what you got.'

'Stony silence at first,' Theodore replied, now carefully wiping his lenses on an immaculate white handkerchief. 'And then a request to hold until they spoke to Head Office.'

'Spare me the details, please,' Cassie said, barely able to contain her impatience. 'Just cut to the chase, will you?'

'Cut to the chase?' Theodore raised his eyebrows as far as they would go and beamed at Cassie. 'I do like that. Wherever do you pick these things up?'

'Theodore—' Cassie said warningly. 'You're just winding me up.'

'Cut to the chase, winding you up, you're beginning to talk like one of your childer,' Theodore chuckled, carefully replacing his spectacles. 'I got a hundred and fifty to one.'

'A hundred and fifty to one,' Cassie said slowly. 'Exactly what Mattie thought we would. A hundred and fifty to one.'

'One hundred and fifty to one,' Theodore echoed proudly, as if he had called the odds himself.

'And did you get the bet on?' Cassie asked him, standing looking at him in the looking glass above the fireplace.

'I did so,' Theodore replied. 'One thousand to win one hundred and fifty thousand, tax paid.'

Now Cassie turned and moved away from the fireplace

to come and stand in front of her debonair guest. 'They actually took the bet?'

'They actually took the bet.'

'Brilliant. Perfectly brilliant.'

'I know,' Theodore agreed. 'You can kiss me all over if you like. I won't mind.'

Cassie gave a peal of delighted laughter before throwing her arms around Theodore. 'I'll just hug you to death instead. One thousand to win one hundred and fifty. And that's just for starters.'

Theodore put his own arms around Cassie's shoulders and gently hugged her to him. 'I hope this is too,' he murmured. 'This is a most excellent *hors d'oeuvre*.'

Cassie said nothing but neither did she try to move from his embrace. Instead she just rested one cheek on Theodore's chest.

'Just think. If this comes off won't that be something?'

'It will, it will,' Theodore replied carefully, lifting one hand gently to stroke the back of Cassie's head. 'But then suppose it does not, Cassie Rosse? What then, may I ask? What then?'

'If I don't pull this off, Theodore,' Cassie replied, moving her head so that she could look up into his eyes, 'I have no business here any more. There would be nothing to keep me. But then if I fail to avenge what they did to The Nightingale, I really have no right to be here any more either.'

Theodore looked back down at her, his hands now both back around her slim waist. 'You are without any shadow of a doubt, Cassie Rosse, the most remarkable person it has ever been my privilege to know.'

And he kissed her.

'I think you could have done better,' Mattie said as Cassie and he cantered their horses down to the start of the gallop away from the other work riders.

'You would,' Cassie retorted. 'And next time you're short of a work rider, remember I have horses of my own to exercise.'

'I wanted to talk to you,' Mattie said. 'It was you that said not to use the phone in case anyone picked up an extension.'

'I'm only teasing,' Cassie assured him, hooking up the horse she'd been given to ride, swinging his head to one side so he would stop tanking off with her. 'This one of the horses you're going to use in the trial? Because he doesn't half pull.'

'That's what I wanted to talk to you about,' Mattie said, easing his own horse back to keep pace with his mother's. 'One of the things, anyway. Obviously we can only use our own horses because as you said—'

'No owner is going to want any horse of his running in an unofficial race without any prize money, right,' Cassie finished for him.

'Someone wants to buy your chap, the one you're riding,' Mattie said as they pulled their horses up. 'And with the way things are and the way we want things—'

'Of course,' Cassie agreed. 'We'll find another.'

'I'm down to only two I can run against you. This one I'm riding, Bohandur, and a rather useless handicapper called Touch Paper.'

'I can still field four,' Cassie said. 'The good thing is one of them's Aperçu, and he's bound for Cheltenham.'

'How come?' Mattie wanted to know.

'His owner wants a touch, and is more than happy to give him his last outing before the Festival in private rather than in an official race where everyone can see the sort of shape he's in. So as long as we organize the outing properly, we should be able to manage a pretty serious trial.'

'Won't Aperçu's owner want to come and see his horse?'

Cassie smiled at her son. 'He lives in Dubai,' she replied, swinging her horse round in the direction of where the other racehorses were getting ready to gallop some hundred yards off. 'Now let's see the sort of shape your fellow's in.'

'I still say we should have done better than a hundred and fifty to one,' Mattie muttered as he picked up his reins. 'A hundred and fifty to one for a second season trainer to land the Champion Hurdle at Cheltenham? We should have got five hundred to one!'

When she got back to Claremore at midday a fax was awaiting her on her private line. It was from Joel's brother and it simply read:

> BEST THIS END A TON TO A SINGLETON SO INVESTED
> POINT FIVE MORE. AMENDED DIVIDEND THUS TO
> READ THE SAME.

'Right on,' Cassie said to herself as she fed the sheet of paper into her shredder. 'The game's afoot.'

# Thirty-Two

The first trial was not a race proper. It was more an organized school over six flights of hurdles. Cassie had thought long and hard about it but although she knew that the longer the cards stayed close to her chest the less was the chance of being *kibbutzed*, she knew just as well that if she wasn't going to give her horse a race in public over the timber, then the more he got the idea of hurdling in private the better.

Which meant letting a bit more of the cat out of the bag.

As he waited down at the start of Peter Nugent's private track checking his girths Liam said nothing when he saw the last horse to join the party come out of the woods with Josephine up. He just smiled a huge broad smile before giving a great whoop of joy.

'What's up, Liam?' Bridie said, swinging round her horse who was standing the other way round.

'Prepare to fall out of your saddle, Bridie Moore,' Liam said. 'Will you just look at who we've come to work against?'

The two of them stared with growing delight as the big black horse walked nearer and nearer. He looked a picture of health, his dark coat glowing like ebony and his eye as bright as one of Erin's saucepans.

'Now listen,' Cassie said from the back of the horse she was riding as Mattie, Josephine, Liam and Bridie gathered around her. 'On the principle that the less you know the better, all I'm telling you today is that we're going to work at a strong but sensible gallop over one and a half miles jumping six flights of hurdles. I don't want anyone doing anyone else any favours. By that I mean this is not a polite school, this is a serious piece of work and I want the best

513

horse to win it. But conversely I don't want any rough stuff or unnecessary scrimmaging. And none of you are to knock your horses about – all right' – Cassie held up a placatory hand – 'OK – I know you won't, I'm just telling you in case some of you get your blood up and think you can take the old boy on. There are no prizes at the end of the day, not yet anyway. And there won't be either, if one word of what we're doing gets out. If it does, I'll know who to come after.'

Cassie gave them all a good long look in turn before picking up her reins. 'OK!' she called, kicking her horse on towards the starting line where Peter Nugent was waiting with a flag. 'Let's go to work!'

As soon as Peter Nugent dropped the flag Mattie set off to make the pace on Bohandur. Coming to the first flight of hurdles the five horses had settled into a sensible gallop, more than a married man's pace but a couple of notches down from a racing one. Even so already Bridie who was riding Touch Paper was a good four lengths adrift with Josephine lobbing The Nightingale whom she had nicely settled a couple of lengths in front of her, tucked in behind Liam on Aperçu and Cassie on Call To Arms, a good hurdler of hers which had won six good races over the timber. The three leading horses pinged the first flight, getting away well, and now that Mattie's horse had come back to them settling into a keen arrowheaded trio, with Bohandur still striding out half a length up.

Cassie took a quick look round at The Nightingale and to her surprise saw he had jumped so big at the first he was now only a length down on her own horse, racing along as always when he was enjoying himself with his head tucked into his chest. Over the next two flights of hurdles there was no change in the order but at the fourth Cassie heard a loud crash and a cry from behind her as someone took the flight by the roots.

'It's OK!' Josephine called. 'It was Bridie! But she's OK! Sounds as if the horse just missed it out completely!'

That really left only four of them working seriously, since

the mistake had made Touch Paper drop a good dozen lengths behind The Nightingale who as far as Cassie could make out when she took another quick look was still lobbing along as if he was taking a hack along the sands.

The second last hurdle had been erected on the top of the turn leading to the home bend and here Bohandur ran very wide, leaving Liam on Aperçu and Cassie on Call To Arms with the lead. Liam was still sitting with plenty in hand as indeed was Cassie on her own mount, both of them a good three lengths clear of The Nightingale as they began their run to the last.

They both met the final flight perfectly, landing neck and neck and kicking away for the winning post some hundred and twenty yards distant. For a moment Cassie had a terrible sinking feeling in the pit of her stomach as it seemed as if Aperçu, whom if they were to get serious looked to have Call To Arms well beaten on the run in, was going to come home as he liked, and then the feeling of despair gave way to one of jubilation as she heard Josephine's cheeky cry of *On your inside, thank you!* barely fifty yards from the line.

Looking over her left shoulder Cassie saw The Nightingale flash by, still on the bridle, still with his head well in his chest. As horse and rider flew past Josephine raised one hand in the air and waved.

'Handstands,' Josephine said for the fifteenth time. 'Cartwheels. Blindfold. Backwards. Have it how you will. Nightie could have done that doing all of those things.'

'It was only a racecourse gallop,' Cassie said, also for what seemed the umpteenth time. 'And only two of the horses have any real ability.'

'Mums – ' Josephine sighed, leaning back in her seat as they sped across the Wicklow Hills. 'Mums, we were still hardly *cantering*.'

'And Cheltenham is still three months away, Jo,' Cassie reminded her. 'There's a long way to go yet, and even if we do get there he'll be facing a dozen or so of the very best hurdlers in the world.'

'They might as well all stay at home,' Josephine said happily. '*They might as well all stay at home.* I mean, what *is* that horse?'

'Hmmm,' Cassie said, and that was all. She knew well enough who she thought The Nightingale was, but she wasn't telling that to anyone. Not even to her daughter.

Under the Rules of Racing horses are not required to be in the yards of their licensed trainers until three weeks before they run their first race for the yard, so The Nightingale did not have to go into training formally with Mattie until after the entries for the Champion Hurdle closed on 1 February. This meant that even when the list of the horses entered was published on that day the horse would not yet be listed as being trained by Mattie Rosse and so the bets on his stable winning the big race should not necessarily make alarm bells ring in the big bookmakers' offices.

Bells would sound none the less. Cassie and her team knew that well enough, but since the horse would not have been seen out over hurdles by that time, it could only be sheer speculation on the bookmakers' and the punters' part as to what sort of chance the horse might have. He had, after all, been subjected to a terrible ordeal when he had been kidnapped and wilfully gelded and on his return home he had subsequently undergone an operation which most certainly would have accounted for a less resolute animal to save him from dying from a twisted gut.

Above all, he would be ridden by a woman, and no woman had as yet even ridden in the Champion Hurdle, let alone won it.

All these things were public knowledge, thanks to Cassie's diligently written broadsheets. Nothing had been hidden from the racing public except the owner's change of plans for her horse, and even those were made public by a press statement from Claremore on the very day the declarations for the big Cheltenham hurdle race were announced:

516

As a result of some extensive schooling sessions over hurdles in private while hopefully preparing The Nightingale to go eventing, the horse's natural ability to jump at racing pace has led to a change in the short term aims for him. Since even more significantly he has recovered so well in his health after his ordeal it is now the plan to see if and how he takes to racing under National Hunt Rules over hurdles, and if he continues to show the same talent as he shows at home on the schooling grounds in his prep races then his entry for the Champion Hurdle will be allowed to stand.

Once again it was headline news on all the sporting pages as all the racing correspondents made the most of the racing story of the year. But this time it was Mattie who was deluged by calls and visits from the press.

'In answer to the tremendous interest shown by members of the racing public and the media,' he said on television on the evening of 1 February, 'I feel it only fair to answer the questions which have been put to us concerning The Nightingale's return to racing as best I can in public, and RTE have very kindly offered me the chance to say a few words here on television. Briefly, because I'm sure there isn't anyone who follows horse racing who doesn't know the story, my mother – who bred and owned the horse besides training him to all his great and famous victories – when she decided to retire him from the Flat very generously gifted him to my horse-mad sister Josephine. Now Josephine is a bit of a rider herself, and some of you might know that too, and one day when she was schooling him she decided to give Nightie a pop, and found he was a seriously serious lepper. Her first plan was to take the horse eventing, but then the more she rode him the more convinced she was he could still win a decent hurdle race, and what more decent race to win if you're going to have a crack at winning a race over timber than the Champion Hurdle itself? So having decided that's where she wanted to go, she asked me to train him for her, we just got the entry in on time, and now it's in the lap of the gods. All I can say is the old horse is very well or we wouldn't even be thinking of running him, and that all still being well he'll have a prep race either at Leopardstown in the Robinsons or going for the Kingwell Hurdle at Wincanton. If he runs a decent race in his trial then we'll definitely have a crack at the Champion.'

'Now?' Theodore wondered when he was invited for a drink the following evening.

'No,' Cassie said. 'They've taken fright and the first show reflects it. He's no better than twelves in most lists, and Mike Gold has him in at tens. If anyone puts any serious money on him now they'll shorten him even more, and tens and elevens and twelves aren't in any way honest to God odds at all. What we do is wait until after Leopardstown or Wincanton. Then we put on our waders.'

'Excellent, excellent,' Theodore agreed. 'Except I thought you weren't planning to run him at either.'

'We're not,' Cassie replied and raised her glass.

Mattie pulled the horse out of the Leopardstown hurdle at the overnight declaration stage, having warned the punters to keep their money in their pockets because the horse was short of a piece of work and was being re-routed to Wincanton where all being well he would definitely run.

A day later he boxed up six horses to take them over for a change of scene to gallop on Tom McMahon's grass the other side of the Curragh. Slightly earlier in the day because she had a longer journey Cassie had supervised the boxing of six of her own hurdlers who were also on their way to the Curragh. When they were all met Mattie pulled three horses from his box, as did Cassie, the six horses being worked twice up the gallops before being walked off and then returned to their horseboxes. Due to the continuing inclement February weather all the animals wore waterproof exercise sheets and hoods to protect them from the elements.

But mostly to disguise them from the eyes of the gallop

watchers, who weren't having the best of mornings anyway, such was the rain which was being swept across the Curragh by a gale from the north-east.

Naturally when all the horses were being reloaded any gallop watcher hardy enough still to be out with his field glasses would not have noticed which horses were returned to which box, or the fact that in the *mêlée* that generally surrounds the gallops at this time the three horses which had been left in Mattie's box were switched to Cassie's so that the unexercised six were driven off in the direction of Kilkenny while the six exercised horses were shunted back to Mattie's yard across the plain.

And then, while the Nightingale team was preparing to run its private trial on the Nugent estate, Mattie's team of lads, each with a bonus of £50 in his back pocket, went off for an early lunchtime drink at their usual haunt where one or two of the lads were overheard dispiritedly talking about the rather disappointing bit of work *you-know-who* had done that morning, the very lads who were already holding ante post vouchers on their newly arrived star horse to win the Champion Hurdle at 20/1.

'Now,' said Cassie as her team once more prepared to go to work on the Nugent racetrack. 'What we're going to try to do this morning is not exactly out of the training manuals. We are not going to have a serious school, we are going to have a serious race. We are going to race over the full distance of two miles and we're going to jump eight flights of hurdles, just as we would if we were on the racetrack proper, and this time I want you to go for it. The horse each of you is riding is as you well know fully race fit, and since only one of them is owned by anyone outside either Mattie's yard or my own, you can rest assured you have the owner's permission to race. As for Aperçu, which Liam is riding as usual, all I can tell you is that this piece of work is exactly what his owner wants, so there's no risk of spoiling any of your horses' immediate chances by asking it all of them this morning.

'You've all also been weighted according to your horses'

latest ratings,' she continued, 'so although Himself over here has been entered up for the Champion which of course is most definitely *not* a handicap, it would hardly be a fair test to ask the likes of Bohandur and Touch Paper to take either him or Aperçu on at level weights. So you've all been weighted in with a chance, even your fellow, Bridie. You're getting over two stone and a half from Nightie and over a stone and a half from Aperçu and the horse I'm riding this morning, Cartographer, who was only just beaten into second in the Glenlivet Hurdle last April remember. Finally, the only other instruction I'm going to give you is to make sure it's a good gallop. They go like hell at Cheltenham in the Champion, so don't take any prisoners.'

'And what exactly are my instructions?' Josephine asked her mother, swinging The Nightingale round alongside her. 'How do you think I should ride him?'

'That's a difficult one,' Cassie replied, hitching up the flap of her saddle to check her girth. 'Since I'm no longer the trainer, you'll have to sort that out with Mattie.'

'Are you serious? You know all there is to know about this horse. Mattie's just a rookie!'

'I think we ought to get just one thing straight, Jo,' Cassie replied, steadying her horse. 'When I put Nightie in Mattie's yard, which I did before I gave you both shares in the horse, I did so not for love but because I know Mattie's going to make a hell of a good trainer. So if you want instructions, you really must go ask him.'

Josephine eyed her mother then walked her horse over to where Mattie was also busy adjusting his girths to get her instructions. Cassie called over young Phelim O'Connell to give him his orders, the lad having been counted in to make up the numbers since Liam was now convinced of his integrity, and while she told him what she wanted him to do on Pipistrelli, the very smart four-year-old he was riding, out of the corner of her eye she watched her son and daughter arguing and saw Josephine as always trying to countermand everything her brother was saying while Mattie patiently talked her down, until finally Josephine sat back with an obvious sigh and listened.

'All right, jockeys!' Peter Nugent called, the big white flag raised above his head. 'Go!'

With the track being just under two miles in circumference they had moved the start to a chute back in the boundary of the woods so that the ground they would have to travel would be approximately the same shape as that at Cheltenham, jumping what would be the last hurdle as the first before passing the winning post for the first time and swinging away up a hill to jump the second, the third and then the fourth before the back straight levelled out flat. The fifth was met at the end of the back straight and then the sixth just before the track began to drop back downhill, very like Cheltenham except that the drop was not nearly so severe. Even so, if they weren't going to fall or make a bad mistake horses still had to be well balanced and come off the right stride as they jumped the sixth and seventh hurdles before swinging left into the home straight to meet the last on rising ground a good two hundred yards from the finishing line. All things considered, in fact, the Nugent course was a perfect test in miniature for the great course in Prestbury Park in Cheltenham.

By the time the field of six horses had all jumped the first, taking good advantage of her featherweight Bridie had shot Touch Paper to the front and was bowling along a couple of lengths to the good. In second place came Pipistrelli, just where Cassie had wanted him to be, followed by Aperçu with Bohandur on his outside, Cassie on Cartographer fifth and the Nightingale two lengths away last. The order stayed exactly the same as they jumped the second and third, Touch Paper making a slight mistake at the third which brought him back to his field so that as they jumped the fourth along the back straight Pipistrelli took it up, with Phelim O'Connell squeezing him on to snatch a quick two and a half lengths over the tiring Touch Paper who was already being scrubbed along by a now vociferous Bridie. By the fifth flight of hurdles Pipistrelli had opened up a three length lead over the ever-improving Bohandur, followed half a length away by Aperçu whom Liam had lying cosily up the inside. Both Cassie on

Cartographer and Josephine on The Nightingale had yet to make a move, although they had closed their horses up on the one in front so that as they raced to the sixth there weren't more than six lengths from the leader's nose to the tip of The Nightingale's thick black tail.

'How are you going, guv?' Josephine called to Cassie from alongside her after they had pinged the sixth hurdle, losing Touch Paper as they did so who seemed to miss his stride and slip over on landing.

'Never you mind!' Cassie yelled back. 'And don't you dare come up on my inside!'

'I won't need to! Don't worry!' Josephine returned. 'I got a ton of horse under me! I can go where I like!'

There were now only two hurdles left to jump, the second last just before they swung into the straight and then the last on the stiff climb up to the finish. Cassie smiled grimly to herself as after they jumped the seventh she saw a gap opening up in front of her on the running rails as both Bohandur and Aperçu ran wide to start their serious pursuit of the free running Pipistrelli who at last seemed to be tiring. Switching her own horse who was still full of running quickly to the left Cassie accelerated through the gap, getting to Bohandur's flanks and to within half a length of Aperçu, who like Cartographer was still on the bridle. As she made her move she heard a yelled curse from Jose behind her but Cassie resisted the temptation to look because her job was to ride as hard as she could for home and not to take prisoners. Driving her horse on into the last she saw Pipistrelli hit the hurdle hard and although both Bohandur and Aperçu jumped the flight half a length up on her, Cassie had them in her sights and as soon as she saw Mattie go for his whip she knew Bohandur was beaten. With a hundred yards to go she and Liam on Aperçu were neck and neck until Cassie saw Aperçu change his legs and as he did she knew that horse's chance was gone because Cartographer was lengthening out under her driving and going away from the big bay who was beginning to hang into him.

Even so, well as she was going, Cassie was waiting to

hear the thunder of hooves on her outside and the appearance of a big black horse alongside her, with his rider sitting as still as a mouse on his withers as her mount quickened and went on quickening until the big black horse would cross the line easing up with two or three lengths to spare.

And sure enough with less than fifty yards to run she saw The Nightingale's head appearing in the corner of her eye. Not daring to look any closer Cassie sat down and rode even harder but The Nightingale simply picked up and flew past her, leaving Cartographer to cross the line a well-beaten two lengths behind him with Aperçu another length and a half away third, and Bohandur a well-beaten fourth. The only trouble was The Nightingale's saddle was empty.

Standing up in her irons as she eased her own horse up, Cassie took a look back down the track and saw Josephine sitting on the ground on the landing side of the final hurdle. She appeared to be perfectly unscathed because she was busily hitting the ground in front of her with her whip before getting up and half turning to wipe the mud and grass off the backside of her breeches. Cassie swung Cartographer round and cantered him back to where her daughter was now striding up the track towards her, with a face as black as the devil in a comedy.

'So what happened?' Cassie asked, having turned her horse round and brought him back to a walk once she'd made sure The Nightingale had allowed himself to be caught by Liam who'd cantered on up the track after him.

'What happened . . .' Josephine sighed, at the same time managing to glare up at her mother. 'What *happened* was you shut me out, that's what happened, thanks a bunch.'

'You mean you were coming up on my inside after all?' Josephine said nothing to agree or disagree. She simply rewarded Cassie with another dark glare. 'Look, if you were trying to get up on my inside—' Cassie continued. 'If you tried that at Cheltenham certain jocks would have you out over the rails.'

'There was a gap, for God's sake!' Josephine protested hotly, particularly now that Mattie had cantered Bohandur over to learn what had happened. 'If there's a gap it's perfectly all right to go for it, right Mattie?'

'There wasn't a gap, Jo,' Cassie replied. 'Anyway, I called to you to tell you not to come up the inside and you said you were going so well you didn't need to, damnit.'

'That was tactics!' Josephine declared. 'I thought you'd move over if you thought I was coming on the outside and I was going to slip up on the inside! Then you went and shut the bloody door in my face!'

'I came across because I was still on the bridle and I had the rail, Josephine! That's the unwritten rule about coming up on the inside and don't you ever forget it!'

'The guv'nor's right,' Mattie said laconically. 'Even so, that doesn't explain how we ended up getting our new breeches dirty.'

'Don't you start,' Josephine retorted, half turning once more to make sure she'd got all the mud off her backside.

'Well?' Like Cassie, Mattie had now jumped off his horse and was leading him at the walk to let him cool off. 'I still want to know what made you go humpty.'

Josephine glared at him, looked at Cassie, then sighed long and deep up at the skies. 'He dumped me,' she said.

'He dumped you?' Mattie echoed. 'He must have had a reason.'

'Ask the horse.'

'Josephine . . .' Mattie warned her. 'The Pony Club this is not. You're meant to be riding in one of the greatest races in the world in just over a month so let's have it, please. Why did Nightie dump you?'

Josephine repeated the process of glaring first at Cassie and then at her brother before dropping her voice to a confessional level. 'If you really want to know why he dumped me,' she said, 'he dumped me because I hit him.'

'Sweet Jesus,' Mattie groaned. 'Holy Mary Mother of God.'

'I take it you had a reason,' Cassie asked grimly. 'At least I hope you thought you had a reason.'

'Look,' Josephine replied. 'You shut the door on me, I had to snatch him up, and when I did he changed his legs.

When I got him back and pulled him off the rails, he changed his legs again just as we were approaching the last. He was going to meet it all wrong! Talk about being disorganized! If I hadn't given him a smack he'd have taken it by the roots!'

'I don't think so,' Cassie disagreed. 'I don't think so for a minute.'

'Fine,' Josephine seethed. 'Fine – so you ride the bloody horse then!'

'That's not such a bad idea,' Mattie said. 'At least she'd ride to orders.'

'I *was* riding to orders! You said to hold him for a late rattle, I had him perfectly placed, we were still on the bridle and then I had the bloody door slammed shut in my face!'

'And then you hit him. I told you specifically not to touch him with the whip. He's never been touched with the whip since he was a two-year-old when he made it quite clear what he thought about being hit. But you knew better. You had to hit him.'

'OK, children,' Cassie intervened, sensing a return to the nursery floor. 'Let's just keep this professional, shall we?'

'He can't have dumped you before the last, Jose,' Mattie persisted. 'We all saw you sitting the landing side, so where and how exactly did he get you off?'

Josephine gave him one last glare before confessing. 'We jumped the last perfectly,' she said. 'And I could have picked you all off any time. But instead when I asked him to go for it – and gave him just a little tap down his shoulder – he suddenly veered to the left and chucked me off.'

Then before anyone could add to her humiliation Josephine whipped off her crash hat, shook out her mane of hair and hurried away to collect her horse.

There was little to add at the post-mortem held over a pot of tea and a plate of doorstep sandwiches Mattie cut them for lunch back in his kitchen. At first Josephine continued with her sulk but soon got bored when both her mother and brother persisted in ignoring her, as they did her continued sarcasm. Finally she came off her high horse and without being prompted admitted that she had been wrong.

'I was trying to be too clever by half,' she said, 'and so instead of winning as we liked, I ended up on the floor.'

'Better now than in a month's time,' Cassie said. 'Because we simply can't afford that sort of mistake. If you don't mind me saying, Mattie—'

'You go right ahead,' Mattie said, reading Cassie's look. 'You know the horse better than anyone will ever know him, and whatever you say we'd be crazy as hell to ignore your advice.'

'Dexter's really the guy you should listen to, Jo. I can only tell you what I've seen. He's lived it all.'

'Even so.'

'Even so, you'll see when we watch Peter's video again. Nightie's still well on the bridle when you have to snatch him up. It's almost too good to be true. We were going some lick too, weren't we, Mattie?'

'According to Liam's stop watch, and even allowing for the fact that the gradient on the track is nowhere near as severe as Cheltenham, Liam reckoned we were three seconds inside a comparative course's average time over two miles. So that makes the pace not that far off a Champion Hurdle pace.'

'In other words if you'd stayed on board you'd have possibly been another second in front of us which if Nightie was still only in third gear—'

'He was, Mums. I hadn't asked him anything in the way of a serious question.'

'Then theoretically you'd have beaten last year's Champion Hurdler by six lengths,' Mattie said. 'On the watch, that is, and as we all know stopwatch times are generally only academic.'

'My elbow,' said Cassie. 'Your father and I both trained on a watch. Split times might not win races, but they sure as anything show you what your horse is capable of. I knew Nightie's split times on the Flat down to a hundredth of a second, and so did Dex.'

'I'm seeing Dex tonight,' Mattie said. 'I'm meeting him in town for dinner.'

'First thing's first,' Cassie said. 'First we have to decide on what we do next. Or rather whether or not the horse had a proper trial. If he didn't, we don't have any option but to organize another one, but—'

'But that might be pushing our luck,' Mattie said, finishing her sentence for her.

'Exactly, Mattie. Besides, what would we work him against? We couldn't give him another "race" for ten days to a fortnight, so we wouldn't have any decent enough horses to run him against, regardless of what weight we put on them. He could give most of your and my handicappers three or four stone and still not be extended, and I'm certainly not going to heap tons of weight on his back. So what do you both think? Do you think we've seen enough, and more important – do you think that's enough ring experience for him? Or will we be throwing him in the deep end without enough rehearsal?'

'He's hardly a novice,' Mattie said. 'All he's got to get used to is jumping hurdles—'

'With other horses around him,' Josephine chipped in. 'And maybe other horses falling around him.'

'Agreed. But he's taken to jumping completely naturally, and as for other horses, well – he's had one good trial and a proper race,' Cassie said. 'The fact that you came off him might be the best thing that happened. To you both.'

'So that's it, then. We go to Cheltenham just as if he'd had his prep race.'

'He has had his prep race,' Mattie insisted. 'Like I said, what happened today could have happened at either Leopardstown or Wincanton. And we'd still be heading straight for the big one without another prep.'

'Good,' Cassie said. 'Then Cheltenham here we come. Now let's go and have another look at the video.'

'I still think you should ride the horse, Mums,' Josephine said, suddenly sounding panicked. 'I mean if I *do* make a mistake – '

'You won't, and even if you did and you go on and lose, that's racing,' Cassie assured her.

'But so much depends on it. I'm not sure I want that

responsibility. In fact I know I don't want that sort of responsibility.'

'Are you serious?' Mattie asked her.

'Of course I'm serious, you dweep.'

'OK,' Cassie said after a moment. 'I think that's fair enough. I guess I hadn't thought this thing through right, not all the way. Just because it's something I want to do doesn't mean I have any right to force it on you, Josephine. No, it has to be your choice, too. This has to be something you want to do more than anything, and if you don't, if there's one doubt in your mind or you think you're being steamrollered, then you get out. It really isn't fair otherwise.'

'Suppose I did. Who would you put up instead? I mean, why not you? You really would ride him better than me. And you wouldn't go getting any fancy ideas.'

'No, I'm not good enough. Besides, you're a far more *talented* rider than I am. I'm OK text book sort of stuff, but I don't have the flair and the natural ability that you have.'

'Just look where my famous flair got me today.'

'That's because you weren't thinking straight. You won't make that mistake twice. But even so, if you're having second thoughts we can easily get somebody else to ride him. As long as whoever it is rides to orders, Nightie's just a steering job.'

'You bet,' Mattie agreed. 'Even Bridie could ride him.'

'Sure,' Cassie said, glancing at Mattie and winking the eye Josephine couldn't see. 'In fact that's one very good idea. We'll put Bridie up instead.'

'*Bridie?*' Jo protested. 'You can't be serious! Bridie rides like a sack of spuds, Mums! And as for her hands! I mean, you should have been behind her this morning on Touch Paper. Talk about a *bumper*.'

'She rides work very well,' Cassie said, keeping her face straight.

'She can't race ride. She couldn't have won on Touch Paper this morning if the rest of you had been riding donkeys!'

528

'OK, so failing Bridie, we could put Phoebe up,' Mattie suggested.

'Now I know you're all mad,' Josephine concluded. 'Anyway, you know Nightie only goes for girls.'

'Careful, sis,' Mattie warned, his tongue in his cheek.

'I thought it was all over between you and Phoebe, anyway?' Josephine said.

'There was never anything to be over.'

'Cough cough.'

'Not that it's any of your business.'

'Now then, children,' Cassie intervened once again. 'Let's all be our ages, OK? But that's a good idea, Mattie, as it happens. I saw Phoebe riding in a Bumper at Thurles the other day, and I thought she rode a very good race.'

'Great,' Mattie said, responding to the goad. 'I'll have a word with her tonight.'

'Over my dead body!' Jo said, getting to her feet. 'Over my dead body do you let that lump of lard anywhere near my third of the horse!'

'We could outvote you, sis,' Mattie reminded her. 'You only have a third to our two thirds.'

'Very true,' Cassie agreed. 'And that's precisely what we ought to do – put this to a vote.'

'Agreed,' Mattie said. 'Jose? Not that you have much choice.'

'You're not serious?' she said, sitting back down. 'You've all lost it completely.'

'No we haven't, Josephine,' Cassie told her. 'We all have a share in the horse, so we're entitled to take a vote. We'll do it by ballot.' Taking hold of the notebook by the telephone she pulled out three of its small square pages and handed them round. Three votes per share. We write down the three names, Bridie Moore, Phoebe McMahon and Josephine Rosse – that's if you're still in, Jo?'

'There are other women riders, you know, besides Bridie and Phoebe bloody McMahon!' Josephine seethed.

'We don't have that much time, Jo,' Cassie continued. 'And since Bridie knows the horse, and we need to keep this to people we can trust—'

'You think you can trust Phoebe McMahon?'

'Phoebe would give her eye teeth to ride Nightie at Cheltenham,' Mattie said, po-faced. 'Of course she can be trusted. Anyway, as our mother was saying, sis, are you still in?'

'Of course I'm still in,' Josephine replied tartly in response to her brother's reminder.

'Then write down the three names and then record how many of your three votes you want against each name,' Cassie instructed. 'Fold the piece of paper up, and give it to Mattie.'

After they had recorded their votes, Mattie opened the folded slips, lifting them so no-one else could see the result.

'And the result is—' he began. 'Phoebe McMahon – *nil points*. Phoebe McMahon – no points. Bridie Moore – *nil points*. Bridie Moore – no points. Josephine Rosse – *neuf points*. Josephine Rosse – nine points. So by the jury's unanimous vote, Josephine Rosse gets the ride.'

'You silly buggers.' Josephine grinned back at the two of them. 'Really.'

# Thirty-Three

'I don't like cheating,' Cassie said to Mattie on the eve of the race. 'But I don't see any other way round it.'

'This isn't cheating,' Mattie replied, finishing the draft of his intended fax. 'It would have been if we'd had to have Niall sign a vet's certificate, but now the weather's come to our rescue we're above suspicion.'

'The point is,' Cassie repeated, 'that even if the ground at Wincanton hadn't come up firm, we were going to withdraw him on a spurious vet's certificate.'

'It happens all the time,' Mattie said, waving the fax under his mother's nose for approval. 'Imagine if we had run him in Somerset tomorrow and he'd trotted up as he most surely would have done, what price the Champion Hurdle?'

'I know,' Cassie groaned, 'but it still would have been cheating to pull him out, it still would have been bending the rules.'

'But this isn't,' Mattie assured her. 'I had two jocks who live near Wincanton walk the course, and they both said even if the sun shines all morning which it won't, they doubt if the frost will come right out of the ground. It's such a drying course, you know that. Even when it's heavy going everywhere else, it's only on the soft side of good there, and so with this dry spell followed by these two heavy frosts – well. It couldn't actually have worked out better. We won't be the only horse to come out, you wait and see. Simon McNeill who's down to ride Jay Arthur and was one of the jocks who walked the track says his will certainly come out.'

'OK,' Cassie sighed, 'but what about the people who might have backed him tomorrow? They're not going to take kindly to the horse being pulled out on the morning of the race.'

'Small beer,' Mattie replied. 'I don't mean to sound hard-hearted but they're small beer. No-one's going to put any sort of sizeable bet on the horse until they've seen him in action, and my guess is that the few people who might have had a couple of quid on him ante post will double their stakes when he runs in the Champion. Last minute withdrawals happen all the time. That's racing.'

'Not my sort of racing.'

'We're not going to throw it all away now, Ma, not now we've come this far. We made it clear all along we'd always have to take a good look at the ground wherever he ran, particularly if it was going to be Wincanton because as we said, we don't want to risk jarring him up at this stage of his preparations. It's hard luck on the track and it's hard luck on Nightie's fans, but really they're only half expecting him to race. As far as they're concerned it's a miracle he's alive, let alone that you've got him fit enough to make a comeback. So let that terrible conscience of yours rest. You've done so much right with your wonderful horse, I'm sure God will forgive you for pulling him out of the Kingwell.'

'Do you think you're right, Mattie?'

'I know I'm right, guv. So just check this fax, will you please? This really is the time to get real.'

Five days later Cassie met Mike Gold for a drink at the bar in the Dorchester. She was more nervous than she could ever remember being but did her practised best not to show it, just as Mike Gold put on a polite show of pretending to be glad to see her.

'To what do I owe the pleasure, Mrs Rosse?' he wondered as he settled down in front of his glass of champagne. 'Might this be in connection with this famous horse of yours?'

'It might, Mr Gold,' Cassie said, crossing her legs and then straightening her skirt. 'Although of course the horse is no longer mine but my daughter's.'

'My mistake,' Gold replied with a smile. 'Anyway, what's the news on him? A pity he missed Wincanton, for the punters that is. I can't say we were unhappy to see him withdrawn.' Gold laughed, followed by a bout of coughing. 'Excuse me,' he said.

'It wouldn't have been worth risking him on that ground,' Cassie said. 'Obviously a lot of other trainers thought the same, seeing how many other horses were withdrawn. Karen Whiteman pulled out all four of her runners at the meeting.'

'So the plan remains unaltered,' Gold said. 'The horse still heads for Prestbury Park without the benefit of a prep race.'

'That is his trainer's intention,' Cassie replied. 'Although he would have been happier getting a race in him. No-one's ever happy to be going to Cheltenham with a horse who's not only a maiden over hurdles but untried.'

'On the racecourse.'

'On a racecourse.'

'On *the* racecourse, Mrs Rosse. I'm sure your son, rooky trainer though he might be, is well enough advised not to send a horse to the National Hunt Festival without giving him *some* racing experience.'

'Of course not, Mr Gold,' Cassie agreed. 'The horse has been working alongside a number of horses. It wouldn't be very professional to send him to Cheltenham without some pretty intensive schooling.'

'Certainly not, Mrs Rosse.' Gold took a drink of his champagne and then shot his cuff to look ostentatiously at his gold Rolex, the *tic* in his cheek twitching twice as he did so. 'Forgive me, Mrs Rosse, but I have a luncheon appointment in twenty minutes so if we could get to what this meeting is about—'

'Of course.' Cassie put her own champagne down and made another minimal adjustment to her skirt. 'Your advertisement in the racing papers has The Nightingale at ten to one ante post for the Champion.'

'That is perfectly correct, Mrs Rosse,' Gold nodded without ever taking his eyes off Cassie in her Chanel suit.

'Hardly the most generous of odds if I may say so, Mr Gold. After all, the horse has yet to race over hurdles.'

'He has yet to race over hurdles *in public*, Mrs Rosse.'

'He has yet to race over hurdles, Mr Gold, period.'

Gold nodded again, but this time slowly blinked his eyes while again the *tic* tweaked his cheek.

'Your rivals have the horse at twelve to one, and the Tote has him on offer at fourteens,' Cassie reminded him.

'Then if you're looking for a bet and there's better value elsewhere why not take it? That is if you are looking for a bet, Mrs Rosse?'

'It would appear from the odds on offer generally at the moment that if I was, I would be one of only a few. Before Wincanton the best you could get was fives across the board. So somebody's whispering.'

'As far as gossip is concerned, Mrs Rosse, I'd say racing beats even show biz, wouldn't you?'

'As I thought,' Cassie nodded. 'People are saying there's something wrong with the horse.'

'There isn't any confidence in the market. When there isn't confidence in the market, that is usually because there isn't confidence in the horse.'

'Yet you still have him two points worse than the other big bookmakers and four points worse than the Tote.'

'Possibly because I'm a better bookmaker, Mrs Rosse, and the reason why I'm a better bookmaker is because I have a better information service. Now if you want to do business, please come to the point, because I really do have to leave in a few minutes.'

'I want to back the horse, Mr Gold.'

'Very well, Mrs Rosse – and why not? That's your privilege. But since you're not happy with my odds—' Gold shrugged and tapped his cigar on the edge of the ashtray, neatly knocking off a good inch of ash.

'I'll take your odds, Mr Gold,' Cassie persisted, 'because I particularly want to back the horse with you.'

'Could this be something personal?'

'As far as I'm concerned this is something utterly impersonal.'

'I see.' Gold breathed in very slowly and then out very slowly. 'What sort of wager do you have in mind, Mrs Rosse?'

'I want one to win ten, Mr Gold,' Cassie replied.

'That makes perfect sense, Mrs Rosse,' Gold said. 'Seeing the odds on offer. One hundred to win a thousand? Or a thousand to win ten?'

'A hundred thousand to win a million,' Cassie said. 'Tax paid.'

Gold's expression changed completely. He cleared the husk again from his throat and shook his head slowly. 'Nobody would lay you such a bet,' he replied, in his flat, rasping voice. 'Least of all myself.'

'When we last met you told me you once laid five hundred thousand to an even five hundred thousand,' Cassie replied. 'I'm sure that was a while ago now, so given inflation, what's half a million more? I'm prepared to lodge the money with a stakeholder.'

'Other firms are offering more generous odds than mine,' Gold persisted. 'I really should try them instead, if I were you. Or perhaps even spread your money about. That way you could be more certain of getting your money down.'

'It's not their money I want, Mr Gold,' Cassie replied. 'It's yours.'

Gold kept his eyes on Cassie for a moment longer then once again consulted his watch. 'Excuse me, Mrs Rosse,' he said. 'I really am going to be late.'

'I think you owe me the courtesy of an answer, Mr Gold.'

'I don't think I owe you anything, Mrs Rosse.' Gold got out of his chair, brushed a few flakes of cigar ash from a lapel of his dark blue suit and nodded to the man who had been waiting for him by the door of the bar.

'I take it that's a "no" then,' Cassie said, remaining in her chair.

Gold smiled, but there was no humour in his pale eyes. 'How you imagined you might get any other answer is beyond me, Mrs Rosse. Good day.'

'Good day, Mr Gold.'

'Oh.' Gold stopped by the side of Cassie's chair as if he

had forgotten something, which Cassie knew perfectly well he had not. 'Your charming daughter. How is she? I trust she is fully recovered from her fall – and there were no painful consequences?'

Cassie's blood froze as the implication of the bookmaker's remark sank in, but she thought better of saying anything in return which would in any way reveal her shock. Instead she smiled back at him as if they were enjoying the politest of exchanges at some informal social gathering.

'No, Josephine is fine,' she replied. 'It was her pride that was hurt more than anything. But how very kind of you to ask.'

'Not at all, Mrs Rosse,' Gold assured her, the smile disappearing from his face. 'Let's hope that nothing else of a similar nature befalls her. It's an anxious business after all, being a parent, yes? Whatever age one's children are.' The smile, not quite gone, flickered back momentarily into life as did the tiny *tic* in his cheek, then he was gone.

Cassie sat for a long while until she was quite sure her heart had stopped racing before calling the waiter over and requesting another glass of champagne. Gold had shaken her to her very core with his final enquiry, so much so that suddenly Cassie's world which she had considered once again to be safely shored up against invasion lay violated at her feet. It mattered not how Gold had found out, nor for how long he had been privy to inside information. What counted was that it now seemed as though everything which had been so meticulously prepared in secret had probably been public knowledge as far as the enemy went ever since inception and that any hope Cassie had nursed of not only recovering her losses but at the same time taking her revenge had been not only inconceivable but totally foolish.

Gold had made a fool of her. Worse, she considered she had made a fool of herself.

*What could I have been thinking?* she wondered as she drank some of her second glass of wine. *What folly ever prompted me to believe that I could get away with such a ridiculous venture? How could I ever imagine that I could secretly prepare the best-known racehorse in the world for a tilt at one of jumping's most prestigious races without anyone giving the game away? Not only that, but then confront one of the United Kingdom's most powerful bookmaking organizations and expect him tamely to accept what to all intents and purposes must seem like a guaranteed winning bet, and not only that but to bet to lose him one million pounds? I must have taken leave of my senses. Pride. Tyrone always used to warn me that my pride would be my undoing, but for once he was wrong. It isn't my pride. It's my conceit. I was conceited enough to think that my one man band could outplay Gold's philharmonic orchestra.*

First things first, she thought as she hurried up to her suite. Before she made any plans to retrench, first she must make sure there were no holes in the fence back home.

'Mattie?' She reached him on his car phone, on his way to the races. 'Mattie, I can't go into details on the phone but I think as they say our cover's blown. Or rather to put it a little more truthfully, I think I've blown it. I'll tell you all the moment I get home but in the meantime it's even more imperative than ever not to leave Nightie alone for one second. Not a minute, not half a minute, not for one unguarded second.'

'I thought that might be the case,' came back Mattie's calm reply. 'I mean, I didn't think Gold would roll over and give up, but there's no need to worry. You know I quadrupled all the security the moment the horse arrived in my yard. And Josephine's staying here so that one of us can be with Nightie twenty-five hours a day.'

'You really should hire more security. I told you to use the firm I use and I'd pick up the bill.'

'And I told you I'm not taking on anyone I don't know. You know my feelings on strangers in the yard. Even if they're the most righteous god-fearing blokes you can find *ha-ha* I don't want anything upsetting the horse. Any changes in his routine—'

'Yes, all right, all right.' She'd run this one by Mattie before and he'd made the same point then and just as well, so well that Cassie had been happy to agree. 'It's just that

Gold really got me worried. I half expect to wake up tonight and find him in bed beside me.'

'So when are you coming back?'

'Soon as I can, Mattie. But I thought before I do, I might drive up and see Joel.'

'What for?' Mattie wondered. 'He's not going to be able to help you.'

'I'm not so sure. Besides, I just suddenly got this feeling that I have to see him.'

But Cassie's reasons for wanting to make the journey up to Oxford were not only intuitive ones. It was now eleven months since Joel had been sent to prison and although they had kept up a diligent correspondence, and hard as Joel had worked on trying to unravel the mystery behind The Nightingale's kidnapping, in the last three months Cassie couldn't help noticing a change in tone in Joel's letters, as if rather than to a lover he was now writing to an old friend. Even more to the point, Cassie thought, turning the matter over in her mind as she drove up the M40 motorway towards Oxford, that seemed to be precisely the turn her own feelings had been taking.

*Not that I could ever tell him as much in those sorts of terms*, Cassie thought as she sat parked outside Radford Open Prison checking her hair and looks in the driving mirror of her hired car. *I couldn't bear his disdain. I can just see the mock tired look in his eyes and hear the sarcasm in his rejoinder. No, if that really is going to prove to be the case I'm going to have to be a whole lot more honest and original than that.*

Cassie pushed her car door open without looking right into the path of a woman who was making her way back through the park towards her own car. The woman stopped, putting her free hand up to grab the top of the offending door in order to prevent it hitting her in the chest. When she saw Cassie, she stared at her for a moment, almost it seemed to Cassie as if she already knew her.

'I'm so sorry,' Cassie said at once, getting out of the car

as quickly as she could. 'That was entirely my fault, I really wasn't looking.'

'That's OK,' the woman replied. 'I wasn't really looking either.'

She turned quickly away from Cassie, briefly examining the hand she had used to stop the door from hitting her, flexing her fingers open and shut. But Cassie had still time to take in the younger woman's good looks. She was tall with a head of long fashionably tangled dark hair styled to fall around her face which, with its high cheek bones, finely chiselled nose, and small butterfly mouth, gave her an admirably Pre-Raphaelite look. It wasn't a beautiful face, but it was definitely a face which would be difficult to forget. Her style of dressing too was free-flowing – long loose fawn linen skirt, a white grandad cotton vest under a finespun black wool shirt, a long loose-fitting grey coat almost as long as her skirt, and a pair of what appeared to be men's ankle boots. Everything about the young woman suggested independence, individuality, and above all feminism, right down to the total lack of make-up and jewellery, except for a twisted horsehair bracelet worn on one wrist.

'Have you hurt your hand?' Cassie asked, out of her car now and beginning to follow the woman who was moving off across the car park.

'No, really,' the woman replied, turning to give Cassie a brief smile. 'I'm fine. It's really no problem.'

She hurried on, leaving Cassie behind to watch her go, walking ever more quickly towards a green and cream Citroën 2CV which she got into and started immediately, as if she could not wait to get away. Cassie watched her until she had driven off, wondered for a moment why the woman had given her such a strange look, then, putting any further thought of her out of her mind, turned and made her own way into the building behind her.

From Joel's letters Cassie had gathered that once he had settled into life at Radford his daily existence was hardly demanding. Once he had fulfilled his allotted tasks he found he had a lot of time on his hands so that soon, thanks to the patronage of the governor who happily for Joel was an art man, he was given a room to himself where in return for teaching sculpture and life drawing he was allowed to start working on his own projects. So it was that when Cassie was finally shown into the art room to meet Joel the surprise was not hers.

Seeing her Joel stared at her for a moment, frowning as always, before quickly throwing a cloth over the bust on which he had been busy working as Cassie had been ushered in.

'I know you don't believe in doing things by halves,' he said, wiping his hands on the sides of his trousers, 'but even for you, that's quick.'

'I don't get it. What was quick? What do you mean?'

'I only posted the letter yesterday,' Joel replied.

'Oh.' Cassie laughed to cover her feelings of awkwardness. For a moment she felt as though it was she who was the prisoner and not he, so apparently unencumbered did he seem by any anxiety or strain. 'No, I mean I wouldn't have got any letter because I've been over here in England the last two days.'

'Really?' Joel looked at her with what Cassie felt was almost accusation, as if to say in that case she should have come to see him first and not last. 'I see.'

'I came over to see Mr Gold,' Cassie said. 'I didn't have time to write and tell you—'

'Why should you? I had a letter from you two days ago.'

They looked at each other for a moment, both of them uncertain as to what to do.

Cassie smiled. 'I guess I don't know the routine here too well, not having visited for so long,' she said. 'What do we do? Can we sit here and talk? Or do we have to go somewhere like we did when I first came over? You know, into some official visiting room?'

Joel shook his head and pulled out a chair at a table near him. 'We can talk here,' he replied. 'I'm a trusty.'

Cassie sat down. 'I see you've been busy,' she said, looking up at a wall covered in his drawings and a shelf full of sculptures.

'Hardly surprising,' Joel returned, fishing out his cigarettes.

'What are you working on? Can I see it?' Cassie nodded at the bust that stood hidden under the cloth.

'Work in progress. I'd rather not.'

'That's OK. Whose are all the kids?' Cassie wondered, remarking on the amount of children's likenesses Joel had been working on, before singling out the head right in the middle of the collection. 'Hey.' She got up for a closer look. 'This is Padraig, right? It's wonderful. You did that in here?'

Joel nodded, examining the end of his cigarette.

'You did this from memory?'

'Nope.' Joel glanced up at her and smiled briefly. 'At least not altogether. Erin sent me some photographs.'

Cassie nodded thoughtfully, returning her attention to the exquisite sculpture. 'You wrote and asked Erin, did you? For some photos?' she enquired.

'How could I have got them otherwise?' Joel asked her back with a laugh. 'We're not telepathic. In fact, now you're here perhaps you could take them back to her?' He took a white envelope from the shelf and put it on the table between them.

'These are all out of this world.'

'The other studies are – well. Some are kids of other inmates, done from photos again,' Joel said, inhaling on his cigarette. 'And those two at the end, the two girls – they're the governor's twin daughters.'

'As I said, you do great children.'

'I suppose because I like children.'

'I think it's more than that,' Cassie disagreed. 'I'd say these were works of love.'

'I wouldn't go as far as to say that.'

'I would. Don't forget, when you finish here—'

'When I'm released from here, Mrs Rosse,' Joel corrected her with a smile. 'This is still a prison, whatever you think, not some glorified polytechnic.' He cleared his throat and tapped his cigarette on the edge of the tin ashtray on the table in front of him. 'Anyway,' he continued, 'enough of how brilliant I am – or not, as it happens. Sit down and

541

tell me what happened with Mr Goldfinger Gold and then I'll tell you how I've been getting on.'

Briefly Cassie ran through her meeting with the bookmaker, going light on the details but not on her sense of having blown it.

'I think you're being unnecessarily hard on yourself,' Joel said when she had finished. 'Your approach lacked a little subtlety, perhaps, but you're bang on target. You want to hear how I've been getting on?'

'First of all tell me how you are,' Cassie replied. 'You haven't even told me how you are.'

'You haven't asked me.'

'I'm asking you now. How are you?'

'How do I look?'

'You look fine,' Cassie sighed. 'I didn't mean exchanging pleasantries. It's just – well. It's just a little odd, cutting straight to the chase without even saying hello properly. After all this time.'

'Who's fault is that?' Joel wondered, taking a pull on his cigarette.

'That isn't fair, Joel, and you know it,' Cassie replied. 'We agreed that—'

'I know,' Joel admitted. 'It wasn't fair, and I'm sorry.'

Cassie smiled. 'So let's start again,' she said. 'How are you?'

'I'm fine.' Joel looked at her and nodded. 'It's just that in my reckoning gaol's a fine but public place, and none I think do here embrace. If you get my meaning.'

'Of course I do,' Cassie said, embarrassed lest she had embarrassed him. 'I just thought maybe we'd jumped the gun a bit. So back to business.'

'The wheel comes full circle,' Joel said, as Cassie's eyes strayed to the covered bust behind him. 'Our friend in Windsor, remember? Our death by misadventure man. He used to work for Mike Gold.'

'I don't believe it,' Cassie said after a moment.

'You're right not to, because strictly speaking he used to work for old man Gold. He worked in shops in south London, before leaving to resurface as a gate man up north.

Doncaster first, then Wolverhampton, back up to Nottingham, Catterick then south to Kempton and then Ascot.'

'What do you mean? You think he was always on the Gold payroll?'

'Once a Catholic, if you'll pardon the comparison. Makes sense, too, doesn't it?'

'How did you find this out?'

'Prison's a great place for making contacts. Bloke doing life class, he's got a bit of talent as it happens. Anyway, he's what's called outside a creative accountant. Has a lot of very useful friends. In return, I give him a little extra free tuition. His contacts also helped me make the last and perhaps the most vital of all connections. Remember on the fateful day at Ascot there was a handful of European runners? Mostly as we found with squeaky clean credentials, but one or two gave me pause for thought. Two in particular, one in the Diamond Stakes and one in the King George itself. They were both in the same ownership, namely a stud farm called Lermont. Guess who has money in the stud farm.'

'Gold.'

'Correct. Herr Brandt *and* – wait for it – your very own Monsieur de Vendrer. So now you has jazz jazz.' Joel looked at her, both eyebrows quizzically raised. 'Want it synopsized?'

'Yes,' Cassie replied thoughtfully. 'Go ahead, although I think I have the picture.'

'Your late husband has a feud with a bookie. Bookie dies of heart attack, son blames premature death on late husband. Bookie's son vows to get even. Some years later, husband also dies prematurely – and in his case tragically – wife assumes mantle and makes a good fist of it. En route she trains for so-called Swiss financier otherwise known as a German currency smuggler who thanks to his trainer's integrity doesn't get his bets on to cover some critical financial shortfall. Languishing in gaol he gets to hate honest trainer. Trainer re-meets so-called charming Frenchman who guess what – unbenownst to honest trainer is an old romping companion of trainer's deadly rival Leonora

Von Wagner – and tried to do *bad* things to honest trainer in his state of the art château somewhere in the Loire. Honest trainer escapes frightful fate by skin of her teeth, locking mad, bad Frog in closet en route and thus humiliating him in front of servants and who knows? Maybe even wronged wife. Sadistic Frog added to list of trainer's deadly enemies, particularly when fuelled by old rival – now Mrs Charles C. Lovett Andrew – who plus mother are refused a share in the syndication of honest trainer's home-bred and owned wonder horse. More?'

'You bet,' Cassie said. 'I'm a sucker for soaps.'

'Let's say old rival fans the flames of discontent. Not so unlikely given Monsieur de Vendrer is an old and close friend. Maybe he and she even still play together, for old time's sake. Certainly someone coordinates all this hatred into something coherent, and if it's not old rival then it has to be bookie's son, although my money is on the fact that he enters last, probably through the offices of Herr Brandt who knows a thing or three. The coup is jointly organized, the stud putting in a no hoper at Ascot to provide the necessary cover to get the stolen horse out and Gold's old employee and still fully paid up mole is on the gate of the racecourse boxes, just to make sure. Everything goes perfectly to plan, except for the untimely death of the gate man.'

'Who you I'll bet still say was murdered and who I still say committee suicide,' Cassie interrupted. 'I just don't see them killing the guy – it simply wouldn't have been necessary.'

'He might have been asking for some more dosh,' Joel suggested.

'I don't think so,' Cassie insisted. 'I think he simply had an attack of the guilties when he saw how far in he was, and so he killed himself.'

'It's not what the evidence indicates.'

'It's not what *your* version of the evidence indicates, Joel. The official verdict was death by misadventure and I think we should go along with that. I really don't see murder as part of the overall plan.'

'Maybe because you don't want to. Come on, Cassie, look what they did to your horse.'

'People like that see horses differently,' Cassie said stubbornly. 'They see them as a means to an end. A murder like that – if it was murder, which I don't think it was – would be pursued far harder than the highjacking of some apparently well-insured racehorse. It's a different sort of ball game, murder, and even if the gate man had been asking for more money, I'd say in this instance where money seems to have been no object they'd have paid up.'

'Mmmm,' Joel said reluctantly. 'I'll give you that point, but only because I don't want us to get hung up on it. I suppose I'm hanging on to my theory because what happened to Mr Waldron deceased was the event that first really got me on to the case, so OK, we'll let that one go and pick up the story at the racetrack. Like I said, everything went according to plan, they got the horse away from the course and into a safe house somewhere where after lying low for a while the animal was taken back to Ireland amongst a whole contingent of horses. We don't know the hows of this particular bit, but this we do know – the horse was not taken abroad. He was taken back to Ireland and returned unceremoniously to you without his vital equipment. As far as they went, that should have been that, particularly when the horse nearly died from a twisted gut. No-one could have foreseen him coming back, and if they did, it certainly wouldn't have been over the jumps. As far as those who hate you were concerned, Mrs Rosse, to all intents and purposes it was a knockout blow.'

Cassie nodded thoughtfully. 'I'll buy that,' she said. 'The way you put it, it's what's known as a slam dunk.'

'It would be, Mrs Rosse,' Joel agreed, 'if we had some hard evidence. All this is purely hypothetical, as you know. It's all one hundred per cent conjecture.'

'To hell,' Cassie said through half-gritted teeth. 'We must be able to come up with something solid.'

'Only if some little birdie sings,' Joel replied. 'And I can't see any of this lot singing. This lot are more like vultures than little birdies.'

For the next half an hour they both examined every possible avenue there was to examine, yet neither of them could come up with anything approaching a feasible suggestion for obtaining the proof they so badly needed.

'Don't despair,' Joel said when they'd finally ground to a full stop. 'Having come this far we're not going to concede now.'

'You said it,' Cassie agreed.

'Something will come up, Mrs Rosse. Now don't think me rude, because if I had my way you could stay here all day, but I have to give a class in about two minutes.'

'And I have a plane to catch,' Cassie said, checking her watch and realizing how the time had flown. 'Look, I'm sorry for spending the whole time discussing the kidnap business, because there were all sorts of other things I really wanted to talk about.'

'Me, too,' Joel agreed. 'But I'm out of here next month.'

'That's true,' Cassie said. 'Maybe everything can wait till then.'

'Thanks for coming. It's been good to see you.' Joel got up and then leaned across the table to kiss her on the cheek. 'I'll let you know what my plans are as soon as I know them.'

'OK.' Cassie smiled back at him. 'Make sure you're out in time for Cheltenham.'

'Even if I have to tunnel out,' Joel said. He smiled once more, then, seeing his students lining up outside the door, he turned back to prepare for his class. Cassie picked her bag up from the table and hurried out as Joel's class began to file slowly in past her. As she walked away down the corridor she realized she had left the photographs of Padraig on the table and hurried back to get them before Joel got too far into his class. She was just about to knock on the glass panelled door when she saw Joel with his back to her unveiling the bust from under the cloth he had thrown over it on Cassie's arrival. When she saw the head Cassie took a step back into the shadows behind her because even roughed out in clay, the woman's likeness was unmistakeable.

Among the correspondence awaiting Cassie's attention when she returned to Claremore there were two letters which, even though she had been half expecting them, none the less all but removed what little wind was left in her sails.

One was from Joel, the letter he had told her he had written and which due to her trip to England she had not received when Joel had thought she would receive it. Had she done so, she would have understood not only Joel's evasiveness and the distance he had put between them but the entire nature of their meeting at Radford.

The letter read:

Dear Cassie

I don't know exactly when I'm going to see you, hence this letter.

Obviously this past year has sorted me out. Even in this sort of prison, porridge is porridge and it gives you plenty of time to think.

OK – now before I write anything more, I want you to know that you're the greatest person I've known, ever, and don't argue. But. What next? What we both want is different maybe, which is why I reckon we can't go on, certainly not like this (if you follow).

What you want is not to marry me. No, it's true – you don't. Whereas I would like to marry you but can't, the main reason being because it isn't possible, and if I can't marry you, then what do we do? Drift on till it's over? I don't think so.

If you want to know why you can't marry me, it is not because I'm always right and you're never wrong but because you haven't let go of the past and the reason for that is because you don't want to.

Look. If it was *me* who'd been married to *you* and I'd lost you the way you lost Tyrone, I wouldn't ever want to let go either. I certainly wouldn't want someone gatecrashing my life and telling me I had no business to go on loving someone who was dead just so that they could have the sole copyright. There's no reason for you to want to get married again. You've done marriage. You've done it better than anyone could ever hope to do it. If I'd had a love like you had with T the last thing I'd want would be to be married to somebody who's going to make me try to forget that love ever existed.

This isn't a criticism, I've loved you all the more because of your honesty and for your undying devotion to T. Trouble is I'm a mite possessive (as you may have noticed?) so I'd want you to myself. I have too inflated an opinion of myself to live in T's shadow – you know that as well as I do.

I know you've given this a lot of thought as well because I reread your letters to me all the time. And some of the things you *haven't* said to me have made it quite clear what's been going through your beautiful head. It seems what you want is the love of someone who's perfectly willing to share what's gone before, and that's not me, as you've found out. Someone maybe who's also suffered a loss and whose whole thing would be more like a drum in tune with yours. My beat's maybe a bit too militant – or rather insistent . . .

There's another reason I think we've come to a full stop and my suspicion is you know this reason already which is why you wrote and told me about that magical thing down in Dingle. Knowing you I'll bet you saw long before I did that there was something else I wanted out of life, something which through no fault of your own you can't give me. Maybe it's got worse since losing my own father, but there you are. Now there's nothing I want more than to have kids of my own.

I wanted to talk to you about all this when I saw you, but funked it. In case I got it wrong and I hurt you. But then when I saw you, I knew you were feeling differently too. We know each other too well now

548

not to get those sorts of vibes, don't you think? I feel
we've settled into a friendship now, a deep one too,
a lasting one I hope, I really do. But that something
else has gone. *The* something else, perhaps.

I've also met someone as well – someone who's been
visiting me here. I don't *feel* for her – or about her –
the way I did about you but then I never will feel that
way about anybody. I just feel that because of the
sort of person I am and the sort of person she seems
to be we might just make it into parenthood. She's
called Polly, by the way, and she's writing a book on
euthanasia, which is why she contacted me in the first
place.

I hope this letter makes some sense. I don't know
where I'm worse at explaining, on paper or in person.
But whatever you make of it, Mrs Rosse, I can tell
you one thing for sure – I really never have loved
anyone the way I loved you and that I never will.

Joel

Cassie read the letter twice and when she had finished
the second time through there were tears in her eyes, not
because it was over but because she suddenly realized
how much she had loved Joel. He had given and helped
her so much. Until he had come so positively into her life
she had been hiding herself away in Tyrone's mighty
shadow. Joel had made her step out of that shadow and
his love and determination had given her the confidence to
live her life as a woman again, yet she knew just as well
as Joel that they could not live the rest of their lives together.
Just as she had always thought and just as Joel had himself
admitted, he wanted Cassie solely as his own, which by
force of circumstance she could never be.

Just as she could never give him the other thing he wanted
from life, fatherhood. She had watched him for so long now,
not just with Mattie and occasionally even with Josephine
but most particularly with Padraig, and while she knew
most men liked to indulge themselves by playing uncle with

other people's children, she had very soon realized this was not the case with Joel. There was a deep longing behind his love for Erin's tousle-haired little boy. Behind his bluster and mock gruffness, Cassie had watched him melt every time Padraig appeared, watched as he never let slip an opportunity to sit the boy on his knee or carry him round the gardens, or tuck him up in bed and read him a story. It was there plainly in his eyes for any woman to see, most of all any woman who loved him and Cassie had seen it all too clearly. Now that his own father lay dead, what Joel wanted more than anything was a child of his own.

Doubtless this was why Cassie had felt herself drawn more and more towards Theodore and perhaps for the very reason at which Joel had hinted in his letter, because like her Theodore had lost but not forgotten the great love of his life, his beloved Bree.

Putting aside Joel's letter, Cassie turned her attention to the second one, which was short and to the point. It was from the bank, pointing out that it was the opinion of the new manager, Mr Ignatius Pomeroy, who had been appointed the previous week, that in consideration of the situation regarding the insolvency of the insurance company which had held Claremore Racing's livestock insured and which was in default of a due payment of one million pounds sterling, the loan made by the bank to Claremore Racing must be called in within a notice period of three months from the given date above.

Cassie was interrogating Erin who was looking, for Erin, just a little embarrassed.

'Now there was never any deception intended in that, I promise you, not at all. Mr Benson was always saying how much he wanted to do young Pad's head, so here was the ideal opportunity I thought to meself. And since we'd had those lovely new pictures taken, what harm in sending him a few? Sure he adores the boy as if 'twas his own.'

'There's more to this, though, isn't there, Erin? I think you forgot to post that letter by mistake on purpose, because you've thought all along that Mr Benson and I – that we weren't right for each other.'

'Now how do yous knows what I'm thinking, Mrs Rosse?' Erin protested vigorously, sticking her hand deeply in the front pocket of her apron as she stood before the fireplace in Cassie's study. 'You couldn't possibly knows what I've been thinking.'

'I can *feel* what you're thinking, Erin Muldoon,' Cassie smiled. 'I always have done. I can pick up what's going through that head of yours as if you were a radio transmitter and I was a wireless. It's nothing to do with approval or disapproval—'

'I should hope not either,' Erin protested again. 'That isn't my proper place, to be approving or disapproving of you.'

'What I meant was I know how much you like Mr Benson, Erin, so that it wasn't a matter of you thinking that he wasn't the right sort of man, it was because you didn't think we were right for each other—'

'Will you listen now?' Erin sighed, sitting down on the edge of the large wing chair by the fire. 'There are some things that are easier for others to see rather than the people involved themselves. And while I saw the good Mr Benson was doing you, as well as the good you was doing him, I knew 'twould never be a match. I knew that when I was looking after him when he locked himself away, because of the way he talked and some of the things he said. I never asked him one single question about himself, but the more I listened the more he told me, and I saw that with his father lying dead, God rest his soul indeed, he'd a terrible longing to be a father himself. And it was 'ating at him, I can tell you.'

'What would you have done if I had decided to marry him, Erin?' Cassie wondered, knowing that if there had ever been any such possibility it was now long past.

'I'd have prayed for you, Mrs Rosse,' Erin replied gravely. 'I'd have prayed for you every day of my life. For when there are two people in a boat and they're both rowing in different directions, sure as I'm sitting here the boat's certain to end spinning round.'

# Thirty-Four

With less than a fortnight to go until the big race, Cassie had all but given up any hope of getting a substantial bet on her horse, certainly one anywhere near large enough to collect sufficient for her now vitally pressing needs. The largest single bet she managed to lay herself was ten thousand to win one hundred and eleven, and once the word was out on that single bet the odds were slashed across the board down to 4/1 at best and in most places (and absurdly so according to the racing scribes) threes, the lowest price being 5/2 on Mike Gold's books. Not that the newspaper experts denied The Nightingale's ability, far from it. To a man they were sure the great horse still had the potential to win a competitive race, but without a proper and competitive race over hurdles, in spite of all the rumours of sensational racecourse gallops, they all considered odds of less than 10/1 about the horse as daylight robbery for a race as keenly contested as the Champion Hurdle, most particularly this year's race which was considered to be one of the best for two decades. Even if The Nightingale was still as brilliant as his legion of admirers thought him to be, he was going to have his work cut out to win since the entries were headed by Glockamorra, last year's easy and fluent winner of hurdling's Blue Riband, Hello Absailor, the champion of the year before and runner up to Glockamorra twelve months later, Butler's Perk, winner of last year's Irish Champion hurdle, and the unbeaten Birdwatcher who had finished his preparations for Cheltenham by breaking the course record at Wincanton when winning the Kingwell Hurdle by a ridiculously easy fifteen lengths.

All four of these exciting horses had the credentials to

be ahead of The Nightingale on the books, yet only Glockamorra shaded him at 2/1, the others being available at up to 10/1 which was the current price of Hello Absailor, despite the fact that The Nightingale had yet to jump a hurdle in public.

And in spite of the fact he was to be ridden by a woman.

'It's perfectly ridiculous,' Cassie fumed one morning after Mattie had given the horse a good piece of work. 'Twelve to one about the horse would be the theoretically fair odds for him, not joint second favourite at threes and five to two.'

'The bookies aren't fools, Ma,' Mattie sighed over his cup of tea. 'You saw how the horse worked this morning, and so probably did they. If you were a bookmaker and I came back to you saying I'd seen a gallop as good as today's piece of work, you wouldn't be as keen as you are to lay the odds now, would you? I certainly wouldn't. In fact knowing what I do I'd say three to one or even five to two was asking for trouble. If he'd had a race in public he'd be evens now, maybe even a shade of odds on.'

'But he hasn't, Mattie, and if I was a punter I'd want to know why the cramped odds,' Cassie replied.

'Oh, come on, Ma!' Mattie threw his head back as he laughed. 'It's the punters' money that's bringing him down! I was talking to Con O'Neill in his betting shop only yesterday and he said he was looking to lay the horse off two weeks ago! There's been a flood of money for him.'

'Hmmmm,' Cassie said, pouring some more tea. 'Well, five to two isn't going to save Claremore, I can tell you. You'd have to lay three and half hundred grand to win what I need and who's going to take that bet?'

'Not a lot of people, I'll grant you that,' Mattie said, putting down his paper. 'But what do you mean about not going to save Claremore? This isn't what all this is about, surely? I thought this was about making up the shortfall in the insurance money.'

'Which is the amount of money I need to save Claremore,' Cassie said succinctly. 'Look, I wasn't going to tell you, but now there's no point not, because if we don't pull this off, that's it.' She looked Mattie right in his large grey eyes and shook her head once. 'The bank has called in their money.'

'They've *what*?' Mattie said.

'They've called in the money I still owe them.'

'They can't do.'

'They have.'

'Your man Dennis would never do that.'

'Dennis is gone. He had a stroke when I was over in England – I didn't know a thing about it, but although he's all right, or rather he's going to be all right, he's out of the bank and a new broom by the unlikely name of Ignatius Pomeroy has decided to call in the money.'

'But why? I mean – *why*? Even if we don't pull off the Champion Hurdle, surely once the Flat season gets going again—'

'No.' Cassie shook her head. 'Think of the interest on a million-pound loan, Mattie. If I can't get hold of the necessary capital now, that interest mounts, and I pay interest on the interest, et cetera et cetera, and at that level of finance that isn't funny. Let alone possible.'

'How long have you got?'

'Three months.'

'Then we had better get serious,' Mattie said, taking a pull on his spinhaler. 'Let's do a few sums, shall we? The race itself—' He grabbed his racing paper to check something. 'OK – if The Nightingale wins the Champion Hurdle for a start there's a decent bit of prize money goes with the race. Nearly two hundred thou.'

'Split three ways.'

'Oh no,' Mattie said. 'Jo's and my shares in the horse are nominal. Particularly if Claremore's under the axe. If he wins the pot goes to you. Jo'll agree, don't you worry. She won't want to lose our home either.'

'No,' Cassie protested.

'Yes,' Mattie replied. 'If the horse wins and your bet stands you'll be a third of the way there. That'll buy you some time, surely. Then there'd be the money from Joel's brother's bet and Theodore's – we're not going to lose

Claremore, Ma. I know it's only a house, and a house is only stone and cement and all that, none of which any of us really believe, particularly in the case of Claremore because of what's happened there. Because of – because of Dad. And you. Claremore isn't a place, it's your life, and if you lose it—'

'It's all right, Matt,' Cassie said. 'I won't go and jump off the cliffs of Moher, don't worry. If I lose this place, I'll survive. We all will.'

'You're not going to lose this place, Ma, I promise you,' Mattie said, getting up. 'I promise you that you won't.'

Grateful as she was for Mattie's resilience and determination, Cassie knew there was little to stop the inevitable from happening. Whether The Nightingale won or lost the Champion Hurdle was academic now she had failed to get her bet in place. That first letter from the bank had been followed up by a much longer one spelling out the cost and consequences of carrying on a prolonged extension of the credit at present carried by the business. Had she got the underwriters to court the bank would certainly not have had to threaten to take such draconian measures, but now they had no alternative, unless Claremore Racing could provide sufficient extra collateral to safeguard the continuance of the loan.

Nor, it appeared, was there any longer any hope that a way could be found to break the conspiracy of silence which surrounded those undoubtedly responsible for the actual act of kidnap and violation. In those seemingly endless small hours of the morning Cassie had sometimes been tempted to throw herself on Leonora's mercy, but by the time she had the whole possible scenario worked out in her head and dawn was peeping over her windowsill Leonora was laughing at and humiliating her, promising only to help bail Cassie out in return for the thing she wanted most now that Tyrone was dead, namely Claremore itself. Whenever the imagined proceedings reached this stage of particular absurdity Cassie either turned on her light and tried to read a book, or if it really was almost dawn got up and went out for one of her long and solitary walks in the hills before riding out.

And then one night, the night of the third of March with the race less than ten days away, Cassie dreamed.

*She dreamed there was a fire. The whole sky seemed to be on fire but when she looked up she saw it was just one tree that was burning, and then only its branches. Yet everything was lit up by it, the countryside, the sky and a building just beyond it, a large house which dominated the skyline. She knew what the building was, but she couldn't put a name to it, and when she looked for someone to ask a man came forward with a clapperboard and he clapped it in front of her face and said scene twenty-one, take one. Then Josephine who was beside her stepped forward and began playing the scene. She was dressed as a doctor in a white coat and Cassie was in the scene with her, but because Cassie had been called in at the last moment she didn't know her lines. She didn't know what she had to say yet everyone was relying on her and she felt a terrible panic overtaking her. The next thing she knew she was inside a hospital, except it was a private house peopled by doctors and nurses who were all speaking so quietly she couldn't make out what they were saying. Help me, she asked them. I don't know what I'm meant to say, but they all shook their heads and walked away from her leaving her in a bedroom and all at once she knew where she was. When she knew she was in the château she had been in once long ago she became suddenly paralysed with fear. She tried to run away but her feet wouldn't move. They felt as though they were glued to the floor. A man began to talk to her, telling her what to do. He was behind her so she couldn't see his face but as soon as Cassie heard his voice she felt utterly safe because her heart told her who it was. Then still standing behind her the man gently took her by the arm and led her to a closet which opened from the panelling of the wall and inside there was a leather-bound book on a shelf. Nothing else. Just a large leather-bound book. Cassie was right in the closet then, with the book in her*

556

*hand, and when she opened it she saw just as she knew she would that it was full of Tyrone's racing and betting entries, all written in gold. And when she saw the entries she started silently to cry but they were tears of happiness because she knew then everything was all right.*

The following evening when Cassie drove over to Mattie's for dinner with both of her children, Josephine opened the door to her in tears. When Cassie found out what had upset her daughter so deeply, she knew suddenly she still had one more life to live.

'You won't remember,' Josephine began as Cassie poured them both a drink since it was Mattie's turn to take watch outside The Nightingale's stable. 'Well, you might, actually. Do you remember a film I made in France about four years ago? An Anglo-French production called *One Twenty One*? It doesn't matter if you don't because—'

'No, I remember,' Cassie said, sitting down beside her daughter. 'You were rather good in it. You played the girlfriend of some ridiculously handsome French actor who you had a crush on, as I recall.' Cassie smiled but she noticed Josephine did not.

'Gérard Fournier,' Josephine said quietly. 'And it was more than a crush. We had an affair.'

'And he was married,' Cassie said carefully, remembering now the aftermath of Josephine's location in France.

'Yes,' Josephine replied. 'I know it's no excuse, but he wasn't happily married even though he returned to his wife. And there's this sort of unwritten law in show business as well. That being on location is like being away at war. It doesn't count.'

'This is a long time ago, Jo,' Cassie said after a moment. 'Why should you be bringing all this up now? He's not come back into your life, has he?'

'No.' Josephine shook her head miserably and then turned her brimful eyes on Cassie. 'He's dead.'

'Dead?' Cassie echoed. 'How can he be dead? He can't be that much older than you are, surely. Not that that makes any difference, of course—'

'He was killed in a car crash,' Josephine explained, leaning her head back on the sofa. 'He had just finished the shoot on his latest film and apparently they were on their way home from the wrap party late at night when the car left the road, hit a tree and burst into flames.'

'Where did you hear this? Was it on the news?'

'Someone rang me. A friend. But it will probably be on the news. Gérard was France's big new up and coming young star.'

'I'm so sorry, darling,' Cassie said, taking her daughter's hand. 'What a simply terrible thing to happen. I really am so sorry.'

'The driver – would you believe? The driver was flung clear. Sophie, this friend of mine, said he was as high as a kite because he'd been doing cocaine all evening, but he drove because everyone else was pretty drunk. This bastard wasn't, he was just out of his head on coke, and he killed them all. And he was the one who was thrown clear.'

'He's still alive, is he?' Cassie asked. 'Who was he? Another actor?'

'No.' This time Josephine shook her head as she wiped her tears away with the back of her hand. 'No, he was the producer. They were all going back to his château where they were staying. They'd been filming there as well. Somewhere down in the Loire valley near Amboise.'

For a moment Cassie felt as if her blood had changed, then she gave herself a mental scolding, telling herself not to be so absurd.

'It probably will be on the news,' Josephine said, looking at her watch and then flicking the television set on with a remote control. 'Not that I particularly want to see it. Except to make sure that it's true.'

'This friend of yours?' Cassie began.

'Sophie. She was in *One Twenty One* as well,' Josephine replied, tuning into the right channel. 'And she had quite a decent part apparently in this picture as well. Though she said it wasn't nearly as much fun. Mostly to do with this sod of a producer, so she said. He made everyone's life a misery, particularly the girls'. Sophie said he was a serious card-bearing sadist.'

Again Cassie's heart stopped and again she told herself to control her imagination. Even if by some outside chance the man in question was who she thought he might be, his involvement in a fatal car accident somewhere in France was hardly going to affect her.

For five minutes the two of them sat through the main part of the news before sure enough an item came up about the death of France's latest young screen idol, Gerard Fournier, killed instantly in a car crash exactly as described by Josephine. While the dead young man's image was on the screen Josephine sat staring at it as if unable to believe the news she was hearing yet again, while Cassie listened for any other details of the fatal accident.

Finally the newscaster arrived at the detail which she awaited. 'Three of the other four people in the car died in the ensuing fire,' he announced. 'Two were believed to be members of the production staff, while the third, a young woman whose identity has not so far been confirmed, is said to have been an actress working on the film. The driver, who was thrown clear before the car exploded into a fireball, has been identified as the producer of the film, Jean-Luc de Vendrer.' Cassie sat bolt upright as she heard his name, staring at the screen in disbelief. 'De Vendrer was taken to hospital and placed in intensive care where he remains in a critical condition.'

'Not for too long, I hope,' Josephine said with understandable bitterness.

'For just long enough,' Cassie muttered, getting to her feet and standing for a moment staring aimlessly around the room, before picking up the telephone.

'Who are you ringing now?' Josephine asked, killing the sound on the television. 'What's the matter?'

'I'm ringing Jack Madigan,' Cassie answered. 'And the matter is I want a lift to France.'

\* \* \*

'What can you hope to achieve?' Mattie asked when Cassie went outside to the yard to tell him of her plans. 'I just don't get it.'

'I'm not sure I do myself,' Cassie replied. 'I just know I have to go over and try to see him, that's all.'

'Along the lines of a death bed confession.'

'He's a Catholic, Mattie. If he's dying he won't want to die with an unclear conscience.'

'That's what priests are for, Ma. If he has anything to confess he's not going to confess it to you. Least of all to you.'

Cassie leaned over the stable door and offered The Nightingale another couple of Polo mints which he received gratefully and slowly crunched to bits. 'It's silly, I know,' she said. 'But it's a last ditch chance. And I feel – I feel as if I have to go. You see, last night . . .' Cassie hesitated, then stopped.

'Yes?' Mattie prompted. 'Last night what?'

'You'll only say what you always say,' Cassie sighed. 'That I'm losing it.'

'Try me,' Mattie suggested.

'Last night I had a dream, and while I know it was only a dream I haven't been able to shake it off. You know the way you normally lose dreams either when you wake up or during the day. I mean they just go, don't they? Back into the ether or whatever. But this one wouldn't go. It's stayed with me, just as if someone got into my head.'

'So what did you dream?'

Cassie told him, in detail, such was her recall of the dream. When she finished, Mattie nodded, chewing his lip thoughtfully.

'So what's the significance?' he said. 'To me that just sounds like a typical panic dream, except for the book at the end of it. Does it mean something special?'

'The house, the château, Mattie,' Cassie explained. 'It was de Vendrer's. The man who was driving the car Jo's friend was killed in. The producer of the film.'

Mattie's mouth fell open as he looked at Cassie. He

pushed himself away from the wall of the stable on which he'd been leaning as he'd listened, frowning deeply. 'You dreamed this last night?' he asked.

'Yes.'

'Jesus.' Mattie exhaled and shook his head. 'That is weird. I mean seriously weird. What do you think it means?'

'That's what I'm going to the Loire to find out,' Cassie said. 'You just take care of everything.'

'I will, don't worry,' Mattie replied, still frowning deeply. 'Don't worry about a thing.'

Cassie smiled and kissed him on the cheek. Then she leaned past him to stroke The Nightingale over the stable door and give a gentle pull on his big ears before going inside to say goodbye to her daughter.

What she had not told Mattie was the last part of the dream. *That the man who stood behind her guiding her everywhere was of course Tyrone.*

She didn't tell Jack Madigan anything of her dream, but none the less Jack thought if Cassie reckoned she had good reason to fly down to the Loire in the hope of learning something about the kidnapping of her beloved horse, that was good enough for him. He also insisted on going over with her.

'I have a friend just outside Tours with his own landing strip, just like mine,' he told Cassie through her headset after he had successfully lifted his twin engine Nightstar into the dark. 'I've already called him to tell him we're on our way and he's going to have a car waiting to take you straight to the hospital in Tours itself. He doesn't know de Vendrer personally, but he knows all about the man and tells me he's not France's best beloved. So how come you know him?'

Cassie told him of re-meeting de Vendrer on her fateful trip to Longchamps and how she had narrowly escaped what would more than likely have proved to be a very distasteful as well as painful experience.

'Well, there you go,' Jack replied. 'And you think that

was enough to get him involved in the hijacking of your horse.'

'Obviously you don't,' Cassie remarked as Jack levelled his plane out at cruising altitude.

'On the contrary, Cassie,' Jack replied, scanning the instrument panel in front of them. 'I've long thought that some men have a spite equal to women when it comes to being rejected. Anyway from what I hear of your man he sounds like the sort of fella who gets his kicks pulling the parachutes off free fallers. He might just have gone along with the whole thing for kicks.'

'Meaning if he couldn't hurt me then, why not a little later?'

'Why not indeed?' Jack agreed. 'Now we should be there in about an hour fifty, so to pass the time away let's have some fun discussing by how many lengths exactly this famous horse of yours is going to win at Cheltenham. Because, you know, that's something else we could have a little bet on.'

After he had switched the plane onto automatic pilot the two of them got to grips with trying to imagine exactly how the great race might be run.

The chauffered car that was waiting for them drove straight to the hospital in Tours. Jack dozed most of the way, tired after the night flight and anxious to build up his reserves for the return journey, leaving Cassie to her thoughts as the car sped through the darkened countryside. Quite what she was hoping to achieve she was not at all sure, but with all real hope apparently lost of finding the missing link she saw no reason not to put herself in the hands of the Fates, or as Mattie was forever saying, going with the flow. There was very little likelihood that her journey would result in her discovering the final truth, yet as long as there was some sort of chance she knew she must take it.

Particularly as long as the dream she had dreamed the night before stayed so vividly in her mind's eye.

There was even something vaguely familiar about the hospital. Not that the building was at all recognizable, because the hospital in her dream had been a huge old house which had become the château, while the one she was now entering was a modern, strictly functional edifice. Yet as Cassie made her way into the brightly lit reception area she felt as if she was retracing her steps, just as she felt that she already knew the woman on duty at the desk.

'Monsieur de Vendrer?' the nurse repeated in answer to her enquiry. 'Madame, I am so sorry, but I regret to inform you Monsieur de Vendrer died early this evening.'

'I don't understand,' Cassie replied hopelessly. 'When I telephoned earlier they said there had been no change in his condition.'

'I gather it was very sudden and somewhat unexpected,' the nurse replied. 'Monsieur de Vendrer seemed to be rallying, but then . . .' The nurse gave a small, sympathetic shrug. 'The doctors say his internal injuries were obviously worse than was first thought.'

'Thank you,' Cassie said, preparing to go and tell Jack their journey had all been in vain. Yet as she went to leave something stopped her, a voice which spoke to her somewhere deep in her head, a voice she knew, a voice she had loved and which now urged her to return to the desk and ask where she might find the person who would finally help her, who held the answer to the questions she so badly needed to ask.

'Madame de Vendrer,' she began, without knowing quite what she was asking for and why. 'I think I really should speak to her.'

'Madame de Vendrer is at the château,' the nurse replied. 'She was here earlier, but went home at midday.'

'I really should like to speak to her,' Cassie repeated. 'To convey my condolences. My problem is that I flew over from Ireland specially and I have to return again tonight.'

'Perhaps you might telephone her?' the nurse suggested. 'There is a pay telephone in the hall over there—'

'I don't think I have her number.' Cassie went through the motions of looking for the non-existent telephone number in her small pocketbook, watched by the nurse.

'It's all right, madame,' the nurse said finally. 'I can give you Madame de Vendrer's number from her husband's record card. It will save you having to look it up, perhaps.'

Armed with the number but with no idea what she was going to say, Cassie went and made the call from the nearby pay phone. When the phone was picked up at the other end it was by Madame de Vendrer herself.

'I am so sorry to hear about your husband, madame,' Cassie began.

'Thank you,' an impersonal voice said at the other end of the line, 'but you have not told me who you are. Are you – I mean were you a friend of my husband's?'

'Not really, no, madame—'

'Then please why do you telephone me now?'

'Your husband and I had a close mutual friend, madame. Leonora Lovett Andrew?'

There was a pause before Madame de Vendrer replied. 'I see,' she said. 'Then you were a friend of a friend, shall we say? Rather than a personal friend of my husband's.'

Thinking she could detect a note of relief in the woman's voice Cassie decided to try to press home her advantage. 'Madame, I wondered if I could come and talk to you?' she said. 'Only briefly. I have to return to Ireland tonight and while I know this is a very sad time for you—'

'*Puh*,' the woman said derisively, just as Cassie had thought perhaps she might. Remembering her brief but telling conversation with the garage proprietor from whom she had rented a car on the night of her flight from the de Vendrer château, Cassie had gambled on there being no love lost between Madame de Vendrer and her husband and the gamble seemed to be paying off. 'If you knew my husband even remotely, madame,' the voice continued, 'then you would know that this time is the very opposite of what you say. Even so, I do not understand why you should want to see me. After all, you and I do not know each other.'

'No madame, we do not,' Cassie agreed. 'But even so—'

'No, please wait a moment,' Madame de Vendrer interrupted. 'You said Ireland, did you not? That you had to return to Ireland?'

'That's what I said, yes. Why?'

'What is your name?'

'Rosse. Cassie Rosse.'

Again there was a silence the other end of the telephone.

'Who sent you?' Madame de Vendrer asked eventually.

'No-one sent me, madame. At least not in a way you would understand. Madame – I can't explain this on the telephone, believe me, but—'

'I know who you are now, Mrs Rosse. As I think I might know why perhaps you want to see me. Do you know where the château is?'

'No,' Cassie said. 'Only vaguely. But I'm sure if I ask here at the hospital—'

'Yes, yes,' Madame de Vendrer agreed, her tone completely changed. 'They will direct you. It will take you no more than twenty minutes by car.'

Exactly twenty-five minutes later Cassie found herself seated opposite Madame de Vendrer beside the remains of a large log fire in the drawing room of the château, while a manservant poured them both brandies before going out quietly and shutting the two women in the room behind the huge double doors.

Madame de Vendrer was much more beautiful than Cassie had expected, remembering only the *garagiste*'s dismissive summary of her when he had described her as a *go-go* girl. Consequently Cassie had imagined de Vendrer's wife to be less elegant and somewhat more *streety*, as her fellow countrymen were fond of describing women who had come from the sort of world from which Madame de Vendrer had been rumoured to have come. But there was nothing *streety* about the woman who was now sitting opposite Cassie. On the contrary, Madame de Vendrer was the epitome of French *chic*, from the top of her beautifully styled blond hair to the tip of her expensive red shoes. She had a perfect peach-like complexion, the figure of a young woman although she must have been well into her forties, and a pair of sensational legs clad in sheeny silk stockings. Only her eyes betrayed any lack of confidence, a pair of oval-shaped dark green eyes which viewed Cassie as Cassie was sure they viewed everything, with distrust and suspicion.

'It is really very good of you to see me,' Cassie said. 'Particularly seeing how late it is.' Madame de Vendrer raised her eyebrows very slightly. 'The time is really of no importance,' she said. 'And I must compliment you on your French. I have met very few Americans who speak French as well as you, madame.'

'I was very well taught at a convent,' Cassie said. 'And subsequently at my finishing school, which was where I met Leonora Lovett Andrew.'

'I am sorry to speak ill of a friend of yours, madame,' Madame de Vendrer returned. 'But I simply cannot abide Leonora Lovett Andrew.'

'No, neither can I,' Cassie smiled. 'Leonora is the very opposite of a friend of mine.'

'Good,' Madame de Vendrer said. 'Then we have common ground. She was a friend of my husband. The remarkable thing is that although my husband had many such friends, Leonora Lovett Andrew was the only one he really liked. Did you know my husband did not like women? In fact my husband hated women, beautiful women in particular. Yet he simply adored Leonora Lovett Andrew. Perhaps, would you say, it was because Madame Lovett Andrew was quite as bad as my husband was, yes?'

'I only knew your husband slightly, madame,' Cassie said. 'But from our brief acquaintance and knowing Leonora as well as I do, I would imagine they would get along all too well.'

Again Madame de Vendrer nodded and smiled at Cassie, although her dark green eyes still showed a degree of mistrust. 'Now,' she continued, 'we are agreed not to waste any time in false sympathy because I assure you, Madame Rosse, I disliked my husband as thoroughly as he disliked me – and if you wonder why I stayed with him, then please look around you. He was extremely wealthy and when I married him I was very poor. I was a ballet dancer, you understand, in the corps de ballet, and came from Paris where my father was a picture frame maker. Once I understood the sort of marriage I was expected to endure, I soon learned to bear it in return for a very good life style. Cynical I am sure you will say, but I would see it as practical.'

'I think you were right, Madame de Vendrer. If you were allowed to lead an independent life, then what harm?'

'Only the harm he inflicted on me, Madame Rosse, and even that you can learn to endure when you have been as poor as I was. Besides, finally he bored of beating me, and began to beat others. I could have divorced him, but I was afraid. He was not a good man, madame. He might well have done me worse harm.'

'All those sayings come to mind,' Cassie sighed. 'Better the devil you know, and so on.'

'Truisms only become so because they are true. At least according to my father. So. What was it you wished to talk to me about, Madame Rosse? Our mutual acquaintance Leonora Lovett Andrew? Or your horse perhaps?'

'Why do you say that?' Cassie asked in astonishment. 'What do you know about my horse?'

'Yes – well. I know about your famous horse from the newspapers, naturally. But I make mention of it because when he was stolen – and maimed, yes?'

'Castrated, yes.'

'Exactly. When all this was happening I remember my husband laughing, you see, and my husband rarely laughed at anything. He only laughed at things which hurt people, so when your horse was kidnapped, he laughed. As did Leonora, as did certain other friends of his.'

'Such as Herr Brandt?'

It was Madame de Vendrer's turn to be surprised. 'Yes, Herr Brandt precisely,' she agreed. 'He and my husband often did business. They also had money in a breeding farm. You know Herr Brandt?'

'I used to train some of his horses,' Cassie replied. 'A few years ago. Before he got caught.'

'I often wondered why my husband found the disappearance and the maiming of your horse so amusing,'

Madame de Vendrer continued. 'I never asked, of course. To ask my husband anything not one's business was generally rewarded with a slap on the face. But you were often mentioned, not directly to me, but when Madame Lovett Andrew visited, and Herr Brandt, the three of them would often talk about you and your horse and I would wonder why.'

'Do you know a man called Gold?' Cassie asked. 'Was he ever a visitor here? A small, heavily built Irishman, with a pair of the coldest eyes you would ever have seen.'

Madame de Vendrer shook her head. 'I do not think so. I never heard the name, and certainly a name like Gold I would remember.'

'When they talked about my horse, and about me,' Cassie wondered, 'did they ever say anything that might have implicated themselves in his kidnapping?'

'No. But why should they? Do you think they had some part in it?'

'Very possibly, madame, but I need proof. That's why I'm here, really, to see if there is anything I could use as evidence. There would seem to be a good case against this man Gold, your late husband, Brandt and perhaps even Leonora Lovett Andrew, but it's all hypothetical. We can't prove a thing.'

Madame de Vendrer drank some of her cognac, thought for a moment, then shook her head. 'I do not think I can help you, alas, except to say these people all knew each other, and that they talked about you. But then everyone who knows you must have talked about this case, yes?'

'I should imagine so,' Cassie agreed.

'Of course if I find anything which will help I will let you know,' Madame de Vendrer volunteered. 'Believe me, I should be only too happy to see my late husband implicated in something like this. So would most people I know.'

Again Cassie found herself in a cul de sac, facing a blank wall. Closing her eyes she racked her brain in the vain hope of coming up with something at the eleventh hour, of finding the one question which would prompt the discovery of the vital evidence she needed.

'Yes,' she heard Madame de Vendrer saying, 'yes, I believe he did. But why do you ask?'

'I'm sorry?' Cassie said. 'What do you mean – why do I ask?'

'You just asked me if my husband had a leather-bound journal,' Madame de Vendrer replied. 'Specifically a marbled leather book with a small gold lock which he kept locked away, and I said yes, yes he did. You don't remember asking me?'

'Yes, of course,' Cassie said hastily to avoid further embarrassment, since her mind was still a complete blank. She had no recollection of even opening her mouth to speak, let alone saying anything. 'I am so sorry,' she added. 'I misunderstood what you were saying. So your husband did keep some sort of journal?'

'I do not imagine it was a journal at all,' Madame de Vendrer replied, putting down her glass. 'He despised people who kept diaries and journals. No no, he had a book in which I occasionally saw him writing, usually at some length, too. I imagined it to be a record of his doings with women, even though he despised such records, but then such was my husband's conceit he possibly could not resist the temptation to write down exactly what he had done to the women who had fallen prey to him. I had very little interest in what he might be writing about and never asked him. All I know is he kept it locked away where he always locked his private papers, in the closet in his study. But please, how do you know about the existence of such a book?'

'I don't *know* about it, madame,' Cassie replied. 'This is going to sound absurd, but, you see, I dreamed about it.'

'You *dreamed* about it? You say you have never seen it, yet you describe it just how it was? Good God, Madame Rosse. You have made my hair stand on its end.'

Now her husband was dead Madame de Vendrer had all his keys, and it took her no more than half a dozen tries before she found the large old-fashioned key which opened the door cut flush in the panelling of de Vendrer's study. But far from being empty as it had been in her dream, Cassie found it was packed to the ceiling with files, papers, drawings, books, photographs and magazines, everything de Vendrer had apparently wanted to keep hidden and to himself.

The two women wasted no time in looking through the dead man's secret papers. What they were looking for they found easily enough on a small shelf along with other notebooks, although none of them were bound in marbled leather and none of them were secured with small gold padlocks. There was just one to fit that description and when they found it they took it back to the drawing room and sat together on the Louis XIV sofa with the smallest bunch of de Vendrer's keys until they had found the one that sprang the lock and opened the covers of the book, revealing the secrets Cassie had so desperately needed to uncover.

# *Thirty-Five*

'You're right, you got the pig!' Jack called to Cassie over her headset after she had finished a brief translation of the story de Vendrer had so painstakingly recorded in his marbled leather notebook. 'Seems you got everything you could have hoped for, chapter and verse!'

'Everything, Jack, down to the last detail,' Cassie answered into her mike.

'What is it with you, Cassie?' Jack wondered, as the plane cleared a bank of cloud and flew into some utterly clear sky. 'You got some sort of extra sense or something?'

'Now and then something speaks to me, Jack, that's all,' Cassie replied, looking out of her side window at the coastline of France disappearing thousands of feet below them. 'Or rather someone.'

'Don't tell too many people that, Cassie,' Jack said with a laugh. 'Remember what they did to Joan of Arc. Now if you'll excuse me for a moment, I have to take a new bearing and call in our flight path.'

While he was busy, Cassie stared out of the side window again and wondered at her luck, then wondered whether in fact this pilgrimage had been anything to do with luck at all. *When I'm gone, Cassie,* Tyrone had so often said to her while she lay in the protection of his arms in the still and dark of the night, *I shall never be far from you. When you need me I shall be there close at hand. If ever I see you troubled or in danger, I shall come to you and if I go before you, I shall always, always watch over you, for ever more.*

She smiled as she remembered how she used to demand to know how he could *possibly* dare to make such promises, promises which he couldn't possibly keep, and how Tyrone had teased her, laughing as he held her in his arms before telling her to wait and see. *I don't want to wait and see!* she had cried in return. *If you die first then I shan't live one moment longer! I shall die with you! I won't have to kill myself – because my heart will just break in two! So don't you dare ever say such things again!*

But he had. She had only been married a matter of months when he first had made her such promises, but then as they grew older and their love matured and deepened he would tell her again and she learned not to fear his Celtic preoccupation with death but rather to understand that what he was promising her was eternal love. She stopped taking him literally and instead took comfort from his words, knowing that since he was older than she was Tyrone might well die before her, but that after she had mourned him she would know that she would indeed always be watched over, never alone.

What then of her dream? And what then of the voice which had guided her? Cassie sighed to herself and stared again out into the night sky. That had to be a bonus, she thought, that was just typical Tyrone. St Peter would probably put him to stand outside the pearly gates for a day or two, but as sure as there was a God somewhere up above the dark blue yonder into which she was staring, He wouldn't be able to stay cross at Tyrone for long. No-one ever could.

Just as no-one but Tyrone could have got into her sleeping head and sent her flying across the Channel in search of something she had seen only in a dreamscape.

For Cassie now knew with certainty that because of the contents of the notebook Claremore could be saved. Not that she was altogether sure how she was going to play out the rest of the game once she got back to Ireland, although an idea was beginning to form. What she did know was she had to be careful not to make any rash, presumptive moves. De Vendrer had recorded every detail of the heist, right from his initial idle discussions with Leonora through to the private party he had thrown for the conspirators once the horse had been loosed in the lanes behind Claremore. Every conversation had been logged, every involvement specified and every meeting itemized and dated. There was not one detail omitted, not even the name of the suppliers in Wigmore Street from whom the conspirators had ordered the wheelchair to be delivered to her suite in the Dorchester.

'Fine,' Theodore said after she had filled him in on all the details over a late lunch the following midday. 'Now tell me, because obviously the thought must have occurred to you, why do you think de Vendrer recorded all his misdeeds so meticulously?'

'I suppose the clue to that lies in what he wrote inside the front cover, Theodore. *In the event of my untimely death.*'

'Ah,' Theodore nodded. 'Of course. He may have been wary of Mr Gold and his connections, yes, yes of course. He was obviously very well aware in what sort of league he was playing.'

'And he may have begun to keep the journal so that if anyone threatened him he'd have something up his sleeve,' Cassie continued. 'If they tried to lean on him, he'd have something which could hurt them in return. And if anything untoward—'

'Untoward,' Theodore mused. 'I've always loved that word when used like that. Anything *untoward.*'

'Seriously, Theodore, he must also have used this as a banker. I'll bet his lawyer knew of its existence—'

'So that if anything untoward happened to him,' Theodore agreed, widening his big blue eyes, '*that would blow the lid off.*'

'I don't think you're taking this as seriously as you should, Mr Pilkington,' Cassie scolded him.

'Oh, but of course I am,' Theodore reassured her in return. 'It's just that much as I may talk about it, I fancy myself really as no sort of detective *at all*. However, all things being considered, you really should hand this notebook over to the police.'

'I should.'

'But you ain't going to.'

'I was just wondering the best way to go about it. You see, with the notebook still in my possession, I reckon I could pressurize Gold into taking my bet and in return he gets the book.'

'Not the most moral of stands, Mrs Rosse,' Theodore sighed, taking off his spectacles and holding them up to the light.

'Of course it's not, Theodore!' Cassie retorted. 'But then we're not dealing with St Ignatius of Loyola here!'

'What on earth made you pick on that particular saint?'

'I don't know! He was the first one who came into my head, I suppose, that's why!'

'Fine, fine.' Theodore replaced his spectacles and smiled at her.

'Now you really think this horse of yours can't be beaten, don't you?'

'Any horse can get beaten, Theodore, one way or another,' Cassie replied. 'If this was a Flat race, sure – it'd be a ten to one on chance of him losing, but a Flat race this is not. This is a race over hurdles and over hurdles any horse can fall, however good a jumper he may be. He might stand off too far, hit the top and good night. He might slip on landing. Most likely of all, he might get brought down by another horse falling in front of him, and that sort of thing happens all the time, particularly in such fast run and highly competitive races as the Champion Hurdle. But if nothing *untoward* goes wrong, The Nightingale won't get beaten. The other horses, good as they are, aren't within two stone of him, not with the conditions of the race. Five-year-olds and upwards carry twelve stone, four-year-olds eleven stone six, and mares are allowed an extra five pounds off their backs, right? While if this was a handicap, The Nightingale would be giving them all two stone. So to answer your question, no, he can't get beaten except—'

'Except,' Theodore nodded, 'by the *untoward*. The next thing we should talk about is the bet.'

'It's taken care of,' Cassie said shortly. 'Jack's underwriting my stake.'

'To the tune of? I know it's not really any of my business, but you'll understand why I ask in a minute.'

'To the tune of two hundred and fifty thousand pounds. I've already used Claremore as collateral. In the event of the horse getting beat.'

'The unlikely event.'

'Precisely.'

'But this bet, Cassie. And I have to know this. This isn't about money, is it? This is about squaring the circle – and if that is the case then surely handing the notebook over to the police would do that nicely.'

'It's about more than that, Theodore,' Cassie replied carefully. 'People like Gold get away with murder the whole time. Who's to say the evidence in this book is watertight? It all has to be vouchsafed, doesn't it? It has to be proved genuine. Everything has to tally. And like an awful lot of other people nowadays I don't have a very high opinion either of the police or of the law.'

'You're still going to have to give the book up, Cassie. You know that. You're far too honest a woman to hold on to it.'

'Yes, Theodore,' Cassie sighed, 'I know, I know. I just wish there was another way.'

'There is another way, Cassie, as it happens,' Theodore replied. 'It involves bending the rules slightly, but it doesn't involve breaking the law. You see, I feel there's something else you should know about Mr Michael Gold.'

# Thirty-Six

No man's land was a private room in the Shelbourne hotel overlooking St Stephen's Green in Dublin, and the elected day was exactly five days before the due date of the Champion Hurdle at Cheltenham. Mike Gold arrived in a large black Mercedes S class, accompanied this time by not one but two minders, watched from the reception hall of the hotel by Cassie, Theodore and the back row of the Lansdowne rugby XV who were all good friends of Theodore's.

The five of them followed Gold and his muscle as they made their way across the hallway to the lifts, where the back row of the Lansdowne rugby XV put themselves between Gold and his two minders, separating the latter from their employer so that when the lift arrived Gold was obliged to take it in the company of Cassie alone.

'Explain, if you would,' Gold said to her hoarsely as the lift doors closed on the two of them.

'We don't need them while we do business, Mr Gold. We're old enough now to look after ourselves,' Cassie replied, and then watched Gold in silence while the lift sped up three floors. More than anything she was now intrigued to see that he walked with the aid of a stick, and that the *tic* he had previously had in only one cheek now seemed to be affecting the bottom half of his face.

The room designated for the meeting was furnished only with a large reproduction dining table, twelve chairs, and a sideboard. Cassie took one side of the table, indicating that Gold should sit opposite her. For one moment Gold refused her offer, standing behind his chair and watching Cassie while breathing in and out very slowly and heavily. During that moment Cassie was afraid he might turn on his heel and walk out, but rather than show any such reservation Cassie pretended to ignore Gold's display of truculence, proceeding instead to take a small package out of her shoulder bag and set it on the table in front of her.

As soon as he saw the package, even though he could not have known what it contained, Gold pulled the chair out and sat down.

'Can you speak or read French, Mr Gold?' Cassie enquired.

'Of course I can't,' Gold replied. 'Why?'

Cassie smiled and opened the cardboard box on the table in front of her, taking from it the marbled leather notebook. 'Because this is in French, Mr Gold,' she said. 'That's why.'

For the first time since his arrival a flicker of emotion showed in Gold's normally dead eyes. It was not a readily identifiable one, but when she saw it Cassie truly believed it was the nearest Gold could get to fear.

'You know about this book then, Mr Gold?' she wondered.

'How can I know about a book when I don't know what the book is, Mrs Rosse?' Gold replied, drumming the fingers of one hand on the polished table top.

'For a moment you looked rather anxious, Mr Gold. Very well, if you don't know what this book is, let me tell you. It belonged to the late Jean-Luc de Vendrer, with whom I understand you were acquainted.'

'I've never heard of him,' Gold replied.

'I think you have,' Cassie contradicted. 'As I was saying, this book belonged to Jean-Luc de Vendrer who is now dead, killed as the result of a car crash last week in France.'

'Tut-tut,' Gold growled, clearing his throat as soon as he had spoken. 'How very sad.'

'It would have been tragic had his widow not given me this, Mr Gold,' Cassie countered. 'Tragic because you might well have got clean away with it.'

'I have no idea what you're talking about, Mrs Rosse.'

Rather than reply directly Cassie chose instead to take a sheaf of typewritten pages from a folder in front of her and push them across the table to Gold.

'Guessing you didn't speak French, I translated the contents of the book into English,' Cassie said. 'It's a word for word translation, and if you read it you'll soon see what I'm talking about, Mr Gold.'

Gold shot her another look of undiluted hatred then fitting on a pair of Armani tortoiseshell glasses began to read the document in front of him. While he did so Cassie got up from the table, poured herself a glass of water from the carafe on the sideboard and went to stand at the window where she pretended to watch what was going on in the famous gardens which lay at the front of the hotel while in fact what she was looking at was the reflection of Gold reading the translation.

As he read it he neither moved nor changed expression. He simply read the pages through from first to last, paused as if fully to digest the contents, and then tapped them back into a tidy shape. Taking her cue from the noise of him tidying the manuscript Cassie returned to the table.

'So?' Gold wondered, drumming his fingers once again on the tabletop. 'Who's to say it's the truth?'

'There's enough that's verifiable in there,' Cassie replied. 'As you well know.'

Gold looked at her, the bottom half of his face suddenly convulsed by a violent muscular spasm. When it was over, Gold shook his head and once again cleared his throat.

'Show me the book,' he said. 'I can soon tell whether or not it's a fake.'

'If you didn't know about the book, Mr Gold,' Cassie wondered, letting him slide the book across the table, 'how can you tell whether it's genuine or not?'

Gold didn't reply. He just glanced at Cassie briefly, then, returning to the book, carefully counted to page thirteen, laying the book open and pointing to the corner of the page which was capped in gold.

'Of course I knew about the book,' he said quickly, his voice now positively larangytic. 'Why else would the stupid sod de Vendrer have written it?' Now he had the book he closed and upended it, holding it in both hands before him on the table. 'And who's going to stop me walking out with this?'

'The person on sentry duty outside the door?' Cassie replied. 'No, you're not going anywhere with anything until you hear what I have to say.' She took the book from him and returned it to safe keeping in her shoulder bag. 'You might remember last time we met, I tried to lay a bet with you and you refused. Now, Mr Gold, you're going to unrefuse.'

'Ah,' Gold said thoughtfully, taking a cigar in a tube from his inside pocket and undoing it. 'What a surprise.'

'It's a perfectly straightforward deal,' Cassie continued. 'You lay me the present odds on offer about my horse—'

'Three to one.'

'Four to one with everyone but you, Mr Gold, and those are the odds I want. I want two hundred and fifty thousand to win a thousand thousand.'

'In your dreams,' Gold said, rolling the cigar now out of its tube around in his fingers.

'I don't think so, Mr Gold, and neither do you,' Cassie said. 'You have no choice, and furthermore I want you to lay the bet personally. If the horse obliges I want the money to come from your wallet, not out of your firm.' She reached into her bag for another document. 'I have here my banker's draft for two hundred and seventy-five thousand pounds, which is my stake of two hundred and fifty thousand plus betting tax at ten per cent. It's made over to you and it's dated the day after the race. Should the horse lose, the stakeholder's instructions are for this to be paid into your private account of which you will give me details. In return you will now instruct your bankers and have them write a draft for one million pounds in my favour, to be held by the stakeholders and paid to me on the day following the race in the event of the horse winning. The stakeholders are to be the National Bank of Ireland on College Green, who have also agreed to hold this book in their vaults until the race is over. The book shall be handed over to you whatever the result of the race, but not until the race has been run and the money paid out one way or the other. Then it will be surrendered simultaneously with whichever is the losing draft. I'm not going to ask you for your agreement because this is not a proposition. It's a statement of fact. However, should you not accept the terms of this statement, this book will be handed straight over to the police.'

'Which it will not be if I accept what you are proposing,' Gold said, striking a match for his cigar.

'No,' Cassie said without hesitation.

'I see.' Gold lit his cigar and stared at her. 'This is in retribution. You're asking me to pay for my alleged crimes.'

'It's a whole lot better than you just sitting there in jail,' Cassie replied. 'That is if they ever get to put you in jail. They bang you up and what do I get? A sense of justice having been done. But I don't get the horse I had back. I don't get the future of my family back. I don't get the life I put in to get this far back. I don't get anything back. As you know from reading your newspapers, I don't even get the insurance money that I'm owed for what you did to my horse.'

'For what I allegedly did to your horse,' Gold replied. 'But no, I agree. Sending me to jail would be a short straw.'

'This way if the horse wins I do at least get compensated,' Cassie said. 'This way at least I get something due to me and you won't have succeeded in ruining me utterly. And as for you, you get the sporting chance you sure as hell don't deserve, not after what you've done—'

'What I have allegedly done, Mrs Rosse.'

'What you have undoubtedly done, Mr Gold. At least you get a sporting chance as far as your money goes, because once you strike the bet – in front of witnesses, of course – whatever happens you still get the book.'

'And get to walk away.'

'For a price, if the horse wins.'

'And if the horse doesn't win?'

'I lose,' Cassie told him. 'A lot more than you lose.'

'Of course.' Gold drew on his cigar, suffered another bad spasm to his face, closed his eyes until the spasm subsided, then opened them again to stare malevolently at Cassie. 'Your friend Leonora instigated all this, you know,' he said. 'Did you know that?'

'I suspected as much,' Cassie replied.

'I think it is important that you know the details, Mrs Rosse,' Gold continued, never taking his eyes from her. 'I think it is important you know how much certain people hate you. And how much certain other people hated your husband.'

'I'm ahead of you there, Mr Gold. We've already worked out the motivations, beginning with what happened to your father.'

'Even so, it's quite intriguing to learn exactly how the whole enterprise came into being and then took shape.' Gold tapped some cigar ash into the tray and smiled. 'I met Mrs Lovett Andrew and her feeble minded husband at the Guineas Meeting at the Curragh, in the spring after your horse had won the Arc and you had refused Mrs Lovett Andrew a share in any syndication as well as announcing your horse was to be kept on in training. We were at a party after the races at a mutual friend's house where your friend Mrs Lovett Andrew proceeded to get extremely drunk and indiscreet. Both de Vendrer and Brandt were at the meeting because one of their stud farm horses was running and fancied to go close. I'm surprised you didn't see either of them that day.'

'I go to the races to watch horses, Mr Gold, not people,' Cassie replied.

'Perhaps they kept out of your way,' Gold suggested. 'Anyway that was where it all began, that night after the Two Thousand Guineas.'

'I'd already had threats before that.'

'You were bound to, Mrs Rosse, when you think about it,' Gold replied enigmatically. 'This was one of the happy things about the ensuing business partnership. Certain of us had already been out gunning for you, but none of us had yet thought of a way to really put you down for the count. That particularly inspired idea came from Mrs Charles Lovett Andrew.'

Cassie matched Gold's stare but said nothing, resisting the temptation to react.

'Yes,' Gold continued, sounding slightly disappointed that he had failed to get a rise. 'The actual idea of taking your horse's balls off was all Leonora's own, but of course she couldn't do anything without the proper effort. She is bright, very bright, but no way could she pull something like that off without expert assistance.'

'Which was where you came in.'

'Which was where we all came in. This wasn't nicking a trolley from a supermarket, Mrs Rosse. This was stealing the best-known horse in the world from one of the most famous racetracks. This was keeping the horse hidden not from a handful of clodhopping coppers but from an entire animal-crazy nation. This was getting the animal properly castrated so that it'd be useless for ever more, and then dumping it back in the owner's back yard without one person seeing or suspecting anything. This was keeping up a campaign against you, your family and your stable without anyone ever being traced, and this was stopping the horse you had so miraculously restored to life from getting to Cheltenham.'

'But you haven't done that, Mr Gold,' Cassie said, managing somehow to keep her voice steady despite being shaken rigid by that final threat.

'Not yet, Mrs Rosse,' Gold agreed, 'but if I were you I wouldn't count my chickens just yet.'

'If anything happens to my horse,' Cassie began, only to be interrupted by the squat, sallow-faced man opposite her.

'The deal's off were you going to say?'

'My very words.'

'The deal's off and the book goes to the police.'

'You got it.'

'I think so.'

Gold got up with difficulty and with the aid of his walking stick made his way across to the window where he stood smoking his cigar in silence. If he pulled out of the deal because he was confident enough to believe this was going to be a hard case to prove in spite of the existence of de Vendrer's journal, Cassie was lost because in getting the bet laid was her last chance of salvation. Even if Gold was convicted and sentenced it would only be a Pyrrhic victory since by then the bank would have called in its money and her beloved Claremore would have had to be sold. What Cassie was banking on was that Gold's conceit would work against him, leading him to imagine that because he had won practically every game so far, the end game was also his for the taking. Besides, he was a bookmaker, a man who had laid odds all his working life, who had examined every eventuality to see how best to profit from it, so at this very moment what Cassie was herself gambling on was that Gold would not be able to resist laying this ultimate wager.

'Very well,' he announced finally, after Cassie seemed to have had the time to review her entire life not once but twice. 'You obviously have arranged for witnesses to the wager?'

'Yes,' Cassie replied as calmly as she could. 'They're waiting outside in the corridor.'

'So let's get it over with, then I'll go to my bank and have them prepare the necessary draft.'

'We'll both go, Mr Gold,' Cassie corrected him. 'Then after that we'll both go to the National Bank and have them hold the stakes.'

While Gold carefully tapped the half inch of ash off his cigar into a large glass ashtray, Cassie went to open the door and call in Theodore and one of his rugby playing acquaintances.

'The best I'll lay you is seven to two,' Gold said from behind her.

'The best you'll lay me is four to one,' Cassie corrected him, then threw open the door.


On the Saturday before the National Hunt Festival opened Niall Brogan announced the horse sound in wind, heart, and limb and ready to do battle with the best.

'I only wish I felt as good,' Mattie moaned after Niall had spelled out the results of all the tests he had run on the horse. 'This month has been a total nightmare. I can't remember the last time I slept right through the night in my own bed.'

'You've done a great job, Mattie,' Niall said, handing Cassie the sheet with The Nightingale's blood count on it. 'As long as no-one takes an eye off him between now and the big day, the horse goes to Cheltenham with the greatest chance possible.'

'Josephine says he's not put a foot wrong as far as his work's gone,' Cassie volunteered, scanning the papers in her hand. 'And as far as his last gallop went, she said she came back with her arms a good six inches longer. Now all that remains for us to do is to get him over there in one piece.'

The plan was to fly The Nightingale over on the Monday morning in one of Jack Madigan's custom built horse transporters to Gloucester and then box him to Cassie's old friends the Mandersons where she always stayed for Cheltenham so that he could sleep overnight in the security of their private stables. The horse would then be taken to the racecourse itself at first light on the morning of the race which was traditionally held on the opening day of the Festival meeting, allowed a good stretch and a brief photo call and press conference, then shut away under the ever-watchful eyes of Mattie and Bridie and young Phelim O'Connell whose services Cassie had loaned her son for the journey to Cheltenham and the meeting proper.

The only problem was that on the Sunday morning Phelim failed to show up for work.

'You've obviously tried his home,' Cassie said as soon as she had hurried down to the yard in response to Liam's call.

'I sent Tim post haste down to the village first thing, guv'nor,' Liam replied. 'He'd told his mother he was sleeping over at Mattie's yard Saturday and Sunday night in preparation for the Cheltenham trip so she didn't think a thing of it when young Phelim wasn't in for his tea or slept in his bed last night.'

'And obviously he's not at my son's.'

'No, guv'nor. But here's a thing now. I called Mattie of course, to find out whether or not Phelim was indeed there, and he said no, he wasn't actually due to arrive at his place until tonight. But then he said at about a quarter to three last night all hell broke loose at his yard, the security lights went on, the dogs all went spare, and the alarm he and Mick his head lad had rigged up on the fence round the top yard went off. Mattie left Mick and Josephine on guard outside Himself's box and went off hot foot in his old truck to see what he could see and sure enough didn't he see a car tear-arsing its way out of the drive? He went after it right enough, but whoever it was doused their lights and be the time Mattie got up to the crossroads he had it lost.'

'You think that might have been Phelim, do you?' Cassie asked carefully. 'I just can't accept that. Phelim's such a gentle lad. Phelim wouldn't let anyone touch a hair of Nightie. He's devoted to his horses. I mean, he seems the sort of lad who'd die rather than let any harm come to any of the animals.'

Liam shook his head and grunted. 'It's not him, boss,' he said, ''tis the company he's been keeping. He's a quiet lad and much as he loves his horses he's never really struck it up with any of the other lads. He's a funny sort of lad, and very conscious of his looks, you know, with them jug handle ears, poor lad, and that no chin of his. But then last spring in Liverpool at the Grand National meeting he got picked up be this lass who was working at the time for Mr Brownlow, you know, who I have to say made a dead set for young Phelim and of course completely turned his head, what with this lass being a bit of a looker all right and poor young Phelim not being so happily endowed. Well.' Liam shook his head again and ran his fingers back through his thatch of hair. 'The long and the short of it was we all thought it was a one meeting wonder, as it were, and that when young Phelim got back home here that'd be that and no real harm done, but not one bit of it. Doesn't the lass show up on his doorstep during the summer—'

'When?' Cassie asked. 'Do you remember exactly when during the summer?'

'I do as a matter of fact,' Liam replied. 'It was June, the morning of our Derby, and I remember because for the first time since he joined us that young Phelim was late to work. I gave him a right earful because we had a full hand of runners, if you remember, guv'nor, and it certainly wasn't the morning to be late to work. And then it all came out, how this lass had turned up early in the evening at his house, how there'd been an unholy row with his father when he announced he was going into Dublin because I don't know if you know but poor young Phelim has the mother and father of all mothers and fathers, believe me. He couldn't breathe without getting their permission and – well. To cut a long story short, Phelim disobeyed them, stayed out the night, and of course cut it far too fine getting back out here first thing in the day.'

'What makes you think this girl is bad company, Liam?'

'Ach you can tell, boss. You could tell Sally was a number the moment you saw her. She's a right floosy, and come on, we all asked ourselves. What's a floosy like that doing with poor young Phelim? She's a real eyeful, if you like that kind of thing, guv'nor. Blond hair, big blue eyes, and a figure like an egg timer. Now what's she doing with the likes of our Phelim? And what's she doing working over here when she had a perfectly good job in a perfectly good yard in England? She was the assistant travelling head lad with her last outfit, yet she's working over here as a plain unvarnished groom for Mick Heaslip, and sure that's not exactly the most creditable place to be.'

'You're thinking what I'm thinking, aren't you, Liam?' Cassie wondered. 'If she was around before Wally's Ascot run—'

'And didn't Heaslip send over some horses to Ascot? And didn't Miss Sally Eastman travel over with them?'

'I still find it hard to believe Phelim would have anything to do with that sort of dirty work, Liam,' Cassie said. 'Don't you?'

'I'm not saying he did, boss,' Liam replied. 'All I'm remembering is what the guv'nor used to say. Your late husband that is that was, God rest his soul. Follow the man home, he'd say, boss, follow the man home.'

'I know what my husband used to say, Liam. In fact I was quoting it to Mattie only the other day. But besides a couple of typically domineering Irish parents, what else would you find if you followed young Phelim home?'

'You'd find that his youngest sister Philomena is spastic, boss,' Liam said sadly. 'She was born with cerebral palsy for which as you know there isn't any known cure.'

'I didn't know that, Liam,' Cassie said. 'All I knew was he came from a large family.'

'And little Phil has always been his extra special favourite, boss. Ah sure they took the poor lass to Lourdes twice, much good did it do her, for over these last couple of years hasn't her condition got a lot worse.'

'I never knew,' Cassie said with a frown. 'If only I'd known—'

'There wasn't a thing you could do, boss, not a thing. Until very recently, that is. Phelim told Bridie – whom incidentally he adores – only a few months back that someone had told him of a place in California where they'd found a treatment for certain types of the palsy but of course it was far too expensive and way out of his family's reach. So he started putting all his money to it, every spare penny, and he began buying Sweepstake tickets and even doing the football pools God help him, anything in the hope that somehow and with some sort of luck he might come be enough money to send little Phil over to America.'

'Dear God,' Cassie said quietly. 'If he'd only come to me directly, Liam—'

'Sure he knew you had troubles of your own, guv'nor.'

'But what sort of trouble is *he* in now?' Cassie wondered. 'If this girl's working him, Liam, he could be in serious trouble.'

'And so could we, guv'nor,' Liam replied. 'Dear heavens, I feel a right ejeet meself now, so I do. Here have I been remarking on young Phelim the whole time, but the thought never crossed my mind that Phelim himself could have been

587

got at. So perhaps it's just as well he hasn't showed up this morning.'

'Yes, but why hasn't he shown up this morning, Liam?' Cassie persisted. 'Don't you somehow have the feeling it might have been better if he had?'

Once she had rung Mattie to make absolutely sure that nothing untoward had happened in his yard other than the alarm of the night before and that The Nightingale had remained under Mattie and Josephine's personal supervision, Cassie set about trying to find out where Phelim might have gone, but without luck. Not only that, but Phelim was not the only person gone missing. When she telephoned Mick Heaslip's yard she discovered Sally Eastman had also failed to turn up for work.

Worse was to follow, as if any further setbacks were needed. Bridie, who it emerged had not been feeling one hundred per cent for the last couple of days, woke up on the morning the Claremore party was due to fly to England with a roaring temperature, a bright red rash on her face and throat and all her lymph glands swollen. Despite her remonstration that it was only a bad cold Dr Gilbert diagnosed measles and forbade her to travel, a decision reluctantly endorsed by Cassie who now faced a real dilemma. She had no other experienced girls working in her top yard, but The Nightingale would only let women near him, and in the *mêlée* that was Cheltenham he was going to need all the steadying influences he could get. Mattie had a young woman working in his own yard who had been given The Nightingale to do as one of her three, but she had only just begun working for him and her racecourse experience was non-existent so Mattie ruled her out as a Bridie substitute.

'We can't leave one thing to chance,' he told Cassie when they were discussing the matter that morning. 'We can't entrust the horse to a complete novice and imagine if the girl was nervous and made a mistake which she'd be highly likely to do and say the horse got loose. God he'd panic in that scrum, particularly if it's a lad who tries to catch him because they're not to know Nightie hates all members of the male sex. So there's only one thing we can do, and that's leave the horse to you and Jo. You're going to have to saddle him up while Jo holds him, and then you're going to have to lead him up.'

'Fine,' Cassie said grimly. 'Except you're forgetting one thing. I can't saddle him up single-handed. It always takes two to saddle a horse as you well know, Mattie, and a third person at the horse's head, so we're not going to make a proper job out of it if it's just Jo and me. Since Nightie won't let you anywhere near him let alone hold his head, that means we're still one woman short.

'OK, so we'll take the girl, we'll take my Deirdre,' Mattie decided, 'but she's not to lead him up. She can hold his head while you and Jo saddle up—'

'That's going to look good at the home of National Hunt racing, right?' Cassie said with a grin. 'Co-owners and jockey saddling up one of the favourites. Just like at an Irish point to point.'

'To hell with conventions, Ma,' Mattie said. 'I'm just trying to cover every eventuality. You'll have to lead him because we can't risk anyone else at his head, and if you have to leave your lucky hat at home, that's tough.'

'What haven't we covered?' Cassie asked, running her finger down the check list yet again. '*Of course*. Down at the start. The starter's assistant who checks the horses' girths—'

'Is a woman.' Mattie smiled. 'I rang David Armstrong, the clerk of the course, because I suddenly remembered that last night – and I also remembered they have a woman assistant starter over there now – and as luck would have it, she's on duty for the whole meeting.'

'So at no point will there be a man anywhere near Nightie.'

'Not unless he gets loose, and since the last thing he'd do would be to dump Jo on the way to the start, with you at his head and Jo on his back, the only way he's going to get loose is during the race if God forbid he gets brought down – and if he does, it's not going to matter then because it will be all over.'

'He won't be brought down, Mattie,' Cassie said. 'That's a fact.'

'How come, guv'nor? There's a big field this year, fourteen runners all told and at least four of those shouldn't be running. There are bound to be fallers, particularly at the pace the race is generally run, so I'd like to know what makes you so utterly sure we won't be brought down.'

'Then if you listen I'll tell you,' Cassie said.

Which she did. In fact for the next three hours Mattie, Josephine and Cassie planned the race in detail, expanding Cassie's plan of action, looking once again at the videos of all their most serious rivals, studying and cross referring the form of every single horse running and finally feeding into Mattie's computer the timings of all the races the entered horses had ever run in over the same distance, making allowances for the weights they had carried and the conditions of the ground.

Whatever permutations they made the result always came up the same.

# Interim

'The last time we talked on camera, Cassie,' the television commentator said, '*was after your horse's famous victory in the Eclipse. Then, like so many millions of racing fans, I was devastated when he was kidnapped and though mighty relieved when he was returned to you simply appalled by what the blackguards had done. Surely on that dreadful, fateful day you could never have imagined you would be walking the course here at Cheltenham on Champion Hurdle Day with The Nightingale not only starting in the race but looking as though he might well start favourite, such is the ton of money the punters have poured on him ante post and today ever since the offices opened?*'

'No, John,' Cassie replied as followed by a camera car on the inside of the track they made their way towards the second last hurdle from home. '*Not for one moment during those very dark days did I think the horse would ever race again. For a time we didn't even think he'd live, first when we found him out the back of Claremore tied to a tree and looking for all the world like something out of the horse hospital in Cairo, and then not so long after that when he went down with a badly twisted gut. I thought if the horse pulled through his operation then the most we could hope for was to get him on his feet, fatten him up and turn him away in a quiet paddock somewhere.*'

'Instead of which,' the commentator said, '*you have a horse which many of us believe will be the first horse ever to win both a Derby and a Champion Hurdle. As well as practically every other Group One race in the book.*'

'There's many a slip, John, as you well know. This is the most competitive hurdle race in the world, they go a heck of a lick, there are eight flights of hurdles to be jumped, and The Nightingale is taking on top class horses who have mostly all well and truly proved their true worth over the timber.'

'But you wouldn't be bringing the horse here just for sentiment, Cassie. And even though he hasn't had a race in public, we've all heard the rumours of some pretty remarkable performances back home in private schooling sessions, and you yourself have as always kept the public fully informed as to the horse's well-being.'

'Yes, and I'm glad to report that the horse travelled well and seems to be very well in himself. I just think the odds aren't very realistic, that's all. If he starts as favourite—'

'Which it looks as though he will, Cassie.'

'OK, so if he does start as favourite, John, they shouldn't have him at anything less than two to one. Anything shorter than that you would have to say was not only unrealistic but unfair on the punters. The Tote still have him at five to two, I understand, and if that's so and I was a betting person—'

'Which you're not.'

'I have to admit to having a small investment on this race.' Cassie smiled at her interviewer and then stopped to look up the long uphill climb towards the finishing post. 'Having got this far, all of us took a little of what was on offer ante post. Even so, as I was saying, anyone who wants a bet today should see if those odds are still available on the Tote.'

'And you can guarantee the punters a run for their money.'

'There aren't any guarantees in this game. A horse can get loose, it can spread a plate during the race, it can be brought down, run out, or just refuse to race. What I can say is that my son Mattie, who now of course is training the horse, has done a wonderful job with him and provided the horse gets to the start and jumps off, he'll give the usual good account of himself.'

'What about his jockey?' the interviewer asked, saving the best till last. 'The one weakness according to the commentators and probably a lot of the punters is that The Nightingale is being ridden by a woman, by Josephine your daughter in fact. Who I'm sure is an excellent pilot – in fact I know full well she is because I saw her win the Diamond Stakes at Ascot last year. But riding a big strapping horse like The Nightingale in a race like the Champion Hurdle . . . If the horse has an Achilles tendon, could this be it, Cassie?'

'No,' Cassie was quite adamant. 'Josephine has ridden the horse in every bit of his serious work and whereas I know many people are worried she won't be able to hold a big horse like Nightie together in the heat of a fast-run race over hurdles, I say they can put those worries to bed. If the horse hadn't shown his disdain for your sex, John, and I could have the choice of anyone to ride the horse, I'd still have put up Josephine.'

'You think a woman really is strong enough for the game then? That what all the male jocks believe isn't so? That a woman isn't made to race ride, et cetera?'

'Tell that to my fellow countrywoman Julie Krone. You've seen her ride. She can hold her own with any male jockey and she does.'

'And you think your daughter's in that league, Cassie?'

'Wait until after the race. Who knows? Without tempting Providence maybe the lady in question just might make a few of the questioning gentlemen in the weighing room eat their safety helmets.'

# Thirty-Seven

The heavens had opened by the time Cassie got to where Mattie was waiting for her back at the bottom of the track down which in six hours' time the horses would be led out to do battle for the first race on the card.

'I don't know whether this is significant,' he said, sheltering under Cassie's large golfing umbrella and showing her the day's edition of the *Sporting Life*. 'Jump For Fun's got a new owner.'

Cassie took the paper and looked at the story tucked down at the bottom right hand corner of the front page and then at the photograph of the apparent new owner.

'Miss Diane Danielle,' she said, with a shake of her head. 'Good luck to her. She'll need it, if you remember. Jump For Fun's that lunatic High Line chestnut who nearly knocked Glockamorra over at the second flight last year. We also watched a tape of his last run at Sandown in the Rendelsham, remember? Where his spectacular fall at the third practically decimated the field.'

'She paid £45,000 for him,' Mattie said.

'Then they saw her coming. That's one of the horses that really shouldn't be running. Who did she buy it from?'

'Some farmer in the West Country,' Mattie said. 'Must have thought it was Christmas.'

'Just remind me to remind Josephine yet again to keep well away from it anyway,' Cassie said. 'If anything's going to take us out, it'll be that horse.'

It was still pouring with rain when The Nightingale had his early morning stretch in front of possibly even more cameras than he'd ever faced before. But as always all the fuss failed to bother him. As Josephine in her wet weather riding out gear sat on him, pulling his ears and stroking his neck, he stood and posed as he always had posed, calmly and patiently as if he earned his oats as an equine model rather than as a racehorse. All the while he was having his pictures taken, however, Mattie and Deirdre were always close at hand to make sure no-one got any nearer than the stipulated fifteen yards' distance, a measure marked by a length of white string Mattie had pegged to the ground. Then as soon as he thought the *paparazzi* had taken enough footage Mattie stood in front of his horse, thanked the press for their help and allowed Josephine to wheel the horse round and away up the track for his last spin before the race itself. As always the track had been perfectly prepared with a good cover of grass and in spite of the heavy rain the going was still perfect racing ground, off which The Nightingale flew as Josephine allowed him just enough rein to stride out comfortably without wasting any valuable energy. Then once she felt he had eased himself out of any early morning stiffness and warmed any aches he might have contracted on his travels out of his muscles Josephine slowed him up and walked him off the course to be met at the designated exit by Cassie, Deirdre and Mattie.

'The others might as well stay in their boxes,' Josephine said with a grin.

'I don't know,' Mattie said as Deirdre threw a sheet over the horse's quarters. 'There's a useful bit of place money to be won.'

'And there's a two mile hurdle race to be run before you two go counting your chickens,' Cassie reminded them.

'What about this rain?' Deirdre enquired. 'I can't remember – does he go in the soft?'

'He goes in anything,' Mattie replied. 'But all the same we wouldn't want too much of this. No one wants to race in a bog.'

'First things first,' Cassie said. 'When we've got him in his stable, I'll take the first watch with Deirdre, because I have to go and meet somebody at eleven.'

* * *

595

He was late but Cassie imagined it to be through no fault of his own. According to those to whom she had spoken while she was waiting the race traffic was already blocking the roads into the town, and taxis from the station were at a premium. As arranged Cassie had positioned herself to meet him at the easiest place on the course, just inside the main entrance from where early arrivals with their reserved entry shields swinging from their lapels and race glasses were already making their way into the grandstand and the members' enclosures, while groups of journalists and photographers having picked up their passes stood around in groups waiting to spot any well-known names and faces getting out of the expensive machinery arriving in the car parks.

The machinery in which Joel arrived was certainly not very expensive. It was a green and cream Citroën 2CV. Cassie saw the car from a distance, as soon as it left the main road and bumped its way up towards one of the unreserved car parks in which there was still plenty of room. Putting up her lightweight race glasses to have a better look, Cassie watched as Joel unwound himself out of the passenger seat, stretched, and then bent back down to say something to the driver who emerged from the other side a minute later.

Before she took refuge under the umbrella Joel was holding for her, Cassie saw she was wearing a variation of the sort of clothes she had worn when Cassie and she had met by chance in Radford prison car park, a long black linen skirt and a baggy red jacket over a blue jumper and white undershirt, with another pair of clumpy black ankle boots and a large black floppy-brimmed hat trimmed with an oversize red paper rose pulled down over her mass of dark tangled hair. Perhaps not only because it was Cheltenham but also since it was his first full day as a free man Joel had chosen to wear a suit, a suit Cassie had never seen him in before, dark green and baggy with a dark blue shirt and yellow tie. He had of course no hat. Cassie doubted if he had ever had a hat other than his old but undoubtedly genuine Dodgers baseball cap, nor could she even begin to imagine him in one, whereupon from the back of the Citroën he produced a large black fedora which he pulled on over his shock of long hair. Cassie found herself smiling at the sight of the two of them, both very tall, long-haired and dressed in odd and colourful baggy clothes. Surrounded by all the incoming racegoers, most of them in variations of the traditional British racing colours of brown and green, they stood out as two apparently carefree individuals, happy with both how and who they were. Then as if to unite their individuality, they leaned towards each other under the umbrella as one and exchanged a kiss, a kiss brief enough not to embarrass any passer-by but long enough to indicate passion withheld.

Seeing their embrace, Cassie instinctively stepped back as if she might be seen by them, which in fact was not possible since it was still pouring with rain, she was well hidden from their view by the fact that she was inside the entrance building and far enough away from them that she had to observe their actions through her race glasses. None the less such was the effect of witnessing this moment of endearment that Cassie found herself looking away as well as lightly colouring, even though she had made sure to invite Joel's new friend to the races when she had written back in reply to his letter. *Dearest Joel*, Cassie remembered writing as she folded her race glasses up and replaced them in her bag,

*Thank you for your honest and touching letter and yes – of course you are right. You have said what we both have been thinking, which I am sure we are both right in our different ways to think. We've always known what we had wasn't really for keeps, however much for our very different reasons we might have wanted it to be. And what you have said so well was always there waiting to be said, but it was never said I suppose because really and in truth there seemed no real need to say it. It was there every time the two of us kissed, every time we made love. Each time we did, there was always goodbye somewhere there waiting to be said, if not this time then sometime soon, just as there was always that feeling that this might be the last time. I hope you find what you want with Polly – I'm sure you will. Now we've both got this far with each other's help, you're ready for what you want. Maybe you weren't before, when you and I were together and maybe that was what was at the back of it. But now after everything that has happened to you, after all you have been through, I think you'll find the love you want, need and deserve so very much. I shall certainly pray that you do, and I shall always think the same of you – that you are a wonderful, vibrant, original and highly determined person, and just as you say you won't stop loving me nor will I ever stop loving you. Please God may we always still love each other as friends. I'm sure we will. That's one of the good things about getting older. Everything doesn't have to be so definitive. You can let the edges blur a little, leave a few emotional ends well and truly loose. What's important now is that we both do the best for ourselves and for those we love, and that includes letting each other be when and where we want to be.*

'Mrs Rosse,' a familiar voice said behind her. 'Look, I must have kept you waiting, but the traffic is a nightmare.'

'Joel,' Cassie said, turning to him and smiling. 'You haven't kept me waiting one bit.' She stood on tiptoes and kissed him gently on the cheek. 'Not one bit,' she repeated and then carefully wiped the lipstick mark off his cheek with her handkerchief.

'Thank you for your letter,' Joel began, taking one of her hands. 'I meant to write back but then as I knew I'd be seeing you again so soon—'

'It's OK,' Cassie said, stopping him by squeezing his hand. 'You know the old motto, never complain, never explain. Your enemies won't believe you and your friends already know. So where's Polly?'

'Just behind. I said I wanted to go on ahead just so that

I could say hello, and well—' Joel shrugged, for once giving a boyish grin instead of a puzzled frown. 'You know.'

'I know,' Cassie said. 'As a matter of fact I knew when I saw the head. The bust you were working on in Radford.'

'I didn't,' Joel said, frowning now.

'You're not a woman,' Cassie replied.

'She's doing a book on euthanasia,' he said, by way of explanation. 'I don't think I told you that, did I?'

'Yes, you did.'

'Oh. Anyway. She wrote and asked me if she could come and see me, and that's how we became friends.'

'She's very beautiful.'

'I don't normally go for tall women.'

'Don't worry about it. She suits you.'

Joel looked at Cassie and shook his head. 'At the risk of being corny, Mrs Rosse,' he said, 'you're something other.'

'Go and get Polly,' Cassie said. 'I like the name Polly. Although I suppose you'd rather she was called something like Brubeck or Ellington.'

'Ellington would be a very nice girl's name,' Joel agreed. 'Maybe if we have a daughter that's what we'll call her.'

'Good,' Cassie said crisply. 'So now go and get Polly and while you're at it, leave that frightful thing you've got on your head in the car.'

# The Race

It was the worst race of Cassie's entire career.

'I have never been so nervous,' she confessed to Theodore who had now arrived to join the party and was accompanying Cassie across the crowded thoroughfares towards the racecourse stables. 'In all the races I've run the horse in, even in the English Derby, I've never been so utterly terrified.'

'Yes, well, you had nothing to lose really, Cassie, when you ran in the Derby, now did you?' Theodore asked her. 'If you'd come second or third, he'd have been a good horse but not the great one he became. But the moment he won that race, then *suddenly* – all at once you were in charge of a *super*horse.'

'I know, Theodore, I know you're absolutely right,' Cassie agreed. 'But that doesn't make it any better. And as for poor Josephine. She was quite literally sick with nerves all night.'

'So it would appear,' Theodore replied, spotting the ashen-faced Josephine waiting for her mother by the security gate to the stables. 'Mind you, I was always the same before a big match.'

'I thought you were going to say before a big operation.'

'No no,' Theodore threw back his head and laughed with delight. 'No, rugby matches were infinitely worse. When I won my first cap for Ireland I neither slept properly nor ate decently for a week. But as soon as I ran out onto the pitch, Dr Sport soon cured my ills. Let's hope it will be the same for dear Josephine.'

He stopped by the gate, knowing that he was unable to escort Cassie any further. Cassie showed the security guard her pass and then turned to Theodore to tell him where she would meet him. Instead she found herself briefly in his arms and almost off her feet as he kissed her good luck. 'Now is the time to be Buddhist, Cassie dearest,' he said to her, putting her back down on her feet. 'From now on think of nothing else but the horse. I am the arrow. I fly to my target. Be your horse, and win the greatest race of your life.' He smiled, raised his hand and was gone into the throng of racegoers queuing up in the still pouring rain outside the racecourse stables gate waiting to catch first sight of the horse which had become their totem.

Liam was poised ready with Deirdre outside The Nightingale's stable, Deirdre with a fresh bucket of water and sponge and Liam with Josephine's saddle, number sheet, surcingle and girth which he handed to Cassie. As was often the case when The Nightingale ran, both Liam and Fred had travelled over with the horse as an extra precaution and as always Cassie was glad of his presence. Liam could sometimes be doleful and often downright lugubrious, but his greatest asset was his quiet strength and his inability ever to panic, qualities which Cassie needed more than ever in those around her that day. He was also good for Josephine, keeping her mind easy with his constant teasing, his observations and his banter, so much so that although he had to stand outside The Nightingale's box as they got the horse ready, Cassie could see that his non-stop patter was finally relaxing Josephine.

As for the horse himself, as always The Nightingale knew he was at the races, pushing both Cassie and Josephine aside with one nudge of his muzzle as soon as they came into his box so that he could stick his head back over the door and survey the opposition. At times like this he always reminded Cassie of a prize fighter before a big fight in the way he seemed to eye up every horse he got in his sight, staring at them fixedly and often pawing the ground with a forefoot at the same time. As Cassie pulled his stable sheet off his back the horse suddenly threw his head back, snorting contemptuously.

'That was Butler's Perk walking by,' Liam called. 'He obviously doesn't give him much of a chance.'

'He's right,' Cassie agreed. 'Glockamorra's the horse he has to beat. I saw him being unboxed and I have to tell you he looks awful well.'

'So does Nightie,' Josephine said, doing up the horse's racing bridle. 'In fact I think he looks about as good as he did when he won his first King George, and that was the best I've ever seen him look.'

'And I'd say he's a little fat,' Cassie said. 'Let's face it, in an ideal world he could have done with a proper race. But then I'd far rather see him carrying a little bit of condition than looking like a toast rack.'

'We're seven to four clear favourite,' Mattie announced, arriving in front of the box, his appearance being greeted by The Nightingale's laying his ears flat and pulling the worst face Cassie had ever seen him pull. Mattie, well used to the horse's tricks, pulled an equally hideous face back which seemed to surprise The Nightingale who immediately repricked his ears and whinnied softly at his trainer.

'Well, well,' said Josephine, stroking the horse's neck. 'Don't tell me we're losing our inhibitions?'

'That's what I thought the other night when he'd got half his rug off,' Mattie replied. 'Fat chance. He wouldn't even let me unbolt the door.'

'Good,' Josephine said. 'We want him still to be angry. As long as he's angry he'll want to make mincemeat of the others, particularly since they're all going to be ridden by men.'

'Now that is something I hadn't thought of,' Cassie said, straightening up from doing up the horse's monogrammed paddock sheet. 'The nearer the other jockeys get to him, the more he'll want to get away.'

'Hopefully,' Josephine said. 'As long as he doesn't try to get away sideways. What about the ground, Mattie?'

'I have to say the way it's rained it'll be more like heavy than soft by the time they're off,' Mattie said. 'But then it won't bother Nightie half as much as it'll bother some of the others. Remember how Dex said he went through it the last time he raced at Ascot? He said he just sluiced through the mud, so in a way, as long as it keeps raining and the sun doesn't come out and start to make it sticky, I'm not that worried.'

'Right,' Cassie said, picking up Josephine's rolled up saddle and girths. 'Time for you to go and put on your party clothes, Jo, and Mattie – you'd better tell Security we're ready to roll.'

One of the main areas of worry had been the distance The Nightingale would have to walk from the racecourse boxes to the pre-parade ring. Without a sufficient escort the team considered that this journey was when their charge might well be at greatest risk on the course proper, particularly since they had guessed – perfectly correctly as it happened – that crowds of his fans would collect around the exit of the stable yard in order to get as close a sight of their equine hero as possible. With that in mind Mattie had asked David Armstrong, the clerk of the course, if he could lay on extra security to act as an escort for the horse, a request which was readily granted in consideration of what had happened to the horse on his fateful appearance at Ascot.

Even so the phalanx of security guards had their work cut out to stop people from pushing through the cordon in order to try to touch the horse. Just as they had so often done before, people had brought their sick and their lame in the hope that one touch of the skin or one hair from the tail of a horse they believed imbued with magical powers would cure their loved one's ills. *Please please, Mrs Rosse!* an Irish voice beseeched her, and then another. *Please God may my child just touch your horse just the once*! But Cassie could not and did not dare relent because she dared not run the risk. Knowing the sort of people she was up against she believed them capable of anything, even of using an apparently innocent child as a shield to get near the horse. Having seen what had happened to Big Wallow at Ascot the last thing Cassie and her team wanted was for The Nightingale to be stopped in similar fashion, particularly when they had all come this far.

Neither was the horse safe when he reached the pre-parade ring, even though security guards positioned themselves at both the entrance and the exit to the ring. Protected as it was like any parade ring by a set of simple rails to keep the horses and spectators at a safe distance, such was the construction of the rails that there was nothing to stop anyone determined enough from ducking underneath them and doing harm to the horse before they were caught. When she saw how many of the horse's camp followers were positioning themselves up against the rails, Cassie knew she dare not risk leading the horse up within an arm's length of them, so instead she walked the horse round on the grass lawn in the middle of the ring, with Deirdre on the other side of the horse to protect his blind side, then the moment Mattie reported the main paddock empty of horses when the eight runners for the Arkle Challenge trophy had been called to post, the team escorted The Nightingale into the comparative safety of the huge enclosure which lay in front of the weighing room and behind the members' grandstand.

The other runners for the Champion Hurdle soon followed, and by the time the field had been sent on their way for the Arkle the paddock had a complement of ten horses. Even so, the Claremore team was leaving nothing to chance, with Cassie leading the horse up and Deirdre still on the blind side with both Liam and Fred following on at a safe distance behind the horse's flanks and Mattie watching from the middle of the grass for anything even remotely unusual. Happily The Nightingale was taking it all in his stride, walking out freely and easily and taking in his surroundings with his old genuine interest, watched by a far bigger crowd than would be usual at this time, since literally hundreds of people had forgone the thrill of watching eight of the best young steeplechasers in the country doing battle for the crown of the year's best novice for the privilege of seeing The Nightingale walk round the parade ring.

'Must be a close thing,' Cassie called to Mattie as the roars from the grandstand reached fever pitch. 'Listen to the crowd.'

'Photograph!' a voice announced over the public address.

'Photograph between horses numbers one, six and seven!'

'Number seven's Dubedat, the FitzPaine horse!' Mattie called back. 'Could be first blood for Ireland!'

While the stands around the paddock began to fill to brimming with returning racegoers anxious now to secure a place to see both the returning horses and the contenders for the Champion Hurdle, Mattie called for his horse to be taken over to the saddling boxes so that they would not be caught in the ensuing *mêlée*, particularly since an Irish horse was involved in the photofinish and as always at Cheltenham there was bound to be pandemonium if it was called the winner. So while the judge called for a second print of the photograph, so close apparently was the finish, Cassie and Josephine, who had now emerged from the weighing room wearing a Barbour over her race clothes and with a face even greyer than before, began the careful ritual of saddling the horse up.

'Two more your side,' Cassie said quietly as they began to fix the girths. 'But first just ease the saddle back half an inch. It's sitting just a little too high on his withers.'

'How are you your side?' Josephine asked. 'I think I could still come up one my side.'

'We'll both go up one,' Cassie said, notching the girths up one more hole. 'Then that should do it.'

She took a step back to judge the all important position of the race saddle with an experienced eye. 'These aren't new leathers, are they Jo?' she suddenly asked.

'Yes. Why?'

'You know what bad luck it is to ride with or in anything new. What were you thinking of?'

'It's OK, Mums,' Josephine replied. 'I rode them in this morning when I gave him a stretch. I know better than to ride in anything new.'

'Sorry,' Cassie said, giving the girth one last check. 'I just want to make sure everything's covered. Right – paddock sheet, please, Deirdre, then do me a sponge.'

After they had rearranged the horse's smart paddock sheet and fastened it with its matching roller, Cassie took the sopping wet sponge and opening The Nightingale's

605

mouth pushed the sponge into it and squeezed it out into his mouth. 'I can never do this without getting it up my sleeve,' she complained. 'Just as well I didn't wear my suede coat.'

Now the horse was ready to do battle. In fact so keen was he to go that he almost pulled himself free of Cassie as for a moment she dropped her guard to turn and drop the sponge back in the bucket. Luckily as instructed Deirdre had a good hold of the paddock strap as well as the side of the big horse's bridle otherwise he might well have got loose and charged into the parade ring unaccompanied.

With the horse firmly back under her control Cassie led him back into the paddock where the victor of the Arkle, the Nicholson horse Fine Man who had just beaten Dubedat by the shortest of short heads into second place, was finally being led away. As she entered the ring she saw Mattie and Liam in the middle of the lawn talking earnestly. While Liam talked Mattie cast a look in his mother's direction, smiled briefly, then turned back to finish listening to what Liam had to say.

Meantime Cassie and Deirdre walked the horse round the parade ring.

Someone they passed began to clap when The Nightingale passed in front of him, and within seconds his personal tribute was picked up by everyone around him and finally by the entire paddock side crowd who it seemed were simply applauding the courage of a horse determined enough to make a comeback after the terrible events which had befallen him, in spite of the fact that he had as yet to set foot on a public racecourse. So moved was she by the tribute that Cassie hardly dared look into the crowd, but when she did she saw many women with tears in their eyes and a whole host of gentlemen raising their hats to her horse. In return The Nightingale swung himself half round to look back at them eagle-eyed, beginning to dance and prance on the spot with excitement. The more he did so the more the crowd applauded until even some of the owners of his rivals who were all now gathered on the oval lawn in the paddock joined in the homage.

Then it was time for the jockeys to get mounted. They had already streamed out in a line from the weighing room, led by Robert McDonagh, last year's champion, who as always made his entrance into the paddock alone, deep in thoughts as to how to ride his race. He was on the second favourite Glockamorra, with his greatest friend and rival Andrew Squire riding the other solidly fancied horse, Hello Absailor. All the jockeys had tipped their hats with their whips to their horses' owners and trainers as they joined their respective groups on the lawn for their final instructions and now that the rain had finally stopped they stood around in groups discussing how the change in the going might affect their tactics. Finally as the bell sounded for them to mount up it seemed the last thing they did before being legged up was all turn to take a good look as the rugs came off the horse they all most feared.

'We're now clear favourite at six to four in most places, except guess-who who has us at five to four,' Mattie said as Cassie brought the horse onto the grass and over to where he, Liam and a now green-looking Josephine waited. 'Glockamorra's taking a walk in the market and you can have him at an easy three to one and probably seven to two by the off. The thinking is we may well start at evens.'

'Ridiculous,' Cassie said, knowing that the very opposite was true. Given an untroubled run, there wasn't a horse in the field who could beat The Nightingale, not even if he gave them a dozen lengths at the start. 'Is that what you and Liam were talking about?'

'Liam didn't think I should tell you, but I disagree,' Mattie said, glancing at Liam. 'They found young Phelim. He's all right—' Mattie added quickly, seeing the anxious look on his mother's face. 'Someone gave him a real going over and left him half dead up on the Military Road but he's going to be OK. He's not in danger apparently. And the reason I'm telling you is because whoever did it to him I'd say did it because Phelim maybe didn't do as he was told. So you can take that worried look off your face, guv'nor, because I don't think we've anything to worry about – other than making sure Jose here brings Nightie home first.'

'I'm to jump off first and if no-one wants to make it, I'm to make it all,' Josephine intoned, trying to control the shakes which were affecting her entire body. 'If anyone does go on and try to scorch the pace then I'm to lie handy, second but no worse than third, not on the inside but on the outside of the bunch, and even if I'm in the lead I'm to lie two or three horses' widths off the rails. I'm to take the hurdles bang in the middle, and if there's no real pace and I'm leading then I'm to have them stretched a good five or six lengths or more by the fourth obstacle, give him a blow after the sixth but not to worry if they start to come at me down the hill, kick him on into the seventh then press the go button on the run to the last. And come home clear.'

'Six clear,' Cassie teased. 'Jack Madigan's got a hundred to win a grand on the winning distance.'

Cassie kept hold of the horse's head while Deirdre legged Josephine up into the saddle. While she slipped her feet into her irons, The Nightingale turned a half circle and began to bounce on the spot.

'Jeez, he knows what he's here for,' Josephine said as she gathered her reins. 'He feels as if he's ready to run for his life.'

'When you think about it,' Cassie said, 'in a way he is.'

'Now remember to let him find his own way into the hurdles,' Mattie said, coming as close as he dared. 'Don't try to show him a stride—'

'I know, I know,' Josephine cut in impatiently.

'Don't try to show him a stride,' Mattie repeated, deliberately slowly. 'Even if he gets one wrong he's so smart he'll fiddle it. Just don't whatever you do ride the rail.'

'No,' Cassie agreed, indicating to Deirdre to pull the horse's number cloth straight. 'Remember not to ride the rail and particularly on the home turn. Time after time the Champion's been won by horses coming up the middle of the track, having jumped the last flight smack in the centre. You come up on the left and the chances are you could get pushed into the wings. So don't come up the inner, don't get squeezed and ideally try to be two or three widths off the rail on the final turn. Jump the last in the centre and if anything try to make your run up the right hand side of the track where the going's better.'

'Good luck, sis,' Mattie said, seeing the other horses beginning to make their way out. 'See you in the winner's enclosure.'

'You bet,' Josephine said, the colour beginning to return to her cheeks now she was up on the great horse. 'I can't tell you the feel he's giving me. Even just at the walk. He feels as if he's going to explode.'

'Don't let him,' Cassie said, following on behind Glockamorra and in front of Butler's Perk. 'We don't want any explosion to happen until after the second last. We know he can still quicken like nobody else, so save it, even in this mud. You'll have plenty of horse under you all the way round.'

In those few final moments as they walked round the paddock before going out onto the course to parade, Cassie noticed little else except how her horse was walking and whether Josephine was relaxing. She knew if the jockey was tense, the horse always felt the tension through the reins, so although she could not order her daughter to loosen up, she kept talking to her about all the other horses and their riders, commenting on their general condition and turn-out, keeping the chat going so that Josephine would not have any time left to brood about the ordeal facing her. As soon as the horse was cantering to the start Cassie knew the worst would be almost over, and that once the race actually started fear would be gone altogether because once the tapes had flicked open there'd be no more time for nerves, only for raw courage and the utmost skill.

So although Cassie was taking in the other horses as they walked in a circle round the paddock, she took no notice whatsoever of their owners, which was why it was not until she was just about to turn away to lead The Nightingale out and onto the long track which wound its way down from the parade ring through the tented village and past a long double-sided line of spectators that she saw him, and then, at first, only out of the corner of her eye.

He was standing with a small party of half a dozen people, by the side of a tall woman in a scarlet coat and hat, and once Cassie had caught sight of him she turned to make sure that it was in fact who she thought it was, only to see that it was. It was Gold's subordinate, the ferret-faced man who had been standing in the corner of the book-maker's private box at Ascot.

*What's he doing in the paddock?* Cassie wondered to herself, her blood running cold from the look he had given her. *What's his connection? Surely to God he doesn't own one of these horses?*

As she walked down the track and on towards the racecourse to the sound of further cheering and applause, followed closely by Deirdre and Mattie, Cassie racked her brains as to who owned which of the horses. Most of the owners she knew well, either by reputation or in some cases personally, and all of them as far as she knew were above suspicion. *He must be just hanging on,* Cassie assured herself. *He's probably with the big party that was going on around Katwandra who's owned by that couple of cheery so-called scrap merchants from somewhere in Essex. Whatever he's doing here, he never got near the horse, so put it out of your mind, Cassie Rosse, in case anything transmits itself to your daughter.*

'OK, sweetheart?' Cassie said as they took their place in the parade which was to lead past the stands. 'So far the old boy's behaving himself. There's not a bead of sweat on him anywhere.'

'He's always loved parades,' Josephine said. 'You know what a show-off he is.'

Once more spontaneous applause greeted their horse as he paraded himself in front of the jampacked stands. In the public enclosure in the middle of the course a party unfurled a huge banner which read: FLY HOME THE NIGHTINGALE in front of another whose slogan proclaimed: MAKE THE OTHERS SING FOR THEIR SUPPER, while a party of Irish all with shamrock pinned to their lapels, it being St Patrick's

Day, began to sing 'A Nightingale Sang in Cheltenham' as Cassie led the horse by them.

'Good luck, Cassie Rosse!' one of them cried. 'God bless your endeavours! And may your horse come home safe!'

Now she let the horse go, with one last call of luck to Josephine who had already set her face to the starting line. The big horse kicked away from her at once, tucking his head down into his chest and cantering his way down the chute which led to the start of the two mile hurdle course set down at the bottom left hand corner of the course but still well in sight of the stands. Cassie stood and watched him go, and failing to move out of the way of the horses behind her might well have got herself knocked for six had not Mattie pulled her out of the way of Demerara who was plunging and bucking his way to the start, trying his poor jockey's skills to their limit.

None of them said anything as they made their way back to the stands to join the Claremore party in their private box. Not until Cassie suddenly stopped dead in her tracks to say out loud: '*Of course.*'

'What now?' Mattie said, taking his mother's arm and steering a way through the crowds. 'Not that it matters because whatever it is you forgot to tell Jo it's too late now.'

'That woman, Mattie,' Cassie said urgently. 'The woman in the bright red coat and hat. She's Jump For Fun's new owner.'

'So what?' Mattie said, still hurrying her along.

'So what?' Cassie echoed. 'She only had Gold's creepy little sidekick on the other end of one of her arms!'

'Are you sure?'

'I'm sure, Mattie. Once seen *never* forgotten.'

As soon as they made it into their private box both Mattie and Cassie pointlessly examined their racecards as if the information contained would offer up a clue, which of course it did not. All they gathered was as indeed the sporting papers had already stated that Jump For Fun now ran in the name of Ms Diane Danielle.

'We told Jose to stay out of Jump For Fun's way,' Mattie said. 'So as long as she remembers that—'

'But suppose Jump For Fun doesn't stay out of Nightie's way,' Cassie came in.

'No way. The horse won't have the legs to lie up with Nightie.'

'He might not need the legs,' Cassie said. 'Remember the way a certain trainer ran a horse in a recent Gold Cup? Deliberately to spoil the favourite's chance? No, I'm serious,' Cassie continued, stopping Mattie's interruption. 'Something's up. You should have seen the look in that man's eyes.'

'Jeez,' Mattie hissed. 'It had bloody well better not be.'

'It is,' Cassie said. 'Look—' She pointed down to where the horses were already being called into line. 'Jump For Fun's been pulled right over beside Nightie.'

'Who's riding it?' Mattie looked at his racecard. 'Goddam. It's that bastard Brian Baker. No trainer in his right mind would put him up on a decent horse in a race like this.'

'Right,' Cassie said, putting up her race glasses. 'So why have they?'

'This could be the Epsom Derby all over again,' Mattie said, following suit with his own binoculars.

'Or that infamous Gold Cup. Just pray that Josephine gets away fast,' Cassie said. 'If she gets a decent break she should be able to leave him cold.'

'The horses are being called into line,' the course commentator announced. 'And they're off!'

Josephine was in a perfect position as the tape flew clear but the man on Jump For Fun had anticipated her, almost causing a false start so quickly did he jump off. He got half a length up on The Nightingale before Josephine could get racing, then as soon as he had the advantage he drove Jump For Fun right across The Nightingale's racing line, hooking his own horse up at the same time so that The Nightingale's head came up and almost hit Josephine in the face, a move which all but stopped the favourite in his tracks.

'Shit—' Mattie swore. 'You're right, dammit. He's in there to stop us.'

'He's done so,' Cassie said, moving closer to the window.

'It's Brown's Gazette all over again. We've lost a good six or eight lengths.'

'Brown's Gazette lost twenty lengths, Ma,' Mattie reminded her. 'We're not cooked yet.'

'We're not,' Theodore agreed from his position beside Cassie. 'He's off and running now, Cassie, and making up ground like the proverbial hot cakes.'

'So's Jump For Fun,' Cassie said. 'For God's sake will you look at that! He's leaning on Nightie all the way! He's trying to run him out!'

The field was already about to meet the first hurdle, packed in a bunch with Demerara leading by three-quarters of a length and pulling hard for his head, the others all tightly packed behind him, all except Jump For Fun who having crossed The Nightingale had now been straightened up by Baker and set to race along the favourite's nearside with the very obvious intention of putting the horse off his stride at every conceivable opportunity. The result was that as the leaders all flipped over the first, Josephine who had been trying to run up to the hurdle on the left found herself being forced with every stride right across the face of the obstacle by the big chestnut who was being driven deliberately into her horse.

'Switch him, Jose!' Mattie cried helplessly. 'Take a tug and pull Nightie in behind!'

The gods must have been listening because at once Josephine sat back to take a good tug at her horse, bringing him back almost to a park canter leaving Jump For Fun to plunge across him and take the first hurdle practically by the wing. But because of this last minute manoeuvre The Nightingale had hardly any room to put down before the jump and had practically to cat leap it from the walk, yet jump it he did, Josephine kicking away from the hurdle as soon as she had landed to try to escape her pursuer as well as catch up the field which had now pulled a good half dozen lengths clear of her. The moment she did Baker gave Jump For Fun a violent crack with his whip, causing his horse to bolt forward, this time charging up on the inside of The Nightingale.

'This is perfectly deliberate!' Cassie announced as she realized what was happening. 'He's been put in to mark Nightie! To take him on at every hurdle to try to either run him out or force him into a mistake!'

'They should call them back and stop the race!' Fiona announced. 'This is an absolute disgrace!'

Without putting his glasses down Jack Madigan called to Cassie. 'He's cooked, Cass!' he said. 'If your daughter doesn't get right away from him, he's going to be run out of the bloody race altogether!'

'She's got either to drop him right out!' Cassie called back, 'or go for broke now! But if she does that there's a chance she'll use up all Nightie's speed and he'll have nothing left at the business end!'

'He's going to have his work cut out as it is!' Mattie yelled. 'That son-of-a-bitch Baker's slowing his horse right up into the second – look! And he's pulling across Nightie again!'

In the race itself as the field swept past the packed to bursting stands Hello Absailor had pulled his way to the front, relegating Demerara to second with Pleaseturnover third on his outside and Vote for Nigel and Katwandra bringing up the rear of the leading group ahead of Glockamorra who was towing along the second group of horses about a length and a half adrift, but it seemed that everyone on the course was more interested in the battle that was going on at the rear of the field where The Nightingale and Jump For Fun looked more like horses engaged in a match on the polo field than racing in a Champion Hurdle. Ahead of them the twelve other contenders all flew the second flight of hurdles, Flaky Pastry making the only mistake and losing half a dozen lengths to drop back only a couple of lengths up on Jump For Fun who was still just shading The Nightingale as they now approached the second obstacle.

Josephine pushed The Nightingale on, anxious to get away from her murderous rival, managing to get half a length up on him as she saw a stride in to the jump, but as The Nightingale took off ahead of his market, when Jump For Fun left the ground Baker quite cynically pulled his horse's head to the right, forcing his horse into The Nightingale's flanks so that the favourite landed crooked with his rival all but on top of him. It was only Josephine's courage and The Nightingale's nimblefootedness which stopped them both from falling in the mud, Josephine giving the horse more rein instead of snatching him up in panic and The Nightingale responding by tucking his powerful quarters right under him so that even though his nose touched the turf he was somehow able practically to catapult himself up off the ground. As soon as she felt him come up Josephine sat to him, gathered her reins and urged him away from the jump as quickly as her horse could gallop, yet Baker who had somehow managed both to stay on his horse and collect it from out of the splits it had performed on landing was still galloping after her, still with the advantage of the inside berth.

Despite Baker's efforts, Jump For Fun could not quite get to The Nightingale, managing instead only to race up as far as his girths. Even so, it was near enough for Baker to begin once again to make his horse lean on his rival and force The Nightingale to run wide, so wide in fact that as they swung towards the third hurdle the racing line of the two horses was set a good half a dozen widths too wide of the fast approaching obstacle.

'If he holds that line he'll run Nightie out!' Mattie called, his glasses fixed firmly on the grim battle that was being fought out at the back of the field. 'Jose'll never get him back from there! Christ in heaven – this is worse than bloody Ben Hur!'

It might have seemed bad enough from the grandstand but it was even worse out in the country where Josephine now was, unable at any point so far to get her horse fully into his stride and away from her marker so that she was indeed facing a very real chance of being run out at the next flight.

And if that happened, The Nightingale's race would be run.

Baker had no doubts that was where she was going. 'Go on, you stupid, silly little bitch!' he yelled at her as again he laid his horse hard into hers. 'Go and see your old granny over in Bourton for tea!'

If Baker had only been content with following his strictly delivered orders, namely to force the favourite to run out, there was no doubt he would have been completely successful for with only about ten strides to go to the third hurdle there seemed to be absolutely no way that Josephine could avoid the disaster short of trying to pull The Nightingale up altogether. But she knew that if she did that, if she managed to slow her now galloping horse to even a canter let alone a trot, regardless of his undoubted courage and his blistering turn of foot they were so far behind the horses in front of them that it would be a physical impossibility to get the horse back in the race proper.

But Baker was not only a conceited and ignorant little man, he was a vicious cruel one too, so instead of being content with forcing the greatest horse ever to have taken part in one of National Hunt's premier races to run out, he had to add a *coup de grâce*, which he did by raising his whip up to his shoulder and then savagely belting The Nightingale as hard as he could across the area just behind the animal's saddle, in the hope of sending him well and truly on his way past the hurdle.

His action had the opposite effect entirely.

Baker couldn't even have seen The Nightingale's head come round, so fast did the big horse pay back this act of barbarous folly. All the jockey knew was first the horse's mouth had him by the leg, with teeth sunk so far into his flesh they cut him to the very bone, and then the next moment he was out of his saddle and crashing to the ground where he received a thorough trampling from Jump For Fun's own hind legs before the horse swerved right away from The Nightingale across the face of the jump. Even though in the *mêlée* the reins had slipped right through her fingers, in that split second of time Josephine saw her redemption, kicking her horse on in the direction in which he had turned himself, back towards the third flight of hurdles which now was only three strides away. Without even looking directly at the hurdle since his head was still half turned towards the direction his adversaries had come at him, somehow The Nightingale saw a stride and cleared the obstacle, landing well clear the other side of it and picking up speed the moment his feet touched the turf as Josephine gathered up her reins.

'Go on, Nightie!' Josephine urged him, now her path was clear. 'Fly, Nightie – you have now got to *fly*!'

All who saw the race said that it had to rank as the greatest display of hurdling of all time, such was the courage and brilliance of the horse. When Josephine and The Nightingale finally shook off the attentions of Jump For Fun and his jockey, they had already jumped three of the nominated eight flights and since by then they were lying at least six lengths behind the next horse, and a full ten lengths behind the leader, even to his most ardent and diehard supporters the day would seem to be well and truly lost.

Yet from the moment the horse touched down on the landing side of the third hurdle that seemingly unbreachable gap began to shorten with every stride The Nightingale took, so that by the time the leaders had jumped the fourth the favourite had already caught and passed Flaky Pastry, relegating him to last place, and unbelievably was actually back on the bridle. Not that his opponents knew that. A look over their shoulders had told the jockeys that the favourite might be back in the race, but such was still the distance the horse had to make up on them, to a man they would all have thought that even should The Nightingale finally get to them, in going as heavy as it now was the effort would surely have totally exhausted him.

Any normal horse would be exhausted by the effort of galloping flat out to catch a field which had slipped him by such a distance, particularly in a race of this merit and with a field of this calibre. For this was no handicap hurdle run on some small country track where more often than not some outsider poaches a thirty length lead while the other jocks sit comfortably behind on the fancied horses knowing full well the leader will tire and come back to them. This was the premier hurdle race in the world, a race which was always run at a full racing gallop, a pace which removes the likelihood of any tailender being able to cruise up on the tiring horses up front and pick them off at random. At Cheltenham, the pretenders for the crown of Champion race at full tilt and the race is invariably won by the horse with sufficient stamina to stay with the pace and enough acceleration to produce a turn of speed to beat off his rivals in that grim uphill struggle to the line.

It is not won by a horse coming from some sixteen lengths off the pace, particularly one which has suffered interference in one of the most crucial moments of the race, namely the start, particularly in heavy going and most certainly of all not when ridden by a rookie woman jockey.

Yet as the field raced along the back straight towards the fifth hurdle, with Hello Absailor still towing them along ahead of Demerara, Pleaseturnover, Vote for Nigel and Katwandra who were all bunched up within two lengths of him and the second favourite Glockamorra still swinging along easily and looking full of running on the rail another length away in sixth, The Nightingale was still closing, fast enough to pick off the back markers which included Hotel Paradiso who had been running in snatches and was about to be pulled up by his jockey.

That left eleven horses to jump the fifth hurdle in front of The Nightingale, the field coming away from the obstacle in the same order as they ran into it with the exception of High Compression who suffered a crashing fall, turning turtle and finally bringing down the already exhausted and out of touch Flaky Pastry. Luckily Josephine, seeing the field bunching up as they went into the flight, had taken a line well to the outside and avoided all the grief which took place on her inside to the left of the obstacle. Both the fallen horses happily jumped to their feet immediately to charge off after the other runners, leaving their jockeys sitting in a daze but otherwise unharmed on the soft ground, but their good fortune presented another very real hazard to the other runners particularly since one of the loose horses had his reins caught round one of his front hooves, giving the animal every chance of bringing himself down if he persisted in jumping any of the rest of the hurdles. The Nightingale was still galloping on the outside of the field, apparently out of harm's way until as the field swung round the top corner to begin the run downhill to the sixth flight of hurdles one of the loose horses suddenly cut across The Nightingale's path, unsighting him completely from the oncoming obstacle.

Josephine knew she could do one of two things – either take a pull and lose her momentum or she could ride The Nightingale into the fence in the hope that the horse which was now charging along dead ahead of her would at the last moment duck out to the right hand side of the flight. There was neither the way nor the time to hook her horse up and round the flanks of the animal in front.

Josephine chose the latter option. She chose to ride at the obstacle in the brave hope that the horse ahead would duck out.

She had no sight of the looming hurdle, at least not a good enough one to see a stride into it. All she could see was a loose horse in front of her and to her left a wall of horses now leaving the ground. So feeling rather than seeing the stride she needed she sat and gave, letting her horse do the work which the great horse did, rising heroically under her in spite of not being able to see his own way into the jump.

Then as he rose the loose horse suddenly ducked out to the right, crashing through the wing of the hurdle and leaving The Nightingale's path clear.

Even at that stage of the race with so much still left to do, a huge and mighty roar went up from the stand when the crowd witnessed what was happening behind the leaders. The Nightingale had flown the hurdle, landing two lengths up on a couple of horses smack on the left of him. Josephine couldn't see which the horses were, so mud-covered were their riders' colours, but as she landed she could sense the horses were cooked, a feeling confirmed by two cheery shouts from their jockeys.

'G'on, sweetheart!' they yelled. 'Go get 'em, girl!'

The two beaten horses were Demerara, which had led

the field a merry dance for the first part of the race, and Vote For Nigel who had seemed to be full of steam yet went out like a wet candle as soon as his jockey asked him the question, breaking a blood vessel as he tried to quicken and covering his pilot with gore.

That left seven horses flying down the famous hill towards the second last hurdle. Hello Absailor still led, but his jockey Andy Squire was already beginning to scrub him along and although the horse was gamely answering his pilot's call, Josephine could tell from the glance Robert McDonagh gave his rival as he ranged up alongside him on Glockamorra that he had the third favourite covered.

Yet still The Nightingale was remorselessly making up the ground, even faster now that some of the field were coming back to him. As she looked ahead of her to make sure of her position at the penultimate flight, Josephine suddenly realized that the devastating gallop the field had gone in such heavy going, prompted no doubt by the realization that her own horse was in such serious trouble, had taken its toll on the horses and that of the six horses left in front of her, at least four were visibly tiring, while by some miracle The Nightingale was still cruising and apparently full of running.

A few strides later Hello Absailor, on whom Andy Squire had been taking the paint off the rails, suddenly rolled away towards the middle of the course as he too began to tie up, forcing Glockamorra out even further into the centre of the track where the two horses then got locked seriously in battle. Immediately behind them Josephine got her first good look at the unbeaten Birdwatcher, who to her horror she saw was cruising, his jockey Philip Dacre sitting with his hands full of horse and apparently looking round for danger. Katwandra, however, who had run a fine race was now fading fast and backpedalling, allowing The Nightingale up on his inside where the big mud-caked horse eased past both him and Pleaseturnover who was already receiving reminders from his pilot.

The move left The Nightingale now in fifth place as the field continued the run down to the second last flight,

Josephine reckoning them to be no more than five lengths off the two leaders who were still slugging it out up front. But with Birdwatcher going so ominously well two lengths up on her on her right and last year's Irish champion Butler's Perk on that horse's outside and also still yet to make his move, Josephine suddenly realized that if she was going to have any real chance of winning she was going to have to disobey orders and creep up on the inside. Following her pre-race instructions to swing Nightie off the rails and come up the middle would now be suicidal since trying to take both Birdwatcher and Butler's Perk on the outside would add at least another two or possibly three lengths to her own horse's journey, so after they had flipped over the seventh flight of hurdles and begun the long left-handed swing round into the home straight, without checking her horse Josephine eased The Nightingale to the inside, even though both Birdwatcher and Butler's Perk were also holding their line to the left side of the track.

This meant as yet there was no gap for Josephine to take.

'Jeez!' Mattie shouted suddenly above the mayhem in the Claremore box. 'We're done! God, she's only gone and switched him to the inside!'

'So what else could she do!' Cassie shouted back. 'She was still a good four lengths down on the front two! She's got to hope a gap will come at the last! It's her only hope!'

'Rather her than me!' Mattie yelled. 'She could end up in the wing!'

The noise from the stands had become phenomenal as the leaders picked up down the hill and now, as they rounded the final turn to race flat out towards the last flight of hurdles, such was the volume of sound it made the relatively inexperienced Birdwatcher suddenly swing his head to look up at the jampacked stands and the moment he did so he faltered and lost his momentum, leaving the others to quicken away from him into the final flight. Glockamorra and Hello Absailor were still a good two lengths up as they measured the flight but then one stride more and Hello Absailor's head came up, his stride shortened and he was done. Sensing the exhausted horse

621

might unintentionally carry him across the hurdle, Robert McDonagh coolly switched his own horse to the left hand line, thus now effectively shutting the door completely in Josephine's face.

Again Josephine knew that if she took even the slightest pull or tried to switch her horse to the right of Glockamorra the race would be lost because any loss of impulsion into the final flight would mean inevitably that she would be slower away from the fence and her chance would have gone. At the last she had to get the sort of jump out of The Nightingale she had got at the second last where he had stood off, pinged the flight and landed running, because coming to the last they were still a good two lengths down on Glockamorra who was showing no signs of stopping. Even more ominously a length ahead of her on her right the Irish Champion Butler's Perk now suddenly ranged up, also looking full of running.

Committed now to making her run up in the inner, however, Josephine knew her only hope was for Robert McDonagh to be unaware that there was danger on his left so that as he jumped Glockamorra would leave The Nightingale enough room to jump the hurdle on his inside. Josephine knew from the way her horse had been making up lengths in the air that if that gap appeared The Nightingale could begin to overhaul McDonagh's horse in mid-flight, a move which invariably disconcerted the horse at the receiving end of the surprise. On the other hand if McDonagh took a peek and saw The Nightingale storming up on his inside it was an odds-on certainty he would tighten Glockamorra up and with nowhere then left to run other than into the wing Josephine would have to take a huge pull just as she was going to jump, which would either effectively kill off her challenge or cause her horse to make a vital mistake and probably fall.

Then six strides before releasing his horse at the last, Josephine's prayers were answered as she saw McDonagh, who was no doubt imagining that no-one would be fool enough to come up on his inner, take one very quick look to his right. What he saw was Butler's Perk at his flanks and beginning to look like his only danger with the now rallying Birdwatcher another head away in third.

What he did not see, sense or hear because of the tumult of noise cascading down from the grandstands was the big muddy black horse a couple of lengths back on his left, with his jockey sitting on him as still as a stone. So thinking himself safe on his inner Robert McDonagh changed his line into the last hurdle, tracking his horse smoothly across to try and clear the flight about six feet from the wing to give himself the benefit of a run home up the centre and most favoured part of the course.

And as soon as Josephine saw the gap she asked The Nightingale to go for it.

He was then only disputing third place, but even so The Nightingale seemed to rise at the hurdle as the leaders did, standing off so far before the wings that it seemed he must have no chance whatever of clearing the flight, yet not only did he clear it the horse made up two of the lengths he had been down, landing only half a length behind Glockamorra. Not that Glockamorra had been tame into the hurdle either. As always Robert McDonagh had seen the perfect stride, the horse had come up just when he should, cleared the hurdle easily and yet still come out of it two lengths worse against The Nightingale, whose prodigious leap had finally buried the rallying Birdwatcher who took the hurdle by its roots and crashed to the ground, decanting his jockey over his head and slithering painlessly but spectacularly on his side uphill through the mud.

Now the race was on in deadly earnest. McDonagh, at last aware of the danger on his left, got seriously to work on Glockamorra, changing his hands and then beginning to urge his horse on up the famous hill with legs, hands, seat and finally whip. In response to the driving force in the plate Glockamorra stuck his head out gallantly and forged on up the hill, but Josephine, who had yet to move on The Nightingale, saw that the leader was not actually gaining any ground.

The crowd also sensed this and roared the big black horse home even more vociferously, particularly now they saw

Butler's Perk unleashing his run. The compact Irish bay had seemed to be biding his time and now his pilot was letting him have his chance the little horse seemed to be catching Glockamorra and The Nightingale with every stride. In response McDonagh hit his horse even harder but Butler's Perk was now flying, with his jockey Declan Powell riding out the big iron grey only with hands and heels.

Yet Josephine still had made no real move on The Nightingale who was showing no signs of fatigue whatsoever. Instead, as Butler's Perk began to get up between Glockamorra and himself, The Nightingale lengthened his stride of his own free will, stretching effortlessly on up the famous hill, sluicing his way through the mud and making Josephine realize in one thrilling, heartstopping moment that as long as the two of them had timed their run right the race was there for the taking.

Then in another stride the whole complexion of his historic race changed yet again. Butler's Perk, who had seemed a moment earlier to have the race at his mercy, now began to shorten as The Nightingale took him on, so dramatically in fact that the bay appeared now almost to be treading water. Sensing this, Robert McDonagh renewed his effort, hitting his horse now on every other stride and pulling back the half length he had lost a couple of strides earlier to Butler's Perk who was now a totally spent force.

'Go on!' McDonagh screamed at his horse. 'Go on, you great bugger! Go on, Glock! G'arn!'

As he well knew his horse was also fast coming to the end of his tether and as Glockamorra did indeed begin to falter the horse began to hang badly to his left, carrying The Nightingale who was racing now at full steam alongside him across the course. In one last effort to straighten his horse out Robert McDonagh changed his whip from his right hand to his left intending to give Glockamorra one final reminder, but as he did so The Nightingale caught one brief glimpse of the hated instrument and thinking it was about to land on him swerved violently away, diving headlong for the left-hand set of running rails.

A huge cry of dismay surged up from the crowd as they saw the favourite suddenly swerve.

'What happened?' Cassie cried up in the box where near-pandemonium was reigning. 'Did McDonagh catch him with his whip or what!'

'I don't know!' Mattie yelled in return. 'But whatever happened he must have lost it now! Just when he had him, too! Just when he was galloping all over bloody Glockamorra!'

From having the race at her mercy, all Josephine could do now was sit and steer, since carrying no whip herself the only way she could try and straighten The Nightingale out was not with a slap down his left shoulder but by trying to ease the horse back into a straight line with left leg and right rein before sitting down to ride him for all she was worth.

But that was not the only problem she faced. On top of her struggle to get her horse back on course Josephine no longer knew how far there was to run. As the field jumped the last one of the horses in front of hers had kicked up a huge divot of mud, most of which hit Josephine full in the face, covering the best part of her goggles which were already half fogged up with condensation. In her race plan she had intended to push her goggles up on her helmet the moment they turned for home, but in the heat of the moment with everyone jockeying for their final positions on the bend she had forgotten all about them with the result that now about all she could see was the shape of the horse on her right and the blurred outline of the running rails on her left. She had no idea as to whether or not they had passed the final furlong marker and worst of all, never having ridden the horse in a flat-out finish before, she suddenly thought she might well have been misinterpreting the signals she had been getting from The Nightingale and that in fact there was nothing left in the locker. If that was the case then thanks to The Nightingale's sudden deviation they were beat.

But on the other hand if her horse had indeed something left to give then if she could only straighten him up and ask him for it there was still a very slim chance they could get up and win. If there was just anything left of his famous flying finish then they could still catch the horse two lengths in front of them. So rather than waste a split second more in trying to get her bearings Josephine locked her left leg well forward of the girths, loosened off her left rein and hauled in her right rein as much as she could. Immediately the horse responded, and the moment she felt him straighten out under her Josephine sat to her horse and did precisely what Dexter Bryant had told her to do only the night before on the telephone from Hong Kong.

*When you're ready to go but not a moment earlier or you'll never get him back*, he said, *just sit down and shake the reins. That's all, Jose, just shake those goddam reins.*

And that is all Josephine did. She sat, she slackened the reins and she shook them just the once at The Nightingale.

One moment the horse was two lengths down on Glockamorra whom Robert McDonagh now had back on a straight line, with his whipless rookie lady rider appearing to have as much chance of winning the race as a man has of learning to play poker on an ocean liner, and the next he was up alongsides the leader. The crowd, witnessing this sudden breathtaking burst of speed, suddenly realized that their hero might not after all be going to taste his first defeat, and they let fly a massive tidal roar of exultation which rolled down from the very top of the stands to the bottom, across the packed lawns from steps to rails and up from the thousands of throats of the masses packed in the public enclosures in the centre of the course. In response to the urgings of tens of thousands of racegoers, the famous horse now stuck out his great neck and fought, with Josephine urging him on with every stride that he took, urging him up the last fifty yards of the hill with just her voice and her hands. For a moment it seemed he had used up all the speed he had to get back to Glockamorra as the two horses seemed to race as one, matching each other stride for gallant stride, so that as they raced towards the line it seemed the only result could be a dead heat. But then Josephine threw away the rule book and shook the reins at her horse again, and incredibly the moment that she did The Nightingale picked up and seemed to turn the last heartstopping uphill muddy fifty yards of the finish into a flat track with perfect going, so quickly did he kick away from the horse beside him.

And as he flew for the line, the thousands of racegoers massed on the famous course and the millions watching on television around the world all witnessed a flight that was to pass into racing legend as the mighty mud-covered horse literally sprinted away from the game, gallant and courageous Glockamorra who now looked as though he had been nailed to the spot, so fast did his adversary fly by. With less than eighty yards to run The Nightingale had still been over a length and a half down, but by the time he had flown those last dozen strides to the line so fast had he raced that when he flashed past the winning post ahead of the now dethroned champion the winning margin was an unbelievable two lengths.

As he finally stormed home clear of Glockamorra, it seemed as though every hat brought to be worn that day was thrown sky high, while every rafter of the vast grandstand echoed with roars of exultation that must have been heard twenty miles away in Gloucester with every punter on the racecourse cheering The Nightingale's triumph as he came home with a jubilant Josephine now standing high in her irons, one fist clenched in the air as a salute not only to her wonderful courageous horse but to all those who loved him and who had never for one moment stopped believing in him.

The scenes in the unsaddling enclosure exceeded by far any other victory celebrations witnessed previously at the great racecourse, even those after the great mare Dawn Run had won her Gold Cup with the brave Jonjo O'Neill piloting her to victory. There was sheer pandemonium, and seeing that there was little or nothing they could do to contain the euphoria, wisely the executive let the party run its course, only making sure that there were sufficient police and security men to provide protection for the hero and heroine of the hour so that they might manage to make their way relatively unscathed through the delirious crowd back to the unsaddling enclosure. As it was Josephine was almost pulled from the horse twice, while at one point such was the level of hysteria it seemed as though an army of shamrocked Irishmen might lift The Nightingale right off his feet to carry him bodily in triumph back into the paddock.

On the television the commentators, finding words after a time when it seemed the entire team were at a loss for them, prepared their viewers to await the roar which was certain to erupt in greeting as soon as the all-conquering horse entered the unsaddling enclosure, but hardly were the words into their microphones when a storm erupted below their commentary position, drowning out the rest of their description. Through a delirious mass of people The Nightingale had finally appeared, this time now that the race was run led by a beaming Deirdre, with Mattie alongside his saddle. As soon as the victors began to cross the lawns, a crowd of his fellow countrymen descended on Mattie and raised him aloft, carrying him alongside his horse as they cheered the victorious party fit to bust. Josephine once again fisted a punch of triumph in the air as the crowds shouted their plaudits to her while practically every man she passed tried either to shake her hand or slap her thigh while dozens of the Irish unpinned their precious shamrock and threw it at the victors, covering the horse and rider in a welter of bright green. Robert McDonagh had been the first to congratulate her as they had pulled up past the winning post, throwing an arm around Josephine to kiss her on the cheek as he had ranged up alongside her on his own gallant mount, to be followed in like fashion by all the other jockeys who had completed the course, most of them having finished strung out like Monday's washing in a line down the hill, but now it seemed as Josephine threw the reins over The Nightingale's head and hopped down off his back that every man at Cheltenham wanted to have the mud-bespattered lady jockey in his arms.

Josephine looked round for her mother but for a moment

was unable to pick her out of the crowds swarming round her horse. While she was warning some of her overkeen male fans not to come too near her horse one of the television roving reporters thrust a microphone at her and began asking her the statutory questions about what it felt like and how the race had gone, but as Josephine bent down to undo her girths and then straightened up to slip her race saddle off rather than give her full attention to the interviewer and the questions he was shouting at her, it was clear that what she was really interested in was where the other heroine of the hour was.

Cassie was already down from her private box and in the enclosure but deliberately keeping out of the limelight. 'This is their moment,' she told Theodore who was by her side. 'I don't want anything to take away from a moment like this, not a thing.'

So while her children were being fêted and interviewed, Cassie remained where she was, surrounded by her circle of friends who respected her wishes and kept her protected from the media.

'What about Jump For Fun, Josephine?' the tall, curly-haired interviewer was now asking Josephine, his interview being broadcast over the public address system. 'What do you think they were trying to do with the horse – worry you out of it? Or do you think like a lot of people were saying before the race that the horse is mad anyway?'

'I'm sure if there was anything wrong in what the horse and jockey did the stewards will attend to it,' Josephine replied, wrapping her mud- and sweat-stained girth over her saddle which she then hugged safely to her.

'If they don't, Josephine me girl, we sure as hell will!' a huge Dubliner close by shouted. 'If I was the trainer and owner of that horse, I'd be on the first bloody helicopter out of here so I would!'

'There seemed little doubt from the stands that Jump For Fun was leaning into you and crossing you at the first two hurdles,' the interviewer continued, 'besides nearly stopping you stone dead at the start.'

'He gave us no room at all,' Josephine agreed, 'and Brian

Baker hit my horse with his whip before the third as the replay will no doubt show, just as it'll show how keen he was to try to run us out.'

'He hit your horse?' the interviewer echoed in astonishment. 'We saw some scrimmaging going on out there in the country, certainly, but no-one had any idea he actually hit The Nightingale.'

'It was the best thing he did,' Josephine suddenly said with a grin. 'Nightie won't have a stick near him let alone on him, so when Baker hit him he grabbed him by the leg and pulled him out of his saddle.'

This revelation was greeted by another tremendous roar by those immediately around the horse, as indeed it was with enormous interest by the television commentary team who were busy studying the action replay in slow motion on screen. The interviewer, who had a small viewing monitor propped up on a camera box near The Nightingale's head, looked down at the screen and indicated to Josephine to do the same.

'My word,' he said in awe. 'You can see it quite clearly on the replay. The Nightingale's got him like an alligator.'

'All this at full stretch too,' Josephine said. 'Now if you'll excuse me, I have to go and weigh in.'

'Just as well the bugger was brought back by an ambulance!' another Irishman shouted. 'Because if he hadn't we'd have made sure that he did!'

At that moment Mattie appeared through the crowd, back on terra firma and with a mouth and two cheeks covered in a welt of well-wishers' lipstick.

'Mattie Rosse,' the interviewer said, grabbing him by the arm. 'You look as though you've made some new friends.'

'I have so,' Mattie grinned in return, fetching out a handkerchief and beginning to wipe off some of the lipstick. 'I've had quite a few proposals of marriage too. Some of them I might well take up.'

Which remark elicited a whoop of delight from the Irish contingent.

'Do you want to talk about Jump For Fun?' the interviewer wondered. 'You must surely have thought your horse was done for when he lost all that ground at the start.'

'I don't want to talk about Jump For Fun,' Mattie said. 'The stewards will sort that out. What I want to talk about is the fantastic courage of this horse here—'

Another huge and prolonged cheer rose from the crowd around them.

'Talk about heart,' Mattie said. 'There aren't a lot of horses who could do what he did.'

At that the crowd went wild, reducing both the interviewer and Mattie to silence. Finally, when the cheering died down, the interviewer continued.

'I don't think *any of us* has ever seen a performance quite like that, Mattie,' he said. 'We've seen a few here, a few truly great ones, but I don't want to make any comparisons because what your horse did was unique. No-one has ever done the Derby and the Champion Hurdle double and no-one has ever won the Champion Hurdle against such impossible odds. Did you *really* think he was going to do it?'

'Yes,' Mattie said happily. 'There was never a doubt in any of our minds.'

'Even after he'd nearly been run out at the third and left trailing by – what? A dozen lengths or more?'

'Yes,' Mattie said. 'This horse doesn't know the meaning of defeat. Think of what's happened to him. If he knew defeat he wouldn't be here today. But before I go off to declare the celebrations open—' Another round of cheers stopped the flow, but only momentarily. 'Before we go and drink the horse's health, first I must say well done and thank you to my stable staff and to the staff at Claremore. This is their doing, you know, they're the people who got the horse here. And as for my sister Josephine – who made all you racing scribes eat your hats I'm glad to say—'

'Three cheers for Jose Rosse!' someone called, and the crowd all duly responded.

'I don't think anyone could have ridden a better or braver race,' Mattie said. 'So chauvinists everywhere – enjoy your

631

hat sandwich. Lastly – and certainly not least – I want to thank my mother Cassie Rosse, for believing in me enough to allow me to train him.'

'Hear hear!' many voices bellowed, led by the still delirious Dubliner who called for 'One hundred and three cheers for Cassie Rosse!'

Then, after the rousing cheers had died away, the crowd started calling for Cassie, and they were not to be stopped until Cassie was found and led from the group of her friends surrounding her to face the cameras and the interviewer.

'They say they don't come back, Cassie,' the interviewer said. 'But this old fella certainly did.'

'They come back all right,' Cassie replied with a smile. 'You're just not always sure what as.'

'I'm sorry, I don't understand,' her perplexed questioner said.

'You're not the only one,' Cassie laughed.

'What I meant was the old saying, you know – like fighters. Horses who have been through what this horse of yours has been through don't come back.'

'This is no ordinary horse, Derek. You saw what he did today. He was dead and buried not once, not twice, but three times.'

'So what makes him so special?'

'If I knew that—' Cassie sighed.

'If you knew that,' the interviewer interrupted with a smile, 'you'd be breeding dozens more of them. Is it the famous Irish grass, do you think?'

'No.' Cassie smiled at the man asking the questions. 'As a matter of fact I really believe that this horse is not something else but *someone* else.'

'Yes. Right,' the interviewer nodded solemnly. 'Like Nijinsky, you mean? You mean,' he hesitated, 'like the great Derby winner Nijinsky who was meant to be his namesake, the famous ballet dancer, come back to earth.'

'Something like that.'

'So who do you think this great horse of yours might be?'

'Now that really would be telling.'

'Well, whatever the secret of the horse's greatness, because make no mistake, folks' – the interviewer turned for a moment to talk directly to the camera – 'this is probably the greatest racehorse you have ever seen or ever will see – so whatever makes the old boy tick, Cassie – what next?'

'Remember the horse was short of a proper race, so he'll be an even better horse next time out.'

'And where and when might that be?' the interviewer finally enquired, with a broad smile also on his face.

'Cheltenham,' Cassie replied with a nod. 'Same time next year.'

*Some weeks later, a month or more after she had returned to Claremore, Cassie, Theodore and Wilkie went on a long walk up into the hills behind the house. They walked where Cassie so often walked, in fact they walked the very route she had taken on horseback that fateful day she had lost Tyrone. As always when they walked into the hills Wilkie was in high spirits and insisted Cassie or Theodore throw him the stick he had brought with him at every conceivable opportunity. It was a fine May day, high-clouded and crisp, with the countryside which lay spread out below them beginning to dress in its spring colours.*

*As they were going through the field where Tyrone had fallen, Cassie stopped as she always did on the spot where the accident had happened, but this day Wilkie grew impatient after a few moments and jumped up at her, which was unlike his normal behaviour. He jumped up so that his paws landed high on Cassie's chest and Cassie scolded him and eased the dog down off her, not noticing that as she did so one of his paws had caught her precious gold locket, breaking the chain and causing the locket to drop into the deep grass, almost exactly where it had fallen so fatefully those many years before.*

*Then once again as she reached the top of the field Cassie reached to the open neck of her shirt, suddenly realizing that the little gold heart no longer hung there. She stopped where she was, still with her hand to her throat, and looked back down the slope to the corner of the field where she knew it must lie, to the spot where she had lost Tyrone.*

*She paused for a moment, with her hand to her neck, and as she did Wilkie sat down at her feet and rested*

*his head against her while above her Theodore leaned on
a stile to stare up at the sky.*

*Then finally Cassie raised the hand that was to her neck
up to her mouth and, pressing it to her lips, let one kiss fly
on the spring breeze that blew gently down the hills before,
ruffling Wilkie's head, she set off once more to walk the
hills which rose majestically behind her beloved Claremore.*

# Postscript

'And what of the loose ends?' her shock-white-haired interviewer asked her. 'What of all that criminality? Was the bet paid?'

'Oh yes,' Cassie smiled as they walked on through the gardens of Claremore. 'There was no way Gold could welsh on that bet.'

'Thus the day was saved.'

'The day was, and with it Claremore, but of course no reparation could ever be finally made for what the wretches did to the horse. No-one could ever give him back his career at stud and I think racing will always feel the loss.'

'And Mr Gold is now dead.'

'Long dead.'

'How did Theodore Pilkington know?'

'Well.' Cassie smiled as she remembered the moment when Theodore had leaned across to her and told her there was something else she should know about Mr Michael Gold. 'When Theodore was a young man, qualifying as a doctor, his father used to sit him down on the bench by the fishpond in the village where they lived and get Theodore to diagnose at sight. His father was a doctor, you understand, a general practitioner with a special gift for diagnosis. So there the two of them would sit and let the village stroll innocently by and guess by sight what was wrong with every one of them. Finally Theodore got as good as his father, finding that he too had the knack. So when he met Gold that first day at Ascot, the meeting when Big Wallow was got at, he knew at once by looking at Gold and listening to him what he was suffering from.'

'Which was?'

'Motor neurone disease. The facial tic, the muscular

deterioration, the hoarseness of the voice, the difficulty in swallowing, it all seemed to indicate motor neurone, and assuming he was right Theodore said Gold's expected lifespan would probably be no more than a year, two years at most.'

'This was why you felt perfectly comfortable letting him have the book, rather than handing him over to the authorities and letting the law take its course.'

'Imagine,' Cassie proposed. 'Suppose they had finally got him to court and suppose they had actually found him guilty. By the time he got sent down, maybe he would have had six months left to live at most. No-one would have benefited. This seemed a much better form of justice.'

'I agree.'

'As it happens, he died only five months after the Champion Hurdle. But not before ironically enough he'd been persuaded to set up and finance a trust fund to investigate the incidence of the doping of horses and to find ways not only to safeguard against its happening but also to trace and analyse the state of the art drugs. It's been very successful too, I'm happy to say.'

'A suitable memorial in the circumstances.'

'Horses happily do not understand irony, J.J. They've just benefited from Gold's apparent philanthropy.'

'And all because of one woman's jealousy,' Cassie's visitor mused. 'Can you imagine? What a story. Yes, and by the by, what happened to your friend Leonora?'

'She's still alive and she's still kicking,' Cassie replied with a rueful smile. 'But that, as they say, my old friend, is another story.'

By now they were headed for the home paddock where a group of horses could be seen grazing peacefully in the cool of the shadows spread by the huge horse chestnuts.

'The lad responsible for doping the horse,' J. J. Buchanan asked. 'Phelim O'Connell, right? Whatever became of him?'

'He made a full recovery from his beating, but he wouldn't come back to Claremore, even though we did everything to try to persuade him,' Cassie replied. 'He was too frightened of what his mates might think of him, or even do to him, particularly since although he didn't actually do the doping of Big Wallow he admitted he had been involved in helping them get at the horse. But then he had what they call extenuating circumstances, so when he wouldn't come back here to work we set up a trust for his sick sister and finally got her sent over to this place in America. Phelim went over there with her and he's working somewhere down in Blue Grass country.'

'And his sick sister?'

'She actually got a whole lot better. She won't ever be totally cured, but she is still considerably better, and needs very little treatment now.'

Cassie whistled gently and held out her hand for the big black horse who was now making his slow way over to them. 'Anyway, enough of that,' she continued. 'This is who you came to see.'

'I came to see you, Cassie,' the man beside her replied. 'Much as I love and admire your horse—' He stopped and looked out across the beautiful scene of the horses grazing in the shadow of the blue mountains.

'You know, you still haven't said whether or not you were going to propose to me that night, Joe,' Cassie said with a smile, slipping her arm through her old friend's. 'The night my mother died. Were you?'

Joe nodded. 'I sure was,' he said. 'You bet.'

Cassie sighed and looked at her famous horse who was now standing before her, right up by the rail. 'Just think,' she said quietly.

'I too often have, Cassie,' Joe replied. 'I've thought about what might have happened almost every day of my life. Imagine – if you had said yes—'

'Which I would have done.'

'There'd have been no Nightingale. The world would never have known your wonderful horse.'

And I'd never have known Tyrone, Cassie thought.

After a moment's reflection, Cassie turned back to Joe, squeezing his arm which was still linked through her own. 'Did you marry?' she asked.

638

'I did, and I got divorced, and I have three fine children. Talking of which, how are your kids?'

'Mattie as you probably know is doing brilliantly,' Cassie said. 'He had his first Group One winner two years after Nightie's Champion Hurdle when he won the Irish 2000 Guineas with Tree House, and three years later he trained Soft Spot to win the Irish Derby. Jo is married to Gareth Plunkett and I'm now a grandmother twice over, with a grandson and a granddaughter. And Erin's beloved Padraig has become an actor, which in a way was always on the cards.'

'What about Mr Joel Benson?'

'You'll meet him tonight. He and his wife Polly are coming over for the weekend with their two children, who are my godchildren, Billie his daughter—'

'Billie?'

'Named after Billie Holliday, I gather. And Red, his son.'

'Named after Red Nichols, I guess.'

'Named after Red Garland, Joel's favourite jazz pianist. He's a very happy man, and Polly, contrary to first impressions, is an absolute hoot. Now are you going to make yourself acquainted with Nightie or aren't you? Because if you are, you're going to need these.' She handed him a tube of polo mints and smiled.

'I thought he didn't like us men?' Joe wondered.

'He didn't,' Cassie replied. 'But now he's retired he's mellowed, and although horses never forget, they do as it happens seem to forgive. Go ahead, he won't bite you.'

Joe fed the big horse a stream of peppermints and in between feeds was rewarded with a friendly but thorough buffeting from the great horse's muzzle.

'He looks magnificent, Cassie,' Joe said.

'He is magnificent,' Cassie agreed. 'He's the most magnificent creature you will ever meet.'

'That includes your husband?' J. J. Buchanan asked, poker-faced.

'My husband's different magnificent,' Cassie laughed. 'Talking of which—' She pointed to the left where an old but absolutely immaculate burgundy Rolls Royce was *arriving up the drive. 'Here he is now,' she said. 'Come on, come on and meet him.' Cassie gave The Nightingale one last mint and a final pull at his ears before turning away, followed by her childhood sweetheart Joe Harris, now the famous American sportswriter J. J. Buchanan.*

*As he fell into step beside her, Joe Buchanan put his hand deep into his jacket pocket to flick open a little ring box which contained a simple little one diamond engagement ring, ran his finger once over the stone, then clicked the box shut for ever more.*

**THE END**